The Magic Crystals

On the String

by

Stephen Hayes

On the String
Book 6 in the Magic Crystals series

Written by Stephen Hayes

Published 2020 by Stephen Hayes, Australia

Formatted by www.eBookIt.com

www.StephenHayesOnline.com

Disclaimer: All characters in this publication are fictitious and any
resemblance to real persons, living or dead, is purely coincidental.

ISBN-13: 978-0-9944-5908-4

Contents

Prologue

I would later learn the horrifying details from two people who survived the hostile takeover. Well, perhaps 'survived' would be the wrong word; one of them escaped, while the other, who saw so much more, would be only physically unhurt. Sometimes, saying a person is physically unhurt is the only positive statement to be made for their condition.

It all happened very suddenly at some point just after eight o'clock on the evening of August 27, 2010, at which point the stabilisation of the world was running according to plan. The Sorcerers had canvassed the United States and Canada, removing the mental influence of the Hammerhearts on all those who were still running their agenda, and now the mission had crossed the Atlantic and had entered Great Britain.

"This really would be a lot simpler if we had a way of just vanishing every Hammerheart device on the planet," Brian said as he cast yet another spell, causing a cluster of agonators, bludginators, and other assorted creations of ill intention to disappear off the display screen. The base, which they no longer needed to leave, was equipped with mobile cameras, and the great part about it was the Sorcerers had the ability to cast magic on those objects visible on the screen.

"We don't yet know for sure that there isn't," said Frederic sadly. He was performing much the same operation on another display screen. "All we know for sure is that nothing we have done so far has worked. It may be that we're not casting the right spell, or more likely our own magic just isn't powerful enough to pull that off."

"Which is why I think we ought to revisit the idea of calling Marc into action," said Lillian for the tenth or eleventh time in the last three days. "He may not have enough power either, but—"

"But nothing," said Frederic, vaguely but firmly (a paradox of sorts, yet he somehow pulled it off). "While I'm sure the Beast of Magic could wield such power, we just don't know what unseen consequences might arise from it."

"You could say the same for your own magic, though," Charlie Thomas argued. "I mean, scientifically speaking—"

"There's nothing scientific about this, mate," Chester laughed. "You're probably right about one thing though: The greater the spell, the greater risk you're taking of causing some sort of unpredictable chain reaction."

"While all that may be true, the risk is far greater with the Beast of Magic, even with small spells," said Frederic, "because unlike our

Sorcerous chips, it has the ability to think for itself and use its best judgement."

"Isn't it required to obey Marc's orders?" asked Alice.

"Yes, but the problem still exists if Marc is no wiser as to what the consequences of his magic may be," Frederic said, as though he hadn't said the same thing several times already. "I really don't think we need to discuss this anymore."

Brian checked his watch and then stood up from his workstation. "Okay, Lillian, time for you to take over."

The workroom was really quite small, with only two workstations (because there were only supposed to be two people working at a time), so the six people present had to do a bit of wriggling around each other so that Brian could get out of his seat and Lillian could get into it. Chester and Charlie, bystanders at this stage (they didn't normally do this sort of work, but the order of things in recent days had left their usual jobs redundant) had to flatten themselves against the back wall to manage it.

"What time is it anyway?" Chester now asked.

"Just after five in the morning," Charlie said immediately, checking his own watch, which, for whatever reason, he hadn't changed since leaving Australia.

"Eight in the evening," said Brian, and he yawned, "although I'm not sure what time my body thinks it is. Honestly, I'll be glad when this is—"

He stopped dead, not just in speech but all motion. This made him look rather peculiar for a moment as he had half turned to leave the room. The others in the room could only see his face in profile but while Chester and Charlie exchanged a confused look, Frederic, Lillian and Alice all widened their eyes in alarm.

"What—" Lillian began, and that was when Brian Fletcher collapsed, crumpling into a heap in the doorway.

"Holy—" Chester and Charlie began in freakish unison, but they too were interrupted, this time by Frederic Woodward toppling out of his seat and onto the floor, hitting his head on a desk leg on his way down. Neither man moved or responded in any way to the shocks to their bodies.

And it didn't stop there. Less than two seconds later, and almost at exactly the same moment, both their mothers went the same way. Lillian only slumped back in her seat, her head rolling to the side but fortunately not enough to affect her centre of gravity. Alice fell forward, catching Charlie and almost bringing him down with her, but she was a fairly small old lady and he was strong enough to catch her and lower her gently to the floor before looking, stricken, up at Chester.

"What just happened?" Chester asked, but he already knew—both of them knew. There was only one remote source that could bring Sorcerers down in this way, and it was clear that all four of them had fainted cold. But how could it be? The Sorcerous Crystals were all safely in Marc Moran's possession, defended by him, Natalie and most impressively, Fewul. Moreover, who was left who could possibly want to take the Sorcerers' power? Sure, there was still one living Hammerson, but surely—surely—

"Let's get out of here," said Charlie, cutting off Chester's train of thought. "We need to check on Amelia. Surely, whoever's doing this won't take all six of them—nobody in their right mind would put the world through that again."

So far as the two of them knew, Amelia was presently sleeping in the bedroom she shared with that woman, the freakishly good-looking one who could do all that weird stuff with her mind. Amelia had been through an awful ordeal earlier in the week, one from which she would never entirely recover, not with all the magic in the world on their side, but she had been put back together only hours earlier and the result, though slightly different according to both the woman and Frederic, was close enough to the original Amelia to pass for a member of their family. She wouldn't be made to work, though; after what she and the other kids had done, she deserved a break.

Unfortunately, Chester and Charlie didn't get to find out whether or not Amelia was still with them. The base in which they had operated from for the last couple of months (since the old one had been infiltrated and destroyed from the inside) was heavily protected with all sorts of magic. It was safer than the old base, and supposedly harder to get into than the Hammerheart network, but none of that stopped a large group of people suddenly teleporting straight into their midst.

Lucien Moran was at the centre of the group, and as they were confronted with him, Chester and Charlie forgot all about Amelia. In point of fact, they no longer cared about anything except for the fact that Lucien, the one true ruler of the world, was going to take care of everything, and that very soon, all would be well. As the rest of the Woodward army got wind of the disturbance and came to investigate, they quickly came to the same blissful realisation.

* * *

May, the Honnie, was lying on her back, staring up at the ceiling of her bedroom, and thinking. She was supposed to be sleeping so that she would be refreshed for action in eight hours' time (she had to be fresh, because she couldn't work as quickly or accurately when her mind wasn't at its sharpest) but this strange situation she had landed herself in over the last week or so had given her so much to think about. The last week or so? Honnies didn't even have weeks in their world, and although she understood the concept from those human minds she had held at various points in her life, she had never found herself thinking of time in the same way.

Tonight, it was another time-related matter that was occupying her thoughts, this thing the natives of this particular land referred to as 'British Summer Time'. The concept of time zones was another one she had known about, and now that she had travelled through several (and so far from the one she had started in), she could understand the sense in them. Still, Honnies (those who didn't care about humans, and that would be ninety-nine percent of them) didn't bother to calculate time in any greater detail than how far the sun had moved across the sky, nor did they measure time passed in weeks, months, years, or anything else. Only those with extraordinary memories, like May, counted days, and so far, she was up to 10,376. Humans seemed to think of their system as an accomplishment, but May herself thought rather wistfully that happiness and simplicity often went hand-in-hand.

She wasn't alone in her bedroom at the moment: Amelia was there too, sound asleep in the bed on the other side of the room, as May herself should be. Amelia's mind was presently the only one contained within her own (she had found that keeping too many active minds around her for too long tended to distract her, so she let them all go when she didn't need to use them) but there was no harm in holding onto Amelia. Part of it was because she was sleeping so deeply that her dreams were thick and would probably have faded into nothingness by the time she woke up, but the greater part was that it was hard not to think of Amelia as being her human after what she, May, had done for her. Her personality may have been made up from snippets of her former self, but it was hard to shake the odd feeling that she, May, had actually created this human. It was also hard not to take some pride in the way she had turned out: Even if she was slightly different, and May could tell that she was, she had still been gifted with all those qualities that her friends and family had always admired in her.

She was lying there, now feeling the beginnings of sleep creeping up, when something in her mind seemed to slip. It was a feeling she had long since trained herself to be prepared for, because normally when that happened (in her own world anyway), it meant that something bad had happened to one of her possessions. She sat up quickly, looking wildly around the room, but she and Amelia were still the only ones there, and no sound from the hallways reached her sharp ears. Amelia was lying just as motionless as before, but May's mind was fully alert now, all traces of sleep gone, and she quickly picked up on the change. Amelia wasn't asleep—she was unconscious.

May allowed herself to relax, because this seemed to be nothing serious. She inhaled deeply, trying to smell if anything unusual had happened to Amelia's body which could have caused this, but there was nothing. If her body was fine, then it had to be a mental thing, so with a sigh of relief, and rather perplexedly, she tried to bring Amelia back to consciousness. But this was where the situation was suddenly more serious: Nothing happened. By all May knew about humans, these things all added up to impossible, and that could only mean one thing: Something magical was going on.

May had promised herself that wherever possible, she would stay away from magic, but there was something about this situation that she didn't like, and if she had to get involved, she wanted it to be on her terms rather than someone else's. Her greatest weapon was her mind, so she cast it outward, taking the rest of the base to get an idea of what might be going on, hoping that something she heard would offer an explanation for what had happened to Amelia. It was perfectly timed: Charlie Thomas was thinking that he and Chester ought to make sure Amelia hadn't fainted as the other Sorcerers had, because that meant that they would all be losing their magical powers.

Okay, this was definitely more serious than she had originally thought, so she got out of bed and went across the room to where Amelia lay. Those two men were on their way back here right now, and when they got here, they would probably take Amelia away, which was fine with her. In fact, the thing May grappled with, for only a few moments, was their present attire. Both she and Amelia were wearing night dresses, and although they weren't exactly raunchy, they wouldn't normally be something they would want men to see them in unless they were sleeping together (that seemed to be how humans thought of it anyway). May herself didn't care—she actually rather enjoyed the way male humans' eyes practically bugged out of their face when they saw her wearing this silky slip with absolutely nothing on underneath—but this might be too serious to allow them to be distracted.

She had just decided to get dressed when something truly horrifying happened. She felt a large mind suddenly appear in the base, teleporting in the way she now understood (as she had done it a few times herself now). She had no idea exactly what this mind was; it was far too large to be human (all their minds were the same size, no matter how intelligent they were) but it didn't seem to be made of the same stuff as Honnie minds either. It was still fairly smaller than her own, though, so she decided to take hold of it, open it up and find out what was in there.

That turned out to be a terrible idea. Once she had safely encased it within her mind, she felt it try to take control of her from the inside. It was like those things in space that humans called 'black holes', which sucked everything into them. This thing created a vacuum within her own mind, so powerful that it began weakening her. With a cry of horror, she re-opened her mind and gobbed it out, just in time too; it had almost taken Amelia with it. What it had taken, though, was some of May's mental strength; she was still stronger than she had been prior to taking the collection test, but not as strong as she had been a few minutes ago.

Meanwhile, that thing, whatever it was, had sucked up every mind within the base and who could say what it was doing to them now. Her mind was still too big for it to take her, which meant that she and Amelia were safe from it, but the mind had a physical form too, and she had briefly seen who it was in the minds of Chester and Charlie before it had taken them. She understood who the boy was, and worse, she knew what magical power he had used to create that horrible thing that had almost claimed her.

She could not fight Lucien—his magic would be too powerful for her. She wouldn't get a chance to tackle him physically, and his mind was protected from her. This left her with only one choice: She had to run for it, and there was not a second to spare. No, that was only half-true: There was only a second for her to pull back Amelia's covers, gather the girl up and bound for the door. She knew exactly how to get out, because Lillian had explained how the magic worked when she had first entered this place. There were two doors that would take her to the ground directly below the base, no matter where it was, and one of those doors was quite close to this room. She only hoped she could get there in time....

* * *

"Leave them where they are," Lucien commanded, smiling as he observed the four fallen former Sorcerers with cold satisfaction. "I'll take them back with me—I have a speech I would like to make when they wake up, and one I intend to make before then—but I need Amelia to be with them. Have you found her yet?"

"We've sent people to check the back rooms now," Cornish told him, a little fearfully, it looked to Chester. Neither he nor Charlie cared how uncomfortable Cornish, their old enemy, was with this turn of events, but if Lucien asked either of them to go and bring Amelia to him, they would most certainly do it.

"What about May?" Lucien enquired. "She must be brought in under any circumstances."

"Er—no one seems to know what to look for, sir."

"Then send people who do know what to look for," Lucien snapped. "You two," he said, turning to Chester and Charlie, and the two men were quickly excited by the idea that they could be offered an opportunity to serve the God that Lucien was, "you know who I'm talking about, right?"

"The good-looking one with the gnarly mind tricks," said Chester at once.

"The Honnie, yes," Lucien said primly. "Where is she?"

"She and Amelia share a room at the back of the base," said Charlie. "They were both supposed to be sleeping now."

"Excellent," said Lucien, a slow grin spreading across his face. It made him look so young and happy, and both men were forcibly reminded of John—the look was so similar to the way he looked when he was satisfied. "Take me straight to that room—lead the way, and don't worry about May attacking you—I'll make sure you're safe."

And he knew all the right things to say, too. Serving him was going to be a great pleasure as well as an honour.

They took off, hurrying through the halls with Lucien right behind them and Cornish loping along in the rear, following his original order to stay by Lucien's side, whatever went down here today. Lucien seemed certain that May was here—perhaps he had magically scanned the place when he had first arrived—but by the time they reached the bedroom in question, the door was wide-open and the covers of both beds had been pulled roughly back. It was clear that both girls were gone, but how could it be possible?

Lucien swore under his breath behind them and rolled his eyes up, concentrating on something magical (they had seen Frederic Woodward do the same thing on occasions). The look dawning on his face now was the very antithesis of what they had seen earlier. Thunderclouds were gathering in his eyes, and they weren't just dark; they were black as a moonless night.

"They're gone," he whispered, his voice clearly audible in the complete silence that surrounded them, and Chester and Charlie exchanged fearful looks. Cornish, too, looked more and more nervous by the second about the direction this might be going.

"They're gone," Lucien repeated, now at a normal volume, but those thunderclouds were closing in. They could all see it in his face, and Chester thought he saw something else there, something that looked less like Lucien Moran and more like Arnold Hammerson, the man they had fought all this time—what an idiot he had been.

"They're gone!" Lucien roared, making them all jump, and the world exploded around them. All three of them threw themselves to the floor as walls fell down around them, crashing and crashing and seeming to never end. The ceiling came down, as did everything on the floor above, and then the floor above that. All over the base, the structure the Woodwards and Fletchers had constructed collapsed and became nothing but rubble, yet somehow, nobody got hurt. After the silence had spiralled out for about a minute, Charlie stood up and helped Chester to his feet. Rubble piled high around them, but the two of them, as well as that pathetic excuse for a human beside them, were completely unhurt.

Lucien was still with them, taking deep, calming breaths. The thunderclouds in his face were gone—they had seemingly exploded, taking the whole base with them. Lucien was back to being himself again, and he looked rather surprised by what had just happened. More than that, he looked disturbed.

"Geez, sorry about that," he said, reaching down to help Cornish to his feet. "Man, I've never lost it like that before. I dunno what came over me. It's just," he stopped, thinking, and then, "I really wanted to deal with May. She could be a real thorn in my side if I let her get away, but I guess I'll have to take care of that at a later date. Hopefully, she'll be completely clueless about how to get back to Chopville in this world, since she can't teleport. Can you guys do me a favour?" he now asked the three of them as they began walking back to where most of what had once been the Woodwards' army were congregated, Lucien magically shifting rubble aside as they went.

"Sure," said Chester at once. "What do you need?"

"Remind me of this the next time I start getting angry," he said. "Going off like a bomb was Arnold Hammerson's thing, and I don't wanna be like him—I'm a better man than that. Thank God I had the presence of mind to protect all the people in the base before it hit me. Well, anyway, it looks like May's taken Amelia with her, so I'll have to settle for taking the other four back. It shouldn't be a problem; they were the ones doing the damage anyway."

The base had been completely trashed, and later, Lucien would come back to vanish the entire thing, but for the time being, he just wanted to get all the people out and to a place of relative safety. He gathered everyone around, the Woodward army and those whom he had brought with him, and teleported them all back to the Chopville Hammerheart base, which was now his. They teleported into there just as easily as they had teleported into the Woodwards' base, as though Lucien had discovered some higher level of teleportation that bypassed the usual protection that was supposed to stop people entering by stealth. That probably explained how he had gotten the Sorcerous Crystals in the first place.

* * *

May and Amelia had gotten out just in time. From the ground (they were in a park of some sort), May could still get glimpses of what was happening inside the base by touching that weird mind that had almost claimed her. She caught just enough to know that Lucien knew she was there (he had felt her mind, no doubt) and that he was coming to get both her and Amelia. They would know about the door at the back of the base and if they went through it, they would drop right into this park, where the chase would be on yet again. She had no hope of outrunning Lucien's magic if it came to that; she needed to go somewhere he couldn't get to, or that he wouldn't think of going to. On that score, she had only one idea.

She moved sideways, not in a way that humans understood but a way that only Honnies could do when they wanted to travel between the worlds. May herself hadn't really understood how this worked until she had done it for the first time recently because normally, Honnies weren't taught how to do it unless they were qualified to be collectors. She didn't go all the way back to her world, though, or even into the nothingness between the two worlds, but to a space in between, the place John and some of his friends thought of as 'their shadow'. It was a little cooler and a little darker here, despite already being cool and dark in the human world, and the air was thinner too. It wasn't a problem for her, though, and it probably wouldn't be a problem for Amelia either whenever she woke up.

And that would be a full twenty-four hours from now. May had got that out of Chester and Charlie's heads in the less-than-twenty seconds she'd had before they had been claimed. May had no idea what she could do for her own good now, so her only option was to wait here for Amelia to come around so they could work out a plan together. She didn't dare go back out there in case Lucien detected her presence and came for her, and she didn't want to return to her own world because the job she had promised hadn't been completed and had now been set back significantly. All she could do was sit on the cold ground, take the unconscious girl in her arms and cuddle her (she was really cold, out in the night wearing nothing but a night dress so thin that it wasn't far from being naked) and wait for the day to pass. Eventually, she slept.

Part 1: The Last Resistance

Chapter 1: You Could Be a Diabolical Evil Genius

Breakfast had typically been the quietest meal of the day around the base because people filtered in and out of the dining room at all different stages during the three designated hours in the morning. The last few mornings, however, so few people had gotten up early that the hour between eight and nine saw the room filled almost to capacity. It still wasn't as loud as lunch or dinner because most people were still waking up, but it meant that there was a greater buzz of conversation. Most of the talk since Tuesday morning (three days ago now) had been about the Hammerhearts, the Woodwards' efforts to overturn their rule (which hadn't become noticeable as yet), and wondering where the oldest of the Moran brothers was now. A little sick of it, Peter, James and I tried to make that morning's conversation a little lighter.

"I'm sure we had that conversation with the parents last year," James smirked at Peter, "and the year before that, and the year before that℟—"

"I know, but we're all older and more responsible now," said Peter, grinning. "Besides, we're not really kids anymore—it's not like they can just tell us no without offering an explanation."

"But they did offer an explanation," I reminded him. "Actually, three: They were too busy, none of us could be trusted to be responsible, and Hilda and Violet almost qualified as pets anyway."

Peter and James laughed; I had invented that last one.

"Well, I guess I'd back you up," James said, "and I reckon my sisters would too. So if we do get a pet of some kind, what sort should we go for? Cat, dog, bird—"

"How about a horse, a cow, and two dozen chickens?" I suggested. "That'd make Dad and Charlie feel like kids again."

The other two laughed again. "Don't forget the sheep," James added.

"I would have stuck with a dog or a cat," said Peter. "I know they're kinda boring but they're still the best pets."

"Make it a dog, then," I said. "Cats are mean; they snub you off, whereas dogs just love you regardless."

"Is that some kind of pussy joke?" Peter asked. "'Cause if it was, I didn't get it."

I shrugged. "You know what I mean. I guess I'm just not a cat person. Remember that old tabby that used to live on Napoleon Road?"

We had never found out if that cat had been a stray or if it had actually belonged to someone. All we knew was that it always hung around our street, and ever since Nicole had made the mistake of feeding it on one occasion, it had frequently come around our house. Most of us had liked it at first, but Jessica had turned out to be allergic to it, and it had scratched me pretty badly after I had, on a dare from either Harry or Simon, yelled in its ear. Eventually we had all gotten sick to death of it hanging around, and no one more so than the parents, but we hadn't been able to get rid of it until one day, while we had been at school, it had been hit by a car near Main Street. That had been about five years ago now.

"Ah, memories," sighed James, smirking again. "Well, maybe you're right. Any ideas for what you'd like to call it if we get a dog?"

"How about Poochie?" Peter suggested. In response, James leaned right back in his seat and stared pointedly at the ceiling, while I covered my mouth with my hand and pretended to yawn widely.

The conversation could have gone just about anywhere after that, but that was when Marc dropped into the remaining seat at our table for four. The look on his face sobered me up at once; there was a deadly calm in his eyes, but his cheeks were completely devoid of colour.

"Morning," Peter said to him. "Got any suggestions for good dog names?"

"What's up?" James asked, concerned, having noticed the same thing I had.

For several seconds, Marc only stared with seemingly dead eyes, and my fear increased. I had hoped that I wouldn't need to think about Lucien at all this morning, but there was no way this couldn't have something to do with our big brother. What else could put that look in Marc's face? Finally, he unlocked his throat and said, in a voice as dead as his eyes, "The Hero Crystal is gone."

The three of us only stared back at him, completely uncomprehendingly. Marc showed no sign of panic, which would have made more sense, but seemed completely resigned to it. My brain had jammed and I couldn't think my way through this. Finally, it was James who recovered first.

"Fewul?"

"Also gone. I got no response when I called him to me, which means he's been recalled, because he's supposed to respond to his master regardless of the location of the crystals."

"But only Fewul's master can call it back, unless they have the Seventh Sorcerer and a Maahoo player handy," James pointed out, "and both of those things would be in short supply for the other side."

Marc shrugged. "All true, but the fact remains that the Beast of Magic and the Hero Crystal are gone."

"Didn't you order Fewul to guard the crystal while you slept?" James asked.

"Yep," said Marc monotonously.

"So the only way that the crystal could have been taken was if Fewul was recalled first," said James, logical as ever in the face of a problem.

Marc blinked—it was the first sign of expression he'd shown since sitting down. "I guess so, but that shouldn't be possible either."

"We don't know that," said James darkly. "After all, the Sien-Leoard Crystal is a very magically powerful tool. Arnold Hammerson may not have thought of every possibility, but he's not the one in charge anymore."

"Is that why you were so late?" I asked, finally managing to speak.

Marc shrugged. "I turned my room upside-down looking for it, yeah."

James stood up quickly. "Be back in a minute," he said, and he marched out of the dining room. Several pairs of eyes followed him, a few faces looking as though they were getting wind that something wasn't quite right, but mostly, the atmosphere didn't change.

"But even if Fewul could be recalled remotely," said Peter, managing to speak (all his good nature had evaporated too), "how could the crystal be snatched out of here? We have protection specifically designed to counter that."

"And Lucien would have been aware of every spell we performed," said Marc flatly. "He's probably smart enough to think of a way through it."

"But that can't be," said Peter, his eyes very round. "I mean, we set it up with everything in mind—"

"Pete," I said quietly, "Arnold Hammerson probably thought the same thing about that dome around the school, and we found a way through that."

Peter opened his mouth, couldn't think of anything to say for a few seconds, and then managed to croak, "So what are we gonna do? If Lucien got in here once, he's probably gonna come back, and he won't do it covertly next time."

Marc nodded slowly. "Probably true, but I just don't know what we can do. I—I just don't know."

Not up to Marc's usual level of quick-thinking, but I couldn't blame him. I was forcibly reminded of my own stunned state immediately after I had been wrested of the Sien-Leoard Crystal. Once you got used to that kind of power, having it taken away from you all at once made you feel greatly diminished. Fortunately for

3

Marc, my brain was moving a bit more quickly. What was most likely to be Lucien's next move? Well, if he had found a way to recall Fewul with the Sien-Leoard Crystal (probable, given the evidence) and he had stolen the Hero Crystal, which would now have taken the form of the Sorcerous Crystals, his next course of action seemed obvious.

"We need to get in touch with the Woodwards," I told them, looking around the dining room for our one remaining source of magic, half expecting her to have fainted since the last time I had laid eyes on her, but Natalie was still perfectly unharmed, eating her breakfast at a table with Jessica, Felicity and Stella. "If they still have their magic, they might be able to stop this before it's too late."

James returned to the table just then, looking cautiously relieved. "The Light Crystal is still here," he told us, "and so is the box with the Villain Crystal in it. I suppose he could have tried to get it out of there, but there's no way to check."

"John reckons we should contact the Woodwards," Peter told him.

James nodded. "If they didn't take us seriously before, hopefully they will now."

"If they still have their magic," I reiterated. "They won't respond if they don't, 'cause obviously they'll be unconscious."

"John, how do we get in touch with them?" Marc asked me, showing me his empty palms. "Even if they've still got their magic, I don't."

He had his back to Natalie, so I jabbed my thumb over his shoulder to make him look around. Peter and James followed our gazes, but Peter frowned.

"If she's still okay, surely the others are too," he said hopefully.

"Maybe, but I wouldn't bet on that," said James, and now he frowned too. "Surely, Lucien would know that we would notice the absence of the Hero Crystal and Fewul immediately, so he wouldn't keep Natalie conscious just to keep us in the dark. I suppose he may be trying to prevent a weather change, but if that had been me, I would have kept Amelia rather than Natalie; that would have served the dual purposes of knocking out all our means of magic at the one time, and leaving only the weakest Sorcerer with power for the next twenty-four hours."

"I'm glad you're on our side," said Peter weakly, staring numbly at him. "You could be a diabolical evil genius, you know that?"

"Unfortunately, so could Lucien," said James, getting back to his feet, "and he's got a lot more evil going for him than I do. Come on, we'd better let Natalie know what's going on."

* * *

By lunch time that day, we were fairly sure of the worst. We had pulled both Natalie and Stella aside and quietly told them what we had already worked out, but the six of us agreed at that point not to let anyone else know until we were completely sure, as it would probably cause mass panic—and in the meantime, we couldn't afford to spend a lot of time thinking about it. Natalie had first tried to communicate telepathically with each of the other Sorcerers, including Amelia (even a broken mind could possibly be steered in the right direction if Natalie gave her the right thoughts), but no responses were forthcoming. She also tried communicating telepathically with May, but that also failed (unsurprisingly, given that Honnie telepathy seemed to depend on proximity, and May was probably on another continent). She then repeated the process, trying to contact anyone at all in the Woodward base, but of course, since no one else had magic of their own, they had no way of hearing her. Finally, out of sheer desperation, she tried to contact Lucien himself (if he was holding the Sien-Leoard Crystal, he would probably get it), but if he did receive the message, he chose to ignore it.

Next, on James's advice, she tried to trace the location of the Hero Crystal (even though we knew it didn't exist anymore). Then, when that didn't work, she tried to trace the Sorcerous Crystals, and this was where things really started to get weird. Every bit of tracing magic she attempted revealed that the Sorcerous Crystals were, in fact, still in the form of the Hero Crystal, and furthermore, said crystal was sitting atop Marc's bedside drawers. There was nothing there in reality, though, visible or otherwise. The crystal hadn't been shrunken or been forced to take on an alternate form either. Finally, we were forced to accept that rather than creating fake crystals as Moran had once done (which would have been a lot easier), Lucien had chosen to thoroughly confuse us instead.

"I think I understand his game," James said slowly, slumping on Marc's bed, "but I can't think why he's going about things this way, unless he's got a camera in here somewhere and is enjoying watching us scrambling around."

"Assume he's not," said Marc, "what other game do you think he's playing?"

"Well, he's not trying to give us a false sense of security," said James, "otherwise he probably would have created a fake Hero Crystal—"

"That would only have stood up until Marc needed to use it," said Stella, "or until he had to use Fewul. Lucien probably knew it wouldn't take long, so he saved us some time."

"Perhaps, but on the other hand, he clearly intended to make us waste more time by fluffing around, trying to work out what the hell he's done," said James. "Also, he may want to induce panic, but again, that could only be for his entertainment. He's taken a lot of our power but he's deliberately left us with some too. I've got the Light Crystal; Nat, you've still got your magic, and to top it off, we still have the ability—and maybe the time—to run for it."

Peter shook his head. "James, you're a lot smarter than me, but even I know that's a bad idea. Besides, who says Lucien won't just turn up here in the next hour? So what if Nat's still got magic—he would probably give himself short odds in that contest."

"Why is running such a bad idea?" Marc asked. "I know we'll be out in the open, and it'll be pretty hard for Nat to create an entirely new base on her own, but we're no safer here than we were in the old Woodward base when Hall got in. The fact is, we've been breached, and when that happens, it's time to go."

"Plus, he knows exactly where to find us," I added, "and there are too many places in this base where he could corner people. In hindsight, we didn't really design it very well to hold up under an attack."

James considered my words for several seconds while the rest of us watched him. Finally, he said, "Marc, is there any way Natalie could use her magic to retrieve at least one of those things we used in the school fight?"

He was referring to the object I had privately called my hero device, because it hadn't been given a properly assigned name. Those things had been very powerful—so much so that Marc had vanished them all after the fight, in case they fell into the wrong hands later. I didn't think they could be particularly useful now, though; those things couldn't stand up against the Sien-Leoard Crystal, particularly when it was being used by a bloke who knew exactly how the hero devices worked.

Marc, meanwhile, shook his head. "I suppose she could create one from scratch, but the ones I made are history—at least, I think so. Besides, what good could they do? If you're thinking of standing up and fighting against Lucien, plus any Hammerhearts if he's joined up with them, what chance do we have?"

James shrugged. "Probably none, but some arms are better than no arms. Look, here's what I think we ought to do. Lucien could turn up here at any point, that may be true, but something tells me that he won't. I think we need to take that chance because if we run out into the open, it'll be a lot harder for us to prepare for what might be coming. In the meantime, Nat, you're going to have to do a lot in the next little while. Since I'm fairly sure the crystal was taken in the night while Marc was sleeping, that's probably how long you've got before your magic goes the way of the other Sorcerers'. You need to unlock the control room, in case we need to make a quick getaway, and then you need to try to think of any new ways to protect all of us. Untraceability can't be relied on anymore because Lucien knows how to get around it, so you'll have to be creative."

Natalie looked utterly terrified by all the responsibility that had suddenly been thrust upon her. "How am I supposed to think like that when I could pass out at any moment?" she squeaked.

"All the more reason why you should stay somewhere where you can be relatively comfortable," said James, trying to smile comfortingly at her. "You just do whatever you need to do to help your concentration, and the rest of us will help you as much—or as little—as you want. Right, guys?" he added, looking most particularly at me, Marc and Stella; all three of us nodded.

"What about the rest of us?" Peter asked, his face very pale.

James sighed. "The rest of us have to make everyone else in here aware of what's going on. We need to try any and all methods of getting in touch with the outside world, without actually going out there, and if we have to sacrifice some of our security in the process, we'll just have to cop it. We don't want to be delusional about our position, like the Woodwards have been on more than one occasion —you can see what good it did them in the end."

So Marc stood up during lunch, at which everyone in the base was present, and announced that a meeting would take place in the lounge room immediately after lunch, to get started whenever everyone got over there. The atmosphere in the dining room had already been a little subdued, as though many people were beginning to feel the foreboding which I, and those others who knew what was going on, had been feeling all morning. The idea of a full-house meeting beginning straight after lunch (as soon as possible, in other words) did not help the situation.

And when it got going, the meeting itself seemed to solidify the tension into something from which nobody was immune. A few questions were asked about what Lucien had been thinking, leaving us with this window of opportunity to act, but most people were far more concerned with what we could do with the time we had left.

"As to that, Natalie will make the most of her magic while she can," Marc said, nodding at her, "but other than that, I'm struggling to think. James?"

"Well, I tried to send an email to my dad before we got started here," he said, "telling him what had happened here and that the Woodwards are probably on the verge of losing their magic. The email wouldn't send because our security system thought I was trying to leak sensitive information about what's going on in here outside the base."

Peter swore. "And to think, we designed it to protect us against traitors, and the computer itself stabs us in the back. What else can we do?"

"Well, as you all know, one of the Sorcerers—I think it might have been you, Marc—installed a blanket ban on mobile phones when we got here. There's a spell on the inside walls of the base which disrupts all transmissions on the inside, while through putting to the other side for transmissions on the outside. It means that the spell won't disrupt transmissions that pass near the base on the outside," he added, noticing several confused looks. "I think now the time has come to lift that ban; it hardly matters if the Hammerhearts intercept our phone calls now. Natalie, do you think you can lift the enchantment?"

"I can try," she said nervously, lapsing into concentration.

"Should we move the base away from Chopville?" asked Katie. "Maybe even away from Australia?"

James considered the idea. "It's something to think about, but I would be worried that if it doesn't work and we need to make a run for it, we'll be in a totally unfamiliar place. At least if we're on the run in the Chopville district, we'll know where the good hiding places are."

"Also, the way teleportation works, Lucien will be able to come straight in here regardless of where the base is," Marc added.

"In that case, definitely no," said James firmly.

"Okay, mobile phones should work now," said Natalie loudly, looking extremely relieved.

But it seemed that nobody had their phones with them. The moment the words were out of her mouth, a mass exodus took place so that a minute later (by the time the logjam in the hallway outside had cleared), there were only a handful of people left in the lounge room, of which I was one.

"Should I try to lower the security for the Internet as well?" Natalie asked James. "I could probably do it—I helped Marc design that content screener."

James shook his head. "Time is too precious. If the girls can't get my dad on the phone, email certainly won't do any good."

And so it didn't. Within half an hour, it could be confirmed that although many people were able to reach friends and family on the outside, we received nothing but radio silence from the Woodward base. By now, this hardly came as a surprise. There was a very good chance that all the Sorcerers in there were unconscious now, but that didn't explain the overall silence. What made me most particularly worried was that I had been inside their base on one occasion (only a week ago, although it felt a lot longer) and although I hadn't seen all of it, there had been enough evidence to suggest that the place could remain operational without depending on the presence of a Sorcerer (not unlike our base, I supposed). Even if they had lost their magic, why was no one else responding?

* * *

Precious as time may be, it was impossible to shake the feeling that we were wasting it. Marc and James ended up spending most of the afternoon in the control room, moving the base around Chopville and using the displays to observe what was going on outside, alert for the slightest sign that trouble may soon be heading our way. They had also taken the Light and Villain Crystals (the latter of which was unusable) and had agreed to hold them from now on. This came only after Natalie had eventually snapped at them (and everyone else) to leave her alone so she could concentrate. So far, she had come up with devices that could spring up shields around each of us (both physical and magical) but unfortunately, they were spells with which Lucien would be familiar. Creatively, she was struggling big-time, and since all our suggestions were making things worse rather than better, she had eventually retired to her bedroom to work alone.

It meant that the rest of us had no way of helping the situation and could do nothing except sit around and wait for word (or trouble, whichever came first). I had gone down to the control room three times already today, bored and restless in equal measure, and found myself repeatedly returning to the lounge room where most of the others were, equally anxious. Siobhan had turned on the news feed and was peddling through article after article, perhaps looking for something positive as a distraction, and she was being watched on by several others. The television had also been turned on for the first time (that I had seen anyway), and in the half-hour prior to dinner, it was tuned to the evening news. I was staring absent-mindedly at the screen, which was halfway through a weather report, when everything changed.

Without any warning whatsoever, as though the station itself hadn't known what was about to happen, the weather report suddenly vanished and was immediately replaced by an entirely new story. Several other people who had been paying attention to the television, perhaps intent on seeing how cold it was going to get tonight, cried out when they recognised the person who now dominated the screen.

"This is an emergency broadcast," a pre-recorded voice (with an American accent) announced, and then Lucien Moran began to speak.

"Sorry to pull you away from your regular programming, wherever you may be or at whatever time you're watching this," he said, smiling pleasantly at the camera. His pleasantness was a lot more convincing than Arnold Hammerson's had been, perhaps because Lucien had always been a pleasant person. "This won't take long—only twenty-four hours," he added, and chortled. "This short message will be shown on a continuous loop on every station around the world so that everyone will get a chance to see it. I would like to take this opportunity to inform you all of a few things that have happened in recent days which, up until now, we thought it best to keep quiet.

"Firstly, a good many of you probably recognise me as a man who was painted by the Hammerhearts as a criminal. My name is Lucien Moran and I was cursed into becoming a Hammerheart, and then similarly freed from the curse so that I became good again. I'm sure you can understand the reason why Arnold Hammerson considered me someone worth hunting after that kind of treachery. However, there has been a shift in governance within the Hammerheart ranks in recent days which has changed the situation.

"Many of you will have heard the rumours floating around that Arnold Hammerson was killed earlier this week, bested by a group of people closely affiliated with the Woodwards. Some of you may even have believed that such a ludicrous thing could actually happen. Well, I can confirm that in this case, the truth is indeed stranger than fiction. Yes, Arnold Hammerson is dead, and I know so because I was there when it happened. I'll spare you the details but suffice it to say that by the time the job was done, you could have painted your car with the contents of his head.

"I tell you this because Arnold was a practical man who had many contingency plans. The group of which I was previously a part knew what most of these plans were and were able to get around them, but one of the last things he had planned was that if he should die, I would take over his role. Why he chose me instead of his own daughter, I can only guess, but it's not up to me to argue with his thinking. I intend to continue his good work and I intend to do an even better job than he would have, just 'cause you know, I like to think I'm a more measured man than he was.

"But there is one other thing I need to tell you, and this is directed to those of you who are still holding onto hope that the Sorcerers, the Woodwards and Fletchers, may come to save you from the inevitability. You all know, of course, that there are certain ways that magic can be taken from one person and given to another. My father was guilty of performing such an act once, and the transfer of power from the Hammersons to the Fletchers was particularly public knowledge. Let it be known, here and now, that the Woodwards and Fletchers will not come to save you this time."

He stepped aside so that the camera had an unobstructed view of the wall behind him. Frederic and Lillian Woodward, and Brian and Alice Fletcher, were lined along the foot of it, all four of them unconscious, the implication clear and far worse than we had imagined.

"That is only four of six Sorcerers, as you can see," Lucien resumed, stepping back in front of the camera. "The two youngest Sorcerers are still on the loose, but that's of no concern to me— they'll be back with their families in short order. I know so because the magic of these four is presently being transferred to—yep, you guessed it—me. I have succeeded in doing the one thing that Arnold Hammerson had wanted to do so badly, the one thing that would have made him invincible. His dream will very soon be realised, and each of you has two options: Accept it willingly, or accept it unwillingly. I don't think there will be any major changes to policy; it just means that you'll have to get used to looking up to a different bloke in future."

He considered for a moment, and then said, "I think that's about it. I'll come back on TV in this manner again if I have anything to add down the track—I find this to be a rather convenient way of getting my point across."

He smiled pleasantly again, and then the screen went black for a second. When it returned, it was only the same message being repeated. I stared numbly at the screen, watching Lucien's lips moving but no longer hearing his words. This was so much worse than we had realised. Most people were, like me, too stunned to outwardly react to what we had just seen. Only Erica and Rebecca were able to jump up and dash out of the room, probably heading for the control room and Natalie's bedroom respectively.

It was only when the message began playing for a third time that Siobhan was able to pick up the remote and turn the television off. A couple of people protested, but she merely said, "It's the same message."

With the screen blank, the rest of us were able to collect our thoughts more quickly. Beside me, Peter had gone about as white as a sheet of paper. He and I stared at each other for several seconds before I managed to say, "We're in big trouble."

Marc, James and Natalie came into the room then, shepherded by Erica and Rebecca, and their appearance seemed to break the overall paralysis. Everyone began speaking at once, the noise getting louder and louder until James cupped his hands around his mouth and positively bellowed for everyone to shut up.

"Look," he said, much more quietly when he had silence, "I'd like to see the message for myself, if you don't mind, but from what Erica told me on the way up, the only part of this we didn't see coming was that he actually got inside their base and captured them. In hindsight, it shouldn't be surprising, since he had no trouble getting in ours."

"But that's 'cause he's been in here," said Marc numbly. "Was he ever in the Woodwards' base?"

James shrugged. "Maybe so, maybe no. The only part of this that seriously concerns me is that our parents may well have been captured too, which would explain why we couldn't get in touch with them, but let's try not to worry about that just now. For us, I don't think the game has changed."

He turned the television back on to the message, which was still looping, and he, Marc and Natalie watched it from start to finish in horror. It was no better on its third rotation—it wouldn't have been any better on its thousandth rotation.

"I can't think of anything good about that," said Marc when it was done, and James had turned the screen back off.

"Neither can I," said James, standing up, "but I don't think it makes things much worse either. It just means that he will come here for us, because he'll want to show the world that he has the other two Sorcerers as well. Do you think there was any reason why he told the world that Amelia got away? We know she couldn't possibly have run for it."

"Especially if she's unconscious," Peter added. "People don't generally get very far in that state. Maybe it was a ruse for our benefit—he would have expected that we would eventually see the message. In fact, maybe he chose to show it to us at that moment, knowing we had the TV on."

If the silence wasn't charged before, it definitely was now as people digested what Peter was suggesting. Finally, it was Jessica who said, "You think he did what Hall did?"

Peter shrugged. "I don't know, but in the event that he did: Lucien, you're a coward. Stop spying on us and show yourself."

Several people cringed, everyone waiting to see if there would be any response. I didn't expect there to be—Lucien wouldn't be quite ready to give up his advantage so quickly—and of course, nothing happened.

James sighed. "Well, if he is doing that, we can use those ghost walls to stop him. Of course, those were his idea in the first place, so maybe they won't be so useful against him. Blimey, I'm only just starting to realise what a disadvantage we're at here, what with Lucien being so familiar with us."

"I think we should just accept that if he's watching, he's watching," said Stella suddenly. "Look, you're probably right; it doesn't mean a lot has changed for us. If anything, it confirms that now we know for sure that we don't have a lot of time. It probably also means that Natalie has to keep her ideas to herself so that Lucien can't plan for them in advance."

"Which by extension means that we can't help you," said James, glancing anxiously at our one remaining source of magic. "Geez, we are in serious trouble."

"So what are we supposed to do?" Rebecca asked anxiously.

All eyes immediately shifted to Natalie, our only chance of survival now. She looked more panicky than ever, and James seemed to notice this at the same time I did. Trying to smile naturally, he said, "First thing you do, Nat, is stop thinking about it for now. It's dinner time now, so let's all go eat."

Chapter 2: Thanks for One of the Weirdest Conversations of My Life

It was easily one of the worst nights of my life. I even put it slightly ahead of that night in Germany, the one which had cost Serena, Jane and Moran (my biological father) their lives, because at least then, although terrible things had been happening all around us, at least I didn't have to sit around waiting for them. The night of August 27 dragged on excruciatingly, everyone sitting around restlessly, waiting for something to happen one way or another. A few people may have dozed off from time to time but for the most part, the situation was just too uncomfortable for that.

For me, much of the evening and very early morning was like the previous afternoon, alternating between the control room, the lounge room, and occasionally other rooms in the base if I couldn't stand to be surrounded by all those anxious people. Marc, James and occasionally Peter (he was about as mobile as me, although we didn't stay together as an unspoken rule) were still in the control room, discussing our options over and over. Those two, basically the brains of our operation now that Lucien and Amelia were out (I supposed Stella could have counted, but her routine tonight had been much the same as most other people), normally agreed on most things; but they couldn't seem to find a point of consensus this time. Marc still wanted to abandon ship while we had the chance, and James still wanted to prepare in the comfort and with the resources of our only refuge.

"What resources?" Marc said scornfully at about half past twelve in the morning. "What refuge? James, are you sure you're not as delusional as the Woodwards were when Hall was terrorising us?"

James shook his head. "Believe me, Marc, I'm making a deliberate effort not to be, but if we do run for it, we have to consider what we do next. You may be right about Lucien finding us more easily here, but being out in the open isn't going to hide us from his tracing magic, even if we are untraceable. Also, there are twenty-seven of us; we'll be a glaring target if we stay together, and horribly vulnerable if we split up."

Marc bit his lip, unsure how to continue arguing. I could see in his face that he understood that James was right, but it didn't change the fact that if we stayed here, Lucien could just teleport back in here and round us up like sheep; and he could probably do it so quickly that we wouldn't even have a chance to think about running for it. It was a horrible dilemma, but not one that could be shirked—a lot of lives depended on it. I looked hopelessly from Marc, to Peter, to James and back again, wishing more than ever that I had some magic at my disposal; I would probably be no better in my decision-making than these two, but at least I wouldn't be a useless bystander.

In terms of power, Natalie was still our only hope, because James had tried to use the Light Crystal on numerous occasions now. For whatever reason, he couldn't get it to work; whether because his thoughts weren't good enough (I doubted that if he were trying to protect everyone in the base) or because our odds of survival were just too long for this kind of magic to beat (far more likely, I reckoned), I knew not. Unfortunately, Natalie had become almost as useless; although her magic was still operable, her ability to use it had been severely impaired by her panic. When James had asked her to create a standard bludginator, all she'd been able to conjure was something that looked like a Hammerheart instrument, except that it was made of plastic and contained no magic whatsoever. There was no nice way to say it: At the most important point of her life, she had frozen like a deer in the headlights.

Strained and stressed beyond endurance, knowing that all our lives depended on her magic, knowing said magic would probably be snatched away from her at some unknown point only hours from now, all her insecurities about her magical ineptitude prior to the school fight came rushing back. She flew into a panic attack, her second one that week, although this one contained a lot less screaming and a lot more hyperventilating, followed by a lot of tears. Marc and James had backed off, telling her, as they had in the afternoon, to take her time and do whatever she needed to do to regain her concentration, but she had snapped at them and shut herself in her room for the rest of the night. That had been about three hours ago, and although she may have been performing magic in there (surely she had calmed down a little by now), nobody had seen her since; and although both Stella and I really wanted to go in there and help her, Marc and James insisted that we would probably only succeed in pressuring her all over again.

That was all well and good for Stella, but I was having a hard time with it. Whether or not I could help her, I didn't know, but I thought that I could probably make her feel a little better if I had the chance, and maybe that would have a flow-on effect to her magic. Also, it made me feel particularly lousy to sit back and let her deal with this on her own, and even more so than it would have at any other time since we were now an item. That was a thought I was still getting used to: All week, whenever I had thought of it, I had felt a warm glow of pride inside me, and the time the two of us had spent alone together had been—there was no non-corny way to say it—like heaven.

The thought didn't give me a lot of cheer tonight, though. I doubted that any thought would under these circumstances. Resigned to remaining in limbo for the time being, and sick of watching Marc and James arguing about it, I left them yet again at around one in the morning and returned to the main building, now alone. The place was still lit up like a birthday cake, meaning that as before, most people were still awake. When I got inside, I found that while a good many of them were still congregated in the lounge room, making much less noise than usual (even Harry and Simon had gone quiet—incredible), plenty were wandering around as aimlessly as I was, feeling an oncoming storm and unable to do anything to get out of its path.

I went around to the gym at first, considering working off some of my restless energy, then thought better of it—who knew if I would need it soon. I sat briefly in the lounge room, listening to the fragmented conversation and watching the pale faces. Erica sat nearest to me, biting her fingernails and looking much less unruffled than her usual elegant self. I didn't last long in there—the atmosphere was just too much. I instead went around to the games room, where I found Darcy playing a game of pool against himself; that pretty much summed up the evening, I thought. I sat down in there and watched him unseeingly, neither of us speaking to the other. Within ten minutes, Darcy got bored and left, so that it was just me alone in there.

And within a few minutes of Darcy leaving, I found myself wondering why the hell I was sitting here. If I wanted to be alone, why didn't I just go upstairs to my room? Well, because I didn't want to fall asleep, assuming such a thing was possible; also, I wasn't sure I really did want to be alone. What would have been ideal was if we could all pull together and be supportive in this nervous time, and many of the others felt the same, but no one seemed to know how to make it work—the lounge room over there was a good example of that. Several people came into the games room while I was there (Sophie, Dean, George, Robyn and Siobhan), looked around at their options, and promptly left again. Jessica came in too, and when she saw me sitting here, the two of us chatted briefly, but it was an awkward conversation that went nowhere, neither of us knowing how to lighten the mood; she hadn't stayed long.

About five minutes after she'd gone, Lena came in, looking lost, scared and confused all at the same time. She also looked quite as aimless as everyone else; she stared blankly around at the various activities in the room, not even noticing me until the third time she had looked in my direction.

"Oh, hi," she said, apparently caught off-guard.

"Hey," I said, not altogether enthusiastically, only part of which I could attribute to the current circumstances. It was impossible to have a conversation with Lena without remembering that she had once been attracted to me, that she may still be attracted at least a little bit (she had implied so more than once since she had begun dating Marc, something that may not have happened if I hadn't deliberately set her free), and that although I hadn't seriously considered dating her, I couldn't deny my own purely carnal attraction to her. It was also very difficult to look at that incredible body without remembering how it had looked with no clothes on, a sight I would never forget. It was all sorts of wrong, particularly now that I had the girl I'd always wanted, but what can I say? I'm as hardwired as any other guy.

"What are you doing?" she asked flatly, staring through the window over my shoulder (it was completely black out there) and seeming not to care how I answered. This conversation was probably going to go the same way as the one with Jessica, I supposed.

"Nothing that can't be observed," I said wearily. "Are you okay?"

I couldn't stop myself from asking because, apart from the anxiety seemingly felt by the walls themselves, she looked like she was preoccupied with other things as well. It could have been my imagination, and it could have been a really stupid question (none of us were ultimately okay), but she didn't seem to mind being asked.

"I dunno," she said slowly, still staring out the window, seeing nothing (there was nothing to see), "I just—" She broke off, her brow furrowing, considering what she was saying—or perhaps what she was thinking. Finally, she said, "Is Marc still in the control room?"

"Probably," I said, losing interest—I didn't want to think about what Marc and James were doing any more than I had to. "I'm not sure that he and James will leave it until breakfast, and even then I'm not sure."

Lena shrugged and continued to look at the glass, while I observed her. All kinds of wrong, John, I told myself again, and somewhere a couple of floors above me, who knew what state Natalie was in. None of that changed the fact that I was within arm's reach of one of the sexiest young ladies I would probably ever see in my life, and even in profile, she was great to look at. It also didn't change the fact that she had stuff on her mind, and my automatic instinct—the thing that held me in place instead of motivating me to get up and leave her to her own devices—was to try to help her with whatever was going on.

"Why do you ask?" I persisted after several seconds of silence.

She looked sideways at me then, a speculative look I knew all too well. I instantly regretted my last words; the last thing I wanted to do was give Lena any reasons to start causing trouble in my love life—I already knew just how capable she was in that department. One of the most difficult conversations I'd ever had with a girl had been when I'd told Lena that she and I couldn't date, but I'd persisted with it because I'd known it was the right thing to do. I had subconsciously kept Lena as the backup option in case I couldn't get Natalie, and I'd been so ashamed of myself that I'd let her go at a time when I really couldn't have gotten Natalie; but now that I finally had Natalie, I didn't want Lena to think that there was even a small chance for her with me.

"I don't really know if I should say," she said cagily, turning away from the window and facing back into the room. She yawned and stretched as she did this, giving me a very direct view of her body shape as she did this. Against my will, I felt a stirring down there, and I had to shift slightly to make sure she didn't see anything. Of course, she saw the shift, which was just as bad.

"Well, okay," I said, as indifferently as I could. She knew exactly what game she was playing, and after having dealt with her on and off for six months now, I had a pretty good idea what my options were, and giving in to her wasn't one of them.

Option one: Be firm and tell her, in no uncertain terms, that she was wasting her time. I didn't think that would work, though; I had already done that once, and if I had anything to worry about now, that proved it had only been a temporary solution. Also, we were both supposed to be in relationships, and if that fact alone didn't stop her, telling her how I was committed to Natalie probably wouldn't do any better, especially since Lena already knew me to be the type who would cheat on his girlfriend under the right circumstances.

Option two: Treat her with absolute indifference and hope that she would give up on her own. I had taken that approach for months, and it had partially worked (she had turned her attention to Marc, after all), but since we were here now, it seemed not to be enough.

Option three: Allow her to continue baiting me until she got some sort of reaction, either another one-night-stand, something more serious, or something much more resentful.

This dilemma wasn't quite as bad as whether or not to stay in the base, and that one could supersede this one, but as before, I just couldn't think what to do for the best. Fortunately, in the time I had pondered this, Lena had been staring straight ahead of her, once again seeming to see nothing. Still not looking at me, she said, "Have you ever wished that someone would just take a decision out of your hands because you don't know what to do about it?"

Was she reading my mind?

I considered the question carefully, trying to guess where she was going with this line and honestly having no idea. Cautiously, I said, "Not really; I prefer to make my own decisions. I usually dread when they're taken out of my hands."

Except when Natalie told me how she thought she might be in love with me—that one had been taken out of my hands and turned out okay. In the case of Serena kissing me, not so much.

Lena sighed. "That sounds mature. I've never really thought about it, but I guess in a real dilemma, I'm a little scared of taking responsibility."

What was it with the word 'dilemma' this evening?

"Good thing you don't have to worry about making too many big decisions, then," I said, thinking I now understood what might be going on. If she was still wondering what Marc was doing, she was probably thinking about the almighty decision he was dealing with. "I found that a lot of decisions were taken out of my hands when I lost the crystal, and it didn't make me feel better—it made things a lot worse. Then again, you're not the first person to be intimidated by responsibility. I guess we're a little different that way," I added before I could stop myself, feeling a little hopeful. That may not have been the most subtle of discouragements I could have offered (about as subtle as a sledgehammer, really), but it seemed to fit.

"Complementary," she said, looking at me again, and she was smiling—it hadn't worked. Then again, if she thought I was being complimentary, she mustn't have understood my meaning unless— unless she meant 'complementary'. My stomach fell—she almost certainly did mean that.

"What decision are we talking about here?" I asked, my mouth going a little dry. If talking about the gloom and doom of our little army was the only way to avoid talking about us, I would settle for it.

She hesitated, glancing back at the window, and I held my breath as I waited. When she spoke, though, my heart sank to somewhere around my naval.

"I think I may have made a mistake," she said slowly, as though measuring each word she said before speaking it. "I'm really not sure, though, so I don't know if I should just accept it or if I should try to fix it."

"And it's a dilemma because you don't know if it was a mistake or not?"

"Exactly."

And if it had to do with Marc, it could only mean…I groaned inwardly.

"If it's not that obvious, it's probably okay," I said quickly, "so you can probably accept it the way it is."

"But what if I'm wrong? What if by the time I know for sure, it's too late to fix?"

"What if fixing it turns out to be a mistake and you end up even worse off?"

I was speaking through my arse, not daring to be any more obvious in case she wasn't talking about Marc, but knowing all too well that the advice I was giving her wasn't what I would have given her if I didn't have a vested interest. If she believed she had made a mistake in dating Marc, then that probably meant that she also believed she should chase me again. I could not have that. Never mind being a good friend and giving the best advice; I could not have that.

Lena sighed. "I know you're right, but I also know that I'm right too. That's why I'd like it to be taken out of my hands, never mind how childish that is."

I shrugged and got to my feet, unable to take any more of this. "If that's the case, you'd better not take too long working out if it's a mistake. I gotta go; there's something I need to do."

"Okay, thanks for listening," she said, smiling at me, "but don't be surprised if I need to talk some more about this later."

"Right, and thanks for one of the weirdest conversations of my life."

She grinned and went back to her contemplation of the games room, while I strode out the door and into the hallway, past the open doors of the dining room (which was empty) and stopped in the small foyer from which radiated the hallway containing my old first-floor bedroom, a door out to the yard, an elevator and a set of stairs. That had been a very unsettling episode with Lena, and right now, there was only one person who could restore my sense of self-respect. I had no intention of telling her what had just happened, not because I had necessarily done anything wrong but because in her current state, there was no way she could take it well.

I looked up at the small screen above the elevator doors and saw that it was already in motion, coming down through the second floor towards the first. I stepped back from the doors and waited for them to open. When they did, I found myself face-to-face with my adoptive brother.

"Hey man," he said, grinning weakly, and then it quickly faded. "Geez, what's up with you?"

"A moment," I said, stepping into the lift and grabbing his arm before he could step back out. When the doors slid shut, it was just the two of us in there, and the relative privacy was an enormous relief. I pushed the button for the third level, and then when the lift had risen a little, pressed the button to stop it midway between floors.

"What's up?" Peter repeated, watching me curiously.

"I've just had a conversation with Lena," I said, speaking quickly. "She's—I think she's thinking about breaking up with Marc and going after me again."

Peter whistled. "Man, how do you do it?"

"I dunno. If I knew, I'd quit it."

"Only after you've taught me how first."

"Trust me, you don't want this; not if you wanna hang onto Rebecca anyway."

"Oh," he said slowly, comprehension hitting, "is that what this is about? You think she might get in the way of you and Nat?"

"It wouldn't surprise me," I said, feeling despair creeping up. "She didn't actually say as much, but I already know that if she decides to try again, she won't let Natalie stop her any more than Serena did."

"Because she already knows that you're capable of cheating," he finished my thought from earlier.

"I don't think she realises just how different this is, though," I said. "Don't take this the wrong way, but Natalie is so different from Serena."

Peter could take that the wrong way, given that he had once had a crush on Serena before he'd started dating her friend Kylie. In hindsight, if Serena had only been interested in Peter instead of me, so much of this (perhaps including Serena's death) could have been prevented. Peter certainly would have treated her better than I had.

Oblivious to these thoughts, Peter shrugged. "Maybe, but if you really believe your relationship with Nat is strong enough to withstand Lena, why are you so worried?"

"Because Natalie's been cheated on once before, remember? Her self-security must have taken a hit from that. Also, she's read plenty out of Lena's mind before it was protected—she knows what she's capable of."

"Hmm," Peter muttered, considering the problem. "Well, I honestly don't know what you can do. Lena's certainly not short on determination, and she's got a lot to work with. If Natalie really is insecure, there might be a problem, no matter how much you behave yourself. Isn't that more or less what happened to you and Serena anyway?"

"It is," I agreed. "I probably would never have done that with Lena if Serena hadn't been so sure I would. Insecure girls are so hard to deal with."

"I guess so," he muttered. "So have you got any idea what to do about it?"

"For now, I'm going to spend some time with Natalie, and never mind what Marc and James say," I said indignantly. "I'm not gonna tell her about this but just being with her ought to make me feel better about myself. As for Lena, I'll wait and see what she does, but if she does break up with Marc, I guess I'll have to talk to her about this—try and stop it before it gets started. If she really cares about me, she won't ruin the best thing in my life."

"She won't think like that," he said. "If she really cares about you, she'll try to prove that she cares more than Natalie does, so that unless Natalie's ready to fight for you as well, you may not get a say in what happens."

"Screw that; I'm not letting girls pick who I date anymore. I've tried that once and it didn't work."

"I hear ya," he laughed. "So, are you gonna let me off this thing or what?"

Unfortunately for Peter, the technology made that impossible. We instead rode back up to the third floor where I got off, and Peter then rode all the way back down for a second time. The third-floor hallway was empty and the bedrooms were silent. I supposed one or two people may have been in their rooms, as Peter must have been (unless he'd been with Natalie, but he would have looked a lot more shifty if he had), but most of them were probably still downstairs, waiting and not wanting to sleep. I could feel tiredness beginning to creep up on me now (it was after two o'clock and I'd been awake for about nineteen hours) but sleep would have to wait.

And in fact, I was only guessing that Natalie was really up here. I walked quietly down the hallway till I reached her door, listened for a few seconds, and after hearing nothing whatsoever inside or outside it, I quietly knocked and said, "Natalie, are you in there? Are you awake?"

After a few more seconds of silence, I heard her voice mutter in the affirmative—it was impossible to gauge her mood or wakefulness from one word alone. I waited, breath held, listening for the sound of her approaching the door to let me in, and when I heard nothing, I opened my mouth to say something. Before I could get any words out, though, the door lock clicked and the door opened a fraction, enough for me to push it open the rest of the way and slip inside.

It was pitch-black; Natalie had apparently been sitting in complete darkness, and she didn't bother putting on a light for my benefit. I knew where she was, though; squinting, I saw her shadow against the wall behind her bed. She seemed to be sitting on it, doing—I could only guess. I considered turning the light on, wanting to see her, but quickly decided against it—I could turn it on later, by which time she would hopefully be in a healthier state of mind. I instead felt my way along the wall, around her bedside drawers and onto the side of her bed, reaching out and finding her exactly where I'd expected her to be. Not only was her room an exact mirror of my own directly across the hall, but I'd been in this room enough times after dark during the last five nights that I hardly needed my eyes to get around anymore.

"How are you?" I asked quietly when I had her in my arms. 'Are you okay?'

She sniffed. "Honestly, a little vindicated."

"What?" I asked, wrong-footed. What was she even talking about?

"I knew I wasn't up to this being-a-Sorcerer business. Honestly, why they all thought I could do it—"

"Stop," I said softly, but there was no point being stern with her now—that ship had sailed. "Okay, it's clear you can't get it to work now. I get it; it's okay. I'm not here to make you do magic."

"I know," she said, and I could hear tears coming, "but it's not okay—it's not. The only reason it's not working is because I can't control my thoughts well enough, because I keep thinking about how out of my league I am here, and everyone's lives depend on it, and if I could only use magic to focus myself then I'd be okay, but if I could use magic to do that then I wouldn't need to do it at all—"

I could say nothing to make a single bit of difference, because everything she said was right, and unfortunately, I had too much experience dealing with tearful girls to know that words wouldn't calm her down. All I could do was squeeze her tightly, bringing her emotions to the top so that she could no longer articulate her words. She broke down then, crying harder than ever, and I just held her, waiting for the storm to pass, knowing it would eventually but having no idea how Natalie would feel afterwards.

"I am so pathetic," she choked after several immeasurable minutes, pulling back from me slightly and freeing one of her hands. "We're all gonna be captured and killed or tortured or cursed, and it'll be all my fault because I can't do anything right."

She snapped her fingers in the air between our faces, but nothing happened. She tried again, moving her hand sideways slightly so that a spark of light flickered from her fingers—I recognised the spell she was trying to perform, and would have been grateful for the light— except that a split second later, it was gone. She let out a frustrated grunt and tried a third time, moving her hand more forcefully. This time, a great big flame burst from her hand, shooting straight up to the ceiling and passing so close to my right cheek that my brain couldn't quite register the burning until a few seconds later.

I cried out in pain, letting go of Natalie and belatedly throwing myself away from the flame, which had already vanished. I slipped backwards off the bed and landed on my arse on the floor, the shock travelling all the way up my spine and making my jaws snap together. The resultant flexing of facial muscles caused my burnt cheek to flare up worse than ever, and I let out another involuntary cry, this time of agony. I leapt back to my feet, turned my back on the bed and headed for the opposite wall, knowing the bathroom was somewhere over there. I must have turned slightly to the left of where I'd meant to go, though, because I collided with the table in the middle of the room, causing me to go tumbling back to the floor, now with absolutely no idea where I was or which direction I was facing.

"Oh my God!" Natalie cried out, horrified and dismayed, and I heard her jump off the bed as I clambered back to my feet, feeling blindly for the table and finding only empty air in every direction.

I still had no idea where I was when Natalie and I collided with each other. She seemed to have some idea, though, because she grabbed my arm and pulled me along with her. I staggered along, feeling like I would trip at any moment, not being able to see where my feet were coming down, and all the while trying not to move a muscle anywhere above my jaw line—it was a hopeless endeavour. A few seconds later, however, Natalie flicked a switch on the wall, and the room filled with a light so bright that both our eyes were temporarily reduced to slits.

She let out a soft moan of despair as she gazed at my face. "I'm so sorry; let me fix—"

But I took a step back, disengaging from her and moving out of her reach. It was nothing personal, but I could see her panic-stricken face all too clearly. Any magic she performed now would do more harm than good, and I would rather it not be directed at my face.

"Water," I muttered apologetically, turning and heading into her small bathroom, leaving the door open so that she could follow—I didn't want to make her feel worse than she already did.

In the bathroom, I ran the tap and soaked the face washer beneath it, but before I touched it to my face, I got a good look at what had happened to me in the mirror before me. It wasn't pretty, but it could easily have been a lot worse. My cheek on the right-hand side of my face had turned very red, but the skin hadn't hardened, blackened, peeled or anything. I could still feel it, though, and it smarted when I placed the cold face washer over it, but within a minute or so, it began to feel quite soothing.

Natalie stood in the open doorway during all this, watching me with a desperate, pleading expression, apparently not daring to come any closer. When my cheek felt almost normal (although I knew it wouldn't look as such when I removed the face washer), I reached out with my free hand and took one of hers.

"It's okay," I said reassuringly. "Doesn't hurt anymore; doesn't even look too bad. It could have been a lot worse."

"Are you sure you don't want me to fix it up?" she whispered, her eyes huge in her beautiful face.

I very slowly shook my head. "Sorry, but if our positions were reversed, would you want me to fix it?"

"Yes, because you were always so much better with your magic than I am with mine, but I see your point. I'm so, so, so—"

"Don't worry about it," I said, turning to face her, letting go of her hand and putting my arm around her instead. She took this as I'd meant her to—an invitation to come closer. We embraced, a much better one than the one we'd had on the bed, partially because we could see each other but mostly because, despite what had just happened, there were no tears this time. Apparently, my forgiveness (as if it had ever been in doubt) had made her feel better about what she had done.

She pulled back slightly after a little while and gently removed the face washer from my hand. I opened my mouth to protest, unsure if I were ready for that yet, and then fell silent in confusion as she pressed and then held it against her lips. When she put it down on the edge of the basin, she leaned forward and very gently kissed my burnt cheek. Her lips were cool and slightly moist from the face washer, making the sensation quite remarkable. As a general rule, I preferred warm lips over cool ones, but on this occasion, Natalie had done it in a way that suited my burn perfectly.

I was deeply touched by the tenderness, but in spite of what had just happened (of the pain I would probably start feeling again very soon), I was also turned on by it. I took her in my arms again, both arms this time, and held her close to me—her reaction made it clear that she had been equally turned on by it. After a while, during which we both undressed and then re-dressed each other, we sat together on Natalie's bed and just cuddled.

We had spent some time doing this during the week, in those times when we wanted each other's company, but didn't have anything to talk about or an immediate desire for sex. I found this to be the height of peace, just being with Natalie, holding onto her, knowing that she wanted to be with me as much as I wanted to be with her, and not needing to fill the silence with mindless chatter. Not that I didn't like talking to her—I'd learnt more about her in these last few days than I'd known in the ten prior years of our friendship. I would have thought that this kind of activity (or inactivity, more like) would have been very boring, and it probably would have been with any other girl (who I probably would have been touching in a more sexual manner before long), but not Natalie. In point of fact, no time spent with Natalie seemed to be boring, no matter what we did. I smiled as I wondered how long it would last, forgetting in my post-coital pleasure that we may not have very long left.

At around five o'clock, by which time Natalie had dozed off with her head against my chest, my mind had turned back to Lucien and the inevitable attack, in whatever form it took. After all this time had passed, we were all still sitting ducks, just waiting for him to turn up and do his thing. The complete lack of activity was utterly incredible; now I found myself thinking that perhaps Marc was right. Surely, doing something had to be better than doing nothing. Of course, James would say that wasn't always the case, even if he had no idea what I was talking about. He would weigh up all the risks against the benefits, and how likely each risk or benefit was. If he had time, he would probably open a spreadsheet and crunch a few numbers on the subject.

We had to do something—anything was better than nothing, but of course, anything could have included a lot of things—which anything ought we to choose? How many anything's were there anyway? I didn't know, but there was one thing I did know: Natalie was still our best chance for survival, even if she used a fireball to light up a room. I also knew that under the right circumstances, she could respond positively to pressure. On Monday, when she and I had almost literally run into my former English teacher, now turned police commissioner, she had backed him into a corner and fought with such precision and determination that she probably could have matched it in a fight with either Amelia or Stella (theoretically, of course; Stella didn't have magic anymore). All I had to do was make her forget about the dire circumstances and the fact that she was pretty much alone and focus on the magic itself.

I gently nudged her awake, smiling in spite of myself as she slowly raised her head. It was hard not to feel affection for her, even when she did the most natural of things.

"Hey, how are you feeling?" I asked quietly. "Tired?"

"Did I fall asleep?" she yawned, not seeming to mind one way or another. When I nodded, she grinned sheepishly. "Sorry; I really shouldn't do that to you."

"I don't mind," I said truthfully. "It feels nice."

She slowly straightened into a proper sitting position, leaning on me for support all the while—something else that felt nice. When we were both sitting, still holding onto each other, we just stared into each other's eyes for several seconds. I could do that forever, except that it made us both self-conscious before too long.

"Thank you," she said quietly, leaning forward and kissing me on the cheek—the unburnt one this time. "You really know how to make me feel good about myself. Here—"

Before I could stop her, she touched her finger lightly to my right cheek. I tensed, expecting the flare of pain, and indeed I did feel something for a moment, but whatever it was had probably been mental because I felt it heal at her touch. I knew it had when she gently kissed that cheek, and the tingling I felt there had nothing to do with irritated skin.

"Hey, thanks," I said, grinning. "You did it."

"Yeah," she said, her own smile fading. "I guess I can do it when I feel good, but what else can I do? I have no idea what I can do that would make any difference. I know I've had magic longer than Lucien, but he's so much more creative than me; he's got all the ideas. He may even have Fewul with him, if it can be called with his crystal."

"All true," I agreed, and then hesitated. An idea had just occurred to me, one that could actually work if Lucien didn't know about it. Obviously if he knew, he would be able to undo it before exposing himself to it, but if it remained an unknown factor, as Arnold Hammerson had meant his greatest secret to be, it could be as effective as that should have been. But how could I convey it to Natalie without Lucien overhearing it, on the off chance that he was somehow watching? I considered the problem for a few more seconds before a second idea occurred to me, one similar to something I had once done with Lena (something which could have been extremely erotic if I hadn't made a stern point of keeping it all above board). I couldn't communicate with Natalie without the message possibly being intercepted, no matter how I did it, but if I could find a way to harness her magic and perform the spell myself...

"What are you thinking?" she asked suspiciously.

"I've had a couple of ideas," I said quietly. "Trouble is, one of them is just good enough to work, but if I tell you and Lucien turns out to be listening, he'll be able to undo it before coming in. There may be a way around that, but it'll involve you performing a very tricky spell which may not even exist."

"Am I allowed to know what that spell is?" she asked drily.

I nodded slowly. "See if you can wrap your head around this. You need to perform a spell which will allow me to use the magic from your crystal chip, without moving or removing the chip itself. I'm not sure if secondary links to the chip are even possible, but the best way to do this would be if I had access to magic."

Natalie looked very nervous by this. "No, I don't think that would work. Stella said a while ago that a Sorcerer can't use their magic to control another Sorcerer's magic. She was talking about the domination charm, I think, but if it's true that the magic has to come from the mind it belongs to, I don't think you'd be able to access it, no matter what spells I try to let you in."

But I still felt hopeful, because at her words, another idea had occurred to me. This one was based on the way that May had fed during the few days she had stayed here. The conveyer belt in the dining room, which provided food by scanning the minds of the people before it, hadn't recognised the different breed of brain, but May had been able to manipulate it into giving her what she wanted by taking complete control of someone else's mind. I didn't have a Honnie mind, though, which probably meant that any similar magic performed by humans would be too much like the domination charm to break through the crystal chip's protection, but it didn't change the fact that if Natalie had the right thoughts in her head, she could perform the magic, and the chip would have to respond to her because it was her will. I could think of only one way to do that.

"There is something else that might work," I said, "that'll mean you perform the magic yourself, and I may even be able to guide you in it. It would mean setting up a link between the two of us so that we can communicate telepathically. Would you be game enough to do that?"

Her mouth opened slightly in surprise as she considered my words. "But you know our minds are—"

"I know they're protected, but Sorcerers with protected minds can still communicate telepathically. I can't do anything like that now because I have no magic, but I don't think I need magic; I only need whatever magical antenna Sorcerers use to make it work. You may be able to give that to me."

"Really?" she said, and I could see hope beginning to dawn in her face. "We would be able to send thoughts to each other?"

"Yeah, if we can make it work, but it sounds like a tricky spell. Do you reckon you can do it?"

"I can try," she began, staring into my face as though willing herself to see something that wasn't there.

I waited, holding my breath slightly, to see what would come next. For several seconds, nothing did, but when her expression changed, it became something that scared me worse than anything that had (or hadn't) happened that night. It was as though her eyes, those beautiful eyes I loved so much, were no longer seeing me, even though they were still pointed in my direction. There was darkness in there, as though they had been granted a glimpse of hell itself, and gifted Natalie with a terrible understanding of something that humans who lived long, prosperous lives were never supposed to know.

"Protect me, John," she moaned, making my blood chill. Whatever was happening to her, it was something she knew she couldn't deal with on her own, and when this thought occurred to me, I knew exactly what was happening to her. A moment later, she slumped sideways onto her pillow, her eyes rolling up into her head as her consciousness was whisked away. It was too late; we had run out of time.

Chapter 3: Less About the War and More About the Bling

I sat motionless for perhaps as long as a minute, digesting the full implications of what had just happened, hardly able to believe that as soon as I finally come up with some magic that might work, the option is promptly taken off the table. Clinging to hope for just a little longer, I held Natalie against me, directing her head to my shoulder, touching her as much as I could without it feeling creepy, but she was completely limp and non-responsive. There was no point in sitting here any longer and pretending this was something else: Lucien had struck, probably immediately after the other former Sorcerers regained consciousness, and now, unless something drastic happened in our favour sometime soon, it looked as though Natalie's days as a Sorcerer were finished.

So what came next? If we couldn't protect ourselves, that left only two options: fight or flight. If we stayed and tried to fight without any magical weaponry whatsoever (everything had been vanished prior to the hero devices, and now they were gone as well), Lucien would overpower us single-handedly. If we tried to make a break for it, we would be out in the open and fully exposed to his tracing abilities, even if we were still under the untraceable spell. There was one thing on which I wouldn't budge, though: Lucien would come for Natalie's unconscious body as he had for the rest of her family, and I would not let him have it. Her last request had been for me to protect her, and that was what I was going to do, whatever consequences came of it for me.

I did a quick inventory on everything I could possibly use to my advantage, and I quickly came up with something that Marc and James had probably missed. Lucien may have four of the crystal chips representing him now (or five, if he'd been lying about Amelia's whereabouts), but he probably wouldn't have adjusted to the feeling of having magic in his body just minutes after it had hit him. I had a clear mental picture of Natalie, staggering from the old Woodward dining room in a world of discomfort in the hours leading up to her first taste in magic. That didn't mean he couldn't use magic (if he were sending Natalie's crystal chip to someone other than himself, he would have access to his magic), just that he might not trust in his own magic right away; and that meant he would probably use the Sien-Leoard Crystal.

If there was one area where I had an advantage, that was it. He had only had that crystal for a few days—enough to know how to use it, but would it be enough for him to use it instinctively? Based on how I'd had to think out every spell I performed with the Sien-

Leoard Crystal for more than a month after I first used it, I didn't think so. If he brought it, then he could have it stripped from him as Arnold Hammerson had. If I could get it off him (a long shot but not an impossibility), then I would probably have the advantage of experience in a one-on-one fight, assuming of course that it would be a one-on-one fight. All these plans would go out the window if he brought Hammerhearts with him, and even more so if he ordered Fewul to protect him and the crystal every step of the way.

But it was my only chance, and it was Natalie's only chance to be a free girl when she woke up. Of course, if it had to happen up here, that would mean that Lucien would get to everyone else in the base first…but if I went down stairs, I could make it easier to work him into a position where I could get at the crystal…and to top it off, I had no idea where he would be most likely to enter the base. All I could do was sit there, frozen into position with Natalie still leaning against me, tossing all these thoughts around in an endless loop and come up with absolutely no scenario where I could protect Natalie and the rest of my friends at the same time.

I gently set Natalie aside and got up off the bed, looking around the room for anything I could use as a weapon. Something small but very damaging if used correctly would be preferable, but it was good to know that if I couldn't find anything else, I could always throw one of the wooden chairs at the first person to come through the door. I looked through Natalie's bedside drawers first, feeling like I was invading her privacy but knowing that I had to do this—she would understand. There was nothing useful in any of them, though, so I moved onto the wardrobe. There were coat hangers in here—my best option so far. I pulled a couple down, removed the tops from them, considered using them as strangulation tools and then rejecting the idea—he would have ample time to use magic if that was all I could do.

I looked once more around the room, but it was so sparse; Natalie hadn't bothered to make it too homely since she'd moved in here a week ago, expecting (or at least hoping) that we would soon be able to go to some more permanent living arrangement. Sighing, I went to look in the bathroom, the only place left to check and which still showed signs of what the two of us had done in here together just hours earlier—that was a memory I would keep for the rest of my life, for sure. There were plenty of things in here that could be used as projectiles—shower products, perfume bottles, a hairbrush, a toothbrush—but nothing that would really help me, until I found the electric shaver.

I had never seen Natalie use this, but I knew she must do so regularly enough—or at least as often as girls needed to do that sort of stuff—as there had been no hair on any part of her body which wasn't enhanced by the presence of hair. I turned it on, hoping for something potentially throat-slitting, but the scariest thing about the shaver was the echoing racket it made. I quickly switched it off, now beginning to despair, but a moment later, an idea occurred to me—probably the best weapon I could have at my disposal.

I dropped the shaver beside the basin, hurried across the room and out into the hallway, dashing straight across to my room and my own small bathroom. There was hardly anything in my room that could do worse than the coat hangers from Natalie's wardrobe, except for a packet-and-a-half of razors which, up until now, had only ever been used to keep me clean-shaven. I knew that if I could get close enough to Lucien without him operating his magic, though, I could use the blades to do considerable damage. They would probably work as well as bludginators, except without the ability to strike from a distance.

I took the unopened packet, ripped the top off and stuck it in the left-hand pocket of my pants, where I could reach them easily. I took those that were left, just three razors (bringing the total to eight) and put them in the right-hand pocket of my pants, along with a bunch of condoms which would be useless in a magical battle but which I couldn't bring myself to drop. Whatever happened tonight, if anything, having them there would remind me of all the good times Natalie and I had shared this week.

And speaking of Natalie, she was still lying unconscious on her bed, the door wide-open, leaving her completely exposed if anyone should sneak in there. I hurried from my room, slamming the door as I went and hurled myself through Natalie's bedroom door, shutting it behind me and hearing the satisfying click of the lock. Natalie lay exactly where I had left her, and I let out a sigh of relief. I couldn't afford to let my guard down again—our lives depended on it. I sat back down on the bed, shifting Natalie to the side so that she lay where she normally slept (and now looked as though she could be sleeping again), and began fiddling with the coat hangers, trying to figure out how best to use them in a fight. Before long, though, I had been reduced to leaning back against the wall behind me, stroking Natalie's forehead and thinking about the dream I'd had the night of Arnold Hammerson's death—the happy ending that would never happen.

I'd been doing this for no more than five minutes when distant sounds reached my ears, jerking me harshly from my state of reflection. A lot of people were shouting and moving around downstairs, some of it sounding like it was coming from the court yard but most of the drama coming from the direction of the lounge room. Generally speaking, the lounge room could be as noisy as a nightclub and you wouldn't hear it up here, but apparently whatever was happening this time was even louder than that.

Of course, there was only one thing it could have been, and my insides chilled—it was happening more quickly than I had anticipated. My first thought was that this was at least partially my fault; I'd had time to raise the alarm that Natalie had passed out, but instead of alerting them to the oncoming danger, I had thought only of protecting her. Great for Natalie if I could do any good, but what a lousy way to treat the rest of my friends. I considered going down there and trying to help, but then remembered my original plan to try to ambush Lucien up here. After all the running around I'd done trying to prepare for this moment, I really had no choice but to stick to the original plan.

I got off the bed, considered moving Natalie to somewhere where she might be less exposed, and then didn't bother. Quite apart from needing every bit of energy I had left, I didn't think it would make much difference if Lucien got past me. I instead went to stand beside the table, directly in line with the door so that I would have a clear shot at anyone who could force it open. Lucien would have a clear shot at me too, but the only way he could expect me to stand here was if he was already watching me; and if he was, it would hardly matter where I stood. I held one coat hanger in my left hand while leaving my right one empty for the time being; the other coat hanger lay on the table beside me, within easy access when the fight began.

I was as prepared as I could be; all I could do now was stand here and wait for the slightest sound in the hallway. It didn't take long: Just moments later, I heard footsteps thunder up the stairs at the opposite end of the corridor (the dining room end, so not where the trouble was) and straight down the hallway towards these last two bedrooms—the ones belonging to me and Natalie. Then outside, someone hammered on my bedroom door across the hall.

"John! John! Are you in there! We have to go!"

My stomach turned over. Not Lucien at all—Stella. None of my plans had factored this into the equation. I hesitated for a moment, trying to consider the ramifications as quickly as possible. If Stella had been able to get up here on the dining room side of the building, that probably meant that if we moved immediately, we could get back down and out that way. Somehow, this was far more appealing than fighting, but even though my own chances of survival had suddenly increased, I had no intention of going with Stella and leaving Natalie behind.

"I'm in here!" I called, tossing the coat hanger aside, bounding forward and opening the door. Stella was standing there, having just spun around at the sound of my voice, her face pale and her bright, blue eyes wide and terrified.

"John!" she gasped, leaping forward and throwing her arms around me. "John, it's happening; I saw them come in through my bedroom window."

"They came through your bedroom window?" I said before I could stop myself. Quit it, John; every second was precious.

"No, they came in the courtyard. We have to go, before they start searching the base for us."

"We have to take Natalie," I said firmly.

"What?" she gasped, dismayed. "John, there's no time ℜ—"

"I'm not leaving without her," I said stubbornly. "We can carry her. We'll still have time to get out if we move fast."

She knew as well as I did that there was no time to argue, and she could see that I wouldn't take no for an answer. She swore under her breath. "Fine, where is she?"

"In here," I said, rather pointlessly, stepping back and hurrying over to the bed. Stella followed me in without hesitation and helped me raise my prone girlfriend off the bed (Stella taking her shoulders, me taking her ankles), but before I turned away with Natalie's legs over my shoulders, I got a look at Stella's face, and in addition to her fear, there had been something in it that had hurt my heart; pain. It hurt Stella to see me and Natalie together, perhaps to think about what we most likely did when it was just the two of us in one of these bedrooms.

"Right," Stella urged me as we went through the doorway, neither of us bothering to close it or turn off the light—time was precious.

I turned to the right and went back along the hallway towards the dining room end of the base, picking up greater speed while we could move in a straight line. About two thirds of the way along, however, Stella seemed to stagger behind me.

"What?" I asked, looking over my shoulder.

"Oh," she said, looking vague for just a moment. She was still holding Natalie up but for some reason, she seemed to have briefly lost her focus. It didn't last long, though; a moment later, she straightened up and urged me forward again. A little confused, I resumed my own walk.

Stella had to nudge the button for the elevator with her elbow when we reached it, and when the button was pressed, we had to wait for the goddamned thing to come all the way up from the first floor, a wait that seemed to go on forever, making me more antsy by the second. Stella, too, looked irritated, though I thought her panic and need to hurry had decreased a little since we had left Natalie's room

—or perhaps since she had staggered back there. What was going on here?

When the doors finally opened, the lift was unsurprisingly deserted; it was still a relief, though. We hurried in, Stella moving sideways so that she could once again use her elbow to press the button for the bottom level. The doors slid shut awfully slowly, and then the descent was even more awfully slow, but eventually, we felt the lift bump gently as it reached the bottom of its shaft. We had been turning around as we descended so that when the doors open, I was ready to charge straight through them towards the outside door, which I prayed would be standing open.

But when the elevator doors slid open, I found myself standing almost nose-to-nose with a grinning Lucien Moran, closely enough to reach out and touch. He'd probably been standing with his nose almost touching the doors before they'd opened. I staggered backwards involuntarily, my backside colliding with Natalie's torso and sending her backwards into Stella, who was forced to let her shoulders go. Natalie went down onto the elevator floor, dragging me down with her and leaving Lucien and Stella standing over us, one still smiling, the other grimacing.

"I have some things for you," Lucien said to Stella, ignoring me and Natalie for the time being, "but I'd like you to be out here when I give them to you."

"What things?" Stella asked, nervous and curious in equal measure. There was something wrong with that tone.

Lucien didn't speak but beckoned her to join him outside the lift. Whether because she really was curious or because she didn't want to get on his wrong side, Stella stepped over Natalie and around me to join him outside the lift, while I simply huddled on the floor, frozen in place—not by magic, but sheer shock and dread. I had a moment when I thought luck might be on my side as the elevator doors began sliding shut again, but Lucien casually stuck his arm out to halt them in their tracks.

"What things?" Stella repeated in a brave but brittle voice.

"Firstly, this," he said, handing her what looked like a Hammerheart weapon of some description (use it on him while you can, I thought, but she just looked at it). "Secondly, a little something you'll get tomorrow, and thirdly, this."

And giving both me and Stella possibly the greatest shocks of our lives, Lucien went down on one knee in front of her, holding out a diamond-studded ring in his hands that looked like it was probably worth hundreds of thousands of dollars.

"Stella," he said solemnly, "will you do me the honour⅜—"

"Holy crap!" she finally managed to squeak, but she was just as frozen-in-place as I was, and it probably took all of Lucien's manhood to continue holding that thing out to her while she didn't put her own hand out to let him put it on her.

It had to be one of the weirdest proposals ever; I was the only observer, as the corridors around us were empty, but that didn't change the fact that it was happening in the middle of a battlefield; I could see a few people out in the yard who shouldn't have been in the base at all, and while there was still noise coming from the direction of the lounge room, there was considerably less of it now than there had been when we'd been upstairs. It sounded as though the Hammerhearts over there (he hadn't done it alone after all) had brought most of the others under control.

"I don't know what to say," Stella whispered, her eyes filling with ironic tears.

"Here," said Lucien, and instead of putting it on her finger, he put it in her free hand, the one that wasn't holding a Hammerheart device. "Don't say anything now—you have plenty of time to think it through, but even if you don't want the ring, I would really like you to use that."

He indicated the Hammerheart device in her hand while jerking his head in my direction. What did that mean? Was he going to let his obvious feelings for Stella get in the way of his common sense? Might we still have a chance to get out of this? Oh John, how on earth could you be so foolish?

"Okay," Stella said slowly, unwillingly, turning the device on me and giving it a single click. Ropes flew from its tip, and the sight of them finally jolted me into action, but there was never enough time. They wrapped around my upper body, binding my arms to my side and then seizing my ankles and pulling them up in front of me so that I was forced into a ball shape, doing to me what I had once seen Hammerhearts do to Rebecca Fletcher to bind her in place. Instead of leaving me there, though, they began floating upward so that I was lifted into the air, more like being carried than levitated. Lucien smiled radiantly at Stella.

"I knew you had it in you," he said bracingly, gently squeezing her forearm, and then turning his attention to me directly for the first time. "Sorry if that's uncomfortable, John, but it won't last too long. We just need to do a couple of things and then you'll be able to rejoin the others."

"Bite me," I said coldly. "What the hell do you think you're doing? Stella, let me go."

Stella raised the device, looking for a moment as though she actually would, but Lucien caught her arm. "Try not to let him get to you. You know he'll try anything to get out of this—he's got great survival skills."

She nodded and lowered the device, her eyes on her feet. What the hell was happening? Why was Stella obeying him? She was clearly unhappy about it, but there was no fight in her at all. Was she predisposed to do what he wanted just because he'd given her probably one of the most expensive pieces of jewellery in the world? Was she responding to the part of him that was her father, the one who had intimidated and bullied her all her life?

"Now, I've got something else for you," Lucien told her, "but I'll need you to work with me to make it happen. Are you up to it?"

"I guess so," she said apprehensively.

"I need you to take John here into my old bedroom," he said, jerking his thumb over his shoulder in the direction of the bedroom in which he had slept up until earlier this week. "Take him in there and wait, but don't untie him and don't let him get to you. I have a bunch of influential charms I need to perform, but I'll send someone in shortly to help the two of you out. Hopefully, I'll be with you before it's finished."

"Okay," she said quietly, raising the Hammerheart device again so that the ropes tightened uncomfortably around me; they seemed to be responding to both her actions and her thoughts. I gaped at her—she was doing exactly what he told her without even asking what he meant her to do in there. Reluctant or not, that kind of ignorance went beyond fear; she was obeying his word because that's what she was meant to do...

The truth clunked into place so forcefully that I imagined that I heard the vibration inside my head. James had been right to be nervous about Stella, because Lucien had clearly done something to her in that graveyard after all. He had let her go in the full knowledge that she would come back to him, and somehow found a way to make it so that her own mind wouldn't betray her to Marc and Natalie. She'd been able to get upstairs for a reason, not out of dumb luck, just as there was a good reason why Lucien had known exactly where and when we would come out on the bottom floor. For all I knew, she had even found a way to take the Sorcerous Crystals to him.

My eyes shifted coldly from Stella to Lucien as he stepped into the elevator, his eyes now on a defenceless Natalie. "What did you do to her?" I asked, forcing as much iciness into my tone as I possibly could.

"I took her magic, John; I think you knew that. It's not coming to me, though; that would make the weather all cold again, and I'd rather not put the world through that again. I'm sending it to one of my most faithful followers, who I think can make very good use of it under my instruction. In the meantime, I'm going to teleport Natalie here to the rest of her family."

"I meant Stella. What did you do to Stella?" I asked, hearing her let out a small gasp behind me and not caring. I needed an answer to this question; how was it possible that he could have done something to her in that graveyard and hidden it from even Stella herself until this very moment? There had been no opportunity since then to curse her, and I was fairly sure that she had been cursed with whatever this was when she had stepped into the lift. If I thought it were possible, I would swear that the curse had hit her exactly when she had staggered slightly in the hallway upstairs, but how could that be possible?

Lucien took a moment to wave his hand at Natalie, causing her to teleport away to wherever the other former Sorcerers were, before speaking. He didn't look at me as he spoke, but I could hear the pride in his voice. "Mary Sien was the first, and Arnold Hammerson was the second. Now, I am the third."

Not bothering to explain the meaning of his proverbial statement, he stepped back out of the lift, pulling something from his pocket and holding it out to Stella. "Here; a key that will open my bedroom door. Go now and remember what I said. I'll make sure you don't have to wait too long."

Stella nodded slowly and took the key in the hand that had, a minute ago, held an object that would have made any other woman weak at the knees. With her other hand, she used the Hammerheart device (which now that I got a closer look at, was a familiar object which spun nets—of course) to direct me out of the lift and into the corridor ahead of her. She was going to do exactly as Lucien told her —take me into that bedroom, shut the door, and wait along with me for someone to come and do something unknown, and all the while she would not untie me. I could think of a few choice words I would have with her once that door was closed, but Lucien, who had just walked past me on his way to the lounge room (I supposed), cast me a knowing look.

"You must know that you can get out of this quite easily without any physical injuries, John," he said pleasantly, "but let me tell you now that if you dare give Stella a hard time in there, I can make no promises regarding your immediate future."

"Don't say that," Stella moaned behind me, but neither of us paid her any attention.

Looking Lucien squarely in the eyes, I said, enunciating each word with absolute clarity, "Go fuck yourself. It's the only way you'll ever get fucked."

He just laughed. "Not bad, but altogether not very creative, John. Go on, Stella; no point dawdling."

He set off again, this time not looking back, and Stella began to move too, directing me ahead of her towards Lucien's closed bedroom door. She had to shift me aside so that she could open it, and when she did, I got a brief look at her face. There was pain there again, only now it was significantly worse than it had been upstairs when she'd been confronted with me and Natalie together. The thought of Natalie drove any sympathy clean out of my mind; I had failed to protect her, and I could blame my failure squarely on Stella's betrayal—oh, and the idiot stupid enough to trust her in the first place, of course.

"Do you have anything to say for yourself?" I snarled as she stepped into the bedroom, by which point I was suspended a couple of metres in, not far from the table. My back was to Stella, so I had no idea what expression she wore now.

"Don't be mad at me," she said in a small voice, shutting the door softly behind us, continuing to follow Lucien's instructions to the letter.

She directed me over to the bed and lowered me onto it, loosening the ropes a bit so that I could move my arms a little more freely, though I couldn't move my knees too far from my chest, nor could I move away from this exact position on the bed. The ropes turned me around so that instead of facing the wall (which I wouldn't have minded), I had to look at Stella. She looked severely torn, knowing that what she was doing was wrong but still not making any move to alter her course. Seeming satisfied that I was as comfortable as I was allowed to be, she pocketed the Hammerheart weapon.

"Don't be mad at you?" I repeated scornfully. Remembering what I'd said to Natalie earlier that morning, I asked her, "If our positions were reversed, would you be mad at me?"

She sat down on the bed beside me, close enough that she could reach out and touch me if she wanted to, though thankfully she didn't. "Probably, but what else is there?"

"Oh, I dunno. How about not sleeping with the enemy?"

"I'm not sleeping with him," she said, apparently automatically —Stella didn't usually say stuff like that, and for a moment, she looked as surprised as I felt. "Look, I'm sure there's nothing to worry about if we just stay put. If you run, you'll only end up in more trouble, and where would you go anyway? You'd be on your own if you got away—I don't want you to have to do that."

"Was this part of your plan upstairs?" I asked. "Honestly, I thought you had better integrity than this."

"No, I really thought we could get out, but that changed when Lucien stopped us. There's no point trying now."

"That's so pathetic," I said, packing as much disdain into three words as I could. I felt absolutely awful, but only one of us here was a traitor and she deserved as much of it as I could give her. "It's a good thing some of us have more fighting spirit than you, Stella, otherwise we would have lost the war months ago. Or is this less about the war and more about the bling?"

Each accusation was like a slap in the mouth—I could see it in her face—but every time my thoughts flicked back to Natalie, I felt the urge to keep on going, to drive the knife in as far as I could. If this was Stella's choice, she had to take the consequences. At my last words, though, she grimaced. "I'm not taking that thing."

I snorted. "Why not? Not enough carats for you? Or do you just think that since he probably used magic to either create it or acquire it, it doesn't really count as generosity?"

"I'm not marrying him!" she snapped, looking away from me and twisting her hands together. She was uncomfortable—good.

"Oh really? Why not? Don't wanna be the first lady of the world?"

"Because—" she closed her eyes hard, struggling with what I didn't know. It gladdened me to see it. Finally, without opening her eyes, she said, "I'm not dating him anymore. I don't want to be with him."

"What?" I gaped at her. "You do every little thing he says out there, but you draw the line here? You really think it's cool to ditch all your friends and break his heart at the same time? How dumb are you?"

"I never said I liked it," she said defensively. "I couldn't have done anything for the others, but I can do something about this. Lucien isn't the type who would force the issue."

"He wasn't," I corrected. "He's changed now, but then I guess you have too, so maybe it feels the same."

She shook her head, still not opening her eyes. "He's the same guy. That kind of magic only gives someone a couple of ideas they wouldn't have had on their own; it doesn't change their entire personality."

I swore in frustration and incredulity. "You're even more messed up than I thought."

That got a reaction out of her. Of all the nasty things I'd said to her, it had taken those words to do more than just hurt her. Except, when she opened her eyes, it wasn't just hurt on her face. There was disappointment there too, and something else I couldn't quite put my finger on. I only identified it when she took a deep breath to speak again; she was steeling herself to say something.

"I thought you would have known exactly how 'messed up' I am," she said quietly, looking directly at me.

It was my turn to shake my head. "Don't even go there, Stella. Reminding me of that creepy mind thing isn't going to make me think good of you now."

"I can see that," she said levelly, "but you can't pretend it's not there, any more than I can pretend I wanna spend the rest of my life with Lucien. He's a good guy, I guess," she said, absent-mindedly running her hand over her pocket where the ring lay, "and he gets me more than most, but I just can't—"

She broke off, still struggling, but my blood had run cold. Déjà vu all over again, I thought. I had an idea where this could possibly be going, but I dearly hoped I was wrong. The second most recent time I had entered Stella's mind during my sleep, she had been contemplating her relationship with Lucien in a new light now that I had returned safely from the Honnie world. Her thoughts had been that although she was mildly attracted to him, and he was being very good to her, he wasn't her top preference; and she couldn't (wouldn't) give herself to him entirely until she knew for sure that she couldn't, in any way, have her top preference. I was the one she really wanted (and it wasn't a case of me getting ahead of myself—I knew it for a fact) and now, it sounded like she was vocalising what she had been thinking that night. Please, God, don't let it be so; not just days after a similar conversation with Natalie (one with a very different outcome) and mere hours after an equally unsettling conversation with Lena. I couldn't take much more of this.

Hoping to derail her train of thought, I said, "Fine—don't date him. Just marry him and take half his stuff. How does owning Europe sound to you?"

It didn't work. "John, I'm serious here," she snapped. "Why are you doing this to me? I would never do this to you."

"Untie me, Stella," I dared her.

She hesitated, her eyes moving from me to the door and back again. After several seconds, during which I watched her, waiting for her to refuse yet again, she surprised me by taking the Hammerheart device back out of her pocket.

"Okay, fine, but on one condition."

"What would that be?" I asked. Considering that since she was the one in control here, I would probably be willing to meet most conditions if it gave me a chance for freedom.

"You have to listen to me," she said simply. "I need you to understand what I'm feeling. If you'd paid any attention to my mind at all, you'd already know."

I stared numbly at her, hardly able to believe my ears. Was she saying that she actually wanted me to be inside her head, thinking her most private thoughts right along with her? I despised our connection—useful as it had been on a few occasions, mostly it was the greatest invasion of privacy under the sun. Well, second greatest —the greatest had been what I'd used the Sien-Leoard Crystal to do to Serena, Natalie and Rebecca, the key difference being that neither Stella nor I could control when we entered the other's mind. I could only assume that her attitude came from sixteen years of being a mind-reader.

Finally, I managed to say, "I paid as little attention as I could, Stella. It's not my business what you think or feel."

"It is when it's about you," she said evenly, and the bottom dropped out of my stomach. I'd been right after all.

I sighed deeply. "What do you want from me?"

She also sighed, crossing her hands in her lap, the thing controlling my binds between them. She looked very pretty when she sat like that, but I hardened my heart. I couldn't let her think there was even the slightest possibility that she and I could ever be happy together, mainly because of what she had allowed to happen to Natalie but also, at least in part, because it wasn't true. I couldn't deny that I cared very much for Stella (at least I had done up until now) and if Natalie wasn't in the frame, Stella probably would be. Of course, so would Lena, but if she'd been taken by the Hammerhearts while I'd been stuck in here, it may not matter. There was, in fact, a possibility that Lucien would take all of Stella's competition out of the equation, but that was where my one hope lay; if he really wanted her, he wouldn't let her have me.

"You may not like the connection," she said quietly, "and I guess I can understand why. Most people like their thoughts to be private, and I'm sure you'd like to stay out of my head—it's a pretty sucky place to be. But it's different for me, John; it always has been, because for as long as I can remember, the time I spent being you was the happiest of my life. You were exactly like I would have liked to be if I'd been a normal person."

I listened to her in wonder, forgetting that I was supposed to be keeping a hard heart. I was unwillingly touched by the way she spoke of me and interested (as I always was) by the thought of Stella as a child. Her childhood was probably one of the most mysterious things in the world, and I'd never been brave enough to ask a lot of questions about it. Reliving these memories brought out a bit more emotion in her too, I saw; her eyes had filled with tears, but she wiped them away impatiently as she continued.

"Back when I was maybe six or seven, I thought of you as my 'real imaginary friend', because even then I could tell that there was something different about those dreams. I would always look forward to being you when I slept, and I would always be disappointed when it didn't happen—which was most of the time," she added, and sighed. "When I got a bit older, I started wondering why I was still having these dreams and noticing more and more details of them every time. I was thirteen when I figured that you were probably a real person, and that it was some weird magic that was at work, and that's when things got ℜ—"

She broke off again, struggling to express whatever she was thinking, but in contrast to earlier, she now looked a bit more comfortable—perhaps getting this off her chest was helping. I was as intrigued as ever, but still nervous about the direction of this story.

"I think you can probably guess what came next," she said, giving me a shy look. "I was"—she swallowed ℜ—"I was sad, lonely, becoming a teenager, and even though you were still mostly a kid at that stage, I fell in love with you."

I groaned, not bothering to make it an internal thing as I would have normally done. "Stella, thirteen-year-olds don't fall in love—they have crushes."

"You're only a year older than I was then, and you're pretty sure you're in love," she pointed out. "People don't change that quickly."

"That's different," I said stubbornly. Remembering my thought from earlier, I spoke it aloud. "If you'd been in my head at any point this week, you'd know just how in love I am with Natalie."

"I haven't," she admitted, "but I do know how you feel, and I've seen how happy she's made you. I also know that my feelings for you are just as strong, possibly even more so."

That wasn't what I wanted to hear, but as before, she'd practically handed me my next line. "If you think your feelings for me are equal to mine for Natalie, you would know that I would no sooner date you than you would date Lucien."

Logic at its finest. Thanks for being such an integral part of my life, James, I thought to myself. Then I remembered that James's brilliant mind was probably warped by an influential charm by now; the thought made me feel sad all over again.

"There may be something in that," she admitted, "but what you don't know is the full extent of Natalie's feelings for you. You can only go by what she tells you and how she behaves around you; that's not as accurate as actually being in her mind, as we're in each other's. There's something else you need to consider, too."

She paused for a moment, gathering her thoughts. I took the opportunity to say, "Trying to discourage me isn't going to work. I feel how I feel."

She took no notice. "She knows about some of the things that you've done, but she's never had access to your thoughts, so how can she understand why you do what you do? She's going to have questions which she either can't ask you, or if she does ask, she couldn't be sure if you would tell her the truth. I've heard enough people's thoughts to know how that stuff can eat away at someone, making them more and more insecure until it hits breaking point. How can you be sure that Natalie will be able to handle a relationship with you when all along, she can have no way of knowing if you'll be faithful to her?"

Damn you, Stella; she was echoing my thoughts from my conversation with Peter earlier. She was right, of course, but she was nuts if she thought that was a good reason to ditch Natalie. When I said as much, she merely replied, "It would be lousy; that's why I don't expect you to do it now. I just want you to bear it in mind, though, because if it does happen, there is still someone who does understand your motives."

She indicated herself, and I almost laughed. I was fairly sure she was telling the truth, but it was hard to get past her sheer boldness to come out and say so. This was a side of Stella I'd known about, but only from her thoughts; I never imagined that I would actually see it. Still, as irritated as I was by her, she'd succeeded in taking the edge off my anger. I let out another deep sigh.

"That's flattering, I think," I said, "but whether or not you understand, I don't think you'd really want to be in a relationship with someone who would do the things I do; and after what you let happen to Natalie tonight, I don't want to be in a relationship with you either."

Pain lanced across her face. I had no idea which part of what I'd said had got to her, but I didn't really care—it was all true, after all.

"You're wrong," she said quietly, "but I can see that you've made up your mind. Just remember what I said, though, 'cause I'm not gonna quit on you, and I'm definitely not going back to Lucien. I'm yours, John, if you want me."

It was hard not to be affected by words like that—I supposed every guy under the sun would respond to them, whether he wanted to or not. Still, though, thinking of Natalie kept me in check without too much trouble. I opened my mouth, trying to think of something else to say (not too hurtful now, but firm all the same) but before such a comment could occur to me, someone knocked on the bedroom door in the hallway outside. It looked like I had once again run out of time.

Chapter 4: Exploding is What These Things Do Best

Stella leapt off the bed, quickly stowing the Hammerheart device in her pocket and mouthing "sorry" at me. If I were to believe her, she had meant what she'd said about letting me go if I'd listened, but she'd banked on more time. In actual fact, I thought it more likely that quite a bit more time had passed while we'd been in here than it had felt. Before she could take a single step towards the door, however, we both heard the person on the other side slide a key into the lock.

I hadn't really thought about who Lucien might send to do his dirty work while he busied himself with even dirtier work, but I supposed I had just assumed it would be Cornish, Hall, Tom Hignat (or possibly his son, Ather, as he had a habit of popping up where he wasn't welcome), or just some other random Hammerheart from the area. I was therefore completely caught off-guard when the door opened and Sebastian Williams stepped inside, sweeping the room with his gaze and grinning as he took in the pair of us. He was holding something under his arm, I saw, an all-too-familiar cubic contraption wrapped in wiring that I had last seen on the night Tulip had died. Now I understood exactly what Lucien intended to do to me today.

"What the hell!" Stella gaped at him. "What are you doing here?"

"Hello to you too," he said cheerfully, kicking the door shut behind him. "I can't remember the last time I saw you face-to-face; must have been months ago now."

"What are you doing here?" Stella repeated the question.

Sebastian feigned surprise—or maybe he really was surprised. Who could tell the difference when you were dealing with an idiot like him. "Why wouldn't I be here? Lucien's in charge now—you know it as well as I do—and he was good enough to invite me along. I was curious to get a look at this place, and I have to say, John, I got a bit of a kick out of the configuration—you know what I mean?"

I knew exactly what he meant. He had been confined to the Woodwards' prison yard for a few weeks earlier in the year when we had discovered that he was the spy working for the Hammersons, and the layout of this base had been inspired by that prison yard. I scowled at him.

"Did Lucien mention how that thing exploded the last time it was used?" I asked him coldly.

"This thing has never been used before, John," he said, moving forward towards the bed. Stella, who stood between him and me, scrambled out of the way, apparently repulsed by the thought of touching him. "Lucien created it especially for tonight, but if you're talking about the model this was based on, this is supposed to be an improvement."

"Told you that, did he?" I scoffed.

"Yeah," he said, unperturbed. "I don't know what it's supposed to do, but according to Lucien, whatever the old model had done wouldn't have worked. This one has been reconfigured to do the job properly. All I have to do is set it up and push the button."

Stella watched all this in confusion. Incredibly, she hadn't recognised the device for what it was. If she had, and if she meant what she said about our connection being so important to her, she would be wrestling that thing out of his hands by now. Unhindered, Sebastian set the thing—what I unwillingly thought of as the undoer 2.0—on the bed beside me, took some of the wiring from the top of the box and wrapped it loosely around my upper body. As it had that night six months ago, once it got the sense of me, the wiring took a much tighter hold around my torso, cutting through the net so that it fell harmlessly away around me.

Sebastian didn't watch to see if he'd done the thing right—perhaps Lucien had warned him that Stella might retaliate when she realised what was going on. He was right to think it, but Stella never got a chance. Even before the wiring had really got hold of me, he had taken some more of it from the box and jumped at Stella, who just didn't see it coming. She cried out in surprise and anger, trying to beat him away, but the wiring had already got hold of her waist. Sebastian simply stepped backwards out of harm's way as Stella was reeled in like a fish on a hook, struggling all the while to loosen the wire and having no success whatsoever.

Seconds later, she was stuck on the bed, the two of us on either side of the box which would shortly disconnect us—assuming Lucien knew what he was doing. If he didn't, it could potentially kill us both. Her face was very white, her eyes huge in her face, her mouth pressed into an angry line as she watched Sebastian approach us, both trussed up and unable to do anything to stop him.

"Lucien didn't want this," Stella said, her voice hitching. She seemed to be even more scared than me, and anguished too.

Sebastian looked surprised by this. He considered for a moment, then said, "No, he definitely did. He told me exactly where to come and what to do, and you two were in here waiting for me on his instructions. That says to me that he wants this."

"He wouldn't do this to me," Stella insisted, desperate tears filling her eyes. "He asked me to marry him out there."

That took Sebastian by surprise. He stared blankly at her for a few seconds before chuckling. "I can't wait to tell Ather about that," he chortled, "but if he really cares about you, then this thing must be good, whatever it is. At least, he must believe it is, and if I were you, I wouldn't argue about it. You start getting argumentative, he might decide to divorce you. Now, I believe I'm supposed to…"

He was examining a switch on the device. It seemed to have three settings—'U' to one side, 'T' to the other, and nothing in the middle. It was currently on the middle setting, which was probably the off position. What did that switch mean, though? What was U and what was T? If this thing was a second-generation undoer, what other purpose could it have other than to undo? I could only assume that Lucien had created this device with an idea that it could have another use in the future.

Sebastian pushed the switch sideways into the T position, and the feeling that followed was both strange and terrifying. A vibration ran through the wiring for a moment before entering my body and travelling straight up to my head, which immediately began to swim. I tried to keep a hold of my thoughts, but they quickly became jumbled. Beside me, Stella had hunched over, shuddering as she experienced the same thing. I knew she was because for the first time ever, I began to actually feel the connection between us; I had a clear sense of a duality in my mind, where the second was the thought patterns I recognised from the times I had entered Stella's mind.

Although the connection had been mostly a bother, I felt a great swell of sadness that it would very shortly be over. It would almost be like having part of myself removed, something way more substantial than a loose tooth or even a malfunctioning kidney. It was something inside the mind itself, and things there should never need to be removed. I didn't feel much surprise that I was feeling the presence of the connection now more than I ever had before; after all, as the old clichÃ© went, you don't know what you've got till it's gone.

Was it going, though? Instead of fading away and my mind becoming singular, as it had always felt, the connection seemed to be becoming stronger. Stella's thoughts were becoming so mixed up with my own that at this rate, they would soon become one. In addition, not only could I feel my own body (my head, arms, legs and torso as I had always known them), but I could feel her body too; feel it in a way that I had never noticed before. Obviously when I had entered her mind, I had entered her body too, but it had never really meant anything because I'd never been there when she had thought about her body. If I'd been in her mind while she'd been standing naked and looking into a mirror, observing herself, that might have been different. Now, though, I could feel the clear differences between my body and hers, and she could too.

"How are we going here?"

In my preoccupation, I hadn't heard the bedroom door open again. Now, however, Lucien stepped forward past Sebastian to have a look into each of our faces. He seemed satisfied by what he saw, but when he looked down at the undoer, his face froze into an expression of utter horror. He grabbed the undoer and tried to flick the switch, but it had locked into position.

"What's wrong?" Sebastian asked, his confidence gone.

"I'll tell you what's wrong, you complete buffoon: You've done exactly the opposite of what I asked you to do!"

"What? But sir, I—"

Lucien didn't listen. He grabbed the undoer and began wrestling with it, desperately trying to reverse what Sebastian had done, but the device wouldn't respond. The wiring around me and Stella jerked from side to side, causing us to bump shoulders every couple of seconds, but in our heads, the process continued uninterrupted. Lucien even began casting magic into the device to reverse it, but it still wouldn't respond—he'd done a damn good job making it foolproof.

"Stand back," he warned Sebastian, who scuttled over to stand by the wardrobe.

A few seconds later, the undoer exploded, sending chunks of glass, plastic and metal in all directions. We all covered our faces but somehow, all the debris missed us, landing on and around the table in the centre of the room. The wiring around me and Stella fell away, allowing us both to straighten up into proper sitting positions. Most relieving of all, when the device had exploded, my sense of the connection to Stella just vanished. If Lucien's intention had been to remove it, though, his expression told me quite plainly that the connection was still very much there.

"I should have listened to you, John," said Sebastian, uncovering his face. "Apparently, exploding is what these things do best."

"This is a disaster," Lucien moaned, taking a step back from the bed and running his fingers distractedly through his hair…

…distractedly?

Lucien had stepped back from the bed, and was running his fingers distractedly through his hair…

I didn't give it any further thought. I jumped off the bed and took off, charging straight past Lucien and towards the door, which stood wide-open to the hallway outside, a hallway which looked empty from here. Sebastian made a startled movement, as though instinctively trying to stop me, but his surprise made him too slow to be effective.

"Hey!" Lucien bellowed as I dashed through the door and swung around the corner, the nearest door to the yard my target. Before I got there, though, the wall separating Lucien's bedroom from the hallway exploded outward, sending great chunks of plaster flying through the air. I was tripped up by one and hit in the head by another but with no worse than a dizzy head, I jumped back to my feet and kept on running. I wasn't sure about Sebastian or Stella, but Lucien was giving chase.

I reached the small foyer, swung around to face the outside door, but before I could get to it, all the glass in the frame shattered, spraying inward in large, jagged chunks. I ran straight towards and then right through it, only thinking of what was behind me rather than ahead. The sight of all that glass coming at me would have been utterly terrifying under any other circumstances. I was struck in several places, the worst one being right across the top of my head, but my eyes—the one thing (well, two things) I absolutely needed to protect, remained unharmed. Ignoring the stinging, barely feeling it actually, I just kept running, kicking clinging glass out of the door frame as I went through it and not letting it slow me up one bit.

"Don't let him get away!" Lucien roared as he too burst into the courtyard, so close behind me that even without magic, he was a good chance to catch me before I got to the control room.

I didn't take a moment to see who he was talking to, but I saw them anyway. There were plenty of Hammerhearts out here, but more importantly, most of my friends were out here too, standing amongst the Hammerhearts as though they were all one and the same. Unfortunately, they were now. Those Hammerhearts who had invaded our base sprang to attention immediately, and I was forced to jump and dodge around flying jets of multi-coloured light as I ran, incredibly lucky not to be hit. My friends (former friends now), not having any of their own weapons, sprang forward to attempt to catch me themselves, a few getting in the way of other Hammerhearts and getting struck down by agonators, stunners and solid-outliners.

Then, almost right behind me, someone collided with someone else, and as more people piled in, they all fell down onto the footpath. Judging by the cry of frustration and the fact that the footsteps right behind me had stopped, Lucien was one of them.

"You're supposed to be on my side!" he roared, struggling with them.

"We are," one of the girls replied, and my heart sank—there was the confirmation, "but John is still our friend."

"You go, Playman!" either Harry or Simon bellowed, now a good distance behind me as I ran around a corner and began the sprint past the outdoor pool Natalie had once created. "Stay safe, buddy!"

So Stella had been right; the influential charm had put them on Lucien's side, but as they were all likely to maintain their friendships with each other under his rule, the charm wasn't going to make them forget that I was their friend too. Lucien probably could perform such magic if he chose, but maybe he would be good enough about not doing something like that.

I was almost distracted by a horrifying gurgling noise to my left, from the depths of the pool, but I didn't let it slow my pace. What did almost slow my pace (stop it, in fact) was the water from the pool suddenly spilling over the sides and running out over the path. It wasn't just wet and slippery—it had a sideways current, intent on pulling me off my feet and sweeping me towards the trees on the other side of the path...and holy crap but those trees were beginning to move!

Suddenly, everything had changed from a sprint for survival (something I was reasonably good at) to a living nightmare. It even felt like a nightmare in that my destination now seemed further away than before, and hard as I ran, I couldn't move any faster. That was actually true because my stride had changed from a sprint to a kind of stomp, the best to keep my balance in the swirling water around my ankles. Some of it had run into my shoes and it was bloody freezing. If any more of it got in there, it might actually affect my feeling down there.

But I kept on relentlessly forward so that before too long, I had moved out of range of the water and, even better, out of range of those reaching, groping branches back there. I picked up speed, veering right and ducking as a park bench suddenly uprooted itself from the ground and hurled itself at me—it passed so close over my head that I felt its slipstream ruffle my hair. I straightened, allowed myself a fraction of a second to properly regain my balance, and pushed on.

I cut to the path on the left and there was the control room, dead ahead with its door still standing blessedly open. The room itself was empty, but I could see something else in there that almost sent me reeling back to the ground. The door on the other side of the room, the one that I would have to go through to get out of the base, also stood open. That meant one of two things: Lucien had entered through the control room (unlikely if Stella had been honest about the Hammerhearts teleporting directly into the yard; also that kind of magic would be a lot more difficult to work than standard teleportation), or whoever had been in the control room at the time had seen the hopelessness of the situation and managed to escape. I pushed myself even harder, now feeling the stitch in my side but spurred on by the sight of my doorway to freedom.

I was maybe ten metres away from it when three things happened almost at the same time. Like they had back at the pool, the bushes on either side of the path suddenly came to life, beginning to creep across the path from here to the control room door on both sides. The ground below me lurched sideways, almost sending me straight into those hungry bushes as, just to my left, so close that I could have fallen straight in if I'd been in the centre of the path, a fissure began to open, the ground rending itself apart with an almighty thunder. Before I had time to react to either of these things, a fireball flew over my shoulder, again so close that my head could have easily been ignited and hit the wall of the control room. To my horror, it burst into flames.

This was Lucien's last ditch-effort to stop me from getting out there, but I didn't stop to think about it. If I had, I probably would have frozen, unwilling to enter the inferno and consequently been either collared and strangled by the bushes, or swallowed by the great big hole in the ground. I instinctively moved to my right, away from the expanding fissure and closer to the bushes, which began scraping the side of my shoe as I passed them. I had to run in big, long strides to avoid them but when I had almost reached the doorway, close enough that I could feel the heat from the flames, my right calf was seized and the horrible, ugly shrub to which now had a hold of me began trying to pull me towards itself—towards a black hole opening in its centre—a hole which looked a lot like a mouth.

It was my own momentum that saved me. I dived forward with such force that the shrub, which after all wasn't made of very strong stuff (if it had been a tree from earlier, this wouldn't have worked), was ripped from the ground and pulled along with me. It didn't stop trying to pull me back but it couldn't be very effective anymore, now that it had nothing else to attach itself to. With the shrub on my leg, trying to claw its way up my body, I fell forward into the control room, almost slipping into the fissure on my way through. The floor beneath me didn't feel very strong, though, and I knew that if I stayed on it for any length of time, it would collapse into the fissure (which had opened directly beneath it) and the race would be lost anyway.

It was very hot in here, but as I was in the centre of the room, my greater concern (particularly as I'd been breathing hard when I'd entered) was the smoke. Holding my breath (with no air in my lungs —I wasn't brave enough to inhale again while in here), I pulled the shrub across the room with me and directed it towards the flames, which were taking hold of the control panel. It instantly went up, relinquishing its hold on me immediately and giving me the freedom I needed to dive through the open door, landing on my stomach on the cool, wet grass outside. I scrambled up as quickly as I'd gone down, spun around and slammed the door shut behind me. The last things I had seen before the door itself vanished, leaving me in a completely deserted paddock, was the blazing control room, shrubs and all, collapsing in on itself as it was pulled down into the fissure. I had also seen, through the door on the other side and distorted by smoke and distance, a white-faced Lucien, looking ready to kill someone.

That last look was bad, particularly if he took it out on my friends, who had done me a huge favour by slowing him up (even if they were no longer on my side), but there was nothing I could do about it now. I didn't have time to reflect on this, or to take stock of my various injuries; I had to get out of here before Lucien took it into his head to teleport straight back into the paddock. I took off at a run in the direction I thought would take me to Main Street, which I could then follow back into town, but I couldn't be sure where it was given that I'd never travelled it entirely on foot; and the fact that it was still pitch-black out here didn't help things. On top of that, I had absolutely no idea where in town I ought to go, but I couldn't think about that right now either.

I just kept running, trying to keep my head empty, but that changed when I ran straight into an electric fence. The shock which followed wasn't very intense, but due to my momentum carrying me forward, it seemed to go on rather longer than necessary. I eventually fell back and collapsed to the ground, but my muscles in my legs had all seized up. The sprint was mostly responsible, but the shock pretty much sealed the deal. I still couldn't afford to rest, though, and certainly not here. I got up on my hands and knees, pulled my sleeves over my hands and reached tentatively outward, hoping the shock wouldn't travel through my clothing. To my relief, when I found the wire, I felt no discomfort—perhaps the shock was too minor to pass through clothing.

It was dark on the other side of the fence, but if I were to trust my night vision, I thought it looked more like an empty field than a small forest I could get myself lost in. If I climbed this fence, I could run through it and if I knew the layout of the district, I would eventually find a road. It may not be Main Street, but any road would be better than being stuck in this paddock. I therefore began to climb up the fence, which actually wasn't very difficult so long as I kept my hands covered by my sleeves and my face well back from the wires. It was probably about six-and-a-half feet high, but when I got to the top, I didn't hesitate to jump off the other side, landing catlike on the ground and breaking into a run again, although now it was more like a trot—I was too exhausted to sprint.

About five minutes later, or a duration that felt as such, I tripped down a gutter and fell forward, throwing out my hands to break my fall. They connected hard with asphalt, no doubt breaking the skin in several places, but I hardly cared; I'd found a road to follow. I got to my feet, retreated back to the gutter (I wasn't about to run in the middle of a road, not even now), and considered which direction I ought to go. If this was Main Street, then Chopville would be to my left; and if it was the highway, going to my left would eventually take me to its intersection with Main Street. I didn't think it was the highway, though; it was only a single-carriage road, and it was just too quiet. Regardless, I turned left and began trotting again.

I loped along for ten more minutes, passing by what could only be farmland on either side of the road, making me feel more and more sure that this really was Main Street and I was heading back towards Chopville. Before I got anywhere near the town though, a sound carried to me on the still and freezing-cold morning air. It was a voice, and it was calling out. I did a double take and stopped, looking around wildly and seeing nothing, but if that voice was calling to me, it couldn't possibly be an enemy—they would have happily snuck up on me in the darkness. I hesitated a moment longer, wondering whether to stay or to resume my trot, but my mind was made up by the voice calling out to me a second time, over what sounded like a distance of at least a hundred metres. It was calling my name, I felt sure of it, and I thought I knew who it must be; whoever had escaped through the control room when the attack had started.

"Who's that?" I called back, cupping my hands around my mouth and directing my voice in the direction from which I thought the phantom voice had come.

A couple of seconds of silence followed, but then the voice responded, "Over here, John; hurry up."

My heart leapt because not only were the words easily distinguishable, but so was the voice itself. I broke into a run, finding yet another small reserve of energy to push me forward—probably excitement this time. I was running across another field but ahead of me, casting shadows of deepest darkness, stood a line of trees and shrubs. My stomach turned over as I remembered the far-too-lively fauna inside the base, but I couldn't allow that one crazy experience to slow me down now. It didn't stop me feeling a thrill of terror as I saw some of them move slightly as I approached, but on this occasion, they were being forced apart by three people stepping out to meet me. I could tell by their outlines exactly who they were even before I reached them: Peter (the one who'd called to me), Marc and James.

"Mate," Marc grinned as I barrelled into their midst. A moment later, the four of us were involved in a crazy group hug, which broke up as we all fell on the ground.

"Back under cover," James said quickly, scrambling up and moving back into the cover of the trees. Marc and Peter followed immediately; I did too, after several seconds of hesitation, during which I once again saw the trees by the pool coming to life and reaching out towards me.

"How did you get out?" Peter and I asked each other in almost complete unison.

"You first," I said quickly. "I reckon my story's longer."

"Wait," said James quickly. "Before you talk, do you know if anyone else is coming? Honestly, we thought it would just be the three of us."

I shook my head. "I'm pretty sure they all got hit by influential charms, but even if they didn't, the control room was destroyed right after I got through it."

The three of them exhaled in disappointment.

"Okay," Peter said finally. "Well, we were the only ones in the control room when they teleported in. We didn't see it happen, but we heard it when all the noise started. We went to have a look but there were a lot of Hammerhearts in the yard near the building and they were all armed, and we knew we had no chance of getting through; all that we could do was let them catch us."

He paused for a moment, unwilling to say the next bit, but I reckoned I could guess what it was. James came right out and said it for both of us. "So we turned around and made a break for it."

"I wanted to fight," Marc mumbled.

"If we'd had weapons, I would have too," James agreed, "but the way it was, we would have done no good trying. At least this way, we've given ourselves an opportunity to reload and go back for them. We can only hope that Lucien doesn't do anything too bad to them between now and then."

"If he's got complete control of those Hammerhearts, he won't," I said, "at least, I think not. I saw him and believe it or not, he's still very much like the Lucien we knew; he's just running Hammerson's agenda now. I thought you were the one who initially wanted to stay and fight."

"I did, when we had a chance of defending ourselves," James insisted, "but when the situation changed, so did my opinion."

"So what about you, John?" Peter asked. "Where were you when it all started?"

I had no intention of lying about any of what I'd been through. "I was in Natalie's room when she fainted, and I was originally going to stay there with her and fight anyone off if they tried to take her body. I got coat hangers and razors and I would have totally used them."

"That's what I'm talkin' about," Marc approved.

I nodded, knowing that in this complete absence of light, it was a wasted motion. "I never got a chance, though, 'cause when it started a few minutes later, Stella came up to find me. She was planning for the two of us to slip out the dining room side of the base, 'cause all the drama was on the lounge room side, but I made her take Natalie with us."

"I'm guessing that didn't work out, since you're on your own now," said Peter observantly.

"Yeah, funny how that works," I said drily. "Anyway, we took a lift down, and Lucien was standing like right in front of the doors when they opened; he knew we were coming."

"Oh no," James moaned. "Please don't tell me he sent Stella to lure you into a trap."

"Actually, that's exactly what he did," I told them, "except Stella herself didn't realise what was happening until it was too late. I don't know how, but he somehow put an influential charm on her—or something very similar—while she was on the third floor with me. I suppose he was mentally watching us from downstairs—he probably could have performed magic remotely by doing that, the same way we fought with the crystals from inside the Woodwards' base when the war started—"

"And the way Hall terrorised us a couple of months ago," James added darkly.

"Yeah, but the thing is, when I asked him what he'd done, he said something like, 'Sien was the first, Hammerson was the second, and I'm the third.' What on earth does that mean? Is it gibberish?"

"No," said James slowly, sounding like he understood a lot more than I did. "It means that even though he's had magic for only a few days, he is one of the most powerful Sorcerers we have ever seen. It has to be because I'm pretty sure that none of us ever told him about the time bomb curse—not just that he had one on him, but about the existence of the curse itself. It makes sense, though; Sien and Arnold Hammerson were the only two Sorcerers who have ever done it, and he turns around and puts one on Stella so that he could call her to him when he saw fit, and none of us would be any the wiser because none of our magic could have picked up on it. He probably did it in the graveyard that night; that must be why he let her go."

I swore under my breath. I would have preferred my theory to be correct, but there was no denying the clear logic in James's words. Lucien had let Stella go even though he clearly wanted her by his side, and the only reason he could have done that was so that he could use her to lower our guard. I supposed there was even a chance she'd had a hand in removing the Hero Crystal from the base and then been enchanted to forget about it. Now, the cat had been let out of the bag, and whatever Stella said to the contrary, she belonged to Lucien, not me.

"Probably all true," Marc said, and sighed. "So how'd you get away, John?"

I hesitated, wondering how much I ought to tell them. It was either a highly abridged version, leaving out all the emotional stuff and most particularly the love quadrangle between me, Stella, Lucien and Natalie; or the full version, including all the details. I decided that under the circumstances, though I really didn't want to think any more about my loss than I had to, these three deserved the full version. So, taking a deep breath, I began relating exactly what had happened, starting with the episode in the open elevator doors.

"Geez, he's gonna marry her?" Marc breathed. "Man, that's out-of-control."

"She didn't say yes," I told them, "and in fact she told me she was going to say no later on, if he lets her that is, but I'll get to that."

I continued, telling them how Lucien had ordered Stella to tie me up, which she had done; how he had teleported Natalie's body out of the base; and how Stella had taken me into Lucien's room to await further instructions. I covered the conversation which followed as best I could, though I probably missed a few details here and there along the way. To their credit, the three boys stayed entirely silent through all of this, which made it easier to keep going. They couldn't contain their silence any longer, however, when I told them exactly who Lucien sent into the room to deal with us.

"That bastard!" Peter exclaimed. "Oh my God, what a bastard."

"Yeah, he's got some nerve, showing up in our base after what he did," I agreed, and then went on, telling them how he'd tied us both up and activated the undoer, which would have severed the mental connection between me and Stella if he'd done it right; but of course, he hadn't.

"It sounds like he actually strengthened it," said James when I tried to describe just how I became aware of Stella's presence in my own head—both mental and physical.

"That's actually kinda hot," said Peter. "Just the body part," he added quickly.

"It didn't feel hot," I muttered darkly.

"I don't know what that means for you and Stella, John, or what'll happen when you enter her mind next time," James went on, "but it certainly doesn't mean the connection is broken."

"I guess not," I said. "Anyway, Lucien hit the roof when he saw what was happening. He tried to turn the thing off, but it was locked, so he had to destroy it. He was a little distracted after that, probably thinking about how he was going to fix this, and that's where I got my chance to make a break for it."

"Really? You just got up and ran away?"

"Yeah, but he gave a pretty good chase."

I described as much as I could remember: the plaster, the glass, the Hammerhearts, our friends intervening,the water, the trees, the park bench, the shrubs, the fissure, and the fireball. In hindsight, I couldn't believe I'd gotten out at all. That was a magical gauntlet with ten barriers (not that my friends had ended up providing much of a problem), and I'd somehow slipped past every one of them. Not without a few injuries along the way, I reminded myself, and on cue, I began feeling those aches and pains much more strongly.

"How badly are you hurt?" Marc asked me.

I shrugged. "I can still run. Well, maybe not now; I'm really, really tired."

"Yeah, we all need to sleep," James agreed, "but still, John, we should get a look at you. Here—"

He pulled the Light Crystal from his pocket, and once out in the open, it illuminated our entire clearing. We weren't very far from the edge of the tree line, but this little patch was still fairly well sheltered. James, who was sitting directly opposite me (a fact which I hadn't known before), set the crystal in the space between the four of us so that it lit up all our faces, and the three of them peered anxiously at mine.

"Is it bad?" I asked, beginning to feel nervous myself. My hands hurt the most where I'd landed on the road, but there were plenty of other pains contributing: around the left-hand side of the back of my head where the plaster had hit me; across my forehead where the glass had cut into me, not to mention another cut on the side of my neck (thank God it hadn't touched my jugular); my right leg, where the sharp brambles of the shrub had ripped my pants and broken the skin on my leg; and the right side of my face, which had passed awfully close to the burning frame of the control room door. Funnily enough, it was the same part of my body that Natalie had accidentally burnt earlier.

"Is it bad?" Marc repeated incredulously. "Has anyone got a mirror on them?"

"I've got one," said Peter quickly. "Just give me a moment to pull it out of my bra."

"This is so not funny," Marc snapped. "Look, I don't think there's much we can do about this. If only we had a first-aid kit or something."

"I suppose we could break into someone's house and steal one," Peter suggested. "You do realise that's how we're going to have to survive now? Assuming of course that Lucien doesn't round us up like cattle before then."

"You're right," said James, "about both things, in fact, but we do have this."

He reached out and put his hand back over the Light Crystal, dimming its glow a bit but not diminishing it altogether. He held it there for several seconds before removing it, looking satisfied.

"What was that?"

"I just made it so that you, John, will make a full recovery," said James, "but I have no way of controlling how or how long it'll take."

"Which means I might have to wait for Lucien to catch me and do it with his magic," I muttered.

James shrugged. "I hope that's not how it goes, but the Light Crystal just won't let me be specific about how it happens. Goodness only seems to stretch far enough to grant you a full recovery, but asking it to be done a certain way must be seen as selfishness or something."

"Well, thanks," I said, grateful in spite of not knowing how long I would have to suffer before being well again. "You should probably put that away; darkness might be safer for us at the moment. Hey," I said, struck by a thought, "how did you see me coming anyway?"

"We heard you before we saw you," said Peter. "You weren't making any effort to be quiet. Then when I had a look, there you were, in plain view on the side of the road."

"Guys," said Marc, looking around at the three of us (James hadn't put the Light Crystal away yet), "what do we do now?"

That was the question which had divided us all night, and which most of us had tried very hard not to contemplate too closely: What do we do now? The question was staring us in the face, and there was no way of avoiding it.

"Well, let's firstly empty our pockets and take stock of what we have," James suggested.

"I've only got the Villain Crystal," Marc informed us.

"I've got some razors," I told them, and I took the three in my right pocket out and handed one to each of them. "Use it to shave, or to cut Hammerhearts' jugulars; whichever suits you. I've also got a few condoms, but I can't think of any use for them now."

That sobered the group up even more. I could tell by their faces that they were all thinking about their lost girlfriends, whose minds had now been taken over and warped by Lucien's magic. I didn't blame them; she was unconscious now, but when Natalie came around in the depths of Lucien's lair, she would be subjected to the same thing. It was James who managed to speak first.

"It's not outside the realm of possibility that the Hammerhearts have at least one unboggler in their supplies," he said carefully. "You know, the ones you created, John. If we could get in there and steal one, then find out where Lucien keeps his prisoners, we might be able to get them back. That's a lot to work out, though, and there are a lot of places it could fall down. Let's not give up on them just yet, though."

"Agreed," Marc and I said in unison.

Peter looked from one face to the other, clearly wanting to share our opinion, but he could only shrug. "I really hope you're right," he said sadly, "but I would be really surprised if we even get a chance to get that far."

"What about you two?" I asked James and Peter.

"Only that," James said, indicating the crystal, "and my memory stick that's got a lot of my stuff on it. It's not much use without a computer, but there's no way I'm chucking it."

Of course not, I thought. James had been working on a couple of private projects before the shit had hit the fan, one of which could end up being the most important thing any of us would ever do. If I knew James like I thought I did, he would find a way to keep working on it, even without a computer.

Peter, meanwhile, held up the one and only thing he'd been carrying in his pocket—a deck of cards. That didn't surprise me either. Maybe he could go into town and win our next meal or something.

"I've also got a watch," he added as an afterthought.

All four of us were still wearing our watches, as it turned out, and although they all read different times spanning about seventy-five seconds, the approximate time was around 6:20. The sun would rise soon, announcing the beginning of our first day on the run from the entire world. Prior to this moment, I'd never felt truly alone in the fight for good, because I'd always had a lot of friends around me, not to mention the adults and the general public, most of whom were opposed to the Hammerhearts. Now, though, most of our friends were gone, the adults were gone, nearly all the magic in the world had been claimed by the side of evil, and to top it off, Lucien had the ability to make the general public think that we were the enemies, turning them against us as Hammerson had tried to do with his whole 'Chopville Quartet' deal. That had only partially worked in the end because even though we had been painted as ex-Hammerhearts out only to cause trouble, a brand of local terrorists as it were, most people took the view that as long as we caused trouble for the Hammerhearts, we must be okay.

Now, though, we were alone in a whole different way. There was no getting around the truth of the situation: The four of us were the last resistance against magical rule. If Lucien caught us, there would be absolutely no one left to fight, because nobody else would know how; and pretty soon, no one else would want to. We had to keep going; we had to survive; and we had to save this thing, no matter what.

The four of us talked for a bit more but we were too tired to get any further in contemplating our next move. Eventually, James said we ought to just sleep here, because we would be so much easier to catch if we allowed ourselves to be tired all the time. If we woke up and we were captured, that would be beyond our control, but it was a chance we had to take. The rest of us were too tired to argue; we simply followed him a little deeper into the trees so that even though the sun was beginning to rise, the light didn't reach us here. I cleared the ground of anything sharp and lay down upon it, shivering in the cold but not daring to take any item of clothing off, not even to use as a pillow—sleeping without a pillow wasn't the worst thing in the world.

Sleep took me very quickly, except that it was sleep unlike anything I had ever experienced before. In fact, although my body may have been sleeping, my mind was far away, once again intertwined with Stella. It was different, though; I was no longer hitchhiking in her mind, unaware that I'd been thinking her thoughts until I woke up. This was different—this was so much more real. I became her, sliding from the life of John into the life of Stella with barely a pause for breath.

Chapter 5: I'm Your Boss, Not Your King

The all-too-familiar room was packed with people, but very quiet. It wasn't so much that we were scared about what would happen to us (Lucien would probably be a firm authority figure, but torture didn't seem to be in his repertoire). I didn't even think he would send us all down to the Basement because after all, we were on his side now. However, it was clear that after so many people had tried to stop him from catching John, he would keep us locked up in some capacity for the time being.

No, the atmosphere was shock, caused mainly by the losses sustained right at the end. Lucien had flown into one of the greatest rages I had ever seen, so reminiscent of my father that it was impossible to overlook the most likely cause. Right after John had escaped, and the magic that should have collared him had instead cut off Lucien's only way of giving chase, the entire building had collapsed into a large, upside-down U-shaped pile of rubble. Nobody in the yard had been hurt because somehow, as had been the case when the undoer had exploded, none of the debris struck anyone. The shock was for the eleven people who had still been in the building when it came down; they'd had no chance.

Since then, Lucien had rounded everyone up in the yard and done a headcount, deducing that we had lost six teenagers (Dean, Joanne, George, Belinda, Robyn and Della) and five Hammerhearts, none of whom I had recognised by name, so probably relatively new recruits. He had then gone back into the rubble and attempted to salvage anything that could be valuable in recapturing the four who had escaped (to Lucien, losing Marc and James had been even worse than losing John—apparently, he'd had plans for those two). There hadn't been anything worth saving, however, and even worse, the Light and Villain Crystals had both been taken out of the base.

After that, Lucien had made us all gather together and then teleported us straight into this room where we were now: the foyer off which were the dining hall and Worship Hall in the Chopville Hammerheart base. The Hammerhearts had separated and begun following Lucien's orders immediately, while the rest of us had been ordered to remain here while he went to tie up a few loose ends. Interestingly, nobody here had considered simply escaping; there were a couple of armed Hammerhearts standing nearby, and they would have been hugely outnumbered. On any other day, this particular group would have fancied their chances of overpowering a couple of blokes, but today, nobody even wanted to. Even more interesting, I hadn't given it a single thought myself until now. I had no intention of leaving, though, because I owed it to Lucien to stay;

and also, because even though I didn't want him the same way he wanted me, I still wanted to be a part of what he was building here.

Right on cue, Lucien entered the room from the stairwell, strolling as casually as if he didn't have the ability to teleport straight into our midst. I must make a note to ask him how he had found a way to teleport in and out of places that were supposed to block that kind of magic.

"Okay, everyone," he called, and we all came to attention immediately. "I know I can trust you all not to get up to anything dodgy while you're here, but I also can't trust you to behave yourselves if I lengthen your leash too much. That is why I think it's a good idea to put you in the Big Room. Don't worry, it's only temporary; I'll be able to arrange proper accommodation for you once Marc, John, James and Peter are brought in. Any questions so far?"

Of course there were, and he knew it, because he had deliberately left one unanswered. Several hands went up; Lucien indicated Jessica, who said, "What's the Big Room?"

"Right through there," Lucien responded, indicating a door I hadn't even noticed until now. It was placed midway between the entrances to the dining hall and Worship Hall, a spot on the wall where there had never been a door before. "I created it yesterday to house our newest recruits. I believe many of your parents are in there."

That changed the atmosphere from shock and nervousness to excitement.

"It's not very comfortable," he said apologetically, "but like I said, it's only temporary. So, everyone in."

He opened the door and stood back, allowing everyone to file in. I followed, not really giving it any thought, but when he saw me, he put out his arm.

"Don't be silly, Stella; you don't go in there."

"I don't?"

Lucien smiled and shook his head. "I'm surprised you even thought so. You're with me…aren't you?" he added, suddenly looking nervous. I was touched that he even needed to ask, because it may mean that he wouldn't use his magic to make me do what he wanted.

"Of course," I said quickly, "but we do need to talk."

"Of course," he echoed me, smiling slightly. "I've got a few more things I would like to organise before we do, though. Are you sure you don't want to sleep first? Forgive me for saying so, but you look like crap."

"That's nice," I said drily, "but yeah, I wanna get this over with. How long will you keep me waiting?"

He considered the question. By now, everyone else had entered the Big Room, although there were still a bunch of Hammerhearts standing around, watching Lucien and waiting for instructions, all the while watching me with curiosity. I could hardly blame them; who knew what these people had been saying about me over the last few months. Hank Cornish was there, and Sebastian stood close by him, looking more comfortable now that Lucien had fixed his broken jaw. After he had the sheer nerve to come out and start talking to those whom he had betrayed, Felicity had hauled off and punched him in the face and broken it. I was surprised that Lucien had fixed it, actually; neither my father nor my grandmother would have been so merciful after one of their people had screwed up as badly as Sebastian had this morning. Then, there was Ather Hignat, looking like he'd only been awake for at most half an hour, but smiling at me in a way I didn't care for at all. In fact, he was looking at me as if he would quite like to take me upstairs and lie me down on someone's office floor. Could I rely on Lucien to pull him into line after I told him what I needed to say? Finally, Lucien said, "You, Stella, I won't keep waiting at all.

"Everyone," he turned and addressed the bystanding Hammerhearts, "time out. We'll take a break from all operations and resume this afternoon, except for those of you who are taking care of them." He jerked his thumb at the still-open door of the Big Room. "Those of you who've been up all night may go and rest; the rest of you may go and have breakfast.

"Stella," he said more quietly, addressing me again as almost everyone else did as he told, "I hope you don't mind, but I would like you to sleep in your old bedroom again. That won't be a problem, will it? It need only be temporary," he added quickly.

"It'll be fine," I said, shrugging. The bed in there was a single, so unless he spun a bit of magic against my will, I wouldn't have to share it with him. Actually, it would be quite nice to be home, the place I had always known as home, without worrying about what my father or grandmother did to me the next time I woke up in the morning.

Hank Cornish had waited until everyone else in the room had cleared out; now he came over to join us.

"What part of 'time out' did you not understand?" Lucien asked coolly.

"I understood," Cornish said calmly (he had too much experience dealing with my father to be even slightly intimidated by Lucien), "but before I head out, can I just ask why you would give those four boys time to escape instead of snatching them up now while they're in the open?"

Lucien considered the question, me and Cornish both watching curiously. I had to admit, I was wondering the same thing. I would have liked him to bring them in sooner rather than later too, but only so that I could see John again. Right now, I could only imagine him and the other three, wandering around aimlessly out there, wondering what the hell they could do just to stay safe. Didn't they realise that Lucien wouldn't hurt them? Didn't they realise that he would, in fact, put them in positions of great power and influence if they wanted?

"We'll get them," Lucien said at last, "but it doesn't need to happen right away. They'll be no harder to find tonight than they are now, so we might as well let them suffer out there for a bit; that'll make them more appreciative when we bring them in, give them a good feed and a few comfortable beds."

"Good plan," said Cornish, looking honestly impressed. "What time do you want me back here?"

Lucien shrugged. "Try three o'clock, but if I'm still sleeping, don't wake me up."

"As you wish," Cornish bowed and began retreating.

"Oh, and Hank," Lucien called after him, "don't ever bow to me again. I'm your boss, not your king."

"Sure thing, boss," he said amiably, and disappeared into the stairwell.

Lucien sighed and beckoned to me. "Come on, Stella; let's go somewhere more private."

I hoped he only meant to talk, but once again, I only wanted to obey him. There was something else I wanted to do first, though. "One moment," I said, and I turned and walked through the door into the Big Room.

Its name certainly described it accurately; it was bloody huge! The ceiling was only three or four metres high, but the walls were so far on all sides that they were shrouded in darkness. The room was completely empty except for lots and lots of people, either sitting on the floor or lying in sleeping bags, because there was no furniture. It was a good thing that the floor was carpeted, I supposed. I gazed around the room, spotting those who I'd come in with having spread out around the place, and a few others I recognised as being soldiers of the Woodwards' army, but none of the former Sorcerers were anywhere in sight, nor was the Honnie, who would have stood out like a beacon in a place like this.

"Satisfied your curiosity?" Lucien asked behind me, making me jump.

"I think so," I said, turning and leaving the room. Lucien followed, shutting the door behind him.

"Does that door lock?" I asked, not having heard a lock click.

"I could use magic to seal it shut, I suppose," he said, "but I see no need. No one in there wants to leave, not that they'll complain when they do."

Rather than taking the stairs, Lucien called the lift, which came very quickly. We stepped in and he pushed the button for the top floor, leaving me in no doubt about where we were going. When the doors closed, however, I was caught by surprise by being suddenly thrust into a small space with him. Apparently, he hadn't given a thought until now either.

"How are you feeling about everything?" he asked quietly.

"I dunno," I said unenthusiastically. I was fine about being here, and I was fine about what had happened back at the base (not counting the deaths), but there was too much not-fine stuff going on for me to say yes; and I didn't want to start discussing it in this elevator. I decided a quick, convenient change of subject was in order. "Are things fixed up on the top floor now?"

"You would never know it was the centre of one of the most powerfully magical battles in history," Lucien replied, grinning with pride. As well he should; when the doors opened on the top level, revealing the corridor to the living quarters, it looked even more polished than it had before my father, Marc and Fewul had almost used it as a nuclear bomb testing facility. In fact, there was no getting around the fact: It looked more like a normal corridor now, instead of some plain, sterile place, the styling my family had always encouraged. I couldn't quite put my finger on what had changed about it, though.

The living room, I saw when we reached it a few minutes later (Lucien put a spell on me so that I could pass through the enchanted wall without his assistance or a number-two uniform), was just as I remembered from the last time I had been in it—only five days ago I had reminded myself, and how things had been very different then. The main difference was that I was in no danger, and I certainly didn't feel any coming from Lucien, although that could soon change depending on how this conversation went. That was what I thought before I sat down on one of the very familiar couches facing the kitchen bench; the moment I sank into the soft material, a wave of exhaustion crashed over me, drowning pretty much all of my resolve to do this here and now. Maybe Lucien had been right; maybe I did need to sleep first.

"Okay," Lucien said, sitting down beside me, close enough that he could easily touch me if he chose but not too close for comfort. "What's on your mind?"

I took a deep breath, still trying to decide if I could have this conversation now. I saw his eyes flick to my hands, crossed in my lap, but only for a moment; I knew he was checking to see if I was wearing his ring, which of course, I wasn't. I had no intention of ever wearing it, but then what was I supposed to do with it? I decided to give myself a bit more time to think about it.

"What was all that?" I asked him.

He shrugged and spread his hands. "You'll have to be more specific."

"Well," I considered, "start with yourself. What are you doing here? What made you choose to take up my family's cause instead of the one we all worked so hard for?"

"I rather think this is a good cause," he said earnestly. "I mean, the Woodwards and Fletchers were doing what they thought was right, I'm sure, but you'd have to admit, the world was pretty badly screwed up before all this started. Would things be any better if they went back to the way they were?"

"No, they'd be the way they were," I said, unable to resist pointing out the obviousness of his words. I took a kind of amused pleasure out of it, something I had never really felt before. Well, no, that was only half true; it was the kind of thing that John regularly felt when he was with his friends.

"Well spotted," he said drily, smiling at me, sharing in the joke, "but I think I get where you're coming from—it was a bit out of the blue. I'm not sure exactly what changed—maybe there was an influential charm placed on me a long time ago or something—I only know that it came to me earlier in the week, when we were standing over your father's grave."

"I guessed that," I said, not wanting to think about that night, "but what came over you?"

"I don't know exactly," he said uncomfortably, looking away from me. "It's—it's kind of scary, actually."

And he meant what he said. Whatever had taken hold of him, the part of him that was still the Lucien I'd known for such a long time was frightened of it. It was hard not to feel a small token of affection for him.

"I think I might know a bit of what it could be," I said quietly. When he looked at me, eyebrows raised, I said, "According to the others, my father put a curse on you that would be suspended until the moment he died—or maybe it was only when you got near his body, I don't know."

"I assumed that was the case," he said. "I know about the time bomb curse; I don't know how I know about it, because I'd never heard of it before, but I know all about it now."

"Was that what you did to me?" I asked, struck by an inspiration I hadn't had before. Where had that come from? That thought hadn't even occurred to me until now.

He measured for a moment before saying, "Yeah, I did. Yours was just an influential charm, though, and as I'm sure you can tell, it was a very minor one."

And that was the end of my small token of affection for him. "You put an influential charm on me?"

"Are you complaining about it?" he asked innocently.

"No," I said quickly. "It's actually kind of a relief not to be worried all the time, but still, don't ever do that to me again."

He spread his hands in front of him. "My word, Stella; no more influential charms. Well, not on you anyway."

I let out a sigh. "Okay then. Anyway, I was going to say, I think I might know what my father did to you—not exactly, though. It's just, the others thought that it was the last line of the prophecy being fulfilled."

"The tyrant falling to the ground?"

"No, the line about chasing him from the soul on which he feeds. They think his soul is mixed up with yours, that's why he still hasn't been defeated."

Lucien considered this for several seconds, going rather pale as the words sank in. Finally, though, he nodded. "That does actually make sense. I've gotta say, I'm not too comfortable with that, but it explains a bit of what's been going on with me. I know a lot of things I shouldn't know, like the inner workings of this Hammerheart organisation and how to control it. I'm also a lot more skilled with magic than I should be, given that I've never used it until the last few days. Also, I think I may have adopted some of his character."

"Really?" I said, a little sickened by that thought. If that were true, there was absolutely no way I could sleep with him; it would be almost like incest.

"I'm finding," he said slowly, picking carefully through his words, "that I have two choices here. I can take his good qualities, or I can take his bad qualities, but I have to take one or the other, and then factor my own personality into all of that. If I take his bad side, I can still be myself, but I'd be a horrible version of myself. I'm still trying to find the perfect balance between all these factors, but as you saw earlier, I'm having a bit of trouble with it."

"I don't really understand," I said vaguely. "Exactly what qualities are we talking about here?"

"Well, your father's vision and ambition were the best things about him, while his temper and utter cruelty were his dark side. I have always been much the opposite; I've hurt a few people in the past, but I don't think I'm any crueller than any other human being. My main problem was that I was always such a pushover; you wouldn't have seen that side of me, but only because in our old group, we were surrounded by people who listened to me. I never stood up to my dad, though, even when I thought he'd killed our mother; nor did I stand up to the Hammersons when they promoted me and tried to give me additional responsibilities. I just accepted their offerings and betrayed them behind their backs."

"Why is that such a bad thing?" I asked, surprised.

"Because I'm not normally the treacherous type. I know I've switched sides in this thing more often than anyone, other than perhaps Sebastian, but none of those times were by choice. I don't like to go and do things behind people's backs, not if I can help it, but I never had the guts to stand up to your family until I had a bunch of people backing me up."

"Okay," I said slowly, still not entirely understanding where he was going with this.

He sighed. "So if you're wondering why I've taken up your father's vision, that's why. I would rather do that than sit back and have to go out and strangle cats just to keep control of my cruel side. By doing it this way, not only can I make the world a better place, I believe I can do so without being a tyrant like your father was. It'll still have to be a dictatorship, at least for now, but maybe not the typical kind. I guess we'll see."

"Okay," I repeated, thinking that I had a better understanding. "So you're saying that you're struggling with it because—"

"Because when things go wrong, I hit the roof like your father did," he said heavily. "What you saw back in the yard there, that was your father, not me. It wasn't the first time either; when I took the Woodwards' base, May and Amelia both managed to escape, and I lost it then too. It seems to take all my self-control just to stay in check when stuff like that happens; I just hope I get better at it."

"May and Amelia escaped?" I said, honing in on that part of what he said. "How?"

"Well, Amelia would have been unconscious," he added, "but May would have felt us all when we entered the base. She especially would have felt me because I used magic from the Sien-Leoard Crystal to create a shield around all our minds that would feel to her like another Honnie mind; that way, she wouldn't be able to break through it. When she tried to take me, I was almost able to turn her mind inside-out; that would have brought her under my control, but she let me go before I had a chance. Anyway, she must have grabbed up Amelia and done a runner before we could get down to where they were keeping her. I've been trying to trace her ever since, but she hasn't shown up. If we're lucky, she would have gotten scared and gone back to her own world, but I'll have to keep an eye out for her just the same; she could do a lot of damage if given an opportunity."

"And Amelia?"

"Well wherever she is, she would have woken up by now. She's about equally as important as my brothers; I'd like to get them back, but they don't pose much of a threat."

"Do you know how Amelia is now?"

"I had a brief chat with the other Sorcerers when they woke up, right before coming to get you, in fact. They said that May had put Amelia back together again a few hours before I stepped in; she's turned out pretty well, though perhaps not exactly how she had been before."

I sighed. That was a sad thought, but as had been said by several people plenty of times already this week, there was no point fretting about what had already happened and couldn't be undone. That the old Amelia was gone, but at least the new Amelia was very similar.

"Can I backtrack a bit further?" I asked him. "How did you even make this happen? You only had the Sien-Leoard Crystal, and Marc had ordered Fewul to attack anyone who tried to take the Hero Crystal by stealth."

Lucien grinned. "You know, you'd be surprised how easy it is to overlook the simplest solutions to life's problems. All I had to do was remind myself that absolutely anything is possible with magic, and no matter what kind of counter-magic is performed, there is always something else that can be tried—something that couldn't be foreseen by anyone else. In this case, I just thought to myself, why wouldn't the Sien-Leoard Crystal be able to call back the Beast of Magic? I couldn't think of any reason why not, so I gave it a try. The rest, as they say, is history."

"That's it?" I gaped at him. "But, my father—"

"Never thought of it," he completed the sentence, still smiling. "Probably a good thing for us, I daresay; we couldn't have beaten him without Fewul. Once it was gone, I just teleported in, took the crystal while Marc was sleeping, and began changing the properties."

"And how did you teleport in? There were spells that were supposed to stop that from happening."

"There were," he admitted, "and it was a tricky spell to crack, but I took a leaf out of James's book; I got thinking about ways I could alter the charm from the outside, and eventually found a way that would allow me to get an air pocket of magic inside. Once it was in, I could perform spells on the charm from the inside of the base, creating a small opening through which I could teleport. I didn't wanna get rid of it altogether in case it showed up on the control panel. I did much the same thing with the Woodwards' base, and even with this base; there's not much need for that kind of protection, now that we're the only ones with magic capable of doing that."

"They have the Villain Crystal," I reminded him.

"And when they figure out how to open that box, I'll do something more proactive to get it back," he said, and grinned. "You know, I'm getting quite excited just thinking about having them all back here with me. The Villain Crystal is an evil thing that needs to be put out of the way, but the Light Crystal may be an important weapon for us."

"I'm pretty sure the Light Crystal isn't supposed to be used as a weapon, and aren't you fighting for evil now?"

I hated the words, but they had to be spoken.

"We're not evil, Stella," he said quietly. "I don't even think your father was truly evil; at least not in the true supervillain sense of the word. The only part of him that was, was the way he enjoyed hurting people. His visions, though, they were good, and I intend to take that goodness and mix it with my own. We're not evil, and we won't be using the Villain or Darkness crystals for that reason. As for the Light Crystal, perhaps weapon was the wrong word, but it will still be very important to our cause."

"Right," I said, and suppressed a yawn.

"You need to sleep," he said gently, patting me on the shoulder. The touch felt good—I wished it didn't.

"I know," I said, trying to think of anything else we needed to talk about—anything other than us, of course. All that remained were the events of the last couple of hours, and there were a few things I needed to know before I could comfortably rest. "Where are the Sorcerers? I didn't see them in the Big Room."

"That would be because they aren't in the Big Room. They will be eventually, when Natalie comes around tomorrow, but for the time being, they are in a place I like to think of as the Small Room."

I shrugged—didn't matter, but he'd just reminded me of another matter of curiosity. "Why did you take Amelia's magic instead of Natalie's? We were all confused because it would have made more sense to take all our magic and leave us defenceless, and Amelia couldn't have been dangerous with hers."

"No, perhaps not," he admitted, "but I had no way of knowing how Amelia was before I took her magic. I wanted all those in the Woodward base defenceless so that I could capture them all at once without having to battle someone with magic, and I wanted their base more than yours because of the damage that May could have done. I couldn't take the chance of her and Amelia teaming up; at least this way, wherever they are, if they're together, they have no magic. As for Natalie, well, I was interested to see how you and the others would spend the time you had; not very well was my observation."

I shrugged—again, didn't matter. "What about that thing back in your bedroom, then? Was that what I think it was? Were you trying to break our connection?"

Lucien hesitated, then shook his head. "Break is the wrong word, Stella; that was what your father tried to do. I was trying to untie you, so that you could get on with your life without having your sleep interrupted by entering his mind, and so that your own privacy wouldn't be intruded upon by him. As you know, though, Sebastian stuffed it up."

"I know," I said hardly. "What's he doing here anyway? He really is a traitor."

Lucien shrugged. "Sebastian is a very simple creature, very easy to manipulate. If I give him what he requires to keep him happy, he'll be loyal to me. I don't really consider him to be necessarily faithful; he's more like a pet, if you get my meaning."

I smiled in spite of myself—that was a good description for him. "Is that why you fixed his face? I thought that was a rather good look for him."

Lucien shook his finger at me. "Cruelty, Stella; I'm not going to enjoy another person's suffering. Sebastian may have screwed up, but it was an innocent mistake; he honestly tried to do the right thing. I've told him that I will reward him with more important jobs if he does well by me, but I'm not going to punish him if he makes honest mistakes that anyone else could easily have made; I'll just give him less important jobs until he's ready for more responsibility. Who would have thought someone could screw up flicking a simple switch."

"Okay," I sighed. "So what did that thing do to me and John anyway?"

"He set it to tie, rather than untie," he said heavily, "a feature I wouldn't have put there at all if it weren't the only way to get the magic to work properly. It means your connection will be even stronger now than it was before. I don't know what that will mean for you both, but I promise you that when we have John back with us, we'll set this thing right."

I shrugged noncommittally. I didn't want the connection to break; it was the dearest thing I had, but now that it had changed, I would reserve judgement. If it could go back to the way it was before, that would be perfect.

"Anything else on your mind?" he asked gently.

I hesitated; the only thing left was the elephant in the room, but if I addressed it now, it might start stampeding and trample me. On the other hand, I couldn't just leave him hanging; I had to let him know that I was at least acknowledging the fact that he'd put his heart on the line for me.

"Listen, about that thing you said to me outside the lift," I hesitated, watching him, but he only smiled, encouraging me to continue, "I—I still need to think about it."

"Okay," he said simply, his true emotions impossible to gauge.

"Can I just ask one question, though?" When he nodded, I said, "You said you had something else to give me tomorrow. Am I allowed to know what it is?"

His smile broadened into a grin. "Stella, this is a side of you I hadn't expected. Are you grubbing for gifts now?"

I blushed; that hadn't been what I'd meant at all. "No, I was just worried that it might make me uncomfortable. You have to know that giving me presents isn't going to make up my mind."

"I would have been surprised if it had," he said. "You know that I could give you anything material, Stella, and you also know how meaningless that is when you have the resources to do that. The most meaningful thing I could give you was exactly what happened outside that lift; not the ring, but the words that went with it, and the intent and emotion that went with those words. Those are the things that magic can't manufacture, as anyone who's ever had magic knows. Regarding the thing you'll receive tomorrow, though—that has nothing to do with this. Actually, it's not really a new gift since it used to belong to you."

These words hung in the air for a few seconds before the implication clunked into place. The bottom fell out of my stomach. "You're giving me Natalie's crystal chip?"

"You don't want it?" he said, surprised.

"No—I mean, yes—I mean, I don't know," I spluttered, honestly thrown by this turn of events. "Why would you do that?"

"Well, I like the idea of spreading magic around a little bit," he said, "but the chips can only go to two families, and neither of us have any living ancestors anymore; and I didn't want it for myself because that would have frozen the world over again. This is the best way, and you're easily the most suitable person for the responsibility. If you truly don't want it, though, I could probably find someone else to give it to."

I didn't know; I really didn't. It might be good to have the magic back, and it might even be good to have the responsibility that came with it (if I could make people actually think good of me, that would make it all worth it), but it would take me back to the life I'd had before—the unpleasantness that had come with being a Sorcerer. That, coupled with living under this roof again, would create déjà vu so strong that I would probably start having nightmares about my father and grandmother rising from the dead so that they could point their agonators at me. Also, didn't having magic mean I would be even closer to Lucien than I would have been otherwise? We would, after all, be the only two Sorcerers; we would be the centre of magic in the world.

"I'll think about that too," I said, "but I don't wanna jerk you around, Lucien. You already know how I feel—we've had this conversation before—and really, nothing has changed for me. I'm not going to let any of this"ℜ—I waved my arm around the living roomℜ—"change my opinion of you. All I ask is that you don't do any magic to make up my mind."

"No mind magic from me to you," he said, smiling slightly. "I believe I already said I wouldn't, and I intend to stick by that. Thanks for not being a bitch about it; few things suck more than a guy putting his heart on the line and having a woman poke it with barbed wire for a while before stomping on it."

"I wouldn't do that," I said quietly, meaning it.

He gave me a hug then, and I returned it, feeling good in his arms. It sucked that I would probably have to turn him down. Maybe I should consider letting him break the connection; that might remove the conflict and let me move on from John…but the moment I thought that, a swell of sadness filled me so suddenly and strongly that I almost broke down. Wanting to cover the moment in case Lucien noticed, I kissed him firmly on the lips, feeling his pleasant surprise and feeling my own small spark of pride. It was good to be able to have that effect on a person, but it didn't change the fact that the whole time we held onto each other, he wasn't the one I wanted to be with.

After that, we both got up and went to bed. For his own reasons, Lucien had chosen to set up in my father's old bedroom. I didn't care —what business of mine was it where he slept? My father certainly wouldn't be back to claim it, and in fact he might feel more at home in there. That was a thought I didn't want to examine any more closely than I had to.

Once shut away in my bedroom, I looked around the place. It was exactly as I had left it three months ago, except that it appeared to have been recently cleaned—at least, it wasn't as dusty as I would have expected. All the stuff I'd left behind was still here too, making me think that my father had always expected that I would eventually come back, and wanted to keep my stuff here so that I could settle right in when I did. It was one of those very occasional moments in which he had done something that a normal father would have, and I felt myself smiling in spite of myself. He was better off dead, but maybe Lucien was right; maybe there had been some good in him after all.

I got undressed, slipped into my favourite nighty (even though it was like nearly eight o'clock in the morning) and climbed into bed, the familiar sheets pleasant on my skin. If being in John's mind had been my favourite place to be during my childhood, lying in my bed (at night anyway) had been second on the list, partially because it was just me here, alone and unhurt, and partially because I would soon fall asleep and possibly get to be with my real imaginary friend again.

I rolled over a few times, very comfortable but sleep seeming to elude me for the time being. Something else had come to me in the last ten minutes or so—it had come to me while I'd been undressing, and had intensified when I'd thought about John. I was a little horny, something that certainly hadn't happened very often in this bed. The second factor was understandable, but why would I be turned on by my own body? I'd heard of girls looking at themselves naked in the mirror and taking enjoyment from it, but I'd never done anything so ridiculously vain. It was annoying, but all I could do was roll from side to side every few minutes until eventually, sleep began to creep up, causing me to drift into...

...a place of nothingness, a place of nothing but a tangle of thoughts. There was nothing else. Where am I? When am I? Who am I?

That last question was easily the most pressing. Am I Stella? The last thing I could remember was lying down in her bed and falling asleep, but I also had a clear memory of falling asleep in the farmlands to the northeast of Chopville. Stella had been awake then, standing with our friends outside the Big Room, so she couldn't possibly remember John falling asleep. That seemed to settle the argument, but it didn't settle everything—not by a long shot, because I wasn't just John. The duality I had felt in my mind when our connection had been tightened was back, only much stronger now than it had been then.

I think we're both asleep, and in each other's minds at the same time. It's like putting two mirrors directly opposite each other; the light in the middle doesn't know where to go. If you assume that the back of one of the mirrors is transparent and you look through it, your vision bounces off the mirror ahead of you and directly into the other. If you look at it on even the tiniest of angles, your vision will bounce from one mirror to the other until it lands on something that doesn't reflect it; but if you look at it dead-straight, you'll see nothing at all except the edges of the mirror; the mirror itself will be nothing. We're in each other's minds at the same time; I'm in yours, but since you're in mine, that puts us both in mine, and then back in yours, and it just bounces infinitely back and forth.

Which explained why nothing else existed, but we can still think, and it was more than that. I had been wrong a moment/minute/hour/ eternity ago when I'd assumed that I must be John just because I could remember falling asleep as John; I could also remember all sorts of things that could only be Stella's memories. I seemed to have access to all the thoughts, feelings and memories of both of us, and it didn't stop there: I was thinking two sets of thoughts at the same time. That meant that both me and the other were here and in equal control. If we could only separate even a little bit so that we could work out which of us was John and which of us was Stella, but the tightened connection seemed to make that impossible.

Or did it? The question now presented itself: What were we to do with this? If time ran normally here (and there was no guarantee that it did), we would be stuck here until one of us woke up, thereby presenting a surface that wouldn't reflect the thoughts of the other. If I woke up first, the other would instantly enter my mind until they woke up, but until that happened, we would remain here in this place of nothingness, capable of doing nothing but thinking at each other, and not even knowing which of us was which. We seemed to be united in wanting to separate enough to work this out, but then what? That was where we were divided; one of us wanted to address the discussion from earlier, to continue it, while the other wanted to cut off that line of communication.

Okay, that was me—that was John. There was no way that I, as John, would want to open that can of worms any further. With that settled, I took control of that set of thoughts while leaving Stella to the others, and the whole thing seemed to become clearer and much easier to manage when we did. I could still access her thoughts, both past and present, as she could no doubt access mine, but they were no longer confused with my own—those which were exclusively John Playman thoughts. That should have been the end of it, but Stella was having her own thoughts on the subject—discordant thoughts.

Demonstrating her ease with our connection, she began stirring her thoughts with my own, not in a way that would confuse us both but simply as a powerful means of communication. It was very similar to telepathic communications, both with Sorcerers and Honnies, except that we could only emphasise certain thoughts; all of them were more or less open to the other. The thoughts I was getting from Stella were memories of sitting on Lucien's bed, looking at me, trussed as I was, hating that she had to keep me there but knowing (honestly believing) that it was for my own good. She was also remembering how emotional she had been, how it had cost her to keep on talking, how important it was that I know how she felt.

How was I supposed to respond to this? It hardly mattered; she would know exactly how I felt. There was my one and only advantage lost; where before I might have been able to convince Stella that there was no chance for us as a couple, she now knew from my own thoughts that I couldn't be completely sure of that. She also knew that I cared very greatly for her, perhaps equally as much as Natalie (though in a slightly different way). To top it off, she also knew that I found her attractive, although she may have known that anyway; she was a good-looking girl, after all.

She felt these thoughts, and I felt her emotional reaction to them —a far too positive emotional reaction to them. I couldn't stop it after that; as before, the thoughts bounced infinitely from one to the other, snowballing all the while and picking up speed. It was all too emotionally positive—both caring about the other, perhaps loving the other—both being attracted to the other—both wanting the other; because at the end of the day, we did want each other. The fact that I wanted Natalie more didn't change the fact that I wanted Stella as well. How could I not? She was right; what we had went far beyond anything that either of us could ever have with anyone else. All these thoughts, and each of our reactions to them, just kept bouncing back and forth until they exploded in what could only be an entirely mental orgasm. That, right there, was the greatest sex I could ever have, and it hadn't been with Natalie.

Remorse…self-disgust…confusion. Those were the feelings drifting sluggishly around my head when I woke up. Had I just cheated on Natalie without even opening my legs? It was impossible to shake the feeling that I had, unless of course I was Stella and not John. It only took me a second to verify that this was not the case: I was lying on the ground, not in a bed; there were two sleeping figures on either side of me; a fourth figure (Marc, by the look of it) was sitting a short distance away, apparently keeping a lookout; and the pain of my escape came rushing back to me in a hurry.

I gave my head a little shake but didn't bother to sit up. I felt pretty well-rested, physically anyway, but my mind was a train wreck. The others would have to know about this, as much as I could tell them, but the last part—the part where Stella and I had engaged in a sort of mental intercourse—could probably be left out. Would we have to go through that every time we slept? If we slept at the same time, probably so. I would need to work out a way to avoid sleeping at the same time as her from now on, but there was no getting away from this issue altogether. Stella wanted me, and far from discouraging her, I had just convinced her that we really could work after all; and through all this, Natalie lay unconscious in the Small Room, wherever that was. I sighed; quite apart from our fight just to survive, I predicted a lot of problems ahead for me.

Chapter 6: A Five-Foot Stick of Wood Between Your Legs

By three o'clock in the afternoon, all four of us were fully awake and ready to go—where, we were still to work out. I seemed to be the most awake out of all of us; tired as they had been, the other three hadn't been comfortable to rest properly out here, whereas my body must have fallen so deeply asleep that seven hours was all I needed to recover from the twenty-four that had preceded it. I still felt mentally weary, as though I couldn't bring myself to face further challenges, but that would probably fade once we got moving.

Before we went anywhere, though, I made them gather around so that I could tell them what had just happened—or rather, what had happened to me immediately when I had fallen asleep, because it looked like the last part, though it had only felt like a matter of moments, had stretched timelessly up to the point when I had awakened. I told them as much as I could, omitting some of Stella's mental commentary along the way (just because I was in her mind, they didn't need to be as well). I could see that the loss of the six who had died in the base had hit them hard, but that was something else we couldn't afford to let slow us down.

"I was thinking before," James told us, "that the first thing we really should do is arm ourselves. If both Lucien and Stella are sleeping, now would be our best chance to sneak in there and find their supplies."

"James, they lay down seven hours ago," Marc pointed out.

"Which is why we would need to move right away if we're going to," James persisted. "Lucien may have set up spells to let him know if we try to get in, but I wouldn't be surprised if it takes him completely by surprise; surely he expects us to keep a low profile. As for Stella, she's harmless until she wakes up, and with a bit of luck, that won't be for a while."

"Or she woke up before we started talking about this," said Peter, glancing uncomfortably at me.

A thought passed among the four of us then. As long as I remained with these three, they would be in even greater danger. All Lucien would have to do is read Stella's mind to work out all she knew about my activities, which if she were still sleeping, would be absolutely everything.

Before James could speak the dreaded words, Marc said, "He's staying."

"Definitely," Peter nodded.

James shrugged. "With a bit of luck, it won't matter. Now, John, a couple of things I noticed that may have changed about your connection. Feel free to correct me." When I only raised my eyebrows, he went on. "It went on a lot longer than a normal dream this time, didn't it? Those visions are normally a lot shorter than that, right?"

"Yeah," I agreed. "It was even more vivid too, which is saying something 'cause they were already more vivid than normal dreams."

"Right, and it sounded like Stella had a few thoughts in there that were yours rather than hers," he went on. "Do you think that maybe you had a very small influence on her?"

I hesitated. That would run in line with what had happened during the undoing (or untying, to coin Lucien's phrase) and that thing that had happened when we had both been asleep. It didn't seem to mean I could take control of her, though; at least, not while retaining John Playman's thoughts and intentions. If I had, I would have tackled Lucien and tried to steal the Sien-Leoard Crystal off him. I highly doubted that could ever have worked. It also explained a bit of what had happened right before Stella had fallen asleep, and it hadn't gone unnoticed by her either; she'd become turned on when she'd gotten undressed, something that had never happened before, which could only mean that I'd been the one turned on by her temporarily naked body. It was probably a good thing that Stella hadn't paid much attention to it, otherwise I'd have a hard time not thinking about it.

"I suppose it's possible," I said slowly, "but if so, then she would probably have the same effect on me. What would that mean?"

"I don't know," James conceded, "but I suppose it'd be a good idea for us to keep a close eye on you. Maybe we can pick up when Stella's most likely watching by observing your behaviour. Do you think she's here now?"

"Fifty-fifty," I supposed.

"In that case, we'd better get on with this," said James, getting to his feet. "How should we do it?"

"I've got an idea," said Marc as the rest of us got up. I looked around on the ground but it looked as though we hadn't left anything there. "Hignat and Wilwog's are the only places I know that are still definitely connected to the Hammerheart Highway, and I'd feel better about going through Wilwog's place than Hignat's."

"I think we've done that before," I said as we left the cover of the trees and began walking quickly towards the road, down which I'd been running this morning. "Also, so you guys know and we don't have to waste time working out when we get there, the weapons and storage rooms are all in the hidden corridor on the top floor; you know, the one where we hid during the fight."

"Then how do we get in there?" Peter asked. "Only number-twos can go through that wall."

"Steal their uniforms," James said promptly, already beginning to huff and puff. "Cornish and Hall are both number-twos; with a bit of luck, they'll both be there, but I think that it would be even better if we can lure them out of the way somehow. There are too many public places in that base."

"The third floor, then," I suggested. "It's residences up there for the important ones; if we have to wait for someone to come, we'll probably have the best chance of fighting up there too."

"Good plan," said Marc. "Now guys, we should probably move faster."

So we did, all of us picking up speed and spreading out as we all reached our differing peaks. Marc led the way, his stride long and quick, while I followed not too far behind, and Peter quite close behind me. James was keeping up by virtue of his own momentum more than anything else. None of us bothered to slow down and wait for the others as we entered Chopville and began winding our way through the streets towards the small, cubical-style houses that Hignat and Wilwog lived side-by-side in, because we all knew where to go.

It was a cool but sunny day in Chopville; still winter but with a suggestion of approaching spring. Combine that with the fact that today was Saturday, and you got a fairly bustling town. From what I understood, the town had been a bit more lively in recent days since the Hammerheart installation in the school had been shut down. It meant that nobody looked twice at the four of us as we ran past, so we had no trouble getting to Hignat and Wilwog's houses. Equally lucky, the yard the two families had jointly developed contained several paths and plenty of bushes between them, meaning that we were able to hide there for a few minutes while waiting for everyone to turn up. James was last to arrive, gasping like an old car engine and sweating like a pig.

"Which one is Wilwog's?" Peter asked quietly.

"Er," Marc hesitated, looking from one of us to the other. "Now that I think about it, we never found out which was which; we just used the one on the right 'cause it was empty."

"Let's do that again, then," James wheezed. "We haven't got time to work it out."

"What if there are people in there?" I asked. "We were shrunken and invisible last time; this time we're undisguised and unarmed."

"I suppose we could use your razors," Peter suggested, grinning at me.

"Seriously, man—"

"We work with what we have," said Marc, staring around at the ground for a few seconds before bending down and picking up a long, sharp, jagged tree branch, at least five feet long. He swung it through the air with all his strength, slamming it into the soft ground just off the path on which we stood; it made a satisfied whooshing sound as it flew through the air.

"Good thinking," I said as the rest of us looked around for similarly effective weapons. Peter and James managed to find smaller, lighter versions of Marc's weapon, while I had to settle for a loose brick I'd found near the pond. It hurt my already painful hands to hold but if I threw it, I could do some damage.

"Right then," said Marc bravely, and he led the way up to the front door of the house on the right. "You guys look around on the ground for likely places they might hide a spare key; I'll ring the bell and if someone opens it, I'll take them down before they know what's going on."

Neither of these things ended up happening. The door remained shut a full minute after Marc had rung the bell, and none of us could find any spare keys concealed nearby. Marc didn't seem put out, though.

"Bet you wish you'd brought one of those coat hangers now, hey," Peter muttered to me.

"I've never used a coat hanger to open a locked door," I told him, "and you haven't either. Even if we had one, how do we know it'll—"

My words were cut off by an almighty rending, crashing sound. We all jumped and stared around at Marc, who stood before the front door, which was now hanging off its hinges.

"What the hell!" James exclaimed. "Marc, now they'll know we got in through here!"

"Yep," Marc agreed, kicking the door out of the way so that we had a clear path into the house, "and we won't be coming back here again, so no matter. Come on, before someone shows up or calls the cops."

"How the hell did you do that?" Peter asked as we piled in and hurried down the stairs.

"I threw the branch at it," Marc said, surprised. "Come on, it's almost as thick as your body, Pete."

Thankfully, the inside of the house was a lot quieter and calmer than its entrance. After a brief look around, during which we found nothing that would be useful to us and in which time we weren't discovered by any lurking Hammerhearts, we followed Marc through to the back of the house where we knew the entrance to the Hammerheart Highway to be. When we got to the laundry and opened the closet door, I was relieved and nervous in equal measure to see the familiar slide.

"Me and John first," Marc told us. "You guys, close the cupboard behind you; they might not work out that we came in here. They might think it was a random burglary."

"We should probably go and steal something, then," Peter suggested.

Marc shrugged. "If you insist, but don't take long, and make it small, whatever it is."

He disappeared down the slide while Peter went back out of the laundry. I waited a few seconds and then followed Marc, who had already pressed the button to summon a Hammerheart cart. It took about twenty seconds for one to reach us, but here was where the problem presented itself: This station was only large enough for one cart to pull up. Marc and I would have to leave before Peter and James could call their cart.

"You get in and enter the ID for my old house," Marc told me. "I'd suggest another one except we'd get lost and waste more time. I've got an idea."

He climbed back up the slide and I heard him tell James to send his and Peter's cart to the Chopville base in exactly five minutes, so that the four of us would get there at the same time and not have to leave half of us waiting for the other half. He and I then got in our cart and went to wait outside the old Moran residence for five minutes. It was an uncomfortable period for us both; the cart wasn't very big while I was a growing boy and Marc stood a little over six feet tall.

"I should have asked Peter to get some gloves," I moaned, nursing my hands in my jumper; the brick sat in my lap.

"Do you wanna swap?" Marc asked me. "You reckon you're uncomfortable; at least you don't have a five-foot stick of wood between your legs."

"I'll manage for now," I said dully. "Besides, you got a pretty good swing with that thing."

"Swinging is what five-foot sticks of wood do best," he said, and we both burst out laughing. The circumstances surrounding us made the whole thing even funnier.

I had entered the ID for the Chopville base as soon as we'd pulled up here, while Marc had spent the time between checking his watch every few seconds, cursing that we hadn't taken the time to syncronise our watches before separating. Finally, though, when the time came, he leaned over and pushed the button, sending us speeding towards the Chopville base—and yes, I know that's grammatically incorrect, but you can hardly call it speeding when it only lasts for about a tenth of a second.

There was no sign of James and Peter when we rocked up. In fact, the spacious hall of tracks was completely empty. There were carts zooming around great distances away, their noises travelling uninterrupted through the tunnels of the Highway, but none of them came in here. We decided to get out anyway; we couldn't spend any longer in this place than we absolutely had to. Good thing we moved when we did, too, because Marc had a bit of trouble getting that tree branch back out of the cart. By the time it had been freed, Peter and James had pulled up right behind us.

"Did you get first aid?" I asked hopefully as they began climbing out.

"A few Band-Aids and a face washer," said Peter, "but that was all I could find. I also got each of us a Mars Bar, so maybe we should get our sugar fix before going in there."

"No time for that," said James, pulling his own tree branch out of the cart, slamming the door, and then pressing the button on the parking meter (or whatever that thing was supposed to be) to send the cart zooming back into the tunnels, leaving the four of us standing on the platform between the tracks.

"If we get through this, we can fix later," Marc agreed. "Come on, we're all here; let's get in there."

So dragging our makeshift weapons, we hurried up the stairs and across the bridge to the doors to the base. All four of us managed to get through them before we met any trouble, but of course, it was impossible to get this far into the Hammerheart facilities without running into a Hammerheart sooner or later. There were no guards standing around, as I had half expected, but the moment we were inside, footsteps in the stairwell reached our ears. Without a word, the four of us stood to either side of the door, waiting to see if the person would go right past this level, or if they would come out here and give us trouble. Of course, it was the latter. Hank Cornish was leaving the base with an unmistakable air of purpose about him, and he was being closely followed by...

I closed my eyes in horror, hardly able to believe what I had just seen. Cornish had been oblivious to the four of us, may have been even if we hadn't lurked out of his line of sight, and that had to be due to the fact that he had none other than May following him. The Honnie was as impressive as ever, still wearing the clothes I'd last seen her in, though her face considerably less expressive than I remembered. In the brief moment I'd seen her, she hadn't noticed any of our presences either, which was impossible, of course; maybe she just hadn't said anything out of loyalty to us. What was she doing here, though? Lucien had specifically said that he was trying to track her down and having no luck with it. Had he succeeded while we had been sleeping?

There was a yell of surprise, a brief scuffle, and then a deep, ringing DONG sound. When I opened my eyes, Hank Cornish was falling to the floor, knocked out cold. Marc let him drop lifelessly, turning quickly to the Honnie to see if she would give us any trouble, but she hadn't reacted at all. What had just happened? When I raised my eyebrows at Peter, who had gone very white, he mouthed, "He just picked him up and slammed his head into the steel rail."

"May," Marc said slowly, carefully, "what are you doing here?"

She didn't respond; she didn't even acknowledge his presence. Marc reached up, seized one of her ears and yanked it, but she still didn't respond.

"Marc!" James hissed. "Have you lost your—your mind?"

But apparently he hadn't, because there was still no reaction from the Honnie. Marc considered for a moment before saying, "Are you Fewul?"

Still no reaction, but this time, Marc only shrugged. "Come on, guys; let's get in one of these lifts."

"What about him?" James asked as Marc picked up his tree branch again, while I pressed the button to call a lift. Our luck was still in because one of them opened up immediately.

"Let him lie there," said Marc indifferently, glancing down at Cornish. "If I had magic, I'd take him with us and keep him prisoner, but since we can't do that, we'll just have to hope he's got a splitting headache when he wakes up."

"What made you think to do that?" Peter asked when the doors had closed and we were ascending to the third floor.

"I didn't really think at all," said Marc, looking surprised by the admission, "I just did it. We probably could have let him go and he wouldn't have even seen us, but maybe this is better. If Lucien ordered him to take Fewul out there, we probably just saved a few people's lives—or at least their minds. I wonder what possessed him to order Fewul to take May's form?"

When the doors opened on the third floor, it seemed our run of good luck was still on. There were no people in the corridor outside, but I could hear a pair of voices not too far away. As we stepped out and the doors began sliding shut, I strained my ears to hear where they were and what they were saying.

"We should probably go that way," said James, pointing to our left, "if those guys are down there." He pointed straight ahead.

"Hang on," Peter hushed him. "If I didn't know better, I'd swear I recognised that voice."

I thought I did too, so instead of ducking for cover, the four of us crept along the corridor, following the sound of the two voices, trying to listen to their words and identify them at the same time. It didn't take long to trace them to one of the suites on this level, but the door was closed, so we could only stand outside and listen. This felt like a dumb thing to do; the corridor was empty, there were no places to hide, and we would be directly visible to anyone who stepped out of the lifts or the stairwell. None of the others said anything, though, so I held my own tongue. I was, after all, curious about those voices.

"Look, I know you've been in this thing longer than I have," one of the men said, his voice vaguely familiar, "but I'm telling you now, this is not something you can complain about. Things have changed, and we have to change with them."

"I don't trust him," a second voice said, and this one was much, much more familiar than the first. I knew exactly who it was, and judging by the scowling looks of the others, they did too.

"Don't trust him to do what?" the first voice countered. "He's already shown that he's got backbone, taking the Sorcerers like that, breaking up the kids this morning; he's done more than the Hammersons have all year. Most importantly, he's carrying on our philosophy of world improvement through magic."

"He's seventeen," insisted our former English teacher, now Commissioner Hall. "Seventeen-year-olds are not mature enough to handle all this power. Trust me, I've dealt with enough teenagers over the years to know how irresponsible they are. Most of them can't even take responsibility for their own genitals."

"Let's see if this door is unlocked," Marc whispered, and very quietly, while the first voice began speaking again, he put his hand on the knob and began to turn it. He met no resistance whatsoever, and adding to our run of good luck, it didn't even squeak.

"You guys ready to charge them?" he hissed.

"How do we know there are only those two in there?" James whispered.

"We don't, and if they don't speak, we can't. We have to try. You guys ready?"

I gripped my brick tightly, ready to hurl it at either one of them if I got a clear shot. Marc took a moment to raise his tree branch over his shoulder, holding it in one hand (how he had enough strength to do that, I could only guess) while Peter and I stood a short way behind him, our own weapons at the ready. James brought up the rear, his unspoken job apparently to make sure they didn't get out of the room after we got in.

"Three," Marc whispered, holding the knob even more tightly while on the other side of the room, Hall began speaking irritably again, "two, one…"

He threw the door open, stepped inside, and flung his tree branch across the room at the two men, seated at the table. It hit the man I recognised as 2L11 (something Lawson was his name), knocking him out of his seat and onto the floor, but not knocking him out. As Marc ducked and charged towards him, I wound up and hurled the brick at the stupidly gaping face of one of my two most hated people in the world (Ather Hignat was the other after what he'd done to Amelia and Natalie, and what he would like to do with Stella). It was my only shot, but it was a good one; it smashed straight into his face, rearranging it and knocking him onto the floor. Unlike 2L11, he was knocked out cold, and covered in blood to boot. There you go, I thought; that's payback for what you did to Serena's body. Now, if I could just find a way to pay you back for ordering Kylie's death… and for torturing Tulip in her final hour…

But there was no time for that. There was no time for anything. Before I knew it, the fight was over. Hall was motionless on the floor, and Marc was straightening up over 2L11, whom he had dealt with quite efficiently by a swift kick to the temple. Peter and James, who'd come in behind us, hadn't even needed to get their hands dirty.

"Shut the door," Marc advised James, who did so at once. "Looks like we've struck gold here; two number-twos, and both of them in uniform."

So they were.

"So we don't need to go back for Cornish after all." Peter breathed a sigh of relief.

"We were never gonna use him," Marc shrugged, "he was in the open. Now come on, you guys; help me with these two."

I helped Marc with 2L11 while Peter and James worked Hall out of his uniform. It was tiring work, but we eventually had the two men down to their jocks in the middle of the floor of what seemed to be a combination living room–kitchen. There were a few doors off the main room but most of the suite's main functions seemed to be in here. After Marc checked the pockets of both uniforms and found them empty (a bit of bad luck, but nothing we couldn't deal with), Marc and I began changing out of our top layers so that we could get into them. We were chosen to do the job because Peter and James had gotten a bit of Hall's blood on their hands; they would remain in the suite, standing guard over these two and taking the opportunity to stock up on anything that might be here. A few minutes later, we were ready to go.

"Should we take those things?" I asked, nodding at the brick and the tree branch. I hoped not because my right hand was very sore.

Marc considered. "Can one of you guys check if there's anything in any of those cupboards we can use as a weapon?"

Peter did the honours, taking only seconds to locate the kitchen knives. Marc and I each took the two sharpest ones he could find, concealing them in our pockets and hoping that they didn't cut their way through and end up perilously close to our testicles. Marc then opened the suite door and had a look out in the corridor to make sure nobody had noticed any trouble. It was still as deserted as before, so we slipped out, promised James and Peter that we would be no longer than half an hour, and set off for the lifts.

"We should probably keep our heads down," I suggested as we ascended to the top floor.

"Why?"

"So that people don't look at our faces. You're the same height as Hall, and I'm more or less the same height as 2L11; as long as they don't see our faces, they probably wouldn't look twice at us."

"Unless we run into someone who needs to speak to Hall or 2L11."

"That's why we've got knives," I reminded him.

The top level was just as empty as the third had been. All this lack of Hammerheart activity was starting to make me nervous. How much of it was good luck for us; how much was lulling us into a false sense of security? Whatever it was, Marc was intent on riding the lucky train as far as it would take us, and then creating our own luck after that. I agreed with that idea, but whatever was going on, I just hoped that neither Lucien nor Stella would be lurking back behind that wall at the end of the corridor. Lucien may well have gone out somewhere, or maybe he was still sleeping, but there was a good chance that Stella would be awake by now, and she had nowhere else she needed to be. What would she do if we ran into her? I didn't think she would hurt me, but that didn't mean she wouldn't turn us in to Lucien.

Marc and I walked side-by-side along the corridor till we reached the end, passing through the enchanted wall as though it weren't there. Nobody was waiting for us on the other side, and I couldn't hear any sounds coming from the living quarters or the downstairs corridor, but the moment we had entered this hidden part of the base, I immediately felt as though we were being watched. I stopped dead, looking carefully around for any sign of life, but Marc and I seemed to be the only ones present.

"I know, I feel it too," he muttered. "Come on, let's do this thing. I don't suppose you know which rooms we need?"

"Haven't got a clue. Let's just check them. You do the ones on the left; I'll do the right."

That would give Marc the room in which Tulip had died; I knew it to be empty, but I still didn't want to have to go in there.

We began our search. The rooms I found were either offices or something else entirely that I couldn't work out. Marc seemed to have much the same luck until he got to the fifth room, which appeared to be some kind of storage room. There were several large boxes in there, each of them packed to bursting with all manner of things, magical and non-magical alike. If I remembered correctly, Hammerson had ordered Lucien to get a camera from this room, and if I also remembered correctly, he had said it was next to the weapons room.

"Check all those boxes," I told him quietly, "grab anything that may seem useful, especially if you can find any bags that expand on the inside. I'll be back in a bit."

"What?" he protested. "Hey, I'm gonna need help here."

"I'll be back," I said shortly, leaving him there and going to check the next room, looking nervously back towards the stairs to the living quarters, unable to shake the feeling that someone was lurking there, watching us.

The weapons room, if that was what this was, was a lot like the room from which I had originally stolen the Darkness Crystal. It was small and contained nothing but a box, but unlike the room with the Darkness Crystal, this box was unlocked. I flipped up the lid and, looking inside, breathed in through my teeth. The box wasn't very big, and it looked like it expanded on the inside, but it was nevertheless packed to bursting with handheld weaponry. Digging in, I found agonators, bludginators, solid-outliners, stunners, vertual killing devices, those net-spinning things Stella had used on me this morning, and a wide range of other things. I felt myself relaxing in spite of myself; we'd found what we were looking for.

"Also, if they've got those belts they wear," I whispered as I rejoined Marc. "The weapons room is next door but there may be useful things in here."

"Yeah, reckon so," Marc muttered vaguely. "I'm pretty sure this'll unlock anything."

He held up a small, silver key for my inspection.

"Yeah, that's probably a master key," I agreed, plucking it out of his hand and putting it in my pocket. "See if you can find another couple of those, and a few extender-cases would be useful too, but those weapons belts︎—"

"Yeah, I heard you. Why don't you help me?"

"Oh, right."

I selected one of the other boxes and began looking through it. Like the one through which Marc was looking, it contained all kinds of magical and non-magical items, but I couldn't find any of the ones I was looking for. This one seemed to have mostly electrical equipment, some of which could have been magical, but none of which I could see being useful to us. I ditched that box and moved on to the next one, where I had slightly better luck when I found an invisibility toggle; a copy of the one originally created by Mr. Woodward. I kept rummaging until I found several more of them, stopping only when I'd stuffed six into my pockets; I couldn't have fit anything else in if I tried.

"Any luck?" I asked Marc.

"Not with what you said, but didn't you have one of these when you raided Stella's hideout that time?"

I looked over at him and saw him holding up something small and nondescript in his hand. I felt a thrill of excitement as I recognised it; it wasn't as good as an extender-case, and not as practical as four belts, but it would serve if we couldn't find either of those things. The pouch didn't expand limitlessly, but it would be enough to carry a selection of weapons out of here. My smile widened; as long as we got moving quickly, our luck was still in.

"Let me take that," I whispered, taking it from him, "I'll go fill it with weapons from next door. Maybe check one of the other boxes—not those two, though; I've already done them."

"What's next door?" he asked.

"A box full of agonators, bludginators, and the like."

I left him there and went back to the weapons room, stopping dead halfway between the doors and looking around nervously again. There was no noise other than Marc's muffled search, and no sign of life other than the two of us, but that feeling remained. Our luck was still in, but if we stayed here a minute too long, it could run out very quickly. We had to get out of here as quickly as we could, whether Marc found anything else useful or not.

Agonators, bludginators, stunners, solid-outliners, virtual killing devices (why don't I just call them 'killers') and net-spinners: those were the weapons that would be most useful. There were probably others in there that we could use but I had to give priority to the ones we knew how to use—unless I found a hero device or two in there. I highly doubted that Lucien would have had a chance to re-create them, though, and even if he had, I didn't think he would; he understood as well as the rest of us just how dangerous those things were. I dug into the box and picked out six of each of the weapons I'd decided on (one for each of us and a couple of extras in case something went wrong) and stuffed them into the pouch. By the time I was done, the pouch was almost completely full.

"Any luck?" I asked Marc as I returned to him.

"Do these look like those gloves that are resistant to thicky prison?"

He held up a pair of gloves for my inspection. I thought they probably were, but there was no way to be sure; they could just as easily have been a normal old pair of gloves. I hesitated, wondering if it was worth taking the chance, anxious to be gone from this corridor. I quickly came to the decision that solid-outliners weren't entirely useful without the gloves, but we still needed to be sure. I therefore took a solid-outliner and a stunner from the pouch.

"Put them on," I told him. "We're gonna find out."

He opened his mouth, apparently ready to ask questions, but I gave him a stern look—there was just no time for that. He shrugged and began putting them on, while I set the stunner on the floor and shot it with the solid-outliner; the thicky prison covered it immediately. I straightened up and gestured from Marc to the stunner with the solid-outliner; he understood what I was planning. He knelt down, hesitated for a moment, then touched his gloved finger to the thicky prison. We waited for a few heart-stopping seconds, but nothing happened.

"Phew," said Marc, getting back to his feet and whipping the gloves off, while I freed the stunner from the thicky prison and stuffed it and the solid-outliner back in the pouch.

"I think we should get a move on," I told him. "I'm getting really nervous hanging around in here."

"Me too. Here, can you fit these in that pouch?"

"I think so," I said, taking the gloves from him and trying to stuff them in. They only just fit, and there was absolutely no room for anything else. "We can distribute these when we get back to James and 9t—"

A door slammed nearby, making me and Marc jump. I felt my insides go icy while Marc went very pale. It sounded like that had come from upstairs—in the direction of the bedrooms, if I had it right—the bedrooms where both Lucien and Stella had gone to sleep earlier.

"Let's get the hell out of here," I said, my voice shaking out of control.

We took off, more quickly than quietly now, tearing out of the corridor and through the enchanted wall into the corridor outside, which was still blessedly and strangely empty. In the moment before we passed through the wall, however, I felt it again: the unmistakable feeling of being watched. It was gone as soon as we were out and sprinting towards the lifts at the opposite end of the corridor. The elevator we'd taken to get up here hadn't been used in the time since; it opened immediately and took us down to the third level.

"Don't attack, it's just us," Marc said as he slowly opened the door to the suite where we'd left Peter and James. Peter, who'd been standing almost right in front of the door, visibly relaxed at the sight of Marc. It looked like he'd been on the verge of slicing Marc's nose off.

They hadn't bothered to clean up the suite in our absence (the brick and tree branches particularly stood out), but what they had done was bind Hall and 2L11 around the shoulders, wrists, waist, knees and ankles, and tie them to the couches. The pair had also been gagged; all they could do was make angry grunting noises while rolling their eyes furiously at us.

"I'm not so sure they appreciate what we've done," said James, flushed. "How'd it go up there?"

"Not perfect, but we've got some weapons," I said, opening the pouch. "Should we hand them out now?"

"Yeah, I'd rather be armed with those things than have to take the tree branches with us again," said Peter. "What are we gonna do with those anyway? Leave them here?"

"No reason not to," Marc shrugged, glancing at Hall, "these two have already seen us."

I picked out one of each weapon and handed them to the boys, who stuffed them in their pockets. I also gave each of them an invisibility toggle before taking a couple of weapons for myself. My pockets were already too full to carry too many, so I selected a bludginator, solid-outliner and invisibility toggle to carry, keeping the rest in the pouch and stuffing them all in my pockets.

"Are we ready to go?" Marc asked.

"One question," said James, looking soberly around at us. "Where are we going? I know there's merit in staying in Chopville, since we know the place, but if we move further away, we may be able to stay safer in general."

Marc shook his head vehemently. "No, we're staying in Chopville, James, end of story. How effectively do you think we'll be able to run when we're lost?"

"But Marc—"

"No, we're staying," he said firmly. "Let's go."

I exchanged a surprised look with Peter and James. What had just happened? I would have preferred to stay in Chopville too, but why was Marc so angry about it? He already had his hand on the doorknob, ready to open it so that we could leave. "Come on," he urged.

"I think everything here is in order," said Peter smugly, winking at Hall as we followed Marc from the room.

As before, the elevator doors opened immediately when Marc pushed the button. Our run of good luck was still in, even this late in the game. He stepped in, waited for the rest of us, then pressed the button for the Hammerheart Highway. As the doors slid shut, he glared at James.

"And I thought you were sensible," he fumed, "but you almost gave away our next location right in front of Hall. What good would it do to run if we tell them exactly where we're going?"

James took a step back, dismay written all over his face. "Shit," he spluttered. "Thank God you stopped me."

"As it is, I agree with you," Marc went on, "but since we don't have time to pick a place before this thing opens again, why don't we just pick the first Hammerheart residence in Melbourne by alphabetical order and meet there."

Right on cue, the doors began to open on the foyer, but that was where our good luck ended. There were two people waiting for us when the doors opened, a male and a female…except that the female had her back to us, while the man was still lying unconscious not far from the door. It was incredible: In the entire time we'd been inside the base, not a single Hammerheart had been through here. Cornish hadn't been found, and the Beast of Magic continued to stand and wait for orders.

"Stupid idiot," Marc muttered as we walked past, "didn't even think to order Fewul to fix him up if something happened to him."

"What was he supposed to go out there and do with Fewul?" Peter asked as we walked down the first set of steps to the tracks.

"Something he's too busy to do himself," said James uncomfortably. "First guess would be to recover what ground was lost to the Woodwards while they had May."

"Probably true," Marc agreed. "You all remember where we're going?"

"First residence in Melbourne," said James as two carts pulled up in front of us. Marc and I got into the one in front while James and Peter took the one behind.

I used the list to find our next destination; 'Oceania', 'Victoria' and then 'Melbourne' brought up the list of places, topped by the base 'B773'. The top item preceded by the letter R was 'R193762', and it belonged to a Hammerheart or Hammerhearts by the name of Adams.

"The Adams family," Marc read as I selected it. "Geez, you wouldn't read about it."

"Hold on," I braced, and then pressed the 'Go' button.

Chapter 7: We're the Thomas Brothers

The journey to Melbourne was a bit longer than those within Chopville's borders, but not by a whole lot; this one was more like a third of a second, rather than a tenth. When we pulled up, the station was nothing more than a small platform, big enough for four or five people to stand on, and with nothing but a door and a button—no slide like the ones I'd become used to. We got out and pressed the button to send the cart away, but if I'd so much as blinked, it would have looked as though rather than the cart disappearing, Peter and James had simply appeared inside it. They were both swaying slightly, as though made much dizzier than me and Marc by the journey, and it took them several seconds to recover enough to get out.

"You guys okay?" I asked, helping Peter out and pushing him against the door so that there would be room for James on the platform.

"What the hell just happened?" Peter moaned; he had gone very white.

"You guys pulled up as soon as our cart left," said Marc, and he looked like he was actually fighting not to laugh. "Did it just do what I think it did?"

"It went on forever," James moaned, equally staggered.

I almost burst out laughing. It looked as though while we had been getting out, there hadn't been enough room for their cart to pull up here, and something in the intelligence of the system must have known it. Peter and James had apparently been put into a kind of holding pattern, like the kind aeroplanes have to do while waiting to land at an airport. They must have been zooming all over Melbourne for at least thirty seconds, getting dizzier and dizzier all the while.

"Okay," said Marc, "don't get rid of that cart then; we won't be disturbed from the Highway as long as it's there. I hope to God that this thing opens inward."

He reached past Peter, took hold of the doorknob, and twisted. It was locked tight, and we no longer had any monumental tree branches we could use to knock it down, nor the necessary space in which to swing such weapons. Peter and James were thinking the same thoughts I was; their faces had gone even paler. Marc, on the other hand, merely sighed.

"Still got that key, John?"

"Oh, yeah."

I rummaged in my pocket, past all the other accumulated stuff in there, until my fingers touched the small, silver key Marc had found earlier. I took it out, put it in the lock, and twisted the knob. The door opened easily after that, but unfortunately, it really did open outward. James and I had to squeeze against the wall just to get the door open wide enough for Peter and Marc to slip through, then close the door almost all the way so that we could move around it and go through ourselves. I hesitated for a moment before going through, looking at the cart on the tracks. I had a bad feeling about leaving it there, but perhaps Marc was right; perhaps it would be harder for Hammerhearts (who didn't have the ability to teleport) to reach us here.

The room beyond was even darker than the dimly lit Highway. The moment I stepped through it, I found myself surrounded by items of soft material on all sides. I flung my arms outward, trying to work out which way I had to go, and located James's shoulders ahead of me. It was only when the softness fell away did I realise that they were clothes, and judging by the rectangular-shaped light ahead of me, we had entered the house through someone's walk-in wardrobe. Marc and Peter were already in the bedroom, watching me and James as we emerged.

"Now I know why they keep the door locked," said Peter. "Who'd want strangers coming through their wardrobe like we just did?"

"Strange place to put the Highway," James agreed, glancing back over his shoulder at it. "It's like a real-world version of Narnia in there; maybe that's what they were going for."

"Come on, then," said Marc, "as long as we're talking this loudly, we'd better see if anyone's home. Solid-outliners and stunners at the ready."

"Should we make ourselves invisible?" I suggested.

Marc thought it over for no more than a second. "Nah, we may need to coordinate with each other; that'll be harder if we can't see each other."

"Shame we don't have something that can do invisibility veils," James muttered as Peter walked to the open bedroom door and looked out in the hall.

The moment we'd all fallen silent, we were able to listen to the sounds around us. My first thought was that this had to be an apartment building rather than a house, judging by the noises coming from both above and below. The near vicinity, however, seemed to be very quiet. The four of us left the bedroom and began looking around the house, determining within a minute that there was no one home. I breathed a sigh of relief, but both Marc and James still looked alert.

"I'd suggest we stay here for a little bit," James suggested, looking carefully around the lounge room where the four of us had met up again, "just so that we can fix ourselves up and recover before going out there and finding somewhere better to stay for the night. We should probably steal from these people too; if they've got anything useful anyway."

"James, I was fine with stealing from Hignat and Wilwog," said Peter nervously, "but these people are strangers. They could be really decent for all we know."

"They've got a Hammerheart Highway in their bedroom," I reminded him, "so they're not exactly world-class citizens either. I'm with James on this one."

"We should also get some food and drink," said Marc. "I dunno about you guys, but I'm famished."

"Hear, hear," said Peter, digging into his pocket and starting to pull Mars Bars from it. Passing them around, he said, "Use them wisely, my friends. How's this for a plan: Marc, you stand guard in the hall in case someone comes through the door; John, you go fix yourself up in the bathroom, 'cause you still look awful; James, you can raid the kitchen, while I look through the rest of the house. We'll meet up in the hall in a bit."

"Pete, you're a fast learner," said James solemnly.

And so we split up, although given the size of the place, we were never too far from each other. The kitchen and lounge room were only separated by a bench, and the opening into the hall was quite large, meaning that James could see Marc from where he was. There was a small corridor off the hall, containing the entrances to the bedroom through which we had come, what looked like a computer room, a laundry, and a bathroom with a toilet in it. I ate the Mars Bar, my stomach complaining angrily that this morsel of food wasn't nearly enough, and took the Band-Aids and the face washer from Peter before shutting myself in the bathroom.

"Don't be tempted to use the toilet until I've been through there," Peter called through the closed door. "I will look in there, you know."

"Sure, sure." I called back, but I didn't need to go too badly anyway, given that I'd taken a piss in the bushes earlier and hadn't drank anything since.

Now that I had a mirror in front of me, I could see just how bad I looked. The cut across my forehead was by far the worst; it was big, jagged, and now scabbed over. It was probably deep enough to require stitches too, although that certainly wasn't an option at the moment. What was far worse was the possibility that there may be fragments of glass embedded in there, and if that were the case, it could lead to infection. What could I do about it, though? If this had happened in a more normal time and magic wasn't an option, I surely would have been taken to a doctor, but how could I go to a doctor now? They would take one look at me, recognise who I was, and call the cops.

I decided to focus on my other injuries for now and return to the serious one last. I ran cold water over the face washer and dabbed it on my right cheak, which was a brighter, harder red than the left. As it had less than twenty-four hours ago when Natalie had burnt it, I felt relief almost immediately. I held it there while fishing a Band-Aid out of the packet and putting it over the cut in my neck, feeling that I was wasting my time; that horse had probably bolted. I repeated the process for the shallow cuts on my right leg, and then straightened up, searching for any head damage where Lucien's bedroom wall had almost taken me out. I felt gingerly around the place that hurt but couldn't find any cuts beneath my hair, so maybe it hadn't broken the skin.

Now, back to the issue at hand. I removed the face washer, ran more cold water over it, and began trying to touch it to my forehead. The pain flared up immediately, making me dizzy. I hung onto the edge of the basin and tried again, but the pain brought tears to my eyes. My heart rate had quickened, the blood pounding in my head so that it sounded like someone was banging a bass drum in time with it. I stared at my reflection in the mirror, my scabbed and probably scarred forehead standing out starkly on my face, which had gone very pale. My eyes were much larger in my face than they should have been, and they seemed to know the thing I now had to come to terms with. I could be in big trouble here.

There was a knock at the door. "John, you okay in there?" Peter called to me.

"Er—not really," I called back, my voice trembling a little.

"What?" he asked, opening the door and looking in.

"I think there might be glass stuck in there," I said, indicating my forehead, though not daring to touch it.

Peter's eyes widened. "Are you serious? James!" he called over his shoulder. "We need you!"

"Did he become a doctor while I was asleep?" I asked vaguely, my head starting to spin as the beginnings of panic set in.

"No, but I'd trust him before myself in handling something like this."

"What's happening?" James asked, and his face appeared behind me, reflected in the mirror. "John, what's wrong?"

"What's going on?" I heard Marc call from the hall, but to his credit, he didn't leave his station.

As Peter spoke to James, I leaned over the basin, feeling like I might throw up. What was going on? I'd never reacted like this before, and I'd been through all sorts of crap. I'd even lost my right arm once; it almost killed me but it never made me nauseous.

"Come on, mate," said James, taking my shoulder and pulling me upright. "If there is glass in there, we need to get it out now. Pete,

I'm gonna need tweezers, and anything that looks like it might help me cut this thing back open; and if you see any penicillin in there, make sure you grab all of it."

"Right," said Peter, now looking appropriately nervous.

"Where are we gonna do this?" I asked as James steered me out of the bathroom.

"Couch," he said shortly. "I hope you don't mind, John, but since there's no natural light coming through here anymore, I'm gonna need to use the Light Crystal to see what I'm doing. You'll need to close your eyes."

"I was gonna do that anyway," I mumbled.

I lay down on the couch, resting my head wearily on the arm and closing my eyes. Maybe this would be a good time to drift off and see what Stella's up to, I thought; at least if it meant I wouldn't have to feel what was about to happen to me. Perhaps if I'd fallen asleep quickly, that might have worked, but there just wasn't enough time. Peter was soon handing James a small blade-like object I never actually saw, but I certainly felt it—I felt it plenty. Worse, Peter hadn't been able to find any tweezers, so James had to do that part with the knife as well. About twenty seconds into the cutting, by which time my throat was locked and my jaws and fists clenched, James stopped what he was doing long enough for Peter to wrench open my mouth and fill it with a balled-up pair of socks.

"Sorry," he muttered, "but seriously, you start screaming, someone might call the cops."

"Just try to relax," James insisted, winding his fingers into my hair to hold my head steady. I could think of a whole host of things I would like to say in response to the utter lunacy of that statement, but having one's mouth stuffed with a Hammerheart's pair of smelly old socks wasn't conducive to swearing like a sailor.

After a time that felt like hours, though was probably only ten or fifteen minutes, James said, "Pete, see if you can find a bandage. I'm a little worried Band-Aids mightn't be enough to deal with this."

"I think he needs stitches for that, James," said Peter from somewhere else in the apartment.

"He does," James agreed, "but we don't have the resources to make that happen here. We have to make do with what we've got. Just see if there are bandages in there; if not, grab some hankies or something that'll do the same job."

"Righto," he muttered, not sounding happy about it, but moving away to do as he was told.

"Did you find anything else useful back there?" Marc asked him.

"Not really, no," Peter said, now even further away. "I was mainly looking for money, but I think these people must have taken their wallets with them. There are things we could probably sell if we had more time—jewellery, electronics, and so on—but that's not gonna help put a roof over our heads tonight."

"Are you sure we shouldn't just stay here?" Marc asked. "I mean, what's the worst that can happen? Not counting Lucien turning up, I mean, and that could happen anywhere. If the occupants come home, we can subdue them easily enough."

"Don't think that's a good idea," said James. "Even if we knock them unconscious, there might be some way for whoever controls this building to know if there's been trouble. The last thing we need is for someone to call the cops."

"And maybe they'll be ready to fight," Peter added, returning to the hall. "Will this do?"

Marc burst out laughing for some reason, but James merely said, "Yeah, that'll have to do. Brace yourself, John."

I've been braced the entire time, idiot, I thought sourly. I couldn't remember the last time I had felt quite this pathetic. I chose to think about this than allow myself to notice what James was doing to me now. Whatever it was, it wasn't as bad as the cutting had been. I was only brought back to the present when he lifted my head so that he could wrap something around it. Whatever it was, I couldn't feel it at all on my forehead, but it seemed to be rather longer than was really required for the job; he had to secure it by winding the ends around my neck.

"Hmm," said James, taking a step back from the couch, "I think that's probably the best we can do for now. Pete, did you find any drugs back there?"

"There is a bottle of penicillin here," said Peter, "except it's almost a year past its expiration date, and there are only five pills left."

"Put it back, then," James said regretfully. "Maybe these people will be stupid enough to possibly poison themselves, but we don't need that. We'll just have to hope that John doesn't have an infection, and if he does, we'll have to get medication from somewhere else. After that, if you don't have anything else to do, Pete, can you help me clean this up?"

"Sure thing, Sensei. I am your surgeon's assistant, after all."

"Bite me, grasshopper," James smirked. "You just lie there for a bit longer till you get your equilibrium back, John. Here…"

He pulled the socks out of my mouth, and I resisted the urge to cough and splutter. "Thanks," I said weakly. "You know, maybe I should have just gone to Lucien; sure, he'd screw my mind up, but he'd probably be good enough to make this go away."

"Get out of his head, Stella," Marc said flatly from the next room, and I smiled in spite of myself. It was good to know that even if I might be a burden, they still wanted me around.

Nobody talked for a short while after that as Peter and James began cleaning up whatever mess had been made here. I could only imagine the skin, blood, and possibly even flesh that had been dug out of my body. There had been a few pieces of glass in there too, James had said, although they had been so small that they mightn't have caused any problems. I didn't believe that; my head had been far too painful to the touch to mean nothing.

I felt a bit better by the time they were done, perhaps even well enough to eat. James had found a box of assorted party snacks in the freezer—party pies, sausage rolls, mini dim sims and spring rolls— which he'd had the sense to put in the oven before taking a knife to my head. We sat in the hall so that we could keep an eye on the front door, eating the best dinner we could manage and sharing a bottle of diet soft drink between us, but I didn't think we were going to have any trouble from the home's occupants; they seemed to have gone out for the Saturday night. By the time we were done eating and removed as much evidence of the meal as we could, it was just after seven o'clock and Marc and James both wanted to get moving.

"We still don't have any money, though," Peter pointed out. "Did you hear what I said earlier?"

James nodded. "I did, and I agree; besides, selling stuff would draw unwanted attention to us. We'll just have to take what we already have and nick some cash off someone on the street."

"You mean we're gonna mug someone?" said Marc, eyes widening. "Are we still the good guys here or what?"

James shrugged. "If they knew that it was the only way to assure their freedom, which it could well be, they mightn't mind being mugged. Besides, we don't have to hurt anyone; we can just use our stunners and pick their pockets."

"I've got a bad feeling about this," Peter moaned.

"Do you have a better idea, Pete?"

"There's no dignified way to answer that," he muttered.

"Where are we going anyway?" I asked, hoping either of them had half an idea.

"The streets, mate," said Marc solemnly. "With a bit of luck, we'll find a roof to put over our heads in the next few hours."

"Should we make ourselves invisible?" I asked.

Marc and James glanced at each other, both looking unsure. Eventually, Marc said, "Better not, for the same reason we didn't make ourselves invisible here. I don't think it matters too much if strangers see us out there, and if Hammerhearts try to fight us…we're no longer defenceless. Are we all ready for this?"

We all looked at each other. I didn't know about myself, but something had changed in their faces, as though they had suddenly aged a few years. I tried to see the boys I had always known through what we were likely to very soon become.

Marc opened the front door and looked out into the hall. After a few seconds, he waved us forward. We piled out after him, Peter bringing up the rear and shutting the door behind him. Our part of the hall was empty, but there were a couple of women further up, waiting by the elevators. After a silent consultation, we decided to proceed anyway. It was probably best; we would look even more suspicious if we didn't walk around the place as though we belonged here. It meant that we had to ride down in the lift with them, but thankfully it was only four floors. In fact, they looked even more relieved than us when we got out on the ground level—they were both destined for the car park.

It was in the foyer where the next problem presented itself. The front doors were dead ahead, and it was only a set of steps between the doors and the street, but both doors—the in and the out—were manned. If it had only been people coming in who needed to be checked, we would probably be fine. What sort of checks did they do on people leaving the building? Would they need identification? Would they need to know which apartment we'd been in if we had been visiting? Which apartment had we been in anyway?

"What's the plan?" James whispered.

"Don't give him a reason to be suspicious," Marc hissed back. "We just came to visit the Adams family on the fourth floor, that's all he needs to know."

If only it were that simple.

"Leaving, boys?" the man said, putting an arm out to stop Marc walking past him.

"Yeah, thanks," said Marc casually, giving him a winning smile.

"Don't remember seeing you come in," he said, scrutinising the four of us. The bloke who was supposed to be manning the other door looked over, eyebrows raised. "How long have you been up there?"

"Most of the day," said Marc, his smile faltering slightly. "I can't remember exactly what time we got in; can you guys?"

We all shook our heads, none of us daring to speak.

"Which apartment have you been in?" he asked, and my stomach dropped. Damn, we'd got an alert one.

"Er—can't remember the number," said Marc shiftily, "but it was on the fl—"

"If you don't know the number, how did you find it?"

This was heading downhill very quickly indeed.

"They were with us when we came in," Marc snapped, "so we didn't have to go looking for it. Can we go now or what?"

"Who were with you when you came in?"

"The Adamses."

"Which ones?"

Aw crap. What now?

Marc raised his arms in frustration. "For God's sake, we're leaving the building! What do you think we're trying to do here?"

"Would you four boys mind showing me what's in your pockets, please?" the man said sternly, and any chance we'd ever had of slipping by discreetly was gone.

It was James who spoke this time. "If we were trying to sneak stuff out of the building, and you're implying that we snuck in in the first place, why would we be trying to leave through the front doors?"

"Empty your pockets onto this table here, please, or I'll call the cops."

"Hang on a sec, John," the other man said, and it took me a second to realise that he wasn't talking to me. "I think maybe I did let these boys in. That one looks familiar," he indicated Marc. "Did I check you in earlier, boy?"

"Maybe," Marc shrugged. "It might have been you, but we didn't stop for conversation."

"Did you give me your names?" he asked the four of us.

"Er—Mor—"

"Thomas," said James quickly. "We're the Thomas brothers— Marc, John, Peter, James," he indicated each of us when he spoke our names. Smart move, I thought; his was the only name that couldn't possibly be linked to the Chopville Quartet.

Or could it? The man's eyes had widened at the mention of Marc's name. Too late, James realised that he should have given entirely fake names instead of only partially fake. He exchanged a stricken look with Marc.

"Sorry about this," Marc said conspiratorially to the man guarding the exit door, and then without any warning whatsoever, he punched the man squarely in the jaw. Peter, James and I goggled; none of us had had any sense of it coming. The man—John, his name seemed to be—rocked back, smacking his head on a pillar behind him and collapsing into a sitting position, his eyes wide and dazed. A group of people had come halfway up the steps in front just in time to see the blow; they cried out in horror as Marc shot past, the rest of us hurrying after him, trying desperately not to trip down the stairs.

Behind us, we heard the other man yell, "I knew he looked like that Moran bloke from Chopville! Call the police! Call them!"

Way to remain inconspicuous, I thought irritably as the four of us turned right and sprinted up the sidewalk. I didn't know about the others, but I had no thought other than to move as quickly as I could away from here, and if we were to stay together, it meant that we would follow Marc to wherever we ended up: our safety or our capture. All along the street, people stopped, watched, pointed, and got out of our way as we passed. Those closest to the incident seemed to understand what had just happened while those up ahead, seeing us coming, considered that we were probably young delinquents anyway, and so didn't give us any trouble.

By the time we reached the first intersection, we could already hear the sirens approaching. They were coming from behind, perhaps heading towards the building, but they were also coming from the left, and dead ahead. Unsurprisingly, they were responding in full force to the four most-wanted people on the planet. I exchanged a terrified look with Peter.

"We have to keep going," Marc shouted at us, turning right and beginning to run again.

It was night-time but the streets were lit up like a birthday cake, making me feel horribly exposed. This street was just as packed with people as the last one; there were a few winos and people who might have been drug addicts for all I knew, but most of them looked like Saturday night party-goers—women in particular, dressed up in short skirts and high-heels in a complete mockery of the freezing temperature. None of these people wanted a bar of us, whether they recognised us or not. To them, we were just a bunch of low-life teenagers, probably homeless (true) and on the run from the law (also true). How did this happen to us? We were supposed to be fighting for all these people to be free of a magical tyranny, and here they were, lowering their eyes and crossing to the other side of the street as we ran towards them. Even in the current desperate situation, it hurt.

The sirens were getting louder, closing in on the scene of the crime now—probably already there, in fact. Worse, there were more coming, this time from directly ahead of us. We had to get off this street right now, or we were history. Fortunately, Marc seemed to be thinking the same thing, for he chose that moment to dart to the right, cutting down a short alley between two buildings which ended in a locked door with a 'Staff Only' sign on it.

"John, I don't care what's in there; open that door!" he demanded.

I fumbled for the key, found it, rammed it into the lock, turned it, and wrenched on the handle. The room beyond was a dark passageway of some description; it smelt like horse shit, but we didn't let that stop us. We piled in and shut the door behind us, plunging the room into total darkness. Now what?

"Now what?" Peter echoed my thoughts perfectly.

"We wait for a bit," Marc breathed, "until we know how intensely they're searching, and how far they'll spread out. We're probably gonna have to go invisible just to get out of here, though."

"We need to find somewhere safe to lie low," James panted. "A few months ago, we probably could have beaten the police in a fight with magic, but now they've got magical weapons too, and they would have been trained to use them."

"They've probably got revealers too," I said shakily. This was looking worse and worse every second.

"So what about finding a roof to put over our heads?" Peter asked. "Is that still in the question?"

"Only if we can shake the cops loose quickly," said Marc, "otherwise we'll just have to settle for not being behind bars."

"God, life sucks," Peter muttered.

"So, invisibility toggles?" James enquired. "How do we stay together? We can't very well pick a place to meet up; none of us knows our way around in this city."

"We'll have to hang onto each other," said Marc unhappily. "James, you take my shoulder; John, you take James's; and Peter, you take John's. You guys are only gonna have one free hand, so pick your weapon wisely."

"Bludginator," said Peter at once.

"Solid-outliner," I said a moment later.

James sighed. "Guess that leaves me with the stunner, 'cause I'm not using the agonator, and I'm definitely not using that killing thing on those officers out there, not after Stella said they'll really kill after a while."

"Okay," said Marc, "and I'll use a bludginator and this net thing, whatever it's called. Make yourselves invisible first—"

He was cut off as a loud, amplified voice boomed from somewhere nearby. The words came through loud and clear: Everyone was to clear the area because they had four extremely dangerous criminals trapped. There would likely be shooting, and no innocent bystanders could be caught in the crossfire. Everyone had one minute to clear the area before the police would lock these four blocks down and nobody would be able to get in or out. In the darkness, the four of us exchanged frightened looks.

"There's no way we can get out in a minute," Peter hissed.

"It's worse than that," said James solemnly. "They know they have us trapped here; someone must have seen us come in here. If we open this door, they'll probably shoot through the opening immediately."

"So what do we do?" I asked, dreading the answer. "Do we have to fight our way through?"

"We go the other way," said James, pointing down the passageway. "I don't know where this thing goes, but there's bound to be a way out. Come on; invisibility."

We shuffled around for a bit, making ourselves invisible and getting hold of our preferred weapons; then we shuffled some more as we worked ourselves into a line with Marc in front, followed by James, then me, and then Peter, bringing up the rear with his back to the door. We began moving forward, slowly at first and then a bit more quickly.

"Any of you guys, let me know if we should slow down," Marc hissed back at us.

"Okay, but don't go too much faster than this," said Peter, "otherwise James mightn't be able to stop in time."

"So not the time, Pete," said James through gritted teeth.

"Sorry; stress brings out the funny side of me. You should have heard what I said to Arnold Hammerson this one time—"

"Will you guys shut up?!" Marc hissed.

The end of the passage was dead ahead now, and there were two doors to choose from, both to the right. Marc must have stopped at the first one and tried to open because to my eyes, the knob tried to turn itself. This door turned out to be unlocked; he opened it as narrowly as he could so that the four of us could slip through. Peter tugged on my shoulder to make me stop long enough so that he could close it behind us.

We were in a kitchen of some sort. It was large and presently unoccupied, although it must have been in full swing only minutes earlier because the heat filling the place was almost overpowering. It must have been a restaurant, but the cooks, like all the diners, were being forced from the premises. We knew this was going on because of the shouting echoing from the next room: "No, sir, you have to leave immediately! Yes, you'll be refunded, now please leave before the police throw tear gas in here."

"Tear gas?" Peter hissed behind me, the panic evident in his voice even without an actual tone to go with it.

"This would be a good time to speed up," James whispered, urging Marc forward.

There were two doors out of the kitchen, not counting the one we'd just come through, which I now saw, when I had looked back unseeingly at Peter, was a fire escape. One of the other doors was open; through it, I could see a hallway with a couple of offices, the toilets, and bright light spilling through an opening that had to be the actual restaurant itself. The other door was closed, but it had a window in its upper half which revealed the outside again. Naturally, Marc wound his way through the kitchen, passing ovens, stoves and a walk-in fridge towards this door. It, too, was unlocked, and we managed to slip through just in time. Barely a second after the door had snapped shut, two people sped back into the kitchen from the corridor and began hurrying to turn everything off.

"We dodged a bullet there," James moaned.

"No we haven't," said Marc, continuing to move forward. "Those two are probably gonna come out this way; we have to keep moving."

We had come out in a small, grubby old car park which was probably for the staff only. Marc turned us to the left and began following the line of the building to the end, but rather than turning onto a driveway as I'd expected, we had to walk through another alleyway between two buildings. Where on earth were we heading now? This one was sheltered by overhanging branches, and the car park behind us had been considerably darker than the street. I couldn't see anything ahead except more blackness; this was a long alleyway, much longer than the one that had got us into this mess. The only good thing was that the longer we went in this one direction, the greater the chance that we might sneak past the police blockades without even having to see them.

It was a very scary environment. Not only were their police sirens in every direction, not to mention the unmistakable sounds of a lot of people moving all around us (I couldn't be sure if I was only imagining that one), but I could also hear the even more unmistakable sound of a helicopter approaching from the distance. I still couldn't see anything, though; the fences on either side of us were quite high and branches were still hanging over our heads, when we suddenly emerged into the open about five minutes later.

We had come out in what seemed to be a suburban football ground, surrounded on all sides by fences and buildings of varying shapes and sizes. There didn't seem to be any people on the oval, but the place was much more illuminated than it should have been. The police had spotlights in the sky, lighting everything up and once again, making me feel horribly exposed. I had to keep reminding myself that we were invisible, and that it was unlikely for anyone, even in this lighting, to see our invisible feet kicking stones aside at this time of night.

"We should still try and avoid those lights, though," James said, as though reading my mind. "I don't know where that chopper is, but I'm willing to bet they're firing revealers down from it to try and flush us out."

"The driveway's over there," said Peter. "Er—I mean, straight ahead and slightly to the right."

I could see it too. Squinting, I saw something even better; it led down onto another street, which was teaming with people. They weren't moving especially quickly, but as we got closer, I could see that they all looked nervous and frightened. I didn't blame them; I felt exactly the same way, though for very different reasons. The good thing, though, was that it looked like we had somehow slipped past the police blockades after all. As long as nothing happened to us between here and that street, maybe we could slip back in with the people and resume our original plan...whatever that had been.

Something very nearly did happen. When we were three quarters of the way across the oval, the helicopter came straight over our heads. They didn't see us, of course, but James had been right about the revealers; a jet of transparent light came down no more than six feet ahead of us, almost invisible in this light. In fact, it had only been visible at all because it had come down directly in front of a spotlight. Marc stopped dead; James almost knocked him over and Peter and I piled into them both. The four of us stood stock-still after that; I didn't know about them but I was looking up at the helicopter, tracking its progress as it zoomed around the edge of the oval. Whoever was operating it didn't seem to believe we would be standing in the open because they swung back the other way and headed back towards the apartment building where all this trouble had started.

Ahead, Marc let out a sigh of relief. "That was too damn close. Come on, guys; we've gotta get over there."

We resumed walking, picking up speed now in our eagerness to leave this part of our unwanted adventure behind. Other than Peter tripping in a gutter as we left the grass and stepped onto the gravel driveway, pushing me and almost causing a domino effect that would have left us all waving our arms around in the air, trying to locate each other; nothing else happened. When we got to the end of the driveway and had moved aside (in the unlikely event that a car tried to pull in), I saw that I'd been right a few minutes earlier. These people seemed intent on getting to wherever they were going—the queue to get on a massively filled-past-capacity tram running down the middle of the street was causing a few traffic problems—but through all that, the cops weren't ordering the people out of the area. They must have seriously believed that they'd trapped us back there; maybe they didn't know about that alleyway.

Or maybe they were all around us, lying in wait, knowing we had most likely taken that escape route.

"I know we probably left them back there," James whispered, "but we can't let our guard down just yet. The longer they don't find us, the wider they'll throw the net."

"What do we do now?" I asked. "Are we still going to try to find a place to sleep?"

"Yes," said James, "but like we worked out before, that's not going to be easy. Come on, we need to find a relatively safe place to work out a plan."

Chapter 8: Excuse Me, Tiberius

The walk along this bustling thoroughfare was a very uncomfortable one. Marc, James, Peter and I were all still invisible, still moving slowly so that we wouldn't lose each other, and having to weave out of the way of people as they approached us. The whole thing was made worse by the continued sounds of the manhunt happening nearby, though thankfully it didn't reach us here. To top it off, we had no idea where we were or where we were going; while Marc and Peter were focussing mostly on moving us out of the way of people coming at us from ahead and behind respectively, and I kept looking from side to side in terror of what might happen if someone came at us from that direction (we couldn't possibly move aside in time), James was apparently looking for a dark, secluded place where the four of us could conference and make ourselves visible again without fear of being immediately struck down.

Eventually, after we had negotiated our way across three busy and terrifying intersections, James directed Marc towards a spot that might serve our purpose. A tall wooden fence surrounded a block of land, on which seemed to sit a convent or something similar, and between the fence and the next building (a cosy little cafÃ©) was a gap, wide enough for two of us to simultaneously step through. It also seemed to be pitch-black in there because not only were both the fence and the building too high to allow the lights from the street to penetrate more than a couple of feet, but further in, overhanging trees from the other side of the fence sheltered it from the sky above. Marc led us into the darkness, which turned out to be a lot dirtier than the street and apparently a good place to hide litter, and didn't stop until we reached a dead-end—not a door this time but the back of another building.

"I think we can be visible here," James whispered, and a moment later, he appeared right in front of me. The rest of us followed his lead, but even so, it was still almost impossible to see each other. The light from the street was nothing more than a distant chink from here, and the trees overhead almost completely blotted out the sky.

The four of us did a bit of shuffling around so that we were all facing each other; then James took the Light Crystal from his pocket and placed it in the middle of us so that it shone upon all our faces. There wasn't any real danger of it being seen by anyone else, not with Marc directly blocking it from the street and James keeping his hand over the top of it.

"Did you guys see the place on that last block?" Peter hissed at us. "I'm almost sure it was a place for homeless people."

"What?" Marc gaped at him. "Why on earth didn't you stop us at the time?"

"Well, we weren't really in a position where we could stop," Peter retorted.

"And places like that require money anyway," said James. "It's probably the worst accommodation you could ever imagine too, but I suppose unless you guys wanna sleep in here tonight, it's the best we can do."

"Money," I repeated the word, my voice sounding dead to my own ears. When you got right down to it, money was the one thing we really needed in order to get by. Having Lucien hunting after us wasn't even as great a worry because if he put his magic into action, we would be helpless to stop him. This, though, would be the difference between surviving on our own and falling apart. We needed a place to stay so that we could regroup, and in order to get a place to stay, we needed money.

"Isn't there any other option?" Marc asked, a little desperately. "I mean, I know that we probably will need money eventually, because we can't steal everything, but do we really need it tonight?"

"What other options do we have?" said James calmly. "Well, I suppose we could stop people out there and ask if they would be kind enough to open their homes to four Hammerheart fugitives. Would you like to give that a try, Marc?"

Marc blushed. "Okay, fine, you've made your point. I don't suppose there's anywhere else we could sleep?"

James shrugged. "The only free places are out here, or perhaps in a stairwell somewhere. No, I don't see that we really have any choice. Don't forget, the police know we're in the area, and if we stay here, they may find us before morning. I think we need to get our hands on some money, and although I don't like it, I think we really only have one way to do that."

"Steal it," Peter said emotionlessly. A cold feeling passed over all four of us at that moment; I felt it and saw it in the faces of my friends. We were all coming to the same realisation—there was no way around it; we were going to have to steal money from someone off the street, and the only way to do that would be to mug them.

We began to work out a plan then, a plan to take a stranger off the street and empty them of all the money they were carrying and anything else useful they may have. The good thing was that it didn't look as though we would have to hurt them, not if we used the magical weapons we had. The bad thing—or at least the thing which made the operation more difficult—was our location. The best place to make the steal would be right here where it couldn't be seen, but it could also cause the four of us to become trapped in here after it was over, particularly if the person began screaming at the top of their lungs. As frustrating as James could be sometimes, he was very good at spotting potential problems.

"It just means that we have to be selective about who we bring in and when we haul them off the street," said James, "just to make sure nobody spots it happening. Afterwards, we can just keep them stunned until we've got a safe distance away. Remember, we can only do this once, so we have to be sure that they'll have a good amount of dough on them."

"What if they have credit cards?" Marc asked.

James swallowed. "Not as good as cash, but if we're quick, better than nothing. Did any of you see if there are any banks around here?"

"No, and I doubt we'll have time to go looking for one," I said.

"Okay," said James, turning towards the street. "Is everyone clear on what to do?"

Marc, Peter and I exchanged looks before nodding.

"I can't believe we're about to do this," Peter muttered as we made our way back towards the light.

We stopped just short of the point at which the light could no longer penetrate into the alley. Marc and I stood side-by-side with James behind us, while Peter made himself invisible and advanced into the light. It was necessary because this far back in the alley, we could only see what was directly in front of us. From here on, it was up to Peter to let us know when to fire. All three of us had our stunners in our hands, and were standing ready, braced for the strike, which would be followed immediately by the scuttle. I strained my ears, waiting for the signal, hearing nothing but the city night-life—music coming from at least three different directions, people walking, talking and laughing, and beneath it all, the ongoing drone of the police chopper. The sirens had stopped. People kept walking past in front of the alley, and several cars passed us, not to mention another tram, but still there was no signal from Peter.

It went on like that for long enough to make me nervous. I wasn't worried that something had happened to Peter because he kept ducking back in and hissing at us that the time still wasn't right; but rather, the longer we stayed here, the more it felt like a different sort of trouble could find us before we were ready for it. I was most concerned about the police, who would take us in and lock us up if they caught up with us. What happened next would depend on what orders Lucien had previously given them; if none, the chain of command would probably see us be brought before Hall, in his most official capacity. That would be far worse than what might happen if we were taken straight to Lucien because Hall, particularly after my brick, would want revenge.

I was also mildly worried about Lucien, who must surely be awake by now and would be considering what to do about us (he would surely be aware of our infiltration of the base by now), but based on his rather blasÃ© approach to our capture this morning, I had a feeling that he was going to take his time with us. He reminded me of an animal toying with its food before eating it, knowing that the food, while still alive, had no chance of escaping. That was us, I thought, and Lucien knew it as well as we did. We could run, but no matter how far we got, he could reel us in whenever he wanted, and exactly how he went about that could end up being determined by Stella. How much of a say would she have if she didn't want to be Lucien's lady? If enough, she would see that we (or at least I) were treated well, but that could also happen more quickly.

James had thought that Lucien had enjoyed watching us scrambling around, lost and worried and confused and not having a clue what to do, and now I tended to agree with him. Although Lucien was undoubtedly a better and more humane person than Arnold Hammerson had been, he seemed to have a rather malicious element about him now that hadn't been there before. Perhaps it was a mutation caused by his merger—or whatever it had been—with Hammerson. For the most part, it seemed to benefit them both (Lucien believed he was now stronger, and he had since achieved what Hammerson hadn't been able to manage) but the consequential mutation had possibly caused a new weakness which, if we were quick and lucky enough, could keep us in the game.

Because he had chosen not to go after us immediately, we had been given an opportunity to re-arm ourselves, which we had been able to take, and maybe if he continued to toy with his dinner (so to speak), more opportunities would present themselves. I wasn't sure what they could be, although I could think of one possibility: If May was still in our world somewhere, somehow remaining hidden from Lucien, and if we could somehow find her and join forces with her, we might be able to cause some more serious problems for Lucien. Then, there was the idea James had had this morning: I hadn't found any unbogglers in any of those boxes this time around, but that didn't mean that there were none left anywhere in the world. All it would take was a bit of luck...

A loud slapping sound cut through my contemplations. A certain invisible someone had just stamped his foot down hard on the pavement just outside the alley, while directly ahead of us, three elegantly dressed women were walking past the alley mouth, chattering excitedly about whatever young women (they looked like they were probably in their early or mid-twenties) talked about. Marc, James and I took aim and, just as we had planned, fired our stunners at our assigned victums.

I caught the one to the far left of the group (the front, as they were walking in that direction), while Marc caught the one at the back. The one in the middle, as it was from our angle, was closer to the street and was more difficult to strike from this position without hitting one of her friends first, which was exactly what happened. As Marc's stunner had hit her a moment earlier, James's had no effect, and the woman in question was able to take an extra step before sensing the wrongness all around her. Whether she stopped and looked over her shoulder because her friends had stopped, or because she had heard Peter's stomp, I didn't know; either way, the backup plan kicked immediately into gear, and before she had a chance to say or do anything, Peter's stunner hit her directly in the chest.

The action didn't stop there. Knowing he had achieved nothing except to put himself directly in our way, James turned and sprinted back down the alley so that Marc and I had room to back up, now holding down both buttons of our stunners so that the women were dragged irresistibly into the alley and out of the lit street. Behind them, Peter was using his stunner to do the same to the third woman so that thirty seconds later, all seven of us were crammed into a space so tight that there was hardly any room to move around each other.

"Phew," said Peter, making himself visible again, but not daring to let go of his stunner. Marc and I were still holding ours too, still holding down the middle button so that our victims could do nothing but stand there, unable to move a muscle in their bodies. Only their eyes moved, looking at us in terror, and I didn't blame them. I supposed women all over the world were taught to expect that someday, something like this could happen to them. Luckily for these three, we weren't going to hurt them, but that didn't change the fact that they would probably be traumatised later. In hindsight, I wished our original plan had included using those killing things—at least they wouldn't remember the most of it.

"Hang on," said James sharply, "just listen for a few moments."

We all fell silent and listened to the sounds around us. The plan had taken so long to put in motion, not because we had to wait for the right people to walk past (although that was part of it), but because we also had to wait for there to be nobody on the street who might see the attack and raise an alarm. The sounds were much the same as they had been while we had been waiting; there was no sign that anyone had noticed anything.

"I think we're clear," said Marc, looking down at the woman he had stunned. "James, you're the only one with your hands free; you'd better do this. Don't worry," he added, now addressing the women directly, "we only need to take whatever money you've got on you. We're not bad guys—really."

"I think you're fighting a losing battle there, Marc," said Peter.

"I know," he sighed, "but it's true. Seriously, most people are against the Hammerhearts, so why do they have to be scared of us as well? It's their own freedom we're fighting for."

"Hurts, doesn't it?" I said, remembering how I'd thought much the same thing while we'd been running. "But Marc, you probably shouldn't be talking about that here."

"Well, way to give them my real name, Lewis," he scoffed.

"Lewis?" I gaped at him. "Of all the fake names you could have come up with for me, you go with Lewis?"

"Well excuse me, Tiberius," he said, and we all laughed.

James, who had been searching through the bag of the woman Peter had brought in, now said, "This one has three hundred dollars in cash here. Pretty dumb to carry around that much cash, but I suppose we should thank you for it. I'll let you keep the pepper spray, though," he added, "that was a good thought, although it didn't help much here."

"Enough talk," said Peter, and he sounded really nervous. "Come on, let's get on with it so we can get out of here. I'm getting the willies just standing here."

That was a sentiment I agreed with. While all I could do was stand here and keep one of these women at bay by holding the middle button of my stunner down, I could feel my own nerves jangling. I also had to contend with the woman I had stunned; she was standing right in front of me, still in a walking pose, and because we were much the same height, her eyes were on a level with my own. There was fear in them, but I thought I could also see judgement, or perhaps accusation. Surely, it had to be my own imagination making me feel guilty for an act I knew was bad. Surely, this woman could be feeling nothing but fear; I doubted that any of what we had been talking about earlier had registered with any of these girls.

James moved on to Marc's victim second and then mine last, while the rest of us stood still and silent, waiting for him to finish and, in my case, thinking about how we were going to get out of here. The plan was to leave them stunned in place, not taking them with us but leaving them here in this alleyway, for long enough for the four of us to get a good distance away. They would most likely scream and raise an alarm the moment they could, and this close to the apartment building where this had all started, the police would know exactly who did this and which direction we had gone. The plan didn't include exactly how we would make this happen, or where we would end up afterwards, but I was almost completely certain that it wouldn't be the supposed homeless shelter Peter had spotted earlier—that was way too close. Somewhere similar, though…

"Okay, done," James finally said, stuffing more money into his pocket and closing my victum's bag. "I'm not sure how much money we've got but it feels like enough for at least a few days. There's nothing else here worth taking, so I guess we'd better go."

"Okay," said Marc, and as he had earlier, he spoke to the women. "Again, sorry about this, but hopefully someday when Australia's a free country again, you'll be glad to have played a part in it. Come on, guys; we'd better move them around."

It was just as tricky as before. Peter was fine, being closest to the mouth of the alley, and James was able to join him without too much trouble, having negotiated the three girls already. Marc and I both had to shuffle and move our women around ourselves in order to get past them. Once Peter had shifted his victim so that the three of them stood together, still in the poses they'd been in when they'd been walking on the street, we shuffled back into a line (Marc, me, Peter and James in the rear this time). James pointed and clicked his invisibility toggle at each of us in turn before we headed back to the mouth of the alley to conference.

"It's even more important than before that we stay out of trouble," I said, "because me and Pete have no spare hands to point any weapons, and Marc only has one."

"It shouldn't be a problem if we're careful," said Peter, "and especially if we're quick, just in case someone finds those girls before we let them go."

"You're both right," said James, and sighed. "I'll hold a solid-outliner back here, and Marc, I guess you go with a bludginator. Hopefully it won't matter."

"Er—guys," Marc said ahead of me, "where are we going now?"

"Out of this alley and to the right," said James (that was the direction in which we'd been going earlier). "It doesn't really matter where we go, as long as it's not back towards the cops, and we don't turn too many times. We should eventually find somewhere to hole up for the night, even if it's a dingy room over a bar or something."

"And you're sure we've got enough money?" Peter asked.

"Like I said, enough for a few days at least, as long as we're careful with it," said James, "and who knows where we'll be by then. Come on, let's get going."

And so we did, each of us with a hand on the shoulder of the one in front, and Marc, Peter and I holding our stunners, keeping the middle buttons depressed. We filed out of the alley and around to the right, back into the light and amongst people going from place to place. There weren't as many on the street now as there had been before, but there were plenty of them around; I could hear them, as though every building in the area was packed and full of noise. This kind of hustle and bustle was alien to all of us; Chopville had only one pub, and no clubs to speak of, and the streets were usually quiet after dark, even on the weekends. Granted you got the usual drunken idiots, but a handful of those couldn't make this kind of noise or create this type of atmosphere.

The time had been just after nine o'clock when we had become invisible again. And the walk that followed, slow as it was, lasted for nearly two hours. I only knew so because we walked past an electronic billboard telling us that the time was 10:54 PM. The meal we'd had back in the apartment had given me enough energy to prepare for this task, but by that stage, I was tired, sore (not just from the walking, but my previous injuries were making themselves felt too) and absolutely bloody freezing. We had only stopped once in that time, ducking into yet another dark and dirty alleyway so that we could firstly release our stunners and pocket them, and then take up other weapons. I was in such an irritable mood by that stage that I went for the killing device; any Hammerheart who gave me trouble tonight was going to regret it.

It was about ten minutes after the billboard that, taking us by surprise, we arrived at the beach. Other than the secluded beaches in Western Australia where we had teleported onto and off of the vessel which we'd transported to Rock Haulter, it was the only time I'd been near a beach in my life (Rock Haulter didn't have any beaches—it would have made the little mountain island perfect if it had). It was even colder here than it had been before, and when I said so, the others all agreed. We therefore turned around, backtracked a couple of blocks and then turned to the right, and it was about five minutes further along this new street that we finally found our accommodation.

It was another homeless shelter, similar to what Peter thought he'd seen on that other street. This one looked dirty and dilapidated, and I could only imagine how shabby and filthy the beds would be (assuming they had any), but by now the four of us were so tired and miserable that it looked as good as a five-star hotel. Before we could go inside, however, Marc led us off to the side so that we could conference out of the way of any people passing by.

"You sure this is accommodation?" James asked, looking up at the place.

"It said drop-in centre on the sign," Peter said, and I felt him looking back over his shoulder towards the sign, but we couldn't really see it properly from this angle.

"I think it is," said Marc, "but there are a number of things we've gotta work out before we go in there."

The first of which was what we should do if they didn't have any accommodation available for us, or if they rejected us. I wasn't sure if they were even allowed to do that, but then again, everything about this situation was completely new to all of us. It was reluctantly decided that if we couldn't get in here, we would look for a park and take shelter there, as we had done this morning. Then there was the money: James finally counted our haul from earlier and announced (in a whisper) that we had just under eight hundred dollars. He handed two hundred (in mostly twenties) to each of us and kept the rest for himself.

Then, we had to decide what we were going to call ourselves. Our real names wouldn't do anymore, and after what had happened back in the apartment building, even half-fake names weren't enough. In the end, Marc became Devin Sandford, Peter became Paul Smith, James would be Jackson Buffalo, and I, my creative streak well and truly shot, went with Marc's earlier suggestion of Lewis Sandford, Devin's younger brother. Lastly, we had to make ourselves visible without drawing unwanted attention; there were no dirty little gaps between the buildings here, so we had to settle for the dark shadows of the shelter itself. Fortunately, there were so few people around that it wasn't difficult.

"Marc, you back me up," James said as we mounted the three steps up to the doors. "You two, just be quiet and don't contribute unless you have to."

"Yeah, I know we're not as quick on our feet," Peter said, and yawned widely.

"We'll have to be very quick on our feet if these people work out who we are," Marc muttered, hesitating on the threshold, "I mean… literally."

James gave the door an experimental push, and for a fraction of a second, I was sure that it would be locked—that the place would be locked up for the night, or perhaps out of business; but it swung forward easily, and the four of us stepped into the warmth. As cold as I had been before, I'd been outdoors long enough to have acclimatised to the chill; so the moment the indoor heat hit my face, I immediately broke out in a sweat. We pressed on, though, looking around the little foyer as the door swung shut behind us. It wasn't dark as such, but it was dimly lit, as though they were trying to save on their electricity bill. There were three other people in here besides ourselves. Two of them were clearly in a similar boat to us, though they were both older and looked like they might be drug addicts, but there was a middle-aged woman behind the desk paying no attention to anyone around her. Her eyes were fixed on the television in the corner. My heart sank when, looking over at it, I saw an irritable-looking Lucien addressing a media throng.

"Excuse me," James said when he and Marc reached the counter. Peter and I hung back, glancing at each other, not entirely sure what to do here. All I knew for sure was that if I looked at that television again, I might give that woman the totally right idea, so it was with some effort that I focussed on the conversation at the counter. The woman, it turned out, was having just as much trouble focussing as I was.

"What's up?" Marc asked her a little irritably, after James's third failed attempt to enquire about free rooms. He glanced over his shoulder to where the woman had been looking a moment earlier; I saw his eyes widen as he registered the TV screen, but he quickly composed himself.

"A police manhunt," she said, looking scared as she glanced back at the screen yet again, "dangerous criminals with magical powers, not far from here."

"How far?" Peter asked, and then clapped a hand over his mouth. His voice was still so much higher and squeakier than any of ours—it hadn't even edged towards the teenage breakage that the rest of us had already been through.

"Only a few kilometres," she replied, and then managed to compose herself. "So, you were saying?" she asked James.

Only a few kilometres? We'd been on the road for two hours and we'd only gone a few kilometres? I wanted to throw something.

"Do you have any money?" the woman was now asking James. "Anything at all?"

James hesitated, and I thought I knew why. The honest answer was yes, obviously, and we couldn't give any other answer if we expected to pay for our accommodation tonight, but the four of us looked so pathetic—anyone would have wondered where we'd gotten any money at all. Finally, James said, "We've got a bit, what we've worked for, but it's not very much."

"A room here is thirty dollars a night," she told him, "and while it's not against the rules to share, if it's all you can aford, each room is not designed for more than a single person. Is that something you can manage?"

I felt a rush of relief. Yes, we could, for five nights if necessary, and perhaps more by then if we were prepared to go out and steal again; but I didn't think we would be here that long. In fact, I doubted we would be here this time tomorrow, not if we were going to continue our war against Lucien's regime after we'd rested.

"Are there any other costs along the way?" Marc asked. "Do you provide meals?"

"Free snacks at designated times," she told him, "meals are two dollars each, but they're quite small. You"—she hesitated for a moment, looking at the four of us more closely℟—"you boys haven't done this before, have you?"

We all exchanged stricken looks before James, with exactly the right volume of emotion and with complete honesty, said, "This is a —a new arrangement for us."

The woman's expression, which had up until now been business-like (when dealing with us, at least; each glance at the television screen made it flicker), softened at these words. We didn't need to try to look pathetic; we managed it quite fine naturally.

"Do you have any money at all?" she asked. "Anything?"

"We can afford a night," Marc said, digging a twenty and a ten out of his pocket and looking around at the rest of us, indicating that we do the same. "After that, I guess we'll see. Mostly, we just wanna sleep."

Once we had all handed over thirty dollars and the woman had put the cash away, she went through a door behind her desk, leaving us standing there with nothing to do but look at the television screen. It looked as though this media conference had happened a few hours ago, judging by the fading light in the sky as opposed to the complete blackness of the present hour. A few minutes later, though, the woman returned, this time through a door to the right of the desk, and she was holding a handful of small keys.

"Follow me," she said, beckoning us back through the door, "we have a number of empty rooms up the back. You'll each have a key but I suggest you don't leave anything valuable in there, if you have anything, 'cause these doors aren't very strong."

We went through the door, down one corridor, then through a door on the left and up a set of stairs, around to the right, then through another door on the right, along another corridor, through a door on the left, and it was here that we finally stopped. This small corridor was dark and dank, devoid of decorations and even carpeting. There were thirteen doors leading off it—six on either side and one, a fire escape, at the other end. Given how close these doors were to each other, I could guess just how tiny each of these rooms was going to be. Sure enough, when the woman unlocked the first one and opened it, I saw it was only as wide as the length of the bed along the opposite wall, and contained nothing else but a small desk, a splintery old chair that looked on the verge of collapsing under no weight at all, a wastepaper basket and a little wardrobe. Like the corridor, there were no decorations or carpeting in here. Even the bed looked like crap, with nothing but a couple of sheets, an extremely flat pillow, and a small layer of foam for a mattress. It was absolute crap, and yet my body yearned to lie upon it.

"Bathrooms are communal," she told us, indicating a door directly opposite our little corridor. It had a very familiar skirted figure on it—the ladies' bathroom. The men's must have been further up the corridor. That probably meant that we would see any people who slept in this area of the building as they entered or left the bathroom, if we happened to be coming out of our room at the same time.

This woman, meanwhile, had given the first key to Marc and moved along to the next door. That turned out to be my room, with Peter in number three and James in number four. Once we all had our keys, she said, "I'm going to need your names before you sleep, though."

As Marc gave her our fake names, I stepped into my new room for the next however long and looked around it. I had a strong urge, born out of habit, to unpack my things and get settled in; except, of course, I had no things to unpack. All I had were my razors, my condoms, and the clothes on my back—oh, and this ridiculous bandage around my head, of course. The woman had given the bandage a suspicious look when we had first come in but thankfully hadn't asked how I'd hurt myself.

"We have a number of activities for people like you," the woman was saying, "social workers and support groups. I suggest you have a look around in the morning and see what's on offer. This is only supposed to be temporary, after all."

"Believe me, we won't be here long," said James wearily.

She left us alone then, and once we heard her feet descending the stairs again, the four of us breathed a sigh of relief. Glancing down at my watch, I saw that it was a quarter to midnight. Even though I had only woken up at around three o'clock in the afternoon, I was absolutely stuffed, and at least some of it had to be due to my connection with Stella. I reckoned I could now understand why Tommy had hated his life so much; he'd had to deal with this every day of his life, from the plane crash right up to the point of his German suicide. I had no idea what the future held for us— everything was so far up in the air now—but one thing I knew was that something had to be done about this. Something must be done.

"Guys," James said quietly before any of us could go into our rooms, "we need to work out a plan."

"Can't that wait until morning, James?" yawned Marc.

"I mean the plan for between now and morning," James insisted. "I'm going to assume that they'll do breakfast sometime between seven and eight o'clock; if not exactly, then that'd be close. Why don't we meet back up here, in one of these rooms, at eight so we can discuss what we're going to do tomorrow."

"What if Lucien does something during the night?" Peter asked nervously.

James shrugged. "If he traps us here, we do the only thing we can—fight with everything we have. Whether he does or he doesn't, though, that's out of our control, like it was this morning. I think we should worry about what we can control, and right now, what we really need is rest."

"I think I'll go have a shower first," Marc told us. "I can smell myself."

And that was what we all did. Once we had hunted around the second level for a few minutes, accidentally waking a poor bloke in the process, we located a linen closet and a towel for each of us. We then went back to the men's bathroom, which we'd found a little earlier, and had our showers. There were only three shower stalls, though, so while the other three stepped in first, I went back in front of a mirror to examine my wounds. Before I had a chance to be horrified by the state of my injuries, however, I was even more horrified when I saw the bandage around my head, tied securely around my neck. Now I understood why it was so much longer than it needed to be: It wasn't a bandage at all, but a Collingwood Football Club scarf. No wonder that girl had been so terrified of me earlier, and the woman downstairs had looked suspicious.

I went about pulling all the Band-Aids off, thinking again that I'd shut the gate long after the horse had bolted. In fact, not only had I shut the gate too late, but the process of pulling them off made me feel like I'd jammed my finger in it as well. There was no longer any pain in any of them anymore, and the spot on my face that had been burnt wasn't too bad either. I only had to rub a bit of cold water on it before turning my attention to the wound across my forehead. Blood had dried there, sticking the scarf to my forehead, and pulling it off caused it to start bleeding again. It looked even worse than it had back in the apartment, as generally happens when an incompetant doctor cuts it open with a knife, but on the heels of that thought, I had to scold myself; James had done the best he could.

The wound was still painful to touch, but at least now it was the pain of the wound itself rather than the glass embedded inside it. There were no face washers here (what had we done with the other one, I wondered), so I had to run cold water over my hand and use it to clean up the blood. It would have been much more sensible to save the Band-Aids for this, I thought, even if I would need three to cover the thing properly. It would scab over by the time I woke up in the morning, I supposed, and all I really needed to do to prevent it getting infected (if it hadn't already) was not put anything over the top of it that had been in this building too long.

I waited until the other three were all out of the shower before I dared stop cleaning up my forehead, even though it wasn't bleeding anymore. By the time I felt ready to take a shower of my own, Peter had already put his clothes back on and was preparing to take his towel back to his room. As he walked past me, however, I lassoed him with the scarf and dragged him back.

"Hey—what?"

I waved the scarf in front of his face. Behind me, Marc and James began to snigger.

"What's the deal?" I asked, not entirely sure if I wanted to rage or burst out laughing myself. "Why didn't you tell me I was carrying this around? Geez, no wonder they thought we were criminals."

"They recognised me, mate, not you," said Marc, but his voice was still trembling with suppressed mirth. "I don't think you were a very convincing Collingwood supporter."

"True," said Peter, tilting his head sideways and examining my face, "too many teeth."

"You can have it," I said, stuffing it into his hands. "You're the one who took it."

"I don't want it—it's got blood on it."

"Most Collingwood scarfs have blood on them," James muttered, and this time, we all laughed.

I was in one of the showers a couple of minutes later, and although it was by no means comfortable (the hot water stung as it ran over my forehead), it was the most refreshed and clean I'd felt since—well, since before we had been chased out of our old base. It had been almost forty-eight hours since my last shower, and I had been in the same clothes that entire time. It was good to feel clean again.

By the time I got out, I was the only one left in the bathroom, the other three having probably gone off to bed. I felt nervous being alone in there, drying myself, naked apart from the borrowed towel. My mind turned back to Lucien, wondering what he was doing now —what plans he was making. Surely, after the events of the day—our daring to enter the Chopville base, our theft of weapons from it, the debacle in the apartment building foyer and our ensuing escape—he would modify his easygoing approach to our capture. And then there was Stella: Had she gone back to sleep and entered my body? Was she perhaps thinking these thoughts right along with me? I looked down at my naked body, wondering if I would feel aroused by it, but I felt nothing. Maybe she was awake after all, or maybe it didn't work in reverse…or maybe I just wasn't sexy enough…

Whatever it was, I couldn't control it, any more than I could control the fact that only hours from now, Natalie would regain consciousness in the clutches of Lucien's band of Hammerhearts, and among her first few thoughts would be the knowledge that I had failed to deliver on her final request. Also, hours from now, Stella would regain her magical powers for the first time in six months. How would she use them? Would she put them into action before I had even woken up in the morning? Well, I thought, if she does, I'll know about it. Maybe I'll be able to wake myself in time to fight back.

Rather than putting all my clothes back on, I only put my underwear back on and wrapped my towel around myself instead. I carried my clothes back to my room, feeling a little chilly but ultimately fresh—it was a good feeling. I put my clothes, my razors and my condoms away in the wardrobe, put the towel over the back of the chair, and got into bed. My watch would remain on my wrist, and the pouch with all my weaponry within would stay by my side through the night. I agreed with the woman's idea to keep valuables on me, but I was far less nervous about drunken thieves than wake-up calls from much more dangerous enemies.

I listened to the silence around me. No noise reached me from the street, but I could hear distant voices from somewhere inside the building. Although I couldn't hear what they were saying, I had a feeling that they weren't talking to each other, but more likely to themselves. I neither knew nor cared; a couple of minutes later, despite all my worries about what was next for us, or what might happen during the night, I slipped straight off to sleep, and immediately slid back into my customary position inside Stella's mind.

Part 2: Struggle of Wills

Chapter 9: He Was an Utter Moron in Many Ways

I was bored. I had been stuck in here all afternoon and evening and had totally run out of things to do. I wanted to sleep, but I wasn't even remotely tired, and probably wouldn't be for at least five or six hours. It was almost one o'clock now, and in a few hours, I would begin feeling the tingling of my old magic returning (at least I thought it was my old chip coming back to me), but for the time being, I could only resign myself to another sleepless night. Perhaps when I had magic, I could use it to get my sleeping patterns back where they should be, but a fat lot of good that would do if Lucien continued to stay up in the night and wanted me to help him… assuming he would after what had happened this evening.

The trouble with the current setup, a trouble which made me want to jump to my feet and start throwing things, was that just as had been the case when I had lived up here before, now Lucien could read my mind far too easily. I could usually control my thoughts, and it had worked at first, but the moment Lucien had found out that I'd been hiding things from him, he began directing my thinking, as though my memories were a rail and he was driving my thoughts along them. He didn't even need to use magic either; he just spoke to me, read my mental reaction, and rinse and repeat until he'd got what he'd wanted.

The cause of my problems had been what I'd done when I had woken up in the late afternoon. After that weird mind thing with John, I had continued sleeping for a little longer, long enough to know how bad he felt about our connection, and long enough to see him and the others planning to come in here. It was incredibly dangerous for them to come back here to where they knew Lucien to be sleeping, but they did it anyway—such fighting spirit. More than anything else, I had wanted them all brought in so that they wouldn't have to suffer (I'd felt John's suffering, both physical and emotional, pretty clearly), but if I could, I wanted to do it on my terms rather than Lucien's.

I had therefore made myself invisible and waited on the stairs to see if they would come, resolving that if all four of them came through, I would use a solid-outliner to bring them in—after which, I supposed I would need Lucien anyway. It was a thin plan, and I wasn't at all happy with it, but in the end, it hadn't mattered; only Marc and John came through the wall, Peter and James having been either caught or gone off doing something else in the base. I found out later, of course, but at that stage I was none the wiser. I had settled on plan B: Watch them until they had left, keeping them and Lucien out of the way of each other should the latter get out of bed while they were still here.

Which was exactly what had happened. All three of us heard him get up, and fortunately, Marc and John scarpered before Lucien had even got out of the hallway upstairs. The moment they had disappeared through the wall, I had hurried back up the stairs and intercepted Lucien, wanting to hold him up for long enough for the boys to get out of the base, and trying desperately not to let my intention show in my thoughts. Fortunately, I was famished by then, so I focussed my mental energy on that. Lucien had also been hungry, so he had agreed to use his magic to supply our breakfast (or early dinner, given the hour), and while we had eaten, I had asked him about his immediate plans, partially to keep him talking but mostly because I was genuinely curious.

"Well, before I slept, I gave Hank his orders," he had told me, "2C7, you know—"

"I know who he is," I had said grudgingly, "I've known him like all my life."

"Yeah, well anyway, he's gonna take Fewul out and reclaim all those minds the Woodwards and Fletchers have been fixing up this week. He was supposed to rest through the morning, but he should have left by now. I'm fairly confident that they can get it done a lot quicker; hopefully they'll be back here by tomorrow morning. You'd never guess what form I gave Fewul, though," he added, grinning.

If he had wanted me to guess, I hadn't been interested. Rather than pursue that line, I had asked, "What about you? What are you gonna do?"

"First thing once we're done eating," he had said, "for me anyway, is to go downstairs and spin some magic in the Big Room. I know it's carpeted, but they've got nothing but blankets and sleeping bags in there. I'm not going to let them leave until Marc and his little band of followers have been brought in, and that mightn't be for days yet."

What made Marc the leader, I had wondered? I would have thought that all four of them would be co-leaders or something. Not wanting to follow that line any further, I had asked, "Days? Why days? Surely you can just go after them any old time?"

He smiled. "You heard what I told Hank this morning. Anytime means anytime, Stella; it could be today, or it could just as easily be…well…anytime; that's why they call it 'anytime'." He had chuckled and then gone on, "I think this is a valuable experience for them. I could probably make all four of them happy with influential charms, and that could possibly work for someone like Peter, but I have my doubts about the other three. The influential charm still allows independent thinking, and someone like James, even with my ideas in his head, could very well use his own logic to get back to his current course of actions. Putting them out in the big wide world for a while with nothing going for them should make them appreciate what I'm doing all the more when I finally bring them in."

"Okay," I had said, wishing it didn't have to be so, but understanding against my will, "but then, how long are you going to leave them out there? I—I don't want them to suffer too much."

Surely I could tell him that much; he knew how I felt about John, after all, but even the others shouldn't have to be scared all the time.

He had only chuckled. "Sorry, Stella, but it'll be worth it in the end. I can't put a time figure on it; it's more a case of how long it takes them to reach rock bottom. Rather than bring them in, I'll just keep them out and, on the run,, making it more and more difficult for them every day. Just think about how vulnerable John will be when he finally gets here—how much you could do to relieve him of that."

That actually was an enjoyable thought, but only for a moment. What sort of person would I be if I allowed the boy I thought I loved to suffer for several days just so that I could be the one to take away that suffering in the end? It was a sickening thought. Then there was the fact that I would be suffering right along with him every time I slept…but I could see that Lucien had made up his mind, and I didn't want to argue with him. Not having paid attention to me for several seconds, Lucien had rolled his eyes up into his head. I had known he was probably looking to see where they were now; I put my fists under my knees and clenched them as I waited.

He had grinned. "It's already working. They're scrambling around in an apartment in Melbourne. I'm guessing they used the Hammerheart Highway to get there, but…oh this is excellent. They fear for their lives enough to get out of Chopville and put themselves in a totally unfamiliar environment. I don't think I need to do anything for them at the moment."

"What do you mean?" I had choked.

"Well, they already look troubled enough as it is. I'll eventually add more to their struggles, but for the time being, I'll just let nature take its course."

He had left after that, leaving me not knowing what I had best to do. I had been tempted to try to sleep again to see where John was now—to connect with him in the way I loved doing—but that had been a close call with Lucien just now, and I couldn't allow him even easier access to the boys than he already had. I wanted to go down to the Big Room to see those who had been such good friends to me over the last couple of months, but if Lucien were down there as well, that would give him even more opportunities to read my mind.

That had been so narrow, but it had worked: John and his band of followers had gotten out of the base and far away in the nick of time.

Lucien had returned about two hours later. His face had been white, his eyes wide and his lips trembling. I had been in the lounge room at the time, having spent most of the time since in my bedroom, trying to think of ways to bring John back safely (and then how to deal with him when he returned) but had been driven out by sheer boredom. The sight of Lucien drove me back a step; he was furious about something, and I didn't have to wonder about the most probable cause of his anger.

"You wouldn't believe it," he had snapped, striding forward and throwing himself down in an armchair, "but it looks like those guys used the Hammerheart Highway for a little more than getting out of Chopville."

"What? What else did they do?"

Lucien had sighed. "Why, they came here, of course. I don't think they went in the Big Room, though—someone would surely have thought about it if they'd seen them. I found Hank knocked out cold on the Highway level with Fewul just standing there looking thick—no chance of the job getting done by tomorrow morning now. Then on my way back up, I hear yelling and screaming coming from one of the residential suites. Can you guess what I found there?"

"No," I had gulped, and it was the truth; I hadn't seen any of what else the boys had done within the base other than what John and Marc had done up in the top floor corridor…

…oops!

Lucien had sat bolt-upright, staring intently at me. Sure enough, he'd heard that last thought. "Stella, what do you know?" he had said shrewdly.

"I don't know what you saw in one of the residential suites," I had told him, again speaking the truth, trying to consume every part of my thoughts with that one question.

"I saw Hall and Lawson, bound and gagged, and apparently beaten senseless with a brick and a tree branch," he had said, staring me down. "After I had freed them and repaired their injuries, they told me that all four boys had been in here, but when they had come around, only Peter and James had been in the suite with them; Marc and John had been elsewhere. If it wasn't the Big Room, Stella, what else could they have done?"

"I really don't know," I had lied, and this time, he knew it.

"Well, Stella, whatever it was, it required them to wear level-two uniforms to access it," he had said, still staring me down. "That, it seems, was the reason why Hall and Lawson were attacked in the first place. I suppose it could have been a premeditated attack," he had conceded, "but I can't think why they would take such a risk in coming here just to attack Hall, especially after what Fewul did to him on Monday."

I didn't say anything—there was nothing I could have said that would have been true, and at the same time not scream my own guilt.

"I suppose we can't know if they specifically wanted level-two uniforms," he had conceded, though his face told me otherwise, "but I'm thinking that they probably knew exactly what they were doing. That they found two level-two Hammerhearts so close together was probably luck—or maybe not," he had added, thinking, while I watched on, increasingly more frightened, "otherwise surely they would have attacked Hank. Well, anyway, it doesn't really matter. Do you know why, Stella?"

"No," I had squeaked.

He had smiled then—it was a dangerous smile, so reminiscent of my father that I had shivered—he was building up to a big bad thing here. "Because Marc and John brought weapons back into the suite, Stella—weapons they had stolen from our reserves up here on the top floor. They organised them before leaving the suite, Stella, and you knew about this, didn't you?"

I had shrugged. Why continue the game after it had been lost. "Yeah, I knew."

"You stood there and watched them stealing our weapons, didn't you?"

I hadn't answered, only looked at him. Surely, if he was still set on his idea of letting them run around for a while before bringing them in, he shouldn't be unhappy about this…surely.

"Why did you do that, Stella? Why did you let them get away with that?"

"Are you complaining?" I had asked, trying not to feel like I'd done the wrong thing. I had been beginning to feel angry myself, now; what right did Lucien have to tell me off like a little girl? I wasn't his daughter, weird soul-binding magic included, and I certainly wasn't his wife.

"You didn't think, at any point, that it might be inappropriate to allow those boys to be armed?" he had asked, and his own anger was beginning to show more forcefully. I had remembered back to the episode in the old base and wondered what were the chances of a repeat offence right here in the old Hammerson living quarters.

"I thought you said you didn't want them brought in—"

"Stella," he had said, his voice quiet and extremely dangerous, "I told you that after they had gone. You did not know my intentions when you deliberately stood back and allowed my enemies to defy me. You are with me, aren't you?"

"I'm on your side, if that's what you mean."

"Then why did you let them get away with it, Stella? Even if you didn't want to hurt them, you made no effort whatsoever to stop them from arming themselves. Moreover, you actually tried to help them —you intended to stop me from getting to them, didn't you?"

I had gulped—so that was why he was so mad. "I—I didn't know if you were going to hurt John—"

That was when he had snapped. Thank God I'd been standing on my feet; I had only a moment, in which I saw his eyes seem to turn black, before I hurled myself towards the corridor into my bedroom, hearing the living room exploding behind me. I had run for my room, slamming the door behind me and collapsing against it. I had sat there, listening to the mayhem from the living room, which only lasted another ten seconds or so before silence fell, but it was long enough to think back to all the times gone by when I would be sitting here like this, and for exactly the same reason. It was my father's rage, I knew, and the fact that Lucien forced himself to take it out on his surroundings instead of those people who had enraged him didn't change that fact.

Barely seconds after the noise had stopped, however, Lucien had called to me. I couldn't identify his mood from his voice, but it hadn't sounded angry anymore. Once again, as it had done when he had blown up our old base and accidentally (more or less) killed eleven people, his anger had self-destructed, leaving no remnants behind and allowing the cool, calm and collected Lucien to take charge again. It was seriously creepy, but I hadn't dared barricade myself in my room—it would only give him a reason to come in here, and who knew where having Lucien in my bedroom might lead.

I had opened my door, stepped out and looked down the hallway to the living room. Lucien had been standing there, well back from the door to the hallway but directly in line with it so that I couldn't miss him—nor could I miss the fact that just as quickly as he had destroyed the place, he had repaired it as well. The two of us had simply stood there, staring at each other for several seconds, before Lucien had raised his hands to chest-height, palms out.

"Anger's all gone now," he had said, trying to smile, but it was a troubled smile. I was still a little annoyed by his attempt, however unintentional, to control me, and to reprimand me like a child or minion or whatever; and I was still a little frightened of what he might do if I stepped out of line (not that I feared I couldn't handle him, after having spent sixteen years living under the same roof as my father), but mostly I only pitied him. He hadn't asked for this, and he was dealing with it the best way he knew how. He was entitled to make a few mistakes, but he would understand soon, if he didn't yet, that no matter how much magic he had, or even if he chose to strip me of what would soon be mine again, I would not let him intimidate me like that again.

"Okay," I had said, forcing my feet to move. I stepped back into the living room and looked around to check that everything really had been fixed—yep, everything in its rightful place. I didn't dare sit down, though, just in case I needed to make a second quick getaway.

"Sorry," he had said, shrugging. "That was—I dunno what came over me."

I had only shrugged; we both knew what made the anger what it was, but it didn't change the fact that he'd had a valid reason for getting angry in the first place.

"I know, I guess I'm being unreasonable," he had said, running his fingers through his hair, "but I do think there are some things we ought to straighten out, just so that we don't have to go through anything like this again. You're gonna have magic in less than twelve hours now, so we need to be on the same page."

"Go on," I had said, deciding to reserve judgement until after I'd heard what he wanted to say.

"Firstly, Stella, I need you to trust me," he had said heavily. "It's great that you're so protective of my brothers and all that, but I've gotta say, it makes me feel pretty crappy that you think I would do something nasty to them just because they were here. I'm not that kind of person, so please, don't try to second-guess my actions."

I had nodded, now feeling like crap myself. I hadn't really thought of it in those terms, but I could understand why it had upset him. Not being trusted by someone you really cared for was painful —I knew that all too well.

"Secondly, I understand how you want to protect John, but you really need to stop letting that get in the way of what needs to be done. I've already told you, I'm not going to hurt him—I'm not going to hurt any of them, only bring them in here in the manner that suits me. Do you believe me?"

"Yes," I had said truthfully, "but I still don't like it."

The manner that suited him would make all four of them suffer plenty along the way, and depending on when I slept, I would be suffering right along with them.

Lucien must have been reading my thoughts because he said, "Are you worried about the connection? I don't think I can get rid of it without John here, but maybe I can block it somehow so that your two minds can't access each other."

"No, I don't want it gone," I had said quickly; I wanted every minute with John that I could get. "Besides, that wouldn't work. The whole reason why it happens is because our minds got merged; it's not a link you can just cut. You might give us both epilepsy or something if you tried."

Lucien had considered for a moment, but before he'd had a chance to reply, footsteps had come hurrying up the stairs outside—surely someone who'd heard the destruction and come to make sure Lucien was okay. We had both looked at the door as Commissioner Hall burst through it, his eyes wide and his face bloodless. Remembering what Lucien had said about him being attacked with a brick and a tree branch, I was disappointed to see that whatever damage had done had since been repaired.

"Sorry if I'm interrupting," he had said hurriedly, "but Lucien, you should know that your brother and his friends were at the centre of an incident in Melbourne."

"What incident?" Lucien had asked.

Hall had hesitated for a moment before saying, "Your brother Marc, he tried to slip past a security checkpoint with a fake identity, and when his cover was blown, he punched out an innocent man."

To my surprise, and Hall's intense disapproval (judging by how quickly the blood returned to his face), Lucien had grinned. "Good on him."

"What?" Hall had snapped.

"Well, I'm sure the innocent man was only doing his job," Lucien had said, still grinning, "but at least Marc's got a knack for survival. It must run in the family; I'm sure you knew my dad, and how he was an utter moron in many ways, but we should give him credit for staying alive as long as he did."

I had giggled then; the sound had slipped out of me before I could stop it. Actually, I hadn't even felt it coming. Both men had looked at me with raised eyebrows, one looking as amused as I felt, the other looking like he wanted to blow the place up as Lucien had done a little earlier.

"So, what's the problem, Dermott?" Lucien had asked.

"What's the problem?" Hall had repeated, his eyes bugging. "What's the problem? Your brother is the problem; he's on the run in Melbourne and the police aren't sure which way he went. We need your help."

"Okay," Lucien had said, and he was still grinning. "Er—question?"

"Yes?"

"What do you need my help with?"

This time, I had burst out laughing—not at Lucien's words, but at Hall's reaction to them. I couldn't remember the last time I had seen someone looking so flummoxed. His face was red, his eyes were round and astonished, his mouth was gaping, and he was making weird, gulping noises as he tried to think what to say.

Lucien had sighed, deciding that he'd had enough fun for now. "Dermott, I can't be helping the police with everything. You could, of course, if you hadn't given up the Villain Crystal, but I'm afraid that ship has sailed. Just keep your good men and women on the job for the evening; I doubt they'll get too far, particularly if the general public recognise them."

"Fine," Hall had snapped, looking extremely disappointed. "Also, you should know that the media expect an explanation from you. I've already spoken to them, but those vultures aren't satisfied with anything; they want you."

Lucien had yawned widely, covering his mouth with his hand. "Ah, it's so tiring to be in such high demand. Fine, I'll go talk to them, while you get back to doing your job. You shouldn't be talking to the media at all, you know?"

Hall had opened his mouth in fury, and then seemed to decide that it probably wouldn't be such a good idea to retort. He had taken a moment to compose himself and then had said, "Of course, sir. I'll be very interested to hear what answers you give them."

He had then turned and left the room without a backwards look, leaving me and Lucien grinning at each other.

"This is going to be an interesting working relationship, I think," Lucien had said, and we had both laughed. "I really should go take care of this, although I intend not to spend long on it. I'm not going to tell you what to do, Stella, but I'd prefer you don't leave the suite tonight. Try and sleep, if you can."

"I think I will," I had said, thinking of that weird place John and I had gone to when we had both been asleep—wanting to get back there tonight. "Can I ask, though, why aren't you going to help them search?"

"Because I don't really want to capture them this soon," he had said, and I could have slapped myself—of course he didn't. "If the police find them, that's fine, but I've got a feeling that they'll stay well hidden—at least for a while. The fear of being caught ought to be worse than the capture itself."

He had left after that, and I had spent the time since trying on and off to sleep and having no luck whatsoever. Now, I was sitting on the couch in the living room, thinking about the day…why was I thinking about the day? I should have been thinking far more about tomorrow—about getting my magic back, and how I would use it. I reckoned I would do what Lucien asked me to do, but any time I didn't have orders of my own to follow, I would use it to watch the boys. Then of course, the other thing I would do was find a way to protect my mind, as I hadn't been able to do for years. The domination charm wasn't enough because of whatever damage my father had done to keep an eye on my thoughts, but if the last two days had taught me anything, it was that nothing is impossible if you perform the right spells.

It was just after one o'clock when I heard footsteps climbing the stairs outside the living quarters. I straightened up as Lucien entered the room. He looked tired but gave himself a magical energy booster as I watched.

"You're still up," he said, looking surprised. "I thought you would have been long asleep by now."

I shrugged. "My sleeping patterns are shot."

"So are mine," he conceded, sitting down on the couch beside me (though not uncomfortably close, thankfully), "but I think I'll just use magic to keep myself going for the next twenty hours or so—that ought to put things right. If you can hang on for another four hours, you can do the same for yourself."

"Is that what time I'll be able to use it again?"

"Give or take," he said, and sighed. "In case you're wondering, Marc and the others haven't been caught yet. I've spent the last few hours talking to all kinds of people, and I'm thinking that it mightn't be such a bad idea if I cloned myself or something so that I don't have to waste all my time with public relations in the future."

"Most of your job is public relations. Besides, wouldn't you be worried about your clone getting power-hungry and trying to assassinate you?"

"That wouldn't happen if I do it right. Maybe I'll just get Fewul to do it; I'm pretty sure the Beast would be capable of taking multiple forms and doing multiple tasks at the same time."

I only shrugged again—what else was there to say? I had nothing, but apparently Lucien did.

"Listen, Stella, we need to talk about you and John."

"Do we have to?" I protested. I wasn't up to this right now.

"I think we do," he said, looking down at his hands for several seconds before raising his eyes back to my face. "This isn't going to go away, and I really need to know where I stand. I'm getting a sense out of your mind, but I can't accept anything unless you actually make a decision and tell me what you want to do."

I swallowed. I had known that this conversation would be coming, and probably sooner rather than later, but I hadn't expected it this soon. What could I tell Lucien? Saying that I preferred John, but would be happy to come back to Lucien if there was no chance I could be with John? How crappy was that? Lucien deserved better, and so did John—he might take me more seriously if he knew I was putting everything on the line for him.

"Okay," I said, making up my mind. "I'm sorry, but I can't accept your marriage proposal."

"And us?"

I swallowed again. I'd never had to have a conversation like this —it sucked the big ones. "We can't date anymore," I said, feeling sad and knowing it was right. "You've been so good to me, but it's—it's not right. I belong to someone else, and you deserve a girl who can give you everything. I'm—I'm sorry."

He smiled—it wasn't a happy smile, but it was nevertheless genuine. "I appreciate your honesty, Stella. No hard feelings? No awkwardness?"

"No hard feelings," I agreed. "No promises about the awkwardness, though; that might be a little out of our control."

"We'll do our best," he agreed, looking amused. "I'll always care about you, Stella, but I guess I can see your reasoning. It wouldn't be good for either of us if we kept dating under the current circumstances. So, tell me, have you worked out how you're going to handle John when we bring him in?"

"Not yet," I admitted, "except that I won't use magic to make him fall for me. Even if nothing else works, I won't do that. I want it to be real or nothing."

"You may have your work cut out for you," he warned. "I know John tries to do the right thing, and he's pretty set on Natalie, but he does have a history of messing his love life up pretty badly if given enough opportunities."

"I know," I said heavily, "but I could accept that as long as I'm his number one."

"He's very lucky to have you," he said.

"What are you going to do to him when he is brought in?" I asked. "I mean, to get him on our side."

"The same thing as everyone else," he said, looking surprised. "A simple influential charm to make them agree that I'm doing the right thing, and then that'll be it for the magic."

"It won't change him, will it?"

"It hasn't changed any of the others," he said. "No, it won't change him; his thought processes and rationality and behaviour will all be the same; it'll only be this one opinion which will be different."

"Then he'll go in the Big Room too?"

"I'm not sure, but I don't think so. Peter will certainly go in the Big Room, at least briefly, but once I have those four on my team, I'm planning that everyone can come back out of the Big Room and back to normal lives on the outside, because by then, there'll be no more resistance. I'm thinking that Marc and John should join me at the top so that after all we've been through, the Morans will be running the world, as my dad had once envisioned. I'll have my magic, you'll have your magic, Marc can have the Hero Crystal back, John can use the Sien-Leoard Crystal; and James, who I'd like to have as a magical adviser, 'cause he's so good at coming up with good ideas, can use the Light Crystal. We'll be a pretty good team, assuming they all agree to it after the influential charms."

That actually did sound good, but there was still one thing I needed to make sure of. "But you remembered what I said? I don't want any magic used against John, other than that one influential charm. I don't want anything else to change for him."

"Not even if he breaks your heart?"

"I'd rather wear a broken heart than do anything else to him," I said stubbornly—it was one fact on which I wouldn't budge, no matter what. "You agree?"

"If you insist," he said, but he was smiling, his eyes twinkling. "What you're saying is, absolutely no magic to be performed on John that will make him more attracted to you."

"Exactly."

"I can dig that," he said, still smiling. He had an idea in his head, I was almost sure of it, though I couldn't imagine what it was. As long as he stuck by his word, and I honestly believed he would, I couldn't think of any underhanded way he could make John fall for me. It was down to me to make that happen, and our connection was probably the best way to do that, but in the meantime...

"Can you do something for me?" I asked.

"Perhaps," he said, grinning cagily at me.

"Check where they are now. I—I just wanna know that they're okay. I'd do it myself if I could."

"And you will soon be able to," he said, "although I hope that watching is all you will use your magic to do for them, at least for the time being. Again, we must stay on the same page here, Stella."

"Don't worry, I'm not gonna muck up your plans, so long as your plans keep working. If they don't..."

I left my sentence hanging, also grinning now. I would have bigger things to worry about for myself if Lucien's plans didn't work out, but that was a worry for another day. We went quiet then as he rolled his eyes up into his head, searching for the boys. It didn't take him long to find them; a grin spread slowly over his face.

"Well," he said slowly, "well—good for them. They've managed to get themselves into a drop-in centre for homeless people."

I let out a sigh—I hadn't even realised I'd been holding my breath until then. "So, they're okay?"

"Seems like it," he said, his eyes still rolled up as he watched them. "They don't have a lot on them, but they're all there. John's nursing a few injuries from his flight to freedom but even he's fairly comfortable."

"Oh, thank God," I said, enormously relieved. I'd been imagining the four of them spending the night sheltering under a bridge somewhere.

"Hmm," Lucien said, opening his eyes and staring at me intently. I felt my face flush—what was he doing? His gaze was so intent that it was almost creepy. "You may be interested to know, Stella, that all four of them are asleep."

"Yeah, fair enough, their day was probably a lot more tiring than ours♌—"

"All four of them, Stella," he repeated, and he took me by the shoulders and made me face him. I could do nothing but stare into his eyes as he leaned forward slightly, as though he was going to kiss me. I actually thought that was what he was going to do until he said, "Hello, John."

I flinched, understanding. If John was asleep there, he would be in my mind now, if it were true that the new state of our connection meant that it was impossible for either of us to sleep without connecting to the other. I cast my mind around, hoping I would somehow feel John's presence inside me, but I got nothing. Of course, he wasn't just with me—he was me, and that made what Lucien was doing now all the more creepy.

"How are you doing, John?" he asked, still staring into my eyes. "Having fun down there? You know it doesn't have to be so difficult for you and the others. I'm not so sure how long you've been with us or how much of our conversation you've heard, but I'm guessing that by the time you wake up, you'll have been with Stella long enough to see how things are running here."

"Do you have to do this?" I squeaked, unable to remember a time when I had been this creeped out. It wasn't as scary as what had happened in the graveyard earlier in the week, but it was certainly creepier.

"Don't mind Stella, John. I'm sure you'd feel just as awkward in her position—oh but of course, you are in her position," he said, and chuckled. "Just some things for you to think about when you wake up: You know that you won't be hurt if you and the others get on the road in the morning and come straight to me here in Chopville. You'd be welcomed with open arms, and if you want it, you, Marc and James can be put into positions of great power and influence—"

"I don't think he would chase that carrot—"

"Don't interrupt me, Stella—or are you John now?"

"Do I look like John?" I retorted, my mind flicking through a list of things I could do that John most certainly couldn't. Pulling up my top and flashing my breasts at him would probably have been the topper, but there was no way I was going to do that, not after the conversation we had just had.

"No," Lucien admitted, "I can't see any of him in your eyes, but I'm sure he's there. If he's asleep down there, he must be with us. Seriously, though, John, you have nothing to worry about. I can understand how you might object to having an influential charm put on you but try to think of it as a form of psychological therapy. All the rest of your friends are much happier now than they were before, knowing that they're safe, that nothing bad can happen to them now, and quite soon, they'll be able to go and live normal lives—better lives, better than they would have been before all this started."

"Enough," I said firmly, pulling myself forcefully away from him—this was just too creepy for my comfort. "I'm pretty sure he's got the message now."

"I would think so," said Lucien, getting to his feet, "and I'm fairly sure he'll pass it on to the others as soon as they're all awake. Whether or not they take my advice…well, we can only hope. Anyway, Stella, I think it's time for me to head out again. Are you going to try to sleep?"

"Yeah," I said, my mind returning to that place where I'd had what John had thought of as 'mental intercourse'—that was a good name for it, and how I hoped we could do so again tonight. "Where are you going?"

"America, I think," he said, yawning and putting his hand in his pocket where the Sien-Leoard Crystal now resided, probably giving himself some more energy. "I have ideas about how I'll put my powers to use in the following few weeks, but for the time being, I want to regain what your father lost after his death."

"His life?"

"No, I mean the territories. I'll catch up with Hank and Fewul and help out however I can—get through the job quicker. I intend to be back here by five o'clock so that I can deal with Natalie when she comes around. See you at breakfast?"

"Sure, if I'm awake for it."

He had left then, and I had returned to my room, whereas I had the last time John had been in my mind, I got changed into my night clothes and got into bed, thinking of sleep, but unfortunately not feeling remotely tired. What if he woke up before I fell asleep? Well, I would fall into his mind as he was in mine now, and that would be better than nothing, but more than watching him and thinking his thoughts along with him, thoughts that would probably be painful to me when I woke up again, I wanted to be able to communicate with him—communication that went both ways—communication which could, perhaps, bring us closer together in what we wanted.

It wasn't going to happen, though—I just wasn't tired enough. I supposed I could lie here in bed, a bed which was probably more comfortable than the one he was lying in and wait for sleep to come. If I lay here long enough, it would eventually come, but I was already bored by the idea. I had never been one to lie in bed when I wasn't tired enough to sleep. There was really nothing else for me to do, though; everything that could be done up here had been done at some point today (or yesterday, as it was now).

I tried to free my mind, to quieten it so that my chances of falling asleep would increase, but as is often the case, it just went where it wanted to go. I found myself thinking back to the ideas that James had had about the connection when John had described what had happened to him the last time—particularly, the idea that he'd had a small influence on my thoughts. It certainly made sense; if that untying thing had done what I thought it had done, John and I were a step closer to merging into a single person, a personality which would probably be a combination of both of our existing personalities, and a physical connection which would probably be identical to what had happened to Tommy with his two bodies.

That was certainly not something I wanted—I couldn't possibly be with John the way I wanted to be with him if we became a single person. The idea that we could influence each other very slightly, though, that wasn't necessarily such a bad thing. I didn't think he'd directed my thoughts at all tonight, though, unless getting me to recap the events of the afternoon had been his wish rather than my own; and I didn't think I'd influenced his thoughts at all in the brief time I'd watched him making his plans with Peter, James and Marc.

If I couldn't sleep, maybe I could do something that John would like or appreciate—something that would make him not dread the times he entered my mind. He had thought that not having an opportunity to mentally recharge would drive him mad, and I actually agreed with that, but perhaps if I had my own downtime while he was with me, he would feel better when he woke up. And that seemed to be the story of my night. I had tossed and turned in bed, my thoughts circling and getting nowhere, for hours.

At some point, I had begun to feel that all-over sensation of tingling which meant that my magic was almost completely mine again. I would feel when the transfer of power would be complete—at least, I had when I'd gotten it back from Moran—and at that moment, somewhere else in the building, Natalie would wake up. She may yet be a problem for me, but as I wouldn't do anything magical to sway John's favour, nor would I do anything else to Natalie—I already knew how that would only get his back up. I sighed, staring at the dark ceiling above me and wishing that things weren't…

Chapter 10: A Nice, Cold Glass of Orange Juice on the Side

…so complicated, but not seeing any simple way to make it so.

I rolled over again, trying to think, and promptly fell right out of bed and onto the cold, hard floor of my upstairs room in the drop-in centre in Melbourne. Damn, I thought, scrambling onto my knees and looking for the pouch containing all my magical items; it had been knocked onto the floor too, but was thankfully still closed. I wasn't entirely sure when I had woken up, but Stella's thoughts had drifted so naturally into my own that I hadn't even noticed—and may have gone on not noticing for longer if I hadn't tried to roll over. Stella's bed, though also a single, was apparently a little wider than this thing I had to sleep on.

I pressed down on my watch face so that the numbers lit up in the darkness, showing the time to be a few minutes before five o'clock in the morning. I pulled myself back onto my bed and sat there, toying with the pouch in my hands and examining my current condition. My forehead was a little sore, and the burn on my face was a little itchy, and it took some discipline to stop myself from scratching it—if I started, I knew I wouldn't be able to stop. Other than that, though, I felt fine, even though I could only have been asleep for four hours. As it had before, my body had been so deeply asleep that four hours was all it had needed.

Stella had been wide-awake too, was probably still wide-awake now, which raised an interesting question: What had woken me up at that exact moment? Had it been something in my body, telling my brain it had rested enough and it was time to wake up? That seemed more likely, because there certainly hadn't been anything on Stella's end forcing me to retreat. If it was five o'clock now, Stella would probably be able to use her magic any minute. If I remembered her thoughts (and sadly, I could remember a lot), one of the first things she would do was spy on me. That wasn't a comforting thought, but I reminded myself that it wouldn't make a lot of difference—if she didn't spy on me that way, she would do so by entering my mind when she slept, just as I had hers, and whatever she missed, Lucien would cover with his own spying. As long as Stella didn't teleport down here and try to communicate with me in person, I could probably deal, and I didn't think she would. Whatever her feelings for me, she seemed to be firm about whose side she was really on in this war.

And when Stella got her magic back, Natalie would reawaken in the Small Room, where she was probably presently tied up alongside the other former Sorcerers. The moment she came around, she would be placed under an influential charm, and then the girl I loved would be just against us as everyone else I cared about. I sighed and hugged myself, partially because I was cold (I was only wearing my underpants, and it was probably only a few degrees out) but mostly out of pain—the pain of missing Natalie. Even though I had only been away from her for twenty-four hours, a twenty-four hour period which had gone on and on forever it seemed, I missed her more than I had suspected it was possible to miss a person. There were a lot of other emotions I should have been feeling more strongly—fear for myself and the other three chief among them—but no, it was Natalie I wanted more than anything else.

I had been sitting there for a silent and immobile half-hour when an idea occurred to me. I got up, got dressed in my clothes from the day before (this place probably had some washers and dryers downstairs, but what on earth would I wear while my clothes were going through?), gathered my things (I wasn't leaving anything other than my towel in my room), and went to the bathroom. After spending a short amount of time looking in the mirror, shaving and making sure I wasn't bleeding anymore (it was ugly up there, but it had stopped, thank God), I washed my face and then returned to our corridor where I knocked softly on the fourth door on the left.

"James, James, you awake? Wake up; I need you for something." I hissed, not daring to make too much noise—not because I didn't want the others to wake up, but—okay, yeah, I wanted to let them rest a bit longer. Through the door, I heard James mutter something as though he were still half asleep, so I tried again. "James, wake up, it's John; I need you for something."

"What the hell," he said, sounding pretty pissed. I gave him a few moments to compose himself, but before I could knock a third time, he spoke again, closer to the door this time. "What's going on?"

"James, it's John. Can you open the door? I need you for something."

"How do I know you're John?" he asked, sounding sharp and shrewd—typical James.

"Well, I've got a pretty distinctive scar on my forehead," I told him. "Not as distinctive as Harry Potter, perhaps, but it's gotta be close."

"You know I can't see that from here. Give me a good reason why I should open the door."

"Er—well, if I were a Hammerheart or a cop, I probably would have blasted it open already. Does that count as a good reason?"

Silence from the other side for about ten seconds, but when James spoke, I wondered for a moment if he'd fallen asleep on his feet. "February the 17th this year, John and I overheard the girls talking about a certain type of enchanted person while they were studying for their history of magic projects. What was that type of person?"

"Say what?"

"Answer the question correctly or I won't let you in."

"Fine," I snapped, and feeling nettled, I lapsed into thought. It cost me some effort to get my brain moving in the right direction, though. How on earth did he expect me to remember something like that more than six months after it had happened?

But I needed to get in there, so I had to answer the question. I forced myself to think it out. February 17—that would have been the second last week of the month—the week before I had been captured by the Hammersons and locked up in the Basement for two days. Stella's party had been on the Saturday, her actual birthday the following day, and that Sunday had been the 21st, which made the 17th a Wednesday. Wednesday—what had happened on that Wednesday? Hall had given me the returnamy that day, and then I had gone home, done some maths homework, and then James had turned up. We had used the network of wireless microphones to listen to the girls persuading Natalie to ask me out on a date, but before they had talked about that, Lisa had been telling them about...

"Itchicans!" I exclaimed in triumph, hardly able to believe my own brilliance in working it out. "Now let me in."

The lock clicked, the door opened inward, and James appeared, grinning at me. "Sorry," he said sheepishly, "but I had to be sure. Hmm—yeah, you're right; that is pretty distinctive."

"Could you have picked a slightly easier question?"

"Not really," he shrugged. "I just assumed that given what else we'd heard on the microphones that day, you would remember it, but I couldn't think of anyone else who could possibly know what we'd heard that day."

"Fair point. Anyway, can I use the Light Crystal for something?"

"The Light Crystal?" he said, looking surprised. "I guess so, but why?"

"I just—I dunno if I can explain it," I said uncomfortably. "It's just—Natalie would have come around in the last little bit, and I just —I guess I wanna see if I can do any good for her from here."

That was a lousy explanation, but I couldn't think of a better way to say it. Saying I wanted to send her my love was too corny even for thoughts, let alone speech. Thankfully, James accepted it without question. He stood back to let me in, shut the door behind me, and then pulled the crystal out from beneath his sheets—he had apparently been sleeping with it, something which would have been pretty nasty in any other situation.

"I don't blame you," he said, handing it over. "I spent the whole time I was trying to get to sleep earlier thinking about Erica. I hate the idea that her mind has been altered."

"So do I," I said, my mind on what had probably already happened to Natalie by now.

The first wish I tried to make was for her to forgive me for not protecting her, as she had asked me to do, but the crystal didn't go warm in my hands. Perhaps that wish was too selfish—in fact, it almost certainly was, but it hadn't gone completely unacknowledged either. I couldn't identify the feeling that spread through me from the crystal—it wasn't very strong, but it was good—positive—made me feel better than I had before. I decided to interpret it my own way; that the wish wasn't required, because Natalie already forgave me.

I then wished that she wouldn't be hurt by anything Lucien does to her, and that one worked. I wished that she be safe—that one worked too. I almost wished that she would wait for me wherever she was, and then decided against it; the crystal mightn't let me get away with something like that, so I just had to hope that she would. Feeling like I needed to make one more wish for her, I wished that she not forget how much I loved her, and the crystal obliged. That was probably the best I could do for Natalie, and it might be enough; other than what would have already happened to her mind, and the possibility that she missed me as much as I missed her, she should be okay. She would go into the Big Room now, and she would have her parents and her sister around her.

I then turned my mind towards Stella, and the oncoming fiasco that would surely happen when she and I eventually crossed paths again, because we would have to at some point. The issue of her feelings for me, and my own reluctant affection for her, wasn't going to go away until we had found some point on which we agreed. So far, I could only see it ending painfully for both of us, but worse for Stella than me. The only way we could end up together was if she changed her mind about using magic to force me into dating her; and unfortunately, I would have no defence if she did.

So I firstly tried to wish that I would be reunited with Natalie in the next few days, but that didn't work. I removed the time frame from the wish and the crystal felt better about helping me out, but when I wished that she and I could end up happy together again, the crystal gave me nothing. Was it too selfish again, or was it physically impossible that Natalie and I could be together again? I didn't know, but for the second time, I had to accept it for now and try to make it work on my own. Finally, I just wished that one way or another, Stella and I both be satisfied by the way this ends, but once again, the crystal gave me nothing.

"Having a hard time of it?" James asked, having been watching my facial expressions as I grappled with the Light Crystal.

"It's being difficult," I admitted, "and I can't work out if I'm being selfish or if what I'm wishing for is just impossible or what."

James opened his mouth to say something, but I raised my hand, wanting to concentrate on what I was doing. If I couldn't use good magic to get out of my romantic situation, I would have to do it the hard, non-magic way. That could be messy but it would have to do, but there were more people who needed a bit of luck on their side. My mind turned to Amelia, and May if they were still together. Where on earth were they? Were they even still in this world? That would be a serious worry if May had given up on us and taken Amelia back to the Honnie world to fatten her up, but I had to admit, May had never agreed to anything like what was going on now.

I wished that the two of them be safe from Lucien and the Hammerhearts, and the crystal obliged. I then wished that Amelia be safe from May, my heart beating faster as I dealt the thoughts, but most fortunately, the crystal obliged for a second time. That could mean that May would do the right thing by Amelia, but not necessarily. I decided to make a third wish, that Amelia be safe from all Honnies, and again, the crystal obliged. Okay, that could only mean that they were still in this world, because Amelia wouldn't be safe in the Honnie world if they were there, even if May kept her around for a while. So if they were still here, where the hell were they?

That was probably all I could do for now, I thought, but then thought of a final group of people who needed a bit of luck. I wished that the four of us be safe today, but the crystal gave me nothing. I wished that the four of us not get physically hurt today, but again, nothing. I sighed, and wished that my friends not be in any immediate danger, and this time, the crystal went warm in my hands. I could only hope that if they weren't in any immediate danger, and I stuck close to them, I wouldn't be in danger either.

"Thanks," I said, handing it back to him and taking a look at my watch; it had just gone on six o'clock.

"You know, it probably would have been more sensible to wait a couple of hours to do that," he said, sitting on his bed while I perched on the edge of the splintery old chair. "I mean, I dunno about you, but I probably got less than five hours of sleep, and today could be just about anything for us."

I shrugged. "Yeah, sorry. I wouldn't have woken you if there were any other way."

"You don't look tired at all," he observed. "You did sleep, didn't you?"

"Yeah, for maybe four hours, but I suppose the only good thing to come out of this enhanced connection with Stella is that I don't seem to need as much sleep as I did before."

"Perhaps, but like I said, today could be just about anything, and you'd better hope you don't have to run on four hours of sleep for another eighteen or so," he said. "So, how is she? Still wrapped around Lucien's little finger?"

"In a way," I said, not wanting to tell him too much of what had gone on in the Chopville base just yet. Unfortunately, my memory of it was very clear indeed, but when I told him what he would need to know, I wanted Marc and Peter to hear it too. "She turned his marriage proposal down, but other than that, she's definitely on his side."

"Did you get any indication of whether or not she'd been in your mind at all yesterday?"

"Yeah, but she hadn't been for long," I said. "She slept a little later than me, so she was with me when we made our plans to get into the Hammerheart base, but she woke up before we got there."

James's eyes widened. "Are you saying that she knew we were there while we were there?"

I nodded. "Not only that, but she watched me and Marc from the stairs when we were getting the weapons. She wanted to make sure that if Lucien came down and saw us, he wouldn't hurt us."

James considered these words for a few moments, then said, "That runs in line with all I know about the influential charm. She may be on his side, but she hasn't forgotten that you and Marc are her friends. Is she still—you know—courting you?"

That was a strange way of putting it, but I nodded. I'd been about to tell him what had happened at the end, before I'd woken up, how Stella had tried to make it so that I would enjoy being in her mind, but that would require explaining how she had known I was asleep, and that was another something Peter and Marc needed to know about. Instead, I said, "She wants to use the connection to persuade me that she's right for me, but I dunno—I just can't see myself preferring her over Natalie, and she's really set on not using magic to make me fall for her."

James let out a sigh of relief. "Thank God for that. What about Lucien, though? How does he feel about all this? Handle the rejection well enough?"

"Actually, he was really mature about it," I said, "probably 'cause he saw it coming—he can read her mind now. He even agreed that it wouldn't be a healthy relationship if they'd continued while she still thought about me. She made him promise not to do any magic on me on her behalf, and he did, so it's only the influential charm like the others I'd have to worry about if he catches me."

James smiled weakly. "And did he give anything away about how he intends to do that? Or is he sticking to that idea of doing it in his own time?"

"Yeah, but I'll tell you about that stuff when the other two wake up," I said, deciding that I might as well let him know why I was being so vague.

"Fair enough," said James, and now it was his turn to check his watch. "I dunno about you, but I'm starving. What time do they do breakfast in this place?"

I felt myself grin broadly. "A pancake for you, sir? Would you prefer golden syrup with that? Or perhaps maple, with jam, cream and a nice, cold glass of orange juice on the side? Perhaps some toast or a few pikelets? Or would you be preferring this lovely, crispy hash brown with these waffles and crumpets?—"

"Dipstick," he muttered, but he was also grinning. "You've been hanging around Harry and Simon too long if you can just reel that kind of stuff off. I only said that 'cause that woman last night said that they did do meals—two dollars each, I think it was."

"Might be a little early," I supposed, "but surely in an hour or so…"

* * *

About two hours later, everyone was awake, dressed, fed, and still under no immediate threat of being caught. Marc, Peter and I had waited in the upstairs corridor, fearing that in the daylight, it might be easier for someone in this establishment to recognise us (surely our faces would be plastered all over the city by now). If they were on the ball, Peter and James would be wanted criminals too (probably, if Hall was calling the shots), but we still felt that James was probably the least likely out of the four of us to be recognised. He had gone about exploring the place, returning with a single slice of buttered toast for each of us (it would have to do) and the news that we were assumed to be seeking assistance for our situations.

"We'll have to stall them," Marc said as James shut the bedroom door. We had gathered together in Peter's bedroom, he and Marc sitting on the bed, me sitting on the chair, and James having to park himself on the floor, so that we could conference. "I mean, it's true that we won't be here long, but we don't have time to be speaking to social workers or whatever."

"True," said James. "We won't be here most of the day, though, so maybe they'll think we're out looking for work—"

"Or they'll work out who we are by the time we get back," said Peter nervously.

"We can get a gauge on that before we let them know we're back," I said. "Anyway, I need to tell you guys what happened last night."

Even though I'd been in Stella's mind for several hours, and she had spent some of that time mentally recapping (perhaps subconsciously for my benefit) the day that had been for her, it only took me about five minutes to recount it to the boys. Marc and Peter both looked confused, but James seemed to have been struck by an epiphany.

"So that's his game," he said, and he was smiling. "He intends to win in the end, but he wants to do it his way. It makes sense too; given the way the influential charm works, he could quite easily get us on his side, but he might have a bit more trouble getting us to want to stand alongside him."

"I was thinking yesterday that if he keeps fluffing around, giving us opportunities, he might accidentally give a chance which we can capitalise on," I told them.

"Exactly," James agreed, "and given how much magic we're up against, that's our best chance. Basically, we have to beat him the same way we beat your dad when he was a Sorcerer, Marc."

"James, this is a very different—" Marc began.

"No, it's not," James insisted. "I mean, think about it. We have exactly as much magic now that we did back then—a little more, actually. Lucien has more going for him than your dad did, but we tricked him in the end, and if Lucien's going to allow us to slip away each time, we may get a chance to trick him too—we just have to recognise it when it comes."

"Stella?" Peter suggested. "She seems kind of unbalanced— maybe we can use her against Lucien somehow."

"Possibly," James agreed. "She was almost going to let you go yesterday, John; probably would have done if Sebastian hadn't turned up when he did. We might be able to use her against Lucien, but it would have to be a very good plan, and we'd probably have to trick you just as much as her, John, if it would work."

"Fair enough," I said, not altogether happy about that, but understanding the rationale behind it.

"Lucien would rather have us come to him, instead of him having to come after us," James mused. "I can understand why—it comes back to just what we would be willing to do for him once he can get us—but as difficult as he intends to make it for us, he can't know for sure that we will come to him."

"He's pretty sure that we will," I said, "and after seeing how it is there, I can see why. I mean, he's made it real clear that influential charms are the worst that will happen to us—no physical pain, no mental suffering, and in fact, he would probably say that he'll take all our suffering away."

"Exactly," James agreed. "He wanted you to see that, John, so that you would believe it, and you could convince us of the same thing. To be frank, I believe all of it; he would really like to have us working with him, because he knows how valuable we can be—how important we all were in taking down Hammerson, and how creative we are. He knows us, trusts our judgement, and he'd like to have us on his side rather than the opposition."

"He didn't seem particularly interested in me," Peter grumbled.

James shrugged. "It's a moot point, Pete. What's far more important is that he believes that by showing us these things, we'll forget why we're bothering to resist in the first place; after all, what he's offering certainly looks peaceful enough. Trouble is, he seems to have forgotten the main reason why we were fighting as well."

He looked enquiringly at each of us in turn. "Anyone?"

"I thought we were just fighting because the Woodwards were fighting, and we're on their side," said Peter, grinning slyly. "Okay, I thought it was because we didn't want the Hammersons to install a dictatorship ruled by magic, and how people would be tortured or killed for stepping out of line."

"Lucien's made it pretty clear that his dictatorship won't be like that," James pointed out, "and we've already seen evidence of that. He would prefer to control people directly in their minds, rather than frighten and bully them into submission. So if that's our main reason for fighting, it no longer applies. Any more ideas?"

"We were doing what we were doing," I said slowly, "because the Hammersons were hunting us specifically, and we were looking for the best way to survive."

"Also no longer applies, since Lucien has already stated he would like to keep us alive," James said, smiling in a way that anyone who didn't know him better might have thought was condescending, but was really more indulgent than anything else. "No, the real reason, the most important reason, and the most basic reason—think back to Smiley's memories we saw on Rock Haulter, mainly the first one when the Hammersons were telling the Woodwards about their ideas."

Silence fell for a few seconds, but it was Marc's face that lit up with comprehension. "We're fighting because it wouldn't work, even with magic."

"Exactly!" said James, grinning at Marc. "Utopian societies never work—human nature makes it impossible for them to work. It's nothing more than a pipedream, and the only way to control it to a point at which you can call it a utopia is by completely enslaving the entire human race. Do you guys remember that book," he now said to me and Peter, "that they made us read for English last year? 'The White Mountains'?"

"The one with the tripods?" said Peter.

James nodded. "That may have been only fiction, but what they had in that book was about as close to a utopian society as it's possible to get, and it only worked because the human race was entirely enslaved, and mind control was used to keep them in order. Does that sound familiar?"

"But they weren't entirely enslaved," Marc pointed out, "otherwise there wouldn't have been a story at all."

"True, the mind control was only used on children when they reached a certain age," James agreed, "and I dunno about Lucien, but Arnold Hammerson intended to perform the first influential charms at birth, and distribute them thereafter using medications and vaccinations. My point is that in order to achieve this, Lucien basically has to eliminate our right to freedom, and honestly, the consequences of that probably won't be anywhere near as peaceful as he imagines. That's a good reason to keep fighting, I reckon, no matter what obstacles Lucien tries to throw at us."

I sighed with relief; for a brief time there, I'd been worried that James was going to try to talk us into giving up. His reasoning was good, but there was another reason to keep fighting. This was what Arnold Hammerson wanted, and anything he wanted, whatever Lucien might say about his vision being the best part of him, was not something I wanted. I couldn't live with myself if I gave up, and no influential charm could fix that.

"So, if we're going to keep fighting," said Peter, "what are we gonna do next?"

"Good question," said James, leaning back against the wall behind him (he looked so strange sitting on the floor). "I was contemplating that in the shower last night—"

"You were thinking about that in the shower?" Peter gaped at him.

"I dunno if I needed to know that," Marc muttered.

"I might as well think about something," James shrugged. "It's not like washing myself requires a lot of concentration—well, maybe it does for you guys, but I just got on with it. Anyway, if we can get in the base as easily as we did yesterday, there are some things we can do."

"What if we can't?" I asked nervously.

"Then we try another base," he replied. "I'd rather do the Chopville one, though, and not just because we know our way around in there. Our families are in there, and given that we'll be more noticeable if all four of us are moving around on the top level, the safest place for the rest of us to be is probably in the Big Room. I think we can trust that the people in there will protect us, even if they won't side with us. So, first plan is to try and get in there, and if we can, I think the first thing we should do is look for the Sorcerous Crystals. I'm sure Lucien will have hidden them somewhere, and probably protected them with magic, but they're the one thing that could put us ahead in the game if we can get hold of them."

"Hang on," Marc said slowly, "James, that may be true, but surely there are other things we can do in the meantime. What about stealing the Sien-Leoard Crystal?"

"Lucien carries that with him everywhere," James shrugged. "The only way we could get near enough to nick it without getting cursed is if he's already unconscious, and what's the best way to make that happen?"

"Aren't there Hammerheart devices that can do that?" I asked. "Those things we used on Monday, Marc, they could knock people out for twenty-four hours at a time. Was that based on an existing device?"

"I'm not sure," said Marc. "It was Stella's suggestion, but whether she took it from something they already had or just made it up because it seemed like a good idea, I don't know. If not, we could use those killing things that we've already got, or if we can find one, those things the Hammerhearts used to nullify Natalie and Amelia's magic."

"I'd bet they'd be protected from both of those things," said Peter, "the second one far more likely than the first, because they both knew about it. As for hitting Lucien with a spell, he'd probably have a shield around him a lot of the time—"

"Not if he gets ahead of himself," said James pointedly, "and it looks as though he already is, but I still think that the Sorcerous Crystals are our best bet, if we can get hold of them. I don't suppose he mentioned their whereabouts to Stella, did he, John?"

"No, he hasn't yet, I don't think," I said, "and in the time I've been with her, she hasn't even given them a thought."

"All right," said James, and sighed. "It's not great, because he could have hidden them absolutely anywhere within their network, or maybe even somewhere outside it, but the best place to look is probably the most dangerous one."

"What if we run into him or Stella in there?" Marc asked.

"We do the only thing we can," said James solemnly. "Those pouches are useful, but I'd recommend carrying at least two weapons at all times, and although I don't think any of you will like it, someone needs to be prepared to use an agonator."

"What?" All three of us had jerked convulsively at his last word.

"I know, it's not great," he conceded, "but again, it's probably something he wouldn't expect—I mean, he was one of us only a week ago—and of all the weapons we've got, that's the most likely to distract him long enough to steal his crystal. I say that because if we do get into a fight with him, taking the Sien-Leoard Crystal will be the only way to save ourselves. If we happen to run into Stella, we may not have to fight her at all, but we should be prepared to, just in case."

"But those killing things, James," said Peter, looking stricken, "surely that would be better than the agonator—"

"He would expect us to resort to that, I think," said James firmly. "By all means, be prepared to try, but also be prepared for the possibility that he'll have an idea for how to deal with it."

"I think it would be a better idea for us to come up with a plan to avoid getting into that situation in the first place," Marc suggested.

"Hear, hear," Peter and I said, almost in unison, and we both laughed.

James considered and then said, "If he's watching us when we arrive, nothing we do will avoid an encounter with him, unless he actually wants to avoid us. I don't think he will, though, not after we got away with it yesterday. If he's not watching, then maybe there'll be a way for us to get an idea of what's going on inside through you, John."

I opened my mouth, about to tell him, as I had once told Mr. Woodward, that I couldn't make my connection with Stella activate on command, but what was the point? I could make it happen—all I had to do was fall asleep and it would happen. I didn't feel remotely tired now, though, so I had no idea how I could make the sleep part happen.

"Stella mightn't be in the base, though," Marc pointed out, "or, she could be asleep. That's actually quite likely if she stayed up all night."

"True, and that'll certainly ruin things for us," James agreed, and he checked his watch. "So how's this for a plan: We hole up in here for the morning, have an early lunch, and head out around half past eleven. We'll have to go back to the same apartment building where we got out from ℜ—"

"There are all sorts of ways that plan could go wrong," I said shakily.

"True," he agreed. "The cops, the residents of the apartment, maybe even those security people we had trouble with yesterday, but do you guys have a quicker way we can get to Chopville?"

Nobody did, of course.

"In that case," I said, also checking my watch, "if you want me to try to connect with Stella, I should probably do it about an hour from now. I dunno if she'll sleep or keep herself awake with magic—

she wasn't thinking about that, but it would probably be better for us if she's asleep when we're in there. She'll know what we did when she wakes up, but at least she won't be able to stop us at the time. As for Lucien, our best chance is if he's back out causing trouble with Cornish and Fewul."

"Well, if our run of luck is as good today as it was yesterday," said Marc, "all that will happen, but I wouldn't lay odds on it running that smoothly."

"What are we supposed to do for the morning if we stay here?" Peter asked. "Seems like a waste of time; surely there's something useful we could be doing around here."

"I've got something I'd like to do this morning," James told us. "I found a few computers downstairs earlier and I'd like to use one of them to do a bit of research—"

"James, I know that project of yours is important," said Peter, "but don't you think protecting ourselves is a little more—"

"Also, there's probably no security on those things," said Marc, "at least, not like what we had in our base."

"All true," James agreed, "but actually, the sort of research I need to do at this point isn't really possible on the Internet. At least, after all the hours I've spent looking around, I don't think there's any more answers freely available that I can use. That's why, if I can, I'd like to speak to a magicologist about it."

"Magicologist?" Peter repeated, stunned. "You mean those people who study magic like a science? James, you know that's all bogus, right? We've seen and done a lot more with magic than any magicologist in the world, I bet."

James shrugged. "The magic we had didn't give me the answers I was looking for, but maybe someone who's studied magic in more depth over a longer period of time might be able to help."

"What answers are you looking for?" I asked, remembering him telling me about his magic project in our old computer room last week (really, only last week?), and how his suspicion was that the only way we could really win this war would be to destroy the Magic Crystals altogether.

He only shrugged again. "I could spend all morning trying to explain it, or I could go and see if I can track down a magicologist on the Net."

"I know there's at least one in Melbourne," Marc said, surprising everyone. "Well, there is," he insisted, staring around at us all. "That article in the Chopville rag earlier in the year about my dad, it had an opinion from a Melbourne-based magicologist. Can't remember his name, but它—"

James's eyes lit up. "Marc, if you're right, you may have just saved me a truckload of time—"

A feeling swept over us all then, almost in a single moment. It took me maybe two seconds to recognise it, but those seconds were long enough for panic to fully form in all of our minds. Even beyond two seconds, both Marc and James still didn't recognise the sensation, perhaps hoping that they had felt nothing more than an unusual draught, but believing (judging by their widened eyes and alarmed expressions) that some sort of magical spell had just been cast over us. Peter and I knew better, though, having felt it at least once before; it wasn't magic, but it could still have been Lucien at work, as I remembered something he had said to Stella the day before. That was the cause of my alarm, but it only took two seconds for me to know better. It wasn't Lucien; it was something much, much better for us indeed.

"Awesome," Peter grinned, understanding as I did.

"What the hell is that?" Marc asked sharply, jumping to his feet and pulling his bludginator from his pocket. One of his feet caught a chair leg, causing him to trip and fall, and his weight caused the chair to tip over, spilling me on top of him and both of us on top of James, whose head bounced off the closed bedroom door behind him.

"Jesus Christ!"

It took more than half a minute for the three of us to separate, during which time James could barely move or speak with our combined weight on top of him, and Marc was trapped in the middle of what Peter later referred to as a 'J-sandwich' (which James immediately claimed as his rapper name). Marc could only struggle with one arm as he didn't quite dare to use the hand still holding his bludginator, what with James's face so close. My primary concern was not touching a part of either of their bodies, which could cause us all permanent psychological damage, but eventually I managed to put my weight on the floor and set the chair to rights.

"Awesome," Peter repeated, trying to control his laughter, and not having much success.

"Hang on," I said, scrambling onto the bed beside him so that Marc and James would have the entire floor space to work it all out. Once seated, I lapsed into concentration, projecting my thoughts outward into the Honnie mind which had just encapsulated the four of us. Lucien did have a Honnie mind to work with now—he had told Stella about it, and what he had used it to almost do to May— but this wasn't Lucien at work. I knew so because of the thought that had been placed in my head (and probably all the others, even if Marc and James hadn't recognised it for what it was). May was here, against all the odds, and if nothing terrible happened to any of us in the next half-hour or so, we could reunite with both her and Amelia, thereby increasing our fighting ability by a thousand percent. Quite suddenly, things were actually looking up for us.

Chapter 11: I Demand Use of the Bed

It would take at least half an hour for May and Amelia to get from where they were (which turned out to be Tullamarine Airport) to the drop-in centre, and that was even factoring our complete lack of knowledge about where the hell we were. The four of us were far too anxious about Lucien seeing what was happening and intervening and knowing we could do nothing to stop him if he did, that we couldn't possibly sit up in our little second-floor corridor waiting quietly for them to arrive. James decided to use the time to do some research on one of the computers, which he did by telling the people downstairs that he was looking online for part-time work; and while he used the computer, an invisible Marc stood behind him, weapons poised, just in case.

Peter and I, both being smaller than Marc and able to get out of the way of passing people more easily, were elected to go invisible ourselves and hang around in the foyer, where we would see May and Amelia come in. There were other entrances to the building, of course (not to mention certain second-floor fire escapes), but if any enemies chose to enter through that way—again, nothing we could do. It probably seemed like a strange approach, but with so much magic against us, our best hope was to rely on them not using it and to instead focus on those things that we could control. May and Amelia would be much more vulnerable wherever they were, as neither of them had any Hammerheart weapons (May had told me so telepathically), but if anyone other than Lucien or Stella intercepted them, May could probably sort them out with her mind.

It was a torturous wait. I wasn't sure about Peter, but I know I spent almost as much time looking repeatedly down at my invisible watch to see how much time had passed since the initial communication. It was incredible how I could keep doing that, knowing I couldn't see the bloody thing and continually forgetting that every thirty seconds or so. It got a little easier towards the end, though; once May and Amelia were in the city, having caught a bus from the airport (interesting trying to imagine May on a bus, but even more crazy thinking of her on a plane), they needed a bit of help finding our exact location, and kept in regular telepathic communication with both me and Peter for the rest of their journey. Of course, we couldn't tell them anything useful, but May somehow worked it out anyway, perhaps by reading the minds of others and comparing them with our own. She ran with Amelia the rest of the way, sprinting Honnie style (probably faster than the slow-moving cars in the area), and probably tinkering with the minds around her so that they thought nothing of it.

Incredibly, nothing at all went wrong. Our run of good luck, which seemed to have gone on ever since the initial disaster that had seen the four of us cast out into the big wide world, continued. (Well, I supposed Marc had punched a bloke in the face yesterday, and he'd rammed another bloke's head into a steel handrail—he'd become a little violent since losing his crystal, our Seventh Sorcerer.) The only complication, we saw when the two girls finally walked through the door, was that they didn't look anywhere near as pathetic as we had looked last night; they were both clean, well-dressed, and although May looked just about dead on her feet of exhaustion, Amelia seemed to be completely alert. She cast her eyes around the room as she entered, perhaps looking for me and Peter (May must have told her we were waiting here) before walking up to the desk.

The conversation lasted no more than twenty seconds, during which May stood behind Amelia and only watched on, holding a plastic bag containing whatever belongings they'd carried with them and looking like her mind was elsewhere. The woman behind the desk (it was a different one since last night) didn't ask any questions of Amelia's circumstances—she didn't even ask for money from either of them. She just went through the door behind her and appeared only seconds later with a couple of keys. Her expression was quite placid, as though all of this made perfect sense to her and didn't require any particular thought at all. Of course, I didn't have to wonder what had caused that, and knew for sure a moment later when a thought pressed itself into my mind, indicating that the two girls had been given the keys to the last two rooms on our side of our little corridor.

Leaving them to their devices, Peter and I linked arms after a whispered conversation and went to find Marc and James. He was still using the computer, clicking away and grinning in a satisfied way.

"Oi, J-sandwich, time to—" Peter hissed, but that was when I walked right into Marc, causing us both to stagger.

"Marc, it—argh!"

Marc had reacted instinctively before he'd realised who I was, acted as though I were an enemy who had accidentally given himself away. His bludginator swung around, cutting horizontally across my chest, ripping my shirt and jumper, and causing me to bleed—as if I weren't already hurt enough.

"Stop!" Peter hissed, and thankfully, the place was just quiet enough for all three of us to hear him clearly, without anyone else around (there was only one other person using a computer) hearing anything.

"Shit," I moaned, clutching my chest—it was very painful.

"Crap," Marc also moaned in front of me.

"They're here, you guys," Peter hissed. "James, whatever you're doing, pause it and let's get going. They're in our corridor."

James did so, shutting down the computer and heading out of the room, the three of us following carefully along in his wake. He ducked into what seemed to be a laundry room, which was noisy with a couple of washers in progress, but blessedly deserted, and shut the door behind us so that we could make ourselves visible without anyone noticing.

"Sorry, man," said Marc, staring at the damage his bludginator had done. "We really should have worked out a system or something."

"It's okay," I said, feeling hurt and irritated, but knowing that I could hardly blame Marc; he'd done the right thing under the circumstances.

"Our corridor?" James enquired. "Talk about luck⅜—"

"I really doubt it was luck," said Peter. "I dunno what May did to that woman at the desk, but those two got through in about thirty seconds—didn't even have to pay."

Marc swore. "So we robbed those poor girls for no reason in the end? Damn, we should try to get whatever's left over back to them."

"Yeah," I agreed, knowing that as good as the intention was, we probably wouldn't have time for it.

"How did they look?" James asked. "Have you had a chance to ask them where they've been all this time yet?"

"We haven't spoken to them at all yet," Peter said. "They just went to the desk and then up to the rooms; they'll be there now."

"How did Amelia look?" Marc asked quietly.

"Actually, she looked a lot better than May," I said, a little curious about that myself. "Well, she wasn't as tired anyway. Should we go up there?"

We slipped out of the laundry and made our way back to our bedrooms. We were only held up at the foot of the stairs by the woman who had just shown May and Amelia to their rooms; she was coming down them, a set expression on her face, and she didn't even notice the four of us waiting to the side at the bottom—the stairs were only wide enough to go up single file. You're just another little human pawn, I thought, looking after her as she headed back towards the foyer at a brisk trot. We then ascended the stairs and, less than a minute later, were back in our little corridor.

Amelia was in the fifth room on the left-hand side of the corridor, the room next to James, and May was in the one next to the fire escape. They both stepped out of their rooms when they heard us arrive, and we almost had a little reunion right there in the corridor before realising that anyone passing by might think it strange (at least for a couple of seconds before May dealt with them), and so ducked into the nearest room, which was Peter's this time. It had been a tight enough fit with four of us in one room; now there was barely enough room to swing a grasshopper. Amelia, James and I all had to stand and lean against the walls (and the door in James's case), while Peter sat on the chair and Marc and May took the bed.

"I was beginning to think you guys had disappeared," Marc said. "Nobody had any idea where you were—not even Lucien."

"We found a rather obscure way of staying hidden," Amelia said, also grinning.

"Good for you," said Peter, "'cause I tell you, Lucien's a lot more creative than Arnold Hammerson was now that he's got magic. He thought of all kinds of ways to take us down."

"But he obviously hasn't," Amelia pointed out. "Where on earth are we anyway? What is this place? And how come you four are the only ones left?"

"You go first," I said, thinking of how very complicated our last forty-eight hours had been, and thinking that most likely, our story would take longer to tell than theirs. "Where have you been, and how did you know to come here?"

Amelia shrugged. "We didn't know to come here; we expected to go straight to Chopville when we landed, but since we don't have magic anymore, and May couldn't find the entrances to the Hammerheart Highway in England, we had to catch a plane. We would have been here sooner if we didn't have to do it the slow way."

Peter grinned. "You know you've taken too much for granted when you can say that flying on an A380 is the slow way to get somewhere."

"So go on, then," Marc insisted. "What happened? How did you escape? We saw that Lucien had taken everyone in your base except for you two."

Amelia shrugged and looked at May. "Your story—I was unconscious."

May had been silent all this time, and for a moment, she looked as though she was going to stay that way. She was clearly exhausted, the first time I had ever seen her (or any Honnie, for that matter) looking so drained and depleted (without being physically injured), and I wondered how much of it was the struggle she'd been through to get here, or the full realisation that the situation had taken a turn for which she hadn't been prepared. It would be a much greater shock to her system than any of ours how quickly everything that had seemed to be going so well had been totally torn down.

After a few seconds, however, and with an obvious effort, she straightened up where she sat and told us about the escape: Amelia passing out in their bedroom; Lucien teleporting into the base with a band of Hammerhearts; everyone else in the base being swallowed by his strange half-human, half-Honnie mind; how May had tried to take the slightly smaller mind within hers, and how it had almost sucked her inward; how when she had quickly let it go, it had almost taken Amelia along with it; how deciding that she had no means with which to fight someone with magic, she had grabbed Amelia and made an escape through the nearest exit not a moment too soon; and how she had moved a step along the fourth dimension to escape, moving into her shadow, to coin Smiley's phrase, and had remained there for a full twenty-four hours until Amelia awoke.

"Wouldn't you have been hungry or thirsty?" Peter asked.

"Oh yes," May said, "but we both fed on the aeroplane."

"Not plane food either," Amelia told us, "but while May was making our path through Heathrow easier than you can imagine, she also stole some stocks from the duty-free shops, including these"—she indicated the clothes she was wearing—"and some snack foods, which were great."

May pulled a grotesque face to indicate her strong disagreement with this statement, but seemed to be too weary to say anything.

"We still have some of them left, if you guys are hungry," Amelia told us, and now I knew what must have been in the plastic bag May had been carrying earlier. "They're back in my room."

"We're fine for now," said Marc, and this time it was James's turn to pull a face—he was clearly hungry again, but I agreed with Marc; we had time for food later.

"I have a couple of questions," said Peter, "and then we'll tell you what happened to us and everyone else." When both females only looked at him, he said, "How come you're so tired, May, but Amelia's wide-awake?"

"She made me sleep on the second leg of the plane trip," Amelia said before May could speak. "There was a stopover," she added in response to several questioning looks. "I don't think May was particularly comfortable on the plane, though; she certainly didn't sleep for any of it, and we left London more than twenty-four hours ago."

"Geez," I said, looking at May and feeling sympathetic. I'd gone long stretches without sleep, but the more recent ones, I'd had magic to help me deal with it. The closest I could come to understanding what she must be going through was prior to the first Rock Haulter camp when I'd gotten something like eight hours sleep in about sixty hours—or something similar (and you can thank that Godless Enlightener for that, friends and neighbours). "I wish I could tell you that you can sleep now, but I'm not so sure that's a good idea."

May shrugged. "I think I can push on."

"What else did you want to know?" Amelia asked.

"Well—er," Peter faltered, and I was sure I knew where he was going. I wasn't sure if I wanted him to ask the question or not, but if he didn't, my curiosity would probably get the better of me anyway. When Amelia raised her eyebrows at him, he managed to say, "Well, you, Amelia—how are you?"

Marc and James both flinched, and I think I may have too, but Amelia seemed fine with the question. She considered for a moment, then said, "I know what you're talking about, but I really don't know how to answer it."

"Well—" Peter looked around at the rest of us for help.

It was James who composed himself first. "Well, how much can you remember about—about it happening?"

"Actually, I can remember all of it," she said, and we all looked at her in surprise. "Yeah," she insisted, "I remember the whole fight, and I even remember how I was after it, but those memories are kind of blurry for some reason."

She looked enquiringly at May, who said, "Those are your memories, but the ones before that are my memories of your thoughts while you were fighting him."

"Lucien said something about you being similar to how you were before, but not exactly the same," I told her. "What does that mean?"

Amelia shrugged. "My dad said the same thing, and even May thinks my thought patterns are a little different, but I only feel like me, if that makes sense. I guess you guys can decide for yourselves how different you think I am, but whatever I was before, you'd better get used to this me."

She grinned, now looking a little more self-conscious, and I decided that we had probably heard enough.

"Would you like to hear what happened to us?" I asked her.

She did, of course, and even May seemed uncharacteristically curious to hear the story (as if she hadn't already pulled the whole thing right out of my head). We started with breakfast on the Friday morning, and worked our way through the fifty-or-so hours that had passed since, leaving out as little as possible (though I remained selective regarding details of whatever was going on between me and Stella). It wasn't a happy story, and both girls' faces showed they weren't enjoying it, but at least it had a relatively happy ending. By the time we had finished, it had ticked past ten o'clock.

"And what we were discussing before you two turned up," said Marc, "is going into the base this afternoon and looking for the Sorcerous Crystals. James reckons that's the best place to start, if we can find him, and since I've had time to think about it, I guess he's probably right."

"When is our ever-enlightened J-sandwich wrong?" Peter asked rhetorically.

"Probably a good idea," said Amelia, glancing at May, "but before you go on, there's one last part of our story that you should probably hear."

"I thought you'd told it all," said Peter. "What else happened? Did you have to sit next to a fat person on the plane?"

"No," said Amelia. "You said before that you couldn't believe our good luck because Lucien didn't know where we were, and he must still not know since he's done nothing to interfere…well, that's not entirely true."

"Aw no," James moaned, covering his face. "What happened?"

"He confronted us in the terminal not long after we landed here," she said, "just teleported right in front of us while we were walking —didn't care about who saw."

"I think he did care," May interrupted, "because even though I could not hear his thoughts, I got an idea that he was thinking that he would just capture us both if there were not so many people watching."

"But why didn't he just use his magic to stop them from watching?" I asked. In fact, I could think of many ways Lucien could have taken them both right there in the terminal with no fuss at all. And just when we thought we'd worked him out…

"Because he thought of a better idea," May shrugged. "I did not get what it was."

"I'm not sure what his purpose was," said Amelia, "but he basically told us much the same thing he told you, John. He wanted me to join with him, and he wanted May to go back to her own world and her old life because she wasn't needed here anymore. He didn't openly threaten us at all—he looked like he was being genuine. I probably would have gone right along with him, 'cause I wouldn't have known he was the enemy now, but May stopped me—she didn't trust him at all."

"That is because of what he almost did to me," the Honnie said in an angry whisper, her face twisting in a way that emphasised her difference from the rest of us. "He wanted me to attack him so that he would have a reason to kill me. He only wants me out of the way so that I cannot help you."

So it's personal for May now, I thought. Her reasons for not leaving when the Woodward base had fallen seemed to be based on not having completed the job she had agreed to, but now she actually wanted to fight this war with us. Lucien had unwittingly made himself a dangerous and unnecessary enemy.

"Anyway, he got out of there before any trouble," Amelia went on. "He didn't tell us where you were, or even that there were any of you left, but I'm pretty sure he would expect us to be here with you by now. If what you say is true, he must be so confident that he thinks he can take all six of us down in his own time."

"If he's that clued in to what we're doing," said James, looking uneasy, "then he may be aware of our plan for this afternoon. He could be setting up an ambush for us as we speak."

All six of us looked around at each other, fear in every face. Even the Honnie looked uncomfortable.

"I have an idea," Marc said suddenly. "Look, we need to know what's going on inside that base before we get in there. Amelia, did you say that May used her mind to put you to sleep on the plane?"

I knew where this was going, and sure enough...

"Yes, she did," Amelia said, looking excited as she turned her eyes on me. "You can go in there and see what's going on—"

"I can see what Stella's doing," I corrected, "and a fat lot of good that'll do if she's not with Lucien."

"It's still the best thing we've got," said James. "You up for it, John?"

I sighed. I didn't want to be back in Stella's head, especially as she could very well be sleeping now (she was asleep at this time yesterday anyway), but I had to acknowledge that doing so was our best way of levelling the playing field. It was far too easy for Lucien to monitor us, and we needed some way of monitoring him.

"Okay," I said, "but you two had better shove off. If I'm gonna be sleeping, I demand use of the bed."

That was easier said than done. Peter had to firstly get off his chair so that Marc and May could move at all; he then had to lean against James, far too close for either of their comfort, so that I would have room to squeeze between Amelia and the now vacated chair. I pushed it over into the corner so that there would be room for Marc and May to move past me as I brushed past Amelia. As I did, my left-hand brushed right across her naval, and I thought I felt her shiver slightly at the touch...or maybe that was my shiver, because the touch had aroused me in a most unwelcome way. When I sat on the bed, I had to cross my legs as I fought to regain my composure before May sent my mind spinning away from my body and into the body of a girl a hundred and fifty kilometres away.

"Okay," said Marc, leaning back against the flimsy old desk behind him, and then moving quickly away as a loud snapping sound cut through the air. "Lie down, John, and whenever May's ready, I guess."

"Just a heads-up, though," I said, addressing May directly, "if it turns out that Stella is asleep, and you'll know straight away if she is, wake me up at once."

"Okay," she said monotonously.

I lay down on Peter's bed, knowing that it would probably happen as quickly as a general anaesthetic, but still not feeling remotely tired. Didn't it depend more on how tired the body was, rather than what went on in the mind? If it were that simple, people could just put themselves to sleep whenever they felt like it. Wait... people could pretty much sleep when they felt like it, because if they felt like it, they would already be tired, or was that too simplistic? I wasn't sure, but I found myself...

...walking through the door and shutting it behind me, before taking a good look around. It was the first time I'd been inside the Big Room since I had seen it for the first time when I'd only just got here. Lucien had said that he'd spent some time the day before making it more comfortable for the residents, and I could now see what he'd done. The room had been organised into rows (or isles) of large compartments, some of which stood open so that I could see their interiors. The mattresses looked comfortable enough, as did the pillows and blankets provided, and they were large enough so that a single person would have plenty of room to spread out. Each compartment also had cupboards within it so that they could store anything they might have, although exactly what any of these people had to store, I didn't know. Far to my right, there was a large dining area, complete with a conveyer belt like we'd had in the other base, and far to my left, a couple of doors, both standing open, and communal bathrooms on the other side.

As for things to do, or even clean clothes to change into, I still didn't know how these people were supposed to cope; but Lucien had told me, for something to do, I should come in here and see if I could do anything to help our guests—that was what he had called them; I could do anything other than kill them or release them. Perhaps he would have done it yesterday if he hadn't been distracted by the discovery of what John and the others had been doing right under his nose.

I'd had breakfast in the dining hall next door (about two-and-a-half hours ago now), by which time I'd been in a pretty crabby mood, trying with increasing desperation to get to sleep before my magic set in and having no luck whatsoever. By five o'clock, I had decided I might as well see the night through and sleep in the day. My mood hadn't been improved by the presence of one Ather Hignat, either, who sat with me all through the meal and tried to seduce me. The sickening thing is, it might have actually worked if I hadn't known what a dirtbag he is, and if I hadn't been so firmly set on someone else, but his persistence despite my continual rejections had tempted me to turn my magic on him; I had resisted with difficulty.

I had then gone to find Lucien, eventually locating him in an office up on level one where he was addressing a number of important Hammerhearts. He had been telling them that he would do his best to coordinate the stabilisation of Hammersonia until Cornish returned, after which Cornish would coordinate the army under Lucien's instructions; during which time, Lucien would focus himself on eliminating the sort of threat that had taken my father down—I didn't have to wonder what that was. I had been a little surprised that he was sticking with 'Hammersonia', though; when I'd asked him about it a little later on, he'd told me that since my family had gotten the whole thing started, they deserved due recognition for their efforts, and he would find a way to work the name Moran into immortality at a later date.

"I've been up all night," he had told me after everyone else had left; he'd looked tired, certainly more tired than I had felt. "How about you?"

"Same. I tried to sleep but it just wouldn't come."

"Yeah. Well, anyway, I know I was originally going to use magic to keep myself going," he had said, "but I've changed my mind on that."

"You're going to sleep in the day?"

"Yeah, but if you're still not tired, Stella, I would suggest you stay up for a while longer; maybe you can sleep when I've woken up."

"How come? I was looking forward to sleeping."

He had smiled. "I know, but I've done a little spying this morning, and there's a good chance that they may come back in here today to look for the Sorcerous Crystals. I'm not worried about them finding anything, but I still think it would be a good idea to have someone with magic ready just in case they cause any trouble."

"Do you want me to capture them?" I asked hopefully, thinking of John—how good it would be to have him here in the base instead of out in the virtual wilderness.

He had shrugged. "Only if you have no other choice. I'm quite happy to let them run around a little while longer. Also, so you know, it's not just the four of them anymore; Amelia and the Honnie have joined forces with them."

"What? When? How?"

"Yes, this morning, and it doesn't matter how. I traced them flying into Melbourne and had a little chat to them in the airport. I was originally going to capture them, deal with Amelia and force May to go home, but I changed my mind at the last minute."

"Why?" I had persisted, not understanding at all why he was taking this approach.

He had grinned broadly at me. "Let's just say, Stella, that I have a bigger plan in motion. I've already performed a little spell that should make things interesting for the six of them today, and that's assuming the police don't catch up with them. I'd like to see how that plays out before I bring them in."

"What spell? What are you talking about?"

He had only spread his hands. "Nothing that has caused them any physical pain. Trust me on that; if you don't believe me now, you can use your magic to check what they're doing and you'll see that I'm telling the truth."

I had almost been tempted to do it, but forced myself to take his word. Trust was very important to Lucien, and I had to trust him; otherwise, who on earth could I trust? He had already told me that he wanted to make them suffer, but not hurt them too badly; he had also promised that he wouldn't perform any mind-altering magic on them until they were here. He didn't even seem to want to perform his own influential charm on them remotely, but I could understand that one a little easier; that kind of magic was much more difficult to get right over a long distance.

"Thanks," he had sighed, and got to his feet. "Listen, I'll be sleeping for the next five hours at least, so you've got the run of the place. I'd prefer you not give any Hammerhearts orders, though, just in case you accidentally muck up the coordination. If you're bored, why not see if you can do anything to help the guests in the Big Room."

And so here I was, but what could I do to help them? Create a public laundry room for them all? A change of clothes? Leisure activities? If I had been in a better mood, I probably would have put the time into doing something like that, but right now, it felt pointless. These people wouldn't be here for more than a couple more days, surely; they could hold out for that long. Still, until I felt sleep creeping up again, I might as well do something in here, even if it came down to sitting down and hanging out with my new friends (hopefully they still considered me a friend).

I moved into the aisles, looking all around me as I went. I passed by plenty of people, mostly adults, either by themselves or in pairs, and I recognised a few as being part of the now defunct Woodward army. Every single one of them acknowledged me as I went by them, and I responded to the first several before it became too uncomfortable. Here was something about the influential charms that Lucien had neglected to mention: These people practically worshipped me. Their expressions when they addressed me, always keeping a respectable distance as though I were too important to approach, were reverent and when I so much as looked directly at them, and even more so when I actually spoke to them, they became what I could only think of as blissful.

I quickened my step, wanting to find those closer to my own age; maybe they would treat me the same way they had for the last couple of months. At least, they had treated me as one of their own in the brief period I had been with them before Lucien had shown them into the Big Room. I was just thinking this when I spotted Frederic Woodward and Brian Fletcher, talking together (joking, by the look of it) and seeming at perfect peace with the loss of their powers. It was the sight of them, combined with what I'd been thinking a moment ago, that made me think of Natalie, and an idea came to me —there was something I could do to help a small number of our guests.

I continued looking around, now knowing exactly who I was looking for, and eventually locating a large number of what had formerly been the Young Army, all gathered together in a setup similar to the lounge room in the old base. There were a number of these virtual lounge rooms throughout the Big Room (they weren't actual rooms, just areas free of compartments and encircled by couches), and a couple of the others had been occupied by adults (the parents of both the Playmans and Thomases had been in one of these), but this one seemed to have everyone I was looking for.

As I had hoped, they did treat me more naturally—like a real friend. Even after nearly two months of it, the novelty of having people who considered me a friend hadn't worn off. They welcomed me with enthusiasm that suggested similar admiration as what I'd gotten from the adults I had passed on my way through, but which they were dealing with differently. I was coaxed into sitting with them for a while, actually being included in the lighthearted banter the four Maivises were dishing out (I had almost always been an observer, perhaps assumed to be too serious to take it the right way).

I was enjoying the whole thing so much that for about twenty minutes, I quite forgotten what I'd been hoping to do. All five of the people I wanted to speak to were right here, and after insisting for the sixth or seventh time that I really did need to get going, I managed to separate Natalie, Rebecca, Lena, Erica and Darcy (the partners of the five who were still on the run) from the throng and lead them a short distance into the aisles of compartments so that we couldn't be overheard—not that it would matter too much if we were, but I just felt more comfortable doing it this way.

I knew I was doing the right thing: While the rest of the group had seemed mildly concerned about the runaways (as Harry had jokingly referred to them), these five were the only ones who didn't look at peace with what was going on. Well, no, that wasn't entirely true; Darcy, perhaps already having adjusted to losing the girlfriend he'd known, didn't seem to be feeling it to the same degree as the four girls—or maybe gender was the difference. I couldn't read any of their minds, but I would have bet on the former.

"What's the matter?" Erica asked me, glancing back over her shoulder the way we had come.

"Listen," I said quietly, looking from one to the other and hoping they would all be relieved by anything I could tell them, "I know you're all worried about—about the guys who got out of the base yesterdayℜ—"

"Do you know where they are?" Lena asked at once. "Can you use magic to find them? Please?"

Again, I was tempted to do it, my own curiosity piquing as well, but again, I resisted the urge. They only needed to know their partners were okay; they didn't need to know they had spent the night in some random homeless shelter in Melbourne, probably in the company of drunks, drug addicts and criminals fresh out of jail and with nowhere else to go. I dearly hoped that was a generalisation.

"I don't know exactly where they are," I hedged, "and I'd rather not search for them now—"

All five of them opened their mouths to protest then, and I raised a hand, palm out, to stall them. "Do not tell me how to use my magic."

I hadn't meant it to come out sounding like a command, but that was exactly what happened and all five of them shrank away from me—another thing that wouldn't have happened before the influential charms.

I inhaled deeply and went on, "I was going to say that Lucien has a big plan for bringing them in, and doing it in a way that'll make them agree to his offers when they get here. He knows where they are, and right now, I'm trusting that he'll take care of things. You agree?" I asked in response to several dubious expressions.

"How long is this going to take?" Natalie asked.

"And what's gonna happen to them in the meantime?" Rebecca added anxiously.

"I don't know either of those things," I admitted, "but it should only be a couple more days at most, and so far as what happens to them, Lucien wants them to be scared, but not hurt, if that makes sense. Also"ℜ—I looked directly at Darcy—"you should know that Amelia's with the boys now—looks like she flew in from wherever the Woodward base had been when she escaped from it."

"Phew, that's a relief." Darcy shrugged, and he did look relieved, but not to the extent I would have expected. What was going on with him? To cap my curiosity, he added, "Anything else?"

"Erm—aren't you curious about what state she's in?" I asked slowly.

He shrugged again. "Her dad told me how she turned out when he got in here a few hours ago. Sounds like it went as well as we could have hoped."

"Well, okay," I said, "as long as you're satisfied that your girlfriend's fine, and that she should be back with you real soon."

"Okay," he said, looking awkward, and turned to go back to the rest of the group. I almost called him back, but to what purpose? He was acting very strange, but it wasn't really my business to work out why.

"You all okay with that?" I turned my attention to the girls.

"Did Lucien say anything about how Peter's doing?" Rebecca asked intently.

"No, only that he'll be brought in here rather than given any power," I told her, and Rebecca scowled. "I think he wants James as an adviser, though, since he's so smart," I told Erica, and she glowed with pride, "and he'll let Marc use the Hero Crystal again," I told Lena.

To my surprise, and slowly impending dismay, Lena only shrugged indifferently. "Good for him," she said, "but I'm not gonna date Marc anymore, I don't think. I'll have to tell him so whenever they do bring him in."

"And you decide that now?" Erica asked, frowning. "Timing seems a little strange."

"Actually, I'd been thinking about it a couple of nights ago," she said, looking down at her feet, not looking particularly proud of herself. "It's the right thing to do, and if the shit hadn't hit the fan when it did, I would have done it already."

"Why don't you want Marc anymore?" Natalie asked, her eyes narrowed slightly, and I could see in her face that she was dreading the potential of this development as much as I was.

Lena hesitated, glancing from Natalie to me, to Rebecca and Erica, and then back again, considering her options. I thought she wasn't going to answer for a moment, but then she said, "He's not interesting enough."

"Really?" I said, surprised; Marc had always seemed interesting to me, and I wasn't even attracted to him.

Lena sighed. "It doesn't matter now anyway. I liked him well enough, but he never thrilled me. I guess it's my own fault; I thought I could tell myself how I should feel, but stuff like that never works. That's why when things settle down, I'll stop living a lie and focus on the guy I always wanted."

"What?" Natalie snapped; she had been staring vaguely over my shoulder, down the aisle behind me, but now she spun around to face Lena, her long hair whipping around her. "What are you saying?"

My stomach had fallen too. So it was what I'd feared; now what? Dealing with Natalie while John was so committed to her was going to be difficult enough—how to factor Lena into the equation. On one hand, she would probably have even less success at pulling him from Natalie than me; but on the other hand, she could use her body in a way that neither me nor Natalie could. We were both attractive enough in our own ways (not being cocky; I'd read enough male minds to see how they appreciated me, even if they were terrified of getting too close to me), but we weren't in the same league as Lena. Worst of all, all three of us knew that under the right circumstances, John could be persuaded physically over emotionally.

While I'd been thinking all these unpleasant thoughts, Natalie and Lena were sizing each other up. Lena said, "You heard me right. Why shouldn't I go after what I want just because someone else has him now?"

"I won't let you get him," Natalie hissed, but even I could see that it looked brittle. She didn't want to lose John, that much was clear, but would she be able to fight for him? Would she be able to compete with someone as determined and relentless as Lena? I wasn't sure, and I didn't think she was either. Perhaps there would be a way to work this to my advantage; if Lena discouraged Natalie enough to make her drop out of the race—destroyed her confidence to the point that she may well break up with John, regardless of what he wanted, then I might only have to compete against Lena—and I thought I could probably win that one if I played my cards right.

Something had to be done to stop this scene from spiralling out of control, though. Turning to Erica and Rebecca, I said, "You two can go back to the others; I need a private word with these two."

They did so, casting curious looks back over their shoulders as they left. Natalie and Lena had stopped staring daggers at each other and were now focussed on me; neither of them looked particularly happy, but Natalie more so than Lena. I didn't like what I would have to do now, but this was a challenge I would not shy away from.

"Lena, back off John. He's already told you he's not interested, so stop causing trouble—"

"No way!" Lena said indignantly. "He is interested—he's just a bit stubborn. I'll show him how serious I am𝔑—"

Natalie made a sound of utter incredulity. "Oh please, you only want him because he's one of the only guys you can't charm just by looking at him. You can't be satisfied; even if you got him, it wouldn't be enough for you."

That wasn't entirely true, I thought, because Lena had succeeded in charming John with her body on a number of occasions, as all three of us knew. The rest of what Natalie had said, though, made perfect sense; Lena seemed to be the type of girl who was attracted to the challenge, and she'd probably gotten so used to guys coming on to her all the time that when John had barely spared her any attention at all, she'd found herself wanting him. If he gave in and gave her what she wanted, it wouldn't be enough; she would either want more, or get bored and lose interest, as she had apparently lost interest in Marc for that very reason.

Lena, meanwhile, only laughed. "He's more likely to get bored with you than I could ever get bored with him."

"He loves me," Natalie stated with such certainty that I felt my own confidence waver a touch; Lena, too, looked shocked.

I'd seen and heard enough of this. Taking a deep breath and steeling myself, I said, "It doesn't matter—none of that matters. You know why? Because I have something with him that neither of you do—something so much stronger than anything either of you could possibly offer him. That's why when the dust settles, John will be with me, not with either of you two."

I then took some satisfaction from the thunderstruck looks on both their faces; my words had rarely caused that kind of effect in anyone.

Lena recovered first. "You have no chance. John hates that connection; there's no way he's gonna base a relationship on that."

"What part of 'he's my boyfriend' do you two not understand?" Natalie snapped, but her eyes had widened; she looked panicky. This kind of competition was well outside her comfort zone and she mightn't be up to it. I wasn't particularly comfortable with it either, but I would do it if it was the only way to get what I wanted.

Lena opened her mouth to retort yet again, and she, at least, seemed prepared for the fight, but for the second time, I decided I'd heard enough. This discussion couldn't possibly settle anything, so I raised my hand and put my magic to work for the first time since I'd gotten it back. Whatever Lena had been about to say, or whatever ideas Natalie was thinking of to press her advantage, slipped away from both of them.

"I've already decided not to use magic against John," I told them, feeling my blood pounding more quickly in my veins, "but I won't rule out using it against either of you two if I have to. I only want him if it's real, but I'll fight for that—I'll fight dirty if I have to, so don't make it more difficult for yourselves."

"He's my boyfriend," Natalie said again, and now she looked on the verge of tears.

I didn't respond—what on earth could I have said? If it had been anyone else in Natalie's position, any guy other than John, I would have been sympathetic, and I would have judged both myself and Lena as bitches for causing trouble for her. This was different, though; I knew what I was doing was right, and I would have to take whatever trouble I caused for a few others along the way. Sometimes, there was just no other option.

I didn't stay there any longer; they'd both gotten the message. I turned and walked away from them, heading back through the aisles towards the door out of the Big Room, now paying no attention at all to the people I passed by as they practically worshipped me all over again. I had to get out of there before my feelings got the better of me and I went and did something to those two girls that I would regret later. I thought that maybe now, I should probably see what John was doing.

I woke up with a start, more suddenly than I'd ever woken in my life. I felt only a moment of vertigo as I went from walking upright to lying flat on my back in an instant, but even that quickly passed. I sat up and looked around; Amelia, May, Marc, Peter and James were all staring at me, waiting, I assumed, for me to tell them what I had witnessed in Stella's mind. I looked at my watch and saw that a full half-hour had passed since May had put me to sleep, and speaking of sleep…

"Lucien will be asleep real soon," I told them, "if he isn't already."

"We know," said Marc drily, "May commentated the whole thing for us."

Oh crap. My stomach dropped; they knew everything that had gone on in there. I flushed as the full repercussions of this development sank in.

"Sorry, man," I said directly to Marc.

"Not your fault," he shrugged, looking unhappy but not accusing —that was a relief.

I cast my mind around wildly, uncomfortably aware of both Amelia and May still staring at me. I didn't dare meet either of their eyes so I wasn't sure if there was any accusation there. The scene between Stella, Natalie and Lena had been bad, but the things Stella had been thinking about as she had entered the Big Room were more important for us as a group. I found it hard to focus on them, though, unable to get my mind around the idea of three girls—all good-looking—actually fighting over me. I'd heard about Natalie and Lena both getting into a cat fight with Serena and Amelia that had had something to do with me, but I hadn't actually seen it. If I had no bias towards Natalie, I might have enjoyed it, but as it was, I found it both frustrating and embarrassing…

…and extremely sexy. The arousal I had felt earlier when brushing against Amelia had returned, distracting me from whatever James began to say then. Thoughts of Natalie, Stella and Lena, all very attractive in their own ways, flooded my mind—thoughts of me with them and the things we could be doing, if I were promiscuous enough to take full advantage of the situation. It took all my willpower to get my mind back on track, and to be totally honest, I wasn't entirely successful.

Chapter 12: I Was Always Against Nutcases

Rather than paying a couple more bucks each for a sandwich, we all decided to get our food fix from the supplies Amelia had brought in. They were mostly sweets but they would serve the purpose of putting something in our stomachs for the afternoon. We crammed into Amelia's bedroom during this time, and as I had in the morning, I opted to sit on the chair. Part of this was due to an awkwardness which had sprung up between me and Marc since I had come back out of Stella's mind; he still wasn't openly accusing me of doing anything to ruin his relationship, but I got the feeling that he had a few unanswered questions about how it had happened. I wished I could be honest with myself and say that I hadn't contributed at all, and indeed I had tried to persuade Lena not to do whatever she'd been thinking of doing, but what if that conversation had actually convinced her of the complete opposite? Then there was Amelia, who hadn't said anything to either of us on the subject, but who had dated Marc before Lena and had, at much that same time, been attracted to me (we had even kissed at one point).

The whole thing was very awkward, but so far as Peter, James and even May were concerned, what happened between me, Marc, Amelia, Stella, Natalie and Lena (was that everyone?) was the least of our collective worries. James's confidence in his original plan had been dashed by Lucien's complete certainty that if we entered the Chopville base today, we wouldn't find the Sorcerous Crystals. Peter agreed that it was bad but for the sake of being thorough, we ought to have a look around in there anyway. James kept bringing up the problem of time, and how much of it we had left before Lucien decided to do more than just watch us with his magic; if that time was coming sooner rather than later (and it would probably be sooner, now that May was with us), we ought not to waste what we still had.

May was concerned about whether Lucien might try to force her to go back to her own world, but she was even more concerned that he might decide to kill her if that would be easier. Amelia's top concern was the spell Lucien had said he'd put on us that was supposed to make our day interesting; we had spent several minutes discussing that, wondering what on earth he could have done, but whatever it was, it wasn't revealing itself to us just yet. All of these things gave us plenty to worry about, so we decided to take a sensible, thoughtful approach to dealing with them.

"We should go right now, before we can talk ourselves out of it," James said firmly. "Lucien's asleep, and if we're lucky, Stella will have disobeyed his orders and gone to sleep as well. Even if she hasn't, I'm not too worried about her causing us any trouble."

"What if we do find the crystals, though?" Marc asked. "She may cause a few problems then."

"Then perhaps you, Marc, should be the one to find them," James suggested. "That way, she mightn't even realise what's happened until you have your magic back and can defend yourself. Remember, she doesn't know where the crystals are either."

"What if she doesn't even watch us looking for the crystals?" Peter asked.

"Pete, I'm pretty sure she will—"

"Not if we only send two or three people to look for them, and the rest go into the Big Room, like you said earlier," he said. "If John is one of them, she might be more tempted to watch him, leaving whoever's looking for the crystals without any surveillance."

James's face lit up. "Pete, that's actually a pretty good idea."

"Unless she's watching us right now and heard you say that," Amelia muttered, "so she mightn't take the bait. What if she does, though, and she does something to John in there? I know she said she wouldn't capture him, and she doesn't want to do anything to his mind with magic, but what if she changes her mind on the spot?"

James sighed. "That's yet another matter over which we have no control, so we might as well not worry about it. The best we can do at any single point is always be ready to fight, but if we're blindsided, like Stella was when we hauled her out of a park somewhere a couple of months ago, there's really nothing we can do. Let's just hope that she keeps her discipline and doesn't do anything to John while he's here."

"You guys do realise that I'm sitting right here," I said, though I was grinning slightly.

It was a good thing that we had stocked up on a couple of spares of each weapon we had stolen; those had been meant to be replacements if we broke or lost one, but now they would serve an even more important purpose. After we had loaded May and Amelia with a weapon of each type, we made ourselves invisible and linked arms along the corridor outside. The plan was to walk like this all the way back to the apartment building from which we had come, go up to the fifth floor, and go through the same Hammerheart Highway entrance to get back to Chopville. We would remain invisible from now until the mission was over, or those of us in the Big Room decided that it was safe enough to be visible in there. May would use her mind to make our passage as smooth as possible, but she thought it might be beyond even her capability if we were visible to everyone we passed on the streets, hence the extra precaution.

Before Amelia had pointed her invisibility toggle at each of us in turn, however, I noticed a couple of unsettling things. Given the awkwardness, I had been careful to link my arms with Peter and James, not wanting to be too close to Marc in case he revealed his true feelings with a swift kick to the gonads. I also did not want any physical contact with either of the females, given that every time I thought about either of them, not to mention any of the three up in the base who were preparing to fight over me, I found myself more horny than I could ever remember being—though it wouldn't matter as much if I were invisible.

May had put herself on the end to my left next to Peter, while Marc was between James and Amelia, who was on the other end, and before she had clicked her toggle at me, she had given me a look—a look which had piqued my arousal all over again. What did that look mean? Was Amelia still interested in me, too? I didn't think she was the chasing, competitive type, but had her attraction to me been rekindled as a result of the other girls bickering? That wasn't the end of it, either. Marc had given Amelia a look in the moment before he'd disappeared too, a hungry look focussed on her body rather than her face. What did that mean? Was he perhaps thinking that since Lena had given him the flick and Darcy had given up on Amelia, he should try his luck with her again? If so, he would have my blessing; perhaps if she were taken, she wouldn't cause me to be aroused just by a look on her face (and admittedly, a hot body to go with it)—that could only be a good thing.

Linking arms turned out to be impractical, however, so we switched to hand-on-shoulder as we had done the night before. We then wound our way down through the building and out onto the street, May leading the way and, since none of us could remember how to get to the apartment building, using her mind to navigate the streets as she had done to find the drop-in centre. We kept a slightly quicker pace today, easier in the daylight, and even more so given than rather than us having to move out of people's way, they were unknowingly moving around us—I could only imagine what thoughts May was putting in their heads. It may have taken us two hours to walk to the drop-in centre last night, but today, it was more like forty-five minutes.

The building looked much as it had last night, but as we approached it, May slipped a thought into all our heads. Police Officers were lurking nearby, out of sight and watching the entrance to the building on the off-chance that we might return to the scene of the crime. Hall, or someone who worked under him, had worked out that we'd probably used the Hammerheart Highway to get from Chopville to Melbourne, and there was a chance that we might try to use it from this spot again. Fortunately, they couldn't see us any more than we could see them, and May had already worked out a plan to allow us to enter the building undetected.

The two doormen had changed since the previous evening. I had to give these two credit for having the balls to do this job after what had happened to John the exit door bloke yesterday, but they weren't going to have a chance to stop us. As we quietly climbed the stairs, the bloke manning the entry door became distracted by an insect that only he could see. He began trying to slap at it, staggering back a step in his distraction, leaving the doorway open long enough for us to slip through. The bloke on the other door looked across at him, eyebrows raised in a what's-gotten-into-you expression, but he didn't come over to cover the door.

The elevators were the next problem, but fortunately, May had a solution to that one, too. We couldn't be seen to be getting into an empty elevator, but the Honnie, describing her actions telepathically to us, took all the minds in the building and learned that the Hammerhearts whose apartment we had used (she picked it out of our minds) were presently at home, apparently enjoying a lazy Sunday afternoon. Quite suddenly, even though none of them had really felt like going out, they all got their things together and decided to go to the movies. As they stepped out of the elevator, one of them (the woman—they seemed to be a childless, married couple) hesitated just between the doors, keeping them open long enough for the six of us to slip past and into the lift.

"That was impressive," Peter said as we began to rise, "getting them out of the way and using them to help us get up at the same time. What reason did that chick have for stopping, though? Did she suspect something?"

"No, she was just giving me her key to their home," May told us, and it sounded like she was smiling (a creepy thought), "not that she knew it."

The fourth floor corridor was deserted and quiet, and the apartment through which we had come last night (apartment 4F, we now saw) was much the same as it had been then. Did the couple know that we had been inside their home while they'd been out? Surely they must, unless there were more Hammerhearts in this building with the Highway in their wardrobes. Once the front door was shut and locked on the inside, the six of us made ourselves visible again.

"So what comes next?" Amelia asked.

"The entrance is in the bedroom," said James. "As soon as we go through there, though, we'll be in enemy territory—"

"This does kinda count as enemy territory," said Peter.

"Only as much as any other place on the entire planet if they decide to jump us," said James, "but it'll be different once we're actually in their base, especially if Stella knows we're coming, and I'm betting that she would have worked it out by now. I think we should work out now what we're going to do when we get there."

"Yeah, I was thinking about that on the way over," said Marc. "You said earlier that only two or three people should look for the crystals and the rest stay in the Big Room—well, I think that I should look for the crystals."

"Yeah, you should," James agreed, "'cause you'll be able to use them if you find them."

"Yeah, but also because—well—I should probably not go in the Big Room just yet," Marc shrugged, looking awkward and unhappy. "I mean, so long as you guys say hi to our friends in there, I mean."

"Sure thing, man," said Peter, patting his shoulder. "I'd come with you, except I was hoping to catch up with Mum, Dad and Rebecca in there."

"Same," James and I said at much the same time.

Marc's grin widened slightly as he looked from Amelia to May and back again. It was an odd expression, both unhappy and a little eager at the same time.

"Me too," Amelia said, perhaps noticing the look and not comforted by it. "I need to see how my family are doing in there, and they're probably worried about me."

"Okay," James said, "so Marc, you and May can look around on the top floor of the base, and I don't think I need to tell you both to be extremely careful—and stay invisible this time. Stay up there for no more than an hour and then come down to the Big Room and wait outside it, whether you've found anything or not. The same goes for us; we'll only stay in there for an hour. Everyone agree on that?"

"I agree on meeting at a certain time," said Peter, checking his watch, "but does it have to be an hour?"

"Yes," James insisted, "unless you want to be in the base when Lucien wakes up and possibly has a change of heart about how to handle us."

Peter shrugged and looked at his feet. "Fine, but let's just say half past two so that there's no confusion. It's one o'clock now, so it'll be about an hour, once we factor in the time it'll take to get down there."

"Anything else we need to work out?" I asked.

There wasn't, but what we all did before taking the Highway was use the bathroom. Marc and May took their pit stops first so that they could get going in their cart ahead of the rest of us—the idea being that if there were any Hammerhearts in the station when what looked like an empty cart pulled up, May would be able to deal with them and clear the way for the rest of us. We took a brief minute or two each in the bathroom before leaving, me taking my turn last, and then we were ready to go.

Five minutes later, we were all invisible again and James and Amelia shot off towards Chopville, leaving me and Peter to call the last Hammerheart cart to the residence. When it came, Peter slid in first, leaving me to shut and lock the door before sliding into the driver's seat. I followed the usual pattern, sending us zooming through the underground tunnels for a fraction of a second as usual. When we pulled up in the spacious and all-too-familiar base station, there was an empty cart just in front of us, its door open as its invisible drivers got out. Peter and I quickly followed, sending the two carts speeding away into the network and following James and Amelia up onto the bridge.

"Where are you guys?" Peter hissed, his voice no more than a whisper and yet still managing to echo around the chamber.

"Here," James's voice responded in the same manner, "but let's get inside before we worry about linking up."

A good thought, but still awkward. Peter and I linked arms and moved forward; I wasn't sure about him, but I had my free hand outstretched in case there was an invisible person right in front of me. I could hear their footsteps along with ours on the stone floor, but I couldn't tell how far in front of us they were—at least not until the door into the foyer opened all by itself. The Hammerheart Highway had been empty of Hammerhearts as promised, and this room was the same, though as the door swung shut behind me and Peter, one of the elevators dinged and began to slide open. It, too, was deserted.

"I thought we would be taking the stairs," said Peter as we crossed its threshold, "but oh well. Level five, whoever's closest to the buttons."

The level five button lit up as someone pushed it, and above it, the level one button was already lit—so Marc and May were still with us, it seemed. That was a good thing, because I'd just had an unpleasant thought: If there were still security guards standing outside the Big Room, we would need them sufficiently distracted before we could open the doors—both to the Big Room and this very elevator.

"I can feel his mind," May said uneasily as we began to rise.

"Lucien's mind?" James asked sharply. "Is he still sleeping?"

"Yes, he seems to be sleeping," she said, "but I do not like it."

"Are you gonna be okay?" I asked her; May panicking would be a very bad thing for all of us.

"Can you take him now before he wakes up?" Peter asked.

"I do not dare; it might wake him before I can do anything. I think I will be okay."

But there were more immediate problems to deal with, as we saw when the doors slid open. Yes, there were two security guards standing opposite the door to the Big Room; they both looked over at the empty lift but, seeming to think it had probably been an accident (someone pushing the button for the wrong floor before getting off somewhere else), didn't move. What was worse than that was the exact positioning of the Big Room door; Lucien must have guessed that we might attempt this when he had created it, because he had put it just on the other side of the line on the floor—the line which had normalised and exposed Tulip the moment she had crossed it. To top the whole thing off, the dining hall to our left was packed and noisy —lunch was in full swing in there.

"Marc, May, step out with us," I hissed at them as the rest of us moved quietly forward. I waited several seconds for the doors to close and the security guards to look away from us before saying, "May, you need to do something about those two guards."

She chose to answer with her mind rather than her mouth—a smart move, but not a great answer. Those two minds over there, along with every single mind in the dining hall, seemed to be non-existent to her, as though while their bodies were here, their minds were being kept safely locked up somewhere else. Of course, that was exactly where they were, in Lucien's version of a Honnie mind. A problem which had already been bad had now become so much worse. If May couldn't use her mind to distract those two guards, how could we get into the room? They would fire on us the moment the door opened all by itself, assuming we weren't exposed by the line before then, and if they made a bit of noise about it, backup would come swarming out of the dining hall.

"What do we do?" Amelia whispered close by. "Should we stun those two while there's no one else around?"

"No, that'll only get us all trapped in the Big Room with no way of getting out," James hissed back.

He was right. Everything we could possibly do to those guards would be enough to get us into the room, but by the time we were ready to come back out, the whole base would know there were intruders inside. They would either have an ambush set up outside the door for when we were ready to leave, or they would come in and hunt us down. Lucien may want to let us run around for a while yet, but I doubted that he had confided that to anyone other than Stella and Cornish; they would probably lose faith in him if he did. If Stella were around, she could probably make sure that we weren't hurt in whatever followed, but she wouldn't stop them from capturing us, not after what had happened the last titime:me she had tried to protect us.

"Okay, problem solved," James hissed suddenly, taking us by surprise.

"What?"

But he only made a hushing sound as two people, having finished their lunches, came out of the dining hall. Hatred rose up inside me as I recognised Ather Hignat and his ever-present sidekick, Ugine Wilwog; they stepped out of the dining hall and walked towards the Big Room, but just as Hignat's hand fell on the door, one of the security guards spoke to them.

"Oi, you two, do you have permission to go in there?"

Hignat turned and smiled disarmingly at the guard, fingering the Hammerheart code emblazoned on his chest. "I was unaware that we faithfuls needed permission. Was I wrong?"

The two guards looked at each other, taken aback. "Does he?"

"Yeah, I think you do," the first guard said, but he no longer looked sure of himself. "Lucien was clear on what he wants for the prisoners; they're not to be hurt. What reason do you have for going in there?"

Hignat didn't look happy about that, but he only took a moment to recompose himself. "Some of my old classmates from school are in there," he said innocently. "Ugine and I were just hoping to catch up with them."

"Oh, okay," the guard said, seeming satisfied, "but no more than an hour in there, 4H53."

Hignat nodded and opened the door, and Amelia, James, Peter and I were quick to recognise our opportunity. Leaving Marc and May to their own devices, we hurried forward as quickly and quietly as we could, bounding through the door just as Wilwog allowed it to swing shut behind him. Nobody seemed to notice anything, and most luckily for us, the line must have been turned off. Once the door shut, we just stood for maybe half a minute, waiting for Hignat and Wilwog to make their way further into the Big Room; having them in here wasn't a good thing for us, but if there was any trouble, we could probably take them in an unfair fight.

"Should we make ourselves visible now?" Peter asked from beside me.

We did so, each of us using our own toggle and then pocketing it. I checked my watch; it was 1:18. A little over an hour before we would have to meet up with Marc and May. I only realised then that we hadn't organised a place to meet with them or a method by which to let them know we were there, but it would probably be as simple as May using her mind to work out our locations—assuming nothing happened to her and Marc up there.

"How did you do that?" Amelia asked James. "Did you see them coming?"

James grinned. "No, but the Light Crystal seemed to think we were doing the right thing."

"Everyone remember to be careful of Hignat and Wilwog," I warned them.

"Should we do something about them?" Peter asked darkly.

"If we have to," said James uneasily, "but let's not pick a fight. We have no idea what those two might be carrying. Who knows— they may have been sent in here to do something to us."

That wasn't a comforting thought at all, but it was certainly the most likely explanation for why Hignat and Wilwog were in here— they surely weren't interested in catching up with anyone and chewing the fat, so to speak. It couldn't be the spell Lucien had talked about putting on us that was supposed to make our day interesting, but it certainly fitted his fear-of-capture approach to dealing with us.

We all armed ourselves with a variety of weapons and moved forward into the aisles of compartments. I had all sorts of questions about why Lucien had chosen to accommodate the prisoners in this way, but none whatsoever about why the prisoners weren't complaining. Well, it may have been cramped, I thought, but it was still a damn sight better than the Basement, and I had to give Lucien some credit for not taking that easier and far more evil approach.

Amelia was the first one to spot relatives; her father, her grandmother and a couple of other former Woodward soldiers were leaning against a wall in an aisle to our left and chatting together. Peter, James and I waved at them and proceeded onward, me leading the way towards the place where Stella had found all our friends earlier. When we got there, though, they seemed to have moved on to somewhere else. We turned to the left and went down another aisle, passing more people (mostly adults) as we went. We met and greeted some people we knew (Rob and Bob, for example) but for several minutes, we couldn't find anyone we were looking for…

…until we saw, looking down an aisle to our left, a small group of people standing and talking between the rows of compartments: Mum, Dad, Marge, Charlie, Hilda and Violet. When Peter called out to them, they all looked around and then hurried to meet us, and the scene which followed was similarly celebratory to the night we had escaped from the Hammerson Basement, though perhaps less exuberant. They were happy to see us, relieved that we were okay, and knowing that at the very least, we hadn't been tortured. That was fine for them, but I felt distinctly awkward, knowing that they were on Lucien's side now, and I could tell from their faces that Peter and James were feeling the same way.

"I'm so relieved," Mum said, taking a step back so that she could properly scrutinise me and Peter. "We were imagining all sorts of things that could have happened to you out there, but at least you're safe now."

"Er—actually," Peter glanced sideways at James, and then decided to push ahead, "actually—er—we're really not. We're only staying for a little while and then we have to head out again."

"What?" Dad's eyes widened. "What for? You can't have been here long—surely Lucien would let you rest. He wouldn't send you straight out again."

"Are you saying that you wouldn't mind if he did send us out, so long as we got rest first?" James asked, grinning slightly.

"I would prefer he didn't," Marge said, but Charlie put his hand on her shoulder.

"I wish you were a little older," he said. "No fourteen-year-old should have to do what you boys have already done, but the fact remains that you did it all. We would still be fluffing around, trying to deal with Arnold Hammerson if not for you. I wouldn't be worried about you working for Lucien so long as he equipped you for it— you've already proven yourselves responsible."

"Thanks, Dad," said James, his smile fading, "but we're not working for Lucien. We came in here of our own free will today, and so far as we know, Lucien's asleep at the moment—he wouldn't even know about us. We'll be gone before he wakes up."

The faces of the four women fell as they understood what James was saying, while Dad and Charlie exchanged a look I had rarely seen before—they were angry. They were insulted by what James had said.

"Stop," I said quickly, looking at James and Peter; this could turn into a serious argument if we let it, and that would be a terrible (and typical) family reunion. "Lucien made us an offer earlier this morning to join him, and we might take it, but letting him put influential charms on us isn't a decision we're gonna take lightly."

"So what will you do in the meantime?" Mum asked, her eyes large.

"Stay safe," said Peter, smiling bitterly. "Don't worry about us. I guess we're still hanging on a little too tightly to the thing we thought we were fighting for. Can I ask you guys what happened when the Woodwards lost their magic? I thought you were all against magic domination."

"I was always against nutcases who wanted my children dead," said Marge.

"And we were against the torture and murder of innocent people," said Charlie. "Those things no longer apply; Lucien is a good young man, incredibly so given—well—never mind. The point is, this is right, boys—this is how it should be—and it'll be a lot better than what the Sorcerers would have put back together if they'd had the chance."

"So don't be messing any of Lucien's plans up," Dad warned us. "He's got a bit of a temper problem; you don't want him to take it out on you."

"What?" James and Peter asked, but I knew what he was talking about—Lucien had said it himself, as had May.

And so they told us the story, the part of it May hadn't been present for. What had happened to the Woodward base was disturbing, but far less so than what had happened to my parents. By the time they were done, I wanted nothing more than to get away from them, but still with forty-five minutes before we would be due to meet up with Marc and May again, I wasn't sure if I really wanted to see any more of my friends. These people here clearly still loved us, but they would not support us in what we were doing, even though they had taught us to take this path. Would it be the same with all our friends? Would they all have adopted the same logic that Dad and Charlie had? Worst of all, would Natalie now think like that? It would just about break my heart if she, too, disapproved of our fight for freedom.

Before things could spiral out of control, however, we were saved by the arrival of Felicity and Jessica, who were just as relieved to see the three of us safe as the rest of our families, and thankfully not so surprised that we were continuing to fight. While James hung back to chat to his sisters, Peter and I decided we'd had enough, and turned to walk down an aisle to our left. There were still a few other people I wanted to see (Harry and Simon, particularly) but more than anything else, I needed to know exactly where in the spectrum of disapproval Natalie had come down. Judging by the look on Peter's face, he was having as much trouble dealing with this as I was.

The next person around our age who we found, or who found us, was Erica. She looked gleeful when she recognised us, but almost immediately dismayed when she saw which two we were, and that her boyfriend wasn't one of us. After pointing her back the way we had come, we pressed on, winding our way in and out of aisles, aware that by now, most of the Big Room must know that we were here. Where on earth was Natalie? How could I have covered this much area and still not found her?

And the moment I'd completed that thought, we turned left at the top of another aisle, and there she was. Only, it wasn't, and I imagined my expression must have been similar to Erica's as I recognised the girl as Rebecca rather than Natalie, but in actual fact, both of our expressions remained frozen on horror as we took in the scene before us. Rebecca was standing with her back to an open compartment, one which belonged to someone but probably not her, and she was pressed in by Hignat and Wilwog. Neither boy was armed but it didn't matter; Rebecca was small, alone and with nowhere to go except back into the compartment, which seemed to be what the boys wanted. Even though Peter and I were standing out in the open, none of them had seen us yet.

"I'm telling you, I haven't seen her," Rebecca was pleading, her eyes wide and terrified. "Maybe she hasn't been brought in or some ℜ—"

"We know perfectly well that she has been brought in," Hignat snapped, his fists clenched, but I doubted he would actually throw a punch at her. Why would he when, if he needed physical force, he had Wilwog under his thumb? "Anyone can be helpful around here if they don't know just whom they're helping. Now, answer the question truthfully this time. Where is she?"

"I don't know," Rebecca wept, tears in her eyes which were fixed on Hignat. She was normally pretty gutsy but for some reason, perhaps the influential charm, this particular scenario had rendered her more timid than usual. "Okay, yes, I've seen her this morning, but not for more than an hour now. I don't know where she is. Why do you care?"

Hignat exchanged a look with Wilwog, one which the latter didn't really bother to respond to (he was too busy holding Rebecca in place with his eyes) before looking back at her. "She and I have unfinished business, but since you won't give up her location, I suppose you can stand in."

I had already been pretty sure they were talking about Natalie, and even more when I saw that look on Hignat's face, because I knew exactly what business he was referring to. Now I understood exactly what he and Wilwog had intended to do in here today, and it made my blood boil and pump more rapidly through my veins. A moment later, however, I had to force those thoughts away as Wilwog moved so quickly into action that both Peter and I were taken totally by surprise—and Rebecca too, judging by the look on her face we'd been given a brief glimpse of. Hignat may or may not have given a signal, but Wilwog seized Rebecca's arm, raised it high into the air and spun her around so that her back was to him and Hignat and she could only see into the compartment before her. He had pinned her other hand to her side with his forearm, leaving one hand free to press against her stomach, holding her against his body.

It was my turn to exchange a look with Peter. It hadn't taken long for horror to give way to fury on his face, and I didn't blame him. I didn't even have to think about Natalie to relate to it—seeing that happen to any girl was enough to set me off. Peter nodded once, and the two of us got into position and dug into our pockets for weapons.

"Hey!" Rebecca gasped.

"Quiet," Wilwog hissed in her ear, "or I'll pull your arm right out of its socket."

Hignat, an ugly scowl on his face, stood up beside Wilwog, reached around Rebecca and took hold of one of her breasts. "This is how it's gonna go," he hissed at her, and from this distance, his words were almost indistinguishable. "You don't wanna frustrate me, bitch; I've already got a ton of stuff doing that. Your sister has a big debt to pay back, and since she's not here, you're gonna put yourself down on that bed there, and Ugine and I are gonna have our way with you, and you're going to enjoy it—because from the things I've heard about you, you normally like this sort of—"

That was as far as he got. Both Peter and I had bludginators at the ready, and now we swiped. It was a better strategy than solid-outliners, which would have bound Rebecca to them, but the closeness of their positions made it impossible to attack the pair of them without Rebecca copping at least some of it. Peter had aimed at Wilwog's raised arm, the one that had yanked Rebecca's up to a length which it hadn't been designed for; it cut both of their arms, but at least had the desired effect of making Wilwog let go of her, pushing her roughly forward so that she fell into the compartment while he staggered back and fell over. The falling was from my swipe, which had been at shin level and had taken both Hignat and Wilwog, but hadn't touched Rebecca given that she'd been shielded from it by the pair.

Despite the attack, Hignat's aim seemed to be to get into the compartment with Rebecca and close it before anything else could happen, but Wilwog had looked around to see where the attack had come from, and had seen me and Peter advancing up the aisle, weapons poised. He quickly dug into his pockets for his own arms but before he could draw, I took another swipe, this time at his face. I hadn't intended any particular damage except to slow him up, but the strike took him at eye level, bloodying them both and blinding him. He howled in agony and began swinging his fists wildly around in the air, connecting a second later with…

(Hignat tried to jump on Rebecca, but she had rolled away from him, jumped out of the compartment and before he'd quite gotten his balance, she brought her knee up into his crotch. Hignat let out a high-pitched whimper of a gasp and sank to his knees, his hands clutching at the place where it hurt. Over his head, Rebecca caught sight of me and Peter for the first time; her eyes widened and an expression of enormous relief crossed her face, but before she could do anything else, she had to dive aside as one of Wilwog's flailing fists came flying over her head, missing her by inches and colliding with…)

...Hignat's head, sending him sprawling on the floor, unconscious. Wilwog may have still been able to hurt Rebecca, eyes or no eyes, but before he could touch her, Peter and I had our solid-outliners out and began peppering him with jets of thicky prison. Within twenty seconds, he had toppled onto the floor, unable to move his legs, his arms frozen into position, his face immobile and the rest of his body quickly wrapped up in the white stuff. Even better, he landed on top of Hignat, so that when he came around, he would be immobile too. They could stay right there until someone else with a solid-outliner chose to free them; hopefully, it would be either Lucien or Stella because I thought I could rely on them at least to make sure that nothing like this happened again.

Rebecca scampered around the two prone figures and flew into Peter's arms, squealing with delight and relief. "Oh my God! Thank you! Thank you!"

"Any time," said Peter, grinning a little sheepishly over her shoulder at me.

"I didn't expect to see you guys so soon," she said, letting go of Peter and giving me a hug, too—a bit of a surprise, but a nice one. "Stella said she didn't think you'd be brought in for a couple more days."

"See ya," I said quickly, and the moment she let me go, I turned and hurried past them, past Hignat and Wilwog, and around the next corner.

"Thanks a lot," I heard Peter call after me, not happy that I'd left him to the task of explaining to his girlfriend that we weren't on Lucien's side.

That wasn't why I'd made my escape, though. Seeing Rebecca jump on Peter like that had forcibly made me think of Natalie, a feeling emphasised by the way the two Fletcher girls seemed to like kicking Hignat in the nuts, and when she had made physical contact with me, a new wave of arousal had crashed over me—this one the most powerful yet. If I had stayed there any longer, Rebecca would have quite likely noticed, and that would have led to all sorts of trouble between the three of us if either of them believed I actually wanted to have sex with her. Unfortunately, in that state, I actually would have liked to have sex with Rebecca, and that was the hell of the thing; in my current state, I just wanted it, and it didn't seem to matter who it was with. Forcing myself to think of Natalie made me feel guilty for having these feelings, but it didn't make them go away.

I continued searching the aisles of compartments, getting increasingly more desperate to find Natalie and uncomfortably aware that I was running out of time. With fifteen minutes left before we were supposed to meet up with Marc and May, I still hadn't found her, but I had at least found a couple of other people I'd wanted to catch up with today: Harry and Simon.

"Dude," said Harry, flinging an arm around me and ruffling my hair, "awesome stuff, mate, awesome stuff."

"'Legendary' would be an appropriate word here," Simon amended. "What a sprint—what a stumble over the finish line. It's only now that we can truly understand why you survived so many attempts to do you in."

"I got lucky," I mumbled, my face red.

"You made your own luck, my dear boy," Harry said in his deepest, most unconvincingly worldly voice. "You sure look like you've done it tough since yesterday, but it's great to see that you're still in one piece. I'm sure whenever Lucien gets wind of this, he'll fix that up for you."

"He kinda has to, since he's the one who did it," grinned Simon.

"He doesn't know I'm here," I told them, preparing once again to have the talk, "and by the time he does, I'll be gone. I only came in with the others to see how you guys were doing, but we're still fighting—we're not gonna stop until we're forced to."

The twins exchanged an anxious look before seeming, by some telepathy only twins were capable of, to reach some sort of agreement. A moment later, they were both beaming at me.

"Awesome," Harry said again, thumping me on the back. "What a testament to the human spirit you and the other guys are, continuing to fight even though it's for a lost cause."

"It's not for a lost cause," I retorted, not angry or annoyed at their bravado but now anxious myself to make them understand— somehow, I sensed that I could reason with these two. "Look, I know Lucien means to make this work, but seriously, he has no idea how much trouble his actions are likely to cause, even with all that magic. Things are likely to be far worse than they ever were under the Hammersons' rule if he's not careful."

"Ah, John," Simon sighed, wiggling a finger at me, "it's exactly that scepticism Lucien wishes to harness by making you, Marc and James his advisers. He's a lot more realistic about this than the Hammersons were, and a lot smarter about it too."

"And don't forget, the world was already going to shit before this started," Harry added. "Yeah, I know it doesn't look as bad as this whole worldwide conquest and all, but you know how things would have most likely ended up further down the track if this hadn't happened: nuclear warfare; countries like America, China, Russia and North Korea wanting to blow each other to smithereens; terrorism—you name it, it would have happened. None of that stuff will happen now, because Lucien is removing all the motivating factors."

"And if new ones come up, he'll deal with them as they do," said Simon. "I know the Woodwards thought they were doing the right thing, but they would only have set the world back on a path to destruction. This is a path to unity and salvation, and even the Woodwards and Fletchers can see that now."

I was utterly dumbfounded by their rationality. I knew that a lot of what they were saying was true, that if the Woodwards had restored the planet to its former state, things would have only deteriorated more slowly. Yet I also knew that everything James had said earlier had also been true: Utopian societies never worked, and unless Lucien planned on enslaving the entire human race and controlling its every thought, idea and desire, this one would fall apart just as surely as any other. Yet Harry and Simon's confidence in Lucien's philosophy was unshakable—the influential charm at its best, I knew, and I had no way of making them see the truth of the matter—I doubted that even James could have reasoned with them.

I sighed, preparing to make my leave and embark on one last attempt to locate my girlfriend, but before I could say anything, we were joined by Katie and Sophie, who seemed to have heard that we were in the Big Room. They were both excited to see me and surprised that I wasn't staying, and even more surprised when without warning, I bid all of them a quick goodbye and literally sprinted up the aisle to my right, now heading back in the direction of the door into the place. Again, I'd needed to escape after Katie had hugged me—she was one of the prettiest girls I knew, and feeling her petite body against mine, her arms around me and a lock of hair tickling my cheek, had been more than I could handle. That had been just as close as my escape from Rebecca had been.

With barely any time left, I had to resign myself to the fact that I wasn't going to see Natalie today. I felt extremely downhearted now —everyone in here wanted to stay; nobody wanted us to succeed; they all wanted us to stay in here so that we would be safe; and Natalie was either avoiding me, or both she and Lena (who I also hadn't seen at all today) had perhaps gotten into a fight or something, and were, for whatever reason, hidden from view as a result. That was a desperate theory, not one I believed at all, but I just couldn't deal with the possibility that Natalie didn't want to see me—it would only confirm what I had feared the most, that she didn't support what I was doing.

Chapter 13: Not Exactly Real Happiness

The four of us who had been in the Big Room met up around the entrance at half past two as planned. I'd been the second one to get to the spot; Amelia had already been waiting there, looking about as sad as I felt, and probably for much the same reason. Peter and James showed up around the same time, both of them still being followed by their girlfriends. I wasn't particularly happy to see them again— well, not so much Peter and James, but my ability to control myself around girls was slipping more and more every time I got too close to one—spending the last five minutes alone with Amelia had been bad enough, even though we hadn't touched.

"Seriously, stop worrying about it," Rebecca was shooing Peter away. "I'll just tie a bandage around it or something."

"Oh yeah, sorry about that," I said, looking at the horrible gash still visible on her arm. "We should have brought the thing these guys used to bandage me up yesterday."

"A used bandage?" she said sceptically.

"It was a Collingwood scarf," Peter told her, and she pulled a face at him.

There were a few last goodbyes, and then the four of us linked up and went invisible once again. Marc and May were already outside the Big Room, also invisible, and May would let us know telepathically when the coast was clear to come out. In the end, Marc had needed to fire two jets of thicky prison into each of the security guards' faces to distract them. By the time they had dug their hands into their pockets, freed their own solid-outliners and then vanished the stuff, the four of us were through the door and the Big Room was closed once again.

The good things were that it had all happened so quickly that the guards had no idea what we had done, even though we had obviously done something, and the room was completely deserted other than the eight of us. Amelia, Peter, James and I dived to the floor as the guards used their revealers to try to flush us out, the jets of magic flying over our heads but not hitting any of us. As we crouched there, May put the thought in our heads that we ought to completely disable the two of them before anyone else turned up. It was probably the best plan; after all, we had left fingerprints of our visit all over the Big Room already.

So while I lay there, I felt in my pocket for my solid-outliner, found it, took aim, and fired. The jet of white light missed the guard, hitting the wall just above his shoulder, and giving my position away. I rolled quickly away from the others, hearing them jumping into action at the same time, jumped back to my feet, and fired again. I wasn't the only one either; at least four more jets of white light flew at the guards, peppering their bodies. Within seconds, both of them had their arms bound, and after a few more seconds, their legs too. They ended up crashing to the floor in much the same way that Wilwog had, and in the momentary silence following the sound of their fall, a bell dinged nearby, announcing the arrival of one of the elevators. I spun towards it, taking aim as the doors opened, but it was empty—Marc or May must have called it to make our escape.

And so we did. I collided with an invisible person on my way to the lift but for once, neither of us fell. We all got on board and then just stood there, waiting to see if everyone was present and unsure how to check. I was just about to point this out when someone pushed the button to send us down to the Hammerheart Highway.

"Hey, shouldn't we make sure—" I said as the doors began to slide shut.

"Everybody is here," May told me, her voice coming from the wall next to the buttons.

It was a sombre group that made its way back through the Hammerheart Highway to the apartment in Melbourne. The residents were still out when we got there, meaning that we could briefly make ourselves visible for a quick break before the trek back to the drop-in centre. It turned out to be only long enough for each of us to take another minute in the toilet. Those of us who weren't using the toilet tried half-heartedly to make conversation while we waited, but it never got very far. Somehow, the events of the afternoon had taken some of the heart out of the resistance.

It was about a quarter to four by the time we got back to the homeless shelter, having had no further scares along the way. Now that we were out of the Hammerheart base and the minds around us weren't contained within Lucien's mind, it was again possible for May to smooth our way. When we were back in our little corridor on the second floor, however, I saw that it had come at a price; the Honnie was now more exhausted than ever, and I didn't think she would be able to see out the day before she crashed.

Most of us wanted to take some time to ourselves and recover, now that we could see just how difficult the path ahead would be for us, but James found enough resolve to keep us together long enough to trade stories of what had happened to each of us that day. After Peter and I had left him with Felicity and Jessica, he had soon been joined by Erica, and the two of them had taken the rest of the time to catch up and enjoy each other's company. When Peter asked if that meant they'd had sex, James had only shrugged.

"Not really, I didn't wanna have to get in one of those cubbyhole things, but let's just say we made out a bit. We talked some as well but—well—you know how strange they are to talk to now."

Peter's time with Rebecca had been very similar, by the sound of it, though in his case, the talk had yielded something a little more positive.

"When I asked her how she would feel if I could get an unboggler and use it to get rid of the influential charm Lucien put on her, she said she would probably thank me, but she couldn't imagine it at the moment. She thinks she's happy now but at least she acknowledges that it's not exactly real happiness."

As for Amelia, after she'd spent some time with her father, during which he had once again lamented his inability to get his daughter to listen to him, she had gone to find Darcy. Unfortunately, when she'd eventually located him, he told her that while he was glad that she was okay, he had to break up with her because she was no longer the person he had fallen for. She'd spent some time trying to persuade him otherwise, until he had eventually snapped and revealed the real reason for the break-up: Apparently, in the time they had been in the Big Room, he had hooked up with Jessica, the two of them believing their former partners were gone forever and realising that they needed each other in this tough time. Distressed, Amelia had gone back to the door and tried to leave the Big Room, but sensing what she was doing, even from several floors up, May had put the mental clamps on and forced her to wait inside.

As for her and Marc, they had eventually gotten into the upstairs corridor, from a stroke of luck more than anything else. 2L11, one of the men who had generously given us his uniform the day before, had been coming through the wall at the moment when Marc and May, invisible, had been approaching it. May had knocked him out with a swift punch to the temple, picked his lifeless body up and fed it through the wall, rather like sliding an envelope through a mail slot, and by holding onto part of his uniform, she and Marc were able to slide through after him.

They had then gone about searching for the crystals, but they had come up empty-handed. They had found Lucien while he had been sleeping, but hadn't been able to get close enough to put him out of action and take his crystal due to the shield he had placed around himself. Fortunately, in the time they'd been up there, he hadn't woken up, but Marc said that like yesterday, he had a vague sense that he and May were being watched.

"I can't see how, since we were both invisible," he said, "but if it really was Stella again, maybe she was using her magic to do it—or maybe she was wearing ghost goggles, I don't know. Either way, it looks like she didn't interfere with any of us in the end."

That was something of a relief to all of us. Even though Lucien had ordered Stella not to do anything unless we were on the verge of causing serious trouble, she had wanted to capture us so that we would be safe—the same reason as everyone in the Big Room, in other words, and that was a such a depressing thought that I quickly stopped it in its tracks.

"Guys," Amelia said a few minutes after we had finished recounting the last story, "what comes next for us?"

As if the mood hadn't been dull enough already...

James sighed. "I'm not sure, I'm really not. I still think that the Sorcerous Crystals are our best chance, but how can we find them if Lucien knows we're looking for them? He's several steps ahead, and he will always be as long as he can use his magic to see what we're doing."

"So we need to figure out something that he won't be expecting," said Peter in an attempt to troubleshoot, as James normally would.

"And once we figure it out, Lucien will be expecting it," James retorted. "Look, I still think that waiting for him to slip up is our best chance, but it's looking increasingly more likely that he won't. Part of me wants to jump back in and try to destabilise things in Chopville, and another part of me wants to sit back for a bit and wait till we've all got our energy back, and I can't work out which part is my head and which is my heart."

"I think that as long as we're always ready to fight, we can probably stay here and figure out a new plan tonight," Marc said. "Er —I mean, figure it out tonight and put it into action tomorrow. As long as we make it a loose plan and be prepared to improvise along the way, Lucien can't predict exactly what's going to happen. Unless he changes his mind about wanting to capture us in his own time, we might be able to get through another night without trouble."

"And everyone should always stay with someone else," I added, "just in case we are attacked."

I was uneasy about this plan, though. How long could we rely on Lucien continuing to let us dangle on a string, knowing that he could reel us in at a later time? How long could we rely on Stella resisting the temptation to take matters into her own hands? I didn't know, but I had a clear sense of our time running out. It was a similar feeling of impending doom that I'd had some months earlier, in the days prior to losing the Sien-Leoard Crystal, followed immediately by all those deaths in Germany. I didn't think Lucien had an exact timeline in mind, but I doubted that we could have much more than thirty-six hours, and probably less, before that string, on the end of which we dangled, would be yanked.

* * *

By ten o'clock that evening, nothing about our situation had changed. May and Amelia had taken showers immediately after our discussion, following which May had gone to her bedroom and had been asleep ever since, and Amelia had sat by her, ready to defend her in case of trouble. Marc and James had gone back to use one of the computers, James continuing his research from earlier while Marc stood nearby, invisible and ready to fight should the need arise. That left me and Peter, and we spent the time between then and dinner playing cards and talking disjointedly about whatever. We had all met up for dinner in May's room so that we could be with Amelia, all of us speaking quietly so as not to wake the Honnie; though without her, it meant that we had to stick to the food we already had. We had hung around each other for a while longer but were totally unable to come up with any plans, and I suspected that we would get nowhere even faster the longer we stayed awake. It had been a long day for all of us, and the only thing that could really refresh us now was sleep.

And so now there was only silence in my bedroom as I tried to sleep. Well, it wasn't total silence; there were still plenty of voices around the drop-in centre, some of them nearby, though none in this particular corridor; the others had all retired to their bedrooms by now. There was also the night sounds of the city but I reckoned I could ignore those easily enough; strange as they were to me, they were still only background noise. No, it wasn't the noise that was keeping me awake, but something else entirely.

For nearly an hour, I tossed and turned in bed, electrified with sexual energy that made it impossible to get anywhere near sleep. As long as my body was stimulated, so my mind was too. At first it had been desperate longing for Natalie, and for a little while, I'd relived some of the more enjoyable and orgasmic moments we had shared over the five nights we had spent together; but as much as I wanted her, far more than anyone else, it was no easier to keep my mind focussed exclusively on Natalie than it had been to prevent myself from being stimulated in the presence of Katie and Rebecca. Both of them, as well as Lena, Stella and even Amelia featured in my imagination in that time, doing all sorts of things with me and all of them in various state's of undress. The longer it went on, the more horny and lonelier I became, and nothing I did could settle me down.

Finally, when it was nearly eleven o'clock, I had to concede that it wasn't going to work for me tonight; something had to be done. I got out of bed, put my clothes back on (I'd slept only in my underwear again) and sat on my bed, trying to make my mind work properly. It was incredibly difficult to think about anything other than female bodies, and I would later put that down to my making a terrible decision that night. Surely, if I'd just gone to James and asked for the Light Crystal, I could have done something that would have enabled me to sleep, but in that state, James was the last thing on my mind.

I got up and tried desperately to keep my mind in check as I lurched to the door and pressed my ear against it, listening for any sounds outside—any sign that any of the others were awake. I knew that I shouldn't do this—that somewhere, despite whatever had happened in the Big Room, Natalie was waiting for me to come to her and rejoin her—that despite a couple of very attractive girls seeking my attention, she was the one I loved and wanted to be with more than any other—but there was just no helping that one simple fact: I needed to be with a girl tonight.

I opened my door, shut it behind me, and moved quietly up the hall, having no idea what the plan was, or even if there was a plan. Well, actually, I didn't even think of trying to come up with a plan; my need completely overpowered any rational thought. Later, I would think back to how Smiley had summoned me to the life assistant when he had been trying to communicate with me; then, my mind had disconnected from my body so that it could be drawn to the device without my thoughts getting in the way, but I had maintained just enough control to make an excuse to the others for my odd behaviour. This was similar, except that I was being dragged by my penis rather than anything magical (unless this counted as a different kind of magic), being drawn to the nearest female like a magnet. And this time, there was no self-control left to make any kind of excuse; if there had been, I probably would have forced myself to walk past Amelia's door and onward to May's, because at least she could stop me in my tracks before I did something I would regret, or make me forget that I had done it at all. But, as Dad used to say, 'Wish in one hand, shit in the other—see which one fills up first.'

I crept past Peter and James's rooms and stopped in front of Amelia's, still listening, hoping that she wasn't asleep and trying to master myself. My need was so great that if I slipped up, I could find myself raping her without even knowing it until it was too late. That would be bad enough to happen to any girl, but especially Amelia. Or, perhaps not; would she remember being raped? She would know that she had been, of course, but Hignat, Wilwog and Cornish had been the only other witnesses; where could May have gotten the memory of the experience? I didn't know, and I would only have time to think about it later. Right now, all I could do was tap softly on the door and see what happened.

I was kept there long enough that I almost gave up on her and proceeded to May's room anyway, but after three knocks, Amelia finally opened it, nowhere near as careful as James had been—though when I saw her face, I knew why. She looked very bleary-eyed indeed, and it took her a couple of seconds to focus on my face. The fact that she had a bludginator in her hand was the only sign that she recognised the potential danger, though she probably couldn't have done much with it.

"Hi," I said flatly, and then, "Sorry."

"John?" she said, confused. "What are you doing here? What time is it?"

"Er—eleven, I think," I hesitated, willing myself to look at her face, and only at her face. I'd already seen her body when she'd opened the door—she was wearing a white nightdress which seemed to hang pretty loosely on her, and what it showed me of her body made it more difficult than I could have imagined to focus on conversation.

"Oh," she said, looking more closely at me now. Her expression seemed to soften as she took me in, and she stepped back to let me enter her room; I assumed I must look pretty wretched, because I certainly felt that way.

"Thanks," I said, making for her bed and sitting on the end of it, immediately crossing my legs in one last attempt to control the situation. Remember Natalie, I tried to think, but as Amelia closed her door and turned back to face me, it became so much more difficult to hold on to that thought. "Sorry if I woke you up, I just needed—"

Needed what? I knew exactly what I needed, but I couldn't very well say, 'I just needed to have sex with someone so that I can go to sleep.' Amelia didn't ask what I meant but came to sit on the bed beside me, not close enough that we were touching, but close enough that we could have touched if we wanted to.

"Are you okay?" she asked gently, seeming to be more awake now.

I shook my head. "No, and I don't really know why, but I couldn't sleep just now, even though I'm really tired and—I dunno."

I closed my eyes tightly—I couldn't look at her and say something that wasn't creepy. I could look at her, and I could say something that wasn't creepy, but I couldn't do them both at the same time. With my eyes tightly shut, I managed to organise my thoughts a little better—enough to make me wonder why the hell I was here and what I hoped to achieve by being with Amelia, but not enough to motivate me to leave. "I guess I really miss Natalie, that's all. It's hard to sleep alone at night once you know how good it is to sleep with someone you love."

Where had that come from? It was true enough, for me anyway, but I'd never actually thought of it until that very moment. Beside me, Amelia let out a sympathetic noise which didn't really give much of her thoughts away. I opened my eyes and saw that she was watching me, her eyes full of that same expression I had seen earlier that day—the one which had made me wonder if she might still be attracted to me. Once our eyes were locked on each other, it was impossible to look away.

"That's really sweet," she said softly. "I—well"—It—she swallowed—"I did sleep a bit, but before that, I was really lonely too. I still feel like the same person—I can't be much different—so why didn't he wait for me, even for a week? I thought that I meant more than that."

"You do," I told her with such firmness and conviction that she blushed. I knew that these feelings of inadequacy were probably a holdover from the self-esteem issues she'd been having post the rape, but that wasn't why I'd said it like that. The truth was, in that moment, and especially while we were staring into each other's eyes as we were, she meant everything to me. Thoughts of Natalie, Stella and all others had completely left my mind. The attraction I'd once had to Amelia, which had been pretty strong right up until I'd left for the Honnie world, had returned in full force. It was impossible to pretend that I didn't mean what I said with every ounce of sincerity, and there was no way that Amelia could think I was only trying to make her feel better.

"Oh John," she moaned softly, her lips parting slightly, "I… you…we…what do you mean?"

That had to be her brain kicking in, trying to put the brakes on, because every part of her body was telling me that she wanted this as much as me, if not entirely for the same reason. Even her eyes were beckoning to me, but like I'd been trying to do back in my bedroom, she was clinging to her rationality.

"What do I mean?" I repeated, wanting to reach out and touch her, but knowing that if I did, I mightn't be able to stop. "I mean that you're a great person, both before and now, and Darcy must have been a fool to let you go. You mean so much more than he appreciated—than perhaps even Marc appreciated in the end—at least I think so."

I was still resisting reaching out to her, my legs still crossed more tightly than ever and my arms pretty much wrapped around myself as though I were cold—which I was, in fact, but it was by far the underwhelming sensation. My body was crying out for her, and my conscious mind had been shoved rudely into a suitcase and locked up for the night; only my subconscious mind was keeping me in check. It wasn't thinking of Natalie—it wasn't thinking of anything really—but it was still slowing me down, trying to prevent me from doing something I would deeply regret later.

At that moment, however, the game was lost. Amelia wriggled forward and put her arms around me, setting off a chain reaction from which there was no return. She had probably only meant to hug me in appreciation for what I'd just said, but when I put my own arms around her and held her to me, she didn't pull away—nor did she pull away when my lips met hers in a deep kiss, to which she responded hesitantly at first, and then more aggressively.

I would never know at what point Amelia decided to abandon thought, caution, rationality, whatever; I only knew that when she finally realised just how horny I was and how badly I needed her, she never hesitated. What followed was, certainly from Amelia's perspective, rather quiet; apparently she didn't want to make too much noise in case we woke either James or May through the walls, and it was lucky I wasn't normally a noisy guy myself because I'd completely lost sight of our surroundings. Barely a minute in, though, before either of us had climaxed, someone tapped gently on the bedroom door—the door which Amelia hadn't bothered to lock after I'd come in.

"Shit!" she hissed, her expression anguished and horrified in almost equal measure (the anguish seemed to be worse). I wanted to keep going—I was almost there—but Amelia pushed me roughly backwards. I rose up off her and rocked back on my ankles, my head swinging around to look at the door as the person on the other side tried turning the knob, not realising that it was already unlocked.

"Amelia? You awake? I—I need to talk to you."

Holy crap—that was Marc's voice—the very worst person to be calling on us at this very moment.

"Marc, no," Amelia called desperately, but it was too late. The door had opened wide enough for him to be silhouetted against the dimly lit corridor outside, and wide enough for him to see everything in crystal-clear detail: In short, the two of us, starkers, with utterly sprung expressions on our faces.

"What?" Marc gaped, his mouth hanging open for a moment before his eyes flew wide. The line, 'it's not what it looks like', sprang to mind; and absolutely ludicrous in these circumstances— there was no way this could be anything other than exactly what it looked like.

The moment hung for a second which seemed to elongate in my mind, and probably Amelia's too, before the full implication of what he was seeing struck Marc with the force of a sledgehammer. He stepped forward, fury on his face, probably meaning to grab me and hurl me away from Amelia as hard as he could, but he gave me a few extra seconds when he stumbled over Amelia's discarded nightwear —a fact which only made him angrier.

"How dare you," he snarled, rounding on me as I quickly regained my feet. I felt horribly vulnerable—he was bigger than me, I was completely naked, my penis was pointing defiantly at his own crotch like an accusatory finger, and did I mention that I was completely naked? Well, completely naked except for a condom…

"How dare I what?" I retorted, my own anger rising.

It was an animalistic anger, just as primal and thoughtless as my animal lust had been and may have had something to do with two bull males fighting over a female—I didn't know. All I knew at that point was that it had been just as rude for Marc to barge in here as it had been when Amelia had done the same thing to him and Lena while they had been doing the nasty—well, a slightly different style of nasty. Marc and I were on the verge of a physical stoush here, and this room was barely big enough for us both to stand on the floor; the only thing separating us was the chair on which I'd thrown my clothes, and it was still a small enough distance for either of us to take a swing at the other.

"She's already been through so much," he snarled, his fists and teeth clenched, "and now you just come storming in here and doing that to her all over again? What kind of person are you?"

His look of disgust was so deep that I cringed away from him. What on earth was he saying? I thought he would be more upset because I'd broken the bro code by doing his ex, but he thought I was doing 'that' to her again—oh…

"You thought I was raping her?" I said, my voice rising uncontrollably, my own anger overwhelming every other sense, including my lust. "You really think I would do that?"

Marc struggled with himself for several seconds, his expression flickering between emotions so quickly that I hadn't a hope in hell of keeping up. Finally he snapped, "You'd better get out of here now, because if I ever see you near Amelia again—"

"Marc, stop," Amelia snapped at him. She had got onto her knees on the bed and was trying to hide herself with one hand—an endeavour both hopeless and pointless, given that both of us had seen her already.

Marc rounded on her, his mouth opening in a snarl of defiance, but whatever he'd been about to say died in his throat when he took her in. For a moment, I thought he'd returned to his senses, finally understanding that Amelia had opted into this, and that I certainly hadn't raped her.

"Amelia," he said quietly, putting his hands up in front of his chest in a gesture of surrender, his eyes wide as he took her in, "you —I—wow…I forgot how great you look without clothes on."

"Hey sleazebag, watch your—" I began, my anger on the point of rising again, but that was when I had glanced downward and registered what I was seeing there. Marc was completely incapable of taking his eyes off his ex-girlfriend, and Amelia was blushing again, not enjoying his regard quite as much as she had enjoyed mine

—she actually looked a little creeped out. Below the equator, though, Marc was showing the same sign, though even larger and more glaring, that he was equally and just as irrationally aroused as I was.

Terrible comprehension came to me then—not all at once, because my mind was only starting to ground back into action after several minutes of being well and truly overpowered by the body— but it was definitely there. Both Marc and I were afflicted by the same mindless horniness, something seemingly more powerful than the strongest aphrodisiac on the market, something remarkably similar to whatever Tommy had once done to Natalie by way of the Darkness Crystal—except that had been targeted towards him, and this clearly applied to any human female—and Honnie female too, I supposed.

Okay, now for the bonus question: Who would have most likely performed this spell on both me and Marc, and for what purpose? Why was it us two and not Peter and James? At least, I had to assume that those two were unaffected, and I didn't think they were, not if the intention had been to use Amelia to turn me and Marc against each other. Now, for the final touch: Lucien had told Stella that he had a larger plan, a plan which involved Amelia and had included a spell which he had already performed that morning—a spell that would be painless but would nevertheless make things interesting.

Marc and I were victims of dark magic here, but the collateral damage done to Amelia was far worse than any consequences that might strike either of us. With that in mind, I gathered every ounce of mental resolve I possessed and turned my attention to Amelia, trying to see the friend I'd had for months inside the woman she had become tonight.

"I'm sorry," I said as firmly as I could. "I've overstepped my bounds. I'll go now."

"John—" Amelia moaned quietly.

"Yeah, get going," Marc called over his shoulder as I stepped around him and out into the corridor. "Go back to your girlfriend."

"Marc!" Amelia snapped, but I closed the door behind me, muffling the sound of whatever conversation—if any—would follow. For a fraction of a second, I wondered if I'd done the right thing by leaving her alone in there with Marc; if he lost control as I had done, and Amelia didn't want to have sex with him also, she could end up getting raped tonight after all. But what could I have done? I couldn't have defended her from Marc, and I couldn't have attacked my brother with Hammerheart devices—what devices? I hadn't taken any with me.

No, leaving had been the best thing to do, so I went back to my room, slipped inside and shut the door, hearing movements inside

Peter and James's rooms as I passed the door. Naturally, the kerfuffle had woken them up, and perhaps they would interfere if the drama continued in Amelia's bedroom, but I didn't want to see it—I had to regain control of myself. It was only when I sat down on my bed that I realised how cold I was, and another moment before I remembered that I'd left all my clothes in Amelia's room. All I was wearing was the condom I'd reflexively put on back in Amelia's room.

I got back into bed and lay flat on my back, wishing I had resisted the urge to get up at all. Perhaps Marc would have gone in there as I had done, and he would have been the one to have sex with Amelia, and that would have been okay; it would have meant that they could perhaps get back together, given that they had both been dumped that day. But I'd gone and screwed things up for both of them, and even more so for myself. I groaned as the full realisation struck home: I had cheated on Natalie. I'd wondered yesterday if I'd cheated on her with Stella in that weird dream place, but now I knew for certain. The fact that neither one of us had achieved orgasm was inconsequential, because we would have done. It was the worst of everything: Not only had I cheated, but I hadn't got full value for my infidelity. If I came face-to-face with Lucien any time soon, I would knock his lights out, magic or no magic.

I had been there for maybe three or four minutes when a door slammed nearby, and someone thundered past my room. It was shortly followed by voices out in the corridor: Peter and James by the sound of it, and about a minute later, they were joined by May, who was speaking so rapidly that with her thick accent, she became just about impossible to understand. I did care a little about what was going on out there, particularly if Amelia were in trouble, and even Marc—he was no more guilty than me (in fact, he was considerably less guilty than me)—but I wasn't about to get up and investigate. Hearing May's voice, however, gave me an idea, and I tried to project my thoughts out to her. They were simple enough: I can't sleep, and I really need to sleep. Can you put me to sleep again, please?

After a few seconds, by which time her voice had faded as she moved further down the corridor (away from Amelia's bedroom, as it were), I felt a thought push into my mind: An affirmative, mixed with sympathy. She may have been asleep during the height of the drama, but she had quickly caught up on what had gone down. I didn't have long to think about this, though, as a moment later, as had happened earlier that day, sleep took me with no warning whatsoever.

Chapter 14: Out-of-Control is Exactly What I'm Hoping For

I was lying in bed, curled up and hugging myself, my mind in a state of turmoil. I had finally been able to sleep, after some thirty hours or so of wakefulness, and that was what I got when it happened. I raised my head and glanced at my clock—just after midnight. Great, I'd only gotten a little over two hours of sleep. Should I use magic to get another couple of hours? John was probably asleep by now, or he very soon would be—we could only have missed being asleep at the same time by minutes. I supposed I would need a couple more hours eventually, but after what I'd just seen—after what I'd just done right along with John—there was something else I wanted to do.

I got up, dressed quickly and left my bedroom in search of Lucien, eventually locating him in a room off the corridor on the next level down. He seemed to be doing something with the Sien-Leoard Crystal, though whatever the result was, I couldn't see it. He looked up when he heard me enter, looking pleased to see me, and I acted so quickly that he had no chance to pick my mood from my mind, let alone react to it. I drew my hand back and before he had time to move, gave him a crisp slap across the face. I didn't throw everything behind it but I certainly gave it enough that he would feel it. His head rocked back and his eyes widened as I made contact, but he must have used the crystal to cheat himself out of the pain of it because he was grinning a moment later.

"My apologies, Stella…I think," he said, raising his free hand and rubbing theatrically at the place where it should have hurt.

"You've got some explaining to do," I snapped at him, meeting his eyes and inviting him to read my mind—in this case, it was easier than talking about what had happened. "What on earth were you thinking? Did you think I would want something like this to happen? I thought we agreed, no magicℜ—"

Lucien waved my words away. "I believe I promised not to use any mind magic on him to make him more attracted to you, and indeed, I kept that promise. That spell was very much physical, and not at all mental, and certainly not targeted towards you."

"You're seriously gonna get yourself off on a technicality?" I said incredulously. "Why, Lucien? Why did you do this? Why can't we just go down there and bring them all in instead of screwing them around like this?"

Lucien smiled wearily. "We've had this conversation, Stella. Yes, I could put influential charms on them, but given what I want from them when they're on my side, I need to break their fighting spirit first. All of these things that are happening to them will combine to do that. It's a slower job, but ultimately it will get me what I want."

"Oh yeah? Well in the meantime, it's got your two brothers ready to take each other's heads off over a girl neither of them would have been dating otherwise. How does that tie in with your plan to get them on your team? Won't they have to work together? And Amelia too, for that matter?"

Lucien was still smiling—it made me all the more frustrated. "I'll make them see eye-to-eye if they can't work it out on their own, but ultimately, I wouldn't be surprised if Marc and Amelia find their way back to each other, and I'm sure John won't be too worried about that —then again, it'll be up to you to work that to your advantage."

I scowled. "And you thought I'd be comfortable watching him doing another girl along the way—that I would have to do her right along with him? As if dealing with Natalie and Lena wasn't bad enough—"

"Ah, but Stella, don't you see, the edge has been taken off John's stubbornness now. He has already cheated on his girlfriend, so his loyalty to Natalie will be a little easier to break in the future. His own guilt will drive him crazy, and that may make him more persuadable, if you like. If not, you can probably sit back and watch John push all the other girls in his life away until you're the only one left."

"But—but I don't want it to be for this reason," I told him, unable to believe I had to say this all over again—this was no more acceptable to me than any other magic, because it was just as fake.

"Stella, by the time you're ready for him, it will be real," he assured me. "Granted, the chain of events leading up to it mightn't be, but how is that any worse than everything else going on around here? If you can bring yourself to let John get a bit more experience with girls before you can have him all to yourself, the end result will be so much better for you. Does that sound okay?"

It didn't—it sounded terrible, and imagining John with other girls was even worse. How could Lucien think I would be okay with standing by and letting that happen? I wanted to argue the point with him, but unfortunately, I could also see his perspective; this really was a good way to cause a rift in their little group, which would make them more vulnerable and may cause them to come to us, rather than necessitate us going to them. I tried to find a positive in this for my prospects with John…could this, perhaps, make him better in bed than he was now? I didn't see how, but I had to hang onto that—it was the only thing I could possibly get out of this.

"No," I said, "but I'll go along with it for now. I'd suggest taking the thing off him before too long, though, in case it gets out-of-control—Marc too."

He only smiled. "Out-of-control is exactly what I'm hoping for. Shall we have a look and see just how out-of-control things are now?"

He rolled his eyes up as he spoke, making his question rhetorical. I almost did the same before deciding that I didn't want to see what was going on down there for myself. I already knew that John had been on the verge of falling asleep when I had woken up, and I didn't particularly care what aftermath had followed for the others. That probably wasn't very nice of me but I just couldn't bring myself to care. Instead, I watched Lucien's face as his expression, first amused, slowly darkened.

"Not good?" I asked.

"No," he said, still watching proceedings in Melbourne, his voice almost as distant as his eyes. "It was good, at first; Amelia must have had a go at Marc, and now he's stormed off into the night, and Peter and James woke up and are now out trying to find him, except…" His voice trailed away for a few moments, and I was about to ask him what he meant when he continued. "May has used her mind to sort the whole mess out. She has put Amelia to sleep, because she tried to go and see John again after the fight, and she's made the other three come back. That damn Honnie has ruined everything!"

My stomach sank, and for a couple of reasons. The whole thing might have been worth it—might—if it had achieved the ultimate goal of splitting up the group, but that part of the plan had failed. That was bad, but if it put Lucien into another destructive temper, that would be even worse.

"Maybe you need to do something about her, then," I suggested.

Lucien opened his eyes, entirely in the here-and-now again. "Yes, I think it has come time to put a plan I was working on earlier into action. I've already given May an opportunity to walk away from this war without any harm done to herself; since she has refused, I'll have to provide her with some motivation.

"Stella," he said, focussing on me now, "I need you to go down to the Big Room and fetch Harry and Simon Maivis, Katie Knight, Sophie Crow and Rebecca Fletcher. Find them, wake them if they're sleeping, and bring them to me in our living room upstairs. Can you do that for me?"

"Okay," I said in surprise, wondering what this was about, but not asking—he would have told me if I was supposed to know.

So confused, I turned and left the room, walking through the wall and out into the rest of the base—the long corridor to the elevators. The Big Room again—I had sure found myself in there a few times in the last twenty-four hours; I couldn't really say it had all been today since it was now past midnight. The first time had been on Lucien's instructions, though I hadn't ended up doing anything to help the prisoners. The second instance had been a short time later, while John and his friends were walking towards an entrance to the Hammerheart Highway in Melbourne; they had been coming here, and it looked like John would be going into the Big Room.

I had panicked, unsure whether to follow him, intercept him, or worry about Marc and May while they were searching for the Sorcerous Crystals; but in the end, I had only stayed in the Big Room long enough to take Natalie and Lena out of it—I didn't want to give John an opportunity to hook up with either of them so soon after the confrontation. I had used magic to locate them, shrink them and place them in my breast pocket—the only pocket I'd had—and then gone to covertly follow Marc and May, choosing not to let them know of my presence unless absolutely necessary. There had been a close call when they had almost woken Lucien, and I had nearly used magic then, but thankfully, nothing had gone wrong.

Then after they had all left the base, all of them pretty flat, I had released Natalie and Lena back into the Big Room. Another argument had ensued, both of them pissed that I had used magic to prevent them from seeing John and how it wasn't 'playing fair'. It was a ridiculous notion, and yet at the same time, I really did want to play fair if I could—again, that would make the victory all the more real, and me all the more deserving of it. Still, not in a good mood myself at the time, I had told them both that they were lucky I had only put them in my pocket when I could just as easily have put them in my mouth and swallowed them like pills.

I stopped then, now directly in front of the lifts, thinking about that last part. For a moment after I had shrunk the two of them, I had considered putting them in my bra, forgetting for a moment that I had a pocket, but had rejected the idea because it would have felt creepy if I'd felt them scrabbling around in there like a couple of flightless insects. There was something about the idea of doing those things to those two girls that was unexpectedly hot. Thinking about it now made me feel pleasantly squirmish in a way I hadn't felt at the time; it made me think of John, and bringing the two fantasies together made me want him even more. And then I understood: If he was asleep, he was in me now, and that was probably the reason why this felt so hot. I had two options here; I could be indignant, or I could roll with it. I had a feeling when he woke up, John would appreciate the latter…

The lift arrived at the top level then and I stepped on and pushed the button for level five, thinking about the rest of the day as I descended. Honestly, not much else had happened; before I had left the Big Room, my attention had been drawn to Hignat and Wilwog, who had, according to Rebecca, attempted to rape her. I had sent them both on their way, resisting the urge to perform yet more magic on them. I had then placed a spell on the door to the Big Room to prevent those two from re-entering; I only hoped that Lucien would understand. Then when he had woken up, I had told him everything that had happened while he had been sleeping, and the part about which he was most concerned was backed up by 2L11. Lucien had sent the man away from the Chopville base, as it was the second time in as many days that he had been overcome.

I'd had dinner after that, during which time I had been once again harassed by Hignat, both indignant about my treatment of him earlier and still finding the nerve to try to persuade me to be his girlfriend; he said he was having trouble accepting that the gift promised him by my father had been snatched away, but he still wanted me and would fight for me until I wanted him too. I had snapped at him, telling both him and Wilwog that my heart was set on John Playman —yes, that John Playman, and he had better not bother me anymore otherwise I would have to do something to him. His face had blackened with rage and he had stormed away, but Wilwog had remained behind long enough to ask me what I would do if either he or Hignat caused any trouble for me and John. I had told him that I would make it so that nobody could ever kick either of them in the testicles again, and that had sent him scurrying away with his tail between his legs.

And the time since dinner had been spent alone, contemplating what I needed to do. How do I go about persuading John that he and I are right for each other? It was so obvious to me—why was he so resistant to the idea? Was it only because of his feelings for Natalie? Was it because of the connection—that he didn't want to be with someone who saw into him the way I did? I didn't know, but what I did know was that whatever was holding him back, I would find a way to deal with it, even if it meant eventually conceding defeat if it would remove the burden of conflict from his shoulders. He had to know, if he didn't already, that I would go to any lengths to make sure he is happy—something that none of the other girls would be prepared to do.

I got off the lift on the fifth floor, nodded to the two security guards (not the same ones who had been so efficiently dealt with earlier, but Lucien wanted this area manned at all hours) and entered the Big Room. The lights were out and all was still. There were no hard rules about when people should sleep in this place, but I supposed that most people would choose to do so when the lights were out, as there were no windows in here. I magically cast my mind around the room for signs of activity before proceeding; yes, most people were sleeping, including all five of those I was supposed to collect. There were a few people awake, though, some of them in their compartments and a few hanging around in the public areas—

and one of the latter, I saw, was Lena. She was in conversation with a couple of other girls who I didn't know by name, but who I thought had been in with the Woodwards ever since the very first battle of Chopville High.

I didn't want to deal with her tonight, so I hurried forward into the aisles as quickly as I could. Where she was now was unfortunately close to Harry and Simon's compartments, as was her own compartment, so if I wanted to get those two out of here before she chose to go and get some sleep, I would need to be quick. I didn't check what was ahead of me magically as I went because it made focussing on the here-and-now more difficult, but I wished I had a couple of minutes later when, hidden by a blind corner and in almost pitch-black darkness, I collided with someone walking in an adjacent isle.

"Sorry," I said flatly, disengaging myself from her, but of course, as had to be my luck this evening, it was Lena. She straightened up and looked at me, her expression calculated and suspicious.

"No problem," she said levelly, her voice quiet so as not to wake anyone sleeping in the surrounding compartments. I cast my mind out to check if there were, but the nearest person to us was a full six compartments ahead in my aisle. "What are you doing here? Come to get up to trouble with us in the night?"

"Actually, Lucien sent me here for something completely different," I said just as levelly, but her words had made me think back to how hot I had felt a few minutes earlier. I looked her up and down, wondering what it would feel like to put her in my mouth and swallow her, but as much as the thought turned me on, I wasn't seriously going to do anything to her—I wasn't that kind of person.

"At this hour?" she raised her eyebrows at me, no less suspicious than before. "Seems a little strange, don't you think?"

"Time doesn't stop just because it's night," I said philosophically. "He's got a job he needs done, and I don't know what it is, but I think it's pretty important, and he needs a few people from in here to help him do it. Go to bed and let me get on with my orders."

I made to move past her, but before I could take two steps, she caught my arm and spun me around to face her with surprising strength. We were almost the same height, and my muscle definition was probably greater than hers (I had bulked up a bit during the weeks I'd spent on the run, although neither of us had had much physical activity for a while), and in any other situation, she probably wouldn't have been able to do that to me; but on this occasion, she had caught me off-guard.

"You won't win, you know that?" she told me, her eyes locking with my own. "He won't stay in a relationship where he can't be his own person, and he already knows that."

"And you think you'd stay in a relationship with him if you got him?" I said, trying to pull away from her, not wanting to use magic, but she was seriously tempting me. "You think you won't get bored with him like you got bored with Marc?"

"After how hard I've had to work to get him, that wouldn't happen," she said stubbornly, "and I'm sure there would be plenty of ways for us to spice things up."

I shrugged, knowing I was right but seeing that arguing with her would achieve nothing good. I made to pull away from her again, but she wasn't done with me yet.

"You know you'll have to get rid of your connection with him, don't you?" she told me. "That's your only chance; get rid of it, and maybe he'll start seeing you the same way he sees other girls. But he's not gonna date someone who can see into his mind and use that knowledge to control what he does."

"That connection goes both ways, Lena," I pointed out, my anger beginning to rise, "and are you telling me that you wouldn't try to manipulate him? From what I've seen, you already try to use your body to affect his thinking."

She looked stung by that and had to take a moment to recover her poise. "I wouldn't manipulate him; I'd let him do whatever he wants, because that's how he is now and I wouldn't try to change that."

I didn't believe that, though; once she had him, she would try to mould him into whatever she wanted her boyfriend to be, I felt sure. I didn't bother saying so, though. Instead, I said, "So would I, and in my case because I understand better than you ever could why he does what he does. He's even had sex with another girl on my watch and I didn't interfere or hold it against him."

Which I didn't, really, because he hadn't been in control of his urges, but would I have let him have sex with Amelia if we were dating? I didn't think so, but then maybe I wouldn't have to; maybe he would be loyal if I gave him everything he needed to keep him faithful.

"On your watch," Lena laughed. "Seriously, are you saying that because you didn't try to stop him hooking up with Natalie, that makes you all holier than thou?"

"No," I said, hesitating for a moment; would John mind if I told Lena what he'd done with Amelia? He certainly would mind if I told Natalie, and I had no intention of causing that kind of trouble again, but I didn't think this would be such a big deal—it might discourage her, and he would appreciate that. "No—I'm not talking about Natalie. He hooked up with Amelia a couple of hours ago."

I took some enjoyment from the expression that crossed her face then, as though I had slapped her as I had slapped Lucien earlier. She took a little longer to recover her poise this time, but when she did, she looked pretty pissed. "That's probably 'cause she's the only girl he has access to; I doubt it means anything. If I'd been there instead of her, that could have been me. I think you know it, too—that's why you don't blame him for it."

She was more right than she knew, and that made my own anger rise. If I responded now, we could dissolve into a full-on catfight, complete with hair-pulling and bitch-slapping, and perhaps even a miniaturised human sliding down my throat, screaming in terror in the moments before she became no more. I chose not to let that happen, knowing that not only would John hate me for reacting like that, but that I would hate myself if I actually did that to another person—even this particular person. I had an idea that could settle things between us for the interim.

"You wanna know a little secret?" I told her conspiratorially. "John's in my mind right now."

Her eyes widened. "Really?"

"Yep," I said, wrenching myself out of her clutches, but rather than pulling away from her, I turned and took hold of her shoulders, staring intently into her face, "so now's your chance. Anything you want to say to him, you can say to me. Anything you want to do to him, you can do to me."

That sounded pretty dirty—exactly as I'd meant it to. I felt tingly again and knew that the part of me that was John was enjoying this, because after all, if he could be turned on by my body, he could certainly be turned on by Lena's. It was a very strange feeling for me, though, because knowing that it wasn't really me didn't make it feel any less like me, and I had never felt this turned on by another girl. Not that I really wanted to fulfil some sort of sexual act with Lena; it was her obvious discomfort that was arousing me more than anything else.

"That's—that's just wrong," she whispered, her eyes searching my face, perhaps trying to locate a sign of John in them, "on so many levels."

I smiled at her. "Just imagine, if you do have sex with John, and I'm asleep at the time, you'll be having sex with me too. Get your head around that one."

It was her turn to try to pull away from me, but I held onto her shoulders a little tighter. "You're crazy, you know that?" she said, beginning to look scared, and interestingly, that made me even hotter. Now, I probably could perform a sexual act on her and get off on it—incredible. I had a moment of indecision, a point at which right and wrong hung suspended in front of me, before I cast them both aside; after all, morality was only an abstract concept, and doing this felt absolutely right.

I cast a couple of spells; the first silencing her voice so that she could speak in no more than a breathy whisper; and the second holding her in place, not completely immobilising her but simply making it so that she couldn't take a single step in any direction. She could still move her body around where she stood—she could even move her feet if she chose—but if she tried to take a step, it would seem to her as though the floor was moving beneath her like a travelator. I had never performed a spell quite like that before, but it seemed to be a pretty good one.

"Do you really think so?" I asked her, gazing intently at her, and she flinched away from me.

"Let me go," she said, only then realising that she could only speak in a whisper, and letting out a long, probably high-pitched scream which came out sounding like a combination sigh-hiss. "What the hell have you done to me, you crazy bitch? Let me go, damn it!"

I smiled at her, letting go of one of her shoulders and raising my other hand to hover an inch above her cheek, amused by the way her eyes followed my hand, as though she were mesmerised. "Why should I? You were the one who pulled me back. Did part of you sense a bit of John in me, and that's why you didn't want me to leave?"

I gently touched her cheek and ran my finger down it, finishing by running across her pressed lips.

"You—what are you trying to do?" she glared at me. "This is sick. Even John wouldn't enjoy something like this."

That made my smile broaden. "But he would if it was your body. He would enjoy teasing you, and you would enjoy being teased by him. You know I'm right, don't you?"

She did, of course, but her glare remained in place. "You're not John," she hissed. "You're Stella; stop trying to pretend to be some sort of—of—hybrid or something."

"But I am," I insisted. "At least, part of me is, and when John wakes up, he will remember this as though it were him doing it."

I was trying to decide what I wanted to do to her next as I spoke —trying to decide as though I were John and I wanted to tease her. Perhaps if I gave him this, he wouldn't feel the need to explore Lena for himself—not that he hadn't already. She was wearing pyjamas but she was also wearing a bra underneath, probably because she was out of her compartment and didn't want other guys admiring her assets when she walked past. I knew there was a line here that I had to be careful not to cross—we were in public, after all, and just because nobody was around us now (I used my magic to check just then, and nope, we were still alone), that didn't mean we couldn't be caught in the middle of something that would be pretty embarrassing for both of us.

"That won't stop him from wanting to do it with his own body instead of yours," she said, as though she had been reading my mind, "unless of course, you plan to use your magic to give yourself a penis or something."

"Nope," I said, sliding my hand up her top, concentrating on what I was feeling. I didn't get any personal enjoyment out of this part myself, but I still found myself excited by the effect the whole thing was having on her. Still, I wanted to do a little more than just feel her bra—I could just as easily do that with one of my own, and how ridiculous that would be.

"What are you trying to do?" she finally managed to ask me, and even though there was no actual tone to her voice, she still seemed to sound like she was trying not to enjoy it, and not entirely succeeding. Her face certainly suggested that she was tingling against her will.

I had an idea then, inspired by what she had said a minute ago. "I'm trying to give John a reason not to feel like he's missing anything with you, and trying to show you that whatever you may think, you don't really want to be with him either. Just think, he's already been inside my mind repeatedly, and hopefully soon, he'll be inside my body as well."

"That's not gonna happen," she snapped. "He wouldn't do that; because of your precious connection, he can't possibly like you the same way he can like me. And you're forgetting, he's already been inside my body once."

I smiled, glad that she had said that, because it meant that I could proceed with my idea. "Yes," I said, withdrawing my hand from her top, "and you're looking forward to having him in your body again soon, aren't you?"

"You'd better believe it," she said confidently, "and I doubt I'll have to wait long."

"I agree," I said, keeping her eyes locked with my own and taking a moment to suck on my finger. She watched me in confusion as I did this, but her expression turned to horror as I slid that finger into the front of her pyjama bottoms.

"Don't do that," she said, and it might have been a moan, but without a tone to go with it, I couldn't be entirely sure.

"Why not?" I said, using my other hand on her shoulder to hold her steady. Whatever her protests, I could tell that part of her was also turned on by this, probably because I kept relating my own actions back to John—she wouldn't have been at all turned on if it had been just me doing this.

"I won't let you get away with this," she said, but they were empty words now—they were the kind of denials a woman would normally give a man if she knew she ought not to have sex with him, even while she were letting him do what he wanted to her and doing absolutely nothing to stop him. Perhaps part of her wanted it to stop —the normal part of her—but the part of her mind that wanted John, as well as all of her body, wanted me to continue.

"This is why I don't need a penis," I told her. "I can do this just fine, as could John if he wanted to. How do you think John would look back on this moment when he wakes up? Do you think it would make him horny when he reflects on it? Horny for you?"

She took several moments to reply, during which she began to pant, now losing control of the part of her mind that was resisting this. Finally, she managed to say, "I think he'll be extremely creeped out by the thought of you raping me."

"It's not—" I began, and then stopped, brought up short by her use of the word 'rape', connecting it with the way Marc had mistakenly thought John was raping Amelia.

I had been about to say that this wasn't rape, and I supposed it wasn't really rape in the truest sense of the word, but that didn't change the fact that I was performing a sexual act on Lena's body, despite her consistent attempts to get me to stop. The fact that she mostly wanted it didn't matter because the part of her which did matter, the part by which she made her own decisions, was creeped out and probably violated by what I had done to her. It was sexual assault at the very least.

That thought completely ruined the fun I'd been having, and now I had to wonder why I had even wanted to do such a nasty thing to her. I had already worked out that it was less to do with my own sexual pleasure, whatever John's influence might have done to me, and more to do with enjoying her discomfort, as I had been turned on by the thought of putting her and Natalie in my pocket earlier. It was power, I suddenly realised, and on the heels of that thought came a couple more: My father had been attracted to power, as had his mother and her father, and look where it had gotten them. Perhaps even worse than that was the memory of something that I had seen in a video during a commerce class at school last year. Many men who rape women do so for the power rather than the sexual gratification, which can just as easily be achieved with the hand.

That was definitely my cue to stop. I let go of her with both hands and wiped them on my clothes. I opened my mouth, about to apologise, and then changed my mind; she may not have deserved what I'd done to her (though part of me thought she'd deserved every bit of it), and more, she had enjoyed it for the most part, no matter how much she persuaded herself that she didn't. To top it off, in this game for John's regard, apologising for taking the advantage over her would be tantamount to conceding defeat, and even though it felt wrong not to apologise, I wasn't going to let her think she had won.

I took a moment to construct my parting shot. "I don't think I need to go any further this time, but if you feel diminished now, imagine how it would feel for me to give you an orgasm, or use magic to make you want to do those kinds of things to me. You know all that stuff I said about you is true, so you must also believe I won't mind doing it again if I have to. John won't mind, because it was almost as much his doing as it was mine, so the smartest thing you can do for yourself is back off him. If it's the challenge you're after, you have to know how this challenge is gonna run you down, because I can do so much more to you than I already have. You don't want him for the right reasons, and I absolutely will not let you fool him into thinking otherwise."

Not bad, I thought as I waved my hand at her to nullify the spells I had placed upon her, before turning my back on her and walking away. She would have had a golden opportunity to hit me from behind if she'd been incensed enough to continue the argument from before, but as I had hoped, she now knew better than to challenge me. In the time before I turned into the next aisle, I heard neither a word nor movement from her, though I had to assume that she would eventually go back to her compartment, and probably wouldn't tell anyone else what had happened to her—it would be a difficult thing to confess. I did feel a little sick with myself for what I had done, but it was only a minor feeling because as much as it had been for fun, it had also achieved what I had wanted. I didn't think she would give up her campaign to get her grubby hands on John again, but she would know better than to cross me in the future.

I finally got around to doing what Lucien had asked me to do. None of them were particularly happy about being woken up, and even though they all obeyed my instruction to come with me, they weren't at all graceful about it. That changed when we got up to the top floor and I led them, two at a time and Rebecca last, through the wall into our living quarters. As he had said, Lucien was waiting in the living room, but he wasn't alone. Cornish and Fewul—who had taken the form of May, of all people—were also there, with the two men in the middle of what sounded like a complicated discussion. When we entered the room, however, Lucien was quick to wrap it up.

"I tell you what," he said to Cornish, "you've been in action for a long time, so why don't you go get some sleep and we'll talk about what comes next in the morning. You've done a good job, but there's still plenty of work to be done."

"Thanks," Cornish said, and he did indeed look pretty exhausted.

He turned and walked past the six of us, nodding at me and ignoring the others completely—I returned it politely, though I still didn't like the guy. Lucien must have given Fewul a telepathic instruction to either go invisible or disappear somewhere, because he (or she, rather—oh hell, I'll just say 'it') vanished from sight a moment later.

"You took a while," he said to me. "Did they not want to wake up or something?"

"No, I—er—did something else in there," I said, meeting his eyes and daring him to pull it out of my mind. He may or may not have done, but if so, it didn't seem to concern him.

"Right, you guys," he said, turning to the others, and they all looked back at him with absolute respect—whatever he asked of them, no matter how foul, they would do without complaint. "Why don't we all sit down so we can go over the plan. Do any of you need to be woken up with a bit of magic?"

All five of them opted in for that, and Lucien provided before launching into the explanation of the plan.

"The version of May that you just saw was only Fewul, taking her form, but the real May is still out there. She teamed up with Marc and the others yesterday and has since been using her mind-power to undermine me as much as possible—and unfortunately, she is capable of doing quite a lot of damage, even without magic. I don't want to hurt her after the integral role she played in defeating Arnold Hammerson, but I can't allow her to continue what she's doing. I have already confronted her and told her that she should leave this world and return to her normal life, which she should have wanted to do right away, judging by all I know about Honnies; but for whatever reason, she has chosen to stay and fight. Since she refuses to leave voluntarily, I'm going to have to give her a powerful reason to go home, and that's where you lot come in."

All six of us listened to this little speech in growing wonder. Finally, it was Katie who asked, "What do you want us to do? We have no clout with May—she doesn't even really know who we are, apart from Rebecca."

"That doesn't matter, because it's not May you'll be dealing with," Lucien said, and turned his attention to Rebecca. "Tell me, how much of their world can you remember?"

"Most of the parts that I saw, I suppose," she said nervously. "I can't recall every minute of every day or anything, but—"

"That doesn't matter either," he cut in. "You only need to remember the most important points about the way they use their powers. I need you to spend the next few hours recalling as much as you can for me, and I don't mind using magic to help you remember if necessary. As for you four," he said to Harry, Simon, Katie and

Sophie, "your job will be to go into the Honnie world, track down May's daughter, and follow her wherever she goes. When I give the order—if I give the order—you will capture her and bring her to me, and that is how we will motivate May to return home. I'm fairly sure that her obligation to her daughter, an evolutionary instinct which is probably the main reason why Honnies still exist, will send her running back."

"How can we do all that?" Harry asked, looking scared. "There's a lot about that plan that we physically can't do—actually controlling a Honnie in their world would be top of the list. Remember what she did to John's arm?"

"I imagine that was like a stroll in the park for her," Lucien agreed, "but that is why Rebecca is here. She is going to provide us with every detail you will need to know, and I will provide you with all the magical equipment you could possibly need—for more than we did for the first expedition, since we now have a better idea how much they're capable of."

And that was pretty much the story for the night. I stayed by to watch the most part of what they were doing, leaving a couple of times to go to the toilet and once to get something to eat, and taking an opportunity to check on John and his friends—all six of them were asleep in their beds. I now understood why Lucien didn't just go and take them all in, Honnie or no Honnie, but it still felt rather strange to be sitting back here doing all this while they were as defenceless as it was possible to be.

In the end, what Lucien provided the interdimensional travellers with was some kind of flying ship. It seated the four of them comfortably, was closed-roofed and provided them with all the oxygen, food, water and pretty much everything else they would need for a long stint over there. It was secured in a different way from the thinking caps in that rather than shielding them, a shield that could possibly be blasted apart by a Honnie strong enough, it hid them entirely. No Honnie would be able to attempt to break in because no Honnie would even know that they were there. It contained weapons which would shrink, knock out and contain an unlimited number of Honnies, humans and half-breeds, just in case Ingi (interesting name, that one) was surrounded by others. Finally, it was equipped with the usual invisibility, inaudible and shrinking charms that were now standard of such vehicles.

At around six o'clock, we all left the living quarters and descended together through the building. Rebecca and I got off on level five while Lucien went to take the others down another level so that he could escort them out of the base—he wanted to personally see them safely into the Honnie world, even though their vehicle was capable of moving from one dimension to the other. I let Rebecca into the Big Room and suggested that she go and catch up on lost sleep, while using my mind to scan the area: Natalie had recently woken up, but Lena was asleep—good. With that done, I decided that even though it was a little earlier than I would normally eat, I would go to have breakfast—getting in there before Hignat woke up seemed like a pretty good idea.

Chapter 15: Already So Conflicted

I kicked the sheets off me and onto the floor as I attempted to take another step, before realising that I was lying flat on my back in a dark room and not walking across a dining hall to get my breakfast more than a hundred kilometres away. I then lay still, allowing my mind to catch up to my senses, and reflecting that nobody could get used to this sudden slamming from one place into another. I remembered how when I had captured Lucien and a few other Hammerhearts in February, there had been no perceptible moment for them in which they had been knocked out, and they had continued moving (and even talking, in Lucien's case) for a moment as though nothing had happened before realising that their entire surroundings had changed.

But I was definitely John now, and as I ran my mind over everything that had happened while inside Stella's mind this time, I realised that for whatever reason, I had been in there for a full six hours—the longest period yet. Maybe my body had been more tired than I'd known, only being allowed to sleep when May forced me down. She couldn't be responsible for keeping me down because she herself had gone to sleep shortly after—I knew so because Stella had checked a few hours ago.

I sat up and swung my legs over the side of my bed, shivering and trying to think. May—that was a significant train of thought to follow at this point. Lucien wanted her to leave, and he had sent Harry, Simon, Katie and Sophie into the Honnie world to hunt down and capture Ingi as motivation. Holy crap—that was bad, and worst of all, it would probably work too. May had been great to stay as long as she had, but I didn't think her loyalty to us would ever supersede her duty to her daughter. There was one flaw in his plan, though: It couldn't possibly work if May didn't know they were doing it. Ah, but of course, Lucien had known that I was there—had perhaps checked that I was still asleep in the moments before Stella had come up the stairs with the others. There was no way that I could keep this hidden from May, which left me with one very unappetising course of action: I had to tell her, the sooner the better.

But that was where the next problem presented itself: I was still completely naked except for a condom, and of course, all my clothes were still in Amelia's room—at least I assumed that was where they had remained after Marc had stormed out. Amelia had probably tried to bring them back to me last night, if Lucien was right about her wanting to come and see me (or maybe she just wanted to claim that orgasm that had been denied), but of course, May had forced her back to bed. So the million-dollar question now was: Where were they now?

And of course, thinking about Amelia trying to sneak into my room at the midnight hour, perhaps to finish having sex with me, brought all those delicious yet unwelcome feelings rushing back. I considered masturbating and then rejected the idea; I didn't want to jizz in my condom because then I would have to take it off, and right now, it was the full extent of my attire. It was just after six o'clock now, so there was a chance that none of the others were awake; maybe I could sneak off for a quick shower and then wrap a towel around myself until I got my hands on my clothes again.

So feeling horny as ever (more than six hours of no sexual release was already piling in on top of my over-sensitised loins), I got up, headed for the door, opened it a crack and looked out into the corridor, feeling horribly exposed by actually daring to step outside like this. It was deserted, so I opened it a little wider and slipped out, shutting it behind me and then going still, trying to listen. All was silent in the hallway of the damned, so I took a few steps towards the adjacent corridor and the bathrooms, but stopped when I heard the sound of a shower running in one of them—the men's room, I felt sure. Odds were that it was someone I didn't know, up early on a Monday morning because perhaps he had a job interview or something (who knew), but it could also be Marc, James or Peter. I didn't want the latter two to see me until I had dignified myself, and I didn't want Marc to see me until I had prepared myself for a very difficult apology (because I certainly owed that to him, along with an explanation).

I didn't want to go in there, but I had to do something—and standing out here in the corridor where anyone could see me if they walked past, or opened their bedroom door, was a terrible idea. I still needed to tell May what I had seen, though, which gave me only one option: I would have to knock on Amelia's door again and hope that she would let me into her room as I was, completely naked except for a condom. If not, maybe she could just pass my clothes through to me without looking at me, which would probably make it easier for me not to want to have sex with her all over again; but I would have to talk to her eventually, and preferably face-to-face, because like Marc, she deserved to know what had been going on last night.

I turned and walked back the other way, hesitating when I reached Amelia's bedroom door. Was this the right thing to do? I had no idea what mental state she would be in this morning, or how she would feel about me after last night; but none of that changed the fact that I only had one set of clothes, and they were almost certainly behind this door. So taking a deep breath and preparing to take the plunge, I knocked.

"Amelia, you awake?" I hissed through the door. "It's John; I need my clothes. You awake?"

I had to do this a couple more times before I got a response out of her, and it was nothing more than a grumbled confusion. When I knocked again, she mumbled, "Who's that?"

"It's John," I told her, still in little more than a whisper, but now feeling confident that she could hear me. "Sorry to wake you, but I need my clothes and I think I left them in there."

If she were bitter, this would have been the perfect moment to say, 'Good—you were so willing to take them off last night, so now you can go without until you wish you hadn't.' What Amelia really said was, "Oh yeah—okay."

"Hurry up," I hissed, uncomfortably aware that a middle-aged woman had just walked past the end of the corridor, pausing as she took in the naked boy up towards the other end and adopting an I-didn't-see-that-and-I'm-going-to-go-right-on-not-seeing-it expression, "I'm completely naked out here—well, except for a condom," I added, grinning slightly and then wishing I hadn't said that. She mightn't let me in if she thought I was making light of what had happened (and what had almost happened) between us last night.

Fortunately, the effect it had was completely the opposite; I heard her scramble off her bed and a second later, she opened the door to see me standing here, looking all kinds of guilty (which I was, of course, but it really wasn't my fault that I was naked—well, kind of). We stared at each other for a few seconds before, smiling slightly, she said, "Hi."

"Sorry about this," I repeated, "but—er—and sorry about that, too," I added as, following her eyes down, I saw that my condom-clad penis appeared to be defying gravity again. "Listen, it's not what you probably think耷—"

She reached out and took me by the arm, causing an absolute implosion between my legs, and pulled me into her room, quickly shutting the door behind me. She hadn't turned the light on this time, and there wasn't enough morning sun at this hour to give us any illumination. I could only stare at her face through the darkness for several seconds, before managing to tear my gaze away and look around for my clothes. They weren't exactly where I had left them—they were on the desk now rather than the chair—and I could just imagine Amelia putting them there after Marc, in a fit of rage after I had left, had knocked them onto the floor.

"Do you feel better today?" she asked me quietly.

"A little," I said shiftily, thinking that it was probably true if I could keep my mind clinging to some form of rationality while standing here, enough to continue doing what I had come here to do and not to get so completely distracted by Amelia.

"Listen," we both said at exactly the same time, before laughing.

"You first," I volunteered out of politeness, wishing I hadn't as soon as I'd spoken—who knew what impact her words might have on me.

"Okay," she said, grinning shily. "Well, about last night, I—I get that there wasn't really anything in it—"

I changed my mind and cut her off. "Hang on, before you go on, there's something you need to know about that, that I found out when I was asleep. You remember how Lucien said he put a spell on us that was supposed to make things interesting?"

"Yeah?" she said slowly, hesitantly, and I had a feeling that she wasn't really sure if she wanted to hear the rest.

"Well, apparently, that was it," I told her, glancing down at my erection and willing it to recede—it didn't work. "He let you rejoin us so that he could use you, and maybe even May, to cause a rift between me and Marc, and he put curses on us both to make us crazy horny. Did"—I swallowed and continued—"did Marc—you know—after I left—"

"No," she said flatly, "we didn't, and now that you've told me that, I guess I'm glad. I don't wanna be that kind of girl. He really wanted it, though, and if he'd got to me first instead of you—" it was her turn to swallow, but I didn't need her to continue.

I sighed. "So, you're right when you say it didn't mean that I—I wanna go out with you or something," I said, treading carefully now in case I offended her, "but I don't want you thinking that it was completely meaningless. I guess I would have wanted you even if it was, but I'd really been struggling up until then—you helped me out a lot."

She smiled again. I couldn't see it very clearly in the darkness, but it seemed genuine enough. "It meant plenty to me too," she said quietly. "I know you're still committed to Natalie—I would have known it even if you hadn't been cursed—but I needed last night too, so you don't have to feel bad about using me or anything. Besides, I would have preferred you more than anyone else I know at the moment, even Marc."

That was an enormous relief. "Thanks. I was worried that it might have affected you worse than either of us; collateral damage, you know."

She shook her head. "That would only have been true if I'd been mistaken about what you really wanted, or if I'd asked you to stop and you hadn't listened. Neither of those things happened; even without this curse, I'm as responsible for last night as you."

"So, are we good?" I asked tentatively, and then grinned sheepishly when she nodded. "Good, 'cause I don't want this to ruin our friendship. You know last night wouldn't have happened if not for the curse—well, I would have been lonely, but I would have been able to control it a little better."

Her face fell then, and I wasn't sure which part of what I'd said had upset her. "Yeah, I know," she said flatly, "you've been pretty set against the whole cheating thing ever since that one time. I guess I'm just a bit easier than that."

"No, you're not," I said, understanding my blunder and wishing I hadn't spoken. I took hold of her shoulders and made her look at me; the physical contact made me want her all over again, and she was wearing exactly the same as she had been last night, and we were so close. Control your mind, John, I thought, and managed to do so with great difficulty, though I couldn't be sure how much longer I could last in here. "Look, you probably remember a good deal of what went on between us earlier in the year, even if you can't remember how you felt about it at the time, but you should know that I was attracted to you then, and still am now. I regret last night because of what it might have done to my relationship with Natalie, but not for anything else if it means that you and I are still friends. Don't go thinking less of yourself because of last night; if anything, not doing that would have been denying yourself something that you needed."

Was that the kind of logic that girls normally used? I wasn't sure, but I hoped it would get through to her.

"I did need it," she said quietly. "Maybe guys would respect me if I didn't give into my needs so easily, though. Maybe Darcy would have stayed with me—"

"I don't think that had anything to do with why he moved on," I said, trying to make my mind focus on anything other than sex. I had meant to do something else this morning, something which had necessitated coming in here to get my clothes, but I couldn't think what it was. I let go of Amelia and reached out to pick up my underpants, but before I could, she caught my arm again.

"Wait," she said, looking as though she were trying to decide if she were ready to take a dive or not.

"Amelia," I said a little desperately, feeling my limited control waver, "the curse, remember? I can't—I can't stop myself wanting to take advantage of you if you touch me like that."

She looked at my face then, her expression not changing as she considered me. Then she said, "I can see that, but you have to know that I appreciate your courage to come in here after what happened last night, and to be so honest with me about what happened."

And against all possible advice I could have given her, she hugged me again, turning me to face her. I stiffened, wanting to return the hug, wanting to do what a good friend would have done, and at the same time not do what my body wanted me to do—what I wouldn't be able to prevent if I gave it an inch. The matter was taken out of my hands, though, when Amelia said, "I went to sleep very unfulfilled last night. I still need you, and I can feel that you need me too. What we've already done can't be taken back, so there's no reason not to finish it properly."

"But the curse," I gasped, "Amelia—I—I want it to be for the right reason."

"But it is for the right reason, even with the curse," she said, her voice slightly muffled against my throat. Still leaning against me, she looked up at me and said, "Please, there's a hole left in me that I need you to fill."

I couldn't resist any longer, and as she had already pointed out, I had already cheated once—doing so a second time wouldn't make a difference now. That was a terrible justification for doing the wrong thing, but it was all I could come up with. I was already naked and already wearing a condom which had tasted Amelia last night, and it only took a matter of seconds for me to get Amelia back on the bed. Nobody interrupted us this time, and we were both able to achieve orgasm in short order. In fact, as I had thought last night, we just kept on going for some time after, until Amelia was absolutely exhausted and I'd managed to rip right through the condom.

I hadn't stayed in there after that, hating to be the type of guy who just runs away after the deed is done, but liking the alternative of being discovered here even less. I had got myself dressed, waited for her to put her nightdress back on, chucked the worthless and extraordinarily gross condom in her little rubbish bin, and then taken my leave, giving her another hug on my way out. Looking back at the door, I had seen her crouching over the bin, rearranging the trash in there so that the condom wouldn't be visible.

I wasn't sure how much time had passed since I'd been in Amelia's bedroom, but the corridor was still quiet and deserted. The building itself seemed to be coming to life, but up here, everyone was still sleeping. Good, I thought, trying to make my mind focus again. Unfortunately, that last hug had made me horny all over again, despite the amount of sex I'd already had. Apparently, as much as I felt like I needed it, actually having it had no effect whatsoever. That was a little disheartening—it made what I'd just done with Amelia seem like a total waste of my fidelity, but I tried not to think like that. As dear as Natalie was to me, making last night into something that it wasn't for the sake of my existing relationship would be doing Amelia a great disservice.

Stop thinking about it, John, I chastised myself. My penis had erected itself fully again, straining so hard against my pants that it was painful. I struggled with myself, trying desperately to think what I had meant to do here. I had gone into Amelia's room to get my clothes, because I had been naked before, and I couldn't be naked around the others. Damn—that didn't help at all. I wracked my brain, sending it back even further; there was the thing I'd seen in Stella's mind, the incident between her and Lena, but that was as awesomely hot as it was disturbing—I would have to examine it, and my feelings about it, later. After that…oh, of course—May!

Yes—that ought to be done now. May would be mighty pissed if I wasted time in delivering her this message. I therefore went down to her door and, without giving myself a chance to think too much about what I was doing, knocked. Like Amelia, May had also been asleep, and it took a minute to rouse her and get her to come to the door, by which time she already knew it was me there. She mustn't have done a thorough investigation of the state of my mind, though, for she seemed to know nothing about the horny curse. When she opened the door and I saw what she was wearing, I took an involuntary step backwards; a nightdress, like Amelia's, except that it was silvery in colour, thin as silk, and only almost opaque. It clung to her in a way that made it look as though it were an extension of her body, and it was enough for me to see that she was almost certainly naked beneath it. I had been in her presence when she'd gotten changed and unchanged in the Honnie world, but I had never actually looked at her naked body—this was definitely the closest I had come to that, and it couldn't have come at a worse moment.

"Hello," she said in her usual expressionless tone. Her face suggested that she was mildly interested in this early-morning call, but no more than that.

"Hey," I said, "can I come in for a minute? I need to tell you something really important. Oh—don't mind that," I added, seeing that she had noticed my erection, which was showing up as a great big bubble in my pants, "Lucien put a spell on me to make me crazy horny, and it's kinda hard to look at you like that without—well, it's nothing personal, trust me. Can I come in?"

She continued to watch me for a few seconds, seeming to consider. She may have been reading my thoughts, but if so, I couldn't feel it in my mind. She couldn't have picked up on my reason for coming here because for the time being, I had forgotten it; right now, since I had laid eyes on her, I could think of nothing but sex all over again. I had to consider it a relief that in this case, if I did lose control, May would be strong enough to prevent me from doing something I would regret even more than what I had already done.

Finally, she stepped back to let me pass, saying, "I do not take it personally. I like how most male humans cannot control their minds when they see me wearing this; it is quite amusing."

"Most?" I repeated incredulously. "How many people have seen you like this?"

"Since it was given to me five days ago, several," she said, shutting the door and leaning against it, watching me. "So what is this that you want to tell me?"

I struggled with myself for several seconds, trying to make myself think properly, but it was no good—my penis was doing the thinking now, and it had only one thing on its mind. May watched me during this time, now listening to my surface thoughts, judging by the look on her face.

When it seemed like I wouldn't be able to remember why I had come in here, she said, "What can I do to help you with this?"

Have sex with me, was my immediate and almost all-consuming thought, but I forced myself to remember what I'd thought just a couple of minutes ago: Sex wouldn't help, because immediately after I'd had it, I would want more. I had the knowledge somewhere in my mind; if she helped me force it into the right channel, I could probably get there. This was what she now did, clearing my mind so that I could reflect back on my thoughts from earlier. I went back as far as what I'd seen in Stella's mind, because that was where it lay, skipped over the whole Lena incident (again, not the right time to worry about that) and finally landed on the thing which had sent me running here: The job Lucien had assigned to Harry, Simon, Katie and Sophie, which would see them go after Ingi, capture her and bring her to this world to use as bait against May.

As I touched the surface of the plan, I felt May take complete control of me so that everything else in my world—all my senses, my body, even my own name—were no longer my own. For a brief time, though I had no concept of time until it was over, I became nothing more than a human receptor, forced to recall everything that had happened from the moment when Lucien had begun explaining his plan to the moment when he had separated from Stella to escort the hunting party from the base. When she let me go and I became myself again, I saw that the Honnie looked more rattled than I had ever seen or even imagined she could be; she was both seriously scared and utterly furious.

I wished I hadn't told her—wished I had waited after all—but it was far too late to turn back now.

"How dare he," she snarled, and it was very lucky Lucien wasn't here right now—she would have killed him on the spot, not quickly and mercifully either but slowly, tearing strip after strip off him with her tongue until nothing remained. I was scared to be alone in this tiny little room with her—what if it had to be the bearer of bad news who suffered here?

"I must go," she said desperately, "I must not let him hurt Ingi—I must not."

And she actually looked like she would do it without a second thought; I saw a very strange thing as she flickered from solid opaqueness into semi-transparency and then back again, as though she were trying to decide if she should step into her world from here or not.

"Wait," I said desperately, and against every instinct I had, I took hold of her arm before she could leave—as if I could possibly stop her. Right on cue, all my arousal returned at the physical contact, but for now I pushed on. "May, wait; you can't just leave. Ingi is thousands of kilometres away from here; if you leave now, you'll never get to her before they do."

She glared at me, and I cringed back, my mind wanting to flee, my body wanting to jump on her. "What do you suggest I do? Wait for him to get her and bring her back here so that I can rescue her? I am not doing that."

"We have time," I insisted, "not much, I know, but enough to work out a plan. The whole point is that he wants you to go back to your world—do you really want to give him exactly what he wants after what he tried to do to you?"

"That would be better than any harm coming to Ingi," she said flatly. "I cannot let him hurt her; she is my duty."

"He won't get a chance to," I said, hoping I was right. "Look, just stay a little longer, okay? I know we're not as important to you as your family, but right now, we need you more than they do. If that changes, then you can too."

She knew my rationality was right, and I watched her struggling for what seemed to be an age, but was probably only four or five seconds, her natural Honnie instincts warring with her logic. It was yet another something that Honnies didn't normally have to deal with in their simple lives, and May couldn't handle it. She turned and sank down on her bed, covering her face in her hands and beginning to weep—now there was something I had never expected to see.

"I'm sorry," I said, sitting on the chair beside her bed and resisting the urge to touch her again, even though I so badly wanted to. "Honestly, it's hard not to hate Lucien right now—the things he's doing to all of us. Try not to worry about it; we'll come up with something."

She shook her head. "Did you not see what he has done? He has created something so powerful that even I cannot stop it. If I find Ingi and he chooses to use it, even I will be defenceless. But I cannot just sit here and let it happen; it would be like…" she broke off, considering an appropriate metaphor, and then going with, "like trying to stay awake after you had been awake for days without any sleep. I might be able to do it, but it is going to be very hard."

Unfortunately, as right as my logic had been, hers was too, but it also gave her a good reason not to get in Lucien's way. Of course, Lucien probably wouldn't attack Ingi if he knew that May had left, unless he thought she might decide to come back with reinforcements. Now there was a scary prospect: interdimensional war, humans versus Honnies. The latter would probably have the edge there, unless of course, Lucien was foolish enough to start it.

"I tell you what," I said, and now I really did reach out and touch her shoulder, once again doing my best to ignore the almost-explosion of pleasure that followed, "you call your own shots. If you absolutely have to leave, I'll understand, and I'm pretty sure the others would too, but try to hang on as long as you can. If we can find a way of dealing with Lucien before he gives the order, the whole problem will go away."

"Yes, you are right, I suppose," she said, turning to look at me again. We were about as close as I had been with Amelia last night before she had hugged me, setting off a chain reaction which had led to—well, we knew what it had led to, and I didn't need to think about it now. Damn it, John, stop thinking about it!

"Do you need me to help you with that again?" she asked me.

I nodded. "Ignore what my mind is doing—my body too," I added, crossing my legs as hard as I could, not really achieving very much. "Trust me, you can do far more with your mind to help than you can with your body."

She obliged, clearing my thoughts of all that sexual tension, my body taking a little longer to get with the program but eventually settling down. I took a moment before uncrossing my legs. It was an enormous relief. "Thanks," I said, wishing that I could hug her in appreciation, or let her taste me, or whatever was her preference; but of course, that would only bring the crazy horniness rushing back. Damn you, Lucien!

"This is his way of paying me back for helping your friends last night," she said regretfully. "This thing he has done to you was supposed to tear you all apart, but I have stopped that from happening—for now anyway. There is still work to be done there."

"Yeah, I gather," I said, now a little curiously. "What happened after I went to bed last night? I heard shouting and stuff."

"Marc got upset and ran away," she said, "and Peter and James tried to chase him. I had to make them all come back and go to sleep. Amelia wanted to see you, too, but that was after I had put you to sleep, so I made her go back to bed. I hope you do not mind."

"No, I don't," I said, thinking that it probably wouldn't have made much difference—if I hadn't finished the job with her this morning, I might have done last night. Damn it—the horniness was already coming back, only a little now, but if I kept thinking sexy thoughts…

"Thank you for telling me about this," she said to me, gazing at me, and my stomach lurched—okay, the horniness was all the way back again. "I know I would have found out soon enough from your mind, but I appreciate you not trying to hide it from me—I would not have liked that."

"I almost did," I said, my voice sounding cracked. I licked my lips in an attempt to regain full control over my ability to speak, but seeing the way her eyes followed the movement of my tongue in that moment only made me even hornier.

That would have been a great time for May to clear my mind again, but for whatever reason, she chose to lean forward and give me a hug instead. It wasn't the first time she had done that but it seemed to be different from the others in its intent, although I couldn't tell what that intent was—nothing more than an extension of her gratitude, I could only assume. I appreciated it, and I even dared to return it, but now I was trusting her to stop me if I did something inappropriate.

"Sorry," she said, not really sounding sorry, but as I couldn't see her face from here, I couldn't be sure if she really meant it or not. "Can I tell you a little secret?"

"Okay," I said, my voice sounding strange as I held onto her more tightly, wanting her so badly and yet wanting her to push me away, preferably with enough force to knock me through the wall and out into the fire escape, or whatever lay beyond this corridor.

"I know this is a bad time for you," she said. "You are already so conflicted, but you must forgive me if I make it more difficult for you. I promise I do not mean to, but I still sometimes have trouble thinking of humans as equals—it is still very strange to me."

"Okay," I gasped, very much on the edge of sanity now. What was her point anyway? If that was her secret, it wasn't really one that needed to be kept to herself.

"Normally in my world," she went on, "Honnies just do with humans what they please, with no explanation required. Our humans are raised to have no complaints, and the ones who do can have their minds changed instantly. I wanted to do this only because I appreciate what you did for me just now, even though you are struggling so badly; I am not trying to make it worse for you."

"Okay," I said for the third time, appreciating her openness as much as she seemed to appreciate me, but still wishing she would either let me go, clear my mind or let me have sex with her. Being held in limbo like this was the worst thing yet.

"That wasn't the secret," she went on, and now she sounded like she was grinning. "I said I know this is the worst time for you to hear this, perhaps, but I admit that I am curious. I have never had recreational sex with a human before."

No—that was definitely not what I wanted to hear. I swallowed, my throat parched, struggling with myself as I understood the full implications of what she was saying. She was curious because she had never had recreational sex with a human before, and normally in a situation like this, she would just take the human she wanted and do it without a thought for the human's circumstances; because of course, in her world, humans didn't have circumstances. I hoped that by telling me this, she was saying that she wouldn't take advantage of my mentally weakened state.

After taking a moment to compose myself, I croaked, "I've already cheated on my girlfriend twice; please don't make me do it again."

May didn't say anything for a few seconds, but she didn't let go of me either. At last, though, she pulled back a little so that we could look directly into each other's faces. Oh hell—how was a man supposed to resist such a beautiful woman when she looked at him with complete attention like this? What she said was, "I will not make you do anything. What I think is that using my mind to help you with this is only as temporary as—well—I do not think it is a long-term solution. I want to help you, though, so if that is what you want, I will do that, until you find a magical solution."

"Thanks," I said, my eyes moving up and down her face, bouncing from her eyes to her lips and back again. She had great lips —the tongue behind them was lethal, of course, but kissing her—and even more so letting her taste me—felt pretty awesome.

"But I have to say, I think it would be in my best interest just to have sex with you," she said, smiling at me, and my stomach fell, "because I think that is what Lucien wants me to do. If I keep using my mind, it will only make him go after Ingi more quickly—but like I said, I will not make you do something you do not want to do."

"So," I said, my voice squeaking in a way it hadn't done for more than a year, since it had been breaking, "are you saying that you're going directly against your Honnie instincts by doing something that ultimately favours me over Ingi?"

"I do not think that it would make a difference," she said, "but I suppose so."

That touched me deeply, and I reacted automatically, leaning forward slightly and hugging her again. I wanted to show her that I appreciated what she had just done, but I had no idea how, until I remembered what she had done to me a little over a week earlier, on the night when we had returned from the Honnie world. I pulled back again, not without difficulty, and before she had time to react (or perhaps she had already chosen not to), I put my lips against hers. I didn't kiss her, but I opened my mouth slightly and licked her lips, liking the feeling and giving her an opportunity to taste me if she wanted to.

It was a mistake, I knew so almost as soon as my tongue touched her skin, because that was when I lost control. I thrust myself forward, raising myself onto the bed and pushing her backwards against her pillow, and it was probably the suddenness of the action (nothing in my thoughts could have predicted it) that allowed me to do this. She could have still pushed me away then, but in the instant before I had knocked her backwards, her tongue had poked out from between her lips and touched my own—it hadn't hurt at all, so maybe it hadn't been the very tip. Perhaps it was that moment, combined with her curiosity about recreational sex, that made her choose to do it.

I had a moment to be reminded of Lena—she was similar in that she and May were both taller than me, the only girls (or women) I had been with who had been, even though their bodies weren't at all the same shape (they were both slim, but Lena was more curvy). That was the last thought I had for some time, though, as May took control in pretty much every aspect of the word. Later, I had vague memories of the sex, but as the first orgasm hit, I was swept away on a tide of pleasure unlike anything I had ever felt before. The orgasm was so much more intense—not just a concentration of ecstasy around my groin, and spreading outward in ripples, but a complete submergence of my body. It was like the pleasure equivalent of an agonator, I would later think, and it blocked out everything else. All I could feel was ecstasy, renewed again and again and the sex continued, and I had more and more orgasms.

It only ended when May had had enough. She lifted me off her as I finally returned to my senses, feeling utterly depleted. That had gone on so long that the sun had actually moved across the sky. I had no idea what time it was, but I could hear voices not too far away— Peter and James, by the sound of it, out in the corridor. I looked down at May, who continued to lie on the bed, not looking particularly tired, but very satisfied indeed. Now I understood why she hadn't pushed me away; she had wanted it too.

"Okay, I was wrong," she said, sitting up.

"What were you wrong about?" I asked flatly, exhausted and extremely ashamed—now I had cheated on Natalie three times with two different people. I wriggled backwards and settled myself down by her stretched-out feet, not wanting to touch her again—for once, even my penis had had enough.

"It was not the worst time to have sex with you," she said, and she was smiling, "it was the best time. Honnies who have done this with humans always say that it does not last long because humans can only climax once, but you gave me more than I could count. You would not have been able to do that without this curse you're under."

"Blessing in disguise?"

"Perhaps, but it was so much more satisfying than I had expected. It was even better than with another Honnie, and they are always supposed to be better."

"Do I dare ask why Honnies are so much better at sex than humans? Especially if they normally only have it for procreation?"

"Female Honnies are much more flexible than female humans," she said, "and we can do so much more with our vaginas—you would be surprised. Males get a lot larger than human males when they are aroused, and they require greater power to make them climax, which makes them last longer. Also, since I had your mind, I could make it even better for you than it would have been normally."

"And why was this better for you?" I asked, my curiosity the only thing keeping me in place, because I had some serious self-examination to do and I needed to be alone to do it.

"Because you did not need to stop after one climax—you just kept going. You gave me more fluid than I have ever had in my body before—it felt good."

That was when I remembered the condoms in my pants pocket, the condoms I hadn't had time to take out and put on. "May, I wouldn't have got you pregnant by doing that, would I?" I asked tentatively.

"No," she said firmly. "Half-breeds are created differently from what we just did. I would need to use my mouth for that."

That aroused both curiosity and horror. "Your mouth?" I croaked, picturing her cutting my penis off with her tongue. She was grinning at me, and as I watched her face, she poked her tongue out in what was probably a playful manner, but seeing how sharp it was and knowing what it was capable of doing to human flesh made me cringe.

"I really don't know how I feel about what just happened," I said, managing to hold on to my self-control for the time being. I still felt exhausted, but that certain part of my body was almost ready to go all over again, and all this sexy talk, however disturbing, wasn't helping matters. I needed to get out of here and start looking around for my dignity.

"Would you like me to clear your mind again?" she asked me.

"It might have been better for me if you'd done that from the start."

"Perhaps, but at least now you know how it feels to have sex with a Honnie."

"True," I said, thinking that I would probably regret not taking the opportunity for the rest of my life if it had been presented to me. "Yes, could you do that, please?"

She obliged, and I took the opportunity to set myself to rights and get up off the bed, feeling extraordinarily tired given that I'd had six hours of deepest sleep not long ago.

"Can you do me a favour?" I asked her. "Keep this a secret?"

"I will not tell anyone," she said, and I could see that she meant it. I sighed, knowing that if Stella entered my mind at the right time, the secret would get out anyway, but honestly, what else was there to do? What I'd done with Amelia had already done the damage; this episode probably wouldn't make much of a difference.

Chapter 16: Eating a Meat Pie

You are the worst person in the world, John. You know that? You can't use this curse Lucien put on you to justify your actions because if you only controlled yourself better, you wouldn't be putting yourself into such close proximity to girls, and therefore wouldn't have had to give in to these urges. You know the difference between right and wrong, young man, and now you have more than once taken the wrong path. Who could say what consequences would follow your deplorable actions of the last nine hours or so, both within this group and in your relationship with Natalie—not to mention wherever Stella and Lena factored into all of this. You can't even put some of the responsibility onto May and Amelia because they were only doing what they wanted; the fact that they knew you were making things worse for yourself isn't of any consequence to them.

I crept up the corridor to my bedroom, feeling like—yes, like the worst person in the world. I just couldn't get my head around my recent behaviour; why had I become so weak? Unfortunately, I thought I suspected part of the answer: Once I had cheated on Natalie the first time, it had become easier to do so again; and the more I did it, the easier it got—exactly as Lucien had predicted, in other words. What if, the next time either Amelia or May got too close to me, I just took them with no thought at all? I could only hope that they would understand that I didn't want it, and stop me before I could do something stupid—as stupid as the things I had already done.

And then there was the thing Stella had done to Lena, which I now contemplated as I stepped into my room and shut the door behind me. The time was just after seven o'clock; a whole hour had passed since I had gotten up, and although I couldn't be sure, I thought I had spent perhaps as much as two thirds of that time having sex—a thought that caused the horny feeling to come rushing back all over again, even in spite of the great shame and physical exhaustion I already felt. Even though it had been more Stella's doing than my own (far more, really), I had to take some responsibility for that too, because surely the slight merging of our personalities had tipped her into doing it. It had to be a combination, because neither of us would have done such a thing on our own.

The worst of it was, Stella's opinion of my reaction to it was a little closer than Lena's. Yes, I was a little creeped out by the way she had responded to the power surge, and I did hope that Lena wasn't traumatised by it (I would have removed her memory of the experience, if I'd had any control of it), but more than that, thinking about how it had felt to be Stella in that time was really turning me on. I probably would have really enjoyed doing what Stella had done —I would have enjoyed it with any of the girls who seemed to want me—but I would only really enjoy it if they did. That was the key difference between me and Stella, apart from the opposite genders: She had gotten off on the power, and I was turned on by the sexual nature of the experience. Conversely, Stella had no physical attraction to Lena, while Lena's discomfort did absolutely nothing for my mojo.

I needed to go and have a shower. I got up, got undressed, and wrapped the towel I had used the last couple of times around myself. I left the room, looking up and down the corridor; it was empty, but not silent. Both Peter and James had been in the showers when I had left May's room, and now they were in their own bedrooms, their doors open as they called out to each other in conversation. Marc and Amelia were presently no-shows, but I knew where they were; I had heard their voices coming from Amelia's room as I had walked past it earlier. Hopefully, they were firstly making up after the fight last night, and Amelia was secondly telling him about the curse—he was probably extremely confused about what was going on with his own body.

The bathroom wasn't empty; there were two people already in there, showering and not speaking. I put my towel down on a bench and stepped into the one remaining shower stall, my mind flicking between girls like they were sitting on a spinning merry-go-round: Natalie, Stella, Amelia, Lena, May. They were all attractive in their way, some more than others; they were all important to me, though each in a slightly different way; and I wanted to have sex with all of them. Yes, I could confirm that cheating made a person a little looser and meant that they were more likely to repeat than if they had never done at all—at least until they were directly confronted with the consequences of their actions. Natalie didn't know what had happened, and until she found out, the pattern may well continue.

Another interesting fact, I noted as I washed myself: All five of them were older than me. Lena, Stella and Amelia had all turned sixteen earlier in the year, and Natalie had caught up with them just a couple of months ago; and here I was, still a few weeks away from turning fifteen. And May—I had no idea exactly how old she was, but when I had first met her, I had estimated that she must be in her mid-thirties at least. That was a little sickening; screwing around with multiple girls close to my own age was one thing, but the whole thing seemed somehow even worse when you included May. She didn't seem to care about the obvious age difference, though, or the fact that I was probably the same age as her daughter; perhaps such things weren't as important to Honnies. Then again, plenty of humans didn't seem to care either. I wondered if there was a way of asking her without offending her…

She said that she'd used her mind to make it even better than it normally would be; that explained why it had felt the way it did, but I was still curious to know how it would have felt without. So May hadn't been entirely right; trying it once was clearly not enough, but if I could help it (and I was by no means sure that I could), I wouldn't satisfy my curiosity any further. After all, curiosity killed the cat, and in my experience, satisfaction only brought back new cats that your curiosity would want to kill.

While I had been in the shower, the two men who'd been in here with me had finished up, dried off and left the room. Someone else had come in while they'd been there; I'd heard a brief and uncomfortable greeting before that person had stepped into one of the other stalls. When I got out, he was still in there, and not wanting to have to see him or speak to him when he got out, I dried as quickly as I could and escaped to my bedroom. There, alone and naked, I dressed myself again, put my watch on, and then stopped, trying to think what came next. The question was answered by my stomach letting out a low, vicious complaint: I was pretty hungry. I had every right to be hungry after the amount of energy I had already expended this morning.

It meant that I had to go and find the others, so I opened my door and looked up the corridor. The place was silent other than the voices coming from James's room, where Peter had now joined him. I didn't know where the other three were but supposed that they would catch up with us soon enough. How much did they know about last night? They knew about Marc, of course, but had they heard what had been happening when Marc had opened Amelia's bedroom door?

"Hey," I said, entering and seeing that they were both on the bed, taking the seat beside it.

"Hey man," said Peter grinning at me. "You okay?"

Yep, they'd heard; I could tell by the dubious and slightly disapproving looks on their faces. The way they saw it, I had just thrown away everything I'd ever wanted because I wanted to have sex with someone now, and who knew what their opinion of Amelia was.

"Honestly, not really," I said heavily, deciding that there was no point trying to pretend that nothing had happened. "You guys heard what happened last night, right?"

"It woke me up," said Peter, frowning, "and I was having a very nice dream about eating a meat pie too, but I suppose I can't really blame you since you weren't the one making the racket."

"What on earth were you thinking, man?" James asked, scrutinising me. "Amelia, seriously? After all that stuff you found out yesterday—why her?"

"Yeah, I screwed up big-time," I sighed, "but it wasn't entirely my fault. I didn't have full control of myself—"

James shook his head. "We all have control of ourselves, no matter how lonely we get. I'm assuming that's what led you to that," he added.

"Partially," I hedged, "but what I meant is that both of us—me and Marc—were driven to do that by Lucien; he was trying to cause a rift in the group by using Amelia to turn us against each other. Remember yesterday when he told Stella that he'd put a spell on us to make things more interesting?"

James's face fell. "Yes," he said heavily, "and I'd started hoping that whatever it was hadn't worked, or it was bulldust. Man, that's actually pretty clever—disturbing. Poor Amelia—does she know any of this?"

"Yeah," I said, "but I'm not sure if Marc does, so that's gonna take some explaining—"

"You've seen her this morning?" James asked sharply, looking suspicious.

"I had to get my clothes, man," I shrugged, embarrassed. "I left them in her room last night."

"Fair point," said Peter, "but what about you? How do you feel —you know—with Natalie and all?"

"Horrible," I said. "Amelia said she wasn't upset about it because she understood why I did it—well, she'd thought so before—but Stella was in my mind when it was happening, and she even went and told Lena about it?ℜ—"

"She was in your mind?" James asked, still suspicious. "Is there a chance her own loneliness contributed to the mix and drove you to do something you wouldn't normally do?"

"Don't think so," I said, though in truth, I couldn't possibly know. "The curse was supposed to make me and Marc crazy horny. Anyway, she was really upset when she woke up right after I fell asleep, and she even went and slapped Lucien across the face for me, but yeah—they were both really upset, so there's a couple more people I've gone and hurt. I don't know if Natalie knows yet, but I don't see how this can be kept from her. She'll never believe I lost control—she'll probably think I was waiting for an opportunity to be unfaithful or something, even if on the surface, I didn't want to."

"True, and Lena would probably tell her too," said Peter, "at least, she would if she's still competing for you."

My stomach fell—I'd completely overlooked that possibility— that strong possibility. Stella had tried to do the right thing by not telling Natalie, but would Lena? No, probably not, especially if she thought it might make Natalie want to break up with me. Well that, I decided, was the surest way to make me fight all the harder to keep Natalie around. I would even resort to Stella before actually dating Lena if she did that; I didn't think I could stomach being in a relationship with a woman who was so devious. Then again, weren't they all to some degree?

"How horny are you now?" James asked.

"Not too bad; you guys are crushing my mojo, so cheers."

"Good. Stay in here then until the other three join us—I'm pretty sure they will. You shouldn't have to be alone with Amelia again until I've had a shot at using the Light Crystal to get rid of this thing —May either, in case it applies to her too."

That wasn't how it worked out, though. I wanted to catch Marc away from all the others before we addressed this issue as a complete group; I wanted to apologise for what I had done, namely playing around with his ex without making sure he was cool with it first— among guys who respected each other, that was a cardinal sin. When I heard people out in the corridor, I got up and looked out; Marc's bedroom door was open, indicating that he must be in there—in fact, I now thought that he'd been in the shower when I had been drying myself. Good thing we hadn't had to confront each other when we were both naked; that could have led to a massive brawl. May and Amelia had also just got out of the showers and were walking past James's bedroom; as they went by, May pushed a thought into my head, having been listening to the ones I'd been thinking before: Now was a good time to go and apologise to Marc; she would keep the others out of the way, and she would make sure that it didn't get out of hand.

I went out into the corridor and down to Marc's room where, sure enough, he was in there, seeming to have just gotten dressed and was loading his pouch and weapons of choice in his pockets.

"Hey," I said, knocking on the wall beside the door a couple of times.

He looked up, and his face tightened. "Hey."

"Listen, I wanna apologise for last night," I said, jumping straight into it; if I'd given it any thought, I wouldn't have known how to say it. "It was a mistake, I shouldn't have done it, and I want you to know, I'll do my best to make sure it doesn't happen again."

"What do you mean, you'll do your best?" he said, his eyes blazing. "You make it sound like you had no control over yourself— what a cop-out."

"I had a bit, but not enough," I said, and sighed—so Amelia hadn't told him. "Look, Lucien put a curse on both of us yesterday."

That derailed some of his anger. "What? What are you talking about?"

"He did something to us both to make us crazy horny; that's why he let Amelia and May come to us, and that's how he's gonna try to break us apart. I only found out when I slept last night. I imagine you feel about as out-of-control as I do, right?"

He swallowed, looking deflated. "A curse? Lucien did this to us? But—but that's just—just—"

"It's pretty low," I said heavily, "especially seeing as we're his brothers, but I think that's why he targeted us. Everyone else knows now, and when we meet up, James is gonna try to get rid of it with the Light Crystal."

"Oh, thank God," he said, sinking onto his bed and putting his forehead in his hand. "I thought I was going crazy. Amelia wasn't the only thing that happened yesterday; did she tell you?"

"Er—no," I said, taken aback. "Did who tell me?"

"May," he sighed, "I guess not; we did agree not to unless it became necessary, and it looks like it did."

"You had sex with May?" I asked, a little louder than I'd intended. How could May have not mentioned that? Oh—but she'd actually said that she'd never had recreational sex with a human before. Had she been lying? I felt stung and angry; the anger was because a woman I'd done it with had now done it with someone else as well, and as irrational as it was, I somehow couldn't control it.

"We didn't have sex," he said quickly, "but when we were finished with the crystal hunt yesterday, when we were coming back through the wall, I accidentally touched her—well—I sort of pressed into her arse." He coloured at that but pressed on, "She mustn't have been paying attention to my mind 'cause she didn't see it coming, and when she turned around, I sort of threw myself at her. I didn't even mean to do it, and the only reason we didn't fall in a heap of torn clothes right there on the floor at the end of that corridor—well—she used her mind to make me settle down. We were both pretty shaken, though; I'd been thinking that maybe she'd made me do it and was having me on, but this makes more sense."

"Okay," I said, recovering myself—that wasn't too bad. "We don't have to tell anyone else about that, but yeah—we really need to fix this. So are we okay?"

He hesitated before speaking. "Where are you and Amelia at now?"

"Well, we talked about it this morning," I said, "when I went to get my clothes. She doesn't blame me, even when I told her about the curse, 'cause apparently she was lonely last night too. It was only a one-time thing, though; it won't happen again. I've got a girlfriend, remember?"

He looked relieved by that. "Thank God, 'cause after last night, I'm starting to wonder…"

He trailed off, sinking into contemplation.

"Wonder about what?" I asked. "Amelia?"

"Yeah—well, me and her," he said. "I—I went to apologise to her this morning, just before actually; it went okay, but after how I reacted last night, I'm thinking that maybe I've got feelings for her all over again."

"You're not bothered by the whole not-being-the-same-person thing?"

"No, not at all. Why should I be? She seems so similar. Besides, maybe I'm falling for this new Amelia rather than the old one."

"You're not gonna fight to get Lena back?" I asked hopefully.

"No," he said quickly, looking a little suspicious. "You sure you're not trying to discourage me from going after Amelia?"

"No, I was just hoping you'd take Lena off my case."

He laughed bitterly. "I know a lost cause when I see one—or at least, when I see it through someone else's eyes. It was probably there all along; I was just too blinded by her body to notice. So—so you're saying that Amelia was okay with having sex with you last night?"

"Yeah," I replied, examining his face. "You don't look happy about that."

"No—well—I dunno," he said, agitated. "I guess it's good that it wasn't against her will, but I'd always thought of Amelia as being a little less𝕽—"

"Do not say easy," I said harshly. "That's the sort of thinking that screws up her self-esteem. Is that what bothers you? I thought I was apologising for breaking the bro code."

"The bro code?" he repeated dubiously. "What's that?"

"You know, what guys do to make sure a girl can't screw up their friendship," I said, surprised that he needed to be told—it was normally one of those things that guys automatically knew. "I know it sounds like it's probably about sex or something, but it's really about respect, and playing around with a mate's ex is one of the big no-nos. I shouldn't have done it; I'd hate if that happened to me."

"Oh yeah, that does make sense," he said, "and I guess it does bother me a bit—I didn't really think of that. But then—you didn't complain about me dating Lena—"

"That was different. She wasn't an ex, and I was happier letting her go. If Natalie finds out what I did and breaks up with me, I'd hate it if one of you guys started going out with her—I'd wanna punch someone."

"I don't like it either," Marc said, "maybe that's also why I over-reacted last night, but I guess I shouldn't blame you—if it had been Natalie who'd escaped with us instead of Amelia, and I'd gotten to her first, I probably would have done the same thing. She mightn't have, of course, but I don't wanna think about that."

That spiked my anger—not the last thing Marc had implied, but the thought that he would have done to Natalie what I had done to Amelia if our positions had been reversed. I couldn't blame him, though, remembering how desperate I'd been to have her—how I still wanted to have her—but knew that I wouldn't, because Marc was my brother, and mates didn't do that to each other. This damn curse had to go.

* * *

Breakfast that morning came specially delivered to us in our corridor, free of charge, and much more substantial than our two dollars had paid for yesterday. Exactly why they thought they were bending over backwards for us, I didn't know, but I knew who was responsible for making it happen. The six of us gathered together in James's room, despite the size, and filled up for the day on a hot meal of bacon and eggs, toast, pancakes and even sausages, and even the Honnie had no complaints about the food. We were all done eating by eight o'clock, by which time we were well and truly ready to discuss the immediate problems facing the group. For the sake of everyone's safety, Marc and I were sitting on the bed, across the room and out of reach of the two females.

"Let's not waste time talking about what happened here last night," James said, looking from one face to the next, "but rather focus on what we know. Lucien is behind what happened, and the overall intention was to cause a rift in the group, weakening our fighting spirit and making us more susceptible to his influence. We suspect that it's only you two who are affected," he said to me and Marc, "because I'm doing fine; and you, Pete?"

"I'm cool," he said, reaching out from where he sat on the splintery old chair and taking May, who was leaning against the wall beside James, by the wrist; she gave no reaction to the contact, and after several seconds, he didn't either. Letting go, he said, "Nope—nothing. Why you two, though? You're his brothers, for God's sake."

"That might be exactly why," I said dully, "and also, he probably thought that we were the two who were most likely to cave. You two wouldn't have done what we did last night, would you?"

Peter and James exchanged uncomfortable looks, both of them glancing sideways at Amelia. Finally, James said, "I can't imagine doing so myself, but then I don't know how it feels to be under that kind of curse. Anyhow, I'm going to assume that it's you two who are affected, so…"

He took the Light Crystal out of his pocket, lighting up the room in a way that reached every corner and defeated every shadow. He held it for several seconds before a relieved expression crossed his face.

"Any luck?" Peter asked.

"Yes," he said, putting it back in his pocket. "Apparently, the crystal thought that curse was bad news, and I was right to want it gone, because it did it straight away. Amelia, can you help us test it?"

"I guess," she said, looking uncomfortable. "What do I do?"

"Sit on the bed between them," James told her. "You two may need to move over a bit so she's got some room. Take her hands and hold them for ten seconds, and we'll see if anything unusual happens."

"And if it does?" Amelia asked anxiously.

James glanced at May, who nodded, then said, "She can use her mind to sort it out."

So Amelia stepped between him and Peter and sat on the bed between us. Both Marc and I took one of her hands each and held them for ten seconds. I did still want to have sex with her, particularly now that I knew how it felt, but on the plus side, there were no uncontrollable waves of lust this time. What I was feeling now was entirely in my mind, the aftermath that Lucien had hoped for. I wouldn't enjoy this, but at least I could control myself. Opposite me, Marc looked as though he were feeling the same way —physically anyway. His eyes told me that he wanted Amelia too, but in his case, I doubted that it was just physical.

"I think it's gone," I said, letting go of her hand and leaning back against the wall.

"Yep, I think so," Marc agreed.

"Problem solved," said Peter, grinning. "Now let's keep it this way; horny people, no more sex."

Marc and I both laughed, and even Amelia smiled, but James's expression was set. "Actually, Peter, that's exactly what we should all agree on, in all seriousness. All of us," he looked from those of us on the bed to Peter, and even to May, "should not hook up with anyone else in this room until we're no longer on our own—whether that's when we win or lose this fight. We have to stay completely united, and there's too much room for things to go wrong if we do stuff like that. Everyone agree?"

"Yep, I'm in," I said, and Peter and May both nodded agreeably.

"Sure," Marc said, a couple of seconds later, glancing at Amelia and not looking particularly happy about it, but I reckoned that he

Stephen Hayes

understood what James was saying. Even trying to rekindle an old relationship under these circumstances wouldn't be a good idea.

Amelia, too, nodded her agreement as she got back off the bed to resume her slightly more spacious position by the door. As James started to say something else (this time about communication), though, May pushed a thought into my head—a thought only I was supposed to know. Even though both Marc and I had meant it (at the time anyway), she, May, and Amelia too, only really meant it partially. When I mentally asked her what she meant, she told me that she'd enjoyed what we did this morning and wouldn't mind doing it again if I wanted it, even though she could see that I didn't; and Amelia, too, was quite likely to be lonely for a little while longer, and would probably spend a bit of time thinking about both me and Marc in the days ahead.

"The good thing for us is that all our minds are protected," James was saying, "and even yours, May—I doubt Lucien would be able to read it from a distance, right?"

"He cannot enter my mind," she said, "because his is smaller than mine. He would need to take me to get in, or I would need to let him in."

"Great," said James, and he was grinning. "Guys, that means we finally have a method of communication which we can use without Lucien being able to listen in. John, didn't you say last week or whenever that you can project thoughts to May?"

"Yeah?" I said nervously.

"Well, if we all do that, May, could that work?" he asked.

She considered for a moment before saying, "Maybe, but you would all need to remember to think with your minds and not open your mouths at all."

"And when we do," he went on, "could you make it so that the rest of us can all hear each other's voices in our minds as well?"

"I think so," she said, "but it might be a bit delayed."

"I don't understand," said Peter blankly. "What exactly are you trying to do, James?"

"This is what I'm trying to do," James responded after about a second, and we all jumped, because James had not opened his mouth; and yet, the words were clear in all our minds.

"Holy—" Peter began aloud, and then completed the sentence without moving his lips. "Holy crap!"

"Are you saying that we can do this without Lucien being able to listen in?" I asked excitedly, also projecting with my mind rather than my voice, but I could tell from their faces that they got the question, if not the background thought that had accompanied it: If we could get away with this, we could make the next plan without Lucien having any idea what it was.

246

"I think so," May said, placing the sound of her voice in our heads rather than thoughts alone.

"Can you guys hear me?" Amelia asked tentatively, screwing her face up as though she were trying to push out a crap.

"And me?" Marc asked, his expression concentrated on trying not to move his lips.

"Don't even move your mouth along with the word," James suggested, "in case Lucien can lip-read. It has to be entirely mental so that we can keep it from him."

"This is a great idea," Peter thought excitedly, and we all agreed. The rest of that conversation, for it was very much as though we were conversing, all happened mentally, with May using her mind to convey our thoughts to one another.

"So now that we've got this, what secret plans are we going to make?" I asked.

"Hang on, I just thought of something," Amelia thought urgently. "This might work for Lucien, but what about Stella? What if she's listening in?"

"Well, I suppose you could exclude me from the conversation," I suggested, grinning, but it was a flimsy thing—I hoped that they wouldn't, but I would totally understand if they did. I really hated that connection.

"No, we'll just deal with it," James thought. "If she's asleep, she can't do anything about it until she wakes up. It's not foolproof, but it should be good enough. Now, as for secret plans, I mentioned this one to you guys yesterday morning, and I've been following it up on the computers ever since, and I'm pretty sure Lucien doesn't know about it yet; he would probably try to stop me if he knew."

"If this is that magicologist plan again, he probably thinks it's as ridiculous as I do," thought Peter.

"I know you do," James persisted, "but hear me out. There's a lot of really complicated stuff going on with magic at the moment, stuff that we can only get around by being really clever. Moreover, as I'd feared before we took Hammerson down, it didn't take long for someone else to step up and try and do what he was doing. That isn't a magic problem—it's a human problem. The lure of power is just too strong for so many people; even the best of us have difficulty resisting it when it's put in front of us. So, I've been doing a lot of research to try to find a way to deal with it definitively, and I think I may know the only solution, but I have a great fear that even the most definitive solution may not actually solve the underlying problem."

"You can't solve the underlying problem, James," I pointed out, "not if it's human nature that's causing it—you can't change that."

"Very true," he agreed, "which is why I'm trying to find the solution which will give us the greatest possible outcome. We don't have a lot of time to make this work, because Lucien's solution to the problem is to basically remove people's desire to go after the power, but that won't stop the power going to his head once he has absolutely all of it, and so the problem remains. The best way to find the right solution is to fully understand magic, and despite what you may think, Peter, a magicologist is the best person to help us do that."

Peter shrugged. "Doesn't change the fact that no magicologist in the world has ever actually had magic."

"Maybe not," Amelia chipped in, "but my dad has consulted with a few of them over the years. He wasn't actually interested in what they studied but he was happy to help them out from time to time."

"What are you actually trying to tell us, James?" Marc asked. "Have you got in touch with a magicologist?"

"Yeah," James told us, "and I can thank you for that, Marc. The one who's based in Melbourne—well, there may be more than one—but his name was in the Chopville Daily Telegraph where you said—Derik Castle. I googled him, got hold of his details and sent him an email, telling him that I was investigating a magical solution to the current conflict and asking if we could meet to discuss some things. He sent me a reply last thing last night saying that I could meet him during his lunch break today."

"You're actually gonna do that?" Marc asked, his eyes widening. "But then what are we gonna do today?"

"Well, I'd like you to come with me," James thought, "just in case something goes wrong. Don't think it hasn't occurred to me that Castle might be under an influential charm too; just in case he is, I may need some backup."

"This really does sound like a waste of a day," Peter thought. "What does that leave us with this morning? There's not enough time between now and lunch to actually do something useful. Did he say what time his lunch break is?"

"Yeah, twelve-thirty, and we might need a bit of time to get there because I have no idea where Clayton is—that's where he works," he added when Marc, Peter and I all raised our eyebrows. "Between now and then, we can work out what our next plan regarding Lucien and the Sorcerous Crystals is."

"I do not like this idea," May thought flatly, and I thought I knew why, but since she wasn't actively changing all our minds, I didn't think she would try to stop us.

"Why not?" James asked, surprised.

"Something happened during the night," I cut in quickly, saving May the trouble. "Lucien's decided to send some people into the

Honnie world to hunt down Ingi, so that May will have a reason to leave us and go to her."

"Holy crap!" Peter said aloud, and then clapped his hands to his mouth. "Oops," he continued mentally, "I mean—holy crap!"

"But May," Marc thought, looking alarmed, "you—are you okay?"

"No," she thought at us, "but I cannot go back now; I am too far from where Ingi is in our world; I would not get to her in time. But if you cannot do something about Lucien today, I might have to go anyway. I am sorry, but I cannot let anything happen to Ingi."

"Totally makes sense," James thought, "and I'm not surprised that Lucien would pull this string too. That's why seeing Castle is so important; you guys might be surprised about what we might get out of it. This guy has a pretty big reputation in his field."

"I have a pretty good reputation in my field," Peter thought, "that of being a typical Playman smart-arse, but that doesn't make the field valid."

"Okay, fine, we'll do your idea, James," Amelia thought quickly, "but what about the rest of the day? We shouldn't just kill time here like we did last night."

"There's something I would like to do too," I thought, and if I'd spoken aloud, my voice would have been quiet and a little hesitant, but I had to stick to my guns. I'd only had this idea a minute earlier, but I knew that it was something I had to do. "You guys mightn't like this, but I really wanna go back into the Hammerheart base again— the Big Room, I mean."

"You wanna see Natalie, huh," Peter thought—it wasn't a question.

"Yeah," I thought flatly. "I found out that the reason I didn't find her yesterday is because when Stella found out we were coming, she went in there and took her and Lena out so that I couldn't see them. Also—she does need to know from me what happened last night, and why it happened."

She wasn't the only person I wanted to see, though; Lena had to be set right too. This business couldn't continue any longer without someone getting seriously hurt, and if anyone had been already, that was Lena. My attempt to set her free some months ago had been one of the most difficult conversations I'd ever had, but it had been the right thing to do, and I would probably have to do something like that again. There was something else, though, that I didn't want to acknowledge, even in my own mind, but that didn't change the fact that it was there: I still wanted to have sex with her, the fantasies that I'd had about her months earlier renewed by what Stella had done last night. Why couldn't I be satisfied with having sex with Natalie? Well, if I found her sometime today and we did have sex, maybe I would be; but unfortunately, I had a feeling that after I'd cheated three times already, it would now be easier to do so again. And what might happen if Natalie broke up with me and I ran into Lena on the way out of the Big Room? Or heaven forbid, what if Stella showed up? I wouldn't mind having sex with her either. Oh John, get a hold of yourself; you no longer have the crazy horny curse as an excuse.

"You might lose her if you do that," Marc warned. "Isn't that more or less what Lucien wants?"

"No, I'm pretty sure he wants her to find out from someone else," I thought, "so that she'll be even more upset and more likely to dump me. I'm lucky that Stella hasn't told her yet, but I dunno how much longer I'll stay lucky. Besides, I—I miss her."

"John, I can sympathise with that," James began.

"But since you've already seen your girlfriend, you reckon my business can wait since there's not a good enough reason for taking such a huge risk," I finished flatly.

James shook his head. "That would be selfish of me, but seriously, if we are gonna go down there, we do need a good reason. Marc, May, is there any part of the top floor you didn't search thoroughly enough?"

Marc shrugged. "Probably; it was a pretty big place and there were a lot of hiding places, but James, I really doubt that we can find them. Lucien was sure that we couldn't, and he would know better than us. Either he's hidden them somewhere else or he's surrounded them with magical protection."

James considered, glancing sideways. "Well, how important is it that you go down there, John?"

"It's important to me," I thought dully, "but I get what you're saying; it might have to wait."

"Well, let's assume that we speak to Castle for about an hour," Amelia thought. "That still leaves this afternoon. We need to do something with that time—preferably something that would actually be useful—but if we can't think of anything else, I don't see why a few of us can't go back into the Big𝔈—"

That was when someone knocked on the bedroom door, making all of us jump. "Mr. Thomas," a woman's voice called through the door, "we need you to come and fill out some paperwork."

Things happened very quickly after that.

James, forgetting to use his mind, said aloud, "Did she say 'Thomas'𝔈—"

May, her eyes widening in surprise as she also forgot to use her mind, hissed at the same time, "Do not open that—"

But it was too late. Amelia, who had been leaning against the door, had reacted automatically to the friendly-sounding voice on the other side. She stepped back and pulled the door open, not understanding that May suspected those on the other side were unfriendly, nor understanding that they must be unfriendly if they were speaking to James Thomas instead of Jackson Buffalo (had we told her and May about our fake names?). The door had been locked from the inside, but when Amelia turned the knob, it unlocked automatically. The moment we heard the click, it was blasted open from the other side, momentarily trapping May behind it and sending Amelia flying backwards into Peter, knocking them both onto the bed and pushing Marc against the wall behind him. James and I were the only ones able to fight as a large group of unmasked Hammerhearts began trying to push into the room.

Chapter 17: I Can't See! I've Gone Blind!

It was incredibly lucky that we were all armed, because we couldn't have been in a worse possible jam. There was no time to even attempt to count the number of Hammerhearts who had just blasted the door open, only enough to see that they couldn't possibly fit into the remaining space without all of us suffocating. That didn't stop them from trying, though, and James and I were forced to swing our bludginators at the first few to push forward. Hall was in the front, solid-outliners in both of his hands, but after a couple of bludginator swipes didn't slow him down, Peter pointed his agonator at the police commissioner and gave it two very quick clicks. He fell, yelling and screaming and thrashing, and making me very glad I wasn't on the floor where he would be kicking my shins.

Ugine Wilwog came next, stepping on and over Hall as he reached the bed, seized Amelia before she could draw any weapons and lifted her cleanly off her feet. I made to swipe at him next, but before I could move, I was distracted by the boy who would inevitably be here alongside Wilwog. Ather Hignat, his face twisted with a rage as black as the one Stella had seen the night before (and reflected upon for my benefit later), grabbed James by the arm and pulled; not expecting it, James lost his balance and toppled over, landing on the still thrashing Hall and almost knocking into the next person to push through the door—Sebastian this time.

I was now a clear shot for Hignat, and it was immediately apparent that I was his target, and I didn't need to waste time thinking of the most likely reason for that. I turned my bludginator on him, but it was no good—I had effectively brought a knife to a gunfight this time. He pointed his agonator at me, the tip already glowing with that ominous, golden light, and in the instant when I knew what was coming before it happened, I glanced sideways into the room. James was still on the floor, unable to rise as Sebastian attacked him with a bludginator, but at least he was still fighting with his own; Wilwog had ripped Amelia's top right down the front, and had now flipped her over so that her legs stuck up in the air as he tried to rip the rest of her clothes off, to what purpose I didn't dare to imagine; Marc and Peter were mostly unharmed, but even though they now had weapons at the ready (and Peter was showing no signs of letting Hall go), they couldn't get a clear shot of any Hammerhearts past Amelia, who was blocking their view. May was trying to push the door shut, still stuck behind it, but something on the other side was preventing it from closing—and worse, someone had hit her with a solid-outliner, and the whiteness would soon freeze her in place.

Then, everything disappeared into nothingness as my brain was seized by an iron hand, torn from my body and plunged into a raging inferno. The pain took me, and I probably screamed just like Hall, but I was completely unaware of it. I tried desperately to remember Hignat's face, but I could only see pain. I tried to get up, but I could only feel pain. I no longer had any arms and legs, nor the senses to control them, because they had all been replaced by blinding, all-consuming agony, and then...

The pain disappeared, and I groped blindly for anything to pull myself up. I had slid onto the floor, it seemed, where I shared it only with Hall for the most part—and Hignat, of course. Hall was taking up most of the available space as he jerked spasmodically, but his consciousness seemed on the verge of failing him. I tried to get to my feet, but Hignat kicked me, the toe of his shoe connecting with the side of my head. I went down and blindly swung my bludginator, which I was still miraculously holding, through the air, but it didn't strike anyone. Moments later, Hignat kicked me again, this time directly to the face. Nothing broke, which was also miraculous, but my God it hurt.

Once again, I tried to fight back, but the knife cut into me—Hignat's bludginator, not mine, and he didn't satisfy himself with one swipe. He stabbed and ripped and tore with his knife, not making any physical contact but still cutting my already mostly ruined clothes and making me bleed pretty much all over. I tried one last time to fight back, raising the hand still clutching my bludginator, but Hignat kicked it, sending the weapon spinning away under the bed and out of reach.

"I know I'm not supposed to kill you," I heard him snarl at me, "but accidents happen, you know. Better to ask for forgiveness than permission, in my opinion. Nobody takes what is mine, Playman—nobody!"

Then he cried out in surprise and anger as someone else attacked him (finally, I thought), and no strike was forthcoming. I heard a loud bang, sounding like someone's head (or possibly elbow) smashing into the wall beside me, followed by the sound of a falling body. I opened my eyes, trying to see, but the blood dripping down my face was obscuring my vision. A pair of hands took hold of me then and pulled me up, and May's voice said, right in front of me, "Come."

Come where, I thought? It seemed a strange thing to say, but not as strange as the thing that followed. I felt May move, still holding onto me so that I moved with her, and if I didn't know better, that directionless movement meant we were moving along the fourth dimension—it was exactly how coming back to this world from hers had felt, and how it had felt in my mind when I had accessed the time axis. I cried out, meaning to demand that we go back, that we not go through to the Honnie world, but I couldn't articulate any words.

When May set me gently down on a surface that felt exactly like the cold floor I'd been on moments ago, though somehow softer, I wiped the blood off my face, ignoring the stinging, and looked around to see where I was. The first thing I registered was that we were not in the Honnie world—we were still in the bedroom, although it was a little darker and a little cooler somehow. To my left, Hall's twitching legs were seemingly occupying the same space as May's feet. All the others were here, though like me, they were the worse for wear. Marc and Peter looked the best, a few cuts and bruises but no worse. May herself also looked unhurt, freed of thicky prison at some point—perhaps she'd had the presence of mind to do it herself. James was in worse shape, but Sebastian's attack mustn't have been executed with the same level of passion and fury as Hignat. Amelia had probably been rescued before Wilwog could do anything really terrible to her, but she was now missing most of her clothes. Only her underpants remained intact and in place, and her bra was hanging off her, still covering her when she didn't move but swinging loosely around her most of the time. Amelia and May were calm, but the three boys had gone crazy, yelling and waving their arms around.

"I can't see! I've gone blind!" Marc was yelling.

"What—I can't—what—" Peter was stammering.

"My eyes! My ears!" James was shouting.

"Calm them down!" Amelia cried out.

May did so, and the three boys suddenly relaxed, sitting there looking blank. Yes, I saw, they clearly couldn't see a thing around them.

"May, make them see and hear what I can see and hear," I managed to say through my pain, and I saw when she obliged by the looks of shock on their faces.

"Why can I see myself?" Peter asked, his voice rising and making him sound like a ten-year-old.

"Shut up a minute," I hissed at them. I was pretty sure I knew where we were, and what May had done to get us here, and now I wanted to see what happened.

"Where'd they go?" Hignat shouted, jumping to his feet and looking wildly around. It looked as though he were standing in James, neither of them feeling a thing.

Looking painfully around myself, I saw that the room was still full of people. Hall was bearly conscious now; Wilwog and Sebastian were trapped on the bed, no longer able to access the door; and two more Hammerhearts had pushed into the remaining space beside

Hignat. One of them was 3K17, the woman who had unknowingly assisted us in our attack on the school a week ago, and probably the one who had called to us through the bedroom door. Even more Hammerhearts were in the corridor, unable to get into the room, not knowing what to do with themselves, and even more confused and anxious at the sound of Hignat's shout.

"They—they disappeared," Sebastian said, goggle-eyed. "I saw it—Marc and James first, and then Peter and Amelia."

"But they don't have any magic!" Hignat snapped, staring wildly around, and then down at Hall on the floor. "Er—what should we do about‬Ꭱ—"

There was a collective gasp from the Hammerhearts outside in the hall. Silence fell in the room at the sound, and then a moment later, the source was revealed as Lucien stepped into the doorway, his expression black with fury. He took a brief moment to neutralise the spell of the agonator, which was still active on a now unconscious Hall, before waking him up and using magic to raise him into the air.

"Welcome back, commissioner," he said in a quiet voice, as chilly as an ice cube.

"Lucien," Hall said thickly, his brain slowly grounding back into action, "IᎡ—"

"I gave you the responsibility of leading this little raiding party, I believe," Lucien said, raising Hall a little higher so that he was now floating vertically in the centre of the room, his feet dangling inches above the floor. "As the most highly ranked Hammerheart here, as one in such a position of importance and responsibility, I felt quite sure that you would follow my instructions to the letter."

"Lucien," Hall gasped, his eyes wide and terrified.

"Could you please remind me what those instructions were?" Lucien persisted, and despite the amount of pain I was still feeling after the assault I'd taken from Hignat, I still had room to feel fearful of what might be about to happen all around us, even if it couldn't hurt us where we were.

Hall opened his mouth, but no sound came out. Lucien smiled unpleasantly at him, his expression becoming more and more like Arnold Hammerson than Lucien Moran with every second that passed.

"What about you, Hignat? Do you remember what my instructions were?" Lucien asked, glancing once at the younger boy before returning his gaze to my former English teacher.

Hignat scowled, but said reluctantly, "To bring the six of them in alive, to not kill any of them, and to perform the operation as quietly as possible."

"Did you bring the six of them in alive?" Lucien enquired.

"Er—no, sir," Hall said, "but—"

"Did you make any effort not to kill them?"

"They're not dead, sir—"

"Did you make any effort to perform the operation discreetly?"

"Well, no, but—"

"No," Lucien hissed, and now there was complete silence in the room and the hall outside. "I watched the whole thing from afar, just to see how you would all perform. Suffice it to say that I am not impressed with any of you. Hignat, Wilwog, both of you were clearly running your own agendas, and you, Hall, made no effort to control your soldiers. Now why was that, I wonder?"

"Sir, I only used solid-outliners myself; I only meant to capture ℜ—"

"That was not my question," Lucien said sharply. "Would you like to know what I think? I think you wanted revenge of your own after what they did to you a couple of days ago, and that is not—"

He broke off suddenly, listening hard. From where I was, I couldn't hear what he could hear, but a sound had reached the ears of all the Hammerhearts, and their expressions made it pretty obvious what it was: Someone had heard the racket and was coming to investigate.

"We'll settle this at the base, you bunch of failures," Lucien snapped, and a moment later, the whole bunch of them teleported and disappeared, leaving nothing but a pretty messed-up bedroom behind.

The moment they had left, I heard the sound of more than one person hurrying up the stairs. Only seconds later, they were in this corridor, and their concerned voices reached our ears.

"It sounded like it was coming from up here," a man's voice said.

"This is where those kids are," a woman said, and I thought I recognised her voice as the same person that had brought us our breakfast earlier.

Following that came the sound of knocking on doors, and then keys turning locks. Finally, though, someone appeared in the doorway of this room. The man took one look at the disarray, his eyes lingering on the spot where I sat (I knew he must have been seeing the blood and possibly threads of my clothing on the floor) and then called over his shoulder.

"There's blood here; I think there was a fight, but nobody's here anymore. Better call the cops."

And the man in charge of the cops was, of course, the one who had started all this. It was an ironic thought, speaking volumes about what might have been considered corruption in a more sensible time.

"Now can I know what's going on?" Peter asked.

"I think I recognise this place," James said slowly, looking around but seeing only the same thing from my point-of-view. "Isn't this where Smiley went when he was in his shadow? It feels the same."

"Yeah, it does," said Peter slowly.

"That's because it is the same thing," said Amelia, looking very self-conscious as she angled one arm across her chest, just to make sure we didn't get an unobstructed view of her. "We were hiding in here most of the time—even for the majority of the plane ride, because if we think about it, we can make it take us along. That's why we're still on the second floor here instead of falling through it to the ground."

"Although we can go through the floor if we like," May added.

"Does that mean that they won't see or hear us here?" Marc asked hopefully, and Amelia nodded.

I felt a surge of relief; this would hide us from the raiding party, and could perhaps hide us from Lucien too, so long as he didn't think of the possibility that we might do this. I tried to shift my body, but the pain flared brightly; Hignat's bludginators had done a lot of damage. Like Amelia, my clothes were pretty much hanging off me, and when I wiped blood away from my eyes, I could see that just about all of my exposed skin was criss-crossed with cuts, most of them thankfully shallow.

"But why couldn't we see or hear before?" Marc asked. "And how much longer do I have to keep looking at myself?"

"I think I know," James said thoughtfully. "John, you can see and hear just fine, can't you? And you too, May?" When we both nodded, he said, "Then that's why. We have no perception of the fourth dimension, so we can't see anything from outside our shadow. Since there is no light here, we couldn't see each other without it, and since there doesn't seem to be anything else here, we couldn't hear each other either. If not for John now, we'd be screwed."

"Is there some way you can make us see and hear things from our own perspectives instead of John's?" Marc asked the Honnie. "I know that's tricky, but it can't be harder than that box thing from last weekend."

May nodded and screwed up her face. It took some concentration, but she managed to allow the boys and Amelia to see and hear just as I could. It wasn't quite perfect, though, as we found out; because of the amount of concentration it required, there was a slight delay from the moment they spoke to the moment the rest of us heard them, and the moment we saw them move. I wasn't affected by it, but it meant that when they spoke to each other, there was a slight delay—no more than a second, usually—before the next one spoke.

"Should we move somewhere quieter?" Peter suggested.

"Let's wait a few minutes," James said as the people in the hallway outside converged, one of them already on the phone. "If they think this is a crime scene, they'll leave it alone until the police come."

A silence fell then—it wasn't a complete silence, but between the six of us, nobody quite knew what to say next. All we could do was look at each other, each of us thinking our own thoughts. I checked my watch in that time and saw that it wasn't even nine o'clock yet.

Finally, Marc broke the silence. "Do you think it will be safe for us to go back out there at all? Or are we gonna have to stay in here forever?"

"We can't stay here forever," James said reasonably. "Look, I suppose Lucien could set up some sort of magical alert to notify him when he can find us, because he's bound to wonder why he suddenly can't, but we're going to have to cop that and put up the best fight we can when the time comes. We always knew it would come down to something like that in the end."

Another silence fell, but James's expression looked calculating, as did almost all the others (May was the only one who looked bland, perhaps too busy to actually contribute thoughts of her own). I was thinking too, in my case about how we could take advantage of the position we were suddenly in. First, we needed to take stock of what we had brought with us to this point along the fourth dimension. After that, we would need to work out a plan, work out how to acquire anything else we might need for the plan, and then how to strike. I could only get that far though; the pain I was feeling was too distracting.

"Okay," James said after about a minute, "we need to work out what comes next. May, can we go anywhere like this? Without moving back into our world, I mean?"

"Yes," she said flatly.

"Okay," James went on, "and how quickly can you move from here to our world and then back again?"

That was a curious question, I thought, and May gave it some thought before saying, "Quickly enough."

Peter's eyes lit up. "So you're saying that if May did dip back into our world, it might be enough for Lucien to work out where she is, but not quickly enough to react?"

"Wouldn't that increase the risk of Lucien working out what May's really doing, though?" Marc asked. "And what would be the point of that anyway?"

"Hang on, I'll get to that," said James, his expression still calculating. "May, can you lean across dimensions?"

Another curious question, and this time, I wasn't even sure what he meant exactly, but May nodded immediately.

"Good, then there's a chance that Lucien won't detect her," said James, "and we're assuming, of course, that Lucien has the foresight to set up a spell to let him know when May becomes detectible again."

"I think it's fair to assume he would," said Marc reasonably. "I mean, once he figures out that no magic he performs can find any of us, and knowing that we don't have any of our own magic, he's going to assume that May took us back to her world. I'm not sure what he might do then, but I imagine one of his top priorities would be to know when we return, or perhaps to tell Harry and Simon to go after us instead of Ingi."

"How do you think he would perform a spell like that?" James asked, looking between Marc and Amelia; he briefly glanced at me too, but perhaps decided that I wasn't up to talking at the moment. I felt a little indignant, and tried to think of an answer to his question, but I couldn't understand what he meant by it. How would he perform the spell?

"Maybe it would be set up to detect the presence of May's mind?" Marc said. "Either that or it would look for her body, and then—I dunno how he would be alerted, but is that important?"

James shrugged and went on. "If he does set it up to look for her body, would it be triggered if it only finds part of her body?"

"It probably wouldn't," Amelia said, now looking excited. "Tracing spells don't usually trigger like that because they're not supposed to pick up dead bodies. Are you saying that if May reached through the fourth dimension without actually stepping along it, she could get around Lucien's detection?"

"Possibly," James said, grinning, "although to be safe, she would have to keep her head at this point along the fourth dimenssion, in case it is her mind that he's looking for."

"You've totally lost me, guys," Peter said vaguely.

James checked his watch; I checked mine too, but only a few minutes had passed since the last time I checked it. "Never mind, Pete," he said. "You'll get it real soon; it's just hard to picture May as a four-dimensional being because you can't see it, but it's there. I still want to see Derik Castle this afternoon, but we've still got a few hours between now and then. I figure we can use that time to stock up on materials; May can pull them in by reaching through the fourth dimension—you would do that for us, right?" he added, looking at her.

"Okay," May said, "but how are you going to talk to Derik Castle from here when he is out there?"

James opened his mouth, and then paused—clearly he hadn't thought that far ahead. I had an idea, though, and glad that my mind was starting to work again, I said, "We can drag him in here too—

briefly anyway. It would give him a whole new branch of magic to research, that's for sure."

"It might also blow his mind to the point where he becomes useless to us," said Marc, "and what if Lucien somehow uses him to work out what we're doing?"

"I don't think he would," James said seriously. "If I know Lucien like I think I do, he would come down much harder on us if he knew of my magicologist plan. That's why I wanted to make sure our communication was secure before I brought it up; as long as he doesn't know about it, he should stay complacent. If he finds out that I'm still researching magic, he's likely to feel much more threatened."

"Did you share your project with him before he went all evil on us?" Peter asked; Marc's face screwed up then, but he didn't say anything.

"A little, but he can't know that I still have it ℜ—"

"James, you've talked about the project with us before— yesterday morning, I think it was," I reminded him, "and you've spent plenty of time on the computers in that place. How can you think he wouldn't have guessed what you were trying to do?"

"Because, again, he hasn't reacted to it," said James heavily. "Yes, I know I'm making a dangerous assumption, but it may be the only way."

A silence fell then. Frowns were exchanged between James, Marc and Peter, but my mind was still ticking. What James was saying did make sense, and as had been the case all weekend, we needed to stay bold in order to keep ahead of Lucien. Derik Castle was a concern for this afternoon, however; we still had a morning to make use of, and so I concentrated my mind into that channel.

"What stuff do we have with us?" I asked the group at large. "And what stuff do we need?"

"Hang on," said Marc, putting up a hand and staring at me, "I just had another thought. All these measures have been great, but what if Stella's watching us now? Even if she's not, it's only a matter of time before she sees all of this and once she does—"

I put my own hand up, wanting to shake my head but not finding the strength. "Stop. Marc, that's not a problem—at least, I don't think it is. Look, when I went into the Honnie world to get May, I didn't connect with Stella at all. I know the connection has changed since then, but there's a chance that it won't work as long as I'm in here too."

James considered this before saying, "That's another risk we're going to have to take. If Lucien does find out about this from Stella, well, we may still have some time to react to him. All I know is that the risk of getting caught in here is no greater than it was out there, so we might as well run with it for as long as we can."

We then did an inventory and found that all we had with us was an assortment of magical weapons, five watches, a deck of cards (Peter's), a memory stick (James's), and some condoms (mine, although for the sake of sparing Amelia embarrassment, I didn't mention them). It meant that we were missing some things, including the bag of goodies that Amelia had brought with her, so before the police or anyone else could get back up to our corridor, May put James's theory to the test and reached back into our world to get the rest of our stuff. I got a good look at it as she picked up the bludginator that Hignat had kicked out of my hand; in one moment, her hand appeared to be occupying the same space as the bludginator, and in the next, the bludginator was firmly in her grasp. It looked funny from here, but I reckoned that it would look even stranger if I were watching it from out there instead of in here.

While May went to the other five rooms to pick up anything we had left behind, the rest of us started brainstorming ideas for anything else we would need. Top of that list was a first-aid kit, followed by all the food and drinks that we could carry, at which point, Peter suggested we try to locate a bag with a magically expanding interior. Those things weren't just lying around, of course, but it was worth a try. When May returned to our little circle in the shadow of James's bedroom, we were all ready to go, except for one thing.

"I—er—I'm not sure I can get very far," I said, feeling pathetic, but still in too much discomfort to care what the others thought of me.

I received a couple of incredulous looks from Marc and James, but Peter and Amelia looked more sympathetic as they looked me over.

"Well, that is one of the reasons why we want a first-aid kit," James said, and then indicated himself. "Hey, you're not the only person who needs it, John, but the rest of us are going. Maybe—er—maybe May can carry you or something?"

Peter shook his head. "I know you're trying to get more done in the same time, James, but—no offence, John—I think he might slow us down if we try to take him with us. He looks like he needs rest more than anything else."

I felt enormously grateful that Peter had understood—just lying down on the floor here for a couple of hours, or what I perceived to be the floor, would hopefully be enough for me to be ready to move on by the time we had to go and see the magicologist.

Marc, meanwhile, was considering. Finally, he said, "Yeah, you're probably right. Do you think it would look weird if May dragged one of our beds through here as well?"

"It would certainly make them ask questions," James said, smirking slightly.

"And Lucien?"

"Er—let him think what he wants to on this one. He might wonder, but I don't think it would lead him any closer to the truth of the matter."

And so May went back to my room and returned a minute later carrying my bed over her head. After some discussion, she went and set it back down in my own room, and then carried me over to it. The thought was that although I might be disturbed in here, James's room was far more likely to be swarming with cops in short order. As long as none of them came in here and had the ability to see ghosts, they wouldn't know I was here. The five of them left after that, walking eerily along in thin air in some places, and through the ground itself in others, as they attempted to correctly picture where to place their feet. I would find out for myself soon enough how difficult that was, but right now, it was time for me to sleep.

And sleep I did, eventually, after some bemused staff came back up to our corridor accompanied by the expected swarm of police officers (Hall wasn't among them, unsurprisingly) and began poking around. They spent a few minutes in my room and asked a bunch of questions, but after a few minutes, they closed my bedroom door and demand that it not be re-opened again until they were done investigating. Interestingly, after hearing our physical descriptions from the staff, the detectives reached a conclusion that was extremely close to the truth: We were Marc Moran and John Playman, and a handful of accomplices (James would love that), and we had probably been attacked either by an attempted citizen's arrest or by Lucien's private army. We had either gotten away through the fire escape or, in the case of the latter, been captured and taken in. Either way, they would find out from their superiors soon enough if it had been either of those scenarios.

While they went off to inspect the rest of the corridor, I fell into a light doze, during which I had a very vivid dream. At least now I knew that my connection with Stella really had been broken, at least temporarily, because there was no way this erotic dream, which included both May and Amelia, could have been anything but a dream. Of course, I didn't think of that until I woke up an hour or so later. My penis was as hard as a rock when I finally did, and I had a panicky moment when I wondered if the curse was still active after all, but I reasoned that it would only be natural to be excited after a dream like that.

It was nearly eleven o'clock, though, and the others would probably get back really soon, so I had to make sure I was decent when they arrived. That was easier said than done, though, because images of May and Amelia kept intruding, both from the dream and how I had seen them in real life. I had many regrets about having sex with both of them, but one of the less savoury ones was that I'd been too busy trying to satisfy the roaring physical need I felt that I hadn't gotten to enjoy their bodies the way I normally would—the way I had in the dream. Ugh—this was no good; I couldn't think like this. It was with some desperation that I turned my mind to maths, specifically the exercises that our intermediate maths teacher, Mrs. Parker, had given us earlier in the year. Thinking about that did the trick, and in a few minutes, I was comfortable again.

The other five returned at around a quarter past eleven, looking a little worn out but otherwise pleased with themselves. The first thing I saw was that they were all wearing fresh clothes—brand-new jeans and jumpers, for the most part. Whatever else they had brought back with them was concealed in the bag Marc was wearing on his back. I opened my mouth in amazement, but before I could ask if that was an extender-case, I noticed a third thing: James hadn't been nearly as hurt as I was, but now his cuts looked clean and he was moving much more freely than he had been when they had set off.

"How do you feel?" Amelia asked me, her eyes intent, and the look combined with her tone brought on my arousal all over again. Really, John? You're not cursed anymore—get your act together. I forced myself to think of Natalie, of the explanation and plea for forgiveness I owed her, and it sobered me up—sort of.

"Better," I said self-consciously. It wasn't just my crotch that made me want to stay mostly beneath the covers of my bed: My clothes had been torn almost completely apart by Hignat's bludginator earlier, and now being the only one without fresh clothes —it was hard not to feel self-conscious.

"Well, you'll feel even better in a few minutes," Peter grinned at me, and indicated the bag on Marc's back. "We've got you some new clothes too, and a decent first-aid kit; and if that weren't enough, I swiped some alcohol as well."

"We won't be drinking that stuff any time soon, though," James added with a frown.

"That bag," I finally managed to say, "is it—"

"Internally expanding," Marc confirmed, "and duplicating."

My heart lifted; so it was one of those bags. That meant that if we put some food in there, we would never run out so long as we still had the bag; nor would we run out of clothes, weapons or—or anything else we couldn't afford to lose.

"And is there food in there?" I asked.

"Yep," Peter said, and grinned even more broadly. "It's probably the most valuable thing we now have, apart from ourselves anyway."

"And it'll stay fresh, too," said Amelia proudly. "The way the magic of these things works, everything inside the bag is frozen in time, when you take something out, it will always be in the state it was when it was put in there."

"We probably would have stayed out there even longer, getting more stuff," Marc said, "but it looks like we're going to have to catch public transportation to get out to where the magicologist works, and that could take a while."

"Public transport?" I repeated nervously. I had never caught public transportation in my life; the trains and buses I had set foot on had all been hired by the school and hadn't been open for public use.

"May could get there in time if she ran," James said, "but she couldn't carry us all, so we're going to have to do it the slow way. We've got time to fix you up before we go, though."

That turned out to be Peter and James's job. I would have preferred to do it myself, but the others wouldn't hear a word of it. Marc, May and Amelia turned their backs and moved off somewhere while Peter and James firstly helped me out of my clothes, apart from my underwear (thanks for a little dignity, I thought), and then began swabbing my most recent cuts with pieces of gauze dipped in antiseptic ointment—an experience which was both embarrassing and painful. Most of the cuts were shallow, which meant they could cover them with Band-Aids (and bandages in the case of my arms), but a few of them—the ones where Hignat had really gone to town— could probably have done with stitches. That wasn't an option now, though, so the boys wrapped bandages all the way around my torso in order to keep them covered. They also took the time to clean up my head wound from two days ago, but apart from wiping it down, there wasn't much else they could do for it that wouldn't make it start bleeding all over again.

Finally, I was then helped into my new clothes, which felt fantastic on me. I felt stiff when I stood up, my movements limited by all the bandages I was wearing, but otherwise, I was in better shape than I'd been since the raid on our base. Peter and James called the other three back then, and as they turned away, I took the opportunity to snatch up my old clothes and transfer my condoms from them to my new clothes. I felt a little dishonest doing it— surely, if I needed them again, that couldn't be a good thing—but I reasoned that having them or not wouldn't make a difference if I cheated on Natalie again, and having them was better than not— especially if I could somehow get Natalie to forgive me.

"Right, are we ready to go?" Marc asked as he entered the room, walking straight through the wall from the room next door.

"Yes," said James, checking his watch, "and we had better hurry —we've got ten minutes to get to the tram stop, assuming the tram doesn't come early."

Part 3: In the Not Too Distant Past…

Chapter 18: Typhoid Marys with Crystal Chips

James said that Derik Castle's lunch break began at half past twelve and lasted forty-five minutes, which meant that we had about an hour to get to his office in Clayton if we were to get all of his time. Unfortunately, James overestimated Melbourne's public transport system, and we ended up arriving at the Commonwealth Scientific and Industrial Research Organisation almost half an hour late. The tram arrived on time and got us to a train station in a place called Malvern in a little over twenty minutes, during which time the six of us did our best to make our bodies stay on the tram despite the fact that we weren't physically attached to it. I was able to master the feat only when I thought about how Smiley had managed it when standing in his shadow—he had actually been facing backwards as he rolled along with the Sydney–Melbourne train. The train from Malvern, however, which eventually took us to Oakleigh, arrived several minutes late, and caused us to have to sprint for the bus at the other end which would take us almost the rest of the way—we almost missed it, which would have spelled the end of our appointment.

Castle had given James a rough idea of where his office was in his email, but we still had to wander around a bit before we finally found the man—and we only knew that we had found him because James, who had done his research, recognised him. The man was leaning back in his seat, looking fairly relaxed and reading a magazine of some sort—something to do with planets, judging by the front cover, but how would I know. The six of us stood together in his office, completely imperceptible to him in every way, wondering what was the best way to do this. Finally, Peter said, "Maybe one of us should just step out there and knock on his door."

We all looked at the Honnie, the only one who could step out there without assistance. She just shrugged and said, "What do you want me to say?"

James glanced from her to Marc, hesitating. "We need to bring him here, but I don't want him asking questions about this place. It'll probably blow his mind if we told him about this whole new dimension—give him too much to think about that might put him off what he already knows."

"So?" Peter said. "May can clamp down on his curiosity, right?"

"Maybe startling him isn't such a bad idea," Marc suggested. "I mean—not in the way you're thinking, James, but just to let him know that we're serious company."

"I agree," Amelia added. "These guys are scientists, and that means they pursue knowledge without much care for what that knowledge might ultimately mean."

James looked uneasy at that thought. "That's exactly the sort of behaviour we should be discouraging when it comes to magic, and that's why I really hope that Lucien doesn't think to get guys like Castle on board."

"I'm pretty sure he wants you to be his source of information, mate," I told him. "Anyway, Marc, what did you mean before?"

"Well, all May really needs to do is step out, knock on his door, and then when he opens it, he'll see her. That'll loosen just enough screws to make him realise he's dealing with something a little out of the ordinary. He doesn't need to know what she is or where she comes from, and he certainly doesn't need to know where we are now. How does that sound?"

There was a silence as we all thought it over. I wasn't sure how the others felt, but I had the feeling that the factors were piling up so high that it was becoming impossible to predict all the consequences of just about everything we did. For one thing, May would have to step all the way out of her shadow to do what Marc was suggesting, and what if that alerted Lucien? For another thing, what if Amelia was right about Castle, and he turned it around on us, learning more from us than we could learn from him? Furthermore, what if he turned that knowledge into something which could ultimately help Lucien? I could only console myself with two things: Both Lucien and Stella had been up all night, so with a bit of luck, they would be either asleep or very tired and unable to act quickly enough; and May would have Castle's mind while he was here, so hopefully she could keep him on track.

"Okay, let's do that," James said decisively. "May, you know what to do?"

"You want me to stun him with how I look?" she said, and when James nodded, she went on. "In that case, I will have to change."

"What?"

Aw man. I moaned internally but couldn't quite suppress a shudder of desire as May took hold of the bag on Marc's back, opened it and began looking through its contents. I thought I knew what she was going to do: As beautiful as May's face was, the effect of it seemed to multiply by however much of her body she showed. The clothes she was wearing now did more for her than the robes which seemed to be the only fashion statement in the Honnie world, but not as much as the tighter clothes she had worn during her time in the Young Army base. I didn't think it would really be necessary to give Derik Castle that much—the poor guy might have a heart attack and die on the spot—but there was another reason why I didn't want this to happen. For whatever reason, I was feeling almost as aroused now as I had been when I had woken up in the morning—almost as much as I had when I had been standing in Amelia's bedroom, so close that I could have…

I shut my brain down in a hurry, even though my body didn't want to listen. The curse is gone! I screamed it in my head, hoping that May would understand what I was going through and change her mind—but she ignored my mental anguish. She had located the clothes she had been looking for—a tight top and short skirt—and was already beginning to take her clothes off right in front of us. I wasn't surprised—Honnies seemed to be quite comfortable with their bodies and didn't particularly care if humans saw them—but I quickly turned away all the same. I didn't turn back until I heard Amelia say, "Okay, boys, you can look now."

"Wow," I heard Peter moan, while Marc and James also let out suppressed noises of admiration. I only dared look at May for a second, but it was enough—more than enough. I quickly closed my eyes, but it was no good—the image had been burned into my memory, and would probably return in full force the next time I slept (if it happened in here anyway). May couldn't have looked any more tempting if she had tried: A fairly short skirt and tight top, even daring to show a bit of cleavage; long legs mostly bared; perfect skin; fresh look. She had surpassed the beauty of models and entered the realm of goddesses.

"Okay," said James, clearly making an effort to get his mind back on the job at hand, and doing a much better job than I was doing. "Okay, May; that should do sufficiently. Er—what next?"

"I guess May goes out into the corridor, goes back into our world and knocks on his door," Amelia said.

"Right," James agreed, "right, and May, be as quick getting him through to here as you can. Remember, Lucien."

"Okay," she said, and she stepped around us to go through the closed door.

I felt slightly better once she had left the room. Even though it would only be temporary, I took advantage of the moment to pull myself together and look around at the others. James and Amelia were sitting themselves down on the floor, looking a little weird but perhaps less awkward than the rest of us. I followed their lead, and Marc and Peter did the same just as a knock sounded on the office door. I'd had just a moment to worry that May wouldn't be able to hold our minds once she left her shadow, but the others never seemed to lose their vision or hearing—May being a four-dimensional creature applied to her mind as well as her body, it seemed. Above us, Castle looked briefly at his watch before calling, "Come in."

He may have been prepared for a nerdy teenager, or for some super-intelligent colleague of his. There was no way in the world he was prepared for May, though, as she opened the door and half-stepped into the room to look at him. His eyes widened, his mouth fell open a little, and he dropped the magazine he was holding. It would have been funny, except that in my current state, I could only feel sympathy for the man and enormous lust for the woman who had just had that effect on him. I was very glad that I was sitting cross-legged on the floor, however insubstantial that floor was, because it made it easier to hide what was happening to my body. Not without effort, I tore my eyes away from the Honnie and looked at Marc and Peter; they were both gazing appreciatively at May, but Marc didn't seem to be feeling any of the uncontrollable lust that I was. That meant that it couldn't be the curse…so then, what was it?

"Hello, Dr. Castle," May said softly, while I was struggling with these thoughts.

"What—er—who are you?" Castle managed to stammer.

"You agreed to see my friend, James Thomas," she said, moving up to his desk and reaching out to him. "Can you come with me, please?"

"Okay," he said, with an amazing lack of curiosity, also reaching out and taking her hand. There could be no doubt that she had put the mental clamps on him already.

Whether under his own steam or hers, Castle got to his feet and stepped forward, expecting May to lead him out of the office. In the next moment, they were both in their shadow along with the rest of us, and Castle's momentum had caused him to walk right into the Honnie. That, combined with the weird feeling he would have just experienced, would have sent him spiralling to the floor if May hadn't steadied him.

"I—what?"

"Okay, now we can relax and be ourselves," James said cheerfully, and the sound of his voice made Castle spin around in shock. It looked as though May had taken his mind and was enabling it the same way she was enabling the others to see and hear each other.

For a moment, it looked like just about anything could happen. The magicologist looked ready to scream, shout and bombard us all with questions all at the same time, but once again, May clamped down on his emotions and forced him to focus on the matter at hand. Whatever she'd done to his mind, it seemed to work, for the man said blandly, "So I assume one of you is James Thomas?"

"Yeah, that's me," James said, nodding. "It's a pleasure to meet you, Dr. Castle."

"Likewise, young man," Castle smiled at him. "It's always good to know that young people are interested in science. Hmm…" he allowed his gaze to wander around the rest of the group. "Well, I didn't realise I would be keeping such interesting company. You're Amelia Woodward, of course," he said, scrutinising her.

"I know I am," she said, and then covered her mouth with her hand as though she couldn't believe she'd just said that.

"Yes, I've seen you before, although you mightn't remember," he said. "Your father and I have met a number of times over the years. I wouldn't say we're friends, but—well—we know each other. You two, I've seen in the news," he said, looking from Marc to me and then back again, "but what about you, boy?"

"Oh, I'm just John's brother," said Peter, grinning innocently at him.

"He's a lot more than that," James said, shooting Peter a reproving look.

"And—" Castle faltered, looking over his shoulder at May, who hadn't moved since stepping back into her shadow, "who is she?"

"Her name's May," James said, "and she's been an enormous help to us, but that's really all you need to know about her."

Castle opened his mouth to ask another question, of course, but whatever it had been, May wiped it from his mind just in time. He considered for a moment, then shrugged and looked back at James.

"So, about your email, James, you should know that I'm only taking time out of my busy schedule to talk to you because you seem to be so educated in matters of magic and science, and now that I know the company you're keeping, I can understand why. However, I can only give you"—he took a moment to check his watch—"ten minutes. Fifteen, at most. So whatever it is you wish to talk about, we ought to make it quick."

"Fair enough," James said, straightening up and seeming to organise his thoughts. After a few seconds of silence, he said, "Well, I would love to pick your brains on all matter of things, but since we don't have time, I guess I'll have to skip to the important stuff. You'd be aware of everything that's happened in the last week—you know, with Arnold Hammerson's demise and now Lucien taking charge—and I'm sure you've guessed that we're the anti-Hammerheart movement—all that remains of it anyway."

He paused then, watching Castle's face for a reaction. I wasn't sure what he was looking for, and apparently neither was Castle, for he said, "Yeah, that goes without saying, I think. Go on."

James shrugged, looking relieved. "I was worried that you might have had an influential charm put on you at some point, but your lack of disgust makes me think that we're okay."

He looked over Castle's shoulder at May, who nodded once. I assumed that meant that Derik Castle was safe to talk to.

"Well, I've been doing research of my own," James went on, "for a couple of months now. I've already seen a lot of magic—have even used some of it through the Light Crystal—so I have some firsthand knowledge of it. I'm also fairly well-read in rational thinking, and have done some preliminary reading of physics as well. Obviously I'm not that far along, since I am only fourteen years old, but enough to know what I'm doing. Anyway, the point of my research is to find a magical solution to the problem of the Magic Crystals and the danger they pose to the world—something that could actually end the conflict once and for all, because even before Hammerson died, I knew that it wouldn't be long before someone rose up and tried to do the same thing he did. Granted, I didn't think it would happen so quickly."

Derik Castle was nodding his understanding, or agreement, I wasn't sure. When James took a breath, he said, "I agree, but what you're describing isn't a problem with magic."

"I know. It's a problem with humanity and its desire to go after power," James said. "There'll always be someone who just can't leave well enough alone. I've had time to think about it, and unfortunately, there is some logic in the Hammersons' philosophy. It does seem like a waste to have all this power and not use it to do good in the world. Trouble is, there's even more sense in the Woodwards' philosophy; it's just too dangerous. So, Dr. Castle, based on what you know about magic, what are your thoughts on this issue?"

Castle took the question seriously. He considered for several seconds before saying, "My initial thoughts are that there is no solution to your problem, James. I know that's not what you want to hear, but like you said, the problem lies in humanity, not magic. If you try to use magic to make mankind less power-hungry, you could possibly tamper with an evolutionary safeguard which is designed to keep us alive. It would only take a few generations for our entire species to die out if that were the case."

"Assuming there's a magic in the crystals powerful enough to do that," Marc added.

James sighed. "That's what I was worried about. I guess humans will always fight over power. There have been wars and revolutions for as long as there have been societies—they even predate the Magic Crystals—so I guess we can't change that. That's why, if we can't change one factor, maybe we can change the other."

"The other?" Castle repeated, and then understood what James meant. The only reason I also understood what he meant was because he and I had had this conversation ten days ago—ten long, eventful days ago. "What are you suggesting you do? Naturally, you can regain power by reclaiming the Magic Crystals and resetting their properties, but what then? All it would take is for someone to take them back off you, and the struggle would be on again."

"Maybe you could hide them where nobody could ever find them?" Marc suggested. "Maybe you could teleport them into the earth's core or something?"

"Or into deep space," Peter added.

James was shaking his head. "Just putting them out of the way won't solve the problem. Besides, there'll still be six Typhoid Marys with crystal chips running around the place, and who knows what they could end up doing down the track."

"I had no idea you had such a high opinion of us, James," Amelia said, smirking slightly.

"How can you know that the crystals would even survive inside the earth's core or in deep space?" I asked.

"It's a moot point, kids," Castle interrupted. "Look, there is still much to be learnt about how magic works. What I and others in my field are trying to do is reconcile what we have undeniably observed of magic with what we already know about science. One thing that we are almost completely sure of, though, is that magic and the Magic Crystals are not one and the same. It seems far more likely to us that magic is a part of nature, and it can be tapped by anyone or anything at any time. The Magic Crystals are merely a line through which our minds communicate with magic in its most natural form, so that we can manipulate it within the limits of what Sien and Leoard were able to tap in their time."

We all listened to this in astonishment. Marc opened his mouth several times but kept closing it as though he kept forgetting his counterpoints. Eventually, it was James who spoke.

"I sort of agree with that. I mean, I know that magic doesn't automatically disprove what we already know about mechanics, but you make it sound like, far from being supernatural, magic is just a higher form of physics that we haven't yet reached in our understanding."

"That is the belief of many in my field, James," Castle said, and the look of surprise on James's face was priceless. "Yes, I'm serious here. So far, our scientific journey has only taken us as far as quantum mechanics, but there is no reason at all why it can't go deeper than that. Magic is quite likely the highest form of physics there is, and when you get right down to it, there may be a purely scientific explanation behind every spell that has ever been performed. Of course, that's just a theory, and we're a very long way from proving it, or even coming up with a way to test it.

"My point is that even if you were able to get rid of the Magic Crystals, or even destroy them—and I'm by no means sure that you could—that would not get rid of all magic in the world. How much of it there is, I have no idea, or if it is a form of energy that is conserved. All I know is that it would still be present, and logic suggests that if Sien and Leoard were able to tap it, someone else might be able to repeat the process down the track. Only you would have to think that if more Magic Crystals were made in the future, they would be even more powerful than today's crystals."

James considered this for several seconds, and then shrugged it off. "If that's true, then it's out of our hands. The only reason we haven't been captured yet is because we haven't wasted energy worrying about things we can't change, and I'm not going to change that now. That doesn't solve our immediate problem, though, and I don't think anyone here is content to sit back and let Lucien have his way with the world. We just can't know what the consequences of such a thing would be."

"I agree," said Castle, "but then what, James? What are you thinking of doing?"

James shook his head exasperatedly. "I don't know—I just don't know. I suppose if we can't get rid of magic altogether, then denying people access to it is the next best thing. So far as I know, there is no other source of magic in the world that can have the same effect as the crystals, so let's focus on that."

"But you just said that putting them out of the way ℜ—"

"I know I said that. Look, Dr. Castle, do you think it would be possible to neutralise the power of the Magic Crystals?"

"Neutralise them?" Castle repeated. "I don't understand what you mean."

"Well, here," said James, and he took the Light Crystal out of his pocket and showed it to the magicologist. "See, it's got magic in it, but if you're right, then it's really just accessing a form of energy that is probably all around us. If that's true, then isn't it possible to do something to it that would turn it into an ordinary old rock?"

"That's—that's the Light Crystal," Castle breathed, squinting at the small sun in James's hand.

"I know that. What I'm saying—"

"That is amazing," he sighed. "I've never seen anything like it."

"Better put it away, mate," said Peter, and James did so. Not until the light had faded did Castle's focus shift back to James.

"I—I don't know if it's possible to neutralise them," Castle said. "Like I said, we just don't know enough about them. I might be able to find out, though, if you would consent to letting me run some tests on that crystal of yours—"

"No!" James said a little too loudly, causing the magicologist to recoil slightly. "I mean, sorry, but it's too dangerous to leave it behind where Lucien might be able to come and get it. Also—don't take this the wrong way, but I think it might be dangerous if people learn too much about the Magic Crystals. The more people understand them, the more dangerous they become. You said it yourself; if this ever happens again, they'll be more powerful next time."

Castle didn't look happy about that. "I understand what you're saying, but are you also saying that it's better to live in ignorance? I mean, not understanding them any better than we do now isn't going to change what has already happened."

It was Amelia who spoke up then. "Oh, don't pretend like you're thinking about the social consequences of your research. Now I understand why my father had little patience for your field; you only care about learning. You don't care that what you're uncovering might destroy us all."

"Amelia!" both Marc and James gasped, clearly mortified.

Castle, too, looked rocked. "Hang on, Amelia; I find that grossly unfair. I care very much about the consequences."

He checked his watch then, and stood up. "I really should get back to work. I'm sorry I couldn't be more help to you, James, but if I may, I do have one suggestion for you."

"What's that?" James said eagerly.

"It is said that the Magic Crystals came from a cave close to where Sien and Leoard lived in their time. Nobody has ever conclusively located it, but since you have one of the crystals, you may have some luck. If you go there and put the crystal back where it came from, perhaps that will settle its power back into the world."

That didn't sound like much of a plan to me. In fact, it wasn't much different from what James had been talking about a week ago. He gave it due consideration, though, before saying, "Okay, but that doesn't sound very scientific to me. Even if we find the cave, we mightn't be able to do anything out of the ordinary there."

"Maybe not," said Marc, but he looked a little more excited, "but if the solution really is to put the crystals out of the way, that cave would probably be the safest place to do it. Then all we have to do is make sure no one can ever get in there and the problem should be solved."

"We would need to have all the crystals to make that work, though," Peter said, "and right now, we've only got two."

"What about the Sorcerers?" I asked.

"I have an idea about that," said James slowly. "It mightn't matter, of course—if the crystals really are neutralised, then the chips should be too—but if they're not, there might be a way to solve that problem too. We'll worry about that later, though. Our next problem is the one we were grappling with earlier: We need to get those crystals off Lucien somehow."

Castle cleared his throat. "Kids, this has been fun, but I have a lecture to give shortly, and since I have no idea where we are— where are we anyway? What is this plaaaaaa..."

His voice faded away as May gently wiped his mind clean of whatever thoughts he had been thinking. That must have been an incredibly odd feeling, to be in the middle of a sentence and then to suddenly forget what you were talking about. In that moment, James looked directly at May and communicated something with her. A moment later, his voice entered our minds.

"How much of this should we let him remember?"

"As little as possible," Marc responded mentally at once. "I don't trust him to keep it to himself. He'll be so thrilled about having met Amelia and seen the Light Crystal with his own eyes."

"Also, he might use this in his research somehow," Amelia added.

"How about, he remembers that he had a conversation over lunch with some people, but he remembers nothing about who we were?" James suggested.

That worked for the rest of us, so May spent about ten seconds organising his thoughts for him, before picking him up and dropping him back in his office as he remembered it. He staggered for a moment in surprise, but May had already retreated fully back into her shadow. Derik Castle was just standing alone in his empty office, the door still standing open somehow. He looked at this in confusion before walking to it, shutting it and checking his watch. The man looked thoroughly dumbfounded, and I wasn't surprised: I only hoped that we had done enough to keep him quiet. James was right; it would be very bad if Lucien found out what we were planning for the crystals.

"Okay, that's done," said James, visibly relaxing.

"That was a bloody waste of time," Peter muttered. "We didn't learn anything that you hadn't already worked out, James."

James shook his head. "I dunno about you guys, but I took a fair bit out of that. I just wish I could have spent more time with him. Anyway, we do need to work out what comes next, and it looks like we do need to find a way to get the crystals off Lucien."

"We've done this before," Marc said quietly. When we all looked at him in surprise, he said, "This is just like when my dad had the Sorcerous Crystals and we needed to steal them. The difference was, we knew where most of them were, and we don't know where any of them are now. It comes to the same thing, though: We need to find them and swipe them, and we need to take the magic he already has. But like when we were fighting my dad, there's no way to do that without confronting him—and Fewul, of course."

"And Stella, too," Amelia added darkly.

"And let's not forget all those Hammerhearts on his side," I said. "It may be similar, but it's so much more difficult than that was this time round."

"We need a strategy, though," said James impatiently. "Lucien's too smart to be fooled by such simple tricks—"

"Maybe not," Marc said suddenly. "I mean, I know he's not like my dad, but maybe that can work in our favour. He's probably thought of all the complicated ways that we might try to get at him, but if he has, he might have neglected something much simpler, if only we could find it."

"What about the Darkness Crystal?" Peter asked. "If we're gonna put them all back, we'll need that one too."

"Seriously, Pete, the Darkness Crystal is on Rock Haulter," James reminded him, still impatient, "and the portals don't open again until November—which is a bugger, 'cause Rock Haulter would be an awesome place to be right now. We're absolutely not waiting around for two whole months for something that only might help us with the real problem."

"If we can just find one of the Sorcerous Crystals, we can begin turning things back in our favour," I said. "Maybe we should take advantage of how we are now to look for them without Lucien knowing that we're looking? What's up with you, Pete?" I added.

My brother, who was sitting beside me, was staring straight ahead with eyes as round as saucers. He had gone completely still, his mouth slightly open, his face a little flushed. When he didn't answer after a few seconds, I gave him a nudge with my elbow.

"Oi, Earth to Peter."

He slowly raised his hand, wiped his sweaty forehead, and then looked around at May. All this time, May had been standing behind me, and as long as I kept looking at James, Marc or Peter, I didn't have to see her or Amelia. That was good, because even during the seriousness of our conversation with Castle, I'd had to work to keep my mind on the matters at hand, and not on the matters that had been at my hands earlier that morning. Now, though, I did look around at May.

"Did you get that?" Peter asked her.

"Yes," she said slowly, and in contrast to Peter, who was now beginning to look excited, she looked acutely nervous.

"Would you give it a try?" Peter asked.

May seemed to weigh the question up before saying, "Okay." Then without explanation, she turned and walked right through Derik Castle's closed office door and out into the corridor beyond so that we couldn't see her.

"What's going on, Peter?" Marc asked. "What's she doing?"

"I can't be sure yet," said Peter excitedly, "but there's a small chance that I might be a friggin' genius."

"What—"

But May was already coming back through the closed office door, only now her expression had changed completely. She looked simultaneously astonished and excited.

"It worked," she told Peter, her voice shaking slightly. "It actually worked."

Peter's face split in an enormous grin. "Awesome!"

"Can someone fill us in, please?" James said loudly. "Peter, what did you just ask May to do?"

"Well," said Peter, and he had to clear his throat to get it steady, "it occurred to me that you were right before, James. It would be awesome to be on Rock Haulter right now, wouldn't you agree?"

"Sure, but what's that got to do with—"

"It also occurred to me," Peter went on, his excitement seeming to build even more, "that the portals don't open again for a little over two months, and that's just too long to wait. So I guess we'll have to settle for doing without Rock Haulter, right?"

"Yeah, but Pete—"

"And a third thing occurred to me," Peter went on loudly, and while all these things were occurring to him, one thing occurred to me: My brother looked beautiful in that moment. If there were more girls around, I had no doubt that they would be attracted to him as he was at the moment. "Earlier on, Amelia said that what we're doing now is the same thing that Smiley was doing in those memories he showed us—the ones where he went into his shadow."

"Peter, will you please cut this out," Marc snapped at him. "Just tell us what you're talking about."

Peter turned his grin on Marc. "Think about it, Marc. Think about the three things I just said, and how they might be connected."

"Er—" Marc faltered for a moment. "Er—Smiley went to Rock Haulter in his shadow, and we couldn't follow him until the portals opened."

Peter grunted. "Seriously, you guys, we're doing the same thing that Smiley was doing in those memories—the same thing."

It clicked. In an instant, I knew exactly what Peter was referring to. I felt my mouth fall open and for a moment, I was helpless to do anything about it. Peter saw the probably thunderstruck look on my face and looked satisfied. "Well, at least someone's worked it out."

So far, I was the only one, though.

"Can you explain it to us, then?" Amelia asked, striving for patience and barely managing it.

It was my corridor paradigm all over again—the means by which I had learnt about the origins of my connection with Stella, and the reason why Arnold Hammerson had wanted me dead. That would be hard to explain to the others, though, so I settled for a simpler version.

"Guys, May can move along the fourth dimension, remember? She doesn't just step from one world to the other like we had to do—she actually moves along it, the way that Smiley did when he went into the Honnie world. You remember what happened to him as he passed between the two worlds, how it felt to be actually between them?"

It took several seconds, but when it clicked in James's mind, we all saw it. His expression became very similar to Peter's had been, but unlike Peter, he got himself under control very quickly.

"Holy crap," he said, looking at May now. "Are you saying you actually did it? You accessed the time axis?"

"Yes, I did," she confirmed. "I went back to this morning and then came back here."

That was enough for Marc and Amelia; they had finally caught up.

"So you see what this means?" Peter concluded. "It's too dangerous for us to go into the future, of course, and it might be too dangerous for us to tamper with the past in ways that will affect what we already know has happened. But it shouldn't be too dangerous for us to go back a few weeks, slip discreetly through the portals to Rock Haulter, outfit ourselves with all the magical stuff there, and then come back to this time—this very day—so that we'll be ready to fight Lucien."

We all looked excited now—even May looked like she was feeling it—but James, ever cautious, kept his head firmly in the game. "There are some complications that we need to work out first. Before we do anything, we need to make sure that May can take us along the time axis with her. It won't be any good if she has to do it all alone."

"Why wouldn't she be able to? She brought us here okay," Peter pointed out.

"Second test we need to do, if the first one works," James went on, "is to determine if we can pass through with her by holding on to her, or if she has to be holding onto us. That will determine how many trips May needs to make. And the third thing, and better we do it here rather than in the past, is work out how the hell we're gonna get to the portals at all. Remember, we don't have magic to create a vessel like we did last time, and the August portals are in the Atlantic Ocean."

"Can you remember the coordinates, James?" Amelia asked.

"I remember the ones for the Indian portal, and the Atlantic portal coordinates are the same, only with ninety subtracted from the longitude," said James. "I don't see what good that'll do us, though."

"It should be easy, actually," I said, my mind racing ahead, already thinking of what we might do once we got back to the Rock. "All we have to do is work out where the students' boat leaves from, and make sure we're on it. May can use her mind to make sure we get there without questions—there won't be any worry about her mind being detected by anyone in that time."

It was all coming together now—all of it. Sure, a fight with Lucien would be dangerous, no matter what magical advancements we came up with, but at least we were in the game now—weren't we?

"There are further problems," James went on. "Firstly, how do we find out where the students left from? Secondly, what if there are Hammerhearts on that boat? Thirdly, how do we get to them without being detected? We might be able to avoid Lucien by going back in time, but then we might run into Arnold Hammerson instead."

I opened my mouth, about to suggest that we go back a week, to the time between Hammerson and Lucien, but then closed it again. There just wasn't a big enough window of opportunity to work with there. Then, a much simpler solution occurred to me: "You could use the Light Crystal to grant us safety. It mightn't work, but it's worth a try."

"Let's take a step back, guys," Marc said loudly, in an attempt to tame the excitement. "Let's take on one problem at a time. First thing's first; who wants to be May's guinea pig?"

* * *

It was amazing how much could happen in such a short amount of time. By three o'clock that afternoon, we had worked almost everything out. May could indeed take us back in time, all at once, and could do so without even needing to enter our world even for a moment. Following those tests, we had left Castle alone in his office and made our way back towards the city, but rather than returning to the drop-in centre, which had pretty much served its purpose, we went back to the apartment of the Hammerhearts whose wardrobe hid an entrance to the all-important Hammerheart Highway. Fortunately, the couple were out again, probably at work this time.

There, we had taken a few minutes to eat a quick lunch of sandwiches and a few pieces of apple each (from the bag), while under James's instructions, May had used a laptop computer which they had stolen earlier while I'd been asleep to do a bit of Internet research. It was necessary for her to do it because the Internet wouldn't work in our shadow, and none of us wanted to step out to do the research ourselves. Unfortunately, the research proved to be fruitless; for whatever reason, there seemed to be no information available about what school used Rock Haulter in August, or how they got there. This left us at a dead-end, and the most obvious solution seemed to be to go back in time and try the research again then, but Amelia had a better idea.

"If there's one person who would know this stuff, it's my father," she said. "You guys were talking earlier about a good reason for going back into the base this afternoon? Well, I think I've just found one. I can go and ask him some questions, and he'll tell me what I need to know."

"Amelia, you do realise that Lucien would grill him on everything you talked about if he finds out—"

"Yeah, he probably would," said Amelia quickly, "but I don't think I need to tell my father why I want the information. I'm not even sure he knows about the time axis, either. Besides, if all goes well, by the time Lucien has a chance to react to the information, we'll be back and ready to take him on."

That last point was a good one. I kept returning to my feeling of being on the end of a string, and how Lucien was likely to pull that string and reel us in, sooner rather than later. The situation couldn't have been set up more perfectly for us: Both Lucien and Stella had been up for the greater part of the night, and Lucien had been up for a few hours longer. There was a chance that one or the other could still be awake, but that chance would always be there. The odds of Lucien being asleep now were as good as they would ever be. By the time he woke up, refreshed, he would probably have had enough of waiting for us, and would put another plan into action to get us to come to him. If we had just a couple of hours, it might be enough for us to be ready for him, but none of it would be possible unless we took a huge risk today. We needed that information too badly to sit back and do nothing.

"Are you absolutely sure there's no way we could get the information we need in the past?" Marc asked nervously.

"No, but I think this is probably the best way," James said. "Remember, Arnold Hammerson is in the past, and in case you've forgotten what he was like, he had spells set up to detect our presence whenever we revealed ourselves. He's got the Sien-Leoard Crystal, as Lucien does, and we can't count on May being able to hold him off."

"There's another factor, too," Peter said. "Remember, what might happen to us when we try to go through the portals to the past that has already happened. That means we won't be able to kill

Hammerson if we meet him, because he was still alive last week, but it also means that he probably won't get to us either. If he had, he would have been much more surprised and unprepared for us last week. You know what all that probably means?"

"If you think it means we can afford to be careless?ℜ—" James began.

"No, that's not what I meant," Peter said quickly. "It just means that we'll probably be okay once we get on their ship. All we need to do is find out from Amelia's dad if anything happened to it before it got to the portals; then we can be prepared for it. And if Arnold Hammerson does turn up, May can just whisk us all into our shadow where he won't be able to find us."

So after all that, we would be going back down to the Big Room this afternoon. I was pleased, because I no longer needed an excuse to do the thing that hadn't been far from my mind all day, but it was impossible not to be nervous about confronting Natalie. That wasn't all, either; Lena would be somewhere in that room too, and on the off chance that she was awake, there was a chance I might run into Stella too, and I didn't think she would hide from me this time. To top it all off, as we went to and fro over the details, I felt almost as horny as I had last night and this morning. May had changed back out of her short skirt and tight top, complaining that it had been too cold for her, but even so, I still couldn't look at either her or Amelia without remembering how good it had felt to be with them that morning. Of course, these thoughts inevitably turned me on in a big way, making me hate myself for thinking these thoughts. Yet as before, I couldn't seem to control it. Come on, John; you're not cursed anymore. There is absolutely no excuse for feeling this way. Get a hold of yourself and man up!

Chapter 19: I Guess That's a Yes

We had already accepted the fact that we would have to come out of our shadow once we were in the Big Room—it would be impossible to communicate with anyone in there if we didn't. Unfortunately, we hadn't banked on the magic around the Hammerson base preventing us from entering it in our shadow. It wasn't the being-in-our-shadow that was the problem (Smiley had been in the base in his shadow more than once) but the shrinking. All the Hammerheart bases, as well as the highway, were shrunken and had what Amelia called a 'proportionism spell' at every point of entry. These spells would shrink people who pass one way, and enlarge them passing the other way, always to the same proportions so that they would never know what had happened to them. This was where the problem lay for us: The magic didn't work on us when we were in our shadow, which meant that we would have to step out of our shadow in order to be shrunken to the right size.

After some discussion, it was decided that May, Amelia and I would enter the base, while Marc, Peter and James would remain here, safely in their shadow where Lucien couldn't get to them, so long as he didn't figure out what we were doing anyway. Amelia and I both had things we needed to do in there (Amelia's more important in terms of our survival, but I considered mine equally important for myself), and May would be there to keep our minds safe from Lucien's Honnie mind, should he happen to wake up and find us there. So after saying a quick goodbye to the boys, who had started a game of cards on the imaginary floor to distract them from worrying about us while we were gone, May took the three of us out of our shadow so that we could step through the wardrobe and into the Hammerheart Highway.

We synchronised our watches again and then Amelia got into the first cart that arrived. Before I had a chance to tell May to get in there with her, she took off, leaving me alone with the Honnie. This was definitely not what I wanted; being alone with the two girls had been bad, especially when I thought about that dream I'd had just a few hours ago, but this was somehow worse. There wasn't a lot of space here, and we still had two full minutes before we had to pull up in the base at the same time as Amelia—plenty of time for my mind to once again be consumed with thoughts too lewd to be spoken of.

Of course, standing right beside me, May was listening to all this in my head, and when our cart pulled up, she was quick to get in and slide across so that I could sit before the controls. There wasn't enough room in here for us to have sex, thankfully, but once I shut the door, the two of us were confined to a pretty small space—a rather cosy space.

"What is wrong with you?" she asked into the silence. "Why are you feeling like this again?"

I checked my watch; the seconds were ticking down, but I still had about fifty before I would need to press the big 'GO' button. After keying in the numbers for the Chopville base, keeping my eyes on the display, I said quietly, "I don't know what's wrong with me. It's so much like earlier, but the curse is gone, so there's no excuse for it."

"Your mind is moving exactly like it did this morning," she said. "Are you sure that the curse is gone?"

"Well, it seems to have worn off Marc, so why not me? Maybe— maybe I'm just imagining it. I just wish I could stop it."

"You mean a placebo?"

"Maybe, I don't know."

She surprised me then by putting a hand under my chin, turning my head to face her, and then pulling me into a hug. I was so touched at her obvious care, while at the same time, I wanted to have her right here in the Hammerheart cart, and never mind the lack of necessary space. Before I could lose control of my body, however, these thoughts were gently swept away as May cleared my mind for me and set me back in my seat to face the controls again.

It was almost time to go. I stared at my watch as the seconds ticked down, and then, on the minute, sat back in my seat and pushed the button. A moment later, there we were in the Chopville base once again. Amelia pulled up within a second of us—she was six or seven tracks away but she was there just the same. There were no people here, but there were three empty carts just sitting on the tracks. I didn't think I'd ever seen that before—normally they were always in motion when they hadn't stopped for passangers. Were there invisible people there, perhaps? That made me think of us, and I couldn't believe we had forgotten to make ourselves invisible for this excursion.

Once the three of us were together, Amelia used her invisibility toggle to remedy that issue, and then we linked arms and set off for the door. Amelia was between me and May now, and although I still felt a stirring of desire for Amelia down there, May's mind trick seemed to still be in effect.

We had no trouble getting into the Big Room today. The lift came quickly for us, nobody was in there, and when we got up to the fifth floor, we saw that the door to the Big Room was actually standing open. Even better, there were no security guards on duty today. There were some Hammerhearts standing around in the foyer, chatting casually to each other, but none looked on alert for anything.

It looked like all we would need to do was slip by them and into the room, but I mentally cautioned May (who would have passed it on to Amelia) that we should be even more careful than we would have been otherwise. It was impossible to forget what had happened to Tulip in this very room, and all because we had both been lulled into a false sense of safety. This time, however, there was no trouble at all; even the line seemed to be switched off. All the same, though, the three of us went a safe distance into the room before Amelia and I dared make ourselves visible again.

"Okay, we'll meet back at the door at"—Amelia checked her watch—"four o'clock. That gives us a little over half an hour, and that should be long enough. Is everyone clear on the plan?"

The plan, so far as it went, was for May to stand invisibly at the door and keep an eye on everyone coming in and going out, and let us both know mentally if any trouble might be heading our way. It wasn't a foolproof plan, and even less so now that the door was open and anyone could invisibly sneak through as we had just done, but it was the best she could do. While Amelia would hunt up her father and grandmother, I would go and look for Natalie and Lena, and as far as I was concerned, that was the full extent of my plan. I had no idea how the next half-hour was going to go down.

We split up, and while Amelia headed in the general direction of the place where she had found her father yesterday, I doubled back and eventually located the aisle I recognised. It was the one in which Stella had confronted Lena in the night, and it didn't take me too long to find the exact location of that little rendezvous. It wasn't what I was looking for, precisely, and it was indeed deserted now, but as I hadn't seen Natalie in here yesterday, I couldn't think where else to look.

I stopped, fighting down an urge to start running, and fighting equally hard to keep my sexual desire under control. I had to be rational here. I knew where some of my friends slept at night; Stella had woken the twins, Katie, Sophie and Rebecca from their compartments, so perhaps I could go and check those out. There was also the public sitting area from which Stella had fetched Natalie, Lena and a few others to tell them about our freedom. Either one of them could be there, or they could both be there. I swallowed, feeling a nervous lump in my throat; finding them at the same time would be disastrous. Finding them together with onlookers would be even worse.

With a sigh, I set off, thinking that I would see if Harry and Simon were anywhere near their compartments—I figured I could ask them for assistance without wanting to mount them. I passed by two aisles on my way to the turn right; the first was empty, but I almost walked into someone as I crossed the second. As we took a step back from each other, my stomach lurched—it was Natalie. The temptation to just grab her and hug her was so strong that I temporarily forgot that I was probably in big trouble with her, and if I wasn't yet, I soon would be; but as I opened my mouth, in the instant before I spoke to her, I registered the look on her face—slight surprise, and yes, some pleasure at seeing me, but nothing like what I would have expected. Then my stomach sank to somewhere around my naval as I took in her complete appearance and realised: not Natalie, but Rebecca.

"John," she said, seeming to catch up with her surprise. "I had no idea you were here. Is this—" she broke off, her face growing concerned. "Er—did you sneak in like yesterday, or were you caught?"

"Not caught," I said, trying to control my physical urges. Rebecca was almost as attractive as Natalie, and with such a similar body shape. My body wanted to take her right here and right now, but I absolutely had to control it.

"Oh," she said, her face relaxing, but not completely. Her expression seemed to have become alert, as though she had realised that I wasn't behaving normally. "So, is Peter here?"

"No," I said, trying to exhale deeply without her noticing what I was doing—it seemed to work, but only if I kept talking. "Just me and Amelia today. I'd tell you why we're here but I wouldn't want it to get around."

"Oh okay," she said, looking disappointed and taking a step back from me. Seeing it made me ashamed of myself; she was looking at me as if I might run at her if she turned her back—and unfortunately, she was right to be nervous.

"Do you know where Natalie is?" I asked her quickly, before she had a chance to slip away. "I didn't get to see her yesterday and I really miss her."

All true. I hoped Rebecca took it as innocently as my mind meant it, and not the way my body wanted it.

"Er—I'm not sure where she is now," she said, "but I know that her compartment is down there, to the left and then further down to the right, so if you wait there for her, maybe she'll come."

She had indicated the aisle that I'd been heading for, except with a turn to the left rather than the right. My spirits lifted; I dearly hoped Natalie would be in the vicinity of her compartment.

A minute from now, I would be wishing for the exact opposite.

"Okay, thanks," I said gratefully.

"Sure," she said, and then walked quickly away from me in the direction of her compartment, leaving me standing there, a little dumbstruck.

"John?" another girl's voice said from behind me; or rather, on the left of the aisle I had been crossing before I had met Rebecca, who had been on the right. I thought I recognised that voice, and both my heart and my crotch leapt up as I spun around to look. Yep, the order in which I had wanted to do this had been totally turned on its head. About four compartments further down the aisle, Lena was climbing out of what must have been hers and straightening up to look at me. Her expression was clearly more surprised than anything else, but I thought she also looked pleased. She also looked absolutely delicious, and I had to swallow before I trusted myself to speak.

"Hi. I'm glad I found you; I need to talk to you. "

That had meant to sound firm. I had tried to pour my indignation into my words so that she would know that I was unhappy with her, but both my voice and my eyes betrayed me. The croakiness in my voice made me sound nervous, even though that was one emotion I really wasn't feeling, and my eyes kept darting irresistibly up and down her body, trying and failing to stay on her face. The only saving grace was that so far, she hadn't moved from her position some thirty feet away.

"Really?" she said, looking even more excited. "Well, that's good, 'cause I want to talk to you too. I would have yesterday but Stella"ℜ—her face twisted distastefullyℜ—"did magic so that I couldn't. I didn't know you were even here until later."

"Yeah, I know," I admitted, intending not to speak a single dishonest word while I stood in this room. "I was in Stella's mind when she was thinking about it."

I glanced up each of the four aisles of the intersection in which I stood, looking and hoping that Natalie would not turn up now, and fortunately, there was no one in sight except for Lena. She had taken a few steps towards me, straight-backed and absolutely tempting me with everything about her that was female. I had to swallow again, hoping she wouldn't see it.

Lena had frowned when I'd mentioned being in Stella's mind, but since I hadn't added anything to it, she seemed to take it as an invitation to speak. "Yeah, well, I really hope you're not agreeing with everything she thinks. I dunno what's gotten into her since we got her, but she can be real mean. Maybe it's the Hammerson coming out in her."

She came closer again as she spoke, so that now there was nothing but the aisle and a single compartment between us. I measured the distance, trying desperately to hang on to my thoughts. There was something I wanted to say to Lena, but what rationality I had left was wondering just how much Lena knew about my connection with Stella. When had she found out about that anyway? I couldn't remember. I had completely lost track of who knew and who didn't know these things, and that couldn't be good.

Swallowing once again, I said, my voice really cracked now, "Try not to be too hard on her—she's not used to having any power, so maybe it's gone to her head."

Lena considered, and then shrugged this off. "Is Marc here, by any chance?"

That gave me pause. Had she changed her mind? I dearly wished Marc had come along; maybe he could have distracted her while I went looking for Natalie. But sadly: "No, he stayed behind this time."

"Oh," she said, looking—what? It looked like a mixture of emotions, but I couldn't identify them. "Well, I would have preferred to tell him myself, but since he's not here, can you pass on a message for me?"

"Okay," I said, thinking that Marc wouldn't be interested in hearing any messages from Lena anymore, but if it changed anything...

"I've made up my mind. It's over between him and me. Tell him that, and that it's not his fault, so he shouldn't try to change my mind."

Okay, maybe it was a good thing he didn't come after all. Not that it would have made a difference at this point. "Okay," I said again, thinking that she didn't need to know all this.

I really had to rally my thoughts here, but it was getting so difficult to remember what I was doing here. The most I could think to do was look away from Lena, and it worked long enough to remember my girlfriend—the one I had already cheated on; the one who I needed to find and confess to—and I couldn't afford to spend any more time standing here talking to Lena; I had to get to the point.

Before I could speak, though, Lena took the matter out of my hands with her next question. "Stella said that you had sex with Amelia last night. Is that true? I thought it was at the time but when I really thought about it, she might have made it up."

I started when she said Amelia's name. Hoping she took that for surprise rather than anything else, I discarded my earlier intention to remain honest in this room. I had to confess to Natalie, but Lena didn't need to know anything. I shook my head and said, "Course not. I dunno how she got that."

"Oh, I think I do," said Lena, and now she covered the rest of the distance between us, stopping at the end of the compartment so that we were now within arm's reach of each other. "Is it also true what she said, that you were in her mind last night?"

This time, unfortunately, I didn't react quickly enough before Lena guessed the truth. She went on: "Well, that makes sense then. She was trying to make me jealous. I think she succeeded."

I disregarded that last part; Lena was too close, and if she took that invitation to get any more suggestive…

"Sorry about all that," I said, trying not to think about it, "but look, you have to—"

"Did you enjoy it?" Lena asked, her eyes fixed on my face, so intent that I couldn't make myself look away. It was almost hypnotising. "I kind of did, although it was a little too weird for me to really get into it. But if you liked it, maybe it wasn't such a bad thing."

"Er—" I stammered, wishing I could have said anything else. Later, I would have come up with a whole host of things I could have said at that point, up to and including the fact that I'd already had sex with her once, and although that incident had been rather quick and had included almost zero foreplay (she'd only wanted me to take her virginity, so I had done the bare minimum for that purpose), I still knew what her body felt like. Unfortunately, that single syllable was all I could manage.

"I guess that's a yes," she said, smiling dazzlingly at me and leaning back against the side of the compartment behind her so that her breasts pointed perkily at me. "Well, if you were really there last night, then I guess you already know what I want to say to you."

I wanted her—I wanted her so bad. My body was screaming at me to just take her, right here, right now, and never mind who might come along. My mind screamed back at it; there was absolutely no excuse for doing the deed now. There should never be an excuse regardless, but even taking the curse into account… But Lena's last words had been like a lifeline to a drowning man. They made me remember the thing I needed to say to her—made me remember the reason why I needed to say it to her—made me remember the person for whom I would be saying this to Lena, and so…

"If this is about liking me, please don't."

Again, it was supposed to be firm. Again, it was anything but. In response, Lena raised her eyebrows. "Not even a chance? Come on, I know you want to do the right thing, but how do you know what it is if you don't at least look at other options?"

"Lena, I love Natalie—"

She held up a hand, silencing me. "What has she done for you? You say all this but you know that actions speak louder than words. What have her actions been? Sitting back for months and months and doing nothing, that's what. Whereas I've fought and fought and fought, and will keep fighting, and will not stop even if I win because that's the right thing to do, John. Look at me—I dare you to look at me and tell me I'm wrong."

She was wrong—I knew it—because Natalie's feelings were no less real just because she hadn't pursued them—right? Unfortunately, it was impossible to deny the passion of Lena's little speech. She believed what she said, and I did too, to a point. I remembered thinking, a long time ago, that if Natalie really had feelings for me, she should have done something, but I had disregarded the thought because I hadn't done anything about them myself. What if Lena was right? What if Natalie's feelings really weren't as strong as hers, or even Stella's? Furthermore, what if mine weren't as strong as I thought they were, given that I hadn't asked her out myself?

All these thoughts went through my head in an instant as I looked at Lena; it takes longer to describe them than to think them. Later, when I had time to reflect, I would identify them as the last of my rationality—the death rattle of my rationality, conceding defeat to the much stronger physical urges which could no longer be contained. Lena was so beautiful, and seeing such strong, outgoing passion just amplified her beauty to something that could have been divine. I exhaled, swaying slightly on my feet, feeling like I might collapse; I had fought as much as I could—I was done.

Lena reached out and took me by the shoulders, steadying me. She probably thought I'd had a dizzy spell for entirely unrelated reasons. For a moment, we just stared at each other; then she let go of me. She put her hands in front of my face for a moment, and then slowly, deliberately, she lowered them both in such a way that my eyes were doomed to follow them. Then she touched me, and the internal reaction I felt almost sent me to the floor anyway. Her eyes widened as she registered, for the first time, just how aroused I was, before she smiled at me.

"You were holding out all this time," she said quietly. "What's really making you resist?"

I couldn't say anything. All I could do, with a deep, shaky breath, was reach out and touch her back, and the resultant thrill I felt caused my knees to unhinge and I went down on them, taking Lena completely by surprise.

"Oh my God," she gasped, falling to her knees in front of me. "John, are you all right? What's wrong?"

I wasn't sure at what point she worked out that it was because of her, but when she did, she smiled again. "I think you need me to take care of you," she said, and she helped me to my feet.

What followed was one of the most shameful times in my life as the unspeakable and unforgivable things happened. I was so far gone by then that Lena had simply led me up the aisle to her compartment and sat me down on the side of her bed. Seconds later, she was also in, sliding the panel shut and plunging us into temporary darkness—temporary because Lena had flicked on a light switch moments later. My memories of the next few minutes are incredibly vivid given how much of my mind had been put on hiatus. They bring back shame every time I think of them, and in my darker moments, when I think back and find myself aroused by the memories, my shame is even greater.

"Wow, you must have wanted to do that for a long time," Lena gasped after it had gone on for several minutes, during which a lot had happened. It had only ended because somehow, incredibly, I had managed to put on the brakes, remembering that this was not the girl I wanted to be with. I pushed myself off her and drew back roughly to the foot of her compartment, trying desperately to regain control.

"Lena, I—this—" I gasped, and then moaned. I closed my eyes as hard as I could and gave my head a shake—I needed not to look at her for at least a few seconds to get my thoughts in order. My God, what a mess—what a terrible, horrible mess. Not only had I betrayed Natalie worse than ever, but now Lena would honestly believe she had a shot with me.

I had to get the hell out of this compartment.

"That's enough," I said, loudly and a bit more harshly than I had meant to.

"Yeah, for now," she agreed, grinning and sitting back down near her pillow, looking down at the state of herself. With her face flushed, her hair all messed up, her jacket almost completely unzipped, a couple of buttons clearly popped off the top beneath it, and her pants and underpants hitched halfway down her thighs—she looked like a woman who has just done—well—exactly what she had just done. Even now, she was tantalising to look at, so I turned my back on her and began scrambling into my clothes, which were piled up beside me, all the while thinking of what I was going to have to say to her to get out of here and trying to decide if I should tell Natalie this. I had mentally prepared myself to confess to doing it with Amelia, but even though she almost certainly wouldn't forgive me, at least I had a flimsy excuse. This time, I had no excuse—or did I?

"I need to go," I told her, not looking at her as I tried to get into my underpants—it was rather harder than it should have been, in more ways than one. "I need to find Natalie."

"Natalie?" Lena said, sounding hurt, but only for a moment. "Yeah, I guess so. That'll be a hard conversation but there's no point putting it off—in fact, I'm glad you're not. Will you come back straight after?"

"What?" I wondered for a moment what she meant, and then it hit me—my heart sank. "I'm not breaking up with her—at least, not if I can help it."

"What?" It was her turn to be confused. "Why not? You—what?"

Yeah, this was going to hurt her, I thought, but was it my fault that she'd gotten the wrong idea? Well, yeah, it was. I should have resisted her. Why hadn't I? It was the curse, I thought. What I'd just done with Lena wouldn't have been possible before the curse, which meant that it must still be upon me. How was that even possible? Had Lucien made it stronger on me than Marc, or had he reapplied it since James had used the Light Crystal? I had all of these thoughts as I was putting my pants on, bumping my head on the roof of the compartment as I did so. That was me fully dressed again, as Lena hadn't bothered to remove my shoes.

I turned to find her waiting just a few feet from me. She was just staring at me, waiting for me to clarify, and hadn't even bothered to put herself together. She looked so incredibly hot, and for a moment, I imagined that I could, in fact, break up with Natalie—who would almost certainly dump me anyway—and Lena could be mine—all mine. Perhaps I could even take her out of here with me, then it wouldn't even matter that I was cursed—I would never need to go wanting. But that would be unfair on everyone: Lena, because it wouldn't be real; Natalie, because I did still love her; and all my friends, who would be handicapped by my preoccupation.

"I still love her," I said, as evenly as I could, the effort to keep my eyes on her face taking just about everything I had. "Lucien did this to me, to make me sleep with Amelia, so that Natalie would dump me and Stella would be free to go after me—that was the whole idea. It's a curse that made me do that. It wouldn't have happened otherwise."

Lena didn't deserve this. Whatever her faults, she didn't deserve this. I saw the knife dig deeper with every word, twisting as it went. Nothing I could have said to her outside the compartment would have hurt as much as this did now. She was a good person, Lena, and maybe someday I could make things right with her, but I checked my watch and saw that I had less than ten minutes before I would need to meet up with Amelia again. This was an appropriate time to be selfish, and not just because I had no idea what Lena might do—cry seemed the most likely, but what if she tried to pull my balls off?

I turned away from her, opened the compartment and heaved myself out, noticing my injuries again for the first time in several minutes—the pain had apparently taken a hike during my time with Lena. It came rushing back now, though, and I had to work hard to get myself back on my feet. As I straightened up, I heard footsteps, and looked up to see a long, dark plait whipping out of sight as the person to whom it belong took to their heels. Someone had been standing right where I had been talking to Lena earlier, and I feared I knew exactly who it was. I knew a few people who had long, dark hair, but only three who tied it like that. But I had also seen the scrunchie at the end of it, and recognised it as belonging to...

My heart sank like a stone as I glanced back over my shoulder to see what she, Natalie, must have seen. It couldn't have been worse; not only had I just climbed out of a girl's compartment looking distinctly dishevelled, but Lena was leaning half out of it, gazing at me with an imploring expression, and she looked like she had only just finished having earth-shaking sex. Lena still looked more hurt than I had ever seen her, and I thought maybe she still wanted me to turn back, climb into her compartment again and try to work this out, but the sight of that plait had driven any other thoughts from my mind.

I set off at a sprint, turning quickly into the aisle I had seen the plait go down but finding it already deserted. I kept moving though, looking into every aisle that I passed until I recognised where I was. With a stroke of inspiration, I spun to the left and tore down the adjacent aisle until I swung around to the left again at a most familiar spot. This was where Peter and I had been standing yesterday when we had seen Hignat and Wilwog molesting Rebecca, molesting her because they had been unable to find Natalie when (or perhaps where) they had expected to. There was a girl right there, standing in profile to me with her head down and leaning against the side of the compartment—the very same one Rebecca had almost been raped in.

She looked up at the sound of my footsteps, and I had that moment I'd had twice already in the last two days. For a split second, I had thought it was Natalie, and then seen that it was really Rebecca. Only this time, it really was Natalie—I would know that face and that body anywhere, and I couldn't believe that I had ever confused Rebecca for her sister. She was even wearing the same clothes as she had been two days ago—the same clothes she'd been wearing the last time I'd had her. And in that moment, I knew that would be the last time I would ever get to be with Natalie...

...because she knew exactly what had just happened. Her face said it all as her eyes bore into me. She even took a step towards me, although there still had to be at least a dozen feet between us. She looked so fierce in that moment I almost took a step back from her, but she also looked so incredibly hot. My penis, which had settled down since I had escaped from Lena's clutches, now rose up and strained against my jeans again. Thinking she must surely see it, I said quickly, "It's not what it looks like—Lucien put a curse on me."

But Natalie hadn't even seen my crotch—her eyes were for my face only. Her voice throbbing with emotions which hadn't quite spilt forth yet, she said, "I didn't believe it when I found out. I kept telling myself that you were better than that—that you'd learned from your mistakes—but I see I was wrong. You're no different to any other guy. You're all just a bunch of cheaters who'll happily stick it anywhere."

"No, that's not—not—wait, what?" I said, backing up. Had she said what I thought she'd said?

"You heard me," she said coldly, "and to think, I was actually going to fight for you. Is that why you came here today, to do—that—with her?"

"No, I came to see you—"

"Oh really?" she said, and let loose a wild laugh that sounded disturbingly like a crazy person. She even looked a little crazy now. "What, so that you could do that with me? That's all you wanted, isn't it?"

It wasn't—of course it wasn't—but as she spoke the words, I imagined her and me together, inside the very compartment she was standing beside, and doing to her exactly what I'd just been doing to Lena. Lucien's curse would be good for plenty if I could do that with her. Of course, my penis responded typically to these thoughts—painfully typically, and this time, Natalie did see it. Even though she was completely wrong this time, my body had seemed to confirm the very opposite.

"Just get out of here," she said, waving a dismissive hand at me. "Don't come back to see me 'cause I don't wanna lay eyes on you. Just go back to Lena, or Stella, or Amelia, or anyone who'll take you."

"Amelia?" I gasped—so she did know. How had she found out about that? Stella had definitely been thinking that she wouldn't tell her, so unless it really had been Lena…

"Oh yeah, I guess you thought I'd be okay with that, huh?"

"I told you, I was cursed!" I said loudly and desperately. I was losing this, as I knew I would, but I had to try—I had to do whatever I could to keep her.

It was no good—she just laughed again. "And you won't even take responsibility for it. I guess those two must be feeling real proud of themselves, huh? Go on, get out of here; we're done."

"Natalie?" I implored, hating the sound of my own voice, and unable to do anything to change it.

She didn't speak again, just gave me a very level look, full of ball-shrivelling contempt, such that my penis actually sagged and deflated at the sight of it. Then she very deliberately turned her back on me and walked away. I called after her once but she gave no sign that she had even heard me—not even a twitch of the shoulders. She turned a corner and disappeared, leaving me standing there, feeling, what I could only assume, was the true pain of heartbreak. Anything, even physical pain, would have been preferable to the pain I felt now as I stood there, stock-still, understanding what had just happened. I had known this would probably happen, but I hadn't really understood the depth of my betrayal until I had seen it in Natalie's face.

And with that, there was no point in me being here anymore. When I was able to move, I set off, dispiritedly, through the Big Room towards the entrance, my way taking me back past Lena's compartment (the way Rebecca had originally told me how to find Natalie) and finding it shut. Nothing I did from here on would matter. I couldn't even muster up the energy to want to fight Lucien anymore—everything had been rendered meaningless by the loss of the one thing I had valued more than anything else. How could I ever recover from this?

Chapter 20: That Usually Results in Someone Falling Down

There was no sign of Amelia when I reached the area where we had agreed to meet up. Strangely, there was no hint of May's presence either; she would still be invisible, but surely she would let me know mentally where she was? Come to think of it, why hadn't May done anything to help me out with Lena or Natalie? Certainly when I had been in Lena's compartment, I could have used her mind-clearing technique not to screw my entire life up. Had she just not been paying attention, or had something happened to her? If it was the former, then that was pretty slack on her part, but if it was the latter, that would be so much worse. I found myself hoping it was just because she didn't feel it was her business to interfere—it wasn't like I had asked for her help, after all.

"John," a voice said, disturbingly close to me, and I jumped and spun to my right. Oh, hell no—as if things weren't bad enough. It was Stella, standing beside a door which I could have sworn hadn't existed the last time I had been here. Inside was, other than the bathrooms, the only actual room contained within the Big Room, and it seemed to be some sort of office—at least, I could see a desk and a chair in there. Had Stella created that? Had Lucien? For what purpose? Did it matter? And above all, why was I even thinking about it when Stella was standing right in front of me, May was missing in action, Amelia might come back at any moment, Natalie had just dumped me, and I'd just had mind-blowing sex with Lena?

"Please, Stella, not now—"

"I watched everything that just happened," she said quietly. "Please, come in here a minute."

I sighed. "Do I have a choice?"

"Yeah, but I really wish you would—it could be your only chance."

My only chance to what? Oh, right—my only chance to talk to her before my mind is altered by Lucien's magic. As if he hadn't done enough. I sighed again and walked straight past her into the office, and it wasn't until she had stepped in after me that I realised what she had just said. I felt furious for a moment, but then it fizzled out. Why would Stella step in and stop me ruining my life when the end result could benefit her? She hadn't been happy about standing back and letting me play around with other girls, but Lucien had talked her into believing that it might be okay. She had no reason to help me with either Natalie or Lena, and certainly not Amelia.

But what did she want with me now?

"I'm sorry," she said sincerely, and I was taken aback.

"For what?"

"For everything. This isn't how I wanted things to go. I mean"ℜ—she considered for a momentℜ—"I'm not sure how I wanted them to go, but I never wanted it to hurt like this. Here, stand still a moment."

"Why—"

But I knew why a moment later when first she used her magic to raise my top and pull down my pants, then vanished my various bandages and Band-Aids. A moment later, I felt—and saw—all my injuries healing and disappearing. A few seconds later, they were gone. She settled my clothes back in place, and I was relieved for more reasons than one—at least this wouldn't be a sexual thing. And of course, the moment that thought occurred to me, I imagined taking Stella right here on the floor of this office. I was strongly aroused for a second, and then my mind flashed back to what had happened just minutes earlier: Natalie, staring daggers at me, and then turning her back on me and walking away. It had the same effect as a bucket of cold water.

"Thanks, I guess," I said a bit awkwardly. I hadn't asked for that, but I did appreciate it. I just didn't want her to think that she still had a shot with me—not now, but if she was offering her magic, it seemed a good time to take advantage. "While you're at it, I don't suppose you could get rid of this damn curse as well?"

Her face fell. "So that's why it happened, huh? I was there when James got rid of it but I suppose Lucien must have put it back. I guess I could try to remove it, but even if I succeeded, Lucien would probably just put it back again. It really would be simpler if you just joined with us, John; then you wouldn't have to worry about any of this."

"Stella, I'm not joining Lucien—"

"At least think about it," she persisted. "It really would be easier —for everyone—"

"Haven't you ever heard the saying that sometimes you have to choose between what is right and what is easy?"

"Because they're not always the same thing, yeah," she said, "but this time, they really are the same thing, John. What can you possibly accomplish by trying to overthrow Lucien? Even if you succeed, then what? Our idea of using a Honnie to put the world back to normal was totally flawed because the world was already falling to pieces; this is our best chance to save it—to actually save it."

"How can you defend him when you know he put an influential charm on you?" I retorted.

She considered this question seriously, which I was glad to see, but then she let me down by saying, "Why not? Ideas are just ideas. I wouldn't have considered before but that's only because I didn't have them. You wouldn't complain if he did it to you either. Besides, what Lucien's doing makes sense—it's certainly better than what my family was doing."

I shook my head and checked my watch—surely Amelia would be out there by now. "I have to go—I'm supposed to meet Amelia."

"Wait, John, just one more minute," she said quickly, putting an arm out between me and the closed door—as if she needed physicality to stop me from leaving, I thought sourly. "I just need to tell you something. I know I already told you how much our connection means to me—"

"Please don't go there again, " I moaned.

"Let me finish, please," she persisted. "Look, I know you don't like it, and I think—if that's really what you need to be comfortable with me, well—I could probably learn to live without it. We would only need Lucien to create another one of those things and use it properly, which I'm sure he would do for us."

I was touched by this, but not enough. "That's nice, but if I can't have Natalie, I don't want anyone, so you might as well keep it."

"But—but surely you don't mean that," she said, and she was probably right. Right now, I couldn't even imagine actually falling for another girl, but that wouldn't last forever. Even in my current state, I knew Stella was right about that.

I shook my head. "I really need to go."

"What do I have to do to convince you how serious I am?" she asked—almost begged, it felt like.

I considered this, thinking that there wasn't actually anything she could do—I already knew exactly how she felt, so what difference would any of her actions make compared to what I had already felt in her mind? They wouldn't, but I had an idea for something to try all the same. "Come with me," I challenged her. "Walk away from Lucien and come with us."

She hadn't expected me to say that. She hesitated for a couple of seconds, and it was long enough for two things to happen in my mind: Firstly, surprise and triumph, because I thought that maybe she really would come with us. Not only could she be useful, but I may actually have someone to support me in spite of the terrible things I had done today, and the fact that I most certainly didn't deserve it. Who could say that it wouldn't be enough to win me over, given time? I couldn't rule it out, but it took less than a second for this fantasy to come crashing down around me; if she cared for me as much as she said she did, she wouldn't have hesitated at all. Her loyalty to Lucien, even if she didn't share his feelings for him, was just too strong. I could never trust her to put me first.

"John, I—that wouldn't—"

I shook my head. "Never mind, you just gave me your answer. Get out of the way, Stella; I have places to be."

She just stood there for a few seconds, long enough for me to think that this meeting could be about to go one of two ways: Either she would give up for now and stand aside, or she would actively stop me from leaving—perhaps even take me to Lucien to have me magically influenced. But what actually happened took me completely by surprise: she burst into tears. I had no sense of it coming and could only stand flabbergasted as she covered her face with her hands, doubled over and then sank to her knees. A wave of guilt crashed over me—it had been bad enough doing this to Natalie and Lena, but I couldn't just leave here without trying to console her.

"Please don't do that," I said, going to her and crouching down beside her. "Come on, don't cry. You must know I do care about you —I just can't go there with you, not while my heart's not—"

I made myself gently pull her hands away from her face and then give her a tentative hug, feeling another wave of arousal building again at the physical contact with a girl, but at least it was at a manageable level. As she threw her arms around me in what felt like a drowning person's grip, I felt more than just her body against me— I felt her emotions as well. It was rejection all over again: She had been rejected all her life, and then she goes and puts everything on the line for the one person who might actually take her as she was, but no—rejection again. I didn't need anyone to tell me that our connection had just manifested itself in a new and unusual way, but it made me feel closer to Stella than I ever had before, because I still had my own thoughts with which to understand her feelings.

In the end, it wasn't just the physical contact which aroused me, but the emotional contact. Stella felt it, physically or emotionally or maybe both, and even though she knew about the curse, seemed to take it as the opposite of rejection. She should have known better, especially since she had already seen what had happened to Lena, but later, I could only assume that she hadn't been thinking clearly. I certainly hadn't been thinking clearly as she had pulled back enough to look at me and I had seen the tears in her eyes, and she had seen the naked desire on my face—desire that, in that moment, was for her. The fact that magic had brought it on either didn't matter or had been forgotten.

I made a brief effort to derail what I knew was about to happen —I tried to think of Natalie, but somehow I couldn't remember what she had looked like in that fateful moment. I thought of Lena, but that had the opposite effect. Finally, I thought of Stella as I had always thought of her—a sweet and misunderstood-by-many person, almost like a sister to me—and reached up to tenderly wipe the tears from her face. But my hand nudged one of her breasts on the way up, and pure male instinct took control of me from that point forth. And so my earlier fantasy of taking Stella right here on the office floor came true after all. She gasped in pain, confirming that it was indeed her first time, and later, amidst all my terrible guilt for a wide array of things, I wished I had been more gentle with her. As it was, I had been totally single-minded and had probably ruined the experience for her. I actually found out later on (after an influential charm had been performed, shall we say) that she had actually used magic to not feel the pain.

After a while, which was probably only several minutes, she'd had enough; she pushed me off of her, and that loosened the grip of my animal lust. The guilt crashed in over me, and as I looked down at her, I couldn't believe what I'd done. A similar expression was on her face; now she was coming to realise that she had made a mistake, that it had been the curse all along and not a true, authentic desire for her and her alone, and that her first time hadn't been the perfect fantasy she had no doubt imagined it would be. I got to my feet, not knowing what to do with myself. Stella just sat on the floor, looking up at me with hope in her eyes—hope that I would stay with her, that I wouldn't turn my back on her, that I too would disregard the curse and give her what she really wanted.

And of course, that meant siding with Lucien—giving in to his magic—sacrificing my freedom in exchange for happy ignorance and bliss. It sounded silly, but it wasn't. I had to fight on, and if Stella wouldn't come with me, I would have to go alone. She couldn't read my mind, of course, not like she could read the minds of those who weren't protected, but she seemed to know my struggle all the same —perhaps sensing it as I had sensed her emotions earlier. Tears fell from her eyes and slid down her face again, and she made no effort to cover them up. There seemed to be no bottom to my guilt, I thought, as I watched her, warring with myself.

"I wish it wasn't like this," I said quietly, "I'm so sorry."

And I left the office, looking back over my shoulder only once. Stella just sat there, watching me, tears on her face, and that was it. I shut the door behind her, telling myself that Stella would want some privacy now while she fixed herself up, but really, I just didn't want to have to look at her like that anymore. I then turned and looked around; Amelia was standing a short distance away with her back to me, bouncing on the balls of her feet in a body language pose I understood all too well. As I took a step towards her, she heard the noise and turned to see me.

"Oh, thank goodness," she said, checking her watch and then looking at me. "You were seven minutes—John, what's wrong?"

I swallowed. "It—it doesn't matter. She knew about us already. I knew it wouldn't be good but—but she just wouldn't listen."

She didn't need to know what else had happened this afternoon. "Oh John," she said sadly, and took a step forward to hug me.

I put my hands up defensively. "Better not, Amelia—I think Lucien's put the curse back on me. I—I feel like crap and I don't know what I'll do if𝔒𝔱—"

She listened to this for a moment, but apparently decided that I needed the comfort more than I needed to beat myself up. She hugged me, and I couldn't stop it from happening; my pelvis thrust forward so that my crotch pressed into her stomach, and I actually humped her like a dog—or rather, like Marc had humped May the previous day. And speaking of May: The humping ended after a few seconds when I felt something clear the sexual urges from my mind. I had never been so relieved to have someone else inside my brain.

"Where are you, May?" I asked while giving Amelia the most apologetic look I could muster. She looked taken aback and a little ruffled, but not seriously offended.

"Here," I heard the Honnie's voice say from just behind Amelia —she was still invisible. I opened my mouth to ask her, a little angrily, why she hadn't helped me, but before I could speak, she mentally provided the answer: Something had happened to distract her, something that had looked like flashing lights but which she now suspected to be magical. I didn't have to wonder what had caused that: Stella had wanted her distracted, perhaps just so that she could get into the Big Room undetected, but perhaps also so that May couldn't stop me from ruining all the good things in my life.

"Okay," I said, "let's go."

"Don't you wanna know what I found out?" Amelia asked worriedly.

"Not now, Amelia; I just wanna get out of here."

And so we did, the three of us leaving the Big Room quickly and completely forgetting to make ourselves invisible. There were still Hammerhearts out there, and as we made for the lifts, I heard one of them say quietly to another, "I thought he said they wouldn't wanna leave. Should we stop them?"

"Nah," someone else responded, "he said not to attack them. I reckon they'll be back."

I couldn't believe that they hadn't recognised Amelia, but then she did have her back to them. The moment we were in the lift and the doors were closed, I took out my invisibility toggle and made sure that we wouldn't have that problem again while leaving the base.

* * *

Less than ten minutes later, we had gone through the Hammerheart Highway and rejoined Marc, Peter and James, all of us now safely hidden away in our shadow. They had been playing cards on the floor (the imaginary floor, given that it required the three of them to imagine it was there in order for it to actually exist), and Peter was the only one who hadn't become bored yet. They hadn't noticed that we'd taken longer than expected, but they did notice that my Band-Aids were gone and I seemed to have been healed of my injuries, something neither May nor Amelia had picked up on.

"What else happened to you in there?" Amelia asked, a little suspiciously but seeing that I was still hurt—perhaps she was now realising that the only way I could be this downcast was if it had been considerably worse than just being dumped.

I sighed—there was no other way. "Stella caught up with me at the end there and she did it for me. No, she didn't do any other magic on me," I said quickly, seeing the looks on their faces. "She did try to get me to join with her and Lucien but she didn't force it."

"How'd you get her not to?" James asked. "She would have to have an extremely high opinion of you not to take the matter out of your hands."

"Well, I had to—well—kinda break her heart, I guess."

And her hymen, I thought but didn't say.

"Sorry, man," said Peter, patting me on the shoulder, "but she was kinda asking for it—she knows how you feel about Natalie."

He paused for a moment, assessing my face, then said, "It didn't go well with her either?"

I shook my head. "She already knew about what happened last night. Stella didn't tell her, but Lena probably did. You were right about her, Pete."

I couldn't take the scrutiny anymore—they were all looking at me with expressions that were somehow sympathetic and critical at the same time. Only May's expression was neutral, no doubt because she could feel my internal struggle. I decided I didn't need to take this anymore; I turned away from them and walked through the nearest wall. A moment later, I was standing in the bathroom in which I had almost fainted two days earlier. I sat down on the floor, buried my face in my hands, and wished that I could cry; but for whatever reason, no tears were forthcoming. Was it just because I was a guy that I couldn't cry, or was I so down that I had descended beyond the point at which crying was possible? I didn't know, and it probably didn't even matter, but it would have been a relief to get some of this emotion out.

The voices of the others were a little muffled, but not as muffled as they would have been if the walls had actually existed in this dimension. I heard James checking with the Light Crystal and confirming that yes, the curse had been put on me again; and since he had felt it work the first time he tried to remove it, he thought

Stephen Hayes

Lucien must have been watching us at the time and decided that he hadn't finished messing with us yet. He suggested they all go around the group (excluding May, because she didn't want a bar to do with the crystal) and try to remove it again, starting with Amelia. When she asked why, he said that after what we had shared, she ought to be the most compassionate. She started to say something, and then seemed to think better of it. Silence fell over the group, but I knew when the magic worked because I felt a subtle yet powerful darkness lift from my heart—and my body. The silence continued as the others attempted to use the crystal, but it sounded as though Amelia's attempt had been the only one to work—the only one that had needed to work.

While this had been happening though, May's attention had been with me, and after Amelia had passed the crystal to Peter, a thought pushed its way into my mind. She recognised that I was still depressed, and that I would continue to be depressed long afterwards, and she was offering to help me by removing the memories of what had happened in the Big Room. I started—I knew that was a big thing for a Honnie to do. May had only done it once, back in her own world after the traumatic events that had enabled her to gain the required permission to come into our world. I had to take the offer seriously, and what the potential consequences would be.

It was not an option for me, and it didn't take me long to figure that out. If I didn't know what had already happened, I would be no better off than I had been before going into the Big Room—I would still feel bad for what I'd done with Amelia (and May herself), and I would want to confess to Natalie and try to make things right. Her heart would already be broken, and she would have to break mine all over again, so I wouldn't actually be escaping from anything. As for Stella, I would find out all over again the moment I re-entered her mind—assuming that would ever happen again, given that our connection didn't exist across dimenssions. May had once removed a memory of mine—a memory of me killing a bunch of Hammerhearts—and she'd had to restore it because when people started talking about it, I had no idea what was going on. That would happen again if she did it now, and that ruled out forgetting about Lena and Amelia as well.

I felt her push her understanding into my mind, and then withdraw, for which I was relieved, though not feeling any happier about things. Once upon a time, I had thought about using the Sien-Leoard Crystal to cheat myself out of depression, and I had rejected the idea because I felt that I deserved it—that I had to deal with it the normal way. I had to do that now—it was the only way I could possibly learn from this experience. No happier but at least resolved,

304

I rejoined the group just as James was putting the Light Crystal back in his pocket.

"Feel any better?" Peter asked.

"Not cursed anymore, yeah," I agreed, not wanting to answer truthfully—no one liked a whiner. Still, I felt that they had a right to know what was getting me down. I considered, then decided that May should fill Peter and James in on the truth of what had happened in the Big Room, but not Marc and Amelia—not now anyway. I only had the idea, but didn't bother to project it to her—either she would get it or she wouldn't. If she didn't, I could send it to her later.

"Good, then let's get down to business," said Marc, clapping his hands, and I was glad for the distraction. "Amelia, how did it go with your dad?"

"Well, I didn't get everything I wanted to know, but I think I got enough," she said. "He told me that a high school in Brazil currently has the rights to use the Atlantic portal, and that they leave from a port in their own country, but he couldn't remember exactly where it was or on what date their ship left. He only knew that the portal opened on the tenth of August, at the same time in the afternoon as the other portals did in local time."

"Brazil," said James—it wasn't a question, but Amelia nodded anyway. "Well, that's okay, but Brazil's a pretty big country. Did he at least know what part of the country the school was in?"

"Oh yeah, a place called Recife, but I don't know where that is."

"That's okay," James said, looking gleeful. "This is going to work out okay. All we have to do is use the Hammerheart Highway to get to Recife—I'm sure there'll be a base or Hammerheart's house in the area—then May can use her mind to find someone from the school and find out when and where they're leaving from."

Marc's face lit up. "James, that could work out well. So we can really go back in time and do this?"

"Wait, hold on," said Peter, "what about Arnold Hammerson? We can't go out there because he'll detect us and that'll be the end of it."

"And should we use the Highway in this time or in the past?" I added.

James held up his hands. "Everyone settle down—we can figure this all out, but one thing at a time. Amelia, did he say anything else?"

"Yes, he did," she said heavily. "He told me that the Brazilians didn't cooperate with the Hammerhearts like the South Africans did, so we won't have to worry about there being any on the ship with us, but It—"

"Awesome," said Marc, punching the air.

"—But the ship was attacked by Hammerhearts about fifty kilometres from the portal," Amelia finished the sentence, and that crushed Marc's spirits.

"Damn it," James muttered. "What could he tell you about that?"

"It's interesting," she mused. "He said that the aim of the attack was to force the Brazilians to take twenty-five of their Hammerhearts through the portal with them. Apparently, the charms my family put on the portal to prevent the Hammersons using it for their own ends prevent them coming through on their own, but not if they come through as part of the registered school. But the thing is, even though they were attacked, none of the Hammerhearts got through the portal; they all returned and told their bosses that they were thwarted, but with no memory of how it happened. Arnold Hammerson was mad and assumed that we—the Woodwards, I mean—must have been there to prevent them doing just that, but Dad says he never had anyone on the ship—only a guard around the portal itself. I tried to ask more questions but that was when he got suspicious of me; I had to tell him that I was just curious, but I'm not sure he bought it. I just hope he doesn't go running to Lucien to tell him; Lucien's no fool and he'll probably figure out what we're doing."

"Okay," said James carefully, and I could see his mind ticking over. "That probably means that we were involved, and that May made them forget whatever it was that we did. That's good—it really means we can do this, but we have to be careful not to screw up the past in ways that will affect the present. I'm not worried about it working because if it had, we would already know; I'm more worried about us getting hurt or even killed in the attempt.

"So here's what I'm thinking, and you all feel free to ask questions, but only after I'm done. We use the Hammerheart Highway in this time, and as soon as possible in case Lucien wakes up before we have a chance to get out at the other end. If there's a base in Recife, we go there, and if there isn't, we agree on another place in the city. If there's nothing in Recife, we'll come back here and figure something else out. Then when we get there, May takes us back to a few days before the tenth like I said before, but she only needs to go out of her shadow—the rest of us don't need to follow. Hammerson doesn't know about her so he can't possibly be on the lookout for her. Also remember, although he had technology to detect untraceable people, it wasn't advanced enough to pick up anyone anywhere on the planet, or he would have found us in our base, so there's a chance we'll be safe when we're on the Brazilians' ship. If not, well, we have our own weapons, and we have May—we should be okay.

"So, any questions?" he concluded, looking around at us all.

That seemed to answer everyone's questions, and everyone looked excited, but for me, a new hope had arisen. Time travel—I had done some horrible things in the very recent past—things I would do just about anything to take back. Could this be a way to undo the damage I had done? I wished it so, but if James was right— and he usually was—then it would be impossible. It was the past, I had to remind myself. My future, perhaps, but still the past, and if I had changed it, I would have seen myself change it—and even if I hadn't, I would know it had changed because none of it would have happened, and I wouldn't be sitting here right now thinking these thoughts. Yes, James was right—it would be impossible to interfere with the past, even what had only happened in the last couple of hours.

"So…when should we go?" Peter asked into the silence.

"How about"—James checked his watch—"right now?"

* * *

The six of us crowded into the Hammerheart Highway, but it was considerably less of a crowd when you could stand in the middle of the tracks without any danger of being poleaxed by an oncoming cart. We only stepped out of our shadow long enough to make sure we were shrunk to the right size, making me feel that maybe we had been better off just staying this size all along. We had waited a few minutes to see if Lucien had detected us; then when nothing happened, May did her reaching-through-the-fourth-dimension thing again to first call a cart, and then use its control panel to check for locations in Recife, Brazil—taking instructions from me, as she had no idea how to use the controls until I told her. It took a little while because we had no idea what state the city was in, but eventually we found what we were looking for.

Our contingency plans hadn't been necessary; there was a base in Recife, along with close to a hundred residences. This sounded like a large number to me but as I would find out later, it was relatively tiny for the size of the city. Peter then suggested a little experiment where we might be able to use the carts without needing to leave our shadow; surely it would work if we just concentrated on the cart, as we had done on Melbourne's public transport just hours earlier. James scuttled the idea by pointing out that if it only partially worked—if the person lost concentration in response to the rapid velocity, for example—they could be stranded at some random point on the planet with no idea where they were or how to find the rest of us.

So we did it the more dangerous way—or as James consoled us, the dangerous but considerably less dangerous way. Quickly as possible, we went in twos: May and James first, then me and Peter, and Marc and Amelia bringing up the rear. We were all in such a rush, worried that Lucien could teleport to us at any moment—or Stella, for that matter—that we had completely forgotten to make ourselves invisible. Fortunately, the station in the Recife Base—which was smaller even than the Chopville base—was deserted. It was still familiar, though, and once we had all arrived, we hurried up the steps to the bridge across the tracks and to the end furthest from the entrance into the building. I had a moment to worry that the guest entrance wouldn't be here—or that it would somehow be blocked from the inside—but no such bad luck. Probably for the sake of the Hammerhearts and not us, the templates for these bases seemed to be the same, and we were able to get out without any trouble.

It was night-time in a strange park in Recife, and it was warm. I was no stranger to heat—even in the middle of night in the height of summer, Chopville could be pretty warm—but what did catch me off-guard was the humidity. I should have expected that it would be a tropical climate (wasn't the Amazon rainforest around here somewhere?) but it still took me by surprise. I immediately felt myself break out in a sweat, but there was no time to worry about it. James had already instructed May to take us back into our shadow, and she was obliging. A moment later, we were all there, where it already felt a little more pleasant.

"Okay, we're here," James said, rather unnecessarily. "Now May, when you went back in time earlier, did you notice yourself in the time axis?"

"Yes," she said.

"Did you get in your own way in the time axis?" he asked.

"Yes," she said.

"How did you deal with that?" he asked.

"I went around myself," she said.

"Do you think you could spiral yourself back?" he asked.

"Yes," she said, after consideration—perhaps reading James's mind to see exactly what he meant.

"What the hell are you guys talking about?" Peter asked.

"Kinda hard to explain, Pete," said James. "Er—well, you know how it's not possible for a person to walk through another person if they're in the same dimension?"

"Yeah, I know," said Peter. "That usually results in someone falling down."

"Yeah, well, the time axis is the same," said James. "If May stands in the one spot and goes back in time—well, she won't be able to, because the moment she goes back, even a split second, she would bump into herself in that split second because she is taking up the same space."

"Oh," said Peter, and although it was costing him more brainpower than usual, I saw that he got it, and so did I. My stomach fell—how hadn't we thought of that earlier? By that logic, it would only be possible to go forward, not backwards. Then I thought about it some more and realised that forward would be just as impossible—in fact, even less possible, because it would create a time paradox of people in every time going forward falling down.

"But it can work if May moves along the fourth dimension at the same time as the time axis," James went on, "because if she moves further than her own body width in one direction, she won't bump into herself going the other way."

"But then she would have to step out of her shadow," said Amelia, "or worse, go into another world along the way."

"Not if she keeps moving back and forth," said James. "That's what I mean by spiralling—it's not much different from moving in a circle, except the two dimensions being used are outside our normal field of vision. She can do the whole thing without ever needing to leave her shadow, and she can take us with her. It just means that the spiral will have to be a bit wider to fit an extra person. Er—" he faltered. "Do you think you can spiral with all of us, May?"

"I can try, but it might take a while," she said.

"Okay," he said. "It won't matter how long it takes—remember, once we get there, it'll be the time we get there, no matter how long it takes to do the travel. So, today is the thirtieth of August—what date do you think we should go back to?"

We all gave it some thought, and it was I who came up with the seventh. We didn't know how long it would take them to get to the portal, but if we were a little late, there would be someone somewhere in the city who would know that we had missed them, and then we could just go back a little further.

"Terrific," said James. "One last thing before we leave then: Where should we hide ourselves?"

"What do you mean?" Amelia asked.

He shrugged. "If we're standing out in the open in the past, we're gonna see ourselves out there. They won't see us, but it's still a little weird."

"Can't May just filter us out so that we don't notice?" Marc asked, looking at her.

She shrugged. "You are making me work very hard here."

"She's right," said James. "She's doing plenty for us already—certainly more than she has to. It'll be easy enough just to get out of sight. So, where should we hide?"

Chapter 21: Tapping Morse Code on Each Other's Fingers

I think it would be fair to say that after travelling more than a dozen time zones around the world, and then travelling backwards through time, the process of time travelling taking an indeterminable amount of time itself, we had lost track of exactly what time our body clocks should be assigned to. James would have a simple yet clever solution to this problem, but before we got to that point, there was the time travelling itself. We didn't have to do anything exactly—at least, Amelia and Peter, who May was holding on to, didn't have to do anything—all the rest of us had to do was keep hanging onto her. If any of us let go, even for a moment, we could be left behind at some point along the fourth dimension, at some point in the month of August 2010, with absolutely no way to get back.

But even though May was doing the grunt work, it was certainly an experience for us—at least, for the first couple of minutes, during which time we had probably travelled back no more than a couple of hours. Being in our shadow was rather like looking at everything through a dark haze, I thought, so long as we were, along the fourth dimension, facing the direction of our world. Since we were only three-dimensional beings, with no control over which way we faced, it only appeared as a haze, rather than being a slight way inside a cave as it had appeared to Smiley, and no doubt appeared to May too. As May moved through the fourth dimension, this haze repeatedly faded to black and then to almost blackness—the closest May could apparently get to our world and still access the time axis.

When the others complained that it was too scary for them, May cut off their sensory perception so that they were once again deaf and blind, but still able to hold onto her. That meant that only May and I were aware of the time actually going backwards. When I could see nothing, I could hear nothing, but when I could see a little, I could hear a little too, and it was very like it had been while travelling backwards along the corridor of time in my mind back on Rock Haulter the last time I had been there—the time I had seen Arnold Hammerson's first failed attempt to kill me. Once upon a distant time (actually, only six months ago), I had thought seeing ghosts was all I was good for, but this was so much more than that.

Time passed, both forward and backwards at the same time (a strange paradox, but definitely a true one), and all we could do was wait patiently for May to get to the right point in time for us to do our business. In my case, I was able to see the backwards progress of the park around us, and from time to time, hear people talking in a strange language—another thing it had in common with the time on

Rock Haulter. Eventually, though, May said to me, "We are in the night-time of the day you said. Should I go back to the morning?"

I thought about this, wishing I didn't have to be the one to make this decision but knowing that it was easier than waking James up just to ask him. Surely, it would take the Brazilians no more than three days to get to the portal, so if it took them a while to get to their port. "Yeah, better go back to the morning, just in case."

"Okay," she said, and so we continued backwards, watching the day get a little lighter and then, eventually, darker again. It was time.

May moved further into the light, stopping when we were back in the part of our shadow now so familiar to us. It was still dark here —night-time dark, rather than no-world dark, but the moon was brighter tonight than it had been twenty-three days in the future. May let out a great sigh, looking very tired now, and let go of Peter and Amelia. She then concentrated and was able to bring the other four back to her own simulated form of awareness.

"Is this it?" Peter asked.

"Yeah," I told them. "This is the morning of the seventh of August. Now what?"

"Early morning, by the look of it," said James, looking around himself. "Good, that's good. Now May, when you found us in Melbourne, how much of the city were you able to take in your mind?"

"All of it," she said, and I was impressed.

"Then you can do the same here," said James. "It'll take a while, but you need to find someone—anyone—who knows anything about the camp, and you gotta do it in a way that they won't notice your presence in your mind—not that they'll know what it is, but why take any chances. If you find someone, find out whatever they know about it, most particularly when and where the ship to Rock Haulter will be leaving from."

"I will see what I can do," she said blandly. "May I let your minds go while I do this? It will be easier for me."

"That means we'll be senseless again?" Marc said nervously.

"We just spent however-long like that," said James, unperturbed. "The five of us can hold hands and communicate with each other by tapping Morse Code on each other's fingers if it'll make you feel better."

"Ha, ha, ha," Marc said drily. "Fine, let's link up."

We did so, although it made little difference to me as I could see and hear them just fine. I took hold of Peter's hand and watched as May moved out of her shadow and into the relative (relative because there wasn't much of it out there either) light. All I had to do was watch nothing happening all around us. Given the moonlight, I could see all their forms quite clearly, and I could even make out their faces (all except James, who was furthest from me). Peter was probably the furthest from calm; he kept blinking, as though hoping to restore vision that had no chance of coming back to him, and I gave his hand a quick squeeze to hopefully let him know that it was okay.

On Peter's other side, Amelia looked fairly relaxed, confident that May would return to us and we wouldn't be destined to spend the rest of our lives in a dimension where all our senses other than touch and taste were completely deprived. Also, I saw that she and Marc were holding hands, and whether to calm himself or because he was just opportunistic, he kept stroking the back of her hand with his thumb, and I could see that he was smiling slightly. Amelia didn't respond at first, but I could see that she was smiling a little too, and slowly beginning to feel more comfortable with it. She knew it was Marc, of course, and that made me feel a little jealous—and then quickly ashamed, followed by depressed all over again. This was going to be hard to deal with.

As for May, she was too busy to pay us any attention, even though she was standing within arm's reach of all of us—or at least she would have been, if our arms wouldn't have gone right through her if we'd tried to touch her. She looked fairly concentrated, but not as though she needed to plumb the absolute depths of her mental abilities to do this job. I thought that she probably could have handled our minds after all, but perhaps it was better this way—or at least quicker. As for exactly how much she could do, this had to be child's play compared to the way we had practised for our assault on Chopville High; on that day, May had created an entire virtual world for us to participate in, based on what we remembered of our surroundings, complete with enemies and even bad weather. She had a big mind, of course, but I thought her ability to create such detail was probably based more on her extraordinary memory rather than the number of minds she could contain.

I lost track of time as she worked but eventually, I saw her face relax. A moment later, she moved back into her shadow and rejoined us. A few more seconds later, I saw the others return to awareness. I immediately let go of Peter's hand, feeling relieved; he was my brother, but it still felt a little weird.

"Any luck?" James asked, stifling a yawn.

"Yes," she said. "We must go to a place called Santos; they will leave there at ten o'clock tomorrow morning—not on this morning. They will travel to the port today and stay overnight near it."

James's face lit up, and for now, all vestiges of weariness left him. "May, that's fantastic! Well done! How did you find out?"

"I found a parent of one of the people going," she said, "and traced the school and found its headmaster to be sure. They were both sleeping but I made them dream about it. I am sure of what I found."

"I reckon so," James said, and he looked around at us. "So, this is gonna be risky, but if they need a whole day to get there, then it's probably too far for us to get there any way other than the Hammerheart Highway. Were they thinking about how they were getting there?"

"Yes," May said, "plane and bus."

"Definitely too far then," Marc said, and sighed. "That means we have to leave our shadow after all, and that means Hammerson might turn up. You remember him, don't you May?"

"Yes," she said, "but I could not take his mind in my own; I could only distract him."

"I have an idea," said James. "May, would you use the Light Crystal to wish for our safety?"

"No," she said flatly.

James sighed. "Then can you take me out of my shadow just long enough to do it? I know it's not a foolproof plan, but it's better than nothing."

"Be careful, J-sandwich," said Peter earnestly.

"Don't worry about me, Pete," James said as he took May's hand and she led him into the night.

There was a time when I thought there was nothing to worry about, but that didn't last long. James put his hand in his pocket, froze in what seemed to be horror, and then on some signal to May, was quickly led back into his shadow.

"What—"

"It's gone," he told us, his expression horrified and—something else I couldn't quite put my finger on. "Damn it, I don't think it came back through time with us. Maybe the crystals can't travel in time or something."

Marc quickly reached into his own pocket and withdrew the box containing the Villain Crystal. His expression mimicked James's. "Yep, it's gone. Feels lighter. How could we not have thought of—"

A Hammerheart teleported into the park just a few feet from where James was standing. Amelia screamed, and Marc and Peter both swore and jumped back, forgetting for a moment that he couldn't see them. And no, he couldn't see us, I saw; his eyes darted around in some confusion, and then frustration as he seemed to assume that the Young Army member had teleported away. I felt cold as I realised who it was: Police Comissioner Hall, back in the days when he had the Villain Crystal, and he was still in Arnold Hammerson's back pocket.

He stood there for a few seconds, considering, and then comprehension seemed to dawn on his face. He tapped his watch and said, "Sir, I have strong evidence that the teenagers are going to Rock Haulter again. May I teleport to you to explain?"

"Crap," James hissed, looking stricken.

"Should I hurt him?" May asked, smiling at Hall in a way that chilled me to the bone.

"No, don't," James said quickly, "we can't let him see you. He needs to be taken by surprise when you turn up in the school."

"Okay," Hall responded to a communication we hadn't seen or heard. "One of them appeared for a moment just outside the guest entrance of the base in the city of the school that is going there in a few days."

There was another silence, in which Marc decided to ask, "How did he figure so much out?"

"He's not an idiot," Peter reminded him. "Mad, sure, but not stupid."

"But—" Hall spluttered, taking us all by surprise. "Yes, I know they didn't do this in South—yes, of course, but—but—doesn't that seem like a risk?"

Silence fell again, and this time it was James who filled it. "This is going to make using the Hammerheart Highway a bitch now. We're gonna have to be ready to fight all the way to the port."

"Perhaps I should take part then," Hall offered, and whatever response he got made him smile. "Thank you, sir. Do you want me to do anything while I'm here?"

Apparently the answer was no, because a few seconds later, he teleported away. The moment he had disappeared, James leapt into action. "We gotta go now, before they can organise."

And so back into the Highway we went, May leading all of us out of our shadow just as we approached the entrance and then back into it on the other side. We hurried back down to the tracks and May reached through the fourth dimension again to call a cart to us. She then repeated the process of using its computer system through the fourth dimension, but this time, there were no bases in the city of Santos. There were four residences, however, and we quickly agreed on one for the six of us to go to.

This time, Marc and James went first, followed by me and Peter, and May and Amelia bringing up the rear. We didn't have time to synchronise our watches this time; May just called two more carts, led us all back out of our shadows, and then we all took off. Peter and I ended up circling for maybe fifteen seconds before we were able to stop in Santos; it was a dizzying experience beyond anything I had ever been through, and if I hadn't gone so many hours without food, I probably would have puked. We quickly scrambled out of our cart and sent it zooming away so that May and Amelia could pull up. Before Amelia could send their cart zooming away, however, Marc stopped her, pointing out that no Hammerheart could pull up here as long as it was here.

Apparently, James had been thinking something at May from the moment she had arrived, because she immediately ordered the five of us to grab hold of her. The moment we did, she led us back into our shadow.

"Er—don't we have to be out there to get out of here?" Amelia asked, staring at the door beside the button.

"Yes, but we need to check what's out there first," James said, watching May as she screwed up her mind in concentration. "Can you do it?"

"Do what?" Peter asked.

"Using her mind to see if there is anyone in the house," he said. "If she can, then she can distract them so that we can get out without any trouble♯—"

"But they won't see anything unless they're like right in front of the door," Peter pointed out, "not if we go back into our shadow as soon as we're through, and what are the odds of that?"

"We don't know what's on the other side of that door, Pete," James said solemnly. "Even if we're invisible, we could give ourselves away just by opening it."

"There are six people in the house," May told us, "but they are all sleeping. If I make them all stay asleep, we can go through without them knowing."

James grinned. "Yeah, that'll work well."

And so it did. The entrance to the Highway in this particular house was hidden in the back of a closet in a hallway, and other than pushing through clothes and stepping over shoes, it was a veritable stroll in the park. May just took us out of our shadow long enough to go through the door, and then immediately took us back again. She then stood outside her shadow for twenty seconds before for the second time that night, Hall teleported straight to our location. He was alone again, this time looking triumphant, but it didn't last long. Not knowing that May was there, he teleported so close to her that he almost landed on her foot. Before he could even react to her, she put an arm around his neck and her mind around his.

He struggled for a few seconds but was unable to make any noise, nor was he able to use magic from the Villain Crystal. I wasn't sure how much she had been able to accomplish with her mind and how much was his own panic clouding his judgement; I did know that she wouldn't be able to completely take his mind in hers, as she hadn't been able to touch him at all when they had fought at the school. The struggle ended when she hit him on the top of the head hard enough to knock him unconscious. We watched her concentrate for a few more seconds, and then she smiled. She dropped him onto the floor and stepped back into her shadow to rejoin us.

"Any trouble?" Marc asked.

"No, he will have forgotten that he ever found you again," she said. "I just have to wake him up and he will teleport away—he will not even be suspicious."

"Not until someone reminds him about us being in Recife anyway," James muttered, "but that shouldn't matter. Let's go."

And so we walked over, past, and in Peter's case, through Hall (he actually stamped on his head a few times but of course, the police commissioner felt nothing) and out of the house. Hall only began to come around just as we passed through the door and into the street outside, and none of us bothered to look back to see if he was okay. We found, when we emerged into the open, that this city wasn't quite as warm as Recife had been, although it still felt fairly humid. It also felt more lively than Recife had, although that may have just been because we were in a residential street here.

"They will not try to stop us leaving here," May said suddenly, and we all stopped and looked at her in surprise.

"What?"

"That was in his mind," she told us. "They do not believe that we would go on the Brazilians' boat because they think we can get there ourselves if we want to. They think we still have magic. But they have not forgotten what you did to them the last time. That is why he"—she waved her hand back at the house—"will lead a group of them to intercept us near the portal."

"How hard was it to make him forget about us?" James asked.

"Easy, once he was unconscious."

"Well that settles it," said James, squaring his shoulders. "We'll have to fight them on the ship when we get near the portal. I don't think they'll try to sink us, not if they want to get through the portal at all, so we just let them come aboard and then we immediately take them out."

"And how do we stop the Brazilians from getting in the way?" Peter asked.

James shrugged. "That'll be child's play for May."

"So what do we do now?" Amelia asked, looking around at us all. "We still have a full day before the ship leaves."

"I could spend all of that sleeping," Marc said, and yawned widely.

"I have an idea about that," James said slowly, looking at May, seeming to run it by her before speaking it aloud—she nodded, whatever that meant. "How about we go forward about fifteen or sixteen hours into the future and then sleep through the night? I know that's a little strange but it would actually help us synchronise our body clocks with the local time without having to go through any jetlag."

There was a short silence as we all mulled this over in our heads. It made sense to skip forward so that we didn't have to wait around a full day, and it made sense to syncronise our body clocks. Yes, it was a good idea, and we all seemed to agree on it at the same time. And so that was what we did, all of us hanging onto May as we had done in Recife, her spiralling through time, forward this time, as the day passed us by. It didn't last nearly as long this time; within minutes, the sun was setting again, and the Honnie brought us all back into the shadow light.

The next question was where to go. This street was packed with activity and didn't seem like a good place to stay, but where else could we go? We knew where nothing was in this city. After some discussion, which became more irritated as by now we were all feeling tired and hungry, we decided to go straight to the port and see what we found there. It was easy enough to find: Pretty much everyone in the area knew where it was, so May didn't even need to leave her shadow to get the information she needed. We just followed the trail, all of us trudging along and not paying much attention to our surroundings, which was a shame because if I had cared a little more, I would have been witness to a whole new culture all around me.

Even though night was setting in, the port was alive with activity. May dipped into the minds around us and found two pieces of good news: There were no Hammerhearts in the area as far as any of the workers knew, and given the boldness of the Brazilian government's decision to tell the Hammersons to bugger off, they were particularly alert for any sign of trouble; and the ship that would be taking us to Rock Haulter was already docked and being prepared for its next sea voyage. There would be people aboard most of the night, cleaning it up, loading it with provisions for the voyage ahead and performing safety checks, but it still seemed like the most sensible place for us to go. With any luck, we wouldn't even need to get off it the following morning.

And when we finally reached the ship (finally because it was a damn big port), we were in for another piece of good news, and certainly a surprise: It was the very same ship that we had seen taking the Russians to Rock Haulter three months earlier. Even though it was night, there was enough light around, including in the ship itself, to make it clearly recognisable. I had seen it up close on the day when we had left Rock Haulter to rescue Tommy and I knew what I was seeing now. I supposed it could have been the same model but a different ship, but somehow I doubted that. Maybe it was owned by some sort of Rock Haulter corporation? I didn't know, but I felt myself smiling for the first time in I didn't know how long: It would be comfortable in there for sure.

"Yeah, we're definitely going in there," said Peter, and he too was smiling.

It wasn't that simple. Even after we had located the gangplank and passed right through a group of heavily armed guards, we weren't quite sure what to do next. This part of the deck, situated near the front of the boat or whatever boat people called it (the bow, as James would inevitably bring us all up-to-date on naval terminology throughout the more-than-fifty-hour sea journey ahead of us) was large, open, and seemed to be a place for passengers to get a look at where the ship was heading. It was surrounded on all but one side by glass barriers topped with what looked like a thick, iron rung, while at the back, doors led into what I supposed was the main cabin. Above it was another deck, from which I assumed the ship was steered. I hadn't noticed any of this the last time I had seen the ship (I had only really seen it clearly side-on, and during the battle around the Indian portal, I'd been too distracted) but now that I got a good look at it, if we could get the Brazilians to stay away from here, it would be the perfect place to battle any Hammerhearts who attempted anything silly.

Although she was thoroughly exhausted by now, we used May again to get an idea of exactly what was going on aboard, and where would be the most sensible place for us to stay the night—and the journey ahead. We learned that the main deck, where we were now, included a large eating area, a kitchen (galley), toilets (heads), the lifeboats, some recreational facilities, and what seemed to be a handful of classrooms—of course, this wouldn't be a holiday for those poor students. There were three more decks above it, each of which was smaller than the one below it and was encircled by a wrap-around porch. Two of these were for passengers, and one was for the ship's crew; and above that, the bridge deck. Below the main deck were the cargo areas and the engine room.

We gleaned a lot of useful information from the minds of the crew members already aboard, and some of it we were able to turn to our advantage. The upper passenger deck only had enough rooms for the thirty Brazilian students, but not enough for the staff members. They had instead decided to invade and share the crew's deck, something which they shouldn't have been allowed to do and which the ship's crew were not at all happy about. The lower passenger deck, which could accommodate more than fifty passengers, was completely empty, and other than sparing checks to make sure there was nothing dangerous going on, the cleaning crew were leaving it alone.

The solution to this problem was so simple that it was perfect. May began manipulating the minds all around her so that they would all know the score. She then took the rest of Santos and began searching for the students and staff so that they too would know the score once they got here the following morning. Now, the crew would have their deck to themselves; the students and staff would be sharing the lower passenger deck, where there would be plenty of room for all of them; and the six of us had the entire upper passenger deck to ourselves.

The cleaners were still busy fixing the deck up for us, but there were already enough facilities ready for us to use, so we went into the main cabin, located the stairs to the upper decks (there was also an elevator, but we didn't need to use it for this), and climbed up two levels to get a first look at our accommodation. We saw immediately why they had chosen to put the students up here prior to our interference—it was quite luxurious. Each room was soft and plushly carpeted, with a spacious wardrobe, desk, chest of drawers, large bed (not as big as the one I'd had back in the Young Army base but not too far behind) and a private bathroom. There were also five sitting rooms (each big enough for a handful of people, and each easily big enough for the six of us) as well as a door closest to the rear of the ship (the stern) which led to an outdoor area which had, we saw when we looked through the window, a swimming pool and sets of lawn chairs scattered around.

Yes, this would definitely be good enough for the six of us, especially when you took into account the bag which Marc was still carrying on his back. All the food we would need was in there, not to mention most other things we could possibly need. We might not even have to leave this deck, at least until the Hammerhearts showed up. For the time being, though, while the cleaners finished up on this deck and prepared to start on the one below (I didn't feel too bad about giving them a bunch of extra work for the night), we sat down in one of the sitting rooms, not leaving our shadow, and settled to a light dinner. Amelia said that we should make it a light dinner if we were planning to sleep almost immediately after it, which I was, and I supposed it made sense. It had been a ridiculously long day, which had simultaneously lasted many hours and three negative weeks, and I was more than ready for it to end.

* * *

It was the middle of the night and I was curled up in my bed in a state of shock and despair. The clock on the wall, which had been set to Atlantic portal time (only one hour ahead of local Brazilian time) said it was just after one o'clock. We were all still in our shadows and while May slept, all the others were stuck in their beds, able to sleep but unable to see or hear anything, and pretty much reliant on me and

May to make sure they woke up on time. Last night, we had eaten, and then when the cleaners had left and wouldn't be coming back up here again, May had dragged the beds from each of the rooms we had selected through the fourth dimension so that we could sleep in them comfortably.

None of that mattered to me now, though. Nothing mattered except for the horrible, terrible person I had become. I had just woken up from a dream in which I had firstly seen Natalie turning away from me, accusing me of being 'just like other guys'. I had then been sitting on the floor of an office, my clothes a mess, while above me, Stella was saying that it hadn't meant anything and that her body had made her do it. I had then been sitting in one of the compartments, and Lena was climbing out, thanking me for providing her sex on tap and saying that she might be in touch the next time she felt horny, if she couldn't get the other guys she preferred. I had then been sitting on a narrow bed in a dingy room as Amelia left the room, thanking me for making her feel better and that she would let me know the next time she needed a bit of relief. Even Serena came back to me, telling me that she didn't want to take a bath with me because she was planning on dumping me the following day.

Had that been how I'd made all those girls feel? Had that really been how they had felt, or was my own guilty conscience throwing that at me? Did it even matter? I didn't know, and I wished I didn't care, but I did. Once upon a time, I had resolved not to get on anyone's wrong side if I could help it, and look at me now? I could blame the curse all I wanted, but would the curse have had any power over me if I hadn't already desired all of them at least a little? Probably not, I thought, which meant that it really was all my fault.

This time, the tears came freely, and I buried my face in my pillow.

* * *

Things got under way very early the following morning. The final checks began at six o'clock, some of which involved alarms and sirens which I supposed were to alert the passengers that something was amiss but succeeding in only waking me and May up a little earlier than we would have liked. Disgruntled, we woke the others, had breakfast, got into a fight over showering (the bathrooms were there, but James insisted it would be far too unsafe to leave our shadow while still docked, and we couldn't access the water here), and then settled back to wait for all the business to be done. There wasn't much for us to do except to sit around, listening to the fuss around the ship and letting May concentrate—she was busy keeping an eye on everyone's thoughts to make sure that they would all stay out of our way, and that no danger was forthcoming.

The argument about the showers led to another argument, less heated but still intense, over whether or not we could leave our shadows at all during the voyage. Once we were under way, the idea was for May to let everyone aboard know that we were representatives of the Sorcerers (true enough) and given that there were no Hammerhearts with them, they ought not to have an issue with that. If they did, May would promptly remove said issue, and all would be well. The problem was our magical traceability, and what that might mean for us if we exposed our location to Hall and Hammerson.

It was tricky to know how they might react. On one hand, they would know for sure that we were on this ship and heading for Rock Haulter. They assumed that if we were going, we would get our own way there as we had done three months ago. Had they set up another blockade around the portal? We knew that their attempt to come aboard the ship had failed, but what if they had decided to sink us rather than let us go through alone? Frederic Woodward hadn't told Amelia anything to the contrary, so we had to assume that was a possibility, but James disagreed.

"First of all, even if there is a blockade, May can make them all get out of our way," James told us firmly. "Secondly, if we manage the attack correctly, they won't even know that they've failed until it's too late. Remember, they couldn't remember exactly how they had been thwarted, so I see no reason why that won't work. I really think it'll be fine so long as we wait till we've left the dock."

He, May and Amelia were firmly in favour of leaving our shadow, while Peter, Marc and I were against, but our resolve was fraying. I asked May later on if she had played a role in that and she had denied swaying our minds, saying that even though we were worried about being discovered, our desire to relax for a couple of days after what we had been through was weakening our resistance. Apparently, we couldn't even wait to get to the Rock to take a break. Perhaps it was this ship that was doing that to us. In the end, we decided that it would probably be okay so long as we were vigilant. We knew that the ship wouldn't be attacked until close to the portal, and we knew that the Hammerhearts wanted us in one piece at least until they could get through, and we knew that they would fail to accomplish that. It seemed to be enough.

The passengers arrived at the port at just after eight o'clock local time, spent the next half-hour going through security checks, and were finally aboard the ship by nine o'clock. They were then subjected to a speech from a member of the crew, followed by a safety drill. Their bags were taken to their rooms but they—even the staff members—were forced to stay in one of the classrooms on the main deck for the time being. The gangplank was removed, the engines were revved up, and then finally, right on time, the ship pulled away from the dock. It took more than another half-hour before we had cleared the port altogether, but soon enough, we were powering through the open ocean, rocking and swaying less than I had expected and wondering why we hadn't been allowed to use this ship on our school camp—the port in Melbourne had certainly been big enough for it.

Once we were safely at sea, May let the other people aboard the ship know that we were here, just as planned, in such a way that they believed they had always known we would be here and were now wondering why they had ever worried about being attacked while there were representatives of the Sorcerers present. What we hadn't banked on was the captain summoning one of us—our leader, to be exact—to join him on the bridge to discuss how we would make sure there was no trouble. We elected Marc to do this job, as he looked the oldest (outside of May, since we didn't want to give him a heart attack), and since the captain spoke English fairly well, it turned out to be fine. Marc assured him that there wouldn't be an attack on the ship until close to the portal, and if even that happened, we were well equipped to deal with it. Convinced, perhaps more by May's assistance than anything Marc did, the captain actually saluted him before allowing him to rejoin us on our deck, assuring him that no one other than himself would be permitted to enter our area of the ship. The rest of us then left our shadow together to enjoy the rest of the voyage. My first order of business was a shower.

Chapter 22: I Started Counting at 804

It was evening and I was alone in my room, feeling like utter crap. The day had been a fairly enjoyable one for all of us; after lunch, we had all gone out to the back of our deck and spent most of the afternoon in the sun—chilling in the pool, baking in the chairs, and repeatedly moving from one to the other as the urge took us. James had told us that we ought to do it now because we may be too far south to enjoy it tomorrow, and as long as we were alert for trouble, it would be fine. Fortunately, the Hammerheart devices were unaffected by being under water. No one bothered us; no Hammerhearts turned up, and the Brazilians left us alone, although a few of the students broke away from the group and came down towards the stern to try to get a look at us. They had been on the main deck, and the angle of the superstructure made it impossible for them to see us, and the distance had been too great for them to hear what we were saying, but they had heard our voices. According to May, who had been listening in on their thoughts, they weren't so much afraid of us as they were curious because, as Peter wasted no time in pointing out, we were the good guys, after all, and they knew it.

I had enjoyed the afternoon, although it had felt like a shadow lay over my heart throughout the day. The dream from the previous night was never too far from my mind, nor were the memories of what I had done in the Big Room and the drop-in centre in Melbourne. Ironically, though, seeing May and Amelia, both wearing bikinis, had cheered me up somewhat, especially seeing that Amelia looked generally happy with everything, seemingly unaffected by Darcy's rejection—and by what I had done with her. But there seemed to be something else going on, though, and that was Marc. I remembered what he had told me in his room, about realising that he still wanted Amelia, and it looked as though he had come to terms with his feelings. Whenever one of them was on the chairs, the other would be too, and same with the pool, and when they were close enough, they were nearly always chatting. It made me feel simultaneously sad and happy at the same time: sad because once again, I had to let Amelia go; and happy because, perhaps, I wouldn't have to feel guilty about what I'd done with her—other than the fact that it had led to everything else I'd done.

As for May, she had originally come out onto the outdoor deck wearing nothing at all, but had reluctantly gone back inside to retrieve a bikini from our supply backpack after all of us, me included, had practically begged her to do so. It was impossible not to look at her and feel attracted to her in that form; Marc, James and

Peter had all looked like they'd been hit over the head with mallets, and even Amelia looked as though she was thinking bedroom thoughts. Even in her bikini, though, May had still been incredibly attractive and difficult not to look at, especially when she had playfully brandished her stunner at me from under her bikini top— when I had asked her where she kept her invisibility toggle, she had smiled suggestively at me in a way I understood all too well. Every time my eyes had tried to pass her, they had always lingered on her for at least a second longer than necessary. Looking at Amelia had been a little easier, although it had made me feel worse and desiring her too and having caused Marc to give me a couple of dirty looks throughout the day, but at least I hadn't totally lost myself. The only relief was that at least Peter and James had been similarly affected by the Honnie as I had.

We had gone back inside in the late afternoon when the weather had begun to cool down. It had been sunny all day with minimal clouds in the sky, and the sun baking off the surface of the ocean had given the air a pleasantly humid feel. By then, though, cloud cover was building overhead; whether or not it would result in rain, I hadn't known (it had, but the ship seemed to be unaffected by it, so perhaps it wasn't too bad). About an hour after we had gone inside, the captain himself had come down to see us, saying that the crew had noticed us using the pool, and if we were done with it, would we like some of them to come down and clean it up in preparation for tomorrow. Marc, who had somehow become our spokesperson, said this was okay, and so down they had come and busied themselves outside.

We had had our dinner shortly after this—a considerably larger one than the night before—and then Marc, Amelia, James and I had got into a game of four-way chess, watched on by May while Peter provided a running commentary to all our amusement. It had finished at nearly ten o'clock, by which time we were all starting to get sleepy. Even though we could hear strange music coming from the deck below as the students enjoyed themselves in whatever was their custom (I couldn't speak for the others, but I thought it sounded pretty hip), we decided to call it a night and separated to go to our rooms. (Oh, just so you know, James had ended up winning the game, mainly because Marc, who'd started off better by checkmating me first, had been unwilling to do the same to Amelia when he'd clearly had the chance. James hadn't had any such hesitation, and even though he'd had a few less pieces for the final struggle, he'd been better at manoeuvring them into position.)

So now it was all quiet. Even the Brazilians had gone quiet, although they may not have gone to bed yet—I neither knew nor cared. All I cared about was the person I had become, and how much

I didn't like that person. For someone who claimed to genuinely care how he made others feel, I was doing a remarkably good job of making people feel bad. There was no doubt that I deserved this, even if somewhere in the world right now, Lena was dating a version of Marc who still had the Hero Crystal, Stella was dating a version of Lucien who hadn't turned into the next incarnation of Arnold Hammerson, and Natalie was sleeping in a hole in the ground with a half-human, half-Honnie beefhead. In the future, those three would be hurt by me, and there was nothing I could do to take it back.

May was still awake, it seemed, because she could sense that I was slowly sinking into depression. She sent me another thought, offering a second time to make me forget the things that were troubling me, and I rejected it a second time. When she persisted, I practically pleaded with her not to take the matter out of my hands. Sure, I was unhappy now; not only did I deserve it, but if I forgot it, I would have to go through it all over again in the future. She then offered to take it away temporarily, which was a slightly better idea, but after giving it some thought, I rejected this, too. Even if she made me think that somewhere in the future Natalie was waiting for me, it wasn't a luxury I deserved. This was a pain I needed to suffer to make sure that the next time I had a girlfriend, assuming it ever happened again, I wouldn't treat her so badly.

Having not gotten any sleep by midnight, I decided to get up and get myself a drink—my mouth was pretty dry. I opened my door and stepped out into the hallway, bare feet making barely any noise on the deck. I went to the backpack, which was sitting on a chair in the sitting room where we'd had all our meals so far, and fished around in there for a bottle of water—I knew there was one in here because I had seen Amelia get one out earlier in the day. My hand found a bottle that felt right, and I tilted the bag so that I could see what I was holding; sure enough, it was the very same bottle Amelia had gotten out earlier. I pulled it out, watching as it duplicated and reappeared exactly where it had just been, a piece of magic I particularly enjoyed watching now that we hardly had any of our own to use.

It was as I was returning to my room with the bottle, already having taken a few gulps, that I heard noises coming from one of the bedrooms. The six bedrooms we had chosen were all grouped together and closest to the set of stairs and elevator at the rear of the cabin (there were two of both). My room was on the port side and closest to the bow, opposite May's room on the starboard side and next to Peter's. Amelia was on Peter's other side, and it was from her room that I heard the noises. I probably would have passed right by anyway except that it had sounded, for a moment, that Amelia was crying. My insides shrivelled up as once again, the guilt came crashing in, but I hesitated there in the hallway to be sure of what I was hearing, wondering if I should interfere at all and knowing that it would haunt me if I didn't at least try.

But Amelia wasn't crying, I realised after a few seconds. Those were not crying sounds I was hearing from the other side of her door. No, I knew what those were, because I had heard them myself not too long ago, on the other side of a different door—only I'd been behind that door along with her. No, I thought, panic rising in me. Please don't let it be what I think it is...but no such luck, because I heard the moan from the other person in there at that very moment. My insides dissolved in despair—this was worse than crying. I knew who was in there, of course, and I also knew that it should be okay with me. Hadn't I thought that Marc would have my blessing if he went after Amelia again? Well, yes, I thought now, but this soon! This soon?

And now I had yet another thing to feel bad about—how Amelia herself would be feeling. Fine now, of course, but what about later? Would she feel like she had once again given it up too quickly? I didn't know, but as I heard the two of them in there heading closer and closer to their climax, I decided I didn't want to be standing here when it happened. I tiptoed past their door and stopped, just past Peter and James's rooms, hearing no sounds from either. All of a sudden, I didn't want to go to my room. I didn't want to be alone in that big bed tonight, knowing that just a couple of rooms away, Marc was enjoying Amelia's company. All day, I had felt better when I had been around people, but what was I to do now when they were all sleeping?

May was still awake, I remembered suddenly, but wouldn't she be tired too? She, like me, had been awake for something like seventeen hours straight, but unlike me, she had no reason to be nagged by guilt. Even Ingi, who must still be a chief worry for her, would be safe now that May knew she could just go back or forth in time to the point at which her daughter would need her most. I hesitated for a few more seconds, and then threw caution to the wind and headed for her door instead of my own. She couldn't have fallen asleep yet, and if she had heard any of my thoughts, she'd had ample opportunity to send me back the way I had come.

She was still awake, and had gotten out of bed to open the door before I had even knocked upon it. When she opened it, I saw that she looked weary, but not unpleased. She was also wearing the same nightdress she'd been wearing two nights earlier (by my body clock anyway) when I had entered her room in the drop-in centre, and we all remember what had happened in there.

"Would you just prefer I put you to sleep again?" she asked me.

I gulped for a moment, thinking of Natalie turning away from me; my rejection of both Lena and Stella; Amelia being no longer an option, if she ever had been; and of the dream of the previous night. I also thought of May herself, when we had been as close as we had ever been. Tired as I was, I wasn't ready to sleep, afraid of what tonight might bring for me, and feeling treacherously horny again. May's offer was a good one, and I appreciated that she was willing to use her mind to assist me at all—something she had been more and more willing to do since she had come to our world, but which she had been hardly willing at all to do in her own. I wanted it, but I wanted something else as well.

"Can I sleep in here with you tonight?" I asked her, looking down in shame. She would know what I was thinking, and that what I actually meant was to literally sleep in here tonight. May and I had slept together plenty of times in her world, and we had done so without there being any funny business whatsoever. Even though she had turned me on, even back then, I hadn't tried anything with her, both because of my physical injuries at the time and because I was so determined to get Natalie that I wasn't prepared to let anything get in the way. Even now, I knew not whether she had wanted it back then (probably not was my guess), but the point was that we were capable of sleeping together without it needing to mean anything.

While I had been thinking, she had been considering. Finally she said, "Okay," and stood back to let me enter her room, which was basically the same as my own.

"Can I ask you a question?" I asked her as she shut the door behind me. When she nodded, I said, "You've read a hell of a lot of human minds since you came here, so you must be pretty familiar with how we all think and what's normal for us. Am I—am I a bad person?"

That had not been an easy question to ask, and May would have known where I was going even before I had gotten the words out, but I felt like I had needed to speak them all the same. Whether I was deliberately punishing myself or I thought that I could honestly grow from all this experience, I knew not, but either way, it felt like the right thing to do.

"No," she said firmly. "I think you are a very young person."

That took me aback. "What?"

"If you were a bad person, you would not even care how you made others feel, or even ask the question," she told me. "I have felt some minds like that, but your mind is good. You just make mistakes, but so does everyone."

True enough, I supposed. I knew I'd never meant to hurt any of them, and when I'd had to hurt Lena and Stella, it had only been because there was no other way. Not hurting either of them would hurt others, so I had effectively been caught between a rock and a hard place (or rather, between a crotch and a hard thing). You could also say that they (Natalie, Amelia, Lena and Stella) had made a mistake by ever being attracted to a guy like me.

I actually felt a little better hearing this from May, who was a relative expert in the field of human thinking. All of a sudden, I felt inexplicably appreciative, and found myself wondering if I would be an imposition by staying with her tonight—even though I still wanted to. When I looked the question at her, she just shrugged indifferently, which seemed to be a green light. Relieved, I sat down on her bed and stifled a yawn.

"Thanks, May, you've really been helpful lately," I said, thinking of the number of times that she had cleared my mind of sexual thoughts for me, and that if it hadn't been for Stella's interference, she might have been able to stop me from doing the deed with her (Stella) and Lena altogether. "Wish I could make it up to you somehow, but all we've managed to do is take you out of your normal life and put you in more danger."

"That is true," she agreed, "but then, I make mistakes too."

I had an idea then, a small payback I could offer her in the meantime, something I had done with her a couple of times before and which she had enjoyed. I knew not why Honnies liked to taste the insides of humans—I supposed maybe it was their way of determining if that human was worth consuming before actually doing so and potentially wasting another Honnie's good meal. I only knew that they liked to do it, and I also knew that May liked how I tasted. Deciding, I looked at her directly and opened my mouth slightly, inviting her to make the call.

She smiled and took the offer, leaning forward so that our mouths touched, an arm encircling me to hold me still, and her tongue sliding over my own and down my throat. It was still a strange sensation, but nowhere near as strange as it had been the first time she had done it. At first I was calm, knowing that she wasn't going to hurt me despite the slight (only slight) discomfort, but as the seconds lengthened, it quickly gave way to arousal. I reached out, meaning to gently push her back, momentarily rejecting the idea, but my arms had instead found their way around her body, and then her other arm had found its way around me. I tightened my hold on her, pressing our bodies together, and felt her gasp and withdraw her tongue a little so that instead of being down my throat, it was only in my mouth, as if we were kissing.

We both pulled back a little then, our mouths anyway, so that we could look at each other fully. She was smiling, having enjoyed the moment, and I had no idea how I looked but knew exactly how I felt —very horny indeed. Only this time, it was regular horny, not cursed-to-the-moon-and-back horny. May didn't say anything, only looked at me, and this time, I knew the invitation was for me. I thought about it for a moment, but only a moment. May knew the score—I wouldn't be leading her on in any way, shape or form. The other girls I had hurt wouldn't have a bar of me anymore, and Amelia was with someone else. I could think of no reason not to.

"Don't do anything with my mind this time, okay," I told her, and she smiled at me to let me know she wouldn't.

* * *

Three hours of sleep—that was all I got. They were three very deep hours of sleep, perhaps, but as deep as they were, I still felt like I could have done with a few more. Through the window of May's bedroom, I could see that it was still dark out, and it was just after five o'clock in the morning Atlantic portal time. I was very warm where I lay in May's bed, curled up in the arms of the Honnie, who still seemed to be asleep. She had ended up putting me to sleep, hence why it had been so deep and dreamless, so why had I woken up now? Had it just been that I was so warm, or had something else woken me? I started as I remembered that we were all out of our shadow, and with May asleep, there wouldn't be any warning of an oncoming Hammerheart attack.

My sudden tenseness seemed to wake May up, albeit slowly. By the time she had come to full awareness, I had already relaxed and was feeling a little silly. There was no noise coming from anywhere; I couldn't even hear the ocean outside as the ship cut through the waves, nor could I hear anything from the engine below, or the crew above. There was certainly nothing going on on our deck; Marc and Amelia would surely be asleep by now (unless they'd pulled an all-nighter or something). No, my worry had been needless, and now I just felt relieved and very comfortable indeed.

And since I was in bed with May, it was definitely a good thing that no Hammerhearts had come a-calling. The intimate time we had spent together, however I had felt about it beforehand, was exactly how sex should be, in my opinion. Sure, when I had been cursed, I'd had a lot of orgasms, and most of them had been rather powerful, but there had been no build-up to them—I could have achieved the same result just by masturbating. For me and May, though, it had been slower, and therefore much more fun for me. I had really taken the time to examine and attempt to pleasure her all over her body, and it had paid off because when it was over, she told me that male Honnies didn't pay the sort of attention to the female form that human males did. By not focussing exclusively on the intercourse (which had been amazing, even without her using her mind to make it better), I had been able to make it as enjoyable for her as I would have if I'd just screwed her for hours. That certainly did make me feel better about myself.

"Sorry," I now said sheepishly. "I dunno what woke me."

She thought for a moment, apparently casting her mind around us, and then said, "Maybe I woke you by accident. There is nothing going on. Only James is awake, and he is still in his room."

"Really? What's he doing?"

"Thinking about magic," she said, "and thinking that he should talk to me about Honnies to learn what he can while he can."

"Would you tell him?" I asked curiously.

"Maybe some things, but only if he asks me."

That sounded about right, I thought, and then yawned. Surely I could get another hour or two of sleep before the others would start getting up, and I should probably do that in my own bedroom. If anyone saw me coming out of May's room in the morning, well, I could tell them that I had only just been in there after getting up to chat with her—perhaps spout some half-truths about being depressed and wanting some insight into my behaviour—but it would be simpler to avoid that whole exchange. Then I remembered that May was undoubtedly hearing these thoughts, and I shuddered with self-disgust.

"Sorry," I muttered shamefully, not knowing where to look for the best.

"It is fair enough," she said, and she actually put a hand behind my head and guided it forward so that it was resting against her chest. It was very tender given how strong she was, and that made me wonder: Was I having a relationship with her? That wasn't what I wanted—was it? My mind returned to Natalie, and the vision of her turning away from me. No, I didn't think I was ready to move on, nor did I want to, if there was any chance—any at all—that she could forgive me.

"May?" I said, and when she responded, asked, "How old are you anyway?"

I tensed for a moment, wondering if she would say that it was rude to ask a woman her age, but she merely said, "I was ten thousand, three hundred and eighty days before we came back in time. I think I am that plus two now."

"Whoa, hang on," I said, trying to work it out in my mind. Three hundred and sixty-five days in a year; 3,650 days in a decade, plus two or three for leap years; so if I were figuring it right, that would mean... "You're not even thirty yet?" And then when I thought about it some more, added, "And were you counting since the day you were born or something?" I was going to need to work this out on a calculator.

"No," she said, and I wasn't sure which question she was answering until she added, "I started counting at 804. That was how old I was when I first learned how to count in our world—which is different from how you count, by the way. Our system is octal, but for us it is normal."

"Octal—"

"We only have eight digits."

That was just too weird for me to wrap my mind around, so I said, "But how did you know you were 804 when you started counting?"

"Because my mother was counting for me up until then."

That opened up a whole new line of questioning, but I decided to save it for another time. There would be plenty of time while we were on the Rock—time in which we were too exhausted to do— whatever we planned on doing when we got there. I decided to think back to the first question I had asked. If May was really only approaching thirty, as my approximate mental arithmetic suggested, then she must have been about my age, give or take, when she'd had Ingi. That wasn't unusual in our world either, but was it normal in theirs? Was Ingi almost ready to have children herself? I didn't know, and I could have asked, but decided to save that for another time as well. All I knew was that I now felt a little better about having slept with May; the age difference was still pretty big, but at least not ridiculously so.

And that brought me back to—whatever this was. I thought back to what I'd thought before we had gotten down to it: May knew the score—I wouldn't be leading her on in any way, shape or form. The other girls I had hurt wouldn't have a bar of me anymore, and Amelia was with someone else. That still seemed a little strange, though; most people wouldn't be content to be another person's backup option unless they themselves had other stuff going on. Exactly what did May have going on anyway?

"Are you okay with this?" I asked her. "I mean—well—you know what's going on with me—well, as much as I do—I don't really know what's going on—"

"Yes," she said firmly. "For me, it is interesting, and fun, and it really felt very good last night." I smiled as she said this. "I am not so concerned with deeper meaning because for Honnies, such things do not normally matter at all."

I thought about this, both relieved and a little uneasy. "Okay, but you won't—like—force me to do anything or—"

"No," she said quickly, and she tilted my head back so that we could see each other's faces in the darkness. "I know what is going on. I will only do this until you say you want to stop, then we will stop. I do not need it, but I do like it very much."

Now I was completely relieved. I still felt like I was using her a little, but did that matter if the person being used wanted to be used?

Not if she enjoyed it, and according to May, she did enjoy it—'very much', as it were. There was just one thing still playing on my conscience: Was this the sort of person I wanted to be? Sure, no one was getting hurt by this (not at the moment anyway), but would this somehow make me feel worse later when I had to own my actions? Maybe, I thought, and then I thought of Natalie again—it was impossible not to think of her. It would be best if I could let her go—there was almost no chance of us going forward anyway—but could I? Did I want to let her go? I didn't know, but what I did know was that I had time—however long we stayed in the past before returning to August 30—in which to figure it out.

"Thanks for being so understanding," I said to May.

I decided to go back to my room after all. I was tempted to stay here with May, but what I really needed was to sleep a little longer while I could. I had left her room and tiptoed across the hallway to my own, taking the almost-forgotten water bottle with me. There were no sounds at all, and I hoped that wherever Marc and Amelia were, whether they were sleeping together or he had gone back to his own room, they were both happy. I felt at peace with the situation between the three of us, for now anyway, and I didn't even feel as if May had manipulated my mind into feeling that way.

Another thing that had been forgotten for too long, I thought as I opened the bottle and took a few swigs, was the packet of condoms I was still carrying around with me. The last one I'd worn had proved to be useless under the intensity of my curse-crazed sex with Amelia, and I hadn't used a single one since. That wasn't an issue with May, she had told me, but Lena and Stella? Now there was a potential problem. There was a good chance that I could have gotten one, or perhaps both of them, pregnant. That was certainly a drama none of us needed, and I could only hope now that they were on the contraceptive pill—or if not that, it wasn't the right time of the month for such things to happen.

Then I had to wonder about myself. With all the sex I'd had lately, with five different people in the last week (let's not forget Natalie before all the shit had hit the fan), was I in any danger of contracting an STD? We had learnt about those in health class just the previous year, and I wasn't an idiot. Well, no, I take that back: I was an idiot, because a non-idiot would have thought of that possibility much sooner than now. I sat on my bed, put the bottle on the drawers beside it and pulled my junk out of my pyjama pants. It looked normal—it felt normal—so was it, or was there something hidden there that I wouldn't know about until later? I didn't know, but I comforted myself with one thing: Maybe there would be some sort of magical solution on the Rock which might help me. It wasn't much, and pretty cowardly, but at least it was something. As for the girls I'd been with, well, Stella could fix herself up if she'd caught anything, and maybe she would be nice enough to do the same for Lena. Natalie would probably be fine in that area—I hadn't been with anyone for a long time before her.

I yawned again and looked at the clock—a quarter to six. I climbed under the covers and curled up in a ball, dragging the pillow over from the other side of the bed and imagining that it was a girl. Such was the state of my mind that I wasn't even sure which girl I was imagining; Natalie, mostly, but I also imagined holding Stella in my arms and telling her that ours was a connection stronger than any other, which was close enough to the truth. Then I rolled over onto my other side and imagined I was holding Amelia, and quite suddenly, I felt a little more jealous of Marc all over again. I knew I couldn't begrudge him for being with Amelia, so why did I still desire her? Could I give myself permission to still desire her if I didn't actually do anything to get in their way?

I decided I needed one more question before I could sleep, and projected outwards into May's mind, hoping she was still awake and would consent to answer. She had been beginning to drowse, but I felt her come quickly awake. I shrugged, feeling sheepish again, but once again she seemed not to mind. I needed to know exactly what had happened between Marc and Amelia the previous evening, and more importantly, I needed to know exactly how Amelia felt—or how she thought she felt—about me and Marc. She didn't answer right away, and at first I thought it was because she was retrieving the information from their minds, but when she did respond, I felt her hesitation: She felt that what was going on in Amelia's mind was her own business and not necessarily mine, but she still seemed to care enough for me to give me an answer.

According to the Honnie, both of them had lain awake for some time after we had all gone to bed. Marc had been thinking about Amelia, wanting her; and Amelia had been thinking about herself, and wondering if she should open herself up to dating me (if I pursued her) or if she should stay away from boys long enough to get her self-respect back. Eventually, Marc had decided he couldn't take it anymore and had gone to Amelia's room. She had let him in, confused, and they had got around to talking. Exactly what they had talked about, May felt I didn't need to know, but it had eventually led to sex and a mutual decision for the two of them to 'try again'. As for how Amelia felt about me compared to Marc, she was more physically attracted to him and more emotionally attracted to me, but was also rightly nervous about how unstable I seemed to be at the moment.

That made things pretty clear for me: She was better off with him than me. Yes, I could still desire her, but I would have to keep it to myself. I cared for Amelia as a close friend as well, and this would be best for her. I also cared for Marc; he was my brother, after all, and he'd just been dumped by one of the hottest girls I'd ever seen so that she could be with me. I couldn't control how they felt, and I had little control over how I felt, but one thing I did have control over was my actions. From now on, no matter how horny I got, I would not have sex with Amelia again.

This resolution would last for less than three days.

Chapter 23: A Nice Big Smacker

Later that day, I dragged one of the lawn chairs from the outdoor deck around to the porch on the starboard side of the ship so that I could sit and have some time alone. As the ship was now travelling in a mostly southerly direction, this meant that from this side of the ship at this time of day, the sun was shining directly onto me, and it was very pleasant to just lay back there, looking out over the endless ocean in every direction (keeping my eyes downward most of the time to keep them out of the sun). It wasn't the first time I had seen an ocean, of course (I had even swam in one a few months earlier) but seeing it like this somehow made everything else seem small.

So far that day, we had all gotten up at different times and had breakfast at nine o'clock. May hadn't treated me any differently from usual around the others, which was a nice relief, but even if I hadn't known before that something had happened between Marc and Amelia, I would have picked up on it that morning. The two of them spent the majority of the morning together, sometimes in the cabin with us and sometimes out on the deck; and although it was clear that the dynamic between them had been altered, I caught Amelia smiling at me a few times. I had smiled back, hoping that our dynamic was only friendly and nothing more.

I spent much of the time between breakfast and lunch with Peter, playing all manner of games in one of the sitting rooms. Cards, chess, and even computer games on a laptop from the backpack were on the agenda. I also filled him in with what had truly been going on with me over the last few days. It turned out that when I had decided, back in the future, that Peter and James should know what had happened in the Big Room, May had picked up on it and had let them know after all, but they had both separately decided not to bring it up with me unless I brought it up first. I also told him what had happened since we had gotten on the ship, and that had certainly taken him by surprise (and I thought maybe he was a little jealous as well). The last time I had filled him in like this, he had been pretty disgusted by my behaviour, but this time, while he still maintained that I was making things more difficult for myself than they needed to be, he was more sympathetic and supportive to my current state of mind.

We'd had lunch at around midday (fairly small given that breakfast had been a bit late), and then I had come out here, and now I was thinking. Naturally, it was Natalie who occupied my thoughts. I kept coming back to the fact that when we went back to the future, several days or even more than a week would have passed for me, but no time at all would have passed for her. It meant two things that

I could see: I would be ready to try again much sooner than she would be prepared to even listen to me, and if I played my cards right, perhaps I could fix things before time could magnify them too much in her mind.

Natalie had been cheated on before she had dated me—Tommy had screwed Rebecca less than forty-eight hours after he had started dating Natalie and had gone back for seconds and thirds. Yet when Natalie had found out about this, despite the fact that she had a crush on me at the time, she still gave him a second chance—a chance which he blew a week later. Was it just because of that experience that she had reacted so quickly to my betrayal? Had giving a second chance that time made her think that guys didn't deserve them after all? Was there any hope that she would give me a second chance? It seemed unlikely to me, because even if she might have given me a second chance after finding out about me and Amelia, it would have been wasted the moment she saw me with Lena. If she somehow found out about Stella (not an impossibility, given how Stella must be feeling), she might actually feel relieved that she dumped me when she did.

If I were looking at this from someone else's perspective, I would say that it was an absolutely hopeless case. It probably was an absolutely hopeless case. There was just one problem that I couldn't get around, I still loved her. I had done so for far too long for it to just disappear all at once. None of my actions of the last few days, not even sleeping with May, changed the fact that Natalie was the one I truly wanted to be with more than any other. I wanted to try to get her back, even if it was a hopeless case, but then why was I having sex with May if I still wanted to get Natalie back? The simple answer seemed to be that she was right about me, that I would have sex with Amelia—or anyone else handy who would let me—if I couldn't be with the one I really wanted. That wasn't the sort of person I wanted to be, but then why had it felt so good to be with May this morning?

Someone was coming around the side of the cabin towards me— a girl, I felt sure, judging by the sound of the footfalls. I didn't look up until the person was maybe ten feet away; when I did, I saw that it was Amelia.

"What's up?" I asked her, unsure if I was pleased with the interruption or not.

"Are you okay?" she asked me, plopping down on the deck beside my chair.

"Yeah, I usually end up being okay," I said, wondering if she would remember the reference—that had been from the pre-memory-wipe days. I was pleased to see her smile fondly, and mentally thanked May for letting her remember that moment.

"Okay," she said, twisting her hands together awkwardly, "'cause I just thought—well—I guess I have to tell you something."

Uh oh, I thought, but didn't say. This was going to be deep, whatever it was, and was probably going to make a confusing situation even more confusing. What ought I to do if she now told me that she wanted to be with me instead of Marc?

Fortunately, that wasn't what was eating at her. "Well, last night," she said, "er—Marc came to see me, and we talked."

I smiled, feeling relieved. If this was a let-down she was about to offer me, I could handle that. It would hurt, in the way that rejections always did, but as I had thought earlier that morning, it would be better for everyone. If that was what it was, I thought I could make it a little easier for her.

"How's he doing anyway?" I asked her. "He and I talked the other morning and he mentioned—well—he said he thinks he might be having feelings for you again."

She hadn't been expecting me to say that, and I saw her flinch slightly. Had I made a mistake? "Oh," she said, her eyes widening. "Well, yeah, he does—that's what he told me last night. He said that there's something about this new me that makes me more relaxing to be around, whatever that means."

"Really?" I said, not entirely sure if I agreed with that.

"He wants to try again," she said, gazing anxiously at me now, "but I wasn't sure if—well—you and I—"

I could have made this more difficult for her too, but for what purpose? "Don't worry about that," I said quickly. "Look, Amelia, I'm a mess at the moment. Marc can make you a lot happier than I can. Mostly I still want to try to get Natalie back, even though mostly I know that there's like zero chance of that working."

"I'm so sorry," she whispered, and I thought there were tears in the back of her eyes. "I was so selfish—I can't believe I was so selfish—"

I shook my head. "If you'd thrown me out, I probably would have gone to May, and if she'd thrown me out, I might have screwed some random person in the building. I'm glad it was you, Amelia."

She smiled a little sadly and sighed. "So you won't be hurt if I date Marc?"

"Hurt?" I said, thinking of the right words to say what I knew to be the truth. "Not hurt, no. Jealous maybe, but not hurt. I'll survive."

Especially if I had May's help, I thought.

"Thank you," she said, getting to her feet. Before she straightened up all the way, though, she leaned forward and gave me a kiss on the lips. It was a friendly kiss, not intimate, and actually it was too quick for me to kiss her back. "I'll see you back inside then when you're ready," she said, and turned and left.

"You're welcome," I said quietly after she had gone, and smiled too. I was going to have to put in a lot of hard yards once we got back to the future, whatever else might be going on in the struggle with Lucien, but for the time being, I felt I'd done the right thing.

I lay out there for maybe another fifteen minutes before deciding I felt good enough to rejoin the civilised world, but when I got back into the cabin, any good feeling I'd had disappeared very quickly. I found everyone in the usual sitting room: Marc and Amelia sitting together and chatting; Peter and James playing Scrabble (that was a new one); and May sitting beside them, watching with faint amusement.

"Hey man," Peter said, waving me over. "Help a brother out, would ya? This guy's killing me."

"It's not my fault I'm astute," said James, grinning down at his letters.

"You doing okay now?" Marc asked me, and when I nodded, he grinned—it looked a little off. "That's great to hear. Was it Amelia's kiss that cheered you up?"

Everything in the room seemed to ground to a standstill. Peter and James both looked stunned, but Amelia looked horrified—clearly she hadn't been the one to tell him what had happened out there. I had looked accusingly at May, but the only response she gave me was a denial straight into my brain.

I gathered myself—it wasn't like we had done anything wrong out there. "No, it was what she said that did that. It was just—friendly, man."

"Really?" Marc said drily. "Friendly, you say? May, when was the last time you kissed John?"

His question had been sarcastic in nature, clearly meant to prove that people who are friends don't just go around kissing each other, but May's hesitation for no more than a second was enough to make his jaw drop. "Oh, you've gotta be kidding me. John, you have a problem."

"Marc, it didn't mean anything," Amelia insisted, looking like she might cry again. "I swear, I was just telling him about—about us, you know. I thought he had a right to know."

"Oh really? And he believes the appropriate way to respond to that is to give you a nice, big smacker—"

"It didn't mean anything!" Amelia shouted now.

But Marc didn't believe her. Glancing to my left, I saw that Peter and James didn't look convinced either. The worst of it was, I wasn't sure that even I believed it. After all, whatever the kiss had been, it hadn't been necessary to have it at all. Amelia and I would have been just fine without it.

I decided to take a different tack. "How did you even see it?" I asked him.

"I had to wonder why the two of you were alone," he said stubbornly, "and now I see I was right to."

"You don't trust me?" Amelia said, stricken.

"I trust you just fine; it's him I don't trust."

"I don't have to take this," I said, my own anger rising now, but rather than get into a fight that could do a lot of damage to our group (if this hadn't already), I spun on my heel and walked away. As I did, I sent a thought to May, asking for help—anything she could do to smooth this over. Her response wasn't at all comforting; much as she would like to, she can't just give me an easy out whenever something went wrong. I sighed—this was going to be another lesson I would have to learn from.

I had originally been intending to go to my room, but then I remembered something that Peter had said a couple of days ago. I backtracked and headed for the backpack, which was now hanging on the knob of the door to the rear stairwell—both stairwell doors were locked from the inside, as were the elevator doors on this level, and the only person who held the keys was the captain himself. I rummaged in the bag, feeling for bottles and finding some that weren't what I was looking for. Eventually, though, I did find it, and I grinned, thinking of Graham—that poor old bugger in the old Woodward base who had been a religious drinker ever since the old war had ended.

I took the bottle of beer back to my room, keeping it hidden from anyone who might be looking by hiding it with my body. Nobody saw me, though, and nobody stopped me from getting to my room. There, I sat on my bed, unscrewed the cap and began to drink, wishing I had bothered to get a packet of chips from the bag as well. Maybe I could go back for one? Nah, I couldn't be bothered. I just sat there, leaning back against the headboard, and drinking. I felt pissed off with all of them: May, for not helping; Marc, for being such a dick; Peter and James, for not backing me up; Amelia, for kissing me in the first place and bringing all this down on me; and everyone else back in the future. Lena had managed to screw things up between me and Natalie. Stella had managed to screw everything up by not stopping it when she could. Natalie herself was being so goddamned unreasonable. And as for Lucien, I would quite happily throttle him. But the person I was most pissed off with was myself.

It took me half an hour to polish off the entire bottle, by which time I was feeling pleasantly buzzed, and also feeling very pleased that this particular bottle of beer could be drunk again and again if necessary. But what to do with the bottle itself? There was a rubbish bin in each of the sitting rooms, but getting to one meant getting up and leaving the bedroom. Could I walk just now? I scrambled to the edge of my bed and got up unsteadily, dropping the bottle as I did so. Thankfully, the carpet was thick enough to stop it from breaking, and also thankfully, I didn't fall down—not yet anyway.

I bent down, picked up the bottle, almost toppled over, regained my balance, straightened up, and headed for the door. I opened it, stuck my head out and had a look around. Peter and James were still in the sitting room where it had all happened before, but I couldn't hear anyone else. More importantly, I couldn't see anyone else anywhere, so I stepped out, shut the door behind me, and headed for one of the other sitting rooms, where there would no doubt be a rubbish bin. As I thought this, though, an unexpected wave of panic hit me. What if one of the others looked in the bins? My bottle would probably be the only thing in there, and they would know what I had been doing. If I wanted to keep this quiet—which I did, for I knew there would be much criticism—I would have to deposit this in some other bin on the ship.

There were only two ways to get off this deck—one would require me to walk right past James and Peter, and the other would require me to walk towards the rear deck where, if Marc and Amelia weren't in one of their rooms, they would probably be hanging out. Since I didn't know, though, and since the thought of Marc made me angry all over again, I went that way, and found that I had been right. They were outside, sitting on the lawn chairs by the pool and chatting away—I couldn't hear their conversation, but it sounded like all was forgiven between those two at least. Unnoticed by either, who had their backs to me anyway, I slipped through the door and tottered down the stairs towards the main deck.

The Brazilian students and staff were down here—I knew so because although there weren't any here where I was, I could hear their voices coming from the other end of the deck—the bow of the ship, probably. I looked around for signs of anyone round me, saw no one, and slipped into the nearest classroom, the door of which was wide-open and looked as though it hadn't been used once since the cleaners had been in back at the port. There was a rubbish bin in the corner, I saw—intended for scrunched-up pieces of paper, no doubt, but just big enough to fit the bottle.

Okay, I thought, straightening up, now what? I could go upstairs and try to rebuild the bridge between myself and Marc (not something I felt up to at the moment), or I could go and talk to James and Peter. That didn't fill me with much comfort either, though, remembering the expressions on their faces when they'd heard about the kiss—really, it had only been a little one. Then there was May, but I wasn't all that happy with her either. She was quite happy to help me when it suited her, when she got something out of it, but all of a sudden, she didn't want to interfere? Or had she only told me that because she thought that in my confusing way, that was what I'd really wanted, to be able to figure it out on my own and learn from it? I didn't know, and thinking about it now made me want to drink another bottle, even though it would probably make me sick and half knock me out.

Another idea occurred to me—a strange idea, one I wouldn't have thought of at all if things had been fine with me and the others. Those Brazilians up there—they weren't much older than I was. They weren't at all like the Russians had been, older, and possibly in league with the Hammerhearts. These people knew we were here and thought of us more as protectors than a potential for danger. Why not go and meet them? Well, there was one possible reason not to: their teachers mightn't let me. I had magic, and I may be effectively a guest of honour on this ship, but that didn't change the fact that I was only fourteen. They probably imagined that we, the Woodward affiliates, were all adults who were skilled in anti-Hammerheart combat. Well, they were half right.

With my decision made, I tottered back out of the room and headed up the hallway towards the bow. The worst that could happen was that the teachers could tell the captain that there was a strange kid speaking English with a funny accent on the ship, and he would know exactly who I was, having met all of us the previous day. When I emerged from the cabin, I saw that pretty much all the students were out here, and they were having some sort of break—at least, they were laughing and smiling like they were on break. A few of them noticed me when I came through the door and pointed me out to their fellows, their open curiosity evident even from where I was standing, but my attention had turned to the three adults who were supervising.

One of them had looked around at the sound of the opening door and had hurried over when he had seen me. His expression was unreadable (not blank, just full of thoughts I couldn't identify) as he spoke rapidly to me in his own language, asking me a question I had no idea how to answer. When he had finished, I said, "I'm with the Woodwards," and jerked my thumb back and up over my shoulder so he would know I was talking about the upper passenger deck. "And I only speak English," I added.

I thought he got the gist of it, because his expression relaxed and he offered to shake my hand, though without speaking a word, so perhaps he had picked up on the English theme as well. I smiled back and accepted the offer, then looked back at the students to see that two boys had approached me, looking a little nervous but still more curious than anything else. They had also heard what I'd said, as had the other two adults, and they had all concluded that I wasn't dangerous. Why should they think otherwise, I thought? I didn't look dangerous at all. Tipsy, maybe, and I had to put in a great effort not to let that show, but not dangerous.

Another thing I learnt quite quickly was that while the majority of the staff members (certainly the few I met) had only rudimentary English skills, most of the students were actually quite fluent in the language, and even the ones who weren't could still speak it disjointedly and understand most of what was being said. I ended up meeting and being introduced to all thirty of them, and although I forgot many of their names by the time I left (and could only remember a small handful later), it turned out that they were all very friendly.

"Do you have magic?" one of the boys—Luis—had asked me at one point.

I had been about to say no, and then I remembered the devices I still had in my pockets. If I said yes, they would probably want me to show them, but they wouldn't want to see the things these devices could perform—except for maybe one.

"Only a little bit," I said honestly, "and most of it is for fighting, but I can do this."

I took my stunner from my pocket, pointed it at the nearest girl —Camila—and clicked. It took about a second for the other students to realise that she was frozen on the spot, and when they got it, one of the boys—Bruno—darted forward and gave her a great big kiss on the lips. Everyone laughed as I released her from the effects of the magic; she glared at me, and then shouted at Bruno in Portuguese, but I didn't think she looked as annoyed as she was making out.

There was one other thing interesting about the short time—no more than half an hour—that I spent with the Brazilians, and that was the girls. The ratio of boys to girls among the students was pretty even but of the girls, a great many of them were extremely attractive. Several of them had tried to kiss me on the cheek when we had first met, though none of their lips quite touching my skin, making me think that I was a little more desirable than I had any right to be and wondering if May was playing a role in that. (I would find out later from May herself that what they had actually been doing was nothing more than a friendly custom in their culture.) The not-quite-kisses aside, though, there were a few of them who had paid me very close attention the whole time, perhaps interested in the power they thought I had. I didn't know, and mostly I didn't care, but there was one particular girl among them who had caught my attention as well, though for a very different reason.

Her name was Larissa, and she looked like she couldn't be more than a year or two older than me—no older than Lena or Stella, anyway. She had smooth, caramel-coloured skin, was slightly shorter than me, very pretty, and slim but pleasantly curvy as well. The most striking thing about her from my perspective, though, was that so many of her facial features looked like Natalie. Her eyes, nose, and even cheekbones looked like they were the same shape, although her eyes were darker, and even her hair looked very similar. She, too, had kept her eyes on me throughout the exchange, and mine had been regularly drawn back to her.

I found myself thinking about her later, after the students had been ordered to re-enter the cabin so they could get back to work— the order had been in Portuguese but Luis had told me what was going on. I was invited to stay with them even after that point, but decided that it was probably time to return to my own deck and face whatever was waiting for me there. As I climbed the stairs, I felt better about things in general, like I could handle myself without flipping out. The alcohol had already mostly cleared from my mind, and now I had another girl to imagine cuddling up to at night. Not fair on Larissa, perhaps, given that it was mostly her similarity to Natalie that made me think of her at all, but did it matter? I probably wouldn't see her again anyway.

Before I met any of them, though, I ran into a totally unexpected problem: I had locked myself out of our deck. It was all very well and good locking the door from the inside when we were there, but none of us had thought to ask the captain for keys of our own. I stood before the door, thinking; should I go to the captain and ask him to let me in? I could, but I didn't really want to disturb him in the middle of his important business, whatever it happened to be at the moment.

It didn't matter; someone opened the door from the other side at that moment, giving me one hell of a fright. It was Peter—how had he known I was here? I hadn't even knocked, and even if I had, we usually hung out at the other end of the deck.

"Thanks, man," I said, relieved as I passed him.

"Hang on, mate, we need to talk," he said, shutting the door and turning to face me.

I sighed. "You gonna get stuck into me too?"

"You know your problem is that you keep making things more difficult than they need to be," he said, "so why do you keep doing it?"

I shook my head, exasperated. "Pete, she kissed me. I was sitting on my chair, she got up, bent down and kissed me—I didn't even have time to kiss her back before it was over. If Marc really saw that and thinks it's my fault, then he's the one with the problem."

"Okay," he said slowly, "but what did you think when she kissed you?"

"I thought it was more like a goodbye kiss than anything else," I said, and the moment the words were out, I knew they were true. "She had just told me that she and Marc are going to try dating again, and I was okay with that because I still want Natalie. That's all it was."

"I dunno if that's all it was to Amelia," Peter said warily.

My stomach fell. "What do you mean?"

"Well, she said that it was important to her," he said, "that it meant a lot because she really cared about you. Mind you, she's been with Marc since then and I think they've patched things up pretty well. My advice to you would be to stay away from them and give them a bit of space."

"Yeah, probably for the best," I said, and sighed again. "Damn, this is not what we want when we all have to be stuck here together."

"I agree," he said, giving me a very level look. "Trust is really important now, since it's only us six still fighting. We can't afford any more of these kinds of fractures if you keep having sex with anything that has a vagina."

I swore. "What the hell?"

He sighed. "Yeah, I shouldn't have said that. Sorry. You're right —this is such a mess."

* * *

Dinner that night was very uncomfortable, with no one talking to anyone and few able to look at me at all. It felt like I had become a bit of a pariah among the group and I couldn't figure out why. I got why Marc was pissed at me, even if I disagreed with his reasoning, and I got why Amelia might think it best not to give me any more signals that could be misinterpreted, but the others? May wasn't looking at anyone, and James too kept his eyes on his plate. I was more than happy when it was over; I told the others that I was going to bed, and none of them argued. I got goodnights from all but Marc, and then by eight o'clock Atlantic portal time, I was alone in my room.

I couldn't sleep. It wasn't a surprise to me, given that I had actually done quite well the previous night—got up less than twelve hours ago, and got three hours of blissful, dreamless sleep when I'd been with May. I could also hear music coming from the deck below, the same sort of stuff that the Brazilians had pumped out the previous night, and rather than putting me to sleep, it made me want to get up and dance. Instead of that, though, I first thought of Natalie (the one I was supposed to be thinking of) but as I listened to the music below, my mind turned towards Larissa.

And then afterwards, as I lay there, cuddling my pillow, it was her I imagined I was lying with. This is okay, I thought to myself. It doesn't matter if I imagine being with her because the odds are that I'll never see her again, and if we do run into each other tomorrow or sometime on the Rock, so what? It doesn't mean we're going to do anything. Even if the opportunity arose to do something with her, or any of the other attractive girls I had met that day, I wouldn't be about to take it. May had already offered to provide the interim intimacy I may need, and beyond that, I had my sights set firmly on Natalie. Peter had correctly pointed out that I made things more complicated than they needed to be; there was no reason to keep doing that when I knew the problem existed. All the same, though, I privately hoped that whatever Larissa was doing down there, whatever boy she may or may not be dancing with at this very moment, that she was thinking about me too.

Around ten o'clock, May contacted me telepathically for the first time since earlier that afternoon, checking to see that I was okay. I was touched and responded that I was. We got into a sort of mental conversation, during which I learned a few things about that day. Firstly, the not-quite-kiss thing the Brazilians had done didn't mean they were necessarily attracted to me. If they were, I would have felt their lips. I also found out that Larissa had, indeed, been intrigued by me, so much that a couple of hours ago, around the time I had gone to bed in fact, she had come up to our deck and tried to come in, only to find that the doors were locked, both in the stairwells and elevators—she tried both. And speaking of doors, I also found out that it had been she, May, who had let Peter know that I was locked out.

When I asked her why she hadn't wanted to help me that afternoon, she reiterated that it was because she didn't want to just smooth things over every time they went a little pear-shaped. She also thought that in truth, I didn't really need to be helped because this time, I hadn't actually done anything wrong. Marc might have a trust issue regarding Amelia at the moment but that wasn't my fault. When I asked her if Marc could forgive me, she told me he probably could, but only if I made the first move to heal the breech between us. After this, she asked if I wanted to come to her room, or she come to mine, and I told her not tonight. Although sex with May again would be truly awesome, I couldn't predict how I would feel about myself afterwards, and I didn't think I needed that tonight. I instead asked if she wouldn't mind putting me to sleep for the night, and this time, she obliged.

* * *

I woke early the following morning, around six o'clock, and felt thoroughly rested indeed. I got up, had a shower, got dressed, and left my room to see if there was anything happening elsewhere on the deck. Peter and James were both up and dressed already, I found, although they were at separate ends of the cabin and doing their own things. In Peter's case, it was playing a computer game on a laptop.

"You're up early," I remarked, sitting down opposite him in the sitting room.

"So are you," he said, not taking his eyes off the screen. "You nervous about today, too?"

"A little," I said truthfully. Yes, we would be getting in a tangle with Hammerhearts within the next seven or eight hours, but that wasn't the main thing on my mind at the moment. Right now felt like the best time to try to make things right with the others, so I took a deep breath. "Listen, I'm sorry about what happened with us yesterday."

He shrugged. "Me too, but we're cool now, right?"

"Guess so," I said, a weight lifting from my shoulders—that had been easier than I'd expected. "Er—what's James doing up there anyway?"

"Up where?"

"Up near the front of the ship—"

"You know they call it the bow, right?"

"Oh, bite me," I grinned. "So you know what he's doing?"

"I didn't even know he was awake. I might have gone to join him, except that I'm kind of in the battle of my life here."

"I'll leave you to it, then," I said, and headed off.

It turned out that James was also using a laptop—the very same one as Peter, duplicated from the bag. Unlike Peter, though, he wasn't playing an intensely graphical shooting game, but seemed to be writing something. He wasn't receptive to conversation at first but eventually, when he realised that I wasn't going to give up, he sighed and shut the lid of his computer, resting his elbows on it and looking at me quizzically.

"I get what you're trying to say," he said. "What's bothering you more, though? Your guilty conscience or how the rest of us think of you?"

"The first one," I said, "but even more than that, I don't want other people to be unhappy or upset because of my actions—not just upset with me, but upset at all. Is that too much to ask?"

"It does sound like a tall order," he said, smiling a little. "Look, I've known you a long time and I know you can't help feeling the way you feel, but Pete's right—you do make things more difficult for yourself. You've been an expert for years at feeling the way you feel and choosing not to act on it. What's changed?"

"Nothing's changed," I said, a little defensively. The only thing that had changed was that I was no longer completely inexperienced with girls, but that wasn't the point. "I know that I did what I did, and it's not great. I can take responsibility for those actions, but I'm not about to behave the same way I did when I was cursed—I'm not so out-of-control."

"And the kiss?"

"She kissed me. Like I said to Peter, if Marc really saw it then he would have seen that. I know how I feel about Amelia: I like her plenty, she's a very good friend, but we're not going to have that kind of relationship. Natalie's still the one I want, and when we get back to the future, whenever I get a spare moment, I'm going to try to get her back."

"And are you sure Amelia feels the same way you do?"

"Fairly sure, since she's agreed to date Marc, but if she doesn't— well, that's not my problem. I know that sounds mean but—"

"No, it's not mean, it's fair," said James, and he grinned at me. "I may be a few weeks younger than you, but I think you're starting to grow up."

I sighed. "Yeah, the damn hard way."

Everyone was up within the hour and we all had breakfast together around seven o'clock. Everyone but Marc was already dressed, and I found myself wondering why he wasn't also—had he just gotten up later than everyone else? The answer came from May, who communicated telepathically to me that the reason why Marc wasn't dressed was because he had spent the night in Amelia's room and then the two had showered together this morning, and since his clothes had been back in his own room, he had gotten back into his pyjamas for now with intent to get dressed after breakfast. That made me feel a little jealous, but at the same time gave me the opening I would need to set things to rights with my biological brother.

So when breakfast was done and everyone went their own separate ways for the morning, I waited until Marc was in his room before following after and knocking on his door. When I heard him call out, I opened it to find him turning to face me, having just gotten himself dressed—that was a relief. His smile faded a little when he saw me and I knew that for a second, he had thought I was Amelia.

"What's up?" he asked flatly.

I took a deep breath and said, "I wanna apologise for what happened yesterday."

"The kiss?"

"The misunderstanding. Look," I said, shutting the door so that the two of us would have privacy, "you don't have to worry about anything happening with me and Amelia."

He didn't say anything, only glared at me.

"Look, I can't control how she feels, but I do know how I feel, and it's Natalie that I want—"

"But who you're not with anymore, because you had sex with Amelia," he pointed out, unnecessarily refreshing my memory of the time that Amelia and I had spent together.

"I'm going to try to get her back when we get back to the future," I told him. "I know it's a long shot, but she's the one I really want. I do care about Amelia, but that's all it is—it's not in that way."

"And what if you can't get Natalie back? What if she doesn't forgive you?" he asked. "Then what?"

"Honestly, I'm not planning that far ahead," I said. "If that happens, I'll worry about it at the time."

He didn't look convinced, and I added, "But it won't be Amelia, okay? I'm not going to get between you two. You'll be better for her than me at the moment—I think we can both agree on that."

"And what if she goes to you and says she would rather be with you than me?" he asked, his temper rising.

This was getting old, I thought, but I really didn't want to fight with Marc. If I retorted now, it could turn into a real fight. So I said, "I don't think she will, but if she does, I won't be taking her up on it. I don't wanna make anyone else feel the way I made Natalie feel, including you."

"You'd do that?"

"Yeah, I would," I said honestly, and at the time, I meant it.

He relaxed visibly. "So why did she kiss you then? It seemed important to her."

"Maybe it was," I said, "but I don't think it meant any more than that, thanks for being supportive, and all that. She'd just told me about you and her and I'd just said I would be okay with it."

"Thank goodness," he said, sitting down on his bed. "Man, I don't know what's gotten into me lately."

"It's okay," I said. "So, are we okay?"

"Yeah, reckon so," he said, grinning weakly at me. "I really didn't wanna fight with you."

"That makes two of us," I said, feeling more relieved than I had since—well, probably since before the Hero Crystal had been taken.

Chapter 24: Through the Portal 3.0

The six of us got increasingly more and more nervous as the morning wore on, and by eleven o'clock, we couldn't stand it anymore. The Hammerhearts must know exactly where we were by now, since we had been out of our shadow for a full two days now, so whatever they tried against us to get through the portal was going to have to be pretty strong in magic. We knew that we would stop them from getting through; though what we didn't know was how much damage we were going to take along the way.

We decided to have an early light lunch and then, since action felt better than just waiting around, we all left our deck. While Marc went upstairs to tell the captain what was about to go down, the rest of us went down to the main deck, through the cabin and out onto the open deck at the bow of the ship, which was deserted this time. Good, I thought; as nice as it would be to catch up with the Brazilians again, especially one particular girl, it would be much better for everyone if they stayed inside the cabin, where they would be safe and couldn't get in our way.

Marc re-joined us after about ten minutes, grinning and saying that the captain had given us the green light to do what we needed to do out here, and he would just continue moving the ship towards the portal unless we sent him some sort of signal that we needed to stop.

"What signal is that?" James asked.

Marc shrugged. "He assumes it'll be some sort of red flash of light, but it'd probably be easier if May just made him stop. Oh, and speaking of May," he turned to the Honnie, "maybe you should be invisible for this."

"I was thinking that, too," Peter agreed.

May didn't have a problem with that, so Marc did the honours with his invisibility toggle, and then the six of us, only five of whom could be seen, were left to discuss what tactics we were going to use in the upcoming fight. If they turned up with anything like the kind of magic they had brought last time, we would be in a world of trouble, since the devices we had could only really take the Hammerhearts on head-on, and even then only in small numbers. May was our secret weapon, but even she would be in trouble if they got a chance to use too much magic early. Worst of all, after what had happened in Recife, all of us agreed that there was a strong chance that Hall or Hammerson himself might decide to check up on us.

We weren't able to settle on anything by half past twelve, but we had to stop talking about it after that because that was when the Brazilians decided to join us on the outside deck for their lunch.

They recognised me, of course, to the bemusement of most of my friends, and I hurriedly introduced the two groups to each other—although it was a slightly embarrassing moment when I couldn't remember half the students' names. Marc and Amelia each said hello, but otherwise weren't interested in getting to know any of them, and ended up walking away towards the port side so that they didn't have to. James was more polite but within a few minutes, apologised and said he was just too nervous to chill with them. Since they couldn't see May, only Peter joined me in chatting to them.

Quite a few of the students glanced regularly at Amelia, apparently having recognised her as a Woodward, and were a little hurt by her not wanting to talk to them. Otherwise, though, they were quite cheerful and as lighthearted as they had been the previous day. Within a few minutes, I could see that Peter had been charmed by them as well, especially when a number of the girls did that kissing thing with him—now I knew for sure it wasn't just me. I especially knew it when Amanda, a pretty, light-skinned girl, actually hung onto his arm for several minutes, although it wouldn't be long before I started thinking that she was carrying a torch for him already.

Larissa was there, of course, but although she smiled and said hello to Peter, she didn't kiss him as she had done to me. That wouldn't have mattered either way to me, but one thing that did matter was the way she behaved towards me. Other than saying hi and not-quite kissing me when she had first come onto the deck with the others, we didn't speak to each other directly, but she did keep looking at me throughout most of that time; and when it seemed none of the others were looking at her, she gave me a bright smile that made my heart lift every time I saw it, albeit out of the corner of my eye. I smiled back at her to let her know that I was seeing her, but that was the full extent of it. I had no idea what she expected me to do—what did Brazilian girls normally want from guys anyway? I was glad I didn't know, really, because it meant that I wouldn't be able to self-sabotage by trying anything.

We had told the students immediately after the introductions that we were out here because there was going to be trouble within the next two hours—by two-thirty, the portal would be closed and everything would have already happened. One of them passed the news onto the teachers who had come out to keep an eye on them, but otherwise, no one seemed nearly as alarmed as they should have. Even when May sent us a telepathic message about fifteen minutes later, letting us know that trouble was fast approaching, and we reiterated that they should all go inside, none of them seemed to want to heed us—they were more excited by the prospect of seeing a lot of magic up close than they were worried about their safety.

This only changed when, from a great distance away but still very loud, an amplified voice spoke to the ship. Even though I couldn't understand the words as they were spoken, I still thought it sounded threatening, and I knew for sure when May translated for us and communicated it telepathically—it seemed that she understood Portuguese as well. It went along the lines of: "Stop, you are being ordered to stop. If you do not stop, we will open fire. Some people are going to board your ship before it enters the portal. You are going to stand back and let them, or you will be sunk. Do not try to contact the Woodward guard; the moment you do, we will hear you and we will open fire. Do not bother resisting, for we have ways of making you comply. Stand back and let us do our business, or else."

The threats to sink the ship were, I knew, empty; the Hammerhearts wouldn't really want to sink their only way of getting through the portal, not unless they had no chance whatsoever of boarding. The effect was to scare the hell out of the Brazilians, and on that score, the Hammerhearts had succeeded. The adults began ordering the students to enter the cabin, and then followed themselves, but after they had all gone, a few of the students came back through the doors and then stood by them to watch (Larissa, Amanda, and the two boys who had first approached me yesterday, Luis and Andre). We never sent a signal to the captain to stop, and so the ship kept on moving forward.

The Hammerhearts were coming—I could now see their vessel approaching, and people—the Hammerhearts themselves—were being levitated above it on ropes, ready to descend onto this very deck, I felt sure. And we still didn't have a strategy to deal with them. I now took matters into my own hands: The ideal solution would be for May to knock all those Hammerhearts out in an instant, and take control over whoever was piloting that other ship to make them turn around and leave us alone. The second part of that would work, but the first part was too risky with those Brazilians watching—they would know we hadn't done anything if it went that way. Later, I would think that we could have just gotten May to make them forget what they saw, but under the pressure of the moment, that seemingly simple idea didn't occur to me. What did occur was the memory of what Amelia had told us back in the future: The Hammerhearts would return to their bosses with no memory of what happened to them out here, and I decided that making them forget what they were supposed to be doing was our best bet.

I projected this thought just as the Hammerhearts closed within a few hundred feet, but the response I got from May was alarming: There was no one piloting the vessel—it was automated. So the Hammerhearts were going to land whether we liked it or not. The first part of the plan seemed to work, though, because when two dozen or so Hammerhearts came down from the sky, landing on the deck before us, they all looked totally confused and with no idea where they were or what they were supposed to be doing—it was a rather funny sight. And yes, I saw, Hall was with them, thankfully just as affected by May's mind as the rest were.

It gave us no more than a couple of seconds of reprieve. The moment Hall saw us, he bellowed at the other Hammerhearts to attack. They had also recognised me, Marc and Amelia, and were quick to leap into action, even if they had no idea where they were and what they were supposed to be doing. And so the fight got under way after all, with us swiping our bludginators and trying to pin them down with solid-outliners, and them doing the same but with a few jets of golden agonator light thrown in for good measure (none of those hitting their mark, thankfully). Hall gave us the most trouble with the Villain Crystal, actually succeeding in hitting Marc and almost knocking him overboard, but May still provided us with the advantage, for the Hammerhearts—Hall included—kept forgetting what they were doing every five seconds or so.

It was this lag in their movements that gave us the leg-up we needed, and although all five of us had been cut up a bit, and James had needed to be freed from thicky prison at one point, we were able to trap the majority of the Hammerhearts in thicky prison. Once they were out of sight, May knocked them unconscious so that each time someone freed them, they couldn't return to the battle. Slowly, by this method, we wore down their numbers until only Hall remained.

"I don't understand why you're fighting like this," he told us, fury all over his face. "Come on, show some real magic for a change."

A moment later, he had forgotten what he was doing, and it was enough for me to take a run at him. Before he had a chance to gather himself, I had recalled everything he had ever done to me, both as a Hammerheart and as an English teacher, and pivoted on one ankle, giving him a good, hard kick in the face. I hit him with such force that I lost my balance and toppled over on my arse, which certainly wasn't how it happened in the movies, but May made it look a lot better by knocking him out at the same time so that it looked like I had done it. Now, with Hammerheart bodies littered all over the deck, all of their minds contained within May's, and the vessel they had used to get here now travelling away on a pre-programmed route, the battle seemed to have been won.

A great cheer went up from the four watching Brazilians, and Peter and Amelia both joined in. James was grinning too, but his head was still in the game. "One of you," he called to the Brazilians, "go and get your teachers."

After what they had seen us do, they didn't dare disobey him. Andre turned at once and ran into the building, but the other three came hurrying out to meet us.

"Nice kick, John," Peter said, slapping me on the back as I reached him.

"Guys, we're not done yet," James hurriedly told us. "We need to sort all this out and get back to our deck before we get to the portal. The Woodward guard will be there."

He didn't dare say anymore within earshot of the Brazilians, but I got the message: We couldn't let the Woodward guard see that we were here. But then, what would they think had happened here? The moment the Brazilians mentioned who we were, the jig would be up…or would it?

That was when the rest of the Brazilians came sweeping through the doors, yelling and cheering and laughing. They were all stunned to see so many fallen bodies and the five of us, still standing and mostly unharmed—although we were bleeding in several places. They surrounded us and gave us what I could only think of as a hero's ovation. I put up with it for about thirty seconds, grinning sheepishly, before extricating myself from the throng and rejoining Marc and Amelia beside the doors. Peter was having a bit more trouble getting away from the pack than I had (Amanda, the girl who had hung onto him earlier, was practically all over him now). James, meanwhile, approached the adults as I watched.

"Excuse me," he said to them, and when he had their attention, "a batalha acabou. Derrotamos os soldados. Nós vamos voltar para nossa sede agora. O guarda Woodward fará exame os Hammerhearts antes que nós atravessemos o portal."

And then they were all smiling and shaking hands, and then James was coming back towards us. Marc, Amelia and I stood gaping.

"Did that really just happen?" Amelia said vaguely.

Peter and James reached us at around the same time, but James walked straight past us calling, "Come on, guys, we've gotta go pack up our stuff."

"What's going on?" Peter asked, hurrying to catch up with James, who was already climbing the stairs.

"Did you just speak Portuguese to those people?" I asked him.

"Yeah," James panted, "I asked May to give me that ability, just long enough to tell them what's going on without any communication breakdown. I can't remember any of it now, though, so I hope they don't try to talk to me later."

"And where is May?" Amelia asked.

"Back down there. I asked her to stay there to make sure there's no trouble with the Woodward guard. The Brazilians will assume they know about us, and they'll assume the Brazilians beat the Hammerhearts, and neither side will ask any questions. That's the plan, anyway. Best thing for us to do is hang out in our deck until we're through the portal, then get off the ship as soon as we dock so that we can get out of the Brazilians' way. I don't think they'll mind, they seem pretty cool."

"Great, just one problem with that plan," I told him as we arrived on our level.

"And what's that?" James asked, putting his hand on the doorknob and trying to turn it, only to find it locked.

"That," I said, and grinned at him.

"I'll go talk to the captain," Marc said, and continued up the stairs to the next level. He was grumpy and seemingly the only one not pleased with the way the afternoon had so far turned out, and given that we had almost lost him over the side of the ship, I couldn't really blame him.

It took another ten minutes before Marc returned, without the captain but with his key. He opened the door and then we all separated to clean up the things we had left lying around the ship. The unimportant things, we just threw in the rubbish bins, but the more important things, such as the laptops, we initially weren't sure what to do. Since the contents of their hard drives had changed, they no longer qualified as the same computer that was in the backpack, which meant that if we put them in there, there would now be three computers instead of one (James and Peter had both taken one out). In the end, we had satisfied any computer-related frustration we had ever had by hurling them off the side of the ship and into the ocean below. It was a few minutes after that that, through the window of the rear door to the cabin, we saw the moment the ship entered the portal.

"Got a bone to pick with you," Marc said to me a few minutes later while the five of us were using our first-aid kit to patch each other up.

"What have I done now?" I asked, getting my back up instantly —surely he wasn't about to accuse me of doing something else with Amelia...

"According to May, when those Hammerhearts were falling down onto the ship, you told her not to just suck their minds out so that we wouldn't have to deal with them at all. You know, we could have avoided all this"ℜ—he indicated his Band-Aidsℜ—"if we had been more direct with them."

"Erm—what?" I said, racking my brain—when had I ever told May that?

"Yeah, how you didn't want to make the Brazilians too suspicious by having them all just fall down in front of them—"

"Oh, right," I said, understanding. "Yeah, well of course we had to make it look like we were actually fighting them. I only meant that she shouldn't knock them out; I never even thought of just killing them, but I'm glad she didn't."

"But May's out there right now making the Hammerhearts forget the whole thing," James said. "Why not make the Brazilians forget it as well?"

"I honestly didn't think of that when they were coming down," I said truthfully. "Would you actually wanna just kill them? What if those guys were only under influential charms?"

"Would you have been that open-minded if I really had fallen off the ship?" Marc retorted. "Remember, you don't have the magic you'd need to save me, so it's all well and good thinking you wanna take the high ground nowℜ—"

"Hey lay off him already," Peter snapped at Marc, and I was relieved to finally have some backup. "If we'd figured all this out before they'd arrived, maybe we could have done just that—maybe May could have simulated an entire battle for the Brazilians, complete with John's face-kick on Hall—but none of us did, and that's on all of us, not John."

"True," James admitted, "but remember, this is war, and other than May, those Hammerhearts had a lot more power than we did. We knew the Hammerhearts wouldn't have ended up dead, based on what Amelia told us her father said, but we have to be prepared to aim to kill, otherwise like Marc said, it could have been us."

"Exactly," Marc said triumphantly. "Remember, this is war—it's about survival, not about who can not kill the most people. You gotta harden up and grow a pair, man."

"That's enough," Peter said firmly as I opened my mouth, my own anger beginning to boil—that had been unnecessarily below the belt. "We won, okay. Hall may have had us on the ropes a bit, but other than that, there really wasn't much danger from the rest of them —not with May knocking them out when they were in the thicky prison anyway."

Marc wanted to retort again—I wished he wouldn't, but given that he had come closest to serious danger throughout that battle, I could see why the end result of the battle was small comfort to him. Instead, he glanced at Amelia for her support, but when everyone else's eyes went to her too, she said, "I think they're right, Marc. Just because the battle might have been easier if we had killed them all, doesn't mean that's the right way to be going about things if we don't have to. Remember, we're the good guys."

Marc's face went red. "You're seriously gonna side with them instead of me?"

Amelia didn't flinch. "I side with whoever I agree with."

And so it was a rather frosty group of teenagers who left the upper passenger deck for the last time and went back down to the main deck. Once again, the outdoor area was deserted; the Brazilians were in the process of packing up their own personal effects from the lower passenger deck. Peter and I stuck pretty close, both of us dismayed at how, once again, the group seemed to be turning on each other. James stood near us but for now, he and I didn't have a lot to say to each other. Marc stared grumpily over the port side of the deck, not far from where he had almost fallen off, and Amelia stood with him, clearly trying to mend the breach between them.

By the time the Brazilians returned to the deck, pushing enormous trolleys packed with suitcases, we could see Rock Haulter pointing out of the ocean in the distance—we would be there in no more than half an hour, and the sight of it from here for the third time lifted my spirits immensely. When they came out, James went over to the nearest adult and began speaking Portuguese again; Peter rolled his eyes at me, and a few of the Brazilian students looked surprised and pleased to hear that one of us could speak their language, but most of them were too busy celebrating our imminent arrival on the Rock, the moment when we could all disembark after more than two days at sea, and the fact that we had gotten past a Hammerheart ambush to do it.

The four students who had watched the fight from the cabin doors surrounded me and Peter for much of this time, laughing and chattering away and asking us questions about all the fights we had been in—there sure had been a few. Peter had a lot of fun with this, describing in detail how he and James had needed to climb up a set of monkey bars to get away from some Hammerhearts in the Chopville High battle—which we pretended had happened a week ago, since the truth about it happening a couple of weeks in the future would blow their minds. I wasn't as comfortable with this kind of attention, but I couldn't help grinning reluctantly at the admiration.

"This was actually one of the easier fights we've been in," Peter said impressively. "I can't wait to tell my girlfriend about it when we get home."

Classy, Pete, I thought to myself, grinning at him. The girlfriend reference hadn't been necessary in the context of the battle, and I couldn't see how Rebecca would be any more impressed with this outcome than any other fight we'd been in, but I knew why he had said it. His admirer, Amanda, was practically gooey-eyed over him now, and he was starting to realise himself that he might actually have to let her down. This was his attempt to stop her crush in its tracks before it could turn into something else. She definitely took these words in—I saw so by the slight widening of her eyes—but other than that, her behaviour didn't change at all. Either she was only going to admire him and that was it, or she was up for a challenge.

* * *

Apparently, James's second dialogue with the Brazilians had been to ask them if we could disembark as soon as we docked so that we could get out of their way. They had agreed, of course, whether with May's assistance or not, and so when we pulled up beside the jetty and the gangplank had been set down, it was the six of us, an invisible May bringing up the rear, who got back on solid ground first. Once we were on the jetty, the five of us waved up to the Brazilians—they waved back—and then we turned and set off up the path towards the main hall.

"Alrighty, everyone," Peter said happily as we climbed the sloping path, "which campsite should we go to?"

"Group F's, I suggest," Marc said, now looking a little happier than he had on the ship. "It'd be the easiest to get in."

"There is someone here," May told us suddenly, and we all stopped dead in our tracks. There was the main hall off to our left, looking so out of place in this wild environment, but the path to our campsites was straight ahead and upwards.

"Someone here?" James repeated slowly.

"Yes, someone else on the island, watching us when we arrived."

"Smiley?" I said hopefully, my spirits rising even more as I imagined telling him everything we had done, the fact that we had come through the time axis to get here, and that we had a Honnie—a real live Honnie—helping us.

"No, not him," she said, and I wasn't entirely sure, but I thought she sounded a little regretful too.

"Underwood," Marc said flatly.

"Yes, that is him."

"Wow, I thought he would have left by now," I mused as we set off again. "Surely he's found the magic he needs to get off the island —Moran did."

"I don't care why he's here as long as I don't run into him," Amelia told us.

"If he can watch us, then he knows we're here," James said, and I felt like making a 'duh' sound at him. "It might be a good idea to let him know why we're here so that he doesn't worry that we want him for something, or that he's in any danger. He might actually know some stuff that might help us."

"And how are we going to do all that without talking to him?" Peter asked, smiling slightly.

"I don't wanna see him either," Marc said. "I don't want him to know I don't have magic anymore."

"He's gonna notice that we're not as powerful as we used to be," I pointed out.

"Maybe May could make him not notice," Peter said hopefully.

"I can make him not give you any trouble," she agreed.

"Okay, good," James said, relieved. "So, I guess tomorrow, we—me, John and Peter—go up and talk to him. I'm guessing he's living in the same cave where Smiley lived. You sure he's not there, May?"

"That is where he is living," she confirmed, "but he is definitely alone."

I couldn't remember the password for the Group F campsite, but fortunately, Marc could. When he opened the door for all of us, we found that the interior was pretty much as I remembered it. I did a walk-around inspection of the three campsites, the carpark and the bedrooms to be sure, but it looked as though nobody had been in here since we had left in a scramble the last time. The keys had been left in the hidden panel in the tree house, and I smiled at them, knowing they would be our way to find whatever we needed from this island.

"Guys, there's something we should quickly try before we settle in," James said to us as several people collapsed onto the couches in the Group F campsite. "Natalie created that carpark to be secure, which means the enchantments around it must be pretty strong. I know I'll be fine, and so will you three, but you two," he indicated May and Amelia, "may not be covered by it. If you two can get out of it but not back in, then we may need to find some other way for you to get around."

This turned out not to be an issue for May who, after testing one of the hover cars, proclaimed that she hated it and would rather get around on foot. Given her Honnie athleticism, I imagined climbing the mountain wouldn't be too much more difficult for her than walking around on the ground. As for Amelia, it turned out not to be a problem either; if she left through the garage, then she was able to enter through it as well, so long as she was in a hover car at the time. When she left the campsite through the Group F entrance and attempted to re-enter the carpark, though, even with a hover car (which Peter had driven outside for her), she was unable to get in. That restriction applied to all of us, it seemed, for James ended up having the same problem. So as long as we left through the carpark, we could re-enter that way, and only the other entrances needed to be really secure with good passwords. So after the experimentation, we set about changing the three of them before finally, at long last, it was time for dinner.

As we ate, we talked about how we were going to begin the monumental task facing us. Without any magic to start with, the only way we could search the caves was by taking our cars out and literally looking in every cave we found. Furthermore, since we only had one of each key, and the enchantments on our extender-case didn't seem to work on them (James put them both in and then took them both out, only to find that they hadn't duplicated), it meant that the six of us would have to search together. Even if we split into two groups and one took each key, each group would only be able to open half the caves they found. There wasn't yet any efficient way to search, so all we could do was keep an eye out for any shortcuts we found along the way, but in the meantime, we would have to do it the long way.

* * *

Later that night, I was alone in my room. We had loaded things into our rooms by way of taking them out of the backpack and watching them duplicate, but other than picking out clothes which probably wouldn't fit perfectly, I hadn't bothered to get much from the bag. Weariness had crept up on all of us not long after dinner, and I had been the first to tell the others that I was going to bed. I was tired, and a little sore from the battle, but mostly, I was beginning to feel depressed and lonely again. Apparently, night-time was when those emotions liked to come out and play.

I really missed Natalie. It wasn't all the time I had spent wanting her piling up on me now, but the brief time that we'd had together—just four days, but four of the happiest days I could remember. Well, I'd spent most of one of those days worrying, but I had still been happy because I'd had her. Now, I had gone and screwed everything up—literally—and I mightn't ever get to be that happy again. Yes, that was a depressing thought.

One by one, I heard the others going to bed over the following couple of hours, and by ten o'clock, it seemed to be completely quiet out there. I wanted to sleep, and maybe I would be able to, but there was something else I wanted to do and that was drink. Careful, John, you're heading down a slippery slope if you get into a habit of drinking when you're down, I thought. The voice was reasonable and, in my emotional state, utterly insignificant. I spent maybe ten minutes wrestling with myself before finally, giving up, I had crept back out of my room to see if there was anyone in the campsite—if there was, I would just get a bottle of water. It was blessedly empty, and so over to the backpack I went.

I began rummaging through its contents, originally thinking of the same bottle I had drunk yesterday, but then I remembered that Peter had said they'd gotten alcohol. He hadn't said it was just beer, so maybe there was other stuff in here that I could try. I kept digging through the backpack, shifting things aside so that I could reach other things, hearing things clinking and rattling and trying to be as quiet as possible. Eventually, I located more bottles, and I knew I'd hit the jackpot. There was wine (both red and white), champagne, vodka, whisky, and even tequila. Had Peter been planning to drink all of this? I thought, and smirked. I almost went for the beer anyway, thinking it seemed appropriate given my reason for drinking in the first place, and then changed my mind. I already knew what beer tasted like; time to mix it up a bit.

I took a bottle of red wine from the bag, watched as it duplicated itself inside, and then began shifting the contents back into place as best I could so that no one would know I had ever taken it out. I then tiptoed back to my room, shut the door behind me, sat on my bed, and unscrewed the cap. I put my nose to the opening and inhaled with satisfaction; even the smell was intoxicating, and I already felt better about doing this. I put the bottle to my mouth, took a nice long sip, and then almost dropped the bottle in shock. It really did go to my head, and a lot quicker than I had been expecting.

As I began to drink again, more carefully this time, I found myself thinking, not of Natalie, but of Larissa—honestly, other than the fact that I hardly knew the latter, it didn't take much effort to make that connection. As I sat here, I now understood why so many people felt like they needed to rebound after a break-up. When my relationship with Serena had ended, I'd had a ready-made opportunity to rebound with Lena, but I hadn't taken it—mostly out of guilt, both for the way my relationship had ended and the way I had strung Lena along throughout. I still felt guilty now, of course, but somehow this felt different. Even though I wanted Natalie back, and fully intended to try to get her back, I was realistic enough to know that the odds were stacked against me. And when I failed, as I probably would, I would want to rebound—I felt sure of this because I already wanted to now.

This was undoubtedly why I was open to May (who I didn't have to worry about hurting), and considerably less open to Amelia (who I really didn't want to hurt), and it also seemed to be why I was now enjoying the regard of an attractive foreign girl. Exactly what Larissa thought of me, I still couldn't be sure, but I did feel sure of one thing: She did like me. In some way, she did like me. I had felt reasonably sure of this since just after the battle aboard the ship, when I had been surrounded by admirers for about thirty seconds, and Larissa had been foremost among them. She had hugged me, which had been very nice; and she had kissed me on the cheek, a real skin-on-skin kiss this time, and in my mind, that was suggestive. Then later, as we were approaching the Rock, she had stood close to me—very close, like in-my-personal-space close. That could have meant nothing—

maybe that was normal in their culture—but it had made me feel tingly all the same.

I put the mostly full bottle on the floor beside the bed and lay down, thinking that I should probably hide the bottle but now feeling like I couldn't be bothered. Mostly, though, I thought that if I had to see Larissa again (I might be able to avoid her here, but you never know), I wasn't sure I would be able to resist her charms for too much longer, especially if she chose to be even more forward with them. I missed Natalie, but when I thought of her turning away from me with such disgust and disdain, it was hard not to be attracted to someone who wasn't turning away.

Part 4: Preparations for Battle

Chapter 25: Shot Down by the Brainiac

That first night on Rock Haulter, something happened to me that hadn't happened, so far as I could remember, since June: I connected with the Enlightener, that supernatural-thing that made me see certain things in my dreams. It usually happened when I was missing something and I needed to make some sort of connection, but this time, unless the dream kept recurring, I wasn't going to be able to figure it out in a hurry. I couldn't tell where the dream was located because the entire focus of the dream had been Lisa Pont; she was telling me something, but the words weren't making sense.

"What are you saying?" I asked her desperately.

"Your focus is all wrong," she said, and this time, I understood the words perfectly. "You need to change your focus, otherwise you won't find what you are looking for. I really need to tell you something, John."

"Tell me what?"

But when she spoke again, her words were totally incoherent. "What is it?" I asked her. "What is it? What is it?"

The desperation in my voice was what woke me up, and it wasn't until I was awake that I realised I had been sleep talking. I relaxed where I lay, thinking about the dream. Lisa was trying to tell me that my focus was wrong, and that there was something important that she needed to tell me.

Okay, what part of that dream ought I to focus on? Firstly, why was it Lisa who was telling me these things and not someone else—like Nicole, for example? Secondly, what was I focussing on that was so wrong, and what ought I to be focussing on instead? Thirdly, what was so important that she needed to tell me? I had no idea about the first one, and the third one—well that probably meant that I would keep having this dream until she told me what she needed to tell me, unless there was something else going on that I was missing. As for the second question, that was probably the most important part—the part I would need to work out in order to stop having these dreams.

I did have one idea about a starting place, though: Lisa and I hadn't been especially close in life. We had been friends, sure, but out of the ten of us who'd hung around the toilet block at school back in the early days, Lisa was probably the one with whom I was the least close to. Perhaps the reason why she was coming to me now instead of Nicole, or Serena, or hell, someone alive, is because the issue to which she was referring wasn't a particularly personal one.

That narrowed it down a bit, but not enough. Did it have something to do with Lucien? Or was it a bigger-picture issue like the kind James was grappling with? Also, and this was a point of curiosity, did the Enlightener know that I had travelled in time and that things were very different in the future? Was what I was seeing now relevant to this present or the present of August 30?

* * *

A little after nine o'clock that morning, Peter, James and I left the campsite in our hover cars—the same ones we had used last time—and followed the familiar path up the mountain to where Smiley had lived, and was now the residence of one Jacob Underwood. We had talked about it over breakfast and decided that we would tell him certain elements of the truth, but leave some other things out. He needed to know that I had lost the Sien-Leoard Crystal, but he didn't need to know that Marc had lost the Hero Crystal. He needed to know that we were on the Rock to magically outfit ourselves to take on the Hammerhearts, but he didn't need to know that Arnold Hammerson was dead and Lucien had taken over from him. Most importantly, he didn't need to know that we were time travellers from the future. Marc and Amelia had the morning off, which they were going to spend in the Group F campsite, and May sat alone on the verandah of the tree house—her favourite location among the three campsites—and kept an eye on things with her mind, ready to intervene if necessary.

As we flew, however, my mind was on a conversation I'd had with May earlier that morning, away from the rest of the group. Seeking some sort of clarity on my feelings and what I ought to do about them, I had asked her, "Does Amelia still feel the same about me as she did yesterday?"

> She hadn't answered for a few seconds, and I had nervously added, "You don't have to say if you don't want to."
>
> "She still cannot work out what she wants," she had said softly. "She and Marc were together last night, but she was thinking about you when they were intimate."
>
> I had felt simultaneously flattered and worried by this. My point in asking her that question was that if she had said Amelia was more set on Marc, it would leave me free to relieve myself of her. Now, though, it sounded like I wasn't going to be able to

do that all at once. All I had was the promise that I'd made to Marc, that if she came to me looking for intimacy, that I wouldn't take her up on it. That would have to do—surely I would have enough discipline and self-respect not to go back on my word on that one.

"Can I ask you another question?" I had asked her.

"You want to know what she thinks of you?" May had asked, and since she had no doubt been reading my mind to see who I was thinking of, I didn't need to wonder who she was talking about.

"Yeah, if you know, or want to tell," I had said, grinning a little.

"You guessed right about her," May told me. "She is attracted to you. She was attracted within a few minutes of meeting you and it has only grown stronger. She thinks you are mysterious and have a lot of hidden depth, but she also thinks that you are fragile—maybe because you are, lately," she had added.

"Mysterious," I had mused, "hidden depth. Well, I can't complain about having that effect on someone."

"Would you like to have her?" she had asked, and that had taken me by surprise.

"What—you mean have sex with her?"

"Yes."

I had thought about it, and then said, "I don't know—no, maybe not. If you were gonna offer to find a way to make that happen, thanks, but I don't need that."

Truthfully, I didn't feel right about May using her mind to get me and Larissa together. I had no doubt that she could do it, but what I had already asked her to do for me was as far as I was willing to go.

Underwood seemed cheery enough when we knocked on his door and then hollered at him through his intercom. As May had said, he had seen us arrive and then separate from the Brazilians immediately—and of course, he had recognised us at once.

"How did you watch us anyway?" Peter asked. "You got some sort of magical thing happening in there?"

"You could say that," he grinned smugly. "My grandfather had set a fair few things up in there already, and when I had the whole island to myself after those Russians left, I went exploring and set some stuff up in there as well, including a way to find out when the next lot of people got here. I could be wrong, but am I right in thinking that there are no Hammerhearts here this time?"

"Yep," I said, "they tried to come but the Brazilians wouldn't let them on their ship."

"Brazilians, you say," he said, and grinned. "That sounds interesting."

"So how come you're still here anyway?" James asked. "Smiley isn't still alive, is he?" he added hopefully.

"No," Underwood said shortly. "He died about two weeks after you guys left. Don't worry, he went in his sleep—it was about as good as it could have been."

The four of us exchanged sad looks, and then Underwood said, "And the reason why I'm still here is because I'm also watching what's going on out there, and honestly, I think I'm better off here— safer, at least. Is it just me or does it look like things have gotten much worse since I came here?"

"Yes, it is," I said, and held up my empty hands, "because they stole the crystal I used to have. Arnold Hammerson has it now."

"Tankom's dead, though," Peter added, "so it's not all bad."

"Well, that would explain a lot," Underwood said. "I don't see all the details, just bits and pieces—a general feel, I suppose you could say. It's been a bit lonely here, but mostly I'm happier to be here rather than out there. So—what brings you guys back here? Not the same thing as last time, obviously. I wasn't really expecting you to come back, although I'm not altogether surprised that you did—less of you, though."

"Basically, we're here to outfit ourselves to take on the Hammerhearts," James said—it was time for the real porkies. "Obviously we don't have the power that we used to have, and we're not working with the Sorcerers anymore—they're doing their own thing, and we're doing our own thing."

"Ah," he said, considering. "I thought I saw Marc and Amelia with you when you were coming up the hill—don't they still have magic?"

"Yeah, but we need more," said James, and there it was, the outright lie. "More than they're able to create with their own magic, if that makes sense," he added, and if I didn't know better, I probably would have believed that.

Fortunately for us, Underwood didn't know enough about magic to understand how implausible that was. "Well, you won't have any trouble with that here," he said, and grinned. "This place is unbelievable. I still haven't seen everything there is to see—I may never see everything there is to see."

"Is that all you've been doing, exploring the caves this whole time?" Peter asked.

"Course not," Underwood said, and grinned. "I've got an awesome entertainment system in there, and I've had plenty of time to watch movies, cricket, drink myself silly. I also play computer games and stuff like that, and if I ever get bored with all that stuff, there are some caves I know of that have some really awesome stuff in them. There's this one cave," he said confidentially, "fairly high up around the western side, that turns into a full-on simulated brothel when you go in there. I guess it can't really be real if there's no one else here, but I tell you what, when you're in there, it sure feels real."

"So you haven't been totally alone after all," I said, grinning reluctantly and wondering if I should go looking for that cave at some stage.

"Well, it's not the same as actual human company, you know," he said, "but I guess you're too young to have ever been to one of those places before, huh. It was okay, though, because the Russians were here for about another week after my grandfather died, and it seemed only right that I have a bit of fun with them before they left."

"Really?" Peter grinned. "You got away with that?"

"Sure I did—they loved my accent," he said smugly. "One of them said she'd been with another English-speaking boy weeks earlier, though, so I'm thinking it was one of you?"

"Marc and Tommy had a bit of fun with a couple of Russian girls before we left," I said, and Peter and James gave me very quizzical looks. "Didn't he tell you?" I added, surprised and hoping I hadn't just spilled someone else's secret.

"Good for them," said Underwood, "but apparently, all they did was make out a bit—I had plenty more to offer them. These Brazilians, are they like the Russians? Same sort of age range and all that?"

"I think they're a bit younger," James said, thinking. "Sixteen and seventeen, most of them."

"Ah," he said thoughtfully, "well, that sounds even better."

Of course it would, I thought, remembering how he had been with Siobhan before we had exposed to her the fact that he had cheated on her. But what irritated me even more was what he had said about the Brazilians—would he try something with them? Any of them? What if he decided to take a shot at Larissa? The thought of him even trying, let alone succeeding, made me feel mad and jealous.

That was when I realised that I did want her to myself after all.

We took our leave not long after that, after getting an assurance from Underwood that he would stay out of our way while we were here. The moment we shut his door behind us and were getting in our hover cars, Peter said to me, "I saw your reaction in there, John. You like Larissa, don't you?"

I started. "Say what?"

"Yeah, what?" James said, looking at me in surprise.

I shrugged, deciding on the spot that it wasn't worth trying to lie. "I got a bit of a crush, that's all. It's kinda hard not to, the way she was all over me—you saw her, Pete."

"Of course I did, that's how I knew which one you were thinking of," he said, "but—er—what about Natalie?"

"That hasn't changed," I said—also truthfully. "I still want her back, and I'm not gonna try anything with Larissa, I just don't want to think about her giving him the same attention she was giving me."

All of that was true. The only part of that I left out was that even though I wasn't going to try anything with Larissa, I wished I could. I remembered then what May had offered to do for me that morning, and then rejected it: If something happened, it happened; I would do it the normal way.

* * *

The next issue facing us was exactly how we were going to go about searching the mountain. The problems we had discussed over dinner the previous evening were still very much present, but we hadn't yet figured out the most efficient way of dealing with the restrictions currently plaguing us. Accepting that we would all have to search together, or a few of us search while the rest bum around here and do bugger-all, the problem seemed to be deciding where to search first, and in which direction to search.

We all had different ideas: Marc wanted to start at the top of the mountain and spiral downwards; James wanted to start at the bottom and spiral upwards; I wanted to start on the northern side and do every cave there before moving around to the eastern side, and so on; Peter wanted to do all the S-caves first, since they were the more serious ones, and finish off with the L-caves since they would be the more recreational ones; Amelia just wanted to get started, since searching anywhere had to be better than sitting around here talking about it; and May had nothing to contribute at all.

"Okay, everyone stop for a moment," James said loudly, and when there was silence, he continued. "Okay, John, Peter, let me explain to you both, in simple terms, why your ideas are stupid—"

"Hey, watch your mouth, man—"

But James held up his hand, and Peter fell silent. "If we do the S-caves first and the L ones later, we would basically be searching the entire mountain twice; and even if we did it like that, we would still need a direction to search in, otherwise we would search in a bunch of them more than once, so that idea would take an incredibly long time. If we search all on one side first, the same problem exists where we may search a bunch of them multiple times because we haven't picked a direction in which to search. There's also the caves that aren't quite on either side but are on the corners—the mountain is basically cone-shaped, not a pyramid, so those caves might get skipped altogether, or searched multiple times."

Peter and I exchanged looks. "Damn it, shot down by the brainiac again," he muttered sadly.

"Every time," I agreed mournfully.

"Marc, your idea would work okay," James went on, "but my thinking in starting at the bottom and moving around and then upward is that—well—the caves are just easier to get to. We may find the sort of things we're looking for without having to go all the way to the top, which will save us accumulated travel time over the duration. It's easy to assume the most valuable caves are closest to the top, but that assumption isn't really based on anything—is it?"

"Only that the most valuable cave is at the very top," Marc said, "but yeah, I guess you're right."

"So are we all agreed?" James asked, satisfied that once again, he had out-logicked the lot of us.

So at a little after one o'clock, the five of us humans took our hover cars (Amelia ended up in Lena's old car) out of the garage and down to the pink ribbon hanging on a branch of a tree on the path up to the Rock at the point where, if we were heading to the tree house, we should stop and enter the trees. May was waiting for us, standing there and carrying nothing but the clothes on her back. We then turned and headed back up to the Rock to begin the search, the Honnie sprinting along beside and easily keeping pace with us.

The first problem came before we had even started searching. Spiralling up the mountain was all good in theory, but the placement of the caves over the rock face made that a bit more difficult in practicality. Some of the caves were at ground level, while others were three, six, ten, fifteen feet off the ground. Exactly how far up should we climb before leaving them to the next spiral? This question resulted in another argument, this one getting even more heated, before I decided to approach it the way I would have done if I had the Sien-Leoard Crystal. What would a magically empowered John Playman do in this situation, I asked myself? It didn't take long to come up with an answer, and it was only a small step to figuring out how we could make it work without magic.

"Guys, stop, I have an idea," I told them, and when I had all their attention, I projected what I was thinking to May so that she would know where I was going with this. Aloud, I said, "Would you be able to remember if we've searched in a particular cave if you saw it again?"

"Yes," she said, and she was smiling—I knew I was on the right track.

"All well and good, John, but what if May's not with us?" James asked heatedly.

I rolled my eyes. "Where else would she be? And even if she's not with us in person, she's always with us in our minds. Do you think you could do what I'm thinking?"

Her response was a loud flapping sound a short distance away. Looking around, we all saw that a flag had suddenly appeared in front of the nearest cave—a flag with a bright, red cross on it. I grinned broadly, satisfied with what I was seeing, and then laughed heartily at the astonished and somewhat horrified looks on the others' faces.

"What the hell is that?" Marc said slowly, his eyes very wide.

"Guys, it's not real," I said, "look—"

And a moment later, the flag disappeared as if it had never been there. A stunned silence followed before, a few seconds later, comprehension hit James's face.

"That could work," he said slowly. "It just means that May needs to be awake and paying attention whenever we're searching, and I guess that's not too much to ask. It's not too much trouble for you to do that with all the caves we search, is it?"

"It is no more difficult than making you see and hear in our shadow," she told him.

"Wait, May did that?" Peter gaped at her. "Do you—do you have magic or ℜ—"

"Not magic, Pete, an illusion," James told him. "What we saw just there was totally in our minds—there was no flag there, not really, but May made us see and hear it as though it were. Would we even be able to touch it?" he asked her.

"Yes, but that would mean more effort," she said, "so better you do not."

"Fair enough," James agreed, and then clapped his hands. "Okay, I guess it doesn't matter how far up we go with each spiral—"

"Hang on, one more problem," Amelia said, staring up at the mountain. "What if we miss some caves anyway? Even if we notice the ones we've already searched, what if there are some that are too well hidden for us to see at all?"

That was a real stumper. Not even May could do anything to help us this time.

"We can't do anything about that," James said finally, "but there may be something hidden in one of the caves that we do find that will help us locate other caves—more valuable ones. I know it's a bit hit-and-miss, but in this case, I think we have to accept that it's the best we can do."

And with that, the search got under way. It was a bit disorganised at first but the more we searched, the more we settled into a bit of a rhythm. At first, we wanted May to carry and use the keys, since she didn't have to get out of a car each time, but after learning the story of Sien and Leoard from our minds (what we knew of it anyway), she only consented to carry the L-key. So it was Marc who took the S-key instead, and whenever he or May opened a door, they would have a look inside first before calling to the rest of us to take a look if it appeared interesting or useful. If we were called in, we would usually drive our cars straight through the door, and only got out if the cave was too narrow to fit the vehicles.

The majority of caves we found on that first day were pretty dull. Many of them led into empty rooms, dead ends, and a couple that were just boring old caves with nothing in them at all. Some of them might have been useful if we had only been here for entertainment or recreational purposes, such as the cave with the hot tubs which we had used the last time we had come here; the cave with the Olympic-sized swimming pool that we had used on the school camp; and similarly functional caves. The coolest of these was a large, tiered movie theatre, which was capable of playing any movie that had ever been created, in surround-sound and 3D if specified—that had to be a fairly recent addition, and I wondered which of the Sorcerers had created it. My money was on Frederic Woodward.

The most interesting caves we found that day, in my opinion, were what I could only think of as simulated environment caves. We got an almighty shock with the first one; when Marc opened the door, rather than finding some dank cave or a well-lit chamber, we were looking through an opening onto a great, big, sandy beach. When we went through the door to look on the other side, we saw that in this location, it was warm, early afternoon, cloudless, and the doorway back to the Rock was against the cliff-face behind the beach. Most of us thought that we had been teleported to some other location on Earth (an idea which James simply couldn't accept), but as we found more of these caves, we came to realise that their environments were magically created from scratch and entirely contained here on the Rock. The giveaway had been when we had gone through a doorway only to find ourselves smack-bang in eighteenth-century Vienna, where according to May, the people all around us didn't even exist.

As we were searching the foot of the mountain on the western side, having almost completed our first lap of the mountain by then, we passed by the Brazilians who were apparently having a mid-afternoon snack break. It didn't look like the entire group—maybe half of them or so. They were all sitting on the ground with notebooks (actual books, not the computers they called notebooks) in front of them, and as per usual, were chatting away cheerfully. They got a bit of a shock as we passed them by, taking in our hover cars in wonder. The boys who were part of that group—eight of them, of whom Luis was one—also got their first look at May as she sprinted along beside us, and the sight clearly knocked them for a loop. Larissa and Amanda were also a part of this group; they both waved at me and Peter respectively, and we both waved back, me feeling my spirits lift in spite of our fruitless search thus far. We continued on after this, and by the time we were coming around for our second lap of the mountain, our cars now hovering about a dozen feet from the ground, they had left.

Shortly after this, we reached the entrance to the Group F campsite below, where the first lap had begun. It was almost six o'clock now and the sun was beginning to disappear over the distant horizon. None of us were too tired to go on yet—not even May, and she was the only one really exerting herself—but it didn't seem practical to keep searching in the dark. When Peter asked May if she could make us see in the dark, she had replied that such a thing would only work if she could see in the dark, and although her vision was a bit better than ours, it wasn't that good. So we decided to call it a night and have our dinner.

"Okay," Marc said as we were parking our cars in the garage, "I'm all for not searching anymore tonight, but that doesn't mean we have to stay here. That movie theatre looked pretty good—wouldn't mind grabbing a packet of chips from the bag and settling in there for a few hours. What say you, Amelia?"

Amelia shrugged. "I don't really feel like that tonight, but we should definitely do that before we leave. Some of those other caves look pretty cool to hang out in as well."

"If Erica were here, I'd totally take her to that beach," said James wistfully.

"And I'd take Rebecca to that cave that had to be a simulation of a Vegas casino," said Peter. "Do you reckon they would have age restrictions here? Hey, do you reckon they'd let me keep my winnings?"

James laughed. "Pete, if they wanted the simulation to be realistic, there wouldn't be any winnings."

"There would if I were there, J-sandwich," grinned Peter.

It was only as we were settling down to dinner, and the others were all starting to really relax, that I remembered something I should have thought of much sooner than now.

"Guys," I said, and the seriousness of my tone made Marc stop talking mid-sentence, "something happened to me last night that you have to know about."

"What's that?" James asked through a mouthful of food.

"I'm pretty sure I connected with the Enlightener again. It's the first time in months that it—whoa, you okay?"

James was coughing and spluttering on his food. Marc began patting him on the back as he got himself under control.

"Okay," Peter said slowly. "I understand why you're telling us this, 'specially if it's important. What I don't understand is why James is just about killing himself over it. What's got into you, man?"

"I totally forgot about it," James said, and took a deep breath. "Okay, we'll circle back to that 'cause it's gotta be discussed, but first things first: What did you dream of this time?"

"Lisa," I told them. "I don't remember anything else about it except that she was there. She was telling me that my focus was all wrong and that I needed to change it, otherwise I wouldn't find what I was looking for. She also said that she had something to tell me, but I woke up before she could."

"What was she referring to?" Amelia asked, her eyes wide.

I shrugged. "Dunno, that's the whole point—I have to figure it out. When I was dreaming about me and Stella here on the Rock, it took three whole months of recurring dreams before I got it. I sure hope it doesn't take that long this time."

James was deep in consideration. Finally, he said, "I wish we could help you with that, John, but other than bouncing ideas off us, I think this one's up to you."

"It's gotta be about Lucien, surely," Marc said. "I mean, what else could it be? Maybe we should be finding some other way to save the world, other than fighting him head-on."

"You mean like destroying the Magic Crystals?" James suggested, and Marc went very still. "I don't think that's it—the point of taking on Lucien is so that we can get the crystals off him in the first place. Once we have them, we can cut him down to size, and hopefully without needing to hurt him at all. That goal doesn't feel wrong to me—I guess it could be, but unless you guys have a better idea, I suggest we stick with that."

"I don't think it's Lucien either," I told him, "because—here's the thing I'm not sure about—how can the Enlightener know that Lucien is even a problem yet? Remember, in this time, he's still hanging out with us in our base."

"But then what could it be?" Amelia asked. "Surely she's not trying to tell us something about Hammerson—if she is, she's wasting her time."

"That's a good thought, John," James said slowly, "but I'm not sure if it's logical. The Enlightener may be an external source, but maybe it's not as external as you're thinking—maybe it's just smart enough to know what we're trying to do. If it knows that, it'll be basing its visions on what you know, rather than what it knows about the present."

"That doesn't sound right..." I said just as slowly.

"It may not be right," James admitted, "but it is a possibility. I don't think it's directly related to what you're doing in the present because if it was, it would have happened to you in the Honnie world rather than here and now; and if the Enlightener couldn't get to you there, then theoretically, it shouldn't have anything to show you because it can't know what you're doing. That's why I think it's more likely to be based on what you're doing now, which means it may apply to the future."

"That's true," Marc said carefully. "Didn't the description of the Enlightener say something about providing information you may need in the future? Maybe that's what this is about. What I wanna know is, why Lisa?"

"I wondered that too," I said, "and so far as I can figure, it just means that whatever she wants to tell me can't be too personal, since that's not the sort of friendship we had when she was alive. That probably means it's either related to Lucien, the Hammerhearts, or the crystals."

"Not necessarily," James said thoughtfully, "there is one other possibility. Can you think of anything about Lisa that doesn't apply to anyone else from the Young Army who's not with us anymore?"

It was Peter who got it. "She's the only one stuck in the in-between."

"Correct," James said, "and yes, I know William and Carl are there too, but ℜ—"

"Do you have to say it like that?" I said, his words stabbing at my heart when I thought about how the three of them were trapped there for timeless eternity.

"Sorry," James said quickly. "It's hard for me too. What I was going to say is, maybe that experience has gifted her with some crucial knowledge that nobody else has, but which we really need to know if we're to win this thing. Maybe that's what she wants to tell you, John. In fact, it mightn't be just the Enlightener creating this out of nothing to send you a message—maybe Lisa herself wants to talk to you."

"What?" I started. "How?"

James shook his head. "I have an idea, but I think the best thing to do for now is wait and see if it happens again. Remember, no time will be lost if we're here—well, at least until we leave."

"You just made me think of something," Peter said suddenly. "John, now that you're here, do you think you could connect to Stella in this time?"

I shook my head. "Doubt it—our connection has changed since then, remember?"

"I know, but that doesn't mean it can't happen. Even if you don't connect with her, she might connect with you and see what we're doing here. What do you reckon she'll make of it if she does?"

"Hopefully she'll see me, Marc or Amelia," said James, "then she'll get up and see us in the base, and she'll think that it was just a crazy dream. I don't remember her giving us any funny looks, though, do you, Marc?"

"Nope," Marc said, "and she certainly never mentioned anything, and I reckon she would have said something if she'd had anything from John in that time—we were all pretty worried."

"She didn't say anything to me either," I said, "but just in case, if it's okay with you guys, I'd like to get back to our own time on or before the eighteenth—that way, we'll be gone before we come back from the Honnie world. It's probably nothing, but it just feels like the right thing to do."

They all considered this, and then James said, "If we're ready by then. Staying a little longer would be better than heading back to the future before we're prepared for Lucien; but if we are ready, then sure."

Chapter 26: Sometimes We Get Lucky

I was having another bad night. It was late, after eleven o'clock, and I thought that everyone had gone to bed—at least, it sounded quiet outside my bedroom. I had retrieved my wine from under the bed and was now sitting with it in my lap, drinking again, and I had already drank more tonight than I had the previous night. I had a pleasant buzz happening, but it didn't seem to be shutting down my brain. I couldn't have been more confused about what I was doing if I were seeing triple of everything.

After we had had our dinner, Peter and I had ended up grabbing the keys and taking our hover cars out for a spin. James had gotten talking with May in the Group F campsite (apparently deciding to ask her questions about Honnies after all), and Marc and Amelia had said they would go into the Group E campsite for a bit of privacy (the tree house turned out to be too cold at night these days), but whether they stayed there or had retired to one of their rooms for the rest of the night, I didn't know.

My brother and I had ended up going back to the Vegas cave, Peter getting his way there, and it had turned out not to be too bad. We had been let in by the imaginary people as if we were ordinary customers, the fact that neither of us had any real money on us seeming not to matter. When Peter had gone to the roulette table, he had found that there was a hundred-dollar bill in his pocket and he had no idea where it had come from. "Wish this would happen more often in life," he said as he began to play.

We had ended up winning a bunch of money, losing nearly all of it, then winning some more, and then we decided to have a few drinks at the bar. It was there that we got talking, me becoming aware that Peter was seriously worried about what I was doing to myself. I had told Peter, truthfully I thought, that the only chance I had of getting Natalie back now was to abstain from anything sexual with anyone (based on the rationale that eventually, if we were to be honest with each other, she would need to know everything), but that I wasn't sure I had the willpower to do it—especially considering that the horse had probably already bolted anyway.

Peter had humbled me when we spoke about the Brazilians. He was no fool—he had noticed Amanda's interest in him—but although he was flattered (and a little turned on, because she was pretty hot), he was happy enough just to enjoy the foreplay but not to actually do anything with her. As long as Amanda knew he was off the market, which he had been quick to make sure she did, then he shouldn't have to worry about hurting her with rejection—surely she wouldn't be so bold as to actually make a serious move on him, so was his thinking anyway. When he had asked me if I would do the same with Larissa, however, I had reiterated what I'd said about her back in Underwood's cave, except now I added what I had left out at the time: I would like to do something with her, and if the opportunity came up (it probably wouldn't, but you never know), I wasn't sure what I would do.

"Mate," he said solemnly, "your life was a lot simpler before you knew how to talk to girls."

I laughed. "What are you talking about? I still don't know how to talk to them."

When we had left the casino cave, all the money we'd had in our pockets vanished. That was fine—I hadn't expected it to remain—but unfortunately, the effects of the alcohol also vanished. That had been very unwelcome, and was the reason why, after I had gone to bed, I had started drinking again—I wasn't ready to be in my right mind again. I couldn't seem to get away from the thought process that whatever I did, I ought to be doing something different. If I wasn't having sex with someone, I would remember Natalie turning away from me, her rejection, and think that I had no chance of getting her back; and then I would wonder why I was bothering to hold myself back. Then when I did it, I would feel utterly regretful and like I had cheated on her all over again, even though we weren't technically together anymore. If only there were some way to move past this limbo…but the only way out I could see at the moment lay in the future, when I would get my chance to try to get her back. At least then, I would know for sure, one way or another, what my chances were.

I was beginning to feel sleepy when a soft knock sounded on my door, startling me. I quickly screwed the top back on the bottle (now only about half full) and rolled it back under the bed, thinking that it was probably May out there (who already knew I had the bottle in here), but not wanting the bottle to be seen just in case it was someone else. I gathered myself and said, in a voice I hoped didn't sound drunk, "Who is it?"

"It's me," came Amelia's quiet voice from the other side of the door. "Are you awake?"

"Yes," I muttered, thinking that was a pretty dumb question, and yet I was the one drinking. "You can come in."

She did so, although it was pitch-black in my room at the moment so other than a movement of the door, I didn't see anything. That changed when, for reasons I couldn't begin to imagine, she switched the light on, causing me to reflexively throw my hands up to cover my eyes. Thank God I wasn't holding the bottle now, I thought, squinting through my fingers at her as she came to sit on the bed, almost exactly where May had sat the previous night.

"Sorry," she said, looking a little guilty, "I just needed to see you —in both senses of the term. Are you—what are you doing?"

She had gotten her first good look at my face, and this time, I was unable to hide the fact that I wasn't myself tonight. Would she figure out what I had been doing? Was the jig about to be up? Should I tell her the truth or should I try to cover it up? If she thought to look under the bed, she would see the half-empty bottle and know for sure what I was doing.

"Nothing, just sitting here," I told her, except I had taken too long to decide, and she seemed to guess pretty quickly that I wasn't telling the truth.

"Hey," she said, and she wriggled forward and gave me a clumsy sort of hug. I hugged her back, thinking of Natalie, of what I'd done to Lena and Stella, of what I'd been doing with May, of what I must be doing to Amelia, and felt like I wanted to cry.

"What's going on?" I asked her.

She didn't answer right away, but continued to hold me for several more seconds before pulling back to get a look at my face. Finally, she said, "Have you been drinking?"

Damn it, I thought—I'd blown it after all. I thought of lying outright and saying no; then I thought of half-lying and saying that Peter and I had been drinking earlier in that casino cave (a truth, but if she caught up with Peter and asked him about it, and he mentioned that the effects had disappeared after we had left, she would know that it wasn't the only truth); and then I thought of telling the truth. I had no choice: Not only did I not want to lie to Amelia, I really wasn't capable of holding a lie together at the moment anyway.

"It makes me feel better," I said sadly, and the urge to cry swept me again—it took some effort to hold it back.

She gave me another hug, and it was getting really hard not to break down. Come on, John, be a man and hold it together, I thought. But right now, I just felt like a scared little boy in way over his head with pretty much everything. Not looking at my face, she said, "I'm sorry, I guess me being here isn't helping at all."

"Why are you here anyway?" I asked her, wanting to put the focus somewhere else—anything not to think about everything rattling around inside my head.

"I have a problem," she said, pulling back again and settling herself on the bed before me. "I didn't know where else to go— everyone else is asleep."

"What about Marc?" I asked her, thinking of how the two of them might go about solving a problem, and then feeling like crap all over again.

"That is the problem," she said in a small voice. "I—I don't know what to do about him."

I gave my head a little shake in an attempt to clear it, but all I succeeded in doing was making myself dizzy. "I don't know what you mean," I said, but my mind flashed back to last night. Hadn't May said something about Amelia thinking of me while she was with Marc? I couldn't remember exactly what it was, but now I had to wonder...

"Well," she said, twisting her hands together, "we—you know we decided to try again—dating, I mean—but—but I'm not sure if I feel it like he does."

"It's only been a few days, you know," I pointed out.

"Isn't that when the feelings are supposed to be the strongest?" she asked. "That's certainly how it was with me and Darcy, and every mind I've ever read who has thought about it; the passion has always been strongest in the beginning. People call it the 'honeymoon period'."

That was too much for me to take in, so I just said, "What about him? Does he feel it?"

She looked sad as she said, "He feels more than I do, I think. I wish—I wish I could remember how I felt about him before we dated the first time, but other than knowing I was attracted to him earlier in the year, I can't remember any of those feelings. I guess May didn't include them."

If she hadn't been thinking about those feelings during the few days between meeting May and losing all her memories, then there would be no way for May to get to them, so it made sense that she couldn't remember them now. It still didn't sound right that Amelia should be resigning herself to this after only a few days of dating, though, unless there was something else going on. The only other thing that could be impacting her now would be...I could have groaned. It was just like Natalie when she'd been dating Tommy; her heart hadn't been in it because she had been attracted to me, and apparently Amelia was too—but hadn't May also said that Amelia was attracted to Marc as well? Maybe this was even more confusing than Natalie's situation had been.

This was all way too complicated to say, so I said, "It still seems way to soon to break up with him, though."

She nodded. "I don't want to do that. I don't want to hurt him again, not after I just got his hopes up, and plus I do care about him. I —I just don't know what to do."

She looked like she was about to cry now, so I reached out and gave her another hug. She threw her arms around me and sobbed against my shoulder, and it was the feeling of her misery which seemed to bring about my own. I thought again of the pain I had inflicted on Natalie, Lena and Stella, the impact I was having on Amelia (if it wasn't for my presence, maybe she and Marc would be okay—maybe), and then I was crying into her shoulder as well. Whether because she was too wrapped up in her own sadness to notice, or she had known that I'd needed a shoulder to cry on as well —whatever it was, Amelia didn't react to my sudden tears. All we did was sat there on my bed and clung to each other, each dealing with our own pain and taking comfort from the presence of the other.

"I'm sorry," she finally managed to say, "I shouldn't be bringing all this down on you when you have your own things to deal with."

I sniffed, and with a monumental effort, managed to regain control of myself. "Don't worry about it, maybe I needed that."

She pulled back again and looked at my face, hers only a few inches away from mine. I would probably see right through her eyes as if they were windows to her soul if my focus was any sharper, I thought, but any leftover tears combined with my intoxication to make her eyes look like blurs. Her vision would be relatively clear, though, and she would be able to see how utterly drunk I was—at least I assumed that was what she was seeing. In that moment, I wanted to kiss her very badly, and I forced myself to remember my promise to Marc—how I would not take advantage of her if she threw herself at me. Hopefully, she would be sufficiently discouraged by what an utter mess I was.

"Do you feel any better?" I asked her, but she didn't answer for some time. The seconds lengthened as we just stared at each other before finally, she leaned forward, covering the distance between our faces, and kissed me on the lips. Part of me knew I should have pushed her back, or at least not kissed her back; but most of me knew I couldn't do that. There were two reasons why: One, I would hurt her more if I rejected her when she was vulnerable like this; and two, I wanted it too—it was just instinctive to respond.

After the seconds stretched on, and the kiss had become long and passionate, she pulled back and then rested her head on my shoulder. "Thank you," she said in a muffled voice.

"For what?"

"For not pushing me away. I know part of you must have thought about it."

That wasn't something I wanted to admit to, so I said, "I think I needed it too, but Amelia?"

"Hmm?" she said softly, in a tone that made me want to kiss her again.

"Are you sure you won't regret doing that in the morning?"

"I'm sure I won't," she said, and now she pulled back so that she could look at me again. "When you and the others went to see Underwood, Marc wanted to get intimate with me. That was in the cold light of day, and I just couldn't get into it. If that's how I felt then, it won't make a difference tomorrow—or the day after."

I held her tighter, wanting to kiss her again, but afraid that if I did, she would push me away. Had she only wanted that one kiss? Had it been a spur of the moment thing, or would she want more than that? Exactly what did she want me to do at this point? Had she even figured that out herself?

"John," she said in a quiet voice.

"Yeah?"

"I—I need you," she said, and my heart skipped a beat—yep, that answered my question. I thought about this for a moment. I thought about Marc. I thought about Natalie. I thought about May. Most of all, I thought about Amelia herself, and how she might feel if I did something with her tonight. Which was the worse of two evils, her being rejected tonight, or her feeling like I had taken advantage of her tonight? Underpinning both was how she might feel about herself afterwards—would she feel like she had let herself down?

Wanting desperately not to hurt her feelings, I said, "Amelia— are you sure you won't feel bad about this afterwards?"

"Are you saying no?" she asked me, putting her head on my shoulder and sounding like she might cry again. I couldn't have that, so I gently took her face in my hands and kissed her again. It was a little clumsy, but it felt like she enjoyed it.

"I care about you too much to want to take advantage of you," I said when it was done, "but I'm always here if you need me."

"Then take care of me," she said. "Make me feel better."

It was literally impossible for me to resist those words, so I gave her what she wanted. I didn't feel like I was doing as good of a job as I would normally do—not that I would say I was a whiz in the sack, but I was better than this. If it was the alcohol, I couldn't begin to understand why so many people insisted on drinking it in order to get laid—the logic seemed the total reverse of what it should be. When we got going, both of us made a great effort to be quiet lest the sound travel through the walls to the other rooms. Marc, the person I wanted least to wake, was several rooms away, and probably out of range unless Amelia screamed or something, but I wasn't prepared to take that chance.

I felt thoroughly exhausted by the time it was over. And it got worse. When she got herself up off me, I sat up with her, intending to kiss her again—I wanted to make this something meaningful for both of us—but before I could, a horrible wave of nausea swept me, making me feel both dizzy and ill. It was in that moment that I knew I was about to be subjected to that other fabled side of drinking.

"Excuse me," I muttered, and stumbled towards the door.

I very nearly didn't make it to the bathroom in time; it was all the way at the other end of the hallway, and there were a couple of moments when I almost fell down and puked right there in the hallway. But I just managed to get my head over the top of the toilet before the heaving started, and a lot of foul-tasting fluids came up the express elevator. There weren't too many chunky bits, thank goodness, but I still remained hunched over that bowl for some time, feeling terrible, my stomach aching, my head spinning, my mouth tasting like a horse had dumped in it, and thinking that I probably deserved this for resorting to alcohol in the first place.

Amelia padded into the bathroom maybe five minutes in, perhaps after deciding that I wasn't coming straight back. She had dressed herself before leaving my room and had brought my pyjamas with her so that I didn't have to walk back to my room in the nude—well, almost in the nude. Just as I had done after my first interlude with Amelia, I had left the room wearing nothing but a condom. I had muttered my thanks, she had stroked the back of my head, and then she had left—to return to her own bedroom, I found when I finally got back to mine.

Had I made her feel worse about this evening by the way I had ended it? I wondered as I lay down on my bed, my room once again in darkness. I didn't know. I hoped not, but the fact that she had gone to bed without waiting for me was rather anticlimactic. I wouldn't know until the morning, I supposed, and that was as much as my poor tortured mind could manage. I dropped off to sleep, or possibly unconsciousness as it was totally dreamless, and when I eventually woke, it was with a splitting headache, a foul mouth, and a stomach that felt like it was full of scrunched-up paper. I leapt out of bed, staggered back to the bathroom and chucked up in the toilet a second time.

There was no chance of keeping this from the others anymore. It was morning now, and when I had charged into the bathroom, Marc had already been in the shower. Even though there had been nothing between me and his naked form but a steamed-up glass pane, and even though he had yelled in horror at the sight of me, my sole intention had been to get to the toilet before making a mess all over the floor—everything else had been secondary.

"Holy crap, have you got a virus?" Marc asked from in the shower, still sounding horrified and affronted that I was in here at all.

"Sorry," I muttered, flushing the toilet and getting out of there as quickly as possible.

I still might have gotten away with it—perhaps I could have convinced all the others (bar Amelia, who knew the truth; and May, who could have extracted it from my mind) that I only had a bug, if it hadn't been for Marc's initial shout. Peter and James had both heard it (Peter from in his bedroom, and James from the Group F campsite) and both had come hurrying to see what was going on. James saw me looking as white as a sheet, and he didn't click right away that it wasn't an illness, but Peter saw my eyes, and he knew exactly what it was.

"Jesus Christ, John," he snapped, his eyes bugging as he put two and two together—I saw him jump to the correct conclusion almost immediately.

"Pete, come on," James said, startled by the harshness of my brother's tone, "can't you see he's—"

"He's not sick," my brother said as two more doors opened, and the two females joined us. "He's hungover."

"What?" James said, confused for a moment, and then realising what he meant. "Oh, but I thought you said that cave didn't—" And then he got it for real. "The alcohol you put in the bag? Oh, Peter—"

Peter rounded on him. "That was supposed to be for fun, not for —this."

He turned to me and said, "I knew you were struggling, but you should have told us you were doing this—maybe you wouldn't be feeling so lousy now."

He was right about that. I smiled weakly and said, "Yeah, I guess I should have. I wasn't ready to be sober last night."

"Wasn't ready to be sober?" James repeated. "What do you mean? Peter, what does he mean? What's going on?"

"Not now, man," Peter said, taking me by the arm and pulling me back towards my bedroom. "We'll talk about it over breakfast. Sorry, John, but we're going to have to."

And so we did. Due to how I must have looked in the eyes of the others, I was gifted the second shower after Marc, but Peter and James decided to delay having their own. Instead, the six of us gathered on the couches, May blessedly clearing my mind of the pounding headache and apologising for not being there for me last night (she had fallen asleep before Amelia had come to me, apparently—a good thing when I thought about it). I hated the scrutiny I was now getting from the others, but I knew I deserved it. I had turned into a bit of a car crash lately and it needed to be stopped now before it became a train wreck.

"So let me get this straight," James said sternly, "you've been drinking regularly since we got here—how many times now?"

"Three," I said flatly. "Once on the boat, twice here."

Peter only shook his head sadly, but James didn't look at all sympathetic. "And why? All this just because you feel bad about having sex with three more girls than you're supposed to be having sex with?"

"Don't talk about Amelia like that," Marc snapped at him. He looked angry, whether at me or James, I couldn't tell, and Amelia had to put a wresting hand on his arm. (Good thing he didn't know that it was actually four more girls than I was supposed to be having sex with.)

"If you're implying that I have no right to feel bad, you can go fuck yourself," I said heatedly. "Do you think I enjoyed cheating on Natalie?"

"I'm sure you enjoyed it more than she did when she found out," he said, and on that point, he was probably right. That made me even angrier.

"James, cut that out," Peter snapped. "The point isn't to judge him—the point is to help him so that he doesn't have to drink."

"Maybe if he thinks about how his actions make other people feel, he'll be less inclined to waste time wallowing in his own emotions," James suggested.

"That's the whole point!" I roared at him, now goaded past endurance. "Do you think I'd have a problem if I didn't care how I made them all feel?"

"Then why do you do this stuff?" James asked warily, perhaps realising that he had pushed me too far.

"He was cursed, man," Marc reminded him. "He wouldn't have done any of that stuff if he hadn't been. He spent months resisting all of them, so I really don't think his morals are in question here."

And now I felt bad that I'd had sex with Marc's girlfriend last night. If only it had been Erica instead of Amelia, I thought, thinking that James deserved it much more than Marc did. Then I thought about how great Erica probably looked without clothes on. Then I felt disgusted with myself.

Peter intervened again. "John, you're gonna get through this in time—it should be a little easier once we get back to the future. In the meantime, though, what do we do about the drinking thing?"

"I have an idea," Amelia said quietly. I had been acutely aware of her presence all through this discussion, conscious that every word I said about my feelings for Natalie—true as they may be—may have an adverse effect on Amelia. Saying I felt horrible about cheating on Natalie was one thing, but saying it right in front of the girl I'd cheated with—especially given that she had been so lonely and still cared about me as she did—now that was incredibly awkward. When everyone looked at her, she said simply, "He can't drink if he's too tired at night. It is in the night that you're doing this, right?"

"Sure," I said, leaving out the part where I had done it during the day on the ship. For the sake of this discussion, saying it had happened at night-time only was fine. "We're too busy during the day."

"Exactly," she said, and looked around at the others. "If he wears himself out during the day, he'll be too tired to do anything at night but drop straight off to sleep."

"That's good thinking," Marc said, grinning at me. "How do you feel about searching the morning without a hover car, John?"

James laughed at that, and I almost got up and punched him, but that was when I felt May finally enter my mind and calm me down. A little overdue, I thought, but at least a disaster had narrowly been averted.

"That just means we have to search really hard today," Peter said. "We should be doing that anyway, but now we have another reason. Now, if you'll all excuse me, I'm gonna go take a shower before James thinks to take it first."

"Oi," James said indignantly.

"You can use ours if you're that desperate to get clean," Amelia said, smiling slightly.

* * *

The searching continued where it had left off the previous night. From just before nine o'clock right up until almost half past twelve. May's imaginary flags had reappeared by the time the five of us re-emerged from the carpark in our hover cars to reunite with May outside the last cave we had tried. We continued around the mountain, working our way upward, but still only a couple of dozen feet from the foot of the mountain—there was still a long way to go yet. Like yesterday, we were finding some amazing caves, such as the one that made us all appear in 2D when we entered it, the one which returned us to an era of dinosaurs, and the one that caused us all to start speaking in Arabic the moment we set foot in it. We were aware of the change in language, and yet when we tried to speak English, it kept coming out in a language that would have been totally alien to me anywhere else and at any other time.

It wasn't until we were just about to give up for the morning and go for lunch when finally, at long last, we found a cave which we could actually use for something. When Marc first opened it up with the S-key, we weren't sure what it was. The interior was lit up and ahead of us sat two large platforms—or rather, containers with clear sides that sat raised off the floor slightly. I estimated that each of them was about five metres long, five metres wide, and maybe two metres high. At the bottom of one of the containers were two buttons; one of them did nothing when we pushed it the first time, but the second one caused the clear sides of both containers to vanish so that they were now open to us.

"I'm going to take a guess here," James said, "and suggest that this is a vanishing cave. Has anyone got something useless that they don't mind losing?"

May's top, I thought before I could stop myself, then I had to mentally scream at her not to do it as in a moment of poor judgement on her part, May had taken the suggestion seriously. In the end, Marc had gone back outside and scooped up a few loose rocks to use for the experiment. Following James's suggestions, he put them on the platform of the container with the buttons; then Amelia, who was closest to the buttons, pressed the button to make the clear walls re-appear.

"Okay, here we go," James said, "Amelia, push that button."

And so Amelia pushed the button that had made nothing happen the first time. This time, though, there was a bright flash of light. When our eyes were able to focus, however, we saw that the stones had not vanished. On the contrary, they had duplicated, their duplicates appearing in the identical location within the other container. A cave that could duplicate things, I thought, but right off the bat, I couldn't see anything useful about it. What could this cave do that our backpack couldn't, I wondered? Probably nothing, which meant that this cave would be very useful to anyone who didn't already have the ability to duplicate things.

James, though, had thought of something else. "Can one of you check what happens if you take that key out of the lock?"

He was referring to the S-key, which was still sitting in the keyhole outside the cave. Marc went and retrieved it, but nothing at all happened. Apparently, this was one of those caves which only closed when you turned the key back the other way in the lock. James was grinning.

"Let's not get our hopes up," he said, "but maybe, just maybe, this will work. May?"

She gave him the other key, and James put them in the duplicate. Amelia saw what he meant to do and pressed both buttons, first shutting the duplicator and then making it do its thing. The flash of light came again, and then we looked. There were two keys sitting exactly where Amelia had left them, and there were two more keys sitting in exactly the same spot on the other platform.

"All right!" Peter said, and punched the air in triumph. "Good thinking, J-sandwich. Get those keys off there and let's copy them a few more times so that we all have them."

And so that was what we did, and when we left that cave and headed down to our campsite for lunch, all six of us had a copy of both keys in our pockets. We had tested them before going too far, and I am pleased to report that the duplicates worked just as well as the originals. Amelia had the honour of having the original keys, but that meant nothing for all the difference it made.

* * *

Forty-five minutes later, we were searching again. Now that we didn't have to search together, we had devised a new organisational system—or rather, James had organised it while the rest of us filled our stomachs. He, Marc, Peter and I each had a side of the mountain to search (me in the south, Marc in the north, Peter in the east and James in the west), zigzagging our way up from the caves we had already searched. Amelia had been given the job of searching anywhere else on the island that wasn't on the mountain—it was unlikely, yet still possible, that there may be other secrets hidden around the place. As for May, now that her job of raising imaginary flags had just increased fourfold, she was allowed to sit on the verandah of the tree house and keep an eye on all of us in her mind, raising red flags for every cave we tried, and a green one if she happened to notice one that any of us missed.

As I went about my searching, I happened along a small group of Brazilians—three students and one teacher. They were occupying a ledge before a cave I had yet to search, and I couldn't see any way I could get in there without disturbing them. I scanned them hopefully, just to see if Larissa was one of them; she wasn't, although Amanda was. I went past them, a couple of them waving at me, and sent a telepathic message to May to scan their brains to see what was in there, and raise an appropriately coloured flag depending on what it was: red if it was no good, green if it was important, yellow if she wasn't sure, or blue if the Brazilians themselves hadn't been in there. I gave her a few seconds, then turned my hover car back on the pretext of entering another cave. Looking back, I saw a red flag waving over the heads of the Brazilians, and smiled to myself. May, I thought, you really are awesome at this.

A little over an hour later, I came across another group of Brazilians—again, three students and a teacher. This time, I saw that Larissa was among them, and for a moment, I had to remind myself that I had a job to do here, especially when she saw me and waved. They seemed to be doing the same thing that the previous group had been doing, only a fair bit higher up the mountain. I asked May to scan their minds as she had done before, and once again, a red flag appeared behind them. Smiling, I pushed onward, my hover car tilting on a forty-five degree angle in order to cope with the tricky terrain up here.

Then without warning, I dropped into a slight crevice, which could have been much worse because just a few feet to my right was a much deeper hole in the ground. I pulled up sharply, my heartbeat quickening in response to the close call. I looked to my right, and then into the cave on my left, and then realised where I was: This was the cave from which we had gotten our hover cars on the last camp. There was the cave to my left, the doorway a short distance into it; and to my right, the hole in which Tommy and I had hidden the Darkness Crystal.

Someone was coming along the angled ledge behind me; one of the Brazilians, most likely the teacher, or quite possibly Larissa herself, perhaps coming to ask me what I was doing—perhaps even to ask where I had gotten my hover car. If so, I wouldn't have to point them far. As I twisted around in my seat to look, I saw that my second guess had been correct, and I had to force myself not to smile. On one hand, Larissa had clearly gone out of her way to catch up with me—even though her group was only twenty feet away. On the other hand, she had almost killed herself trying to do it on foot.

"Hey, be careful," I said in a panic, but she had already crossed the worst of it. A second later, she stepped lightly down into the crevice behind my car.

"It's fine," she said, and smiled. "What are you doing?"

"Erm—" I hesitated, feeling much more nervous than I ought to under her gaze. It wasn't just that I couldn't tell her the true nature of what I was doing. With a shrug, I said, "Looking for stuff that might be useful to what we're doing."

"Finding anything useful?" she asked, touching the rear of my hover car with some envy, I thought.

"Well, yeah, this thing is pretty useful," I said, and then I remembered what I had been thinking just before and jerked my thumb into the cave. "They're right in there, if you ever wanna get one yourself."

She glanced into the cave, but then looked back at me. "It must be very interesting, the things you get to do."

"Yep," I said, glancing down at the scabs on my arm from the battle aboard the ship—the Band-Aids had come off that night over dinner. "Sometimes we get lucky and things turn out okay."

She giggled at that—I wasn't sure what part of it was funny, but then what did I know. She started to reach out for a moment, as though she wanted to touch my arm—the one with the cuts on it— and then she didn't. It would have been within reach, if she had stretched her arm out all the way, but perhaps it was a little more forward than she was prepared to be. Instead she said, "You're funny."

I smiled a little giddily upon hearing those words coming from her. I could have been misreading the signals, but when a girl said a guy was funny after giggling at something that really wasn't very funny at all—it did seem like she was letting me know that she found me attractive. I gazed more closely at her face, trying to see past her slight resemblances to Natalie. So pretty—such great skin—eyes you could get lost in. I wanted to kiss her. I wanted to touch her. I wanted to do all kinds of things to her. What I did was say, rather lamely in the end, "Er—thanks. I hope that's a good thing."

She grinned, her eyes twinkling in a way that suggested she had seen me checking her out. "Do you think I'm pretty?" she asked me.

Yes, was what I wanted to say. It sure was the truth, and then some. I had to remind myself that letting Larissa in now might be a bad idea—for me, surely; and for her, almost certainly. But then, I had to remind myself of something else: Larissa must know that she and I would probably never see each other again after we left this place, and after I'd had sex with both May and Amelia since coming here, not to mention Lena and Stella before, a little flirtation with this one barely made a blip on the radar of my sins. All the same, I wouldn't feel right in my head if I didn't give her some sort of indication of the sort of messed-up fool she was dealing with.

"Listen, you don't wanna—I'm not the sort of guy you wanna get too close to."

She didn't look particularly bothered by that. "How come? Are you worried I will get in the way of your magic?"

I shook my head. "No, but you—well, let's just say I'm kinda messed up."

She considered this for a moment, and then said, "You didn't answer my question before."

I smiled, realising that she was deliberately not heeding the warning—that made whatever happened next her problem, not mine. "I think you already know the answer to that."

If I wasn't awkwardly twisted around in my car, I might have actually done something at that point—touched her shoulder, or even kissed her, but I would have to go without for today. That was what I thought until I was interrupted by a telepathic communique from May, telling me that Peter had found something and that we should all go to where he was. That gave me a chance to move, and that gave me an opportunity I wasn't going to miss. I would have a better idea of what was really going on in Larissa's mind in just a few moments...

"I have to go," I told her, turning away from her and adjusting the controls of my car. "One of my friends has found something."

I moved forward a bit and then swung backwards into the cave so that I was facing forward. Then I moved forward so that I was right in front of Larissa, whose mouth was open slightly in what looked like simultaneous surprise and disappointment. Because she was now side-on to me, it meant that we were much closer together than we had been before, and I was able to lean over and give her a quick kiss on the cheek before taking off, moving fast enough so that my momentum carried me right over the hole in the ground with nothing more alarming than a metre drop before my car righted itself. Once on the other side, the track ahead of me straight for a couple of hundred metres, I looked back over my shoulder to see what had become of Larissa; she was standing in the same spot, looking after me, and smiling very brightly at me.

Yep, I thought to myself as I sped up again. That girl likes me, and I like her too. I may not get a chance to really check her out, but even if I don't, at least I can enjoy this feeling in the meantime. As for what it meant in the long run: Did it matter?

Chapter 27: I Don't See How That Justifies Totalling My Car

Marc, Amelia and Peter were gathered in a cave on the eastern side of the mountain, not too far below the location where we had done rock climbing on the school camp six months earlier, but in a spot that would have been just about impossible to get to without some sort of magical assistance such as the kind we had. It was a fairly spacious cave, lit from an unidentifiable source, and other than the four of us and our hover cars, completely empty of anything. No, not quite empty: There was a rope on the floor, coming out of the wall in one place, looping around and retreating back into the wall in the same spot. Peter was looking mildly pleased with himself, while Marc and Amelia only looked impatient.

"What's going on?" I asked as my hover car lowered itself to the floor.

"He won't say," Marc rolled his eyes at Peter.

"Let's just wait until James gets here," said Peter. "Don't get too excited—it's not a real game changer—but it's still worth having."

James arrived in another five minutes, looking excited, and the first thing I said was, "Don't get too excited, it's not a game changer, but according to Pete, it's still worth having."

Peter stuck his middle finger up at me and said, "Okay, that thing"ℜ— he indicated the rope on the floorℜ—"can make us untraceable. It's only the old kind—the kind Hammerson figured out how to get around—but it's better than nothing."

"Yes, that is good," James said slowly, examining the rope on the floor. "May, you'd better get up here—we're all going to have to do this."

"What's so good about it if they can still find us?" Marc asked.

"They might be able to locate us," James said, "but they— Lucien and Stella—won't be able to spy on us. In order for them to see what we're doing, they'll have to teleport directly to us."

"What if Lucien has found a way to go beyond just locating us?" Marc asked, unconvinced.

James took the question seriously, but after some thought, he said, "I don't think he can. At least, I can't think of any way he could do it, not unless he taps an entirely new level of magic beyond the power of this spell. I think this is worth doing."

"So how does it work?" Amelia asked, also looking down at the rope.

"Well, let's all get over here," Peter said, picking it up and looping himself with it. The rest of us followed his lead, finding that it stretched sufficiently to fit all five of us easily. Peter was closest to the wall, so he pushed the button; I felt a slight dizziness for a moment, and then nothing. Peter looked pleased, while the rest of us just looked at each other.

"Did it work?" James asked.

"It worked," Peter told us. "We're now under a single untraceability spell, and all we have to do to turn it off is press the button again."

"And why would we do that?" I said rhetorically.

That question was immediately answered when May came bounding into the room, colliding with James's hover car and sending it flying through the air; it hit the wall to the left of the cave with an almighty smash and crumpled to the floor. She looked around wildly, then relaxed as she saw that all five of us were here. Smiling, Peter said, "That's why."

"Okay, so May has to be untraceable as well," James said. "Fair enough, although I don't see how that justifies totalling my car."

That wasn't the full story, though. It turned out that when we had become untraceable, we had popped out of May's mind with such suddenness that it was like we had all been killed. May had known that the magic itself hadn't killed us because apparently, before we had arrived, Peter had tested the feature, and then assumed that nothing had happened and tested it a second time. The moment his mind had reappeared, May had practically ransacked it to see what he had done and to make sure that he was okay. She had known we were about to disappear again, but apparently she didn't like not knowing where we were at any given time.

"So wait," Marc said slowly. "May, can you sense our minds now?"

"No, I cannot," she said, looking rather unhappy as she came over to where we were standing.

"Which is exactly why I'm going to push this button again," Peter said, and did so. A moment later, I felt May wrap her mind around my own again; it really was one of those things you only noticed when she first did it, I thought.

"Yeah," James said slowly. "May being untraceable wouldn't have been enough; she needs to be under the same untraceability spell as us. At least, I think that'll work. Er—guys? What if it doesn't work?"

"What?"

"Well what if when all six of us are untraceable, May still can't sense our minds?"

"Well, let's find out if we have anything to worry about," I said, picking up the rope and looping it over May's head. "When you're ready, Pete."

He pushed the button again, nothing happened, and then we all looked at May. She appeared to cast her mind around for a moment, and I felt a slight flutter of alien thought in my own mind as she touched it. She smiled and said, "Okay, it is fine."

"Excellent," Peter said, and clapped his hands. "Let the record show that I was the first one of us to find anything useful."

"You wouldn't have found it if I hadn't found the cave to duplicate the keys," Marc said.

"You didn't find that—we all did," James said indignantly. "Just because you had the S-key at the time—"

"That's enough, you two," Amelia said, checking her watch. "We've still got a couple more hours of useful daylight left, so we might as well keep looking."

"Yeah," James agreed, also checking his watch. "Which one of you is searching on the southern side?"

"That would be me," I told him.

"Great, then you can give me a lift to the cave with the hover cars so I can get a new one—"

Peter burst out laughing, and not wanting to imagine what that was going to be like, I said, "Er—I don't think so. Even if it did manage to get off the ground with both of us, where would you sit, on my lap?"

James flushed and said, "Actually, I assumed I would take the seat and you would just hang onto the bumper and run along behind."

We exchanged middle fingers, and then Peter said, "Just go back to the campsite with May, J-sandwich—there are still a few spare cars in our garage."

* * *

The searching continued for the rest of the afternoon, but there were no further communications from May until six o'clock, when James used her to call a halt to proceedings for the day. I had returned to the hover car cave where I had left off, but by the time I got back there, the Brazilians had moved on—although I did see a different group of four a little later on, and used May to determine if the nearest cave to them was useful or not just as I had done twice already. I was able to cover another couple of hundred vertical feet that afternoon, and although I was still finding some very interesting and imaginative caves, still none were useful to the group in any way I could think of.

We settled down to dinner in the Group E campsite that night, and the feeling around the room was fairly optimistic. Although there was still a lot of the mountain yet to search, we were covering the ground much more quickly than we had expected since we were able to split up. The fact that we had been able to find two useful caves already made the task seem very much possible, instead of highly improbable. And it wasn't only the useful caves: It was all the interesting caves that we had all stumbled over as well. I was particularly intrigued by the one Marc had found which enabled a person to translate between any two languages that had ever existed when they went inside. James, too, was very interested in this.

"How did it work?" he asked Marc.

"Well so far as I can tell, all you had to do was think of something in one language, and at the same time think of another language, and then it would just come to you," he said, shrugging. "May helped me test it out—I was even able to speak Honnie language for a bit in there."

"Does it work for written materials?" James asked.

Marc considered this. "I think so," he said slowly, "but we didn't test that. I don't see why it wouldn't, though. Why do you ask?"

James shook his head. "I'll let you know if it turns out to be anything, but I think I might go check that cave out later on."

And that was what he did shortly after dinner, taking Tommy's old deep crimson car (which he had now claimed for himself) out with his keys and some other strange piece of wood or stone or clay or whatever it was. I had been about to ask him what it was but he had taken off too quickly. Marc and Amelia, meanwhile, had retired to the Group F campsite for some alone time, Marc telling the rest of us that we would be risking death or serious injury if we disturbed them—he was joking, of course, but there was warning in his eyes. Amelia didn't look particularly enthusiastic about the impending alone time but she went willingly enough.

That just left me, Peter and May. May sent me a telepathic message just as Marc and Amelia were leaving through the car park, asking me if I might like to spend time with her tonight, and if I was thinking about drinking again. My answer to both questions was that I wasn't sure, but although Peter wasn't privy to our communication, he seemed to get part of my internal struggle. He told me that we were going out tonight, to some cave or other, and that he wasn't taking no for an answer. Thinking that it would probably be the best thing for me, I agreed willingly, and so the two of us took our cars out after James and set off around the mountain. (May had been invited to come along but she had opted out.)

After checking out a few of the caves that had been mentioned over dinner, we had eventually gone into one that seemed to simulate the moon; the gravity was low, the sky was dark, and the planet Earth was hanging large above. The ground was rocky, and there were dominating cliffs all around. But that was where the realism ended: The temperature was comfortably mild and the atmosphere was Earthlike in both substance and weight. There was also a nearby canteen filled with packets of potato chips, chocolates, ice creams, hot dogs, pies, kebabs, and who knew what else. The topper was all the sporting activities that seemed to be available here: swimming, tennis, basketball, baseball, a bike track, a running track, an obstacle course, and yet more further on.

Why on earth hadn't we come in here on the school camp, I wondered. Had the school not known of this place? In fact, there were many things that the school could have done around here that they hadn't. If things ever get back to normal, I decided, I would pull every string I could to make sure that future camps to this place would be far more interesting. And if the school didn't comply, I would threaten to tell all the students about the hot tub cave. That ought to scare the pants off them—possibly literally.

We started off playing tennis, but the first rally went on so long that we both resorted to doing trick shots to make it more interesting, such as hitting the ball around our bodies while our backs were to the net, hitting the ball with the handles of our rackets, hitting it between our legs, and so on. I had eventually hit the ball into the net deliberately just as an excuse to end it and move onto something else. We then tried one-on-one basketball, which turned out to be more interesting, especially given that both of us were able to jump up to the ring and slam dunk the ball. Peter had even tried to jump right through the hoop himself, but it caught him under the arms and he had to hang there until I jumped up and lifted him back out. We settled into a very acrobatic basketball match, which I eventually won, twenty points to fourteen.

It took a while to wear ourselves out, but fierce direct competition seemed to somewhat make up for the lack of gravity. Eventually, when our heart rates had increased and we had begun to sweat, we headed back to the cave's entrance, got ourselves an ice cream each, and sat back in lawn chairs with a good view of all the facilities before us, the lunar landscape beyond, and the Earth above.

"So," Peter said, leaning back and looking across at me, "feeling good?"

"Yep," I said, taking a big bite of my ice cream.

"Feeling tired?"

"Fairly, yeah."

"Feeling down at all?"

"Nope, not at the moment."

"Think you'll drink tonight?"

"Doubt it," I said, and yawned. "It's been a pretty long day."

"Good," he grinned. "You're not thinking too much about Natalie, are you?"

I shrugged. "I'm always thinking about her a bit."

"What about Amelia, thinking about her at all?"

I hesitated for long enough for Peter to say, "I guess that's a 'yes', huh."

I considered for a moment, thinking of how much of the truth would be best in this situation. I decided to run with most of it and leave out the only really bad part. "She came to see me last night after everyone else had gone to bed. I was pretty drunk by then, and actually I didn't drink anymore after she left—that's why she wasn't surprised this morning," I added, in case he'd been wondering. "Anyway, she said something about—about—"

I stopped for a moment, trying to remember exactly what she had said—those memories were blurry, partially because of the drink and partially because they were totally eclipsed by what had happened afterwards. My silence was long enough for Peter to say, "Was she worried about you?"

"Well yeah, but that wasn't the main reason she came. It was Marc—something about not feeling as strongly for him as he does for her, but at the same time, not wanting to hurt him, because she still cared about him. It made her cry, and then I cried—'cause I was drunk, you know," I added, in case he started thinking I was a total softy. "Well anyway, I dunno if either of us helped each other, but— but she still likes me, Pete," I told him. "She told me she does, and she's so confused, and I'm so confused, and her confusion is making mine worse, and mine is making hers worse, and the whole thing is pointless because I still want Natalie back."

"Ahuh," he said vaguely, looking pretty stunned. "Okay. All right. Okay. Hmm."

"If you're trying to think of advice to give me," I said, "don't bother. You probably won't think of anything I haven't already thought of myself."

He shrugged. "If you say so. Let me ask you this: If you can't get Natalie back, will you still want Amelia?"

"I don't know," I said, thinking hard, and not feeling so great anymore. "I'm sure part of me will, but what about Marc? Does it make me a bad guy to date Amelia, even if she wants to date me, if she breaks up with my own brother to do it?"

"Yeah, that's not great," Peter nodded. "That's the sort of thing that could make a rift between you and Marc. It might be different if he didn't care so much—"

"Would it?" I asked, unsure.

He thought about this too, and then shrugged. "I'll give myself a headache if I think about this any longer. Where are you going?"

"Getting some chocolate," I said, heading over to the canteen. "Seems like the right thing to be eating when talking about this stuff."

When I returned to my chair with a king-sized Mars Bar, Peter said, "While we're on the subject, have you thought much about Larissa today?"

I grinned a little and tried to hide it with the wrapper. "I didn't have to think about her, because I ran into her this afternoon. There were groups of four doing stuff on the mountain—"

"Yeah, I know, I saw them on my side too," he said. "They were blocking the caves they were in front of, but luckily they knew what was in them, because May automatically put the red flags up."

"It wasn't automatic; I told her to do it."

"That was you?"

"Yeah, they were in the way on my side too. Anyway, I saw Larissa in one of those groups, and when I parked my car to check out a cave—the cave where we originally got the cars, incidentally— she separated from them and came to chat with me."

"They let her do that?"

"I dunno if she got permission or if she just did it. What do you think it means when a girl asks you if you think she's pretty?"

"I would have thought it meant that she was interested to know if you think she's pretty, and the only reason why she would care— unless she's an egomaniac—is that she really cares about your opinion of her."

"Hmm, yeah. And what do you think it means when a girl waves away your warning that you're not the sort of person she should get close to?"

"I'd say it means she wants you to park your hover car in her garage and kickstart it."

"Right," I said slowly, not wanting to imagine that too closely. "Well, that's not gonna happen, but maybe a little harmless flirting will get me through this period of limbo until we get back to the future."

"You know you'll eventually have to tell Natalie about all of this if you're gonna have a good, healthy relationship, right?"

"Yeah, but I don't think either of us is ready for that, no matter how much we want to be totally honest," I said. "And if she doesn't give me a chance—then she need never know about all this other stuff, and hopefully that means I can stop feeling bad about it."

"But you don't really want that to be the case, right?"

"You know I don't."

A silence descended for a moment before I added, "Oh, and I kissed Larissa as well."

"What?" he yelped, and if he hadn't mostly finished his ice cream, he would have spilt it all over himself. "Geez, you kept that quiet. What was it like? Did she give you tongue? Did you get to feel her—"

"No, not like that," I said quickly. "It was right at the end, when May let us all know you'd found that cave. I didn't even get out of the car; I just leaned over and kissed her on the cheek before I left—she didn't even have time to react. I only know that she looked happy about it when I looked back over my shoulder."

Peter shook his head and said, "Man, you may have missed an opportunity to really check her out if you hadn't been coy."

I laughed. "Firstly, we weren't exactly out of sight from her classmates—all two of them anyway, plus that one teacher. Secondly, I did kinda have to catch up with you guys. And thirdly, I wanted to do it that way. If she really is interested, maybe she'll be interested in more tomorrow or the day after. Besides, I'm not interested in taking it much further."

"But do you think you will take it further if she lets you?" he asked.

"I don't intend to, but I dunno if I'll be able to say no—or even put the brakes on," I admitted. "Every time I'm faced with that kind of decision, I think to myself that Natalie won't give me another chance anyway, and then later, I'll think to myself, what on earth did I do that for when I still might have a chance with Natalie. So yeah—I dunno what I'll do."

Even though I'd had ice cream and chocolate, I was still pretty tired by the time we got back to the campsite at around ten o'clock. Everyone else was in, we saw when we parked our cars in the garage, but the Group E campsite—the one we went through—was empty. We didn't check the others, just in case we ran into Marc and Amelia in the middle of thrashing ecstasy—or whatever else they might be doing. All we did was say good night to each other and then head straight off to bed. I yawned as I changed, thinking about the bottle of wine under my bed, wanting it, but also feeling tired enough that I might be able to sleep without it. With some discipline, I thought, I got into bed and rolled over, ignoring those thoughts of the wine. It didn't take long for me to fall asleep this time.

The dream was almost exactly the same as the last time, only this time, there was a little more. I couldn't tell where the dream was located because the entire focus of the dream had been Lisa Pont; she was telling me something, but the words weren't making sense.

"What are you saying?" I asked her desperately.

"Your focus is all wrong," she said, and this time, I understood the words perfectly. "You need to change your focus, otherwise you won't find what you are looking for. I really need to tell you something, John."

"Tell me what?"

But when she spoke again, her words were totally incoherent. "What is it?" I asked her.

This time, she gave up trying to tell me whatever she had been trying to say, and instead said, "Remember my diary, John. Remember what I wrote in my diary."

"What?"

But that was when I woke up.

* * *

The searching continued the following morning. I continued where I had left off the previous evening on the southern side, already fairly high off the ground and considerably higher by lunchtime. I found some more interesting caves, although none of them were as interesting as some that had already been found lower down; and more importantly, none of them had been useful. There was still a lot of mountain left, but was there as much left to search as it looked? Given that the mountain got smaller as it went up, I wasn't so sure. If we didn't find something in the next few days, we might be out of luck.

I probably could have searched more than I did in that time if it hadn't been for May, who was sitting on the balcony of the tree house once again, and although she was doing the job assigned to her (that of monitoring all of us and raising the red flags for every cave we searched and discarded), she was also in almost constant telepathic communication with me. It was a bit strange to actually have a conversation in this way, but that was what we did. She was mostly trying to see that I was okay, at least that was what I thought at first, but it eventually became apparent that she was starting to miss me a little after I hadn't had any involvement with her in the last two days.

That made me feel pretty hot, and maybe I would use May to distract myself from drinking (if Peter didn't hog me first), but the momentary feeling was dashed by the other thing May had to tell me. With nothing else to do last night, May had mentally spied on Marc and Amelia, and according to her, Amelia had told Marc that she couldn't stop thinking about me, and that she thought I needed her more than he did. Marc hadn't been happy about that (nor was I particularly happy about it, as I didn't think it was the truth), but now that I knew this, it explained why Marc had been giving me wary looks over breakfast. I remembered my promise to him back on the ship, that I wouldn't take his girl if she offered herself to me, and then I remembered that I had already broken that promise, and felt ashamed all over again. May promptly cleared the shame from my mind, and I was able to continue my searching without carrying the guilt around with me.

At around half past twelve, May put out the telepathic word that someone (either Marc or James, the two most predisposed to take charge) had halted proceedings and declared lunchtime. Since the cave containing our car park was on the southern side, I had to descend all the way down the mountain and then go all the way around it to the other side before climbing back up to reach the garage. Around the time I passed the original entrance to the Group F campsite, however, I stopped short when I almost ran right over the Brazilians—all thirty of them plus several adults, who were having their lunch at the foot of the mountain, less than twenty feet from one of our campsites.

I smiled, waved and responded to several shouts of greeting (most particularly from Luis who actually came up to my hover car and shook my hand), before I skirted around the group and continued onward, now smiling to myself as I remembered the great big smile and exuberant wave I had gotten from Larissa. But that was only occupying half of my thoughts; the other half were trying to think how I was going to get up to the garage without the Brazilians tracking my progress, as I was sure they would still be interested in watching the hover car. Looking up, I could even see the entrance to the car park from here, but that wasn't all I could see: Not quite as high up and maybe fifty feet to the west (closer to me, in other words), another hover car was parked, and Jacob Underwood was sitting beside it, apparently eating his lunch and watching the Brazilians below. When he saw that I had noticed him, he waved, and I waved back. Then, on the spur of the moment, thinking that it might get the Brazilians to lose interest in me for a while, I decided to go up there and talk to him.

"Hi," he called as I pulled up on the other side of his car. "What brings you to my neck of the woods?"

"What makes this your neck of the woods?" I asked as I scrambled around behind his car to get to where he was sitting.

"My neck of the woods is anywhere I happen to be at any given time," he shrugged and grinned. "Want one?" he added, holding out a plate of what I now saw were sausages.

"Nah, I'll be eating with my friends in a few minutes," I said, sitting down on the rock beside him. "Nice lunch."

"Dinner for me," he said, and started on a fresh sausage. If he had been a woman, I might have been turned on by the way he ate it. "Hey, I notice you're pretty chummy with those folks down there." He pointed his sausage in the direction of the Brazilians.

"Yeah, well we came on the same boat as them," I said, "and we had to defend them from some Hammerhearts just outside the portal."

"Why'd you come on the same boat as them?" he asked. "Didn't you keep that thing we came in last time?"

That brought me up short. What had happened to the vessel we had come in last time? I cast my mind back, trying to recall what I'd done with it. Eventually, it came to me: "We lost it when the

Hammerhearts destroyed the old Woodward base—that happened back in June. I suppose we could have tried to make a new one, but it just seemed easier to hitch a ride, since we knew the Hammerhearts weren't allowed to come with them."

Good story, I thought, and luckily, Underwood bought it. He then proceeded to ask a few questions about what had happened to the old Woodward base, and I had told him about how Hall and Hammerson had orchestrated its demise, and about how we teenagers had taken advantage of the chaos to split from the main army and set up a base of our own. I didn't bother to tell him any more than that, though; he didn't need to know, and I certainly didn't want to tell him, what was going to happen to that base a few weeks from now.

"How long did the boat ride turn out to be?" he now asked me, putting another sausage in his mouth.

"Er—the boat ride—about two days," I said.

"Two whole days," Underwood said, looking from me to the Brazilians and back again. He had noticed that my brain was on a different track, and perhaps something about my face had given him a clue about exactly what that track was. "That's a fair while to be trapped in a pretty small space with all those people. Did you get a chance to get cosy with any of them?"

"Say what?" I said, startled, my mind first flicking to Larissa, who I hadn't been cosy with; to May, who I certainly had been cosy with on the boat. "Uh"—I took a moment to get my mind back on the right track—"no, it wasn't like that. They stayed on their deck and we stayed on ours. We only met them right before we went through the portal."

Not strictly true, in my case, but close enough for government work. I wasn't sure if he believed me this time, but he acted as though he did.

"Your loss," he said, and stuffed the rest of the sausage into his mouth—there was now only one left on the plate. When he had swallowed it, he said, "I've been watching them since I came up here —some of those chicks are hot."

"Yeah, I know," I agreed, and that was certainly the truth.

"I like that one," he said, picking up his last sausage and pointing it at Camila, the girl who I'd stunned on the boat, "and that one there," he indicated another girl on the other side of the group, whose name I couldn't remember.

"You gonna try to get in with them like the Russians?" I asked, not really interested in what he planned to do. I felt a spike of jealousy as I imagined him flirting with Larissa, but with what I hoped was resolution, I shoved it aside. Maybe that would be the turn-off I needed to give myself one less thing to worry about.

"Can't hurt to try," he shrugged. "Even if I can't get any of them, it'd still be fun to see what I can do." He then whistled and pointed his sausage directly at Larissa and Amanda, who were talking with their heads together, neither of them looking up in our direction. "Those two look pretty all right—a bit of caramel and a bit of cream." He laughed. "You reckon they might dig a threesome?"

There was the spike of jealousy again, especially when I imagined myself with both of them. I knew Amanda had no interest in me, and that whatever Larissa might have thought, it was unlikely that her and I would actually do anything together—but both of them were attractive in different ways, and it would definitely be hot to have the two of them together. A threesome was something that I hadn't yet had, and at this rate, never would. But Underwood was still watching me, probably well aware of what he'd just done to my brain, and I had to answer him with considerably more discipline than I would have expected.

"I dunno—maybe. I'm not sure how early girls in their culture get into that stuff, but they could be into it if you charm them the right way."

"And you don't know what that way is?"

"Wouldn't have a clue," I said, and it was true—I had no idea what I'd done, if anything, to get Larissa's regard. "Maybe go on the net and search how to seduce Brazilian girls."

"I did that last night—got a lot of stuff about waxing. Some very disturbing images too, I don't mind telling you."

I laughed in spite of myself. "You never know, it could be useful."

"Sure, sure," he said, and finished the last of his sausage. "So how's your searching going? Found the brothel cave yet?"

"No. Well, I haven't—one of the others might have. We have found a lot of interesting ones, but none that are really useful yet."

"Do you even know what you're looking for?"

"Not really—we're just looking to outfit ourselves to fight the Hammerhearts, anything we can't do with our own magic might be useful."

A lie, but one I had to tell.

"You seen the one near my cave yet?" he asked.

"The what?"

"I guess not," he said, and smiled warily as he slowly pulled himself to his feet. "It probably wouldn't be useful anyway—it's not very magically powerful, I don't think—but it does allow you to use magic to make pretty much anything. I've used it a lot here—it's almost like having my very own Magic Crystal, except that I just can't take it anywhere with me."

Now that did sound interesting, but for the sake of the backstory, I had to contain my excitement. "You could be right, but for the sake of thoroughness, I'd better give it a look over anyway."

"Okay," he said, "and as for me, I'm gonna go to my joint and watch a few movies. I would appreciate it if you don't come calling."

"Any particular reason why not?"

"Mostly because I'm not sure when I'll go to bed, but also—well —you don't know what I could be doing."

"And by the sound of it, I wouldn't want to," I agreed.

We said our goodbyes, and then he took off in his hover car. I watched him out of sight and then looked down; the Brazilians were still there, and both Larissa and Amanda were looking up at me. They waved when they saw that I had noticed them, and I waved back, torn in a few different directions. Part of me wanted to go down there and talk to them both and see if I could get them to have a threesome with me, or to at least prevent Underwood from getting a shot at them. I wasn't actually going to do that, though, and not just because they were surrounded by their classmates. I also wanted to rush back to the campsite and tell the others what Underwood had just told me, but that would mean entering the car port in plain view of the Brazilians, so that was out of the question as well. I certainly didn't want to go to the tree house or the Group E entrance and get in that way, so what I really needed to do was bide some time until the Brazilians moved on. If I couldn't spend that time with the Brazilians themselves, then there was only one other place I might as well do it.

I got in my car and set off, passing right by the car port and heading for the eastern side of the mountain, in the direction of Smiley's cave, but with no intention of ending up there.

Chapter 28: This is Gonna Be Fun

The first thing I realised, when I got around to the eastern side of the Rock, was that May had been listening on my conversation with Underwood. I knew she had been because she had dispensed with all the red flags and replaced them with a single green flag, which was placed just outside a cave a few hundred feet above and to the right of Smiley's cave—the location of which I assumed she had gotten out of his mind while we had been talking. I wasn't sure whether or not she had told the others yet, but just in case she hadn't, I sent a quick telepathic message to her not to tell them until after I'd checked it out. Part of it was me wanting to be the one who discovered what could be the best cave we would find, but I also didn't want to waste their time, just in case Underwood was full of hot air.

I steered my car up towards the cave and into it—my car just fit. I then wound my way through the tunnel which followed, my car taking the twists and turns on its own without any trouble, the air cushion beneath it keeping it a safe (small) distance from the walls and floor. Eventually it opened into a small chamber which contained enough space for a few hover cars, and nothing else as far as I could see. Surprised, I turned my car off, waited till it sank to the floor, and then got out, staring around in the almost-pitch-black darkness. This cave was obviously meant to be something, but there didn't seem to be anything here. What was going on? Was this the right cave.

Yes, it was, according to May, who had gotten more than the cave's location out of Underwood's mind. The room suddenly lit up, not a whole lot but enough for me to see more clearly. I wondered, for a moment, if I had done anything to trigger it, but I knew it was May's doing when an arrow appeared in the wall ahead of me, pointing me towards the right. I followed it and saw a small light in the wall, and it was only when I got right up close that I realised the light, too, was only in my mind. It was coming from a small hole in the wall—a keyhole-sized hole in the wall.

I put the L-key in the hole and turned it; it didn't work. I tried the S-key, and this time it worked. A small panel opened beside the hole, and it too had a keyhole in it. I tried the L-key, but once again, it didn't work. Nervously, I removed the S-key from the panel, hoping that it wouldn't close, and it didn't; I then put it in the second keyhole and turned it. A second panel opened, and it had a third keyhole in it. I tried the L-key in this one, and finally, it worked, opening yet another panel. It went on for some time, and I would learn later that I could close the whole lot at once by putting the S-key back in the first keyhole and turning it back, but after ten keyholes—five S and five L—a door finally appeared. I was able to open this door by the exceedingly simple expedient of turning the knob and pushing it open.

The room beyond was dark, but at least this time, there was a light switch inside (well, a light keyhole). That made me wonder how Underwood had figured out how to get in here in the dark, but then he probably had a torch or something—that would be much simpler than having a Honnie making me believe it was light when it was really dark and providing the light, I assumed, from Underwood's memories of what the cave looked like. There was a second keyhole, and when I tried it, it closed the door from the inside. This chamber was about the same size as its antechamber, and it was empty except for some strange contraption against the back wall. It was a tiny bench, about waist-high, with a small hemisphere, about half the size of the Sien-Leoard Crystal, sticking out of the top of it.

I looked around a moment longer, and then approached the contraption warily, wondering how I was supposed to work it— wondering if May would put a sign on the wall giving me step-by-step instructions. I probably wouldn't need it though; I already thought I knew how it might work. Underwood had compared it to having a crystal, and although he never had one of his own, he had seen both me and Marc using ours, and probably figured out how we went about it. If he came in here, not knowing what this cave was, it was pretty obvious what his first assumption was likely to be.

I thought for a minute or so, then put my hand on the device and said, "Unboggler," as if it were like the conveyer belt in the Woodward's dining room back in the day. (If I could create anything here, an unboggler would be one of the most useful things to start with.) Unfortunately, it didn't work, so I stepped back and gave it a bit more thought. Thirty seconds later, I tried again, this time focussing on thinking of how the device had been rather than just the word, remembering my thought processes in creating the device all those months ago.

Something clattered to the floor beside the bench, making me start. I lurched back away from the contraption and looked down to see what it was…and there it was, just as advertised. I gingerly picked up the unboggler and inspected it closely. It looked exactly as I remembered it. It felt exactly as I remembered it. What about the magic within it, though? How could I possibly test that? Well, I couldn't test it, not here, but I would get plenty of chances to test it once we got back to Chopville—assuming I got to my friends before Lucien got to me. As for this contraption, though, I thought I'd seen enough to believe that it could be used to make other useful devices, and I imagined the six of us would pack into this little room for the rest of the afternoon to find out.

* * *

May had held off telling the others about this cave at first, even while they were continually asking her why the hell I was so late for lunch, but she filled them in as I was winding my way back out of the cave and back to the campsite. The Brazilians had finally moved on, so I was able to get into the carport without being seen, only to find a reception committee waiting for me right there. May looked pretty bland, but the other four all looked excited and a little pissed at me for making them wait so long. We bustled into the Group F campsite, and while I settled down to a belated lunch, the others got talking about what we could do with this new discovery.

"This could be the most useful thing we'll find," James said, "but it mightn't be the only useful cave out there, so we shouldn't give up searching just yet."

"But we should see what we can do with this one before we get back into it," said Peter. "Do you think we should re-create those things we used when we broke into the high school?"

"The ones that could do almost anything?" Marc said, screwing up his face. "We probably could, but I'm not so sure we should. Those things could barely stand up to a large number of Hammerhearts; they won't have a chance against Lucien or Stella."

"When you look at it like that, creating our own virtual crystals wouldn't do better than an even chance against those two," Amelia pointed out, "and if we start thinking like that, what's the point in even trying?"

Marc looked stricken by that comment, but he was rescued by James. "You're right, Amelia, but so is Marc. I think the best thing we can do is somehow put enchantments on ourselves that will protect us—something new that Lucien doesn't know about yet—but this cave mightn't be able to do that; that's why we shouldn't give up searching just yet."

"Maybe we can create devices that will put enchantments on ourselves?" Peter suggested.

James shrugged. "I doubt that'll work, but it's worth a try."

"So what other things should we create?" Amelia asked.

"I would suggest things to help us survive," said James. "I'm talking general survival, not stuff we can use in battle—although it can't hurt to have a little of those as well. If we could come up with a way of disabling their crystal chips that's different from what the Hammerhearts used to do, that would really help."

"And maybe something that could have an impact on the Sien-Leoard Crystal," said Marc, "to maybe get it out of Lucien's hands."

"What if he's not holding it in his hands?" Peter asked.

Marc shrugged. "I dunno, I'm just throwing it out there—I didn't say it doesn't need a bit of work."

There was some more discussion along these lines between the four of them, while I ate quietly and May just sat and listened. It wasn't until I was finishing up that it changed a little.

"Feel free to disagree with me," James said, "but I think we only really need two people to go down to this cave, while the rest of us continue searching as we have been doing. I volunteer myself, if no one's got any objections—anyone want to join me?"

Marc, Amelia and I all raised our hands. Peter looked from one to the next, shrugged and said, "I guess I won't put my hand up."

"James, with all due respect, you don't have experience in doing this sort of thing," Marc pointed out, "whereas Amelia and I do."

"And me," I added.

"Well, okay," James agreed, "but if you guys don't do an amazing job, I'll be going back there tonight."

"Suit yourself," Marc said, and grinned at Amelia.

"You don't look like you're going to keep your mind on the job," Peter observed, looking at Marc, and I thought he might be right. Marc looked eager to go, and he seemed set on going with Amelia... to do what, I wondered?

"Sure I am. What are you talking about?" Marc said indignantly.

"Pete's right, you two can have plenty of time together tonight, if you like," James said. "I suggest John goes with either one of you. I'll take his side of the mountain; Pete, May, you two just keep doing what you're doing. As for you two, figure out which of you wants to do it more."

"Hey, what gives you the right to just decide for us all like that?" Marc retorted angrily.

James shrugged. "Nothing does, but the man doth protest to much, methinks, Marc."

"Just let it go," Amelia said quietly, touching his shoulder. "He's right, we can have plenty of time together tonight. Besides, John's kind of earned the right to do this—he sat through another conversation with Underwood to get us this far."

"True, that would have been a real costly endeavour," Peter said, grinning at me.

"Fine, maybe all three of us can do it," Marc suggested, giving me a rather distrustful look.

Not that I necessarily had a problem with doing this with Marc, but being alone with just those two sounded far more awkward than I was prepared to be. Fortunately, I didn't have to look too far for a get-out clause. "I don't think that cave is big enough for all three of us to park our cars—it's pretty small."

"And that would really deplete our searching capabilities," James added.

I didn't want to beg off this job—the searching had been pretty boring, and I was glad for an excuse to do something else—but I was even more sick of this drama. I was about to suggest Marc and Amelia just go and do it themselves anyway, when fate (or possibly May) intervened on my behalf. Peter suggested the two of them play rock-paper-scissors for it, which they agreed to do, and after five consecutive ties, Amelia was able to wrap Marc's rock up in a paper of victory. Marc scowled, but at last, it was decided.

"That's actually better," James said, "because I'm thinking that Amelia's found bugger-all where she's been searching."

"Something like that," she agreed, looking pretty pleased with proceedings.

Shortly after, we left May at the campsite and set off in our hover cars. While Peter, James and Marc went off to the left, I led Amelia to the right and towards the cave of magical creation, all the while trying to think of things the two of us could create in the next few hours, and trying hard not to think of other things. It was hard not to think of how it had been when the two of us had been alone in my bedroom two nights ago, or what May had mentally told me about Amelia just that morning. She and I were about to be alone for a few hours, in a cave, as it were, but a fairly tight and cosy one.

I thought of Marc. I thought of him and Amelia. I thought of myself and Amelia. He was my brother, and he was dating her, and she was thinking about me. He knew this, and was insecure, and justifiably didn't trust me as a result. I had no right to feel indignant with him, for I had proven beyond a shadow of a doubt that I shouldn't be trusted, and yet I did. It would definitely be better for me not to do anything with Amelia, for several reasons, and I reminded myself that if I felt too horny to cope, I only had to wait until later, and perhaps May would help me again. All the same, I hoped Amelia would keep her mind on the job at hand, because I had a feeling that if she allowed it to get even a little bit intimate, I wouldn't put the brakes on. It no longer took much to send my morals flying out the window, it seemed.

With Amelia close behind me, I turned right and into the long tunnel leading to the cave of creation. A minute later, we were pulling up in the almost pitch-blackness (at least I was; Amelia almost rear-ended me). A moment later, the insides lit up again, as they had done earlier, and I mentally thanked May for helping out again. I could see Amelia clearly now, but apparently she couldn't see me—May hadn't extended her the same courtesy. She was still sitting in her car, looking around nervously, no longer even sure where I was, judging by how her eyes kept roving right over me as though she couldn't see me.

"Er, John, how do we do this?" she asked nervously.

"Just wait there for a minute," I said, busying myself with the sequence of keys and locks. Only when I had gotten the door open did I go back to Amelia and help her out of her car, enjoying the feel of her pressing herself close to me in, what was to her, impenetrable darkness. I took a moment to enjoy this feeling before taking her by the wrist and leading her into the inner chamber.

"Are we gonna have to do this all in the dark?" she asked. "And how can you see anyway?"

"I just remember from earlier," I lied, not wanting to make her feel jealous that May had chosen to help me and not her, "but there's a light switch in here, so it'll be better in just a minute."

I guided Amelia to the contraption at the back of the room, placed one of her hands on it, and then went back to the two keyholes just inside the door, fitting them both so that the light turned on and the door shut and locked from the inside. Now, we could see each other clearly, and it was just the two of us in this little room, all alone. I immediately regretted having shut the door, but then, it wouldn't have made much of a difference if it was wide-open; the room was still small, and it would still be the two of us.

"Okay, that's it," I said, and indicated the hemispherical object atop the contraption. "You just put your hand on that and think of what you want to create."

"Well at least that's familiar," she said, smiling and moving around to the front of the device.

She put her hand over the pseudo-crystal, as I would come to think of it, and seemed to be creating something in her mind. Whatever it was, it appeared in mid-air beside the contraption and fell to the floor with a loud crash that made me jump. Amelia started and bent over to pick it up (giving me a rather fetching view of her from behind in the process). When she straightened up, I saw that whatever it was, it had broken in several places on contact with the stone floor.

"Well, this is gonna be fun," she said flatly.

"My turn," I said, approaching the contraption and putting my hand on the pseudo-crystal, trying to keep my mind on what I needed to create and not on the fact that I was standing almost right up against Amelia. She could have taken a step back, but she hadn't... shut up and concentrate, John. With some effort, I managed to do so, and a few seconds later, the thing I had created fell to the stone floor with a soft flump sound. I wasn't exactly sure what to call it, but it was soft, thick, foamy, and would safely catch anything else we created without it breaking on the floor.

"Good thinking," Amelia said, giving me a charming smile that made my knees feel a little watery. "My turn."

She attempted to re-create whatever it was she had done the first time, and when it appeared and fell onto the cushion (yeah, let's call it that), she picked it up and showed it to me. It took the shape, size and appearance of a tablet (as in a computer tablet, not the kind you might swallow in an attempt to get a longer-lasting boner). At the moment, it showed a map of the world, and there were pins of light glowing on it in various places. One of them appeared to be somewhere in China, but most of them were in Australia—right around Chopville, I thought.

"Some sort of tracker?" I asked, and when she nodded, "for who?"

"Not who, what," she said. "The crystals. It'll help us find them when we get back to our time. Look, that must be where Hammerson is with the Sien-Leoard Crystal," she indicated the pin of light in China, "and that must be all of us there, in our base. Looks like Hall's in Canberra at the moment. Hmm."

"This is pretty good, but I think we might have a hard time actually using it," I said warily. "For one thing, there's no way to be sure which light is which crystal—"

She stopped me with a grin. "You think I didn't think of that? Try touching one of them and see what happens."

Cautiously, I did so, touching my finger lightly to the screen at the point where the lights were clustered together right around Chopville. Immediately, the screen zoomed in, revealing that there were six lights (two brown, two blue and two green) all clustered together in one spot, and that spot was presently walking somewhere. There was also a yellow light, not too far away, which appeared to be stationary. I didn't need Amelia to tell me that they were the Hero and Light Crystals, and although they appeared to be close together, it was possible to tell them apart, even though they were likely shrunken and in our Young Army base. I grinned back at Amelia; yes, this would be useful.

"Okay, you sold me. Now, my turn again."

Next, I created a vanishing device, which I pointed at the ruined crystal tracker and clicked once, causing it to vanish into thin air. Amelia was nervous about having such a powerful device, but I showed her its restrictions: Not only would it not work on people, but there was another button on it which acted as a sort of undoer; if pressed, it would bring back the last thing that had been vanished. After some persuasion, Amelia agreed that it would probably be useful, and with her next turn, she created a device which took the same size and shape as the vanisher (only a different colour) that would duplicate objects. Seeing how the next little while was likely to go, I used my next turn to create an extender-case with which we could carry all these creations back to the campsite.

It was Amelia's turn next, but she took some time over it, trying to think best how to create what it was that she was trying to create. I tried to ask her what it was a couple of times but she kept shushing me. Finally, she put her hand on the pseudo-crystal and thought at it for about twenty seconds before a new device appeared and fell onto the cushion. With a great sigh, she smiled and let her hand fall away from the contraption.

"Can I talk now?" I asked. "What is that?"

"The best way I could think to disable Lucien's magic," she said, picking up the device and dropping it into the extender-case with the others. "It won't actually disable it, it'll just put a one-way shield around the person it hits so that any magic they perform can only impact anything inside the shield, and the shield can only be removed by the device that created it. It will repel any magic I can think of, except possibly Fewul, but I can't think of any way we can deal with that."

"Then, we need some way to forcefully get rid of Fewul," I said, thinking of how Lucien had forced Fewul away when he had first come to power.

Oh, but he'd had the Sien-Leoard Crystal, and the power of these creations would only be as great as whichever Sorcerer had created this cave in the first place—at least, I was pretty sure that was how magic worked. But then I had another idea, a better one, and I put my hand on the pseudo-crystal to create the device. It took the shape of the signaller Mr. Woodward had once created for me to call for help, except this one only had one button, which, if held down for five seconds, would cause the Beast of Magic to vanish as if it had heard Leoard's Lament played on a nearby Maahoo. The five-second rule was only there so that we didn't accidentally vanish it here and now, perhaps right when Marc might be using it.

"You know that mightn't work," Amelia said nervously.

"Yeah, I know, so we'd better not rely on it when we get back. Your turn."

Amelia's next attempt at a device didn't work; at least, the contraption refused to create whatever it was. She had to amend it, which she wasn't happy about at all, but when the device was finally created, it looked pretty neat to me. Like the crystal tracker, it took the shape of a tablet, and on it was a list of various foods and drinks that the device was capable of creating out of thin air, along with a quantity specifier. I tested it by selecting a chocolate bar from the list and watching as it appeared in my other hand.

"Excellent," I said, unwrapping it. "Out of curiosity, what were you trying to do?"

"I wanted something like what we used to have in our dining room," she said sadly. "This is almost as good; it just means that it can only create the foods I could think to put in the list."

"No complaints here," I said through a mouthful of chocolate. "My turn."

I took a moment to think of what to create next. It didn't take long; the thing I had struggled with most since our flight from the Young Army base, apart from my rogue banana, was physical injury. We needed some sort of magic that could help us stay healthy. Ideally, we would have a device that could cure literally anything, but that would probably suffer the same issues as the device Amelia had just tried to create. I had to try to think of all the things that could go wrong—cuts, bruises, broken bones, pulled or ripped muscles or tendons, foreign objects in the body—and create a device that could heal all those things just by being clicked while pointing at a person. I racked my brains, trying to think of anything else that could go wrong—any injury I had ever seen or heard of—before putting my hand on the pseudo-crystal and finally creating the device.

"Definitely a good idea," Amelia agreed when I explained what I had just done. "My turn."

She created a similar device, only this one could create all different items of clothing out of nothing, in all different sizes, dimensions, colours and quantities. I probably wouldn't have thought of creating something like that, but given how often my clothes had been torn apart under Hammerheart assault, I was sure glad she had. That gave me an idea for a device to create with my next turn: something that could put up a shield, both physical and magical, that no Hammerheart would be able to break through. Lucien or Stella probably could, but it might slow them down while they tried to figure out what it was, and that could be advantage enough.

"Good idea," she said approvingly, "that would have been useful in the school fight."

We both fell silent then, me waiting for her to have her turn and her—well, I wasn't sure what she was thinking. After about fifteen seconds, I said, "Something wrong?"

"I'm trying to think what else we might need," she said vaguely. "James said we should focus on things we might need to live and survive rather than fight, but I'm not sure what else to create."

"Well, what other problems do you think we might run into once we leave the Rock?" I asked.

"Problems," she repeated, and her tone made me look more closely at her face—she looked a little sad, but she quickly composed herself. "Well, I suppose we need a way to get off the Rock to begin with, so…"

She put her hand over the pseudo-crystal and created something else. When she held it up, I saw that it was a shrunken duplicate of the vessel we had used to get to and from Rock Haulter back in May, small enough to fit in the palm of her hand, and with a single button on the side which, I assumed, would enlarge it to normal size— which Amelia confirmed when I asked, only with the five-second rule like the vanishing device I had created earlier. Thinking of the vessel gave me an idea for something else to create, and I put my hand on the pseudo-crystal. The device which dropped onto the cushion a few seconds later could create furniture out of nothing— tables, chairs, couches, beds and other assorted furnishings— including a toilet and shower.

The shower it could create, complete with a never-ending water supply, was big enough for two people—that design was intentional. Perhaps it wasn't a good idea for me to intentionally allow for such a thing, especially given that we had all promised that no one should have sex with anyone else in the group (a promise which four out of the six of us had already broken), but I hadn't been able to help myself. I wished I could try it with Amelia; that thought made me feel aroused all over again.

"Nice," Amelia said, dropping the new device into the bag along with the others. "My turn again. Hmm."

"Still having trouble thinking of new things?" I asked.

She considered for a moment and then said, "No, I just can't think of any way of dealing with the sort of problems I'm having."

"Oh," I said, thinking I now knew what she was thinking of and not knowing what else to say. True, awkward social situation was the greatest problem our little group could face, short of being captured anyway, and I didn't think there was any magical solution to that. I hesitated for a moment, and then deciding, I turned to Amelia and gave her a hug. It took her by surprise, but she returned it gratefully —and when I let go, she didn't.

"I guess for some things, we really are on our own," I said quietly.

"Yeah," she said. "Hey, can I ask you something?"

"Sure."

"Have you drank again since the other night when we—you know—"

I shook my head. "Peter kept me busy so that I wouldn't have a chance."

"Oh good," she said, and put her head on my shoulder. Her arms were still around me, and I now felt a little weird just having mine by my side, so I raised them and put them lightly around her again. I tried not to be too conscious of her body so close to mine, but that was definitely not an easy thing to do.

When it seemed like this moment would just keep going on, I said, "Do you wanna keep creating stuff or have you had enough?"

"It's okay," she said vaguely, "I just like this."

"Ah huh," I said, now feeling nervous. As much as I liked this feeling too, there was one thing nagging at me. "Can I ask you something now?"

"Sure."

"Do you still wanna date Marc?"

"I'm really not sure. Do you still wanna date Natalie?"

"Definitely, if I can."

I felt her shrug. "Same here. If I didn't have feelings for you, I would date Marc."

"I don't like messing with your head," I told her. "I know it's gonna hurt to hear this, but as much as I like you Amelia, Natalie's my first preference."

"I know," she said sadly, "but you know she mightn't take you back. I know you do, because you wouldn't have done what you did with me if you felt sure you could get her back."

That was probably true. What I'd done with Amelia back in Melbourne had been terrible, but everything that I'd done since had been brought about, at least in part, by the knowledge that I might have already lost Natalie. I didn't want to say any of this, so I said, "I guess it's possible that I'll eventually move on if she doesn't."

And if I did, there was a chance Amelia would be waiting for me. May wasn't an option for a girlfriend, Lena probably hated me now, and Stella—well, I wasn't so sure about her, but what I did know for sure was that I wouldn't date her while she was in league with Lucien. But what about Marc? If I stole Amelia from him now, he would never forgive me. He probably wouldn't forgive me if he found out about the two times we'd had sex since he had walked in on us, but it would be so much worse if I actually made her my girlfriend.

Confirming this, Amelia said, "And if you do, you have me. I don't like being a backup option, and believe me, if I could feel about Marc like I do about you, I would be with him, but I can't just pretend I don't feel how I feel. I know you've messed up pretty bad lately, but I still think you're a pretty good guy, and you'll be an even better guy when you've grown up a bit and gotten past all this."

That hurt a little, like she had given me a swift punch to the gut, but it was exactly what I deserved, I supposed, so I wore it. "Thanks, Amelia, but if it doesn't go like that, you should move on from me. It doesn't have to be with Marc, if you can't have those feelings for him, but it can't be for me either—that'll end up hurting all three of us."

"Yeah, I know," she said, finally raising her head from my shoulder so that we could look at each other, "but..."

She kissed me on the lips, taking me by surprise, but instigating an instinct I was powerless to stop: I kissed her back deeply, holding her close. It went on for several seconds before we finally separated, although we didn't let go of each other. Still catching her breath, she said, "I know I shouldn't have done that, but I really wanted to."

"I guess I went a little too far too," I said, "but—I wanted to, too."

"Among other things?" she said, smiling slightly in a way that made me want to kiss her again. When I recognised that want, I went ahead and did it. As we kissed, one of her hands dipped to my waist and, whether accidentally or on purpose, she became aware of exactly how aroused by her I was. She stopped the kiss then, and for a moment I thought she had been turned off by it—something that I both wanted and didn't want—but actually, she had something else in mind.

She put her hand on the pseudo-crystal again and created a new device. I said, "Ah, so we're ready to get back to—" and then she pointed it at me and gave it a click. I didn't feel any different at first, although looking at Amelia's body, I did want to kiss her again—among other things, as she had said.

"What was that?" I asked, taking the device from her.

"A kind of magical Viagra," she said, grinning cheekily at me. "Will keep you wanting something without fail for a whole hour."

I considered this, trying to ignore a feeling of arousal that seemed to be building inside me. It didn't seem too bad, other than the fact that it was disturbingly similar to what Lucien had done to me—though thankfully, it didn't seem to have taken away my rationality. One thing I did rationalise, though, was that unless Amelia was particularly cruel, she intended (or at least wanted) to utilise the next hour of my time in a way that was directly related to what she had just done to me. There was only one fair thing to do: I pocketed the device, thinking it might be useful someday when I had an official girlfriend again, and put my hand on the pseudo-crystal again, thinking of what I wanted to create. I quickly snatched up the device when it appeared, turned it on Amelia and clicked it. If all went well, it would have the same effect on her, and for the same length of time.

"And that was?" she asked, taking the device from me.

"Let's just say, I just paid you back in kind," I grinned at her.

She just stared at me, her face flushing as her body began to speak to her; and I stared back, wanting to have my way with her, wondering if I ought to create anything else to make it more exciting. I wasn't so sure I would be able to work the pseudo-crystal in this state, though, so I decided on a different course of action.

"What are you doing?" she asked me as I began rummaging through the extender-case.

I didn't answer until I had found what I was looking for. When I had located the vanisher, I took it from the bag, turned it on Amelia, and gave it a click. She gasped when the jet of light hit her in the stomach, but as advertised, she didn't vanish—but her sweater did. I clicked it again, vanishing her T-shirt, so that now, her bra was her only remaining item of clothing above her waist. Before she had time to react, I pointed the vanisher at her pants and clicked again; they, too, vanished, leaving her standing in her shoes, socks and underwear.

"I don't think you need that stuff," I told her, smiling as I regarded her body.

"Oh really," she said, smiling and posing for me. Then while I was distracted by her body, she snatched the vanisher out of my hand and turned it on me.

"What—" Before I had time to react, my jumper, T-shirt and pants vanished into thin air, leaving me standing in my shoes, socks and underwear too. "Give me that—"

And that was how the two of us ended up naked together in that cave. I then rummaged in the extender-case again, finding something else I had created, and pulling it out. It was the furniture creator, and for a moment, I was going to create a large bed—almost the size of this chamber—for us to bounce on for the remainder of the hour before our horny ran out and we could get back to work. But almost all the sex I'd had lately, though in various locations, had been on beds. During the time I had been with Natalie before the shit had hit the fan, we had almost always done it in our bedrooms, but in many places around those bedrooms. It was only one scene with Natalie, which had taken place in an elevator, and the interlude with Stella— that had been so different. I wanted this time with Amelia to be unique, so rather than a bed, I turned to the corner away from Amelia and created the large shower I had been thinking about earlier.

"I like the look of that," she said. "Lead the way."

And so, Amelia and I showered together. Then while she used the vanisher to re-create our clothes, I created a few more devices specifically for us: The first one would instantly dry us; the second was a normalising device which could set us to rights once this was done; and the third device was a secret I intended to take to the grave if I could. I used the drying device to dry us both, and then used the furnishing device to create a large bed for us—it may be standard, but at least it would be comfortable and functional for us. That was where we remained for the next forty-five minutes.

When it was all done and the effects of the magic we had placed on each other were finally wearing off, we both got into our clothes and I vanished the bed. I considered vanishing the other devices I had created, and then didn't; the normaliser would be useful, and maybe someday, the other two would be, too. I put them in my pocket next to the two arousal builders.

The last hour had been incredibly enjoyable, but it came at a multifaceted price. Firstly, I knew that nothing Marc did with Amelia would match up to what I'd just done—not unless Marc got creative and tried to do something similar, but then maybe she would end up just being reminded of this time and that would make her want me all over again. On one hand, it made me feel proud of myself; on the other, I couldn't think of any way it could be good for anyone. The second price was that although I had just done what I felt like doing, my rationale when we had started out, there was no way I could reconcile this with what little remained of my morals. Not only had I screwed Marc's girlfriend in ways he couldn't imagine, but I had cheated on Natalie in a way that was considerably worse than what I'd done while I was cursed. Natalie herself probably wouldn't see much difference, if she ever found out, but I would know the difference.

"Amelia, can I ask you something?" I asked her when she came over to me, standing beside the contraption.

"Sure."

"Do you think Natalie could ever forgive me for the sort of person I am?"

She smiled tenderly at me. "I think that if I can still think good of you, knowing what you've done, she can too."

"I'm not a good person," I said flatly, but she stopped my mouth with a soft kiss.

"You know what I think," she said, "I think you are a good person if you want to be but don't quite get it right. Besides," she added, grinning more broadly, "you sure took care of me today. I don't think I've ever felt so good in my life."

Chapter 29: It's Hard to Know What's Real

Amelia and I returned to the campsite at around four o'clock, a full two hours before everyone else was due to return. We might have stayed in the creation cave longer, but after we had created several more devices on top of those we had made before the session had dissolved into a veritable warehouse full of orgasms, we had finally run out of ideas. I still felt like there were more things that we might need, but neither of us could think what they were, so perhaps it wouldn't be such a bad idea for the others to try their hand up in that cave as well. We had, of course, vanished all traces of those other things we had done in the cave, so that the only record of them was in each of our heads—and no doubt May's, as she would have ridden all the highs right along with us while simultaneously supervising the other three as they searched.

With two hours before the others would come back, we found ourselves in a slightly awkward situation. There wasn't a lot to do at the campsite without the rest of the group present, and as pleasant as Amelia's company was, I was nervous about being with her now. What if we got intimate again? What if we got caught again? It was a risk I wasn't prepared to take. Even just sitting and chatting to her would no doubt make Marc jealous when he got back and found out, so I decided to go to my bedroom and take a nap. After the workout my body had gotten that afternoon, that was a much more desirable option than getting back in my hover car and going out to search. Amelia first went to sit with May on the tree house verandah, but after that, I didn't know.

The three boys were pretty tired when they got back to camp, but they quickly became excited when they saw all the cool stuff Amelia and I had created. James used the food device to create a few large pizzas, some garlic bread and bottles of coke, and then we all sat down to eat and examine all the devices. Marc was most interested in the crystal tracker; Peter was particularly interested in the furniture device (he had noticed the shower); James couldn't stop going through the items on the food device, and I thought he might want to try all of them at some point; and May had taken notice of one we had created later on in the session, one which could knock a person unconscious through the fourth dimension. That is, if we were in our shadow, we could use it to attack someone in the regular dimension.

But although he did marval appropriately over our creations, Marc wasn't in a particularly good mood over dinner. He kept shooting me covert, untrusting looks across the group; and although he was sitting next to Amelia, and was holding her hand throughout much of dinner, he kept frowning whenever she spoke to someone else in the group—and especially when that someone was me. When the dinner was over and we used the vanisher to get rid of the rubbish, Marc asked if Amelia would spend the rest of the night with him in one of the other campsites. She went with him without argument, but not with a whole lot of enthusiasm either, I thought. I didn't mind so much that she was going with him (after what had happened that day, I no longer felt jealous towards Marc) but I wished that Amelia could really enjoy it, and not just pretend to.

The rest of us settled down to a game of four-way chess in the Group F campsite. May had seen enough of the game to know how to play it, although she didn't really see it as her version of fun, but for the sake of fairness, we got her to agree to release all our minds from hers for the duration of the game—or for as long as she was part of it, anyway. That turned out not to be long: It only took ten minutes for James to checkmate her, her king locked in by most of her own pieces, and I tended to think that perhaps she had deliberately lost so that we could go on without her, only playing at all because we needed a fourth person. Unfortunately, I was the next person to lose, so that it was down to Peter and James to fight it out. James usually did well in these situations, but on this occasion, he and Peter had roughly the same number of pieces still on the board, so it was anyone's game.

At around eight o'clock, Marc re-entered the campsite from the car port. He was alone and looked pretty pissed. We all looked around at him in surprise—at least, us three boys looked surprised. May just looked bland. My heart sank at the sight of him—I didn't think Amelia had told him what we'd done, but clearly something had happened.

"What's up with you?" James asked.

"And where's Amelia?" I asked.

Marc grunted as he took a seat beside James. "I believe I may have upset her. She went out in her car and demanded that I not follow her."

"Geez, man, what did you do?" Peter asked, returning his gaze to the chess board.

Marc shrugged, his head down as he considered. Finally he looked up at me. "Okay, I know we came to an understanding on the boat—"

I sighed and prepared to tell an outright lie—that I hadn't broken my promise to him, that we hadn't done anything during the hours we had spent alone together this afternoon—but before I could, Marc continued.

"Does it make me nuts that I still worry about how she's feeling?" he asked, looking around at the group at large.

"Er—you mean if she's thinking about John when you're knocking boots?" Peter asked.

Marc and I both cringed. "No, not that," he said quickly, "and God—now I probably will worry about that. I mean, I know she still likes you," he told me, "not just because she was willing to sleep with you in Melbourne, but she actually told me, just last night, that she thinks you need her more than I do."

"I don't," I said quickly, and that, at least, was the truth. "Look, I've thought about this a lot since we came back through time. I like Amelia, but I have no intention of actually going there with her, and I really regret what happened in Melbourne—don't tell her I said that, though," I added quickly.

"Then why would she think you need her more than I do?" Marc asked.

"Well, I have been kind of a mess lately," I said, looking down at my lap. "I actually think you need her more than I do. I still want Natalie, and if I can't have her—well I guess my next girlfriend will have to be someone entirely different."

"Not Lena or Stella?" Peter asked.

"Not while they're on Lucien's side," I replied, and when James opened his mouth to say something, I added, "and yeah, I know we might get a chance to bring them back to our side. I just think if it's not Natalie, it should be someone who wasn't around for all this crap."

Peter and James swapped looks, and Marc said, "Well, if you're serious about that. What about now, though? What should I do? She's got feelings for you, man, and even if you don't feel the same way, it still drives me crazy."

"I think the thing to remember is that it's not Amelia's fault that she feels the way she feels," James told him. "I know I'm not a girl, but it seems to me that if she agreed to date you again, she must still have some feelings for you. Try to focus on those, and let Amelia sort out her own mind in her own time."

"So basically, I have to wear it," Marc said flatly. "What if she dumps me because she can't feel for me what she feels for John?"

"Then she'll be the loser," I told him, "but if that does happen, you probably just have to let her go—again," I added, feeling terrible for him. "Can I ask a favour from you?"

"What's that?" he said warily.

"Can I go out and talk to her?"

That made his shackles rise. "Why do you wanna do that?"

"I'm still her friend, Marc," I reminded him, "and maybe I can get her to come back. She won't respond to you right at the moment, but maybe she'll respond to me."

He pursed his lips, not looking happy about it, but seeming to see sense in my words.

"Be careful, John," Peter warned me. "If she's feeling vulnerable at the moment, she might want to kiss you or something."

"Oh, I hope not," I said as I got up. "I don't want to have to hurt her."

I headed out to the car port without looking back at the others. I didn't want to see the mistrust in Marc's eyes, nor did I particularly want to look at May. She had been sitting silently beside me throughout that entire conversation, and she had spent all of that time watching me closely, and no doubt listening to my every thought. She had the full picture of what was happening on the Rock better than any of us—what did she make of it? Given the terrible things I had done since I'd been here (cheating on Natalie three times, cutting Marc's lunch twice, messing with Amelia's mind and leading her on, using May for sex, and even kissing Larissa—can't forget that), I wasn't sure I wanted to know.

I jumped in my hover car, started it up, and tore out of the garage without any idea where I was going. Amelia had an immense head start on me, and it wasn't like hover cars left any tracks. I called her name into the night a couple of times, and then when I accepted I wasn't going to get a response, I stopped, hovering over a thirty-five degree slope in the rock, and racked my brains. Amelia could have gone anywhere, but if she was that upset, she probably would have wanted to go somewhere familiar. The most obvious place I could think of was the place she and I had had so much fun that day, so I turned and headed in that direction.

But that cave turned out to be empty—at least, the antechamber was, and she couldn't have fit her hover car through the door into the inner chamber. I considered going in anyway, perhaps to create a device that would show me where Amelia was on the island, and then didn't—that was a little too creepy for my liking. So I left that cave and continued my search lower down, checking out various caves which we had found as a group, before we had all had our own keys. Half an hour of this turned out to be entirely fruitless, and I was on the point of mentally asking May to tell me where she was, when finally, I saw someone entering a cave someway below me. Was it Amelia, perhaps ditching her car and continuing on foot?

I took my car down to the cave in question, only to find that it wasn't Amelia who I had seen. Whoever it was, they were carrying a torch in one hand and some other clunky-looking object in the other, and there was no hover car in sight—and to top it off, when I had brought my car down in front of the cave, I had startled them.

"Sorry, I thought you were someone else—"

The person—a girl, I now saw by the shape of her body—raised her torch so that she could get a look at me, and when the light reflected off her face, I saw who it was: Larissa. Somehow, I wasn't surprised. Wasn't it appropriate that out of all the Brazilians who could have been out exploring, I just had to intercept this one? What did surprise me a little was the thing I now saw clearly in her other hand: It was a tracker, the very same type of tracker that the school had forced all the students to use back when we had come here in February; it would enable her superiors to come and find her if she got into trouble.

"Hi," she said, smiling and relaxing when she recognised me.

"What are you doing out here?" I asked, a little nervously. We weren't very high up, and this spot wasn't especially dangerous, but exploring the Rock on foot at night seemed like a real risky thing to do. It wasn't like she had any magic to protect her if something went wrong.

"Just looking around," she said, holding the tracker up so that I could see it, and taking a step forward towards my car. "We're allowed to look around a bit if we take these with us, and if we don't go too high."

"Found anything interesting?"

"Quite a lot," she said. "What are you doing out here?"

"Oh, I—I thought you were someone else," I said, feeling a little embarrassed. I didn't want to tell her about Amelia—I didn't want to possibly make her jealous—I was enjoying her regard and as confused as I was, I didn't want to possibly ruin it. All the same, I had to say something. "One of my friends left our campsite and didn't come back, so I'm just looking to make sure she's okay."

"Amelia Woodward?" she asked, startling me.

"Yeah. Er, how'd you know that?"

"Aren't the rest of your friends boys? Well, except for that—uh —other one."

"Wow, you pay attention," I said, torn in two directions at once. There was something awkward about sitting here in my car while she stood out there. On one hand, I wanted to stand with her; and on the other, sitting here made me want to take off and continue looking for Amelia, who surely needed me more than Larissa did.

"Do you want me to help you find her?" she asked, startling me again.

"Er—that's nice, but I'm not sure you'd be able to do much," I said unwillingly. "She could be just about anywhere—I've already wasted half an hour looking for her."

"Then maybe you should wait for her to come back on her own," she suggested, taking another step forward so that now, she was standing right beside my car, as she had done the day before. "She has magic, doesn't she? She can probably look after herself."

"Er—yeah, I guess," I relented, feeling very uncomfortable. That may not be true, but I couldn't tell Larissa that Amelia was no longer a Sorcerer—that didn't fit the narrative of this time.

"You want to come look at some caves with me?" she asked. "Maybe we can go a little higher if I sit on the back of your car-thing."

"Er—" I faltered, torn in more than two directions now. I wanted to say 'yes', but I didn't think this car would support both of us. I wanted to get out and check out a few caves on foot, perhaps settle down with her in one of them (the hot tub cave would be a good one for that, even though that was around the north-east and we were on the western side of the Rock), but that thought made me feel very guilty for Amelia. I wanted to say 'no' to Larissa and take off in search of Amelia, but I didn't want to hurt Larissa's feelings. I decided on a compromise. "Did you get a chance to look in that one right there?"

"I was about to when you came."

"Maybe we can check it out then," I said, turning my car off so that it sank slowly to the ground, and waving her back so that I had room to get out. I couldn't remember what was in this cave, but it looked familiar and I thought we had probably looked in it as a group two days ago.

"Okay," she said eagerly, and when I was on my feet, she stepped up beside me—right beside me, in what I considered to be my personal space, just as she had done on the boat. It made me very aware of both of our bodies, but I didn't mind.

Following the light from her torch, I led the way into the cave, only to find a locked door a short distance in. Larissa sighed despondently. "I have found these doors everywhere. The teachers have keys, but they won't let us take them."

"Almost all the interesting things are locked away," I agreed. "Here℟—"

I took hold of her wrist, feeling a tingle of excitement at the skin-on-skin touch, and moved it around until the torchlight fell on the keyhole. I then withdrew the appropriate key from my pocket (the L-key), put it in the lock, and turned. The door opened before us, and dazzling sunlight hit our eyes. It was the sandy beach cave we had found on our first day here. The sun was warm, bright and high; the water was clear and stretched endlessly ahead; the cliff behind us as we stepped through the door was big and tall, but somehow not intimidating; and the beach itself was just about overwhelming in its beauty. There were many caves in which it would have been interesting to find myself alone with a girl, but this one was right up there with them.

Beside me, Larissa let out a long sigh of pleasure. "Wow, this is magical."

"Well, yeah, literally," I said, grinning.

She switched the torch off (we hardly needed it now) and set off towards the water, taking me by the wrist and dragging me with her. I thought maybe she would go right in, but she stopped about halfway between the water and the cliff, looking down towards the waves. The sound of them breaking was loud, but the waves themselves weren't very big. Clearly, whoever had created this cave hadn't meant for it to be used by surfers. The radiant smile on Larissa's face would have made any guy weak at the knees, and I was no exception.

"I wish I brought better clothes," she said wistfully. Personally, I thought she looked pretty good; she was wearing jeans and a dark jacket, both of which fit her body pretty snugly.

As I thought this, she proceeded to take the jacket off, revealing a sleeveless top beneath. She was also revealing a certain amount of cleavage, which I had to quickly look away from (I couldn't be sure if that would offend her, but had to assume it might). I didn't think she was doing it for my benefit, though; the temperature back on the Rock had been pretty chilly (especially for someone who would have been used to tropical weather), and now that we were suddenly in a summer environment in the middle of the day, even I found myself feeling rather hot. Normally I would wear board shorts and a T-shirt in a place like this; as it was, I pulled my sweater up over my head so that I had accomplished half of the typical outfit.

"I normally wear bikini on the beach," she told me, her eyes on my face as though watching for a reaction. If so, she would have got it, for I had been unable to stop myself imagining her in a bikini at her words. I couldn't be totally sure what reaction she was hoping for, but in this case, I didn't see any point pretending that hadn't just happened.

"I kinda wish I could see that," I admitted, and her smile broadened—that had been what she had hoped for.

"Should we walk or sit down?" she asked.

"Walk, I guess, but only for a bit," I said, checking my watch—it was nearly nine o'clock. "We had better not lose track of time."

"Yeah, I have to be back before ten o'clock, and it will take a while to walk back from here. I wish we could stay longer, though."

We turned and set off to the left, me looking back at the cliff only to see that the door back to the cave was following us as we walked. The clothes we had left behind remained where they were, but that was okay—we would have time to come back for them as long as we didn't go too far.

As we walked, I found myself feeling incredibly refreshed—more so than I had for a very long time. I looked around as we went, even though the scenery wasn't changing at all, and periodically back at Larissa because, well, she was the most interesting thing here. Only once did I catch her looking out towards the waves—every other time I looked at her, I found her watching me. After about two minutes of walking, on a stroke of inspiration, I reached out and took her by the hand, feeling a moment of anxiety when she could have pulled back, but she didn't. In the minutes that followed, I had time to reflect that, although we weren't talking, there was something romantic about walking along a beach with a girl. The most obvious clue to this was my increasing desire to kiss her the longer we touched.

"We should probably go back," I said after a depressingly short time.

"I don't think we have to," she said, pointing up ahead. I followed her finger and saw something on the sand directly ahead of us; when I looked more carefully, I saw that it was our discarded clothes. Apparently, this beach wasn't so never-ending as it looked; it just kept coming back to the start. It would only take us another ten minutes or so to get back to them from here.

"Oh good," I said, and so we kept walking until we arrived back at our clothes. I checked my watch—it was now twenty-five past nine. Larissa should have just enough time to get back to the main hall before ten o'clock if she hurried, and Amelia had been out on her own for over an hour now. That thought filled me with guilt, and I roughly shoved it away; she didn't know I was here, and meanwhile Larissa deserved my attention.

"I know, we should go back now," she said, picking up her jacket and shaking the sand off it.

"Yeah, we should," I agreed, "but this was nice. I dunno if we'll run into each other again, but if we do, we should—"

She stopped my mouth with a kiss, taking me by surprise and confirming that I wasn't the only one affected by this place. My desire to kiss her hadn't waned at all, and so I instinctively kissed her back. Her body was close to mine again, and now I put my arms around her; and even after all the sex I'd already had that day, it made me feel horny again. Fortunately, thinking of Amelia again in that context made me feel somewhat less horny, and that made it easier to regain my composure when we finally broke apart. At least, our mouths broke apart—she continued to stand close to me.

"If you hadn't done that, I probably would have," I said, and it may have been true—I had certainly wanted to.

"I do like you," she said, putting her head on my shoulder.

"Larissa?"

"Yeah?"

"You remember what I said yesterday? It's not really a good idea to get close to me."

"Why not?"

"Well—I have a habit of hurting people who get too close. I'm trying to change that, but I don't to hurt you."

"Hmm," she said, raising her head off my shoulder. "Okay, I hear your warning."

And then she told me exactly what she thought of that warning when she kissed me on the lips again.

"Can I see you again tomorrow night?" she asked me as we made our way back up the beach to the cave.

"Er—maybe," I said, a little reluctantly. A big part of me wanted to, but what if I couldn't? I considered for a moment before deciding, I could figure something out tomorrow night. "Let's say we can, and I'll find a way to let you know if we can't. Don't worry about meeting somewhere; I'll find a way to find you."

"With magic?"

"Yeah, probably."

She smiled. "I was kind of hoping you would let me visit you at your campsite, wherever it is."

I shrugged. "You wouldn't be able to get in even if I wanted to show it to you; there's a lot of magical protection around it."

We said our goodbyes and parted ways outside the cave, she heading down towards the ground and the path back to the main hall, I in the opposite direction. I still had no idea where Amelia was, but now free to wallow in my guilt for not thinking of her when I was with Larissa (while she was probably sitting somewhere in tears), I had no intention of wasting any more time looking for her. I did what I should have done in the beginning: I contacted May telepathically, asking her where Amelia was and how she was doing, hoping that she (May) hadn't gone to sleep. She responded quickly, indicating a cave on the western side of the mountain (so not far from here but high up). Letting May guide me, I went up and up and up, until I finally found Amelia's car, which sat empty on a shelf of rock.

I found Amelia in a nearby cave, sitting on a rock and staring blankly ahead of her. I hoped that she hadn't become virtually catatonic as she had been months earlier when she had been distressed, but fortunately, she stirred when I sat down beside her.

"I would ask if you're okay, except obviously you're not," I said flatly.

"Hi, John," she said dismally. "I suppose Marc told you what happened?"

"He told me what he thinks happened," I said warily. "You know he can't help feeling insecure about us, right?"

"Yeah, I know, and I know he's right not to trust me," she said, looking at me directly now. "I just don't know what to do anymore. I really care about him, but how can I be happy with him when I feel like I'm living a lie when I'm with him?"

"I don't know, but I do know one thing," I said, and I took her by the face so that she had to look at me. "Amelia, whatever this is between us, it has to stop."

She sighed. "I know, I can't hold a torch to Natalie."

"I'm sorry," I said, feeling horrible. "If I could change how I feel, I would—it'd make things a lot easier for me. But then if you could do that, you'd be back with Marc."

"This is really messed up, isn't it," she said sadly.

"Couldn't agree more," I said, "but it is what it is. I think you should come back to camp with me."

She sighed. "Actually, I'd rather stay out a little longer. Don't worry, I'll come back when I'm ready."

"And you're not gonna quit on Marc?" I prompted.

"I won't, if he doesn't quit on me."

"And I won't quit on you either," I told her, getting to my feet, "as a friend, I mean."

"Thanks, John. When you get back, tell Marc that I'm okay, and that I'm sorry for being such a difficult girlfriend."

So after all that, I went back to camp alone, feeling worse than ever. I'd had such a great time with Amelia that day, and she had enjoyed it just as much as I had, and now it had made things much worse for her, me, and even Marc. Now there was Larissa to think about; I had inadvertently started something with her, which might still be nothing (and would definitely be nothing once I left the Rock), but now she would have expectations, and I had an undeniable attraction to her. Then there was still my overarching desire to be with Natalie; I had to remind myself that she was the one I loved, that I would feel much worse without her once I got back to the future, and that all the fun I was having now didn't change that.

I returned to the Group F campsite in a state of high confusion to find all the others waiting for me. They had started another game of four-way chess, and most incredibly, James had been eliminated—it was now between Marc and Peter, and it looked like Peter had the upper hand. They all looked around at me when I entered the room.

"Should I be worried about how long you were gone?" Marc asked, his eyes narrowed.

"Don't look at me like that," I said wearily. "I only spent a few minutes with her; the rest of the time, I was trying to find her."

Marc grinned. "I know that, mate; May told us you asked for help finding her."

"Oh," I said, relaxing. "Well, yeah. She'll be coming back soon, but she told me to tell you that she's sorry for being a difficult girlfriend."

Marc flinched. "Okay, thanks. I hope she doesn't stay out too late; it must be freezing out there."

"What's that?" James asked, indicating something on the floor. I looked down, saw what he had seen, and my insides shrivelled up in embarrassment. I had tracked sand into the room. It wasn't much, barely visible in fact, but there was no mistaking what it was.

I had a moment of indecision, and then decided on the truth—or, most of it. "That's sand. I went into a cave that had sand in it while I was looking."

"I don't remember any caves with sand in them," Peter said, frowning over the chess board.

"Actually, it was the beach cave we found on Wednesday," I said. "I forgot that's what it was when I went in, though. I think I might go to bed, feeling pretty tired and all."

"Aren't you going to clean up the mess?" James asked pointedly.

"Oh, right."

Fortunately, Amelia and I had created just such a device that afternoon. The vanishing device could have gotten rid of the sand, one grain at a time, but there was another device which could clean up any sand, dust, dirt, stain, or just about anything else that needed to be cleaned, with a single push of a button. I retrieved said device from the extender-case I had also created that afternoon, got rid of the sand, put it back, and then went to bed, waving to the others as I went.

Being alone with my thoughts was not a good thing for me. I undressed, got into my pyjamas, got into bed, and lay there, feeling miserable and horny. I thought of Amelia and Larissa. I thought of Natalie. I thought of Lena and Stella. I even thought of May. I thought of the things I had already done with all of them, the things I would probably do to them, and the things I wished I could do— things such as have sex with them, and simultaneously not have sex with any of them, as that was what had gotten me into this mess in the first place. Perhaps someday, when I was older, I would look back on this time in my life and feel pleased that I had taken all the opportunities that had presented themselves to me, and a couple which hadn't really. I knew that I would regret the things I'd done less than I might have regretted not trying some of them, but had I really needed to do them all?

One thing I hadn't done was have sex with Larissa, though, so it was her I thought of first—and when I felt bad for not thinking of Natalie, I thought of her instead. I lay there, listening to the silence in my room, eventually hearing one person come to bed, then another, and then another. Had Amelia returned to the camp yet? Was she still alone out there, or perhaps alone in her room? Or was she perhaps making up with Marc...perhaps being intimate with him...

I sat up, bent over the side of my bed and rolled the half-full bottle of wine out from beneath it. I had enough sense to stop and consider what I was doing, knowing that the drink would be bad for me, knowing that I would be in all sorts of trouble if the others found out, and knowing that I did not want to be in my right mind tonight. So I unscrewed the top and began to drink, sitting back against the headboard of my bed and thinking about the girls in my life. If I could just accept that I was a terrible person, I could think sexually about any and all of these girls without feeling guilty for doing so. That made it easier to imagine myself with them—to imagine them here. I particularly thought of Lena, the most attractive of them in many ways (certainly everything about her body seemed to scream sexuality) and although it seemed unlikely that she would ever forgive me for what I'd done to her, it was still fun to imagine what I might do to her now if she were here.

Yes, I could now confirm that my morals had completely gone by the wayside ever since I had cheated on Natalie with Amelia. Everything I had done since had made me more and more loose, and that was exactly how Lucien had planned it. The only part of his plan yet to materialise was the part about Stella being the only girl left who would have me, but there was no reason why that wouldn't happen eventually. If Marc had gone to Amelia before me, perhaps that would be the case right now.

May was alone in her bedroom, and now she contacted me telepathically, causing me to put the wine (only a quarter full now) back under the bed. Then I realised that she had made me do that, and I felt indignant with her. I asked her what she wanted and she asked me if she could come to me tonight; she had recognised how horny I was, and maybe that meant she was offering herself to me. I told her it was okay, but that we probably shouldn't have sex because I would no doubt feel even worse afterwards—worse than I felt now? What was the point of feeling bad if I couldn't at least get some sex out of it? That was a strong argument in favour of just doing what I felt like and be damned to the consequences. Oh hell, sometimes I hated my brain.

May opened my bedroom door without knocking and slipped through, shutting it softly behind her. My head down, I said, "Did anyone see you?"

"No, they did not," she said, sitting down on my bed next to my feet. "You know, Peter and James are worried about you."

I sighed. "That's nice, but I'm fine."

"No, you are not," she said firmly. "We both know it, and you should not be drinking anymore—you will make yourself sick again. If I had one of those magic things, I would make your drink disappear, but I am a bit scared of those things."

"I'll be fine, you stopped me before I could drink enough to make myself sick—I think," I said. "In fact—"

I still had a bunch of the devices I had created in my pockets. Now I leaned over, picked my pants up off the floor and began rummaging through the pockets, eventually finding the normalising device. I turned it on myself, gave it a click, and immediately I felt better. I hadn't known if that would vanish the alcohol from my system, but I was glad it had. Now I felt both better and much worse —worse because I was free to think about all the things I didn't want to think about.

"See, no problem," I said, putting the pants back on the floor. "No problem."

"I do not think you should do that anymore," she told me. "I feel what it does to your brain, and it might feel good to you, but it makes things worse. You are not as bad as you are making yourself think you are."

"Nice that you think that, but it doesn't change things," I said flatly.

She sighed. "If you drink any more, I will tell the others that you have started again."

That took me by surprise. "You wouldn't do that—would you?"

"Yes, I would," she said firmly. "It is for your own good."

I sighed and got out of bed, rummaging through my pants pockets until I found a vanisher—the first one I had created, but which had been duplicated since. I pointed it at the wine bottle, clicked it, and the wine was gone.

"There you go. No more wine. Problem solved."

"I will know if you get more from that bag," she reminded me.

"Yeah, 'cause you know everything, I know," I said, and then a thought occurred to me. "Hey, did you have something to do with me running into Larissa tonight?"

She smiled. "Yes. Amelia was too upset when you left, and she would not have wanted to see you, so I had to slow you down. I thought it might give you a chance to examine how you feel about her too."

"Did you make her kiss me?"

"No, she did that on her own, and so did you."

I gave my head a little shake. "It's hard to know what's real when you're around."

"I know, I can distort reality for people," she said, and poked her tongue out me in a way that was both scary and arousing. "If I had all the minds of everyone you have been with, I could make everyone forget what happened and create a whole new history for everyone, all in your minds. It would be so real to everyone that no one would know any different."

That gave me food for thought. If everyone, including myself, didn't know that I had cheated on Natalie, would it have really happened? "And why can't you?" I asked.

"Lucien," she said simply. "He knows it all, and I cannot overpower him."

I sighed. "Just as well, that would seem like cheating."

"You would not know that it is cheating," she said, smiling at me.

I settled back against my headboard and looked at May through the darkness. "Is that what you wanted to come here to do?"

"I wanted to give you the choice," she said. "Would you like me to help you get to sleep?"

What I really wanted was to have sex with May while she was here, but I might feel better about things in the morning if I didn't. Then I remembered what I'd been thinking right before she had turned up, and knew that was what I really wanted. But what about May herself?

"Or would you prefer I stay here with you tonight?" she added. Of course, she had picked up on all of this.

"Maybe the second one, then the first one," I said, "er—if you don't mind doing all that for me. I kinda feel like I'm using you a bit."

"Believe me, if I did not want to do any of this, I would not do it," she said, wriggling up the bed so that she was sitting in my lap.

After, we lay down in the bed together. I had room in my mind to hope that nobody had heard us, and in response to this thought, May said, "No, Peter and James are asleep, and Marc and Amelia are in the campsite."

"Is she okay?"

"She is doing better. They are cuddling."

"Okay," I said, feeling relieved.

Chapter 30: We're Really Gonna Do This Again

I had an extremely vivid dream that night—more vivid even than my usual ventures into Stella's mind, perhaps even as vivid as the more recent times I had connected with her since our connection had tightened. There was no chance that I was Stella now, though, for the dream had nothing to do with her or anything she had ever known. No, I dreamt of me and Larissa that night, an extremely vivid dream that started with the two of us kissing on a sunny beach, and ended in an orgasm before I woke up with a start. May had spent the night in my room.

"May," I said slowly, my face still pressed against the hollow of her shoulder, "you're awake, aren't you?"

"If I was not awake before, I would be now," she said, and even though I couldn't see her face, I could tell that she was smiling.

"You made me have that dream, didn't you?"

"I wanted to give you a little more than I did last night," she told me. "You liked it, right?"

"One of the best dreams I've ever had," I agreed. "I just have to remind myself that it's not real."

"It is a little bit more real than you think."

"Why do you say that?"

"Because I used her mind to help construct it," she said, and I stiffened. "Do not worry, she knows nothing," she added quickly. "I just used what she knew about her body to give you the detail. I also—well—made her have a very similar dream, only less detailed so that it would seem like a normal dream to her."

"You made her dream of having sex with me?"

"Something like that."

"Well—thanks," I said, and grinned. Even though May had done it, it still made me feel good. "What time is it?"

"Not long until we get up," she said. "We already slept most of the night."

"Okay," I said, and lapsed into silence, relaxing my body against her. "You should probably go back to your room before the others get up, or at least have a shower, but I'd like you to stay a bit longer—I don't want to move."

"Neither do I."

"Listen, May," I said, coming to a decision, "I don't think we should do this anymore."

"I see," she said, and she was still smiling as she spoke. "You're sure that you're ready to stop?"

"I think I am. Now I know what it's like to play around, I shouldn't feel the need to do it anymore."

"You know I have felt a lot of minds in my time here," she said, "and from what I can tell, males always feel a need to play around. Regarding sex, men seem to think about doing the same things to lots of different women, while women usually think about doing many, many different things with the same man."

"Are you trying to tell me that I'm just behaving the way I'm meant to as a guy?"

"That is one way to look at it."

"And if we were cavemen, maybe that would be okay, but we're not. Even if I can't get Natalie back, I still need to get my worth back, and in the long run, I need that the most. Eventually, you'll go back to your own world to be with your own children, and I'll have to look after myself. I should get used to doing that while I can."

She thought about this for a moment, and then said, "Yes, you are right. I have helped you a lot—which I was happy to do," she added quickly, "but once I am gone, you will be on your own. Well, you will have magic for some things, I suppose."

"There are some things I just don't do with magic," I said, "like control another person against their will. I've got a lot of mess to sort out, and I have to get used to confronting the consequences of my actions."

"Okay," she said. "I have liked doing these things with you, though. It has been fun for me, and very different from how we do things in my world. It has been eye-opening."

"Good, I'm glad."

* * *

The general mood over breakfast was rather hopeful. May didn't have much to contribute, although she did smile at me rather a lot, understanding that while the good thing between us had come to an end, there was still a good amount of affection between us. I felt good, not just because I'd had great sex that night, but because whenever I thought about our chances against Lucien, I now felt like we had a genuine shot at taking him down. No doubt, there would be more magic to come in that cave today, and who could guess what it would be. Peter, James, Marc and Amelia all seemed to feel the same way, judging by the mood and conversation over breakfast. Marc and James had decided to be the two to go to the cave of creation that morning, while the rest of us continued searching in whatever untested caves we could find.

I also had a good look at Marc and Amelia over breakfast. They were sitting together, and both looked fairly comfortable with each other. I spoke to Amelia only a couple of times, and when I did, there was no sign of jealousy from Marc, whether because of what he and I had said to each other, or what had happened when Amelia had finally returned to camp, I didn't know. Both looked happy and content, and although I felt a pang of sadness for what I had lost with Amelia, I knew it was best. All the same, she and I hadn't said much to each other when I had found her up in that cave, so I needed to make sure she and I were still feeling the same way.

Marc and James were the first to leave, and May was the next, going back through the garage and into the tree house as she had done every other day since we had started searching alone. Peter and Amelia went out into the garage at the same time, and I followed them. Fortunately, Peter left first, giving me a chance to call Amelia back before she took off.

"What's up?" she asked me as she settled herself in her hover car.

"Are we—like—okay?" I asked, feeling unaccountably nervous.

"Yeah, we are," she smiled, "and so are me and Marc. Look, John, I'm never gonna forget about what we did yesterday—"

"Do you feel bad about it?" I asked, unsure what answer I wanted to hear.

"I'm not sure," she said, and she got back out of her car to join me beside mine. "I do feel a little bad, for cheating on Marc, I guess, but I also feel like it resolved something in me. I'm not gonna stop thinking about you, John, and I still wish I felt the same about Marc, but I don't feel like I need you like I did before—now that I had you, I mean. Is that—is that okay?"

"Yeah," I said slowly. "Yeah. I guess, that's okay. I—er—I'm glad you're happier with Marc, though—"

"No, I'm not," she interrupted, "not yet. I wish I was. I don't know if he and I will last, much as I wish we could, not while I still keep thinking about you."

"But you and I won't do anything anymore?"

"Yeah, that's the plan. But John, thanks for being there for me when I needed you. You could have pushed me away more than once, but you didn't."

"I'm too weak to do that," I said sadly.

She gave me a hug and said, "You're too hard on yourself."

"Maybe," I sighed. "Just promise this won't wreck our friendship. I've heard that can happen when friends do what we did."

She shook her head vehemently. "No, I won't let that happen. I promise."

She then went back to her hover car, started it up, and took off into the morning, leaving me with a lot to think about. I was glad that we'd had that conversation, even if it made me feel a little sad to think that I wouldn't get to do any of those wonderful things with her again. And yes, on that score, I would end up being right: I would never have sex with Amelia again either. The time I spent with her in the cave of creation would be the last intimate time we would ever have.

I started my own car up and took off, circling the mountain on the west to get back to the south side and continuing where I had left off the last time I had searched here. When I got there, I found more red flags waving than I remembered, before I recalled that James had searched up here yesterday afternoon while I'd been in the creation cave with Amelia. I mentally asked May how far James had gotten, and she guided me up to the point where he had left off.

I continued the search from there, but only had time to go into a handful of caves because these ones, like the one that had contained the Sien-Leoard Crystal, contained short obstacle courses to get to the treasures within. Those treasures, when I got to them, included a map of the world, something that seemed to be able to bring people back from the dead (knowing what that did to those poor souls, I got out of there in a hurry), and even the Sien-Leoard Sapphire, the key to the Sien-Leoard Crystal. I decided to take it with me, just in case it had some other powers that might come in handy someday.

When lunch was called (by Peter this time), I headed back around the western side of the mountain towards our car port, but stopped when, as I had yesterday, I saw Jacob Underwood eating his dinner atop a ledge, overlooking the trees below. There were no Brazilians in sight this time, which made me wonder why he was eating out here when he could have picked just about anywhere else that would have been warmer. I hesitated for a moment, then deciding I didn't need to hurry back to camp, took my car up to where he sat.

"Hey," he said through a mouthful of chicken. "What brings you to my neck of the woods?"

I grinned. "We're really gonna do this again?"

"Might as well," he said. "What's up? Want to know if I know of any more interesting caves?"

"No, but—er—do you?"

He shook his head. "I know that all you guys have searched most of the mountain by now, so you've probably found them all. Did you check out the one I told you about yesterday?"

"Yeah, we did. It was pretty much like you said, but I think James and Peter enjoyed getting a chance to use magic for a change."

A real porky, that one, so I would have to tip those two off when I saw them, in case Underwood caught up with them at some point.

"Oh good," he said, and took another bite of his dinner. "So—what do you want?"

"I'm just curious about something. Aren't you cold? I mean, I'm cold, and it's the middle of the day for me. Wouldn't it make more sense for you to have dinner—like—anywhere else?"

He shrugged. "I'm from England, mate; this is nothing to me. Besides, these clothes I'm wearing are enchanted to adjust to make me feel comfortable in any temperature between fifty and minus fifty degrees Celsius."

"Wow, where'd you get that?"

"Created it myself, I think you can guess where."

"Oh, right. So why here then?"

"I was interested to see if those Brazilians would come back up here for their lunch, but it looks like they're eating in the hall down there," he said. "I did see them a few hours ago, when they were getting set up for the day—actually got to talk to a couple of them."

"Oh, okay," I said, thinking of Larissa, who had, thanks to May, dreamt of me last night. Even now, she might be thinking about seeing me again tonight. "Did you like them?"

"Yeah, they seem friendly," he said. "They recognised me from yesterday—thought I was your friend or something. Most of them weren't interested in talking, but that would have been because they were getting ready to start their work."

Or because other than the fact that he was British, there was nothing else interesting about him—nothing magical anyway.

"But that's okay," he went on. "You remember those two I pointed out yesterday? The ones who would be good for a threesome?"

"Yeah," I said slowly—Larissa and Amanda.

"Well," he grinned, "it's on." My heart leapt—was he serious? "I mean, it's not on yet," he amended, "but they were the only ones who stuck around to chat for a few minutes. That means I'm in their heads…let the dance begin."

"Well maybe, if you see them again," I said, feeling very conflicted. On one hand, if he actually did something with Larissa, that would make it easier for me to move on from her, because I would be forced to think of her as easy. On the other hand, the jealous male part of me didn't want him to lay a hand on her voluptuous body. But why had she and Amanda taken the time to talk to Underwood in the first place? Were they actually interested in him, or were they only taking notice because they thought he might know something more about me (and in Amanda's case, Peter)? And on top of that, the question I would probably ask myself every time something of any substance happened: Did May have anything to do with this?

"Oh, I'll see them again," he said smugly. "Obviously not right now, but they'll be back out here, and I don't mind staying up a little late. I've got plenty of time to work my will on them like I did with the Russians."

"Well, good luck," I said, half meaning it and half hoping one of them kicked him in the nuts. I got to my feet. "Well, I've gotta get back for my own lunch. I'll see you around."

"Sure, see you," he said, digging back into his own dinner.

I got in my car and took off, not telling him the other reason why I had to leave. May had contacted me telepathically just then, right when Underwood was mentioning the Russian girls, telling me to come back to camp immediately because something very important had just happened. What could possibly be happening that would make May sound so urgent? My heart was racing, because while it might be good news, it felt more likely that it would be something bad—something very bad.

When I pulled up in the garage, I looked around and saw that all the hover cars were present and accounted-for—a good sign. I went into the Group F campsite, only to find it empty, so I checked out the other two, finding them in the Group E campsite this time. I only noticed then that the tree house was going very under-utilised lately, mainly due to how damn cold it was at this time of year. Having it there had been a fine idea in February—not so fine now.

"Oh good," Peter said as I entered the room, "now you can tell us what's going on."

The attention in the room was on Marc and James; Marc was holding the extender-case in his lap, which he and James had taken to the creation cave with them and, I assumed, loaded a bunch of freshly created devices into it. James was holding one such device in his lap, one which took the shape of the digital tablets Amelia and I had created, but he was holding it in such a way that I couldn't see anything else of it.

"Lunch first," James said, looking over at Marc, who reached into the bag and pulled the food-making device from its depths. "Once we're eating, I'll tell you what we've done."

The device was passed around and we all used it to provide ourselves with lunch (a sandwich, in my case), and then James began to talk.

"Well, you know that we made a bunch of stuff up in that cave, and you guys can check it all out later—we just dumped them in the bag with the stuff you two did yesterday," he said to me and Amelia. "The thing is, though, I had an idea for something else to create right at the end, and when we examined it before coming back here, we believe it's given us the answer—the thing we may need to take on Lucien with some degree of confidence."

He put his hotdog on the table beside him (next to his second hotdog) and picked up the device in his lap. He showed us the screen, and I saw that it was an aerial map of Rock Haulter. It didn't take a genius to guess what that device must do, and now that I could see it, I was a little surprised that it had taken so long for one of us to think of making it. If I was right, there wouldn't be a need for any of us to search anymore.

"As you can see, it's a map of the island," James said, "and it's capable of telling us what's inside each and every cave, including the ones that are really hard to get into, complete with directions to get inside them. It even has instructions to get to where the Sien-Leoard Crystal was, and that's the hardest one. I got it to do whatever Fewul was doing that night in order to know what it needs to know. All we have to do to search is touch the screen to get the magic spots to light up, and then touch one of it to see what it is.

"But that wasn't all I got it to do, because that would still involve a lot of searching. I also put in a search feature right up here at the top," he indicated an empty rectangle at the top of the map. "All we have to do is touch it and think of what we want, and the map will light up the caves that might contain the magic to help us get what we want, and it was by doing this that Marc and I found the cave that might give us the final thing we'll need before going back home."

"And what was it?" I asked hopefully.

"A cave that will enable us to put enchantments on ourselves," he said. "Marc and I had a look at it before we came back here and it seems to do just what it says it can do. The only thing it can't seem to do is give us an ability to use its magic once we leave, which is obviously a shame, but not really surprising."

"The thing is, though," Marc went on, "James and I both think that when we do put charms on ourselves, it's also important to make it so that we're capable of turning those charms on and off with our minds, to give us some sort of control over them once we leave the Rock."

"That's not bad thinking," Peter agreed, "but some of us may need to practice working them before we go back. Unlike you guys, I've never used magic."

"Well you'd better get used to the idea," James grinned at him. "So, we should go back to that cave later today, but before we do, we should brainstorm what we should do once we get there. Remember, some ideas we might have might be more suitable encapsulating inside a magical device like these," he indicated the map, "so we can still use the creation cave before we leave."

And that was how we spent the afternoon. We firstly wrote down all the devices we had so far created (there were thirty-two of them, not counting the two horny-inducing devices which Amelia and I had kept secret), and although Marc and James hadn't created very many, they had come up with some good ones. There was one which could make people immune to thicky prison, the substance of solid-outliners; one which could create a number of different electronic and computerised devices, all of which could use the Internet from inside our shadow; one which could allow a person to see backwards through time (on the screen of a tablet, and only through the attached camera); a new and improved untraceability, which according to Marc, eliminated the drawbacks of the existing form of untraceability; but best of all, one which could extract a human mind from inside a Honnie mind (May hadn't been happy about it, but she recognised that even with the unbogglers, it would be the only way to get our friends back from Lucien).

Once we finished that, we began trying to think of other things we might need and deciding if they ought to be done with devices or enchantments on ourselves. There wasn't much left to do, it seemed; Amelia wanted to give herself the ability to read minds, as she had had all her life, but the rest of us were quite happy not to have to deal with everyone else's thoughts babbling away in our heads. The invisibility veil was another piece of magic we wanted to be able to use, but none of us could think of a way to encapsulate it in a device, so it was decided that Marc, Amelia and I would have the ability to perform it just as Natalie had done (Peter and James had opted out). There were two devices we decided to create, one to make magic performed against us pass right through us, and another to shrink and enlarge us with a Transgation Charm in proportion to the charms around the Hammerheart Highway, so that we didn't have to leave our shadow to enter the Hammerheart bases (these had to be devices because the most important feature of them was the ability to toggle them, and perhaps to give the abilities to our friends when we got them back). The most important piece of magic, though, also to be contained in a device, would make us four-dimensional beings, like May was, and like Smiley had been. It would give us all the ability to move in and out of our shadow, and to see and hear in our shadow; but after some discussion, we decided not to give ourselves access to the time axis—it just seemed safer that way.

* * *

The mood over dinner that night was hopeful. We all felt as though we had accomplished a lot. The magic had been performed that afternoon (I had been elected to go back to the creation cave alone to create the last few devices before, with guidance from May, meeting up with the others at the enchantment cave—which was just below the moat high upon the Rock). We now felt that we could get back to our own time and place, survive for quite a while (for as long as it took Lucien to figure out how we were surviving), get our friends back, and even get rid of Fewul—assuming it worked. The only area we were lacking in confidence was in dealing with Lucien himself. After some circular discussion of this issue, James suggested we stay on the Rock a little longer so that we would have some extra time to think about it.

One other thing on my mind over dinner that night, far removed from what everyone else was focussed on, was Larissa. She would be hoping that we could meet up tonight, but honestly, I no longer really wanted to meet with her. Well, part of me did, but the greater part of me felt that I would feel better about myself if I didn't. Natalie was now on my mind more than ever, now that we had devices which could get her back on our side once we got back. It wouldn't be enough to make her forgive me—I would have to do that the hard way, if it were even possible—but it was time to set my mind back on the thing I really wanted, rather than the instant gratifications that ultimately wouldn't make me feel better about anything.

James decided to go back to the creation cave to think of ways to deal with Lucien, and after some inner debate, I decided to go with him. I mentally asked May if she could keep Larissa busy for me, perhaps make it so that her superiors wouldn't let her come out to explore tonight, and she agreed. She also told me that she would make it so that Larissa would fret about this all night, worried that I would think she had stood me up, thereby increasing her affection and desire for me. I asked her not to; she apologised and told me that she wanted to do it, and I would just have to suck it up. I asked if this was in response to me resolving not to have any more sex with her, and she filled my head with an image of the two of us the previous night, reminding me just how good it had felt, in such a way that I almost crashed my car (James and I were out by then). Thereafter, the communications ceased.

James only stayed in the creation cave for about an hour before, mildly satisfied for now, he decided to go back to camp. I would have liked him to stay, but even more, I didn't want to go with him, so I ended up in that cave all by myself. We had brought the extender-case, containing all the devices we had created so far, and I told him I would bring it back when I was done up here. It was for possible inspiration that we had brought it, and I wanted to keep it up here just in case it gave me some fresh ideas. We had been able to create a number of weapons, all of which could be used through the fourth dimension, and not all of which used magic to attack a person. There were weapons designed to disable Lucien, to confuse him, and to get the Sien-Leoard Crystal out of his possession. None of them were guaranteed to work without knowing what protection he put around himself, but just having them was a good start.

We talked a little while we worked, and as Peter had done when I had hung out with him, James asked how I was doing and if I had been drinking lately. I almost told him no, and then thought better of it; he may rebuke me, but I would rather cop that than tell another lie. Fortunately, I could honestly say that I hadn't had much, and that May had mentally made me put the brakes on.

"I'm not the only one missing my girlfriend here," I remarked at one point, "so how come I'm the only one struggling so much?"

"Well Marc has Amelia, and Lucien didn't target me or Peter," James said reasonably, "and after what I've seen you go through, I think I can wait a few more days for Erica."

"You were never in danger of cheating on her, were you?"

He shrugged. "Honestly, no. I mean, I don't know what it was like, being cursed like that, but I've got no desire to be with anyone else now, and I can't imagine ever wanting to. She's my girlfriend and I love her—going even months without sex seems like a small price to pay to keep that."

That made me feel extremely ashamed. I loved Natalie, didn't I? Why couldn't I be as faithful to her as James was to Erica? Was it just my doubts about my chances with her that had made me so loose? I suspected so, but seeing as I supposedly hadn't given up on her, it made no sense at all that I would ever go back to May or Amelia and do what I'd done with either of them once the curse had worn off. I could only conclude that I thought with my penis, and then of course, my mind turned back to Larissa. I was glad I hadn't met with her tonight, but even so, part of me still wanted to see what I could do with her—the part that was only interested in instant gratification, and continually overpowered the rest of me by reminding me of how Natalie had looked as she had turned her back on me.

After James had left, I created a comfortable seat for myself with the pseudo-crystal (it was easier than looking through the bag for the furniture device I'd made yesterday), and sat down, trying to keep my mind away from females and on the issue of things I could magically create to help us after we left this place. We had a vessel to go through the water, and we had a device which could create rooms to give us privacy, and we could create our own furniture, clothing, food, drink, and entertainment. All these things were good, but they lacked the flexibility that we had taken for granted when we'd had our own magic. The obvious solution to not being able to use my own magic was to use the contraption to create devices which would perform the magic I wanted to use—it was a lengthy process, but it was doable.

I decided that the best thing I could create was a whole new base for us—an improved base, with new protections around it, the ability to move through the fourth dimension, perhaps even the ability to move in time (though I eventually decided this would be too dangerous), and one which would be self-sufficient without relying on people within it having their own magic. It would also need to stand up to an attack, just in case Hammerhearts did manage to get it. Obviously, such a thing was far too complicated to create all at once —my brain just wasn't big enough to contain all the details in it at once. So I would have to settle for creating devices to use to build the base, and use them one by one.

I then spent the following ninety minutes or so constructing the base, contained in a palm-sized box as the vessel had been, capable of shrinking and enlarging on command (given from its control room). The key difference between this base and the previous one, though, was that rather than having shrunken innards, it internally extended, just like the extender-case; meaning that there was virtually no limit to how much it could contain. The box also contained the same atmospheric charms as the original base had, complete with sky reflection and anti-rain magic, so that wouldn't be an issue either.

I never went inside the base while I was building it; I stood beside the contraption, one hand on the pseudo-crystal, the other catching devices, pointing them at the base and clicking them. The devices were programmed to create the interior features of the base just by being pointed at it; and once they were used, they were useless, and by the time I was finished, I had a large pile of devices which I had to vanish. Since there was no way to get inside the base from the outside unless someone on the inside let you in, I had to create two last devices to complete the security: One which would let us get in, and another which would disable the magic of the first so that no one else could use that kind of magic to infiltrate.

The control room in this base was underground, and it would only admit people by scanning their brains and determining, according to the rules I had programmed into it, if their intentions were for the right cause. There was a central elevator, with doors on two sides of it, and it went from the control room (with only one door able to open on that level) up to the very top level. There was also a stairwell beside it. The bottom level (above the control room) had the dining room (which integrated the food and drink making device from yesterday), lounge room, gym, games room, computer lab (with the same security as our old base), and all other public facilities.

The upper levels had the bedrooms, and since we didn't know how big this base would need to get, there was magic in the control room which could add more floors to the building if necessary. The building was in the middle of the base, and the yard was around it— the opposite of the old base. However, every single room in the base had an emergency escape, which would permit anyone in danger (which would be determined, again, by brain scanning) to get out of the base without being trapped by its geography. As for the bedrooms, I had just duplicated the ones from the old base; they had done just fine.

There were even more features, but I would get around to telling the others about them later. They would find, though, that once they got around to exploring this new base, it would be almost as interesting as Rock Haulter. Granted, the magic of the pseudo-crystal wasn't powerful to duplicate some of the caves I had found (the Vegas casino cave, for instance, relied on original magic to create such a lively scene), but there would be no shortage of entertainment here.

As I had been working, however, my mind had strayed to other things I could do with magic—things I couldn't incorporate into the base, perhaps, but which I might be able to incorporate into myself. I had a moment of indecision as I thought about it. Would it be dangerous? Would it be unfair to do this for myself but not to get the others so that they could do it too? The thing that settled me on doing it now, by myself, was the hero devices Marc had destroyed because they were too powerful. Maybe it wouldn't be such a good idea to do to the others what I was thinking of doing to myself.

I vanished all the leftover devices, put the last two base-related devices in the extender-case, pocketed the base itself as if it were a mobile phone, got into my hover car with the bag of treasures, and took off into the night, now heading for the enchantment cave. There, I proceeded to perform spells on myself, giving myself a host of magical abilities to save myself the hassle of going for any number of magical devices. I couldn't make myself a Sorcerer, but if I performed the spells one at a time, by putting my hand on the pseudo-crystal (this cave was much the same as the last one, other than the magic it did), I could come fairly close. All I had to do was think, like I did when I had the Sien-Leoard Crystal, and I could perform the magic I was thinking of.

By the time I was done, I could stun people just by looking at them; I could shoot thicky prison from my fingertips; I could cut people just by wiggling my fingers; I could separate my mind from my body, both to spy and mind surf, as I had done back in the day; and, because I hadn't been able to resist, I could make girls horny for any specified amount of time just by looking at them—though to make myself feel better about it, I made it so that it wouldn't necessarily be for me. I knew it was incredibly self-indulgent of me to do that, and it would test my powers of discipline, but if I did get another girlfriend, she wouldn't regret it. In short, I had given myself the ability to do just about every piece of magic we had integrated into the devices in the last two days—not quite everything, but many things—as many as I could think of.

Did this make me a bad person, I wondered? Did this make me as power-hungry as Arnold Hammerson had been—or still was in this time? Maybe it did, or maybe it would depend on how I used the gifts I had bestowed upon myself. I wasn't sure, but I did know one thing: I had to make sure this didn't go to my head. I had to make sure I didn't abuse these powers while I had them. I definitely had to make sure I didn't use them for instant gratification purposes. If I did, I would have to find some way to hold myself to account. Still, even with all these questions running through my mind, I headed back to the campsite feeling fairly positive about things. It was very late by now, and everyone seemed to have gone to bed, so I was able to get into my room without having to answer any awkward questions.

I didn't have sex with anyone that night, but I did think a lot about Natalie. I wished I could drink, but one thing I hadn't done to myself back in that cave was give myself the ability to create alcohol. All I could do was first sit, and then lie in bed, and imagine that she was here. I asked her how she was going. I asked if she was okay. I imagined I could tell her about the things that were happening here on the Rock, and that I would come to get her from Lucien's clutches very soon. Eventually, I fell asleep, imagining that someday, I would be able to fall asleep beside her again.

Part 5: The Greatest Struggle of All Begins…

Chapter 31: Some Sort of Slave Labour Camp

There were no sexy dreams that night; instead, the Enlightener was back for round three.

"What are you saying?" I asked desperately.

"Your focus is all wrong," Lisa told me, frustrated. "You need to change your focus, otherwise you won't find what you are looking for. I really need to tell you something, John."

"Tell me what?"

"A very important secret. You need to know, you all need to know, but you're the only one I can tell."

"Then tell me!"

"You have to come to me, only then can I tell you."

"And how the hell am I supposed to do that?" I said desperately, feeling the dream beginning to fade, and Lisa's voice along with it.

"Remember my diary, John," she said, her voice almost incoherent. "Remember what I wrote in my diary."

"What?"

And of course, that was when I woke up.

* * *

I told the rest of the group about the base I had created over breakfast. They were fairly dubious at first, which didn't surprise me, but once we had all finished eating, I went into the base with the device I had created, and then used the controls within it to snatch them out of the campsite and drop them into the control room. They were imprisoned at first, as per the magical rules I had imposed (so that we could use it to capture Hammerhearts—there was an underground prison as well, accessible from the control room), but I quickly freed them so that they could look around. May wasn't particularly entertained by it, but the others were. Peter and James, in particular, seemed thrilled by all the features I had included—even the lack of a casino didn't seem to bother them.

Marc and Amelia were also fairly impressed, but neither of them showed much enthusiasm as they looked around. I mentally asked May what the deal was, and she told me that they'd had another discussion last night. Amelia was feeling that as much as she cared about Marc, it was hard to be with him when she knew that she was capable of feeling more strongly for someone else; and that even if she couldn't have me, maybe she would feel this strongly down the

track for someone else altogether, and that would be worth waiting
for. For his part, Marc was feeling that he was doing the best he
could, and it was depressing to him to know that despite his
concerted efforts to put the business between them and me aside, it
probably wasn't going to be good enough for Amelia.

This was dismaying to me for two reasons: Amelia being single
would make it harder to resist her, whatever flimsy resolutions I
made to myself; and I would be plagued with yet another source of
guilt if I was responsible for the demise of my brother's relationship.
Somehow this felt even worse than the simple fact that I'd had sex
with her; it was on an emotional level that the damage had been
done, and learning of this from May crushed any good spirits I might
have carried over from the night before. So once we all left the new
base, James telling us that we might as well use that to leave the
Rock, I detached May from the others and led her into her bedroom
—at least here was one place in which we hadn't had sex.

"If you are wanting me to make you feel less guilty, I can do
that," she said, "but I think you would not appreciate that."

"You're right—that wouldn't solve anything, but that's not what I
want," I said, surprised that she hadn't picked up on exactly what I
wanted. "Look, I know you've already helped me a lot more than you
needed to, and you don't interfere with our lives unless it's some sort
of benefit to you or other Honnies, but if there is one last thing you'd
be willing to do for me, this would be it."

I fell silent, letting her see clearly what it was in my mind. She
considered this, looking bland, then said, "I really feel like you are
asking more from me than you should."

I sighed, unsurprised, but not ready to give up. "Remember, you
made Amelia into who she is now. I know you used what was
already there, but the way she is now is very much based on your
work. Don't think of it as meddling; it's more like—putting her back
on the rails."

She hesitated for a moment. "I did feel like she was my creation
at first, but I have not influenced her mind since, so she has grown
into her own person now."

"I only want her to feel more strongly for Marc than she does for
me," I said. "I don't feel like it's too much trouble; it certainly
wouldn't disadvantage anyone."

"What about you?" she said. "What if she is the only person left
for you, and you give her to Marc?"

"It's still better," I said, "for all three of us. Besides, she's really
not mine to give away—at least she shouldn't be."

"You do see that you are selective in what things you wish to do
the proper way, right?"

"Yeah, I know, it's cheating," I said heavily, and sighed again. "Is there anything I can say that'll persuade you to do this? For me? For Amelia? For the group as a whole? For the balance of the known universe? Whichever is more important."

"What about for me?" she asked. When I looked at her in confusion, she added, "What is in it for me?"

That brought me up short. "Er—fewer conversations like this? I dunno, what do you want? Do you want to taste me again or something?"

"Taste you," she repeated, beginning to smile. "That would be enough for me to make them enjoy the morning together; it would not be enough to make them last longer. I think I will need a bit more than that."

"Then what? Not sex again, right? I know you liked it a bit, but not that much—oh, wait," a thought occurred to me then, something that she might be talking about—something she had only gotten to enjoy once. I pictured it for her, mentally adding the question mark.

Her smile grew. "Well," she said slowly, "that would make her feel quite passionately for him, but there may still be some nagging worries in her mind. And of course, there will still be nagging worries in his mind."

I sighed a third time. "Then tell me what you need."

She told me mentally, putting the knowledge directly in my head: She wanted everything. Everything we had so far done together, and more. She would keep the others busy for the morning: Marc and Amelia would go out to enjoy each other's company in some romantic cave, perhaps even the beach cave; Peter and James would also go out, to do what, May hadn't decided; and none of them would give me or May a single thought, not just during the morning but thereafter. There wouldn't be any questions to answer, today or any day, about what we did together that morning. That was May's price for helping me with Marc and Amelia, and it was a pretty big one. But the benefits: Things with Marc would be good, Amelia would finally be happy with him, I would have one less person to be attracted to, and to top it off, I would get three hours of more mind-blowing sex. The drawbacks? Suddenly, I couldn't seem to think of them, and I hoped May hadn't just done that, but I did have one question.

"Why me?" I asked. "You could have anyone you wanted—literally anyone here, but it's always me. And even if it wasn't me, you can wait till you go back to your world and then have crazy-wild sex with a man who won't be in danger of getting crushed to death."

"Honnie men have no interest in creativity; they only have sexual intercourse," she said. "Normally that would be fine, but I did not know how much else there was to enjoy until I met you. I cannot get it from any of them, and since I have already bred, it is unlikely that I will find a man in my own world."

"Even though you know I'm like half your age, right?"

"Do you think I care about your age? I know your mind, and your body, so what difference does that make?"

I had no answer to that, so I said, "You know how much I enjoy it, but—what's got you to trust me with this instead of anyone else?"

"Because you made the most effort to communicate with me when we first met," she said simply. "You opened my mind, so obviously you were the one I let in."

That actually was pretty flattering. Not only that, but now I actually felt a bit bad for May; she would go back to her own world eventually, whenever that was, and she would never be the same person she was before. This experience would have changed her forever. (I would turn out to be totally wrong about that last part, but that's a story for later.) For now, I had a decision to make, and with May standing right in front of me, dressed in warm but skin-tight clothes that showed off her body, her Honnie beauty topping off the picture, the decision seemed exceedingly simple.

"If you really want to do this, there's something I'd like to do first," I told her, picturing it in my mind so that she could decide if she wanted it or not. It really seemed like a good idea to me, but May surprised me.

"No, I do not want that; I like it just the way it is."

"Well—er—okay," I said, a little awkwardly. What was supposed to come next?

"Good," she said. "Give me a minute to sort things out with the others, and then you will have me to yourself for the rest of the morning. You had better take good care of me."

Those words were very hot, and I already felt myself beginning to get horny. "Okay, but you'd better take good care of me too."

* * *

Peter and James had spent the morning exploring in caves that we had already found, but now for entertainment rather than searching for something. The intention had been to relax so that their minds could wander, perhaps coming up with more possible ways to deal with Lucien; but sadly, it hadn't come to much. Marc and Amelia didn't tell us where they had been, but they didn't need to; I knew what they must have been doing. Marc was grinning, Amelia was glowing, and even Peter and James noticed that they'd had a very good morning together.

"Well, I have been thinking," James insisted as we ate, "and maybe we're approaching the Lucien thing wrong. Yeah, we do need to get the crystal off him and the chips out of him, but beyond that, we still need a way of dealing with him. I keep coming back to the prophecy—particularly that line, 'chase him from the soul on which he feeds'; that's obviously Hammerson, and the soul in question is obviously Lucien."

"It's a pity we didn't figure that out before we killed him," Marc said. "We could have put him into an irreversible coma instead, and that would have kept Lucien free."

"It also would have defied the prophecy, which would explain why we weren't able to work it out," Peter said. "We would never have been able to prevent it coming to this point, but I don't think there was anything in the prophecy that said Hammerson has to win. Not that I can remember it word for word."

"The last line was something about a tyrant falling irrevocably to the ground," Amelia said, "so it actually does sound pretty good."

"My point," James went on, "is that if we can just figure out a way to separate Lucien from Hammerson's influence, maybe then we can finally end this thing."

"Great, then I can get my brother back," Marc said hopefully.

But I didn't feel so confident. "James, that thing that happened to Lucien happened hours after Hammerson died. If whatever is left of Hammerson can wait that long, it probably isn't restricted to haunting Lucien—Lucien's presence was just the trigger that set off that timebomb curse."

James considered these words, then nodded slowly. "Yes, you may be right. That means we need to find out exactly what Hammerson did to Lucien. I mean, I know it was a time bomb curse, but I mean the curse within the curse. Exactly what is left of Hammerson? How does it work? And most importantly, how do we access it? Knowing that will tell us both how to get it away from Lucien and how to destroy it for good."

"But how do we find that stuff out?" Peter asked. "We saw Hammerson cast that spell in Smiley's memories, remember? He didn't tell anyone what it was when he did it, so whatever the secret is, it died with him."

I felt an enormous click of understanding in my mind right then. It was Peter's use of the word 'secret' that had brought the memory back in a rush, and I started with the force of it.

"You okay?" Marc asked me.

"Remember when I told you guys about seeing Lisa with the Enlightener?" I said, and when they all nodded (bar May, who just watched and listened), I went on. "Well, she did say that my focus was all wrong, and that she had to tell me something, but I woke up before she could tell me what. I've had that dream twice since, though, and I've worked out that there's an important secret that we all need to know, but which I'm the only one she can tell, and that I had to come and talk to her. When I asked how I was supposed to do that, she told me to remember what she wrote in her diary."

"Okay," James said slowly, "so I was right—she does want to talk to you. It has to be you because her only way of getting to us is through the Enlightener, and you're the only one who can connect to it. Perhaps the secret has something to do with Hammerson—perhaps what he did to his life form is similar to what's happened to hers—"

"James!" Amelia snapped, her face stricken.

James flinched. "Sorry, I don't mean to sound heartless, I'm just trying to work through this. John, is that all you can remember?"

"Yeah, that's all there is."

"Then, for all our sakes, let's hope you have at least one more dream," he said solemnly, "because my interpretation of that is very, very bad."

"Why? What is it?" Peter asked.

"She wants him to come to her, Pete," said James quietly, "and it's the stuff she wrote in her diary that is supposed to tell him how. You remember those entries we read that day, don't you?"

He fell silent then, letting us all reach the conclusion in our own time. Marc got it first, then Amelia, and then me. The bottom dropped out of my stomach as the realisation hit me: What James was saying was that someone would need to die and then be brought back to life. They would need for their soul to be trapped in the in-between where they would be able to communicate with Lisa—in a time when we were both alive anyway—and then that person would die for good, and be trapped in the in-between forever. Someone here would have to sacrifice their life and their soul to a fate worse than death to get the information we needed.

"No," Peter whispered, as he finally got it, "no."

"Yeah, I know," James said heavily. There were dismayed faces all around the room; even May was showing emotion for a change, and it was hard to look at.

"There's gotta be another way," Peter insisted. "She can't possibly mean for John to have to do that. What secret could possibly be worth doing that?"

"Not even for the very existence of the human race?" James asked. "Not even for our very survival? I think we all know that if Lucien continues on his current trajectory, he's likely to damage the world beyond repair, and maybe even destroy it."

Peter had no response to that—he just stared blankly ahead, unwilling to look directly at me. In fact, other than May, none of the others could look at me. Several seconds passed in silence before, thankfully, Marc came to the rescue.

"There might actually be another way to get to her. Didn't Smiley say that ghosts are actually people in their shadow when they're called back? I think he said something to that effect, anyway. If that's true, then the in-between—what we think of as the in-between—is probably just a place between worlds, and you know, we can get there now."

That sent everyone's minds off in a totally different direction. I tried to recall everything everyone had ever said about the in-between, ghosts, death and whatever else. "We would have to go back in time again," I said, "all the way back to when Lisa was alive. If she really does exist there, she can't exist at any point outside her life span. I'm pretty sure Smiley said something like that, too."

"Where, though?" Amelia asked. "I mean, where should we be when we do this? I know they say there is no space or time there, but surely, we have to be somewhere when we do this."

"Well, the most likely spot would be the Chopville High gym," said James, "since that was where—where it happened."

"I don't wanna go back there," Peter said quickly. "Please, no."

"We can't go back there, anyway," I said flatly. The idea had been a good one, but I had to hit it on the head before they got carried away. "If any of us had been there, I would have seen you at the time—as ghosts, I mean. I'm pretty sure I got a look at the entire gym that day, except for behind the big pack of students, and I didn't see anything, so there's no point trying to go back there—something will stop us."

That dampened the mood in a hurry, as everyone's thoughts turned back to what James had said, but Marc was quick to ralley. "Maybe you can go back in your mind, John, like you did last time you were here. You saw my dad in there, right? Do you think he saw you?"

"Er—I don't think so," I said slowly. No, I didn't think Moran had seen me when I'd come back to watch what had happened in the main hall when I had been a baby, and if not, that meant I could go back to the gym battle the same way.

"John, if you could communicate with Lisa in that form, it would solve everything," James said eagerly.

"I'm not sure I could, but maybe," I agreed. "I'm not wild about seeing all that stuff again, but I could do it. I might see what happened to her when she died, and I might be able to hear her if she has something to say to me. I probably won't be able to talk back, though, but it's still worth trying."

"Okay," James said, and clapped his hands. "I suggest we make that our first port of call when we get back to our time—well, right after we retrieve the Light and Villain Crystals from where we left them in Brazil."

"Would it be better to stay in this time and do it?" Amelia asked.

We all considered this. Privately, I thought it probably would be better; Lucien would probably wake up not long after we got back, and we needed to be ready for him. The trouble was, Arnold Hammerson was in this time; would he catch us if we tried anything? Would he be able to? I feared Hammerson more than Lucien because unlike Lucien, Hammerson wouldn't hesitate to kill me, but I also thought that Lucien would have a better shot at figuring out what we were doing.

"I think it's okay to go to our time," James said. "I know it would be more time for John to work through, but if we have to defend him while he's doing it, I think it'll be a little easier to defend him against Lucien than Hammerson and Hall."

"And Fewul?" Marc reminded him.

"We have a way of dealing with Fewul in the future that we can't do here," James said, "and remember, if we do run into Hammerson or Hall, we can't go all-out against them here, not when we'll be killing one of them eight days from now. We're more prepared to deal with Lucien, who has less experience with magic, so if we have to choose between the two of them, it should be him."

We all mulled this over before, one by one, we agreed with him.

* * *

As we had that morning, we all went our separate ways after lunch. James settled himself down to his notes in privacy; Marc and Amelia also sought privacy; while wanting to get out for a bit, Peter and I decided to go out together in our hover cars. I felt great after how I had spent the morning, even though part of me knew I should probably feel bad for doing those things with May while I still thought so much about Natalie. Still, I felt great, great enough that I might be able to do even more of that stuff with May—perhaps for four or five hours this time, right up until dinner. It would be a very exhilarating way to work up an appetite. That was why I wanted to get out, where May could (but probably wouldn't) follow me; I knew not how she would spend the afternoon.

We wandered aimlessly around the bottom of the mountain, bickering about which cave we should while away the hours in, heading clockwise around the east, then the south, and then back up the western side. As we went, I noticed a group of Brazilians high up on a ledge on the eastern side (I recognised Luis among them, but no sign of Larissa); and then as we were veering west around the southern side, I noticed Marc and Amelia, sitting in front of a cave several hundred feet above us and holding hands. We passed by another group of Brazilians not long later, quite close to the beginning of the track which led up to the hover car cave (I counted eight of them, plus a teacher, and I thought the first group had been the same size), but again, Larissa wasn't among them. I wasn't sure how I felt about that at first; part of me wanted to see her again (the part that got a thrill out of whatever was between us); while the sensible part of me thought it would be much simpler if I didn't see her again.

Before I could decide which of these feelings was more prominent, we came across a third group of Brazilians, this time at the foot of a sheer cliff against which we had done rock climbing back on the February camp. I scanned them as soon as we caught sight of them, feeling that this time, Larissa had to be among them; there could only be four groups of them at this size. There were seven of them this time, I saw as I scanned, and one teacher. I quickly saw that Amanda was among them; she appeared to be trying to dig something out of the rock wall with some strange-looking tool, and she was being supervised by a fellow student. And yes, I thought Larissa was there; she had her back to us now, but it really did look like her.

"See anything green?" Peter asked, having noticed my attentiveness.

I shrugged. "I just wanted to see if Larissa was with them; that might be her there, but I can't tell. Look who else is there, though." I jerked my thumb at Amanda.

Peter grinned. "How about that. You reckon we should stop and say hi?"

He had been reading my mind; I wondered the same thing. If only they didn't look so busy, or have a teacher with them. We were getting a little closer now, and I saw that it was the same teacher I had shaken hands with when I had first met the Brazilians on the ship. Not only that, but the girl I thought was Larissa had just been told to take something over to one of the other students, and as she turned to do so, I saw that—yes, it really was Larissa.

"Why don't we get a little closer and see what they're up to," I suggested.

"Might as well, since we're basically killing time while the others come up with something." He grinned and began accelerating.

Several of the Brazilians noticed us as we approached and waved to us (both Larissa and Amanda were among them), and the teacher, also noticing, told them to get back to work. As we drew within earshot, however, Peter called, "Well, well, well, am I right in thinking this looks like some sort of slave labour camp? If you guys start making cheap T-shirts, I want one."

There were a few laughs, and one of the boys called back, "No friend and family discount."

Their teacher again called them back to order in Portuguese, and they reluctantly went back to their business, but Peter and I drifted our cars over to the foot of the cliffs next to the area in which they were concentrated, so that we could watch them and be close enough to talk to them—which we did every time one of them went past us. Their teacher kept throwing us disapproving looks, but seemed unwilling to actually tell us to go away.

It was Amanda who positioned herself closest to us the most, only moving when she absolutely had to, often demanding that someone else get something for her if she needed something; and although she continued to work on whatever they were trying to do to the rock, the greater part of her attention was on Peter, and there was no doubt that she was becoming more and more flirtatious by the minute. She even managed to coax him out of his hover car, and since I felt rather silly remaining alone in mine, I had to get out as well.

Now that I was here, I found that I did want to be with Larissa— to at least talk to her. She seemed to want the same thing, as I found her watching me almost every time I looked at her, but her job seemed to be to move things between the other students, so she was kept too busy to stop. It was about half an hour before she managed to get a moment, and she was quick to use it to get over to where I was standing with Peter. Seeing what was happening, Amanda was able to get Peter to come with her to the other side of the work area, leaving the two of us alone.

For about thirty seconds anyway. It was long enough for her to apologise for standing me up last night, and the clear anxiety in her face told me plainly that May had been all too true to her word last night. I told her that I'd known that was the case and so had done other things instead, and that it wasn't a problem. She looked relieved by that, and was about to say something else, but her teacher had called her back to him, needing her to do more work, and she'd had to hurry away.

I'd been about to go back to Peter, but then stopped, observing him from a distance. He was still with Amanda; she was talking rapidly, her eyes seeming to sparkle as she stood close to him and held his arm, and he was watching her and grinning like an idiot. He said something, then she said something, then he said something, and then she kissed him on the lips. That was bad, but then it got worse: He kissed her back.

It might have been hypocritical of me, but I couldn't allow this. I hurried around the other Brazilians until I reached them, unnoticed by either, and tapped Peter on the shoulder a few seconds after they had broken apart. He started and looked around at me, while she gave me a dirty look that told me plainly that she didn't appreciate the interruption.

"Need to talk to you," I said, looking what I hoped was an apology at Amanda, but she ignored me. I took Peter by the arm and practically dragged him back to our hover cars.

"Dude, really?" he said, but he looked awkward.

"Yeah, really," I said tensely. "What are you thinking? Take it from someone who knows, nothing good can come from that."

He flushed, but to his credit, he didn't look too happy with himself. "Shit, yeah, I know. Man, I can't believe I did that. She—she got to me. How do you resist a girl when she does something like that?"

"Don't ask me, I'm hopeless at it," I shrugged. "Just try thinking of Rebecca. You know you don't wanna cheat on her, right?"

"I don't," he agreed. "I'd better let her know that was a mistake."

"Okay, but go easy on her," I said. "It probably won't hurt much —it's not like you've known her long—but I dunno."

He nodded and went back to her, where she stood beside the cliff, digging at it with renewed vigour. He began talking to her too quietly for me to hear, so I sidled around the group again, winking at Larissa as I passed her (and where I might have felt guilty about even that much in the past, now it felt like barely anything), and ending up on the other side of the work area, now a short distance away from Peter and Amanda. Peter could see me standing there, but he didn't seem to mind, and Amanda's back was to me, so she had no idea.

Although I'd missed the start of the conversation, it didn't take long to pick up on the dynamic: Amanda really did like Peter, had been attracted to him since the first, and had really been into him since seeing him take on all those Hammerhearts on the boat. She knew that he had a girlfriend, but she seemed to want him anyway— she was one of those girls who thought she could win him. Even the distance didn't phase her; she believed he would have access to magic that would make it easy for him to see her any time he wanted. By this point, Peter had had enough; he told her that he could, and that he would be willing to if she really wanted that, but it would only be as a friend because he loved his girlfriend and was totally committed to her.

I couldn't see Amanda's face, but I saw her body go rigid at these words. She put her head in her hand and asked him, in a voice I barely heard, why he had kissed her back. He told her, with some dignity I thought, that he missed his girlfriend, and he did like Amanda and found her attractive and charming and all that, but he could never actually commit to her. He apologised, but Amanda had checked out by then. Having seen enough, I sidled away from them and back around the group to our hover cars, and when I reached them, I got a good look at Amanda; there were tears on her face. A moment later, she turned and hurried away, leaving Peter standing where he was, looking utterly ashamed of himself.

A few people noticed Amanda's retreat, and Larissa was one of them. She looked a question at me, and I could only shrug. I was pretty sure Larissa knew how Amanda felt about Peter, so she could probably guess what had happened. She looked after her friend, and it looked like she was considering going after her, but before she could, their teacher called to them all. I couldn't understand what he'd said, of course, but judging by what the students started doing at his words, it was time for them to move on to another location.

Peter and I decided we might as well move on to another location as well; namely, the campsite. James was in the Group E campsite and May was sitting on the verandah of the tree house, so Peter and I settled down to a game of cards in the Group F campsite. While there, we got talking.

"You gonna be okay?" I asked him.

"Yeah, I'll be fine," he said. "Feels like crap when you have to do that to someone, but it would have been worse for everyone if I'd let it go any longer."

"Yep," I agreed. "Are you—er—gonna tell Rebecca about this?"

He hesitated, then said, "I don't want to, but I guess I should, and probably sooner rather than later. Do you think she'll be mad?"

"Well I don't think she'll be happy," I said, smiling a bit unwillingly, "but you did push her away straight away, so maybe that'll help. I reckon she'll forgive you."

"I guess so," he said doubtfully.

"Are you—" it was my turn to hesitate, but I was honestly curious. "Do you really love Rebecca?"

He grinned. "You know, I think I do. I hadn't thought about it before, and I'd only meant to say it to put her off, but when I said it —I dunno, I just knew it was the truth. That's probably why it affected her the way it did—she must have seen something in my face."

"Well whatever it is, make sure Rebecca sees it as well," I advised.

"You reckon I should tell her?"

"Er—yeah, of course. Why not?"

"Well it's kind of soon, isn't it? Also, what if she doesn't say it back?"

I considered. Yeah, her not saying it back would hurt, no doubt, but on the other hand… "But she might say it back, and it might be the clincher that makes her forgive you for this. Just think about it between now and when you see her again."

"Maybe," he said flatly. "Did you say that to Natalie?"

"Yeah, I did, but remember, what I did was a hell of a lot worse than what you did, so don't beat yourself up."

"Are you gonna do anything with Larissa, do you think?" he asked.

I hesitated, then said, "I don't know what to do about her. I'm trying to keep my mind on Natalie, but—well—I do like her, and I would like to do something with her. I mean, we're not together anymore, so I shouldn't be so hard on myself, right?"

"I think most people would agree with that," he said, "except you want her back, so it doesn't matter what most people think; it only matters what she thinks. I imagine if you do anything with Larissa, on top of everything else, there'll definitely be no chance. I guess you have to take a punt on whether or not you think she'll forgive you as it stands."

"That was always going to be the case," I agreed, not liking my chances. How could she possibly forgive me now? If she had done something like this, there would be no way in the world I would be able to forgive her. That made me think that if I got the opportunity, maybe I shouldn't hold myself back with Larissa after all.

Chapter 32: We Wouldn't Wanna Be Safe, That's Way Too Boring

Dinner that night was a quiet affair: Peter and I were both lost in our own thoughts; Marc and Amelia were both eating feverishly, although they did smile at each other every few minutes; May was looking as bland as ever, never one to start a conversation herself anyway; and James, too, was deep in thought. I expected he would be the one to break the silence, and about halfway through dinner, he proved me right.

"Guys," he said, "I've been thinking—"

"Whoa, I didn't see that coming," Peter muttered through a mouthful of food.

James grinned. "Sorry, but this is serious and I don't think you guys are gonna like it, but it needs to be said."

"What's up?" I asked him.

He took a deep breath and said, "I think we should leave here tomorrow, probably before lunch so that by the time May gets us back to the future, our body clocks will be fairly close to Chopville time."

"Good for you," said Marc. "I think we should leave on Thursday, so that we can be gone by the time you two," he nodded at me and Peter, "get back into this world—perhaps in the morning, like you said."

James smiled slightly. "Is that your way of saying my opinion doesn't really matter in this situation?"

"Oh good, I'm glad you picked up on that," Marc grinned back.

The conversation could have gotten heated after that, but Amelia was quick to step in. "James, why do you think we should leave tomorrow when we still don't really have a plan to deal with Lucien? Three more days really could be decisive if we use them well."

"You mean as well as we used today?" James asked, looking around the room. "Put your hand up if you feel like you've accomplished something today."

Marc and Amelia were both motionless, but I thought that they were probably both thinking that they'd accomplished a lot that day. I felt the same way simply because of what I'd done with May, and how that had solved their problems. Perhaps Peter, too, felt he had accomplished something today, although I couldn't think what. Nobody had anything to say to James, though, because we could all see his point, and James knew it too.

"Okay," he said. "Well I didn't really get anything done either, and that was with my mind focussed on it most of the day. We have a lot of tools that we can use to defend ourselves against him; we have a few ways of attempting an attack on him; and we have a lot of stuff that'll help us survive and stay hidden. I really wish we could have a direct source of magic so that we can create more stuff if we think of it later, but with the magic we have available to us here, that's just not possible."

"All the more reason why we should give ourselves a bit more time to maybe think of some more stuff," Marc insisted.

"I think we all know that any new ideas we have at this point will come to us after we've tried the ones we have," James said reluctantly. "We're not going to know how this stuff really holds up until we're out there relying on it, and extra time here isn't going to change that. There's another reason why we should leave sooner rather than later, too: We're too safe here."

"Er—did I hear that right?" Peter said blankly.

"Oh, I get it," Marc said, grinning and clapping his hands. "We wouldn't wanna be safe, that's way too boring."

James looked unperturbed. "There's a lot of danger out there, and it's perfectly reasonable to want to stay here where it's safe, but the longer we stay, the harder it will be to leave, and the more difficult it will be to make ourselves as alert as we're going to need to be to face Lucien. There's no doubt that we needed this break after everything we went through since we lost our base, but the fact is that we have to go back out there."

Nobody looked very happy about that. Peter only looked worried, while Marc and Amelia looked as though they were trying to come up with some sort of argument for the contrary. Unfortunately, I could see what James was saying, and while I agreed with the logic of it, I hated it too. I didn't want to go back and place myself in that kind of danger again, to deal with all the problems that were waiting for us two weeks in the future, and that was exactly the reason why we needed to hurry up and get on with it.

"I don't like what I'm hearing," Marc said flatly. "Are you absolutely sure there's no benefit to staying just a little longer? We're gonna be kicking ourselves if we come up with some good ideas after it's too late to do anything about them."

"And I'd put money on that happening," James said, taking us all by surprise. "I think that'll happen anyway, despite our best efforts to prevent it. I actually think the stuff we already have is pretty good, probably good enough to start with. I know it'll probably get messed up at some point 'cause—well—it almost always does. But we proved when we took on Hammerson that we can adapt to that if we have to, and I think we'll be able to do that with Lucien as well."

"So you're saying that we have to do this because we've done as much as we can do here, and stuff is gonna go wrong anyway and we should deal with it when it happens instead of sitting around here worrying about stuff we can't control in the future?" I said, trying to wrap my mind around it. Again, it made sense, and again, I hated it.

"Pretty much," James said simply. "I actually think we already have most of what we'll need; the only thing we don't have is a way to break through whatever magical protection Lucien has no doubt put around the Sorcerous Crystals, and without knowing what that protection is, there's no way we can prepare for it. We do have a way to locate the crystals, though, as well as a way to trap Lucien's magic, a couple of ways to shield ourselves from it, a way to knock him out from inside the fourth dimension, a way to get rid of Fewul—hopefully, a way to make ourselves truly untraceable, a way to heal ourselves if we get hurt, and a way to get our friends back on our side. Then we've got that new base that John created, and that'll keep us much safer than the previous one did because of the most important fact of all: Lucien doesn't know what magic we've performed, so it's going to be much more difficult for him to figure out how to get around it."

"When you put it like that, I actually feel better about going," Amelia said, "and I actually thought of an idea we might be able to use. Once we know where he's hidden the crystals, the first thing we should do is get Stella back on our side. Once we've got her, she might be able to use her magic to get through his protection. I know he'll strip her of her magic as soon as he figures out what we've done, but not if we can get the crystals off him first."

A brief silence followed this little speech. I felt incredibly anxious when I thought about Stella, who will no doubt be somewhat of a wreck when we return to the future, no time having passed for her since I'd taken her virginity and then left her on the floor. The others looked much more impressed, though, and James said, "That's a pretty good idea. That ought to be the first thing we do after we retrieve the Light and Villain Crystals, and John does what he needs to do in the gym. We might be able to avoid fighting Lucien altogether if we can get the Sorcerous Crystals that quickly, but I doubt it'll go that well; he'll probably have some sort of alarm set up to let him know if the crystals are in danger."

"Okay," Marc said, looking reluctant. "So that's what we're doing now? Leaving tomorrow morning?"

"Is everyone okay with that?" James said, looking around at us all.

Amelia and I both nodded, putting the vote at three-two. Marc and Peter looked at each other and then both shrugged.

"You're right, J-sandwich," Peter said dully, "no time like the present—or in this case, tomorrow."

"Should we let the Brazilians know we're leaving, or just go and let them think whatever?" Amelia asked.

"Just go," Marc shrugged. "Who cares what they think?"

"Probably right," James agreed, "but I'd actually take it one step further: I think we should make them forget we were ever here. Ideally, they would never have needed to know we were here at all, and as it stands, the ones who are on the island now are the only ones who know about us being here at all. I don't know if they have any way of communicating with the outside world, but even if they can't, it still seems safest to remove all traces of our presence here."

"Do we really need to go that far?" Peter asked, glancing sideways at me, and I knew that he knew what I was thinking.

"I don't know, Pete, but are you prepared to take the risk, however small, that word of this gets back to Lucien before we can act on what we've done?"

"Hmm, yeah, I guess not," he said unwillingly, glancing at me again.

"Can you do that, May?" James asked, and she agreed that she could do so. "Good, but maybe wait until tomorrow, right as we're leaving; simplest thing to do."

"Should we make Underwood forget about us as well?" Amelia asked.

James considered and then nodded. "We haven't seen that much of him, so losing those memories shouldn't affect him too much."

"Wait, I have a better idea about him," Marc said quickly. "We should come up with some sort of way to communicate with him after we leave, like he did with Smiley before he came here. He knows about that creation cave, after all, so he might be able to create stuff for us and magically send them to us—you know, if we create the devices to do that stuff before we leave."

James beamed. "Marc, that really is a great idea! And it solves the problem of not being able to create more stuff after we leave; it just means that we'll have to wait for him to do it for us, but that's definitely better than nothing. Do you think he would agree to do it, though?"

That brought us up short. Nobody was really sure about that, and Peter said, "I guess we just go back up there tomorrow and ask him."

So while the atmosphere at the start of dinner had been fairly flat, by the time we were done eating, it was much more upbeat and optimistic. I felt it myself, though a shadow was cast over my mood. I could deal with going back to the future; I could deal with being back in a world where Natalie probably hated my guts; and I could deal with maybe having to deal with Stella again, so soon after I had done—well—after I had done her. The thought that haunted me now, though, was Larissa. It wasn't knowing that I would miss my opportunity with her after all that bothered me; I could deal with that too. What I had trouble accepting was that by this time tomorrow, she wouldn't even remember that I existed.

As we were finishing up dinner, I mentally got in touch with May, asking—practically begging—that she spare Larissa from the mental purge. She understood my distress, but she also pointed out the logical problems with letting her remember me: If she remembered me, she would have to remember everything about our group that she currently knew, otherwise what she and I had done wouldn't make sense; and if she remembered, everyone else would have to remember, otherwise they might think that she'd lost her mind—and for her part, she might start to question it all herself.

It was difficult for us to find some middle ground, but we were eventually able to find a compromise: If I saw Larissa tonight and let her know that everyone else would be forgetting about us tomorrow, she would know to keep her mouth shut, and then perhaps she would be allowed to remember. If I couldn't do that, then either I would have to accept the status quo, or May could close the circle by removing Larissa from all of our minds, thereby nullifying my distress. I wasn't particularly wild about that either, but I understood that in the present situation, it was the best that May could do, and it was rather more than she needed to do.

Unable to settle, I decided to go out in my hover car after dinner, by which time it had already gotten dark, whether to try to find Larissa (assuming she herself was out) or just to wander, I hadn't decided. Peter, James and Marc had asked me to play four-way chess with them, but when I had told them I didn't feel like it, they had asked Amelia—who had been about to start painting her nails— instead. I got in my car and began roving around, doing a full lap around the mountain before deciding that, as long as I wasn't doing anything, I might as well go and create a device with which we could keep in touch with Underwood—save us the trouble of doing it tomorrow morning. Mostly, though, it would take my mind off the whole Larissa dilemma for a while.

So, I turned my car around and headed clockwise around the mountain, passing a few hundred feet below our car park as I went. My thoughts now were that the best thing I could do would be to find Larissa and tell her what was going on, and then hopefully, she would be spared. At best, May could compel her not to speak about us after we left, although she would have no way of keeping an eye on Larissa once we were gone. The hardest part of that would be telling her at all…

I turned right and began to climb the mountain as it slowly curved around to the right, meaning to climb steadily as I went so that by the time I reached the creation cave, I would be at the right elevation as well as the right position—'cause you know, I thought I was being so smart. Before I had gotten more than fifteen feet from the ground, though, I passed right above a person standing at the foot of a mountain near a cave only a short distance to my left. If I hadn't begun climbing, I might have hit them before I even knew they were there. My heart skipped a beat as I looked over my shoulder, thinking that it couldn't possibly be Larissa, not when I had literally just been thinking about her. It was actually too dark to see who it was, but I could see her (or possibly his) outline, and that outline was waving me down. I didn't even hesitate before gliding back down and approaching the person, and as I closed in, I saw that I had been wrong a moment ago. It could possibly be Larissa, because it was Larissa, and as she had a couple of days ago, she was carrying a tracker—but apparently not a torch this time.

"You gave me a fright," she said, and I thought she was smiling at me. "I wasn't even sure it was you until just now."

"I didn't see you at all until I went past you," I told her. "I could have hit you if I'd still been on the ground. What are you doing out here?"

But I thought I knew the answer to that, and sure enough: "Just looking around again. I didn't know if I would see you again, but you said you would find me if I was out."

I shrugged. "I might have actually done that, although I had been on my way to do something else just now."

There was a click, and then there was light. Larissa did have her torch after all, and now she held it between us so that, although there was a little glare in my eyes, I could see her face—and presumably, she could see mine. She really is pretty, I found myself thinking.

"Really? Would you take me along?" she asked.

That made me nervous. I had two reasons why I wanted to say yes: It would mean I could spend more time with her, and it would probably mean I would have to find a way to get her into my hover car with me, which might be uncomfortably squishy, if not very, very close. Then between those two reasons, if I took her to the creation cave, I could take her on a journey like the one Amelia and I had embarked on in that same place. But there was a big reason not to take her: Giving someone I barely knew access to that much power could have unpredictable results. I hoped I wasn't being possessive of that magic, since it wasn't mine to be possessive of, but it still felt like a bad idea to let her in on that secret.

"I'd love to," I said, hoping she didn't notice my hesitation, "but I don't think I can. It's dangerously high up, and I don't think it would be safe to take you up there with me."

"Oh," she said, looking disappointed.

There was a moment when I thought she might back away from my car, perhaps to go off exploring on her own, or to go back to the main hall. I didn't want that at all, especially given that I had something I needed to tell her, so I decided the best way to keep her here was to keep her talking.

"How's your friend doing?" I asked her, not needing to point out that it was Amanda, or even to let her know that I remembered Amanda's name.

She knew who I was talking about, though, and she shrugged. "A little hurt, but she'll be okay. She said your friend said he loved his girlfriend."

"I know, I heard," I said, "and he's actually my brother, but yeah."

"Do you love your girlfriend?" she asked me now.

That brought me up short. Had I told her I had a girlfriend? I didn't think so, because obviously I didn't, but then what would make her think I did? Was she just fishing to see what I would say, to find out if I had someone else in my life, to prevent her making the same mistake Amanda had made? I didn't know, but I knew that there was only one honest way to answer the question.

"I don't have a girlfriend anymore," I told her, "but I am in love with someone."

Her face fell a little at those words, and I was sorry to see it, but I was glad I'd had the courage not to lie about it. "Does she love you back?" she asked.

"Well, she used to," I said unwillingly, any good feeling I'd had about being in Larissa's company evaporating as I recalled, for the umpteenth time, the expression on Natalie's face as she'd turned her back on me.

Larissa must have seen something in my face then—an indication of the pain (or more likely a fraction of it) that I had been feeling since leaving the present. Her face softened as she smiled, and she leaned forward and kissed me on the lips, taking me by surprise, but only momentarily. I kissed her back, tentatively at first as my mind was still at least partially on Natalie, but as the kiss lengthened, so did it deepen as I was brought back to the here-and-now.

And in the here-and-now, Larissa was the one I wanted. My mind returned to the beach on which we had walked hand-in-hand a couple of nights ago, of how intimate that had felt, of how good she had looked in her sleeveless top, and how good she might look in only a bikini—or less. The fact that I was still sitting in my hover car and she was standing beside it prevented the kiss from getting much deeper, but she still put her arms around me. But that was when my mind finally snapped back into gear, and I remembered that there was another issue at hand—an issue Larissa ought to know about before this went any further.

Reluctantly, I ended the kiss, taking a deep breath of the cool night air to help my body return to a state of balance and equilibrium. She too took a deep breath, and by the light of her torch, I saw that she looked exultant. I switched my car off so that it began sinking to the ground, looked up at Larissa as I sank with it, and said, "Before we do that again, there's something I need to tell you. Step back so I can get out."

She did so, now looking a bit nervous. When the car bumped on the ground, I jumped out and leaned against it for a moment, looking around. There were a couple of caves nearby, but not really anywhere to sit unless we sat on the rock itself. I looked a moment longer, then realised that there were actually some places to sit if we went a little way into the bushes, where there were more trees and branches around. I took her by the hand and led her forward, leaving my car for now (it ought to be fine in the dark), moving bushes and branches aside with my free hand so that she didn't have to—although she did anyway. Once I'd found a nice big log to sit on, I stopped, sat her down and then sat down beside her.

She still looked nervous as she said, "What's this about?"

"We're leaving here tomorrow," I told her, "me and my friends. We always knew this was going to be a short visit here, but we've accomplished what we came here to do, and now it's time to go."

She opened her mouth to say something, and then didn't. I could see the emotion in her face, but it looked as though it hadn't solidified into something concrete yet. She tried to speak again, failed again, tried a third time and then said, "Okay. Where will you be? Will you be going back to Australia? Isn't that where the Sorcerers live?"

"Well, yeah," I said, a little nervously—why would she ask that? "Er—when do you leave here?"

"Second of September," she said eagerly. "Maybe we can keep in touch when I get back? I do have a phone with Internet on it."

"Oh," I said, brought up short again—that could complicate things even more. I racked my brains, trying to think if her having a way to contact me could cause trouble. Unfortunately, I just couldn't know if she would unwittingly tip off Lucien to my location or whatever, but maybe there were ways around that.

"You don't want to?" she said, looking a little hurt. The time I'd taken to think through all the possibilities had given her the wrong idea.

"Actually I do," I said, and it was true. Although there was no good reason to keep in touch with Larissa after this (we would be too far apart to actually have any kind of relationship, and it would be much more dangerous by the time she returned from the Rock), I still wanted to leave the door open to that possibility. "Let me think on a safe way to do that. By the time you get back to Brazil, a whole lot of stuff will have probably happened. We're planning a big move against the Hammerhearts next week or the week after, and I don't know how it will go"—that was a lie—"but if it goes well, you'll hear about it."

"Wow, really? What are you going to do?"

"I can't say, and you can't tell anyone I said even this much," I said quickly. "There's something else you need to know, though, something that concerns you and all your classmates—even your teachers."

"What is it?" she asked.

"My friends think it will be safest if we make you all forget that we were ever here. They want to prevent any possible word getting back to our enemies of what we're doing, and the only way they can be sure you won't accidentally say something to the wrong person is if you never knew us at all."

"What?" she looked appropriately alarmed by that. "But we don't even know what it is you're doing here. What could we say to put you in danger?"

"It doesn't matter that you don't know: If the Hammerhearts found out we were here, they would be able to guess what we're doing, and they would take steps to prevent us striking at them."

"So you would do magic on us? Is that even safe?"

"It wouldn't be me," I said quickly, "and it's perfectly safe. You wouldn't forget anything else—"

"I don't like that," she said, looking like she might cry. "I don't want to have never met you. I've never met anyone like you before."

I shrugged unhappily. "That's only because I've been through more unusual crap than most other people."

"I don't want to forget you, John," she said, and a tear fell from her left eye.

"Okay," I said, and made up my mind—if she really didn't want to forget me, she would agree to what needed to be done. I opened my mouth to tell her, but before I could, she kissed me again. She was full of emotion this time, and the kiss was correspondingly fierce. Taken aback, I could only respond to it in kind.

"I don't care what magic you and your friends do," she panted, clinging to me, when it had ended, "I will not forget something like this."

"You won't have to," I said, taking hold of her. I still wasn't sure how far she wanted this to go, but my body had now taken over from my confused and conflicted mind, and it wanted to take this as far as it could. And although we did have to get up at one point, that was how it had happened, right there in the bushes, on a makeshift bed made from our discarded clothes. We had tried to be quiet, as it was a pretty much silent night, but neither of us had been able to prevent crying out.

I had completely forgotten, yet again, to put a condom on beforehand, and I mentally scolded myself for not having thought of it until it was well and truly too late to do any good—not that it would have mattered, as I wasn't carrying them with me anyway. I wasn't carrying my normaliser with me either, but that was okay, because in a way, I was carrying that—and many other things—all the time now. Sanity was returning for both of us now, and in Larissa's case, desire had been replaced by nervousness. She got onto her knees, looked down at them and frowned, noticing that they would now be dirty, and then realising that all of her clothes would now be dirty—in more ways than one.

"My clothes," she moaned softly. "Oh, I won't be able to hide this. What am I going to do?"

"Nothing," I said, taking her by the hands and pulling her to her feet. I put my arms around her and kissed her again, wanting the goodness to continue, but although she kissed me back, it was more perfunctory than passionate. Stopping the kiss, I said, "Get dressed, and I'll fix it up."

"I wish I had condoms," she said a little sadly. "Don't worry, I won't get pregnant, but I wish—you know—"

"Don't worry, I don't have anything," I said, hoping it was true— I didn't feel like I had anything.

I picked out my clothes from hers, and then once I was dressed, thought of my clothes becoming clean, just as I would have done if I'd been holding the Sien-Leoard Crystal—and just like that, my clothes became clean. Larissa, who'd been standing there watching, gasped when she saw the magic.

"You can do that?" she gaped. "You never said you had magic. I thought it was only the Sorcerers who could do that—"

"Don't get excited," I said wearily. "I don't actually have magic; I can just do a few things with it, just in case there isn't a Sorcerer around. They don't have the power to create new Sorcerers. Go on, get dressed, so I can do it to you too."

She did so without a word, apparently too stunned to speak, and I took advantage of the silence by saying what I'd been about to say before the sex had driven everything else from my mind. "You may not have to forget about me. All you have to do is keep the secret from everyone else. They'll forget all about us—even your friend will forget what happened to her. You'll be allowed to remember as long as you keep it to yourself; I only have enough control over the situation to get you that much."

"That's good enough for me," she said, sounding very happy now. I could no longer see her face clearly, as her torch, still lit, had been left on the log, but I could imagine it.

When she was dressed, she stood before me, looking dirty, dishevelled, and somehow even more attractive than she had been before—perhaps because of the knowledge that I had done that to her. I cast the spell to clean her, applying it to her body as well as her clothes, and cast another one to normalise her, so that no harm could come from this. For several seconds after that, the two of us just stood, staring at each other. I didn't know what came next, but I also didn't want to let her go on that note. It wasn't very late yet, I could afford to spend more time with her, and she wouldn't have to be back at the main hall for at least an hour and a half yet.

An idea came to me then, and I immediately latched onto it. We weren't very far away from where I had parked my hover car, and just beyond that was the foot of the mountain. There were two caves nearby which Larissa had been about to explore before I had come, and although she didn't know it, I knew what was inside both of them, because I clearly recognised the location. One of them led down a large flight of stairs and ended in an enormous hall containing an Olympic-sized swimming pool. The other led down a smaller flight of stairs into a chamber filled with compartments, each of which had a hot tub. Two nights ago, I'd fleetingly wished that I could have taken Larissa into the hot tub cave, and now, it looked as though I would get the chance, except…

"Do you wanna do something else with me?" I asked her.

"Something as good as that?" she asked, smiling, sounding sexy as ever.

"Maybe," I said, and told her about the hot tub cave, not forgetting to mention that I'd never actually been in one of the hot tubs before, although several of my friends had. I was a hot tub virgin, and she could be the one to take my hot tub virginity, and as I had hoped, she was plenty eager to oblige.

So she retrieved her torch, while I went back to my hover car, which was still where I'd left it, got in, and drove it into the bushes, parking it beside the log so that it would be well hidden (I really should have done that to start with). I then took Larissa's hand and led her back through the bushes, into one of the caves, and down the flight of stairs to the chamber at the bottom, which I unlocked with my L-key. The chamber was silent and empty, although it wasn't dark; like many of the Rock Haulter caves, it contained a magical source of light that was unidentifiable. Each of the compartments had a panel, which could be closed so that the people in the hot tub within could have some relative privacy; and right now, all of the panels were closed and silent.

Still holding Larissa's hand, I led her forward to the third panel on the right and raised it, revealing the hot tub within. The sides were about waist-high on the outside, but the inside looked a bit deeper than that in places. There were plenty of shallower spots though, most of them around the sides of the tub, so that its occupants could sit in it without drowning. There were a number of jets hanging over the side of the tub on the back wall for filling the tub, which was a good thing, because it was presently empty and bone-dry. There was also a raised platform off to one side (the left, from where we were standing), raised to the height of the edge of the tub, which looked as though it served two purposes: A place for people to put any discarded clothes within the compartment; and a place for someone to sit if they only wanted to put their legs in the water.

We both climbed into the tub, I shut the panel behind us, and we scrambled up onto the platform, where we proceeded to undress. Larissa settled herself down on one of the seats in the tub and watched as I began fiddling with the knobs, testing them all to see what they did. The one in the middle took care of the water, and it had presets to control temperature. I set it to work filling the tub with nice, hot (but not too hot) water, while I experimented with the other knobs, which seemed to provide bubbles and scents and other such things. These tubs were built to arouse people, there was no doubt in my mind, and it was already working on Larissa. It was working on me, too; I couldn't wait till the tub was full, just so that I could sit with Larissa and begin playing with her body.

The tub filled in remarkably quick time, and by the time I turned all the jets off, it was also full of such thick bubbles that I couldn't see a thing below the surface, and all I could see of Larissa was her head. They weren't ordinary bubbles either; whenever any part of my body touched one, rather than popping, it felt as though the bubble were somehow massaging my skin. It was through this sea of massaging bubbles that I practically swam across the deepest part of the tub to join Larissa.

With the water no longer running, the chamber was once again quiet. The only sounds were the sounds Larissa and I made, which consisted of a little bit of talk, a little bit of splashing, and a little bit of giggling as I did something to her that excited her. I didn't want it to end, although I knew it would have to soon, and although I wished we could have sex again, I didn't think we would be able to. I supposed I could live with that because really, the best part of all of this was just being with her. Being able to enjoy her, even in this way, was more fun than the blaster-cannon sex I'd been having with Amelia, May, Lena and Stella while I'd been cursed—not that Larissa would ever know that.

I had been about to suggest that we get out and start drying off (I knew the goodbye to follow would be difficult, and I wanted to allow time to get through it), when voices reached our ears, and we both fell still and silent, listening intently. I couldn't believe our bad luck: People, a boy and a girl, were coming down the stairs into the hot tub cave. They were young voices, and they were speaking English. I already thought I knew who they were, and when they were closer, I was sure of it: Marc and Amelia. Marc had known about this cave, of course; he had even been in one of these hot tubs with a Russian girl. Now, he wanted to share the experience with Amelia.

Larissa looked at me, eyebrows raised, perhaps noticing my alarm. Whether or not she wanted to be caught here, I wasn't sure, but I knew I definitely didn't want to be found here by Amelia. Yeah, she and Marc were fine now, and she and I were done as far as that stuff went, but how would she feel about me if she saw me with Larissa in this context? Depending on how well May had worked on her, it could be okay, or it could be not so good; Amelia could feel jealous, renewing her attraction and undoing May's good work. Or it could be even worse—she might accuse me of being out-of-control and with no morals at all, which would probably send Larissa running in addition to embarrassing the hell out of me. No, I didn't want to be found here, and I zipped my finger across my lips as Marc and Amelia came into the chamber and got into one of the tubs closest to the door.

"What should we do?" Larissa whispered, making me jump, but with our panel muffling the sound, I didn't think it would carry down to Marc and Amelia. A moment later, they began running water into their tub, which would give us a few minutes of relative reprieve.

"That's Marc and Amelia," I told her, "and—well—I don't really want them to catch me like this."

"Which one is Marc?"

"Er—the tall one," I whispered, and she nodded to tell me she knew who I was referring to.

"How long will they be here?"

"I'm not sure. They're a couple, so it could be a while, and—well—"

I didn't want to say it, but the fact was, we might have to listen to them doing all kinds of stuff together, perhaps up to and including sexual intercourse. I hoped that wouldn't be the case, and not just because of how uncomfortable it would be, but I couldn't see any way around it.

"I don't think I can wait that long; I'll be in so much trouble if I'm late."

"Hang on," I whispered, and I carefully stood up and walked along the tub, glad that I wasn't tall enough to be seen over the top of the panel (although one would have to be at least six-foot-eight to be seen from here). I carefully opened it a fraction and tried to see down to Marc and Amelia's tub, but the angle wasn't right—I could only see the panel directly across from this one. I didn't know if they had their compartment open or closed, and without that knowledge, we had no choice but to wait it out.

"Sorry," I told her when I returned to her and sat down beside her. "Don't worry, you won't be in trouble when you get back; I know a way you can get in without them even knowing."

"How?"

I shook my head and smiled. "You leave that to me; I'll tell you about it later."

I took her in my arms again and kissed her. As earlier, she kissed me back without much excitement, and I thought it was probably because she was now too nervous to get worked up. I too was nervous, especially a moment later when the water stopped and I could hear Marc and Amelia's voices again, but it wasn't enough to dull my excitement. It was this tub, and these bubbles, I supposed, that were keeping me going, and I had a way to keep Larissa going as well. I didn't use it at first, but eventually, as the two down there began doing something similar (I could only imagine, and I wished I couldn't), I just got more and more excited. It wasn't just the bubbles now: It was this whole situation. It was exciting to be here, to possibly get caught being naughty, and it made me want Larissa all the more.

Wanting to bring her into my world, I decided to use my self-given magic for the first time to sexually arouse a girl. I justified it to myself by thinking that at least she was already here in the tub with me; if I'd used it to get her here, that would have been harder to live with. She didn't notice any difference at first, but it didn't take long to work her up. Her breathing got heavier, and a few times she let out involuntary moans, making me put my free hand over her mouth each time. She gasped and splashed around a bit, but there was little danger of Marc or Amelia hearing us. It wouldn't have been impossible, but fortunately, they seemed to be too wrapped up in each other to pay any attention to the noises, even if they did reach their ears. I thought maybe they had started out doing much the same sort of stuff that Larissa and I were doing, but I'd heard them get up on the platform—Marc first, followed minutes later by Amelia—and the noises that followed told me quite plainly how it ended.

Fortunately, that was all we had to put up with. They had spent most of the day together, those two, and it seemed that they really had worn each other out. They didn't get back in the tub, but spent drying themselves and each other as the water drained, before getting dressed and then leaving the chamber. Larissa and I fell still as silence descended again, neither of us moving or speaking again until we hadn't heard any other sound for more than twenty seconds.

"Oh wow," Larissa said, turning to look at me, and her eyes were practically sparkling. "That was amazing."

I wasn't sure if she was talking about the sex or the circumstances in which the whole thing had happened, but either way, I agreed.

"I know you have to get back," I said, "and so do I, but there's something I want to do first."

"I've got something I want to do before we leave as well, but you go first."

It turned out we both wanted to do the same thing, and it didn't end until the spell I'd performed on her finally wore off, by which time it was past eleven o'clock. We had well and truly overshot the mark on that one.

"Don't worry about it," I assured her as we climbed the stairs out of the cave together, holding hands again. "You'll be able to walk right into that hall without anyone asking any questions."

She'd better be able to, I thought, and I mentally contacted May to make sure she would be on the same page. I knew I was taking her somewhat for granted by making these promises before I'd even asked her, but at the time, it had felt like the only way to calm Larissa down and prevent her from giving us away. It turned out that she was on the same page as me, for she immediately responded, telling me that it was fine by her, that she'd made sure Larissa was in the right place at the right time when I'd found her, and that she had gotten Marc and Amelia to leave quickly so that we could, too. She hadn't made them come down to the cave, but she hadn't stopped them either.

The goodbye was still to come. I'd forgotten about it in the excitement of the hot tub, but it quickly came home when we got back to my hover car. There were tears in Larissa's eyes again, but before they could fall, I kissed her again.

"Remember, you can't talk about me, or any of my friends, after we're gone," I reminded her.

"I know," she said sadly. "How can I get back in touch with you? I really want to. I'll miss you."

I hesitated again, having forgotten about this thorny point as well. I had to remind myself that Natalie was still the one I wanted, that in spite of all the terrible things I'd done, I was still holding on to hope of getting her back. Any chance I had with her would be utterly dashed if she found out about Larissa, which might just happen if I stayed in touch with her. Then, there was the matter of safety…

"I tell you what, I'll get in touch with you after you get back," I told her. "It's safest that way, since I have no idea where I'll be or if it'll be safe to be in touch with you."

She shook her head. "Not good enough. I need something, just in case. What if something happens to you? I would never know. I would go on thinking you'd ditched me."

That was a fair point too, but what could I do about it? What channel of communication could I give her that would be safe? I couldn't think of a single one, unless I went up to the creation cave and made it myself. In fact, now that I thought about it, that was actually a good idea.

"Leave it with me," I told her. "I can make something that will be safe to use to get in touch with me. It will be telepathic. Do you know what that is?"

"You mean like mind-reading?"

"Yeah, a bit like that. We'll be able to send thoughts to each other long-distance, which will be safer than the Internet. It'll do for the time being until someday when we can maybe meet again."

"I hope so," she said. "So what is this thing?"

"I'll have to make it and give it to you later."

"Give it to me when? Aren't you leaving tomorrow?"

"Yeah, we are. I'll get it to you before we go. I'll find a way."

"Promise?"

"Yes, I promise," I said, and kissed her again.

And indeed, when I got back in my hover car, the first thing I did after Larissa and I parted ways was to go up to the creation cave and create two separate life assistants. Four devices, two red and two blue, which communicated on completely separate magical channels. Underwood would get a red device, while the other red device could be duplicated and passed around to anyone who needed to contact him. He could also, by holding something in his free hand, teleport it into the free hand of the person using the corresponding device, which would enable the transfer of magical items. Larissa would get a blue device, which she would keep secret and protect with her life; and I would have the other blue device, which would also remain secret from everyone except for that Honnie who knew everything about everyone. It was closing in on midnight by the time I was heading back to camp, and although my emotions were torn between satisfaction at the magic I'd just performed, contentedness after having had more great sex that evening, and sadness at the thought of not seeing Larissa again, mostly I was just worn out and eager to get to bed.

Chapter 33: So Much for the Vote

The following day promised to be a very long one for me, and that wasn't counting the fact that it would span two weeks. The first thing I did when I woke up at seven o'clock was go to find May, who was herself just getting up, as was everyone else (Amelia and one of the other guys had already snagged the first showers, while it sounded like the other two had gone into the campsite). Well, actually, the first thing I did when I woke up was mentally lament the fact that I'd only gotten six hours of sleep.

"I need to talk to you—quickly, before we join the others."

"Okay," she said, sitting down on her bed and looking at me, standing near the door which I had just closed behind me. "You should know I did not make any of those things happen last night. I only made it so that you would find her, because I knew you would eventually want to."

"I know, and thanks for that," I said, grinning as I thought back to the time Larissa and I had spent together. "So then you know I've made up my mind about her; I want her to remember, and I really think she can keep the secret. I only need one more thing from you, but I understand if you've had enough of me asking for your help. I promise this is the last time."

She smiled slightly. "I do not think you can make a promise like that; you do not know if you will have to break it later. But okay, I think I know what you want."

"To be able to see her this morning and give my thing to her, yeah," I confirmed. "Can you make that happen?"

"It will need to be around nine o'clock, when they are leaving their hall. That will be the easiest for me to work."

That probably would be best for me too, but what about the others? What explanation could I give them for why I was leaving the campsite when we were about to pack up and go home? May had an answer for that: "You are going to see Underwood this morning as well. Just go and see her on the way to him."

I shrugged. That would mean taking Peter and James along, and they wouldn't approve of what I was doing with Larissa (Peter would probably understand, but James certainly wouldn't), but if necessary, May could make them forget—or not even notice what I was doing. Getting this too from my mind, she nodded, and I relaxed; I was still in some control of the situation.

I left her room after that and was just in time to snag the second shower. Once I was done, I left the bedrooms and found Amelia, Marc and James in the group F campsite, where they were settling down to some magically created breakfast. Figuring I could catch

Peter up later, I told the three of them about the telepathic communication devices I had created last night—or rather, two out of the four devices I had created, so that we wouldn't have to worry about doing it this morning. James suggested that he, Peter and I go and see Underwood straight after breakfast, while Marc and Amelia went inside our new base and got started loading all our stuff into it, and May dealt with removing the Brazilians' memories of us. If all went well, we would all be done with those things around the same time, and then we would be able to leave the Rock as early as possible. Marc and Amelia both agreed to that plan, and so did I, publicly anyway.

May had been listening to this whole exchange from her shower, of course, and she had even telepathically filled Peter in on what was going on while he was showering (something that made him acutely uncomfortable, especially as he knew that May was naked while she was sending him these messages, but I didn't mind knowing all these details). I mentally asked her if she could hold off on wiping the Brazilians' memories until after I had spoken to Larissa, and she told me that she would have done that anyway.

"You okay?" Marc asked me.

"I'm fine," I said, "just a little nervous about going back—not just because of Lucien, but—you know—all the crazy shit I did before we left."

Marc patted me on the shoulder. "You'll be fine, mate, one way or the other. I know you've had more time than she has, but I'm sure she'll be a bit more forgiving when she has time to think it through and understand that you couldn't control yourself."

True, maybe, but I had also done plenty of crazy shit while I had been in complete control of myself—shit that Marc didn't know about. There was no good reason for Natalie to forgive me if she found out about any of that stuff, but she may not ever find out about it if she didn't give me a second chance. Well, these are happy thoughts to start what could be a monumental day, I thought sourly, and smiled in spite of myself.

* * *

We actually got going with our plans at a quarter to nine, which was a little earlier than I needed to be at the main hall, but not enough time to see Underwood first. I asked Peter and James if we could go down to the main hall quickly before we saw Underwood so that I could see Larissa one last time before we left. Both of them frowned, but agreed, and I mentally thanked May for yet again smoothing my path—assuming she had this time.

"I still think it would be easier to just let her go," James said as we swung our cars around to the left, heading for the path that would take us past the tree house en route to the main hall. "I mean, it won't hurt her once she's forgotten all about us."

"I know, but it would hurt me to think she'd never been attracted to me at all," I said, not looking at either of them but keeping my eyes on the path ahead. I didn't want either of them to see my face and understand that I was so obviously keeping something from them.

"Wow, you really do like her, huh," Peter observed.

"A bit more than I thought," I admitted. "A bit more than I should, but I'll be able to put her behind me if I can say goodbye. She'll just think we're leaving the Rock; she won't know she's about to forget me."

"If you say so," James said, still disapprovingly, but at least he wasn't objecting. "What do you want us to do?"

"Stay on the path out of sight, I suppose. If you wanna avoid being seen and spoken to by the rest of them, better to stay out of the way."

Not to mention, that would keep them out of my way as well.

We ended up timing it perfectly: The Brazilians were just getting ready to set off when I turned the corner and saw the main hall, its doors standing open, ahead of me. A few students were carrying some supplies from inside and stacking them in what looked like golf carts, while other students were making sure the contents of each cart were secure and well balanced. Larissa was in this category, and she waved at me when she saw me, as did a couple of the others. I smiled at them and made my way over to Larissa's cart.

"How you doing?"

"Really great. You were right, I didn't have any trouble last night. I don't know how you did it but thanks. And—and thanks for seeing me again. I hoped you would but I didn't think you would."

I smiled, reached into my pocket and pulled out one of the blue telepathic communication devices. Handing it to her, I said, "I made a promise, and I'm usually pretty good about keeping them. All you have to do with that is put a finger on that soft bit there and think hard at it, and if I'm holding mine"—I showed her that I had an identical device—"I'll get the message in my mind. And I can contact you the same way."

"Wow," she said slowly, turning it over in her hands. "This is real magic? Wow."

"Yep, it is," I grinned at her. "If I don't respond when I get a message from you, it'll be because I'm not holding mine, but I'll get any missed messages as soon as I pick it up, as will you. I need you not to use it for the next two weeks though: I'm gonna be very busy and I won't have any time to use it. Can you do that for me?"

"I guess," she said slowly. "How will I know if it works?"

"Trust yourself," I said simply. "Here…"

I put my hand back on my device, touched the soft pad and imagined the hot tub in which she and I had had so much fun the night before. I knew she'd gotten it when her eyes widened and her face flushed. "Was that—was that?ℜ—"

"Yeah, that was me to you. Go on, give it a try."

She did, and it didn't work very well at first. She sent me a picture of the two of us on that beach, walking hand-in-hand along it, and how good it had made her feel. It wasn't a very clear picture, and it was tinged with doubt and anxiety that she wouldn't be able to make it work properly.

"That was a nice beach," I said, letting her know that I'd gotten it, and she beamed at me. "Now, I don't think I need to tell you, but I will anyway: No one else is allowed to know that thing exists. Don't let anyone see it, and definitely don't let anyone use it. It's yours and yours only."

"I'll protect it with all I have," she said, pocketing it.

I hesitated, because that was the end of it, but there was no point putting it off. "I—er—have to go now."

"Can I have a kiss before you leave?" she asked, glancing around surreptitiously. We weren't alone, and in fact a few people were watching us with interest, but she didn't seem to mind. Given that they were all minutes away from forgetting all about me, I didn't mind so much either. I leaned out of my car and kissed her on the lips, and it was a good kiss. It might have gotten deeper, as our kisses had last night, if a teacher hadn't come out and shouted something in Portuguese, causing Larissa to start and jump back from me, looking guilty but pleased with herself. "It was worth it," she said to me, and then shouted something back in Portuguese that made several people laugh.

"Yep, it was," I said, and thinking that would be a good note on which to leave things, I turned my car around and sped off. I only looked back once, right before I turned the corner onto the path where Peter and James were waiting. Most of the students were no longer paying me any attention, called back to order by their teachers, but Larissa had been watching me out of sight. We exchanged one last smile before the bushes shielded her from my view.

Spoiler alert, don't read the following bit unless you really, really want to know what happened after that. Skip over this paragraph, don't read any of it. You have been warned. If you're still reading, here it is: That was the last time I ever saw Larissa.

* * *

Underwood was our next order of business. May had once again intervened on our behalf, making Underwood feel like staying at his place this afternoon and watching movies, rather than going out and doing whatever he did in the caves. We let ourselves into his cave, James briefly spoke to him through the intercom, and after a few minutes, he came out to join us, looking grumpy that we had interrupted him.

"What's up this time?" he asked, looking around at us.

"This won't take long," Peter said. "You can get back to your business in a few minutes."

"We're actually on our way out," James told him. "I mean, we're leaving the island today. We've done what we came to do. We wanted to let you know that, and to ask a little favour of you before we go."

Of course, those words immediately put him on his guard. "A favour," he said slowly. "What might that be?"

I took the two red telepathic devices from my pockets, looked down at them, and handed one of them to him. He took it mistrustfully, and then comprehension dawned on his face as he realised what it was.

"Not a chance," he said, holding it back out to me, but I didn't take it.

"Yeah, it does work like that," James confirmed. "Look, we're not gonna bug you all the time. We just want a way to communicate with you after we leave—just in case."

"And why would you want to do that? And more importantly, why would I want to do that?"

Now this presented a problem, one I was surprised none of us had foreseen: What good reason could we give him for wanting to stay in touch? Would he believe that it was so that he could use the creation cave on our behalf? Why would he believe that if he thought we still had our own magic? All three of us hesitated for a moment, and I would have gone on hesitating for probably a few more seconds, but James was the first to take decisive action.

"We may not have to," James said. "If all goes well, we won't, but there's always a chance we could lose our magic. You know that Sorcerers' magic can be transferred to other people, and you know that crystals can be stolen. If that happens, we could find ourselves in real trouble. All we would need from you is to use that cave where you can magically create stuff to create some magical solutions for us, we'll tell you what if necessary, and a way to send them to us."

Underwood frowned. "I suppose that is possible, but it still sounds like a lot of trouble."

"If you care about your survival, you'll help," Peter said boldly. "Remember, if we lose, there'll be no one to stop the Hammerhearts coming to get you. It'll be like cutting off a loose end, as far as they're concerned."

That made Underwood blanch, but he got the message. "Fine, fine, I'll take the damn thing. But you'd better not ask me for much: I've got a good thing going here. I'm only gonna help you as long as you keep me out of the fighting and all that shit."

"That won't be an issue," James agreed. "In fact, we would prefer it if you just stayed put right here. I hope you're still not bored of the place."

"Nah, you can never get bored here," Underwood said, and then frowned again. "No, maybe that's not quite true. I mean, I will eventually want to go and do something with my life, but I'd rather wait until the war's over before that. And I've got plenty to do right here in the meantime."

"Good," I said, standing up, "then we'll let you get back to it. Don't lose that thing, okay?"

"Wouldn't dream of it," he said, a little sarcastically, and we parted ways at that point.

No, Underwood wouldn't lose his device, and for a reason that no one but I knew: Unlike the blue telepathic devices, the red ones weren't completely identical. When I had taken both devices from my pockets and examined them before giving one to Underwood, I had been sure to give him the one with the finger pad a tiny shade darker than the other. The magical difference between the two devices wouldn't be obvious to anyone on our end, but it would be very obvious to Underwood when one of us tried to contact him, because it would do the same thing Smiley had once unintentionally done to me. If he wasn't holding his device at the time, he would be magically compelled to go and pick it up, so strongly compelled that the need would be irresistible, no matter what he was doing. The only reason I had placed that burden upon him and no one else was because if we needed to contact him, the chances were good that it would be urgent.

* * *

Getting into our new base was our next order of business. When the three of us returned to the campsite, it was to find all of them pretty much as they had been when we had gotten here. The furniture was still in place, but our bags and everything we had created was gone. The keys remained, a set hanging in each of the three campsites, and the three of us added ours so that there would be two sets in each site. Then what? The other three were nowhere to be found, and I assumed that the base was shrunken—it could have been anywhere. The device I'd created so that I could get in from outside, I'd given it to Marc before we had left, so what were we to do?

That was when Marc, the person at the controls, used them to snatch us right out of our campsite and drop us in the control room of our new base, imprisoned by its magic. Amelia and May were also there, Amelia examining the controls with interest and May just looking blandly at the wall (I supposed, anyway). A moment later, Marc pressed a button, releasing us from the magical imprisonment and leaving us free to roam the base. This control room was larger than the one in the last base, and it had three doors: The emergency escape, which couldn't be opened unless there was real danger; the prison, which could only be opened by pressing a button on the control panel; and the one which led to the elevator.

"Okay, now we're all here," Marc said with satisfaction. "Now what?"

"May, have you taken care of the Brazilians?" James asked, and when she nodded, he said, "Okay, then since we've taken care of Underwood, it's time to go. Marc, do you wanna drive?"

"Sure," he grinned. "It's pretty straightforward stuff—well, maybe not once we try the teleportation."

"We'd better make sure we're in our shadow before we leave the portals, though," I suggested. "I dunno if that would work here, but‽—"

"I imagine it would," James interupted confidently. "I mean, you were able to do that mental thing in the main hall, John, so that would suggest that there is something here. Go on, Marc, give it a go —just a little, though."

Moving through the fourth dimension could be done by pushing a slider either to the left or to the right, depending on which way we wanted to go (from here, the Honnie world was to the right). Marc edged this slider slightly to the right, causing us to move very slowly through the fourth dimension (this could be seen through the six display screens, which showed our surroundings becoming darker and darker). He released the slider when it looked the same as it had when May had first brought us through, meaning we had reached the right point.

This was where we could be safe from both Hammerson and Lucien (although truthfully, the untraceability 2.0 spell Marc had created would probably do just as well in our regular world). It was also where, two weeks into the future, the Light and Villain Crystals were hovering in interdimensional space in Recife, and I supposed our next order of business would be to go and get them. Before that, though, we all made ourselves into four-dimensional beings; we would need to be so at all times if we were going to stay in our shadow, otherwise it would be up to May to use her mind to keep us in communication again. It just seemed to be a lot of unnecessary work for her, now that we had an easier option.

"Okay then," James said, "let's go."

"Hang on," I said quickly as Marc turned towards the door to the car park, "going through there won't work, remember? We're not affected by those transgation charms in here. We'll have to use the regular entrance."

Fortunately, here in the Group F campsite, beyond the regular entrance was only a small cave, beyond which was the foot of the mountain. Marc turned us in that direction and flew us straight through the door, through the darkness beyond, through the rock itself, and even briefly through some other random cave before we finally came out in the open. He then turned us to the path towards the main hall and the jetty, and as we flew down it, I watched the displays in hopes of seeing Larissa again, but no such luck. She and the rest of her classmates seemed to have moved off to some other location, and we saw no signs of human life until we reached the jetty itself, where the Brazilians' ship was anchored and two people (the captain and one other crew member) were on the deck.

"Two questions," James said as we shot down the jetty. "Firstly, May, did you make them forget about us as well?"

"Yes," she said. "Everyone except Underwood has forgotten you."

And Larissa, she added mentally to me, and I was glad she had left that detail out of her comment.

"Good," he said, and then turned to me. "Secondly, John, is this thing going to let us know when we have left the portals, or are we going to have to guess?"

"Er—" I looked at the controls and the displays, making sure that I knew what I was talking about before answering. "Look at the coordinates; they're not moving at the moment, but once we leave the portal, they'll start moving."

"Okay," James said, satisfied. "Now, one last thing we need to do, John?"

"Yeah?"

"That device you used to get in—"

"I have it," Marc cut in. "I was thinking before, maybe we ought to keep it, you know, just in case all of us need to leave the base. We'll need a way to get back in."

"If we take that thing out of the base, we'll be risking it falling into enemy hands, exposing all of us," James insisted. "John, you gotta remove the magic that makes that thing work. It's better to always have to have someone here than take the chance."

Marc shrugged. "What if we don't have a choice?"

"We make it a choice," James said. "Look, we were forced to hide in the Woodward's base, then we were forced to flee it and make our own base, then we were forced to flee that and hide in a crappy homeless shelter, and then we were forced to flee that and hide in the fourth dimension. I don't know about you guys, but I'm done running: This time, we make absolutely sure that no one can get into this base except the people we want."

"I agree," I said, going to the bag which had been deposited on a seat at the back of the room (there were about ten seats in here, as the room was more than big enough), and which contained all the devices we had created. I fished through it until I found the two that I wanted: The first, which I pointed at the control panel and clicked, removed the power of the device Marc had used to get in here; and the second, which I pointed at the device in Marc's hand and clicked, made that device disappear (I then made it vanish the device in my other hand as well). I could have performed that spell without the device, but I wasn't quite prepared to give that secret away yet.

"Well, so much for the vote," Peter grinned. "Don't worry, I think you're probably right. We've had to run for it too many times."

Amelia nodded her agreement, followed by May, who had also been forced to flee when Lucien had infiltrated the Woodwards' second base. Marc looked around at them, shrugged and said, "Well you usually know best, James. So, since this base can't travel through time, how are we all going to get back to our normal time without any of us leaving here?"

A stunned silence followed this before Amelia shouted, "Why didn't you say that before John vanished the fucking thing?"

"Relax," James said, much more calmly. "We don't all need to leave the base to do that. In fact, only May really needs to leave; the rest of us can just sit back in here and let her do her thing. All we need to do is make this thing large enough that she can hold it, or put it in her pocket. You do have a pocket?" he asked her, and she nodded and indicated her right thigh. "Good. So, may I suggest, and feel free to debate it if you will: Once we're out of the portal, we teleport to Recife, go to that park, and then we let May out so she can take us forward until she sees the crystals—"

"She'll see us first," Peter said. "In fact, how are we gonna make it so that none of us from then notice her now?"

"Does anyone remember seeing anything?" James asked, and everyone shook their head—except for May.

When we all looked at her, she said, "I did not see myself, but I felt another Honnie mind that I recognised as my own. I touched it briefly and I told myself I was returning to this time, so I will just do that when the time comes. That is how I will know to stop, so we do not even need to go to the same place."

"And you had the foresight not to panic or mention it to any of us so that we would panic," Marc said, looking impressed. "Good on you. So I guess once you get to that time, you go to the park, get the crystals, and then we bring you back in—"

"No," May said loudly. "No, I will not touch the crystals."

James sighed. "I'd expected that. How about we just bring you back in once you're in the right time—you'll have to give us some sort of signal—and then we use these controls to go and get the crystals?"

That idea seemed to work for everyone.

"Then what?" Amelia asked. "We'd better work it out now, 'cause things are probably gonna move pretty fast once we get back there. We won't have a lot of time—or maybe no time—before Lucien is back in action."

"I think we would have enough time to have a quick meal," James said, "if we're hungry, anyway. If we're not, then I suggest we teleport to the Chopville High gym and let John out so he can do his thing. The rest of us can keep an eye on Lucien and Stella while he's working, and quickly bring him in if there's any danger—although I don't think there would be."

A brief silence followed this as we all considered the plan. It sounded pretty good to me. I said, "I can probably even go into our dimension if I use one of those untraceability things you created, Marc; that'll give me access to both sides."

"Yeah, that should work," Marc said, and then indicated the coordinates on the display. "It looks like we're out of the portal now."

* * *

The teleportation of this base was different from the vessel we had once used to come to the Rock. Rather than enter coordinates to teleport to, this used the same magic that I had become so adept at performing with the Sien-Leoard Crystal when I had needed to get around. All one had to do was grip a handle on the control panel, think specifically of the location to teleport to, and the teleportation would happen. It wasn't quite instantaneous (we went through a short period of immobility, during which all the displays had gone dark), but mere moments after Marc gripped the handle, we were back in that park in Recife where we had almost run into Hall. It was morning, the sun a little lower in the sky than it had been on the Rock, and it was empty.

We went a short distance away from the familiar tree, through which one could access a certain Hammerheart Highway if they had the right credentials, and then with some trepidation, May allowed herself to be deposited on the grass—though still in her shadow. Marc then enlarged the base until it was the same size as it had been when I had created it—small enough to fit in the palm of May's hand, and big enough to easily hold onto. May plucked the base out of the air and pocketed it, and although no G-forces were transferred through to us within (the magic I had originally cast around it protected us from that), we saw the result of it on the screen. It was a little frightening in the moment when an enormous hand was coming towards us, appearing to wrap around us and smother us in darkness —for that was what it was, as from that moment onwards, the screens revealed nothing of what was going on.

In fact, we neither saw nor felt anything as May began moving forward through time. Whether it was because the base could easily move through the fourth dimension or because we had all made ourselves able to perceive the fourth dimension, I didn't know. All I knew was that it left us free to do whatever we wanted, as it was going to take May a while to move forward two whole weeks. After a few rounds of rock-paper-scissors, James was elected to remain in the control room and wait for some sign that May was ready to be brought back in, while the rest of us were free to go and set up our bedrooms and then get some lunch.

The four of us took the bags from the control room, agreeing to leave them in the lounge room so that we would all have access to them, and took the elevator up to the ground level. We then began sorting through them, taking some of the things that we wanted to store away in our bedrooms. I only took a few things on my first run because I wanted to be the first to pick my room—not that it mattered much, as they were all identical, but given that I had created this place, I did feel like I had a right to do that. So far, there was only one level of rooms, and since each level had twelve rooms, there wouldn't be a need to create any new ones yet.

Since there was no concrete direction within the base (no north, south, east or west), I now thought of the directions as front, back, port and starboard (taking inspiration from the boat ride), where front referred to the direction one would be facing when one was seated at the controls in the control room. On the ground floor, the lounge room took up the entire back of the building, with four doors: One leading to outside, one leading to the main room (containing the elevator shaft and stairwell), one to the dining room (on the starboard side) and one on the portside that led to a small hallway with public bathrooms in it. There was also a computer lab on the portside, a games room in the front portside corner, a gym in the front starboard corner and an indoor swimming pool connected to the gym, with another outside door within it leading to the outdoor swimming pool.

I took the elevator to the first floor alone and began looking through each room to see which one I liked best, settling on one of the four front-facing rooms, the second from the portside, which gave me the best view down to the swimming pool below (there was a tennis court and a basketball court around the back, even if none of us used them—it just looked awesome to have them). Surrounding the building, pool and limited sporting facilities on all sides were other, smaller buildings (basically just a brick appendage big enough for a door on one side), and within each was a Rock Haulter-inspired magical wonderland. I was gazing out at these wonders when I noticed how quickly the sky was darkening outside, and I had a moment to wonder if I had screwed up the magic somehow before remembering that the sky here reflected how it appeared outside the base where (and when) the base was presently located, which in this case was Recife—and whizzing forward through time in May's pocket. Even though my watch couldn't sense what May was doing, apparently the magic of the base itself could.

The devices I put in my top bedside drawer on that first run included three separate telepathic communication devices (the blue one to contact Larissa, the red one to contact Underwood, and the white one, which Marc had created, to keep in touch with the others, wherever they were), my bludginator, my solid-outliner, my stunner, my agonator, my invisibility toggle, my untraceability 2.0 device, my thicky prison immunity device, my unboggler, my mind-extractor and my vanisher. I figured I might as well go down and get some more devices (they were my priorities, because many of the others either weren't as important, were programmed into the base itself, or now programmed into me), but before that, I needed to secure this bedroom.

The inner security in this base was different from previous ones, which ran on magical keys. I had created a control panel by the wall, one which would either allow a person to enter, or reject them, by scanning their brain and determining if they were supposed to be allowed to enter. Before it could make any such call, though, the room needed to belong to someone, and ownership could only be created by the first person to use the controls. I therefore opened the panel, put my hand on the handle (it was much like the one Marc had used to teleport us to Recife), and told it that I was the owner. Now, I would be able to open it any time I wanted, and other people could only enter if, according to my thoughts, I thought it was okay for them to enter. In my case, that would be nobody unless I was already in there. They would know it was my room because there was a display on the door, which had been blank when I had first entered it, but would now show my full name.

I made another trip after that, this time bringing back a duplicator, a food and drink creator, a health maintainer, a clothing creator, a shield creator, a furniture creator, a cleaning device, a room creator, an easy shaver, a spyer, an electronic generator and a spell skipper. They were all magical devices that we had created, and they seemed to do the job. I no longer felt like I needed to get any normal stuff from the other bag, the duplicating extender-case the others had picked up in Melbourne and which had served us so well up until now. After I had deposited this lot in my room, I went back downstairs to the dining room and used its controls to make myself some lunch. It wasn't a conveyer belt like we had had in the previous base (I hadn't had enough magic to create such a marvel), but practically another food and drink creating device embedded into the counter.

A melancholy mode came over me as I ate, listening to the others traipsing from the lounge room to the elevator and back. I wasn't really alone, but somehow I felt lonely in that moment. What was it that I was really missing? I wasn't sure. I missed Larissa, fair enough. I missed Natalie too. Was it just females I was missing? Maybe, I wasn't sure. In that respect, I certainly was alone, at least for the time being: Amelia was well and truly off the table now, and although it cost me some pain, I knew it was for the best; and May was presently busy. I might be able to have her again, to use her to fill a hole in my life until there was someone else, but that was hardly fair on her, even if she was okay with it. It would also leave me unwilling to move on, and if it turned out that Natalie and I really were finished, I would need to be able to do that.

After lunch, I decided to relieve James at his post; he would have a chance to set up his room, and I would have something to do while I waited for the next step in our fight against Lucien—even if that something was just sitting around and watching a blank screen. James, who looked thoroughly bored when I entered the control room, was happy enough to swap places with me, and so that was where I remained for a good few hours (at least, that was how much time my watch thought had passed) before May finally took the base back out of her pocket.

I was caught off-guard when I saw that it was night-time outside the base, before I remembered that in Recife, before we had gone back in time, it had been night-time—or rather, very early morning. It looked as though May was done, and I knew it for sure a moment later when she let go of the base, leaving it floating in midair, and put her hands up to either side of her face—the signal we had agreed on. I pressed a button on the panel, and she vanished from the screen, appearing a moment later in the corner of the room near the door to the prison—the regular entry point. I pushed another button to release her from the magic binding her, and then sighed.

"It is done," she told me. "We are back. Less than twenty seconds after the time we started going backwards."

"Great," I said, taking the controls and moving the base through the darkness towards the entrance to the Hammerheart base. "You might wanna get out of the way; I'm about to bring the crystals in."

They were very easy to find, thanks to the Light Crystal illuminating everything in the area as if it were a small sun—not that any of the locals would have seen a thing, even if they had been out at this hour. I closed in on both of them, used the controls to select them (just to make sure I would bring them through and not a nearby tree or something), and pushed the button. They appeared in the corner a moment later, clattering to the floor and rolling away from each other (May cringed away from them).

I paused a moment longer, thinking, and then got to my feet. "Come on, let's go upstairs and tell the others it's time to go."

If I'd thought to bring a telepathic communicator with me, we wouldn't have needed to make the trip.

Chapter 34: Do As You're Told, Grasshopper

It was evening in Chopville; a cold, slightly breezy, overcast but dry evening. We saw this on the display screens when we teleported right to it, appearing in microscopic form hanging high in the air over the footpath just outside a dark and deserted Chopville High. All six of us were seated in the control room: me at the controls, May just beside and behind me, and the others clustered around us. All but me and May were carrying at least one magical device on them, and probably had plenty more in their pockets. James and Marc had pocketed the Light and Villain Crystals respectively. In other words, we were ready for our next assignment.

"So everyone's clear on how we're gonna do this?" James asked, and when everyone nodded, he proceeded to explain it anyway— typical James. "We'll let John out in the gym so he can do his thing, and we'll hover over him so that we can protect him. May will be in charge of pushing the button to pull him back into the base if anyone comes into the gym and looks dangerous, or if they're in Lucien's mind, and Marc—"

He broke off, thinking, and then said, "You know, Marc, you mightn't have to go out there with him if you use the Villain Crystal."

Marc considered this, while everyone else gaped at James. Finally, Marc said, "Maybe, but I don't know if my protecting John would be evil enough for that crystal, even if I do use it to attack Hammerhearts. I'm not so comfortable taking that chance."

James sighed. "Okay, so the two of you go out there, invisible and untraceable—"

"Untraceable 2.0," Peter said, grinning at Marc.

"Yes, that," James pushed on, "and we'll make the base do the same. That new untraceability should be enough to fool Lucien if he's paying attention. As for the rest of us, I'll keep an eye on Lucien with this." He held up the spyer. "Amelia will keep an eye on Stella, and Peter will keep an eye on Harry and Simon. Perhaps the three of us had better test our spying capabilities before we actually start this thing."

The spyer was a magical device that I had created while I had been with Amelia. Basically, I had thought of a number of significant people that we may need to spy on (Lucien, Stella, Hignat, Wilwog, Cornish, Hall, and yes, some of our friends as well) and programmed their identities into the device. So long as they weren't untraceable, the device would be able to magically locate them and show them on a screen. It would also play the surrounding sounds on an in-built speaker. It wouldn't transmit their thoughts to the spyer, but given that they were in Lucien's mind, plus most of their minds were probably protected anyway, that was hardly a weakness in the device.

Now, James, Peter and Amelia turned on their respective spiers and began selecting the people on whom they would be spying. I knew why James wanted to test it before relying on it; not only did we need to know what Lucien and Stella were doing before we potentially exposed ourselves to them, but we needed to know if they had set up any magic to prevent us from being able to get to them magically—traditional untraceability being only one possibility. As for Harry and Simon, given that they were in the Honnie world, we needed to know if the device's magic could reach that far through the fourth dimension. Personally, I thought that probably wouldn't be a problem; I had considered the possibility that we may need to use it for this purpose when I had created it, after all.

"Lucien's in his bedroom," James told us. "Looks like he's still waking himself up."

"Stella's in the Big Room," Amelia said, "so it looks like they're both gonna be alert then."

"Better that Stella's alert," I said. "If she slept while I went out there, she would know what I'm doing."

"I got the twins," Peter said. "They're with Katie and Sophie and they're in a control room a bit like this one, only way smaller. Looks like they're flying over Ingi and—"

He broke off, an expression of utter shock on his face.

"And what?" Marc asked sharply.

"Tommy," Peter whispered. "She's still got Tommy. He's still alive, and she's carrying him. Those two half-breeds are following her as well."

"Dan and Gob," May said sharply, looking affronted at the way Peter was talking about her children.

I didn't say anything, and only partially because I actually wasn't so surprised that Ingi had kept Tommy alive. While they had been talking, May had pushed some thoughts into my head, thoughts that she had got out of Amelia's head, thoughts that Amelia had chosen not to speak aloud. All Amelia had said was that Stella was in the Big Room; what she hadn't said was that Stella was very upset, had probably been upset ever since I had left her (that was my assumption), and she was presently berating Natalie for breaking my heart, and as it was happening, Natalie too was crying, sorry for what she had done, but saying that she still can't bring herself to trust me. As the conversation around Tommy continued, Amelia kept watching and listening to the device, holding it up to her ear so that she (and no one else) could hear it, but through May, I got the gist of what was happening.

"So I guess we'd better get started while Lucien's still waking up," said James, looking down at his spyer. "In fact, it looks like he's going to eat something before he does anything else, so that's perfect. You ready to go, John?"

"Er—yeah," I said quickly, jerking my mind back to the here-and-now.

"Me too," Marc said. He paused a moment, and then took the Villain Crystal from his pocket. "I reckon we should keep this in here, just in case, you know."

"Fair enough," James said, taking it from Marc and promptly giving it to Peter, whose eyes widened in horror.

"Hey, why do I have to carry—"

"Do as you're told, grasshopper," James said sternly.

He took a couple of devices from his pockets—I recognised them as Marc's new untraceability device and a traditional invisibility toggle, originally created by Mr. Woodward. With them, he made me and Marc both invisible and untraceable.

"I never get used to seeing that," Peter said, squinting at where I stood, but not right at me.

"I no longer have their minds," May said, and James nodded, satisfied.

"Time to send them out," he said, taking my vacated seat in front of the controls and beginning to drive us into the school. "Marc, since you're armed, you go out their first. We'll wait maybe thirty seconds to see if anything happens, and if it doesn't, we'll send John out there to join you—and John will have to say something so that Marc knows he's there. You got that, you two?"

"Yep," we both said, but only half of my mind was on it. Right before May had lost my mind, she had told me the last thing that had happened in the Big Room between Stella and Natalie. Stella was presently leaving the room, but she had just told Natalie (and by extension, Amelia) that I had had sex with her just after she (Natalie) had dumped me, but that I had been ashamed of myself afterward. Unsurprisingly, Natalie had been terribly upset by that, but Amelia thought that she had also looked a little satisfied, and I thought I understood why. Natalie now thought of me as an uncontrollable cheater, utterly faithless and untrustworthy, and what Stella had just told her pretty much backed that theory up. What Stella had been thinking, I wasn't sure, but I knew what it now meant to Natalie: Even without knowing what I'd been doing with May and Amelia on Rock Haulter, Natalie would almost certainly never take me back.

So when we were finally in the gym, not far from the spot where Lisa had died, and James let an invisible Marc out of the base, it was with some effort that I attempted to wrench my mind back to the issue at hand. How was I supposed to clear my mind so that I could go back in time when I now had so much to think (and worry) about? All I could think about was Natalie's face, and how she had looked when she turned her back on me. As the seconds lengthened and the others watched their spiers for any trouble, and May stared at the displays (which showed that the gym was still empty—I hadn't thought to make them show invisible people), my heart began to pound wildly. Finally, before I ran out of time, I whipped my own untraceability spell from my pocket, pointed it at myself and gave it a click. Only May noticed what I had done, and she looked questioningly over towards where I stood, still invisible. I sent the request to her, begging her to clear my mind before I had to step out, and she obliged.

"Okay, looks like we're good to go," James grinned at my general position. "You ready, John?"

"Yep," I said, having just made myself untraceable again and pocketed the device.

And so it was now with a remarkably clear and serene mind that I positioned myself where I needed to stand in order to be released, and James pushed the button. A moment later, I was standing in the Chopville High gym, no longer in my shadow but in our regular dimension, and no longer shrunken either. The gym still felt completely empty and deserted, but I knew it wasn't.

"Marc, you here?" I whispered, and even though it was only a whisper, it still sounded rather loud in the utter silence.

"Yeah." I heard his whispered reply from a few feet to my right. "You good to go?"

"I think so," I whispered back, but I now had a new thing to worry about.

When I had done this on Rock Haulter, I had always been leaning against something—hadn't I? At the time, I'd thought it was necessary to prevent myself from falling over when my mind seemingly left my body in the present. Was it absolutely necessary, though? Could I do this without needing to lean against something? I sure hoped so, because I would need to. There were no walls behind me where I stood now, and although I could move back to one, James would have no way of knowing I'd done so and wouldn't be able to find me to let me or Marc back into the base.

In fact, as I thought about it, I suddenly realised that there was a gaping flaw in this whole plan. If Marc and I were invisible and untraceable, how were we supposed to let James and the others know that we were done out here? They would know if we were in danger, and they would be able to let us back into the base if we remained exactly where we were standing, but what if there wasn't any danger? Even if we had worked out a signal, no one would see it, and worse, we had no way to let any of them know what I'd just worked out, because we couldn't get back into the base on our own. I opened my mouth to tell Marc of this horrible realisation, but before I could, another invisible person materialised a few feet to my left, and then I heard Peter's whispered voice.

"Psst, you guys, James said to let you know that you need to make yourselves visible again before we can let you back in, otherwise we won't be able to find you."

My stomach relaxed in relief. Trust James to come to the same understanding. It probably occurred to him the moment I was out, and he suddenly realised he couldn't locate either of us.

"What if there are other people here?" Marc asked.

"Then we'll let you back in straight away," Peter hissed back.

"Pete, let James know that I have to stand against a wall," I whispered, glad that I had an opportunity to solve the other problem facing me.

"Okay, no worries," he hissed back. A second later, Peter suddenly became visible, and then another second later, he vanished altogether, presumably pulled back into the base.

"Grab onto me," I told Marc, waving my arms around in his direction until one of them connected with his forearm. The two of us linked up and I led him over to the nearest wall. From here, I would have a clear view of the final stages of the first Chopville High battle. I would see the back of the door that they had used to capture students, the area where they gave said students an opportunity to join them, and, of course, the place where Lisa had been shot.

"Okay, I'm gonna do this now, so just wait for me to talk before you do anything," I told Marc.

"Okay, no worries," he said. "Just do what you gotta do and I'll be here to make sure no one comes in here and tries anything."

I thought it was beginning to look like we were gonna be okay, but since I couldn't count on that, I was very glad I had Marc here to fight any Hammerhearts who noticed anything odd. I settled back against the wall, put my hands by my side, and stared out at the empty gym before me. How exactly had I initiated the separation last time? I thought back, vaguely remembered slow counting, and so I did that. I counted slowly in my head from one to ten, and then stopped, as the counting had pretty much driven all else from my mind…

Then it happened, that directionless tug that meant my mind had drifted into the fourth dimension and could now drift along the corridor of time. Except, now that I felt it again, I understood, as I hadn't three months earlier, that it wasn't entirely directionless after all. I'd only thought it was directionless at the time because it hadn't been a direction with which I was familiar, but possibly, because I had now moved through the fourth dimension physically a number of times, I recognised the direction in which I had actually moved. On the scale of the fourth dimension, I had moved towards the Honnie world, rather than the other way; but if I wanted to go the other way, I felt confident that I could.

A thought bubbled to the surface of my mind, and I almost began to raise my hand to hit myself in the head in shock before remembering that that would break my trance. We could have solved just about every problem we'd had if, before Marc and I had left the base, we had opted for an invisibility veil rather than separate invisibility spells. They wouldn't notice any difference in there, we wouldn't notice any difference out here, and they would be able to see us...or rather, they wouldn't, because the base itself would not be part of that veil. So, it was a good thing I hadn't hit myself in the head, as the idea turned out to be a sloppy one after all.

Enough of this, John. I got to work sending my mind backwards, knowing I was doing it right when, in my mind, it felt as though I were moving backwards, when in actual fact, it was just my mind moving backwards through time. The gym continued to be deserted and silent, and would have been totally dark, too, if there weren't a number of windows lined along the highest point of the walls. The first time I found people in the gym was a week earlier, when the Young Army had gathered there after our triumph over Arnold Hammerson, and mourning what we thought would be the loss of Amelia. I saw myself among the group, along with Peter, James, Marc and May. Lucien and Stella were also there, before they had acquired magic and gone over to the dark side. Natalie and Lena were there too, as were people such as the Abbodis (Dean and Joanne), Belinda and George, all of whom had since been killed by Lucien's uncontrollable temper. I wanted to stop and watch them in my own private mourning, but I had to push on.

The gym became empty again as I continued backwards, and remained empty for what seemed like a long time. In this time, the Hammerhearts had turned the school into an on-ground base of local operations, and it looked as though they weren't using the gym for anything. I sped up my backwards movement, watching the light come and go as day turned to night and then to day again around me, cycling faster and faster. When I finally saw people in the gym again, they were moving very quickly. I slowed down so that I could see them more clearly. By the time I was going forward again (so that I could see what was happening), I had skipped right over the cleanup and was now witnessing the third Chopville High battle.

Well, sort of; where I stood, I could mostly see dozens of students sitting at desks, their heads inside Transgators, going about their schooling and completely oblivious to the battle that was going on. My friends and I were way over at the other side of the gym, surrounded by Hammerhearts, who were raining spells upon spells down on us—although a few of us (me, Peter, Erica and Serena—my heart leapt at the sight of her) had broken through the circle and were confronting Hall on the other side of it. I couldn't really see what was going on over there, but that was fine—I remembered how it had been. I also saw a group of male Hammerhearts carrying Sophie away to the side, and I remembered thinking at the time that they might have sexually assaulted her over there, but I hadn't seen it then and thankfully, I couldn't see it now either as they moved too far to my left for me to see them.

I could see Moran too, standing in the doorway to the foyer, and I remembered thinking that I had seen a ghost behind him at the time. I couldn't turn my head to see more clearly over there (how I wished I could, how I wished I could go and stand over there and do all this again so that I could see her), but I could see a little bit. And yes, there was something over there behind him, but it wasn't shimmering as it had done last time. I focussed all my attention on it, and my heartbeat quickened as I recognised it. A woman was standing a few feet behind Moran, looking over his shoulder in the direction of the battle, her arms held out slightly in front of her as though operating some sort of ghostly magic—except, she no longer looked like a ghost. To me, over here, she looked utterly solid and very much alive.

And I knew who she was, because I had seen her before, in a large photograph on Moran's bedroom wall, and in Smiley's memories. I had seen her horrified death, ordered by Arnold Hammerson and carried out by Tom Hignat, and although I knew she was a ghost, she didn't look like one to me here, and the reason was obvious: We were in the same dimension. But with incredible frustration, I realised that she wouldn't see me, as I could see her, because I was nothing more than a mental projection. If I were with May, and we had travelled back in time and come out in our shadow here, perhaps we could see each other, maybe even give each other a hug, but there was nothing to do for it now. I could have stayed there for the rest of the battle, just watching her, but I had two good reasons not to: The fight was going to get much more bloody very soon; and I still had a job to do, and time was precious.

Reluctantly, I began moving backwards, passing back through the battle, back to before it happened (I actually got to see the Hammerhearts sneaking into the gym and surrounding my class), and then onwards and upwards. The previous few days were much of the same, with students just crouched over desks with their heads inside the Transgators. The gym emptied again for a while after that, and the next time I saw people in there, it was being used for what it was supposed to be used for. In other words, classes of students were doing gymwork in here.

I didn't have too much further back to go, now. The school's regular usage had ended when the Hammerhearts had launched their coup in Australia, which had been about two months after the first Chopville High battle. Although the school had certainly been affected by that battle, and to a lesser degree the second Chopville High battle (that had been in late March, and the gym hadn't played a major role in it). In other words, I had only two months further to go, but I had to do them more carefully, lest I pass right over the battle without even seeing it.

I began counting the nights as I passed over them, thinking that once I counted fifty-five nights, then I would have to slow down and really pay attention. As I began speeding up and days and nights passed, I also thought that I could identify what day it was by recognising when the gym remained completely empty for two days at a time. A good theory, but it didn't work because even through March and April, the Chopville High gym was used on weekends for smaller local sporting events. Chopville did have a small indoor stadium just south of the school that could hold 500 spectators, but some local teams (particularly junior basketball and netball teams) preferred to use this gym instead, as it cost less to open it.

Nevertheless, I pushed on with counting the days. Twenty… twenty-five…thirty…thirty-five…forty…forty-five…fifty…fifty-five…I still didn't know what day it was, but I knew I couldn't afford to move fast now. On this day, people were using the gym as normal, so I skipped back to the previous day. It was still being used normally, so back I went. The previous day, the same thing, so once again, I went backwards. This time, the gym was deserted—completely deserted. No students, no teachers, no local sporting events. I had to be close now. I went back to the previous day, and it was still completely deserted. Another day back and it was still completely empty.

Now I knew what day it was. In the aftermath of the battle, the school had been closed down by the Woodwards, and they hadn't allowed it to re-open until the following week. The battle had taken place on a Thursday, and the gym had come back into use the following Monday. In other words, it had been empty for three days, and this day—the one I was in now—was the first of those days. Therefore, I only had to go back one more day. And so I continued backwards, skipping quickly through the night, evening and afternoon. Suddenly, there were people before me, moving around very quickly—moving backwards, as it were. I slowed down and then reverted to normal forward speed so that I could see what was going on.

There were plenty of students still in the gym, organised by Mr. Woodward, but it was clear that the battle was over and the worst had already happened. I had to keep going backwards, but not by much. I watched the scene before me until finally, I saw some very familiar people—namely, myself and Marc. I had a few Woodward soldiers with me, and Lisa's father Greg was one of them. Among a group of nearby students who had been on the verge of being imprisoned by the Hammerhearts were Rebecca and (my stomach backflipped at the sight of her) Tulip Naval, who had been killed by one of Hammerson's monsters just a couple of days later—and, of course, who had taken my virginity that very night. Among the nearby fighters, though, I could see two more people who were dead in the present: Lisa, still living and breathing; and her killer, Candice, who had turned out not to be such a bad person after all.

As I watched, the John Playman of February 2010 was able to get Rebecca, Tulip and the other closest students out of the way of the fighting so that he could focus on the closest enemies. Someone fired a gunshot, the sound causing John to spin around wildly and almost topple over, but he quickly regained his balance and performed some sort of spell with the Sien-Leoard Crystal (that had been the day after I had first acquired it from Tommy, I recalled). There weren't many Hammerhearts left standing—a dozen, perhaps—most of them either unconscious or caught up in white piles of thicky prison. John was able to drop a few more Hammerhearts before someone managed to hit him with a stunner. He was able to break out eventually, and punch the offending Hammerheart in the head as it were, but the moment cost him dearly, and I clearly remembered how the next bit went down.

This was the moment when Lisa had been shot, and my concentration sharpened even more as I watched. I didn't want to see the final stages of the battle, but I knew I had to see what happened to Lisa when she died; and most importantly, speak to her. If I had any chance of learning whatever it was she needed me to know, this would be the only way she could tell me. There were only two Hammerhearts left: Candice and some other kid, who looked remarkably like Hignat but wasn't him. Marc and Lisa were the only people other than myself from our side still fighting, and both of them had just been hit by stunners. Candice had her gun out, and as I watched, she cocked it and pointed it at Lisa.

The shot was fired. The bullet hit Lisa at exactly the same time Candice fell, knocked out by me and the Sien-Leoard Crystal. Lisa went down, blood spewing out from her neck where it hit, disintegrating most of her neck in the process. I wasn't sure if it killed her instantly, but I knew she was dead when she hit the floor—the way her head rolled, she couldn't not be. It was horrible to watch, but I had to do it, waiting for whatever was left of her to join me in this dimension.

And indeed, I did see something that no one, me included, had seen at the time. A flash of light had burst from Lisa's body, and something had risen from it like mist. But by the time the flash was gone, the mist had already dissipated. Whatever was left of Lisa had already gone off to the in-between. I watched the horrible aftermath for a few more seconds, my stomach clenching as I realised that the experiment had failed. Most unusually, I felt like I wanted to cry, not in sadness as I had at the time, but utter frustration that this had all been for nothing. Still, I waited there for a couple more minutes, watching the horrific scene before me, hoping and hoping that something—anything—would happen. Finally, though, I had to face the truth: It hadn't worked, and now it was time to go back.

I raised my hand to my face, feeling my consciousness being hurled back through time until it rejoined my body and I staggered slightly against the wall. Marc sensed the change and hissed at me, "You okay, John?"

"It didn't work," I said dully. "I went back and saw the end of the battle, and I did see something leave Lisa when she died, but I couldn't talk to her."

Marc swore. "That's a bugger, but I guess I'm not surprised. Maybe you needed to be in her body to actually communicate with her."

"Yeah," I said, thinking of how I had seen my mother's ghost as well and not wanting to tell Marc, even if he probably deserved to know. Still, if she couldn't see me, then it made sense that Lisa wouldn't be able to either.

"I guess we'd better make ourselves visible now𝔑—"

"Wait," I said quickly. "I wanna try it again, just in case."

"Er—what difference would that make?" Marc asked.

"There is another way that I can try it," I told him, unsure how to explain how it actually worked. "Er—there are two time axisesℜ—"

"Axes," Marc said automatically.

"Yeah, James, axes," I said sarcastically. "Anyway, there's two: one between this world and the Honnie one, and one between this world and whatever world is in the other direction in the fourth dimension. I tried the one between here and the Honnie world; I think I should try the other one before we write this thing off as a failure."

"Okay, but try not to take too long," he said warily. "We haven't had any trouble, but I'm sure Lucien is fully awake and alert by now."

He had a point. The gym was very gloomy now; it wasn't completely dark, but it was darker than it had been when I'd first stepped out here. Given that it was August, I assumed that it was probably about six o'clock now, give or take, which meant that it was probably less than six hours ago that we were visiting with Derik Castle in his office in Melbourne. A lot sure had happened in those six hours.

"I'll try to be quick," I told Marc, and settled back so that I could do the whole thing again.

Slow counting up to ten…done. The directionless movement which would follow when my mind was blank…done. Once again, it wasn't entirely directionless, but I knew, given that I'd been thinking about it, that I'd gone the right way. I was now in the other corridor, one in which I had never been before, bordering on a new world about which I knew nothing, although I had to admit, I was curious. I swept that wondering from my mind for later contemplation and began going backwards through time, skipping quickly over the previous days, weeks, and even months until I began seeing a lot of people in the gym again. I recognised Transgators and kept going, resisting the urge to see if I could see my mother again. Once I saw people using the gym for sports again, I began counting the days and nights as they passed, except this time, I counted all the way to sixty, by which time I found the gym to be completely empty again.

I wasn't sure if this was the Friday, Saturday or Sunday after the battle, but I went back a day anyway, finding myself once again in the midst of fighting. I'd gone a little further back this time, so I sped forward until I saw Candice. I waited until I saw her stun Lisa, and then I paid close attention to what happened next. I saw Lisa get shot —I saw her blood flying—I saw her body fall to the floor—and I saw the light and the mist. Once again, though, I saw nothing more. I still didn't know exactly where whatever was left of Lisa had gone, but I now thought I understood why I couldn't get to her. Yes, it was true that she could only exist in the in-between, but according to Smiley, it was also true that she could only exist in her own timespan. Yet supposedly, there was no time in the in-between. I couldn't wrap my head around this paradox; all I could be sure of, was that Lisa was not here, and I would not be able to talk to her this way.

I raised my hand again, returning quickly to my body and the present, and gave a great sigh.

"Any luck?" Marc asked, hearing me.

"Nope, nothing at all," I said solemnly.

He too sighed. "Okay, let's make ourselves visible so we can get back in there and get on with whatever comes next."

We each used our invisibility toggles to make ourselves visible again, as I held my breath in anticipation of some sort of attack. Untraceable we may be, but if anyone had thought to put motion cameras in this place, they might know to come and investigate. It was a long shot, of course, and nothing whatsoever happened. Well, nothing happened until I was suddenly sucked in and up, appearing a moment later inside the control room of our new base, where Peter, James, May and Amelia were all watching me curiously.

"Just let me out of here so we can bring Marc back in," I said, and James obliged a moment later.

As I stepped away from the corner so that James could move onto Marc, I said, "It didn't work. I saw her death again, but I couldn't talk to her."

Peter's face fell. "Damn, so what does that mean for us?"

"Let's not think about that now, Pete," James said quickly, pressing the button to recall Marc to the base.

I didn't want to think about it either. In those dreams, Lisa had said that it was important for me to know whatever it was she needed to tell me—important enough that I had to go to her so that she could tell me. If she was stuck in the in-between, then it looked like I would actually, really, have to meet her there, and the only way to get to the in-between was through the acts of death and partial resurrection. Wrapping my mind around the possibility that I would have to sacrifice both my life and my soul in order to proceed was even worse than trying to wrap my mind around the in-between itself.

"No good," Marc said dully as he reappeared in the control room.

"We know," Peter said. "So, what now then?"

James looked at May, who scowled at him, and he said, "I think May wants to have your minds back, so you two had better make yourselves traceable again."

We were happy enough to oblige.

Chapter 35: A Certain Biological Brother of Mine

"Okay, so what comes next?" Marc asked. "Do we talk about how we get to Lisa, or do we focus on Lucien and the crystals?"

"Definitely Lucien," James said, snapping his fingers. "We've been watching him and Stella while you were out there, and it's not good."

"He knows," Peter said softly.

"Knows what?" I said sharply.

James sighed. "After you guys left, he called Stella to him—telepathically, we assume. She was upset about you, John, and Lucien got pissed at that, and he was even more pissed that Stella knew that Amelia was with you but that she didn't pay attention to what Amelia was doing. He was going to take it out on Natalie and Lena, but Stella refused to go and get them, so he did it himself, and while he was in the Big Room…"

He faltered slightly, perhaps noticing how dismayed I was. And I was: Not only had Lucien found out about everything I'd been doing, but now everyone else had as well. Worst of all, though, he was going to take it out on Natalie and Lena. Even if it had only been Lena, that would have been bad, but it was so much worse to think that Natalie might be in danger.

"And what?" Marc prompted.

"And he decided to go and talk to Mr. Woodward first, to see if Amelia had come to see him," James said quietly, waiting for Marc and I to understand the implications.

"What?" we both yelled in unison.

"He found out that I'd asked my dad about Rock Haulter and the Atlantic portal," Amelia told us. "It didn't take him long to assume that we had somehow gone back in time to go through, and he somehow confirmed it with the crystal. He also found out from the crystal that he couldn't follow us because of the paradox that would exist between his crystal chips and ours—since we had ours back then."

"Anyway, he flew off the handle again," Peter told us, "and just about everyone in the Big Room ran for cover."

"I still can't believe Dad sold us out," Amelia said, looking tearful.

"Don't beat yourself up, Amelia," Peter said gently. "Or your father; Lucien pretty much forced him, probably with magic or mind control."

"Anyway, he went for Natalie and Lena and hauled them out of the room anyway," James went on, "and I think he's hoping to use them to lure you to him, John. He tied them up in the Hammersons' living room with Stella𝔑—"

"She's not tied up, though," Peter said, "and she's not untying them."

"They talked a bit," James said, "and Lucien seems to have decided that you'll pick Natalie over Stella, but not Lena. They still want you to end up with Stella, John."

I sighed. "That's so not gonna happen. So—are they okay now?"

"Well, Stella's upset, Natalie's still mad at you, but Lucien is much angrier," James told me, "'cause he hates that Stella's upset and he's mad at Natalie for not caring about it. And Lena's not really saying much at all, so I have no idea what's going on with her."

"And that's pretty much where we're at now," Amelia concluded.

"I have to go," I said, feeling light-headed. "I can't let him hurt them𝔑—"

"He's not going to hurt them," Peter said sharply.

James shook his head. "He might, Pete; he's really mad, and Stella might be upset enough not to stop him. But John, you can't go to him; that's what he wants. Do you really think he's gonna settle down if you give him what he wants?"

"Hammerson wouldn't, but I think Lucien might," I said, "although I guess I'll have to—"

I'll have to let myself be put under an influential charm, I thought to myself. That wouldn't be good at all.

"He's right, John," Amelia said quietly, looking sympathetic but firm. "You're not going to accomplish anything by going to him, except make it much harder for us to stop him."

Marc and Peter both looked unconvinced. Peter said, "You know, if that were Rebecca, or our parents, I'd probably be about as headless as John is now. I get why he wants to go."

"So do I," Marc said, "but guys, there's a big flaw in Lucien's whole theory: He can't have any way of knowing that we know what's going on. He can assume that we've figured out a way to spy, and he can assume that maybe John is asleep now and is seeing it through Stella's eyes, but he can't know for certain. If we go, we'll be practically giving our own secrets away."

"That's true," James said slowly. "Still, perhaps we'd better watch them and see what's going on."

James and Amelia both held up their spiers, and we all gathered around so that we could see. We had two clear perspectives of the events unfolding in the Hammersons' old living room. Yes, Natalie and Lena were tied against one wall, side-by-side, I saw, and Stella was presently looking at them, her expression upset and very confused. All three of them were wearing the same clothes they'd been wearing when I had seen them that afternoon—in the case of two out of the three, the same clothes I had taken off them that afternoon. Lucien was standing a short way from them, gripping the Sien-Leoard Crystal in one hand (his fingers appeared to be clenching thin air) and looking pissed and frustrated. The audio that came through the two devices wasn't as loud as I wished I'd made it, but it was just loud enough to hear what was going on.

After several seconds of watching, Lucien grunted in annoyance. "This just doesn't make sense," he said through clenched teeth. "How are they avoiding my detection? It's been like this all day."

"They're probably just untraceable," Stella said a little fearfully.

"I thought that too, at first," Lucien said, "but the way they got away from Hall's raiding party this morning tells me that they have more going on than that. Whatever it is, they were doing it since before they may have gone to Rock Haulter, and I can't for the life of me figure it out."

"What are you getting from the crystal?" Stella asked.

"That they're still alive," he said, "but other than that, I'm getting nothing from them at all. They can't just be untraceable because we know how to detect signs of untraceability, and I'm not getting any of those either."

"Thanks to our Hero Crystal hero," Peter said, slapping Marc on the back, and the rest of us quickly shushed him.

Thanks to Peter, we missed what Stella said next, but we clearly heard Lucien's response. "That—hmm," he pondered for a moment. "That seems unlikely to me, but it is a possibility. Of course, I would have thought that they really would be dead by now if May had done that, and I'm sure I'd get an indication of that, since we knew exactly when Candice Young died."

"Well whatever," Stella said, shaking her head. "Whatever they're doing, I don't think they're coming here."

Lucien began to smile. It was a slow smile, and it made him look more handsome than ever. It also made him look utterly lethal. "If I know John like I think I do, he would be very upset by what's going on here, but maybe his friends are persuading him not to jump into action. That's fine—I can deal with that, because I can think of one thing that they can't possibly ignore."

"What?" Stella asked, looking nervous but also interested.

Lucien only smiled. "Just give me a moment."

"What's he doing?" Marc whispered into the silence that followed. On the screen, we could see that Lucien had lapsed into concentration, performing some sort of magic. I tensed up, knowing that this couldn't possibly be good. What was he doing? Had he thought of some way to detect us? Was he doing something that might somehow impact us where we were, even if he himself didn't know where that was? I didn't know, but I feared the worst. As the seconds lengthened, it seemed that nothing was going to happen, but none of us could relax until…

"Okay," Lucien said, relaxing and smiling at Stella. "John and his friends will be on their way to us shortly."

"How do you know?" she asked.

He continued to smile. "Although I don't know for sure that they're watching us now—we may have to wait a few hours for them to get wind of what's going on, but when they realise what I've done, they'll be here in triple-time. Don't you worry about that."

"Well, okay, but what is it that you're doing?"

Lucien shrugged, "You'll see in just a few minutes."

"Oh shit," Peter said, and when we all looked at him, we saw that he was no longer watching the spiers.

At least, he wasn't watching the ones showing Lucien and Stella. He had switched his focus to the one showing the twins, where they were presently hovering over a path that seemed to have no one on it. As I watched, Katie—the smartest of the group of four—was pressing buttons rapidly, and it took only a fraction of a second for me to figure out what was going on: Lucien had just pulled the trigger that he knew May would be instinctively driven to respond to. He had ordered them to capture Ingi and bring her to him, and judging by the empty path on their screen, they had captured Dan, Gob and even Tommy as well.

We all looked at May then. She hadn't needed anyone to say it out loud to understand what was going on, and just as Lucien had expected, she was in a real panic.

"May, calm down," James said quickly. "He's not going to hurt Ingi—he's just baiting you."

May shook her head. "I have to go to her. I cannot even take the chance that he will do something to her and the boys. I must go."

"We can't lose you, May," I said quickly, panicking myself now. May had helped us invaluably since she had returned to us with Amelia; we would be goners already if it hadn't been for her.

"Besides, what'll you do if we let you out of here?" Marc asked.

May thought for a moment and then said, "We go in here. We go right now."

"But shouldn't we—" Amelia began, but that was when May shut the debate down in spectacular fashion. The thought she pounded into all of our minds was like a mental canon blast, utterly eclipsing all other thoughts, and the thought was nothing more or less than absolute urgency. We had to go right now—no ifs, no buts, no coconuts.

Overwhelmed by May's urgency, James took the controls and began driving us rapidly from the gym, taking us into the fourth dimension so that we could go through the walls and shrinking us to the default Hammerheart size. At least, he'd intended to do that, but since we were already that size, that button didn't do anything. We then sped through Chopville towards Marc's house, the nearest entrance into the Hammerheart Highway that we knew of (there was a nearer entrance in the Stretch, but none of us were sure which tree it was hidden in).

"Maybe we should go through Hignat's place like we did last time," Marc suggested, watching the screen. "I mean, ours was disconnected, and I suppose Lucien could have reconnected—"

We're not turning around now! May pounded the thought into our heads again, and we all immediately shut up and let James get on with driving us to Marc's house. We shot through his front door, down the stairs, across his living room, into his fireplace, down the tunnel, around the corner and down the slide towards the Hammerheart Highway. Was it reconnected? No, it hadn't been, but it didn't matter; since we were still in the fourth dimension, we shot right through the wall at the bottom of the slide and ended up in the Hammerheart Highway.

Now, we were normal-sized, and that meant that the base couldn't fit in the tunnel at all. In fact, the control room itself couldn't even fit in the tunnel, and only two screens—the front-facing one and the back-facing one—showed something other than earth. It was a damn good thing that we'd been in our shadow when we'd done that; if we hadn't been, there would have been some sort of calamity that, one way or another, would have resulted in all six of us being crushed to death. Seeing this, James pushed the shrink button again, and the spell that would make us shrink to Hammerheart Highway size made us shrink again, as it hadn't done when we'd been outside, as if the two spells had piled on top of each other.

"They're in there," Peter told us.

He was the only one watching the spiers. Looking over, I saw that Harry, Simon, Katie and Sophie were now being sent out of the living room, having just been told to wait over in the den for further instructions. Lucien had extracted Tommy and the three Honnies from the compartment in which they had been captured. All four of them were unconscious, and Lucien levitated Tommy's body over to the couch. He then woke the other three up, and it was immediately apparent that he had taken their minds within his Honnie mind, and had over-ridden their impulse to run or fight. A moment later, the three of them were upright and tied right beside Natalie and Lena.

"Faster," May shouted aloud, pounding the urgency into all our minds again, and James sped rapidly down the tunnel ahead of us.

James may not have known exactly where the base was from here, but I'd done this once before (travelled the Hammerheart

Highway not in a cart), and May seemed to have gotten the knowledge out of my mind and placed it in James's. It didn't take him long to find the base, shoot through the station and up to the main doors. They were shut, but we were still in our shadow, and we went straight through them. Into the stairwell we went, up to the top floor, and straight along the long hallway we went, straight at the wall at the end of it. Heartstoppingly, I remembered that I hadn't put any specific enchantments on this base to make it capable of going through these walls, and that was something I really, really should have thought of. James, however, got around the problem by simply flying through the wall as though it weren't there. In my panic, I'd forgotten that we were still in our shadow, so that wall didn't affect us.

We went quickly up the stairs, swung around to the right, swung to the left and went through the door, and then stopped as the scene unfolded before us, just as it was on the spiers. Stella was standing directly across the room from us, leaning against the kitchen bench and watching Lucien. Beside her stood Fewul, whom Lucien must have recalled, and that was going to make whatever came next be considerably worse than it might have been otherwise. Lucien was standing in the middle of the room, presently staring at the open doorway through which we had just entered, and for a moment, I thought he could actually see us. He didn't react to our entrance, though, so it was apparent that he was just anticipating that we would soon stroll through there to confront him. The five victims were all tied up, all of them looking at least worried by what was going on, but the fear was most apparent in the dark-skinned face of Ingi; she looked utterly terrified.

"You will send me out there now," May told James.

"Okay," he said, "but May, just wait for us—don't do anything stupid. Give us a chance to try and put Lucien out of action first."

"Fine, but you had better not take too long," she said, stepping into the corner where she could be vanished. James pushed the button a moment later, and May disappeared from the room, appearing on the display of the screen a moment later, now back to normal size. She could step out of her shadow and reveal herself if she wanted to, but to her enormous credit, she resisted the no-doubt screaming urge to leap into action.

"We'd better get out there fast," I said hurriedly, getting into the corner so that I could be released from the base.

"Wait," James said quickly. "Before we go, what devices do we have? Does anyone have the thing that'll trap Lucien's magic?"

We all shook our heads, and my stomach sank.

"Does anyone have the thing that'll get rid of Fewul?" James asked.

We all shook our heads, and my stomach sank even further. James swore. "Okay, well, we'll just have to watch and hope it's not too bad. Who's gonna stay here?"

"I will," Peter offered. "You guys just get out there before May loses her shit."

James pushed the button, sending me whizzing from the base to stand beside May. I rummaged through my pockets to see what devices I had, but the only one that might be useful in this situation was the solid-outliner, and I couldn't even use it from here—I would have to leave my shadow to take the shot. A moment later, Marc appeared beside me, and then Amelia on his other side, and then finally James.

"You had better act now," May hissed at us, as though Lucien could hear us, but where we were, even though we were less than ten feet from where Lucien stood, he had zero chance of hearing anything.

"Relax, May, he's obviously just waiting to see what comes next," James said, pulling a device from his pocket. I squinted and recognised it as the interdimensional KO. I had created it around the same time that I had created the spyer, and I was very glad James had it with him. If he could use that to hit Lucien, it could give us a flying start in this battle—and even better if we could hit Stella as well. As for Fewul, we just had to hope that Lucien hadn't given the Beast of Magic any specific instructions for what to do if he (Lucien) was attacked.

"Good idea," Marc said, and he took the same device from his pocket. Amelia and I looked at each other and shrugged, wishing we were carrying that device. James took aim at Lucien and fired.

His plan came heartbreakingly close to working. It probably would have worked, too, if it hadn't been for Fewul, who clearly had been instructed to protect Lucien. A moment after the jet of red light entered their dimension, and a moment before it hit Lucien, it was deflected sideways by Fewul, flying across the room and hitting Lena squarely in the chest. Everyone other than Fewul started at the disturbance, and Lucien hurriedly sprang up a shield around himself. I knew he had because Marc and James immediately fired on him, but the jets of light were absorbed into it. Marc also took a shot at Stella, but she had also shielded herself.

"Damn it," Marc snapped, and he actually stamped his foot before letting out a string of obscenities.

"Now they know we're here," James said solemnly, "even if they don't know exactly where we are."

Confirming this, Lucien spoke to our group. "I don't know where you are or how you're hiding yourselves from me, but you're obviously here, and that makes two things clear to me: You were watching us, and now you know exactly what's going on here, and what the stakes are. I have a bone to pick with you, John, but before I do that, I hope you're listening hard and good, May."

Confident that he had absolutely everyone's attention, he walked over to stand beside Ingi, who was squirming in her binds. He glared at her, and she whimpered. Beside me, May cringed at the sound, and I knew it was costing her every ounce of discipline not to fly out of her shadow and attempt to throttle Lucien. It would only be an attempt, of course; no way known could she actually lay a hand on him.

"As you can see, I have taken Ingi into custody," Lucien said, looking in our general direction. "I don't know if you expect to feel her mind wherever you are, but if you're hoping to do so, I'm afraid I'll have to disappoint you. I have taken her mind into my own, along with these two"ℜ—he indicated the two half-breeds. "I'm sure you would like to have them back, and I'll be happy to give them back to you, but there is just one little condition: You and your children will have to go back to your world, never to return to this place again."

"Don't do it," I hissed desperately at May.

Lucien paused for a moment, letting his words sink in then, and then added, "Oh, and the longer you keep me waiting, the weaker Ingi is going to get. In case you can't tell, I am presently sucking her mind out of her—slowly at the moment, but even so, at this rate, she'll be dead in a few hours or so."

May's eyes widened in horror, and she looked at me and the others. Her face was tortured like nothing I had ever seen before.

"May, don't do it yet," James hissed at her. "Just give us a chance to go back into the base and get more devices to take him on."

"Come on, May, you know you can't stand by while I harm your children," Lucien called to her. As if he knew what James had told her, he went on, "Even if you think you have time to regroup and think of some way to stop me, by the time you do, she will be weaker than she is at this very moment. Surely as her mother, you can't just let me do that to her…"

He paused again, letting his words sink in, and even in the desperation of the situation, I had to admire the way he was going about it. He had really backed us into a corner, not physically attacking us, but nevertheless hurting us in a way that was impossible to ignore. And in the end, that was what it came down to: What he was doing to Ingi was impossible to ignore, and I knew what May was going to say to us before she said it.

"I am sorry, but I must do what he says," she told us, and although I wasn't watching the others, I could feel their horror. "I am glad I knew all of you."

Then she took a step forward so that she was a couple of feet in front of us, and a moment later, she had left her shadow. I knew it had happened when I saw Lucien's face light up with excitement.

"Do not hurt her any—"

That was all May got out before something stopped her. A second later, she collapsed in a heap in front of us. All four of us let out cries of surprise that no one else heard. I wasn't sure what I'd expected to happen, but it hadn't been that.

"Beautiful," Lucien said, levitating May's body into the air and making it float over to him. Beside him, Ingi and the half-breeds looked even more frightened by the sight of their unconscious mother.

"What are you going to do with them?" Stella asked, her eyes wide.

"Exactly what I said I'd do: send them back to their world," Lucien said, staring down at May's body and screwing up his face in concentration. "The only thing I didn't tell her is that I'm going to make her and these three forget all about us. As far as they know, they will never have met or known any of us. They will never know that they had ever been into our world. No time will have passed for them, and I'll even return their minds to the size they were when they first met you, Natalie," he said, smiling at her. "In short, they'll know and suspect nothing, so there is no chance of them ever returning."

I felt my heart breaking as he spoke. Yes, I would remember May—I would never forget her—but for her, I wouldn't even exist. Everything she had experienced in our world, up to and including our sexual adventures, would never have happened as far as she was concerned. Even in our present danger, I couldn't help dwelling on this depressing aspect of our situation, but James's next words brought me back to the here-and-now.

"He's gonna browse her memories before he wipes them," he said, "so he's gonna know every little thing we've been doing, including the fact that we're using the fourth dimension."

"How do we stop him?" Marc hissed, his face agonised.

James shrugged, looking more defeated than I had ever seen him. "I don't think we can, Marc."

"But we have to. If he knows that, everything we do—every bit of magic we've created—will be utterly useless against him."

Lucien hadn't spoken through all of this, so focussed as he was on what he was doing to May's mind. He was frowning down at her lifeless body, looking more and more pissed with every second that passed.

"You done?" Stella asked.

"I cannot believe this," Lucien said in little more than a whisper. "Somehow, she's done half the work for me. Her memories jump straight from her lying on her bed in the Woodwards' base right before I turned up there, to the moment she appeared here just now. There's nothing in between, nothing at all. It doesn't even give me an indication of where she was when she decided to reveal herself, and it certainly hides all the tricks that they've been using to defy me."

"I didn't even know Honnies could do that," Stella said in amazement.

"Neither did I," Lucien said, in almost unison with Marc, who was now grinning like an idiot. "Thank God May thought to do that before she went out there," he added.

Lucien sighed. "It looks like I'm not gonna get anything from her, so I'll have to get to wiping her memories of the battle against Hammerson and so on. Before I do, though…"

He got to his feet, looked at Ingi and the two half-breeds, and they immediately fainted, hanging limp in their binds. He then looked at Lena, causing her to regain consciousness. She straightened up in her binds and looked around, realising that she was still in the same place, then noticing that May's body was lying at Lucien's feet.

"That's her?" she said, glancing over at Fewul, who was still in May's form.

"Yes, this is the real May," Lucien said, nudging her body with his foot, and then stepping over her so that he could move towards the centre of the room. "Now that we've got that out of the way, it's time to address the next issue at hand—namely, a certain biological brother of mine who can't seem to keep his dick in his pants."

"Don't talk about him like that!" Stella snapped at him, which was nice, but depressingly, neither Natalie nor Lena did anything to come to my defence.

Lucien grinned over his shoulder at Stella. "Sorry, but face it, you knew who I was talking about, so it must be true."

"You know perfectly well that if you hadn't cursed him, he would never have done any of that," Stella said, and in the ropes, Natalie and Lena's eyes widened in surprise. I only knew then that neither of them had really believed me about being cursed. I was both relieved that they now knew I hadn't been making excuses for myself, but disappointed that they hadn't believed me in the first place.

Lucien just shrugged. "Just means to an end, Stella. Anyway, John, since I'm confident that you're still here, I am going to address you directly. Since I know that you've spoken to Stella today, and been inside her mind recently, then you'll know what she wants for the two of you—and of course, what I want for the two of you, since I do still care about her. Since I'm also confident that you're not going to do as I suggest without motivation, allow me to provide some for you."

He turned towards Natalie and began performing some sort of magic. I looked worriedly at her to see if she was hurt, but so far, she hadn't been touched. A few seconds later, what looked like a thin strand of wire appeared hanging over Natalie's head (like several feet over, barely coming out of the ceiling). As I watched, though, it began to descend towards her.

"You see that thing up there, John," Lucien pointed to the thing over Natalie's head, "that is magically enchanted to kill the first person it touches, at the instant of contact. I'm sure you don't need me to explain the ramifications here, do I?"

He didn't need to explain anything, but of course, he did anyway.

"Natalie is going to die the moment that thing touches her, and as you can see, it is going to touch her very soon. I can't be sure exactly how much time you have, but I would estimate perhaps seven or eight minutes. Reveal yourself to me, as your Honnie friend did, and Natalie will be spared. She and Lena here will be free to live normal, happy lives, and you'll get to live a very happy and privileged life with Stella. That would be much more preferred to continuing this pointless fight and sacrificing Natalie in the process, now wouldn't it?"

Across the room, Stella buried her face in her hands in what was either devastation or humiliation at what was going on, I couldn't be sure which. Lena had gone very pale, but she didn't say anything. Natalie had also blanched, and there were tears running down her face, but mustering her courage, she spoke to me.

"Just do it, John. I don't wanna die, and she'll make you very happy."

"You can't do it, John," James said flatly, his eyes kind but very firm. "We'll be in the same position if we lose you; Lucien will know everything we've been doing, and we'll be powerless against him."

"But he's gonna kill Natalie!" I squeaked, hardly recognising my own voice.

"Just wait," James insisted, but my eyes were on the wire over Natalie's head. I was almost transfixed as I watched it slowly descend towards her.

"We don't have time to figure this out, James," Amelia said frantically. "We have to do something; we can't let him kill Natalie."

"I dunno if he'll have the stomach to go through with it," Marc said thoughtfully. "At least, I hope he doesn't. I know he's under Hammerson's influence now but I still don't think he's got killing on purpose in him—not yet anyway."

"But there's nothing we can do," I said. "We have no way of attacking him, and once we're out, we'll be disabled. We have no choice."

"There is one other option," James said. "We can negotiate with him."

"James, didn't you hear what John just said—" Marc spluttered, but James quickly cut him off.

"We don't go out there, Marc; we write a note and send it into their dimension. We can just lean through it like May did when we were doing all that shop-lifting; we are all four-dimensional now."

"Er—does anyone have such mundane things as a pen and paper on them?" Amelia asked.

We all shook our heads, and my stomach fell.

"I'll only be a moment," James said, spinning on the spot and raising his hands to either side of his face. A second later, he vanished into thin air, and I assumed that was the signal for Peter to let him back into the base. I was very glad that Peter was still on the ball.

"What the hell is he doing?" Marc hissed, and now his eyes too were on the wire over Natalie's head. It had already progressed a quarter of the way towards her.

"He'd better have thought of something good," Amelia said, and a moment later, James reappeared beside her.

"Here," James said, handing me a pen and one of Peter's playing cards. It was the jack of hearts, and I thought it suited me perfectly; I'd jacked a lot of hearts around lately. "Tell Lucien you'll think about it and decide very soon, and to wait for your decision, but be as brief as possible—you don't have a lot of time."

He didn't have to tell me that, and I didn't waste any more of it with a response. I crouched down, put the card on my knee, and scribbled a very brief note on the back of it:

Pls wait for decision. 3–6 days max. JP

"I've got a few more cards in case we have to go back and forth on it," James said as I sprang back to my feet.

"You got this, John?" Marc asked me.

"Yep," I said, hurrying forward so that I was close to Lucien. I picked my spot, a spot where everyone would see it, held the card over my head, and pushed my arm out of my shadow so that I could let the card fall to the floor. I quickly withdrew my arm, and just in time as Fewul sent a jet of light flying at it; it hit the wall just beside the door to the hallway containing Lucien and Stella's bedrooms. That had been close, but even if no one had noticed the card, everyone had noticed what had almost happened. As I hurried back to the others, I decided that if I had to do this again, I would make sure Lucien was standing directly between me and the Beast of Magic.

Lucien stooped to pick up the card. He frowned as he read the message.

"What does it say?" Stella asked eagerly.

Lucien didn't respond for several seconds, and as he thought it over, the wire continued its downward journey towards Natalie's head. I clenched my fists as I watched him, willing him to make a decision of his own; and finally, he did.

"No, John, not three to six days maximum. You have one day, that is all. If you don't give me your decision by"—he glanced at his watch—"by nine o'clock tomorrow evening, someone you care about will die. It might be Natalie, or it might be someone from your family. It might even be Lena here, although by your recent behaviour, I doubt that she is important enough to you to be worth taking the chance. Just remember, I won't hurt you or any of your friends if you turn yourself over, but if you don't…"

He left his sentence hanging.

"So he's not coming?" Stella asked, looking devastated all over again.

"I probably could force the issue," Lucien admitted, pocketing the card, "but I think he gets the message."

He turned his attention on Natalie, and I was more relieved than I could say to see the wire over her head vanish. I had saved her—for now anyway. Tonight wasn't a total loss after all. It was only an almost total loss; May was now out of action, and we wouldn't be able to get her back. It was a good thing we had created so much magic while we'd had the chance, and even better that we still had a connection to Underwood who could create more; it looked like we were going to need every bit of it.

"And now," Lucien said, turning his attention back to the prone Honnie, "I'd better get down to resetting the minds of these meddling Honnies. Stella, if you're up to it, could you take Natalie and Lena back to the Big Room? Also, tell Harry and Simon to come back around here before you leave. After that, you've got the night off."

Stella only answered with a shrug as she walked around him and the Honnies to approach the two girls.

"Is there anything else we can do here?" Marc asked.

"Don't think so," James said, "but we're gonna have to act fast from here. Tomorrow's going to be a very big day, I feel."

It was on that note that we all turned and raised our hands to either side of our heads so that one by one, Peter could let the four of us back into the base. Before I had turned around, however, I had taken one last look at the scene before me, trying to take it all in. I knew that it could be the last time I saw either Natalie or Lena alive, but I was even more certain that I would never see May again in any form. And on that score, I was right: None of us did ever see May again, and I could only assume that she had gotten on with her life as though none of this had happened, just as Lucien had planned.

Chapter 36: The Opening Shot

It was a very sombre atmosphere in the control room of our sparkling new base as, still in our shadow, Peter drove us back down through the Chopville Hammerheart base and back into the Hammerheart Highway. Presumably everyone, like me, was trying to wrap their minds around the enormous loss we had just suffered. In our first encounter with Lucien after we had spent days preparing for it, Lucien had called all the shots, and if it hadn't been for a moment of mercy on his part right at the end there, it would have been a total defeat for us. In fact, the only real victory that we'd had was that even after capturing May, Lucien still didn't know exactly what we had been doing and how we were keeping ourselves hidden from him. All he knew was what Mr. Woodward had told him under what I hoped was considerable duress: that we had enquired about the Atlantic portal, and that we had most likely figured out a way to go back in time and go through it.

But I had one more thing to worry about than the rest of them, and that was Lucien's response to my written note. Yes, he had let Natalie live another day, but if I didn't hand myself over to him by nine o'clock tomorrow evening, someone I cared about was going to die. I felt certain that Lucien would not show mercy a second time; not only would he not want me to start thinking I had any measure of control over the situation, but the Arnold Hammerson part of him that was still struggling for control wouldn't let him go soft. I had twenty-four hours or so (actually a little more than that, as it was presently about a quarter to nine) to figure out how I was going to respond; and right now, my mind was utterly empty of possibilities.

All three spiers were still turned on, and even though we were now in the Hammerheart Highway, navigating towards the nearest exit out of the place, we still had a clear view of what was going on inside Lucien's lair. Two of the spiers showed Lucien sitting on the couch opposite Tommy's prone body, the equally prone bodies of the four Honnies and part-Honnies laid out on the floor in front of him as he tinkered with their memories; and Harry, Simon, Katie and Sophie sitting in chairs clustered around him. Fewul remained exactly where he had been the whole time, still guarding Lucien from any possible attack we might launch against him, none of them knowing for certain that we had already left.

The other spyer was focussed on Stella as she led Natalie and Lena back to the Big Room. All three of them were upset to varying degrees as they stepped into the elevator, and as the door closed, Natalie spoke directly to Stella.

"As far as I'm concerned, you can have him, 'cause I would never be able to trust him now."

Stella glanced at Lena before replying. "I would, 'cause I know everything he does is for a reason, even if some of them are mistakes. I just wish Lucien wasn't trying to blackmail him, though; I want him to come to me because he wants to."

"Whatever. I'm sure you'll be so understanding when he cheats on you too," Natalie shrugged.

That broke my heart a little more than it already was, and I shoved the spyer away from me (up until then, I'd pressed it against one ear so that only I could hear what was being said). Right before I had looked away from it, though, I had noticed something else about Stella's face: She wasn't just sad, she was exhausted too, and that made me think of something very important to our security.

"I dunno where you're going, Pete, but whatever you do, we have to stay in the fourth dimension," I told him.

"No reason not to," Peter said, not looking away from the displays as he searched for a tunnel to either side of the Highway.

James, who had been watching me, nodded his understanding. "Certainly. It wouldn't do for Stella to learn what's in your head when she goes to bed tonight, John. Now that you mention it, though, where exactly are we going to go?"

"Somewhere where Lucien won't think to look," Marc suggested. "That means, not any of our houses, not the school, not the Stretch, and not the farm where we hid before taking on Hammerson. Not the drop-in centre in Melbourne either, but I don't think I need to explain why we should stay in this area this time."

Amelia and I both nodded our agreement at his words.

In the end, Peter settled us in a very unusual position: Hovering in mid-air about a foot under the Main Street Bridge. He had enlarged us to the size we had been back in the Chopville High gym, so that if we were to let anyone out of the base, they would return to their normal size as they plummeted into the Jade River below. I had to admit, I quite liked the position; not only was it difficult to get to without knocking down the bridge (and I sincerely hoped that didn't happen), but it was nice and sheltered, and it had a pretty good view of the river as it flowed beneath us.

It was well after nine o'clock by the time we were in position, which left us free to do…what? Most of us weren't really sure, but James, whose mind almost never stopped, had been thinking ahead to this moment the whole time we had been on the move. He advised us that we should all have something to eat, and then try to get some sleep. Yes, time was short, but when we had been in even greater danger in the drop-in centre, we had understood the importance of good rest. Being well-rested was going to be even more important, as he, like me, suspected that tomorrow—Tuesday, August 31, the last day of winter—was apt to be a big one.

* * *

I did eventually sleep that night, but it wasn't until well after everyone else had gone to sleep. By then, I was alone in my bedroom, and employing some of the magical abilities I had given myself to keep an eye on things. I had seen enough within our base that only Peter had gone straight to bed after dinner, taking about an hour to fall asleep; James had gone outside, located the hot tub room I had installed (identical to the hot tub cave on Rock Haulter), and soaked for an hour before going to bed; and Marc and Amelia had gone to his room and made love before falling asleep together.

These magical abilities I was using were no longer a secret from the others. Back in the Hammerson living room, James had been the only person to notice that I had been strangely unarmed during the encounter, and although the urgency of the situation had prevented him from asking questions at the time, he hadn't forgotten about it. He brought it up over dinner, and seeing no way to dodge the issue and not wanting to outright lie to my friends, I had told them what I'd done. Marc had been a little jealous that I hadn't shared this secret with them while they'd had a chance to follow my lead; and Amelia, most familiar with using magic, had been even more annoyed at this; while James, though not wanting the power for himself, had shared the same concerns I'd pondered over at the time—that I might let the power go to my head. Only Peter had been pleased about it, saying it had been good thinking on my part, that perhaps I'd be able to react more quickly with that kind of magic than magical devices if I was in danger, and finishing by pointing out that he was glad it was me and not him.

Over dinner, among other things, we had agreed that the first thing we would try in the morning, after we'd had breakfast and showered and such, was teleport into the Big Room and use our unbogglers and mind-extractors (the devices that would extract a person's mind from within a Honnie mind) to recapture a small, hopefully unnoticeable number of our friends and bring them back here to be briefed on what was going on. We would also need to carry the devices that would get rid of Fewul—something we weren't prepared to try until such time as we were prepared to take down Lucien as well, lest he call the Beast back again. In case we ran into Lucien, we would also carry the device that would trap him in a magical prison.

Before leaving, we would make ourselves untraceable again, and just for good measure, apply the magic of the spell skippers. The spell skipper was a device that would cause any magic directed at us to pass right through us without touching us; it was a device I had created while I'd been with James in the creation cave, and it was a damn good one, if I may say so myself. It should also mean that we wouldn't need to be invisible either, which would make dealing with our friends a lot easier. Our top target would be Stella, but if we couldn't get her, we would settle for Mum, Dad, Marge, Charlie, Mr. Woodward, Lillian Woodward, Natalie, Rebecca, Erica, Felicity and Jessica—and then if we still had time, other members of the former Young Army as well.

After a very serious and sobering discussion over dinner, I separated from the others and went to my room. Once I'd established (by spying) that none of the others were going to do it, I opened my top bedside drawer and pulled out the two mind linkers that would enable me to contact Larissa and Underwood. I weighed them in each hand, trying to decide who to contact first. In the end, I settled on Underwood; if I had the time right, it would be about ten in the morning on Rock Haulter for Larissa, and about four in the afternoon for Underwood. That meant that Larissa was probably too busy with her class to talk, and probably wouldn't even know that I'd contacted her until she thought to pick up the device (assuming she still had it). Underwood, though, would be unable to resist the pull of the thing once I made contact with him, so I put the blue mind linker down and put my finger on the pad of the red one, ready to think at Underwood.

Before I could even begin to assemble a thought, I was bombarded with messages that he had attempted to send to us over the last two weeks; messages that had started out irritated, then become concerned as we continued to ignore him, and then irritated with us all over again for wasting his time. Once I'd absorbed the flow of thoughts, and had a private grin to myself (whatever he said to the contrary, I now thought Jacob Underwood actually did give a damn about our fight against the Hammerhearts), I put my finger back on the pad and asked him how he was doing. It took him a couple of minutes to respond, but when he did, it was with a quick fine, followed immediately by a question: Where the bloody hell have you been?

I gathered myself, not wanting to tell him that we had time travelled but knowing that he would sense a lie if I sent it to him as a thought, so I settled on the closest thing to the truth that I could. Now that we were back in the present, it wouldn't hurt him to know.

Arnold Hammerson is dead. We managed to kill him a weak ago, but Lucien has defected again and taken control of the Hammerheart army, and he's even more dangerous than Hammerson was. He's managed to steal the powers of all six Sorcerers and give them to himself and Stella; she's pretty much his next-in-command now. He's also stolen all of Marc's crystals, so now the only magic we have is the Light Crystal and the Villain Crystal, neither of which can be used much in combat against them, and all the magic we managed to create while we were there.

It took another couple of minutes for him to respond, but when he did, it made me think that he was a lot smarter than any of us had given him credit for. His double question was tinged with suspicion: Did you have some sort of feeling or premonition that something like that might happen when you were here? Is that why you were so interested in that one cave?

I couldn't lie, so I just told him: We didn't suspect it might happen—we knew it was going to happen. That's why we wanted to prepare on Rock Haulter. When I sent the thought, I hadn't been thinking specifically of time travel, but he must have gotten that idea somehow himself, and to my relief, he was much more understanding about it than I would have expected. I should have given him much more credit, given that he was a descendent of Rafael Smiley. When he responded, he told me that he understood, told me that he was doing fine, and asked if we needed him to do anything. I told him that we didn't yet, but we would be in contact again if anything changed. He asked me to let him know of further developments in the war, and then we ended our communication.

I put the red mind linker back in the drawer and then hesitated before picking up the blue one. I was unaccountably nervous about talking to Larissa again for some reason, remembering that two weeks had passed, wondering if she still thought about me or if she had moved on with her life. If she hadn't moved on, then she might be pissed at me for not responding to her in all that time, even though I'd warned her that I wouldn't be able to. Finally, after mustering my courage, I put my finger on the pad, and for the second time, was hit by a barrage of thoughts. Like Underwood, Larissa had been trying to contact me, but unlike Underwood, she seemed to know that I wasn't going to respond for a while. Her motive for communication seemed to be that she wanted to share her thoughts with me while they were still in her head, knowing (hoping) that I would eventually get them.

Prominent among Larissa's thoughts were how much she missed me, and confirming that her classmates really had forgotten all about me and my friends. Another thing she told me, though, was that she had met Jacob Underwood (my English friend, she had thought of him, thinking that since she had seen the two of us together, that we must be friends). True to his word, he had tried to set up a threesome with her and Amanda, but as I had hoped, it hadn't gone down. Amanda had told him, quite frankly, that he wasn't her type; and Larissa had snapped at him to leave her alone, thinking that it was incredibly creepy that one of my friends would try to hit on her.

When the thoughts finally subsided, I put my finger back on the pad and thought at it. I didn't tell her what was going on with the Hammersons and Lucien; not only would the personal side of it mean nothing, but her classmates and friends might get suspicious if she suddenly knew that Arnold Hammerson was dead. I did tell her that we were still in great danger, that it looked like I had zero chance of getting my girlfriend back, that I was single now, and that I missed her very much. I completed the thought with a picture of my bedroom, focussing mainly on the bed so that she would get the message, and hopefully be consumed with thoughts about wanting to be in that bed with me—because there was nothing more true than the fact that I wanted her in this bed too.

I waited a few minutes to see if she would respond, not really expecting her to, and that turned out to be right. I therefore put the mind linker back in the drawer and settled back on my bed, sending my mind out from my body as I used to do easily and fairly often when I had been in possession of the Sien-Leoard Crystal. I didn't need to know what Peter, James, Marc and Amelia were doing, but I was curious to know what was going on in the Hammerheart base— assuming Lucien hadn't set up spells to make it impossible for me to get in in this form. What I found when my mind did leave the base was that it was scarily similar to how it had been when I'd been standing in the gym and looking through time, the main similarity being that my mind wasn't in the same world as the things I was looking at, but the key difference being that I wouldn't be pulled back to my body if I so much as wiggled my finger.

Back when I'd had the Sien-Leoard Crystal, I'd been able to direct myself to a person just by thinking of them, and I had given myself that ability now. Heading for the top, I decided to begin with Lucien. I was pleased to find that there was nothing stopping me from seeing into his lair, and seeing exactly what he was doing there. (Perhaps he was so confident of his magical superiority that he didn't feel like he needed to be untraceable anymore.) It appeared that he had finished with the Honnies and had already instructed the twins and their girlfriends to drop them back into the Honnie world, probably exactly where we had first found them months earlier (Rebecca would have no doubt told him the exact location, or what she knew of it anyway).

Now, Lucien was sitting on a couch beside Tommy, who had been brought around and, judging by the look of it, returned to some semblance of sanity. He was looking around him in some confusion, a slightly dazed look on his face, while Lucien watched him patiently.

"What day is it?" he asked, a little groggily.

Lucien checked his watch and then said, "It's the thirtieth of August, 2010, half past ten in the evening. How do you feel, Tommy?"

"Kinda like I've been hit by a bus," he said vaguely, looking around himself. "Where am I? I know I recognise the place, but I can't think where from. Isn't Stella around here somewhere?"

Lucien grinned. "Yeah, she's in her room at the moment, I believe. This is the Hammersons' living room—don't worry," he added quickly as Tommy started. "Arnold Hammerson's dead, and I've taken over his army, which you are now a part of. We're continuing their work, only we're doing it without killing half the world."

Tommy shrugged; this seemed to mean little to him, and if Lucien was still manipulating his mind, as I felt sure he was, then I wasn't surprised. Tommy looked around him, and looking a little panicky, said, "Where's Ingi?"

Lucien's eyes widened in surprise at that. "You remember Ingi? I thought—you weren't supposed to—"

I grinned to myself. So there was some part of Tommy that Lucien couldn't reach, but then my stomach sank as I understood the truth of the matter: The only part of Tommy that Lucien couldn't reach was that part that Ingi had permanently damaged—the part of him that would always belong to her, even if Ingi herself had totally forgotten about Tommy.

Composing himself, Lucien said, "Don't worry about her, Tommy. She's been put somewhere where she can never hurt you again."

Tommy looked stricken at that. "But I love her—I need herℜ—"

Then he fell silent as Lucien worked his will on him. "You'll be fine, Tommy. In time, you will forget about her, and I'll help you every step of the way. How about I show you to your room?"

"Well, okay," Tommy said, getting a little unsteadily to his feet.

I thought Lucien would take Tommy to the Big Room, and I was curious to see how he would be received by all those people who thought he was dead, but instead, Lucien took him down the hallway to Tankom's old room, directly across from Stella's. While Lucien was doing magic to turn the bedroom into something that didn't look like it belonged to a wrinkled old lady, I checked in on Stella, to find that she was in her bed, fast asleep. If I'd been out of my shadow, she would be taking this journey right along with me, but there was still enough doubt in my mind to make me worry that perhaps she was somehow here with me all the same. I therefore drifted across to her, saw that her face was slightly transparent (meaning that I would be able to enter her mind and see her thoughts), and drifted down into her.

I found myself surrounded by darkness, as I had every other time I'd done this. If I'd wanted to, I could have gone back through Stella's memories, experiencing everything right along with her—all the stuff that I hadn't already experienced right along with her. I didn't want to do that, though; all I needed to know was what was going on in her mind right now. I therefore settled into her mind and a few seconds later, found myself in her dreams. I had become Stella, except Stella seemed to be dreaming of herself as a small girl playing jump rope. I couldn't see her, but being her, I didn't need to see her to know that she was young, enthusiastic, and hadn't yet had all the joy crushed out of her by her evil family.

That was enough for me; I drifted back out of her head, and then just hovered over her, watching her sleep and thinking to myself. Stella may not have liked the way that Lucien had gone about things, but she would be happy with the result if she knew it in its entirety: Amelia was now settled on Marc; Lena seemed to have been turned off me as a result of how I'd used her that afternoon; and Natalie had been completely turned off me after learning that I'd screwed Amelia, Lena and Stella all in one day when I was supposed to be her boyfriend—and she hadn't even known about May, or anything that had happened on and en route to Rock Haulter. Stella didn't know all the details either, but she knew enough to know what sort of person I was—enough to think that she could understand and trust me, no matter what I did. She would be happy with this result because in the end, it looked as though she was the only one left for me. Whatever else, as much as I still wanted Natalie, I had to admit that I did like Stella, and that I would be happy with her as a girlfriend—just as she wanted me to be happy with her—if it weren't for how much I was still hurting over the whole mess with Natalie.

I sped away from her and went to check on Lucien and Tommy, only to find that Lucien had left Tommy in his bedroom. I sent my mind out to find Lucien, locating him walking down the corridor on the floor below towards the elevator. He stepped into it, pushed the button for the fifth floor, got out on that level, and entered the Big Room. I tensed up as I worried about what he might try to do in there —whether he'd changed his mind about waiting a full day and would take his anger out on someone I cared about—and this worry continued on as I watched him locate Lena, pull her aside, and order her to follow him from the room. I intended to watch whatever he had planned for her, but before I left, I had a quick check on Natalie. She was lying in her compartment, her arms folded beneath her pillow, apparently trying to sleep, but her eyes were wide-open—and they were red, as though she had recently been crying.

Feeling more guilty than ever, I sped away from her just as I'd left Stella, located Lucien and Lena again, and followed them back up to the top floor of the base, where Lucien made her sit down opposite him. It was only then that I noticed that Fewul had finally departed, perhaps sent back into Cornish's service. Meanwhile, Lucien spoke to Lena, who didn't seem particularly interested in looking at him.

"I know you're not particularly thrilled with me at the moment—"

"That's an understatement," Lena scoffed, still not looking at him.

Lucien's face twitched, as though her words had hurt him, but he pushed on. "I normally don't care how people feel about me, but I'm going to make an exception for you, since you and I were part of the team that beat Arnold Hammerson. I don't want you to keep going around like this, remaining loyal to my cause but continuing to hate me as a person. What can I do to make this right?"

Lena finally looked at him; it was a very level look. "Well, since you're so powerful, maybe you can go back in time and stop yourself from killing my brother."

"I thought that's what it was," he said, leaning forward and staring into her eyes. Where a minute ago, she hadn't been able to look at him; now, somehow, she couldn't look away. It was as though he had somehow locked her eyes on his as if they were magnetic. It seemed to have a hypnotic effect on Lena, whose face began to flush. Surely he was using magic to do this…

"I wish I could take that back," he told her earnestly. "Believe me, not a minute has gone by since that morning that I haven't regretted my outburst, killing all those people. If there was any way I could go back and change what happened, I would do so. But as you know, there is no magic that can permanently bring back the dead."

"I know," she said softly, and then licked her lips. "I guess I'm glad you're really sorry about it; that means maybe you're not such a bad person."

"I'm really making a great effort to be a good person," he told her. "I want to do this thing right, and I don't want to be responsible for people losing their lives—"

"Not even Natalie?" Lena asked suddenly, seeming to break the spell over her for a moment.

Lucien smiled at her, and then told what I was absolutely certain was a bald-faced lie. "That thing was never going to kill Natalie. She was part of our group as well, remember? I wouldn't want to kill her, or even hurt her, after all the good she's done for us. I just did that so that John would be forced into position, and I fully intend to do it again if I have to."

Except next time, he really would kill. I knew it, and so did Lucien, and perhaps deep down, Lena knew it too. Lucien was just saying what he wanted Lena to believe, and he was surely prepared for the possibility that I was listening, even though he wanted me to believe the complete opposite. On that score, he had succeeded, but it hardly mattered. When it came to people's lives, I couldn't afford to assume Lucien was bluffing. There was just too much risk in dealing with a man possessing some of Arnold Hammerson's traits in that fashion.

"Okay, good, 'cause you had me worried there," Lena said, appearing to relax for the first time.

"I don't want you to worry; I want you to be comfortable with the way things are going here," Lucien said, leaning forward and taking her hands in his.

Suddenly, I knew exactly where this was going: Lucien was going to seduce her. It all made sense. He was killing three birds with one stone: Bird number one, it would be absolutely sure to take Lena out of the running for me; bird number two, it would enable him to move on from Stella's rejection in spectacular style; and bird number three, people would see the leader of two thirds of the world with an awesomely stunning young woman on his arm. Even I could see how Lena was the perfect arm candy for Lucien; I just hoped that Lucien would appreciate that he would also have a really great person by his side in Lena.

I watched a little longer, just to confirm my suspicians, and then when I had seen enough, I returned my mind to my body and lay down in bed. My mind was full of images of Marc having sex with Amelia; Lucien having sex with Lena (although I hadn't actually watched that, but I could imagine how it would look); Natalie, Stella and Larissa all having sex with nameless faceless strange men; and even May, who would be wandering through the Honnie world as though none of this had ever happened. I did feel horny and lonely, but as self-punishment, I resisted the urge to take care of it. In time, I drifted off to sleep.

* * *

As planned, we had gone straight back to the Hammerheart base the following morning, around eight o'clock, this time by teleporting straight into the Big Room, managing to dodge every bit of magical protection around and within the base simply by being in our shadow. We then adjusted ourselves to the right size so that we would be normal-sized when we left the base, and then finally drifted out of our shadow and into the real world.

Before we had come here, we had checked to make sure Lucien and Stella were otherwise occupied. Lucien was asleep, which was very good news, and as we all saw through the spyer, Lena was asleep in bed beside him. Even better than this was the fact that Fewul was nowhere to be found, probably helping Cornish to do his dirty work. Stella was sitting alone in the living room where so much had happened the previous evening, seeming to be occupied with some sort of magic. None of us were sure what she was doing, nor were we particularly sure how we would go about capturing her. My opinion was that we would only need to use an unboggler and a mind-extractor, just the same as the rest of our friends, so long as we did it before she could use her magic on us.

"So are we all agreed on how we're going to do this?" James asked. All five of us were standing in the control room, except for Marc, who was sitting; he had been elected to remain behind in the base while the rest of us went out there.

"Unbogglers, mind-extractors," Peter said in a bored voice, holding the two devices up for James to see. All four of us were carrying the devices—even me, although I didn't think I would need either of them.

"And," James prompted.

"This thing for Lucien or Stella if they turn up," Peter said, digging into his pocket and pulling out the magical prison shield device.

"Great," James said, checking his watch. "We'd better synchronise these things before we get started. I don't want us to be in there any longer than twenty minutes."

We all followed his instructions, and then Marc said, "And when you're done, come back to this spot where we are now, and give me the regular signal, and make sure you're holding the arms of anyone you want me to bring in with you."

"Good idea," I said, "except it won't work—you have to bring each person in separately. I made it that way to stop any unwanted stragglers getting in."

Marc shrugged. "Okay, a little more work for me. Are you guys ready to do this?"

"Hang on, let's make sure we don't double up on who we're going for," Amelia said quickly. "I'm focussing on my father and grandmother. What about the rest of you?"

"I'll do our parents," Peter said quickly, "and Rebecca. John, you just focus on Natalie and Stella—I have a feeling you're gonna need to be focussed to get them two."

I shrugged unhappily. "You're telling me."

"And I'll try for my parents and sisters," James concluded. "If you see any of our other friends, like Harry or Simon or whoever, if they're not with someone else in this room, bring them in too."

"And I'll keep an eye on the whole thing from here," Marc added, "including those two." He nodded at the two spiers, still tuned into Lucien and Stella.

"Okay," James said, clapping his hands. "This is pretty much the opening shot of what could be our main battle against Lucien—what could even be a greater battle than anything we faced from the Hammersons. Is everyone ready?"

"Let's get going," Peter said grimly.

And so the four of us were let out of the base, one at a time, to drop into the Big Room. We were all untraceable and protected by the spell skippers as planned, but as I sent my mind back up to look at Stella, I wondered how I was going to go about getting her while she was up there and I was down here. I supposed I could go up there and grab her there, but something about that idea didn't appeal to me—perhaps it was nothing more than the close proximity to Lucien that put me off. I had an idea how I might be able to attract her, though: Before setting off into the room, and still with my minds-eye on her, I felt in my pocket, withdrew my untraceability device, pointed it at myself, and gave it a click, making myself totally traceable again.

As I had hoped, Stella started instantly, confirming my suspicion that she had been attempting to track my location. She just sat there for a few seconds, probably seeing that I was just a few floors below her in the Big Room. Then she jumped up and tore across the room, out into the hall and down the stairs. She was coming here, just as I'd hoped, and she wouldn't take too long. I quickly checked to make sure Lucien was asleep, just in case he had an alarm set up to let him know if any of us appeared, but thankfully, he and Lena were still asleep. Perhaps he was too exhausted from seven or eight hours of mind-blowing sex to be bothered waking up for me, I thought, and smirked before returning my mind to my body and hurrying further into the room in the wake of the others.

I sent my mind out again, thinking that I could locate Natalie more quickly if I did it manually, and found her sitting alone in her compartment—the same one I'd seen her trying to sleep in the night before. I hurried off in that direction, turning corners here and there and waving to Darcy as I sprinted past him (I would have stopped to bring him over, but I was in a hurry—I wanted to deal with Natalie before Stella got here). Eventually, I reached her aisle and hurried down it until I found her compartment. She looked around at me in surprise and then jerked backwards in shock and astonishment as she registered that it was me, actually banging her head on the back wall of her compartment in the process.

"John? What the hell—"

I hit her with the mind-extractor first, simply by pointing my finger at her, and then with the same finger, hit her with the unboggler. She felt nothing when I extracted her mind from Lucien's, but when the unboggler hit her, she fell sideways and would have toppled right out of her compartment onto the floor if I hadn't caught her. I steadied her and then helped her to her feet, and by the time I had her upright, enough of her sense had returned to her that she could stand on her own.

"Natalie, are you okay?" I asked her urgently.

She nodded, and then as I had expected, began to cry. I took her by the arm and began leading her back through the Big Room towards where we had parked our base, hoping that I could get there before Stella found me. Wanting to make it a little harder for her, I made myself untraceable again (with my hand this time, rather than the device), and continued leading Natalie onward.

"I'm sorry," she kept sobbing into my ear.

"It's okay, it's okay," I kept saying in response, and then, unable to tell if she was talking about defecting to Lucien's side or about not believing me about being cursed, and being unable to take it, I made myself ask the question. "Er—Natalie, are you and I gonna be okay?"

She didn't answer for several seconds, and I didn't dare look at her but kept my eyes firmly on the path ahead—we weren't far from the base now. Finally, she said, "It was an unboggler what you just did to me, wasn't it?"

"Yeah, that's right."

"It doesn't change anything between us," she said flatly, and my heart sank. "It doesn't change what you did."

I nodded but couldn't bring myself to speak. I wasn't surprised to hear her say it, but I was still saddened by it.

We got back to the base, and Marc let me in, followed shortly by Natalie. There were three more people in the room with Marc, three people who had never been in this base before: Erica, Rebecca, and a very impressed-looking Mr. Woodward. Natalie and Rebecca threw their arms around each other as soon as Natalie was released into the base, and Mr. Woodward threw me a very grateful smile right before Marc sent me back out again to find more people. As I hurried back into the Big Room, I saw James leading his two sisters back to the base, all three of them looking tearful, and a short time later, Amelia leading her grandmother. I didn't see Peter or my parents, or anyone else for that matter.

I stopped, a little confused as to why I hadn't seen Stella yet. Had she made herself invisible before coming into the room? Was she lurking around somewhere, waiting to catch me off-guard? I sent my mind out again, looking for her, and to my surprise, found her going back up to the top floor. She didn't look excited anymore; she looked very distressed. In some puzzlement, I entered her mind to get an idea of what was going on, and was smacked with the reality of what she had seen: She had entered the room just in time to see me leading Natalie and to hear her continually apologising to me, and she certainly hadn't been invisible. If I hadn't been so distracted by wanting to know about my future with Natalie, I would have surely seen her.

Now, she was heading back to her living room, with no idea of just what we were doing in the Big Room—she seemed to have seen nothing except what I had done with Natalie, and had no sense that there was a bigger operation in play. As for Lucien, he was still fast asleep, continuing to have no inkling of what was going on down here. Satisfied, I drew my mind back to my body and resumed hunting for people to bring back to our side.

Epilogue

When the twenty minutes were up, we had regained a substantial number of our army. Plenty of people, mainly those recently recaptured, wanted us to continue bringing people back, nervous about leaving them in the Big Room lest they become the focus of Lucien's wrath once he discovered what had happened under his nose. Still, even though some people had been left behind, we had regained a considerable flock: Natalie, Rebecca, Erica, Felicity, Jessica, Mum, Dad, Marge, Charlie, Hilda, Violet, Harry, Simon, Katie, Sophie, Mr. Woodward, and Lillian Woodward. The control room did get pretty packed, but at least it was big enough to hold all these people.

Marc, the man at the controls, took charge very quickly. "Peter, Amelia, can you show everyone around the base and help them pick out rooms and get themselves settled in as quickly as possible. John, James, you two remain behind for a few minutes. The rest of you, try to take no longer than half an hour."

The room quickly emptied as, awestruck, everyone crowded into the lift and went upstairs. Nobody spoke again until it was just the three of us left in the control room. Marc had already teleported us back under the Main Street Bridge and moved us back into our shadow.

"We don't have a lot of time to enjoy our success, do we," Marc said—it wasn't a question.

"Nope," James agreed. "Now that we've shown our hand, we have to act against Lucien right away—preferably before he wakes up. John, what happened with Stella?"

"She saw me with Natalie and assumed the worst," I told them. "Last I saw, she was—"

"Running back upstairs in tears," Marc finished the sentence, and I remembered that he would have seen it all on his spyer. He glanced over at said device and added, "And it looks like she still is. Do you think she has any idea what we were actually doing down there?"

"No, she didn't even stop to think about it," I said.

James grinned. "Good, one point to us. Hopefully she doesn't stop to think about it any time soon, then she won't think to tell Lucien. Okay," he clapped his hands. "It's time we bring some devices down here—namely, the one that'll track the crystals, and the one that'll get rid of Fewul. We won't be able to plan what comes next until we see where the crystals are and how they're protected."

"I still think we should try to get Stella back," Marc said. "If we still had May, we'd be able to take her mind off John—"

"But we don't have May, so even if we do recapture Stella, she mightn't be much use to us until she cheers up on her own," James pointed out.

"We will have to deal with her, though," I said reasonably, "so even if we don't do it right away, we have to be prepared for it."

"Okay, but let's focus on the crystals first," James pushed on. "If we can get the Hero Crystal back in your hands, Marc, we'll officially be back in the game."

"Okay, I'll go get my tracker," Marc said, getting to his feet.

"I'll get some of my devices as well," I said, and we both left the room to head up to our respective bedrooms, leaving James to mind the fort.

As Marc and I ascended, I thought back to the previous evening and the conversation we'd had over dinner. Once we had had enough of talking about the calamity of losing May and almost losing Natalie, we had gotten back around to Lisa and the Enlightener, and the issue of what Lisa needed to tell me. We had gotten talking about the in-between again, but where on Rock Haulter we had been hopeful that we might be able to reach the in-between without dying by simply going between worlds and back to a time when Lisa was alive, now none of us were confident that there was any way to get there other than through the worst means possible.

"The fact remains that John saw only a light and a mist when she died," James had insisted. "He didn't see her soul go anywhere, which leads me to think that it can't exist anymore except for in the in-between."

"You know, Lisa did write about seeing Mary Sien when she was in that cave in her diary," Amelia had reminded us. "If that was supposed to be representative of the in-between, how come she could communicate with Sien? They certainly never existed at the same time."

"Well, Sien's not exactly a normal Sorcerer," Peter had said. "She was the first one, so it might be different with her. Besides, how could she have gotten stuck in the in-between in the first place? Maybe Lisa was wrong about it being Sien."

James had shaken his head. "She seemed pretty sure of herself when she'd been writing it, and yeah, I know she'd been scared and freaked out at the time, but in my mind, that just makes it even more believable."

"So, what does it mean?" I had asked.

"I think it means that once you're in the in-between where time doesn't exist," James had said, looking around the table at the four of us, "then it doesn't matter if you lived at the same time as someone else who's also stuck there. That would explain why Lisa could see Sien, and probably anyone else who has ever somehow gotten stuck there."

Including my mother, I had thought, but hadn't said.

"And that means, if one of us did get into the in-between," Amelia had said slowly, "then we would be able to converse with Lisa without any trouble."

"But that would only be useful if that person was alive at the same time," Marc had added, "which is all well and good, since a person has to be brought back from the dead just to get there. But guys, you understand what this means, don't you?"

"Someone has to die and sacrifice part of their soul to see Lisa," Peter had said solemnly. "James, are you absolutely sure it's the only way?"

James had slowly shaken his head. "Pete, I'd be lying if I said that it was definitely the only way, but I'll be perfectly honest with you and say that I think it probably is the only way. I just don't know enough about this to be sure, and I doubt that Mr. Woodward, or even Smiley when he was alive, knew enough to make this call."

A brief silence had followed this, and then Amelia had said quietly, "John, you were the one who had those dreams. Do you think what Lisa wanted to tell you is important enough to pay such a high price?"

"Yes," I had said without hesitation. "At least, in the dreams, I'd been full of desperation."

"And although I don't have any firsthand experience of the Enlightener as John does," James had said, "I tend to think that sense of urgency was put into the dreams for a reason. It's supposed to spur you on, John, and I don't think we should disregard that."

Another silence had followed this, and then Marc had said, "I remember this feeling. This is how we all felt the first time we went to Rock Haulter, and Fewul told us that someone had to sacrifice their life so that we could get the Sien-Leoard Crystal. Ironic that it turned out to be Lisa who did that for us."

James had then stood up so suddenly that we had all started. "James, what?—"

"You guys talk amongst yourselves," he had said, hurrying from the room. "I'll be back in a couple of minutes. I've got an idea."

The four of us had just looked at each other. It was Peter who said, "Let's just wait for him. You know James; whatever he's thinking of is probably sheer brilliance."

James had returned within a couple of minutes as advertised. What he hadn't advertised was that he would be carrying some heavy-looking stone thing and a piece of paper on top of it. He had plonked the stone tablet (that's what it looked like) down on the table so that we could all see it, and then had sat down, still holding the piece of paper.

"Told you," Peter had grinned, "sheer brilliance."

"Er—what is this, James?" Marc had asked warily.

"This," James had said, indicating the stone tablet, "I found on Rock Haulter on our second day of searching. I picked it up almost right after you showed us that cave that made us untraceable, Pete. Then when you told me about that cave that could translate languages, Marc, I had to take this along and see if I could work out what it said."

And yes, now that he had mentioned it, I could recall seeing that tablet just once on Rock Haulter; James had zoomed off with it in his hover car before I'd been able to get a good look at it. Now that I could see it clearly, I had been able to see that it did indeed have what looked like a positively ancient script engraved into it.

"And did you?" Marc had asked. "Work out what it says, I mean?"

"Yes," he had said, and then had clarified. "Well—whether I got every word, I'm not sure. The language is so vastly different from English that you can't just translate each word out of context and expect it to have a corresponding word in English: you can only translate entire chunks into broad concepts. In any case, I got enough to understand how to activate the spell it describes, but if there are additional details of the spell, they escaped me."

A brief silence, and then Amelia had said, "As someone who has been using magic all her life, can I point out how foolish it is to try to perform a spell without fully understanding it?"

"Hear me out," James had insisted. "Look, we all know that we're barely hanging on here. Lucien has basically been toying with us for most of the time that he got his magic, but we can't expect that to continue much longer, especially after last night. We do have this new base, which is good, but if Lucien finds a way to break our defences here like he did with the last base, it's all over. We don't have any magic other than that which we gave ourselves on Rock Haulter, and we no longer have a Honnie to fight with us."

Another brief silence, and then Marc had said, "You're trying to say that this may be a choice between fighting and surrendering?"

"Almost certainly yes," James had gone on. "This spell, basically says that we may invoke the full power of magic to reach a desired outcome, and it was made in such a way that potentially, anyone can use it, because it doesn't require the crystals or anything else. Basically, this stone is almost as old as the crystals themselves. It was created by Sien and Leoard when they were on Rock Haulter and left there, either before or after they hid the Sien-Leoard Crystal there, I'm not sure. It's probably been picked up since then, but it doesn't look as though anyone else has bothered to investigate its meaning—or its power," he had added, "and given all the magical studying that goes on there, that surprises me a little."

"The full power of magic?" I had said, a little dubiously, my mind racing. What could that possibly mean? The full power of magic was, for the most part, under Lucien's command, so how could we use it?

Either missing my scepticism or choosing to ignore it, James had nodded. "Basically, if you have a group of people together who are intent on a cause, if those people possess enough belief in magic, they will be able to use this stone to invoke the true depth of magic to serve their intent. It supposedly reaches within the Light and Darkness Crystals in equal measure, combined with the power Sien and Leoard possess within their very souls—that's what it implies anyway," he had added doubtfully. "My point is, I think this may be our only hope. We need to use this to make sure that we are able to learn what Lisa needs to tell us."

"How do we do that?" Peter had asked hopefully.

"Well, the tablet says that the spell requires three things," James had told us. "It basically reads more like the kind of ritual you would see in a movie or read about in a book than the sort of magic we're used to. What we'll need is a promise to activate the spell, belief in magic to carry the spell, and a sacrifice to complete the spell. I know that sounds bad," he had added quickly, seeing the looks on our faces, "but there is a way we can work this."

Everyone had just looked at him, waiting with bated breath. Finally, James had said, "We all have to agree that if one of us is killed in the fight against Lucien or the Hammerhearts, that the rest of us will bring that person back from the dead. That's not saying that we go out and try to get ourselves killed, but if someone is killed, the first person who is killed, that person must be brought back from the dead so that they can get into the in-between. All five of us need to agree to this, just in case it's us. That promise will activate the spell, and the loss of part of one soul is a sacrifice which may complete the spell."

We had all looked at each other, and I had seen judgement in three pairs of eyes. I had known exactly what they were thinking: Why must we make that sacrifice when it's John who Lisa wants to talk to? Without needing a prompt, James had answered that very question: "The fact is, even though she did say in John's dream that she needed to tell him something very important, the thing in question is something that we all need to know. John was only on the receiving end of her request because he's the only one she could reach through the Enlightener. I think all five of us need to agree to do this, because if we have less, then we mightn't have enough belief in magic between us to make this thing work. Hands up, who's prepared to make the sacrifice?"

James had been the first person to raise his hand and feeling as though I were sliding down a laundry chute, I had raised mine shortly thereafter. The idea that I might have to make such a sacrifice made me sick to the stomach, but whatever James said, the dreams had been mine, and I couldn't expect my friends to make the sacrifice without doing it myself. I felt a little better when Peter had raised his hand shortly after me, making it three out of five. Marc and Amelia had both looked terrified, but when Marc finally raised his hand with obvious reluctance, Amelia had stoically followed suit.

"Okay," James had said, letting out a deep sigh—he had been holding his breath. "So, the people in question are supposed to be connected and encircling the stone, so everyone link hands."

I had reached out and taken hold of Peter and Marc's hands, and they had each taken hold of James and Amelia's hands respectively. James and Amelia had then linked up, completing the circle around the table and the stone tablet still sitting on it.

Â "Okay," James had said, "now everyone just focus on Lisa, what we need to learn from her, and the promise that we just made. I'll do the rest."

And so that was what we had all done, thinking of Lisa and, in my case, the dreams I'd had of her while on the Rock, and the promise that if I did, I would be the one to enter the in-between and acquire the needed knowledge from Lisa. While we were all focussed, James had begun speaking, haltingly at first, and then a little more confidently, reading from the piece of paper which he had placed beside the stone tablet. The words sounded ancient and were utterly incomprehensible to my ears, but as James had grown in confidence, they seemed to take on a more ringing tone. Finally, for a few seconds, there had been a tangible and undeniable sense of power building around us, a power which I thought had to be older than Sien and Leoard—a power as old as the Earth itself.

On the last syllable, there had been a thunderclap. It wasn't visual or audible, nor could it be physically felt, and yet we had all felt it. At the same time, I had felt a stinging sensation in both of my hands, and had gasped in pain, and only just managed to avoid letting go of Marc and Peter. I hadn't been the only one; in fact, everyone had let out a similar gasp of pain, and as I had watched, mesmerised, I saw blood begin to trickle out from between James and Amelia's linked hands. I had looked around again and seen blood trickling from between James and Marc's hands, and Peter and Amelia's hands, and…I had looked at my own hands and seen the same thing.

Without anyone daring to let go, James had spoken into the shocked silence. "It's done—not quite how I expected, but it's done. We have the power on our side, we just had to lend it our blood for it to work properly."

"Maybe that was the sacrifice? We won't need to do anything else?" Marc had asked hopefully.

James looked incredulous. "A few drops of our blood for this spell? Well, that would be nice, but I doubt it. I think we should resign ourselves to it being one of our souls."

"So, what does it mean for us?" Peter had asked, finally dropping his hands and staring at them. I had stared at my own palms in considerable wonder; both of them were now sporting identical circular cuts, like nothing a stone or knife could have done. Whatever magic James had somehow invoked, there was no denying that it had been incredibly powerful.

"What does it mean?" James had repeated, looking around at us all. "Well, to put it bluntly, it means that through the will of Sien and Leoard, we will succeed in our endeavour, provided we live up to our promise."

Now that James had said it, and now that I could look back on it the following day, I understood exactly what James had done. Magic as powerful as what we had used required a sacrifice, a port of accountability, so to speak. The promise had been that, and if we kept it, if one of us died and came back, sacrificing part of their soul in the process, only then would the incredible might of Sien and Leoard's magic align itself with the five of us—the five who had believed in magic, and who had been willing to make the call. I got that James had been right, that we didn't have to go looking to get ourselves killed, but I had a horrible feeling that we wouldn't have to. Whether it was because of the promise, or simply because we were walking straight into a world of danger unlike anything we had faced before, it seemed only natural to feel that it wouldn't be too long before one of us got the chance to come back from the dead.

The Magic Crystals Series

www.TheMagicCrystals.com